My Aunt is a MONSTER

Reimena Yee

RH
GRAPHIC

NEW YORK

My Aunt Is a Monster was conceptualized in a Moleskine notebook, sketched and penciled using Procreate on an iPad Pro, then colored and finished in Photoshop. It was lettered in the author's hand.

My Aunt Is a Monster was written, illustrated, and published on the respective lands of the Wurundjeri people of the Kulin Nation, the Lenape, and the Orang Asli.

Copyright © 2022 by Reimena Yee

All rights reserved. Published in the United States by RH Graphic, an imprint of Random House Children's Books, a division of Penguin Random House LLC, New York.

RH Graphic with the book design is a trademark of Penguin Random House LLC.

Visit us on the web! RHKidsGraphic.com • @RHKidsGraphic

Educators and librarians, for a variety of teaching tools, visit us at RHTeachersLibrarians.com

Library of Congress Cataloging-in-Publication Data is available upon request.
ISBN 978-0-593-12546-5 (hardcover) — ISBN 978-1-9848-9418-2 (paperback)
ISBN 978-1-9848-9420-5 (ebook)

Designed by Patrick Crotty

MANUFACTURED IN CHINA
10 9 8 7 6 5 4 3 2 1
First Edition

A comic on every bookshelf.

Also by Reimena Yee
Séance Tea Party

The author expresses their gratitude for the time,
labor, and kindness from members of the blind and
visually impaired community and their allies in the
collective act of creating an accessible world for all.

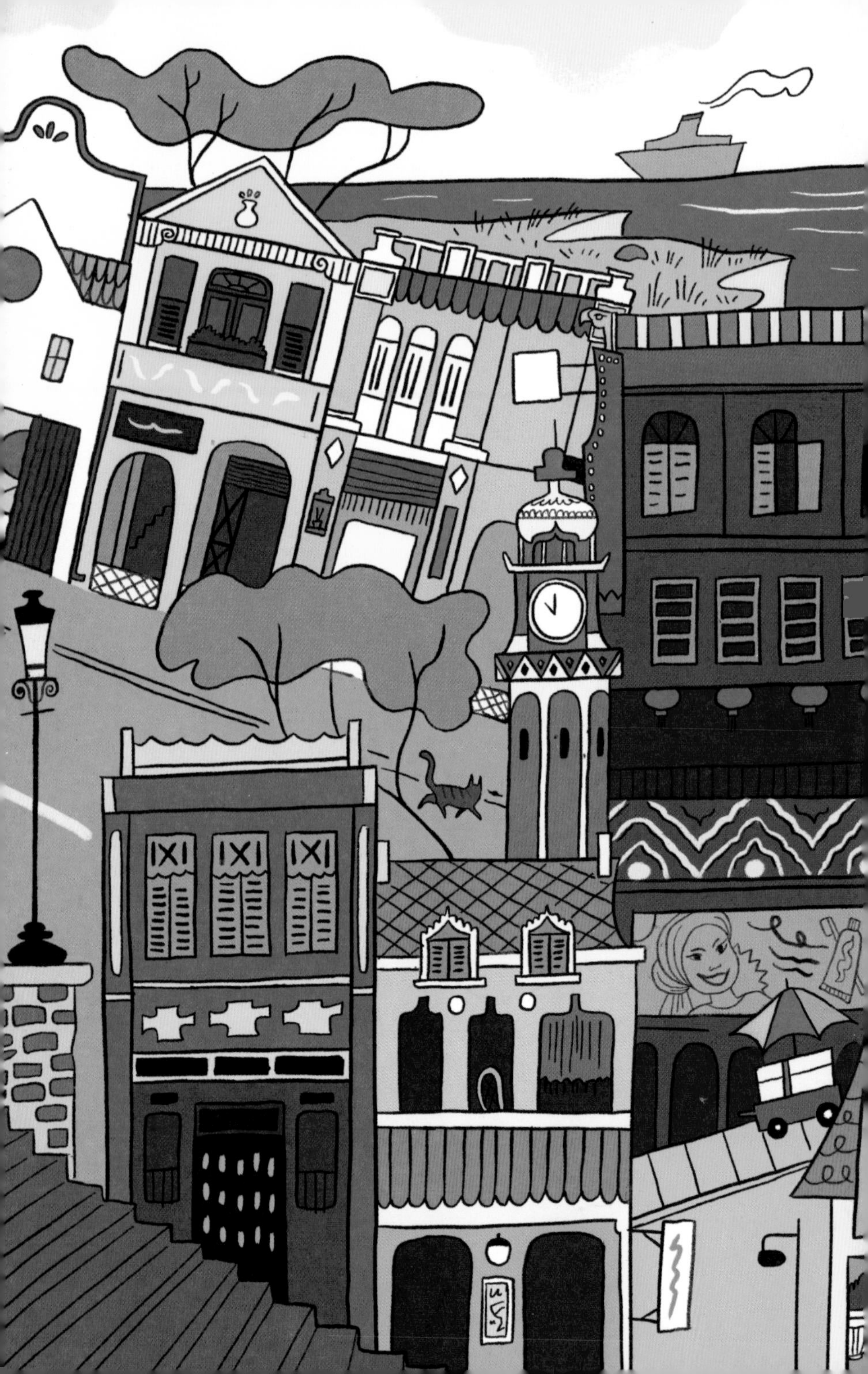

Prologue

Once upon a time,
there was a blind little girl named Safia
who lived in a little bookshop
on a laneway that smelled
of roasted chestnuts
and pine leaves
opposite the lamppost
where the cobblestones
were uneven.

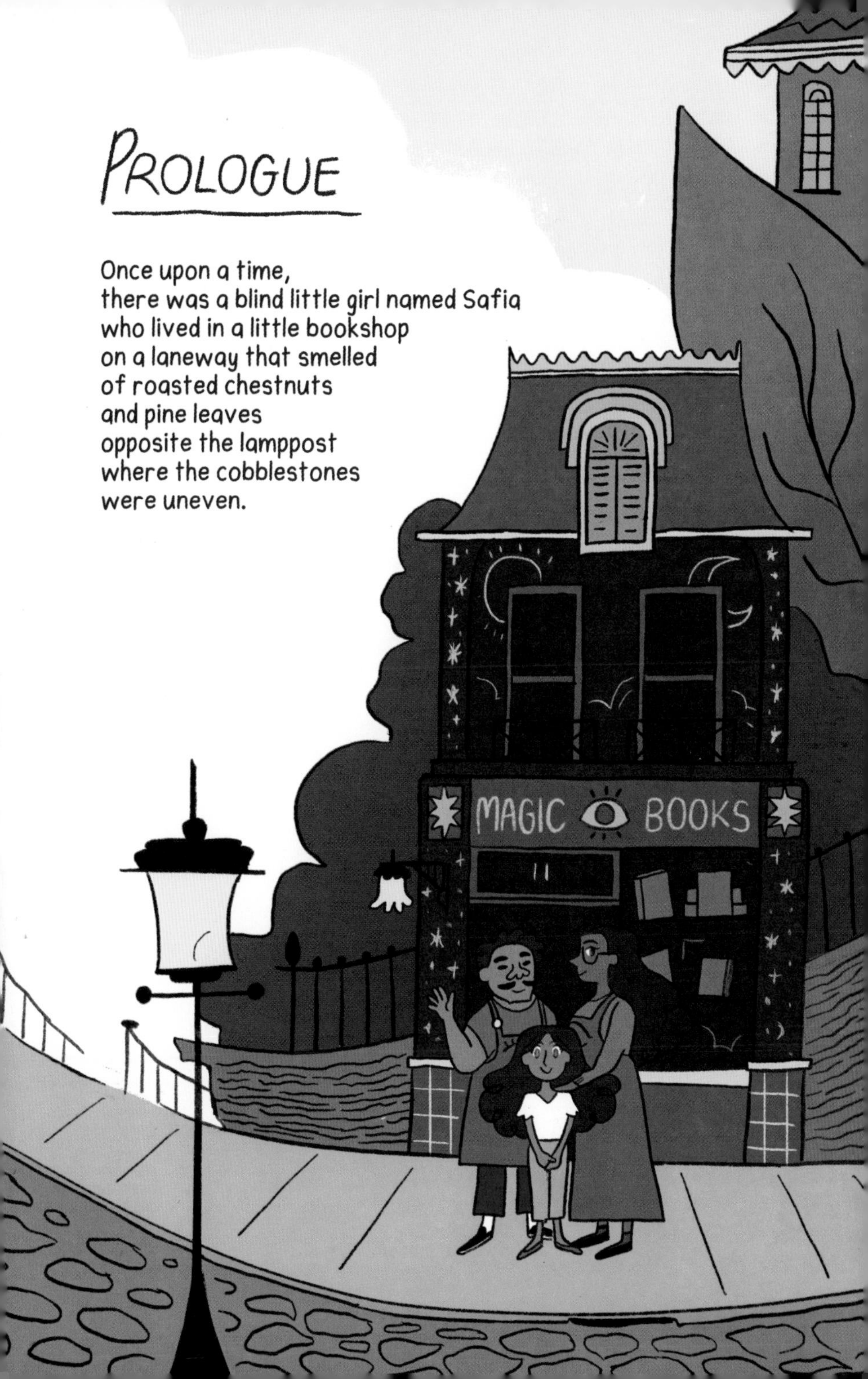
MAGIC BOOKS

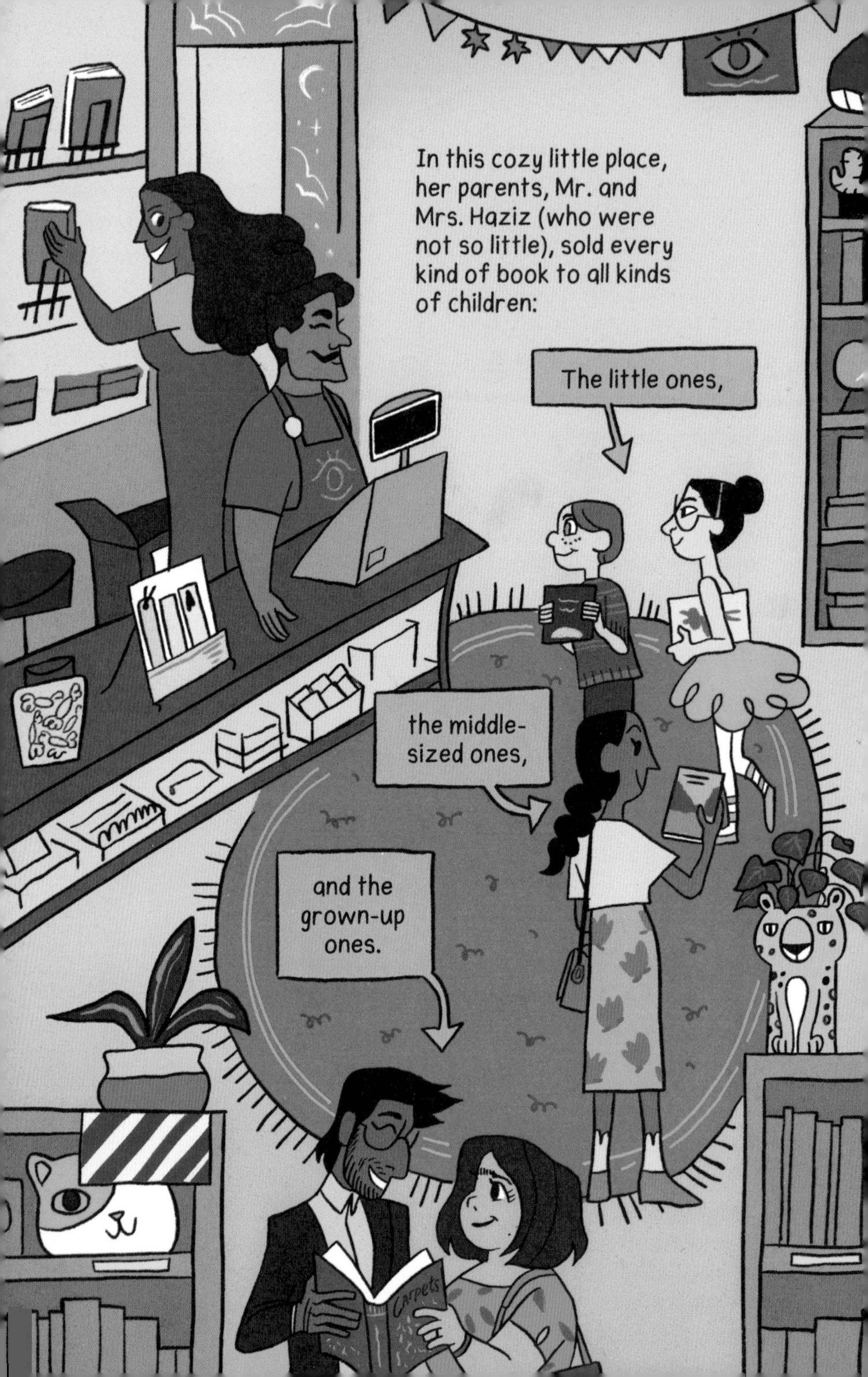

In this cozy little place, her parents, Mr. and Mrs. Haziz (who were not so little), sold every kind of book to all kinds of children:
The little ones,
the middle-sized ones,
and the grown-up ones.
Carpets

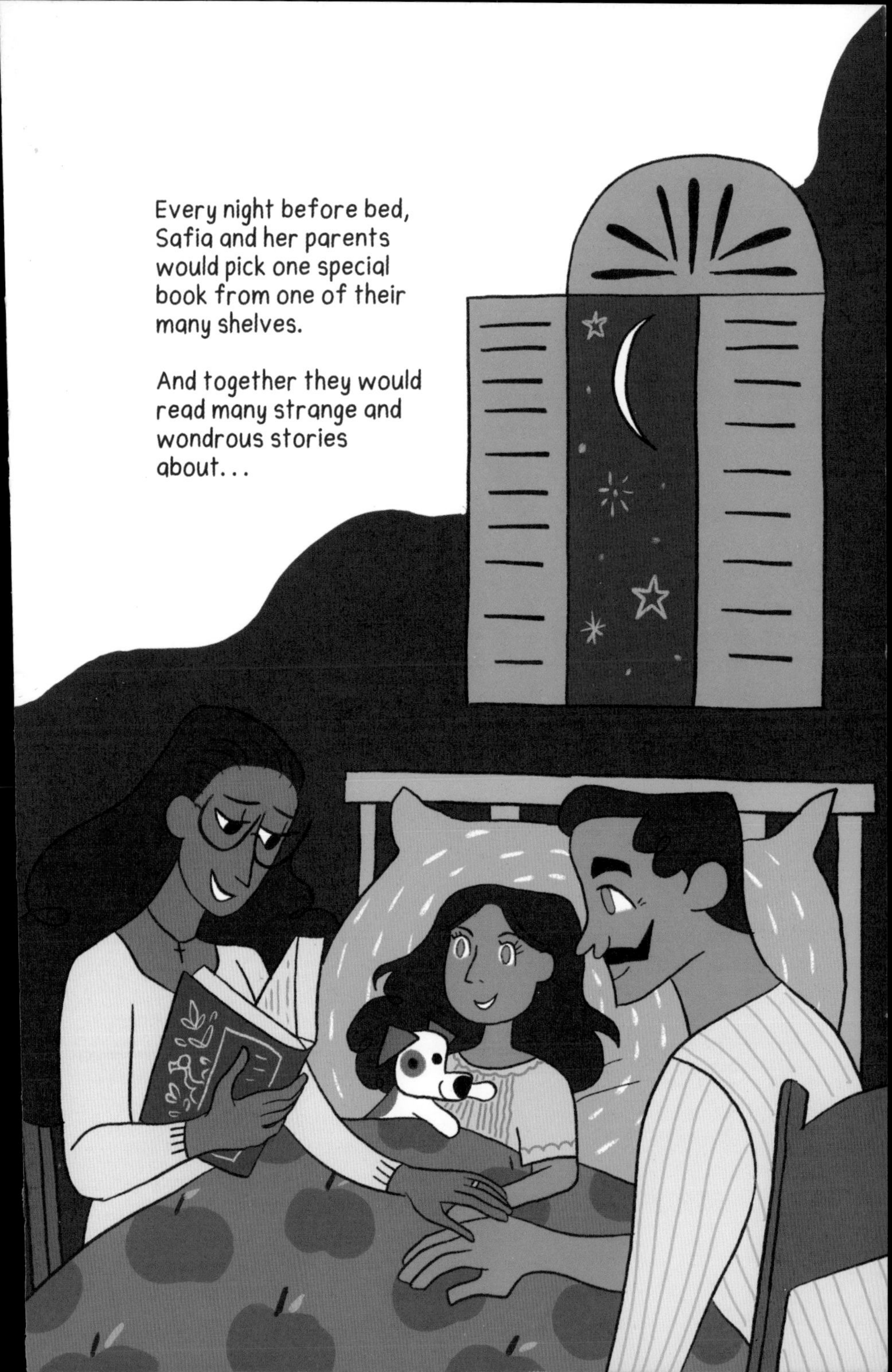
Every night before bed, Safia and her parents would pick one special book from one of their many shelves.
And together they would read many strange and wondrous stories about...

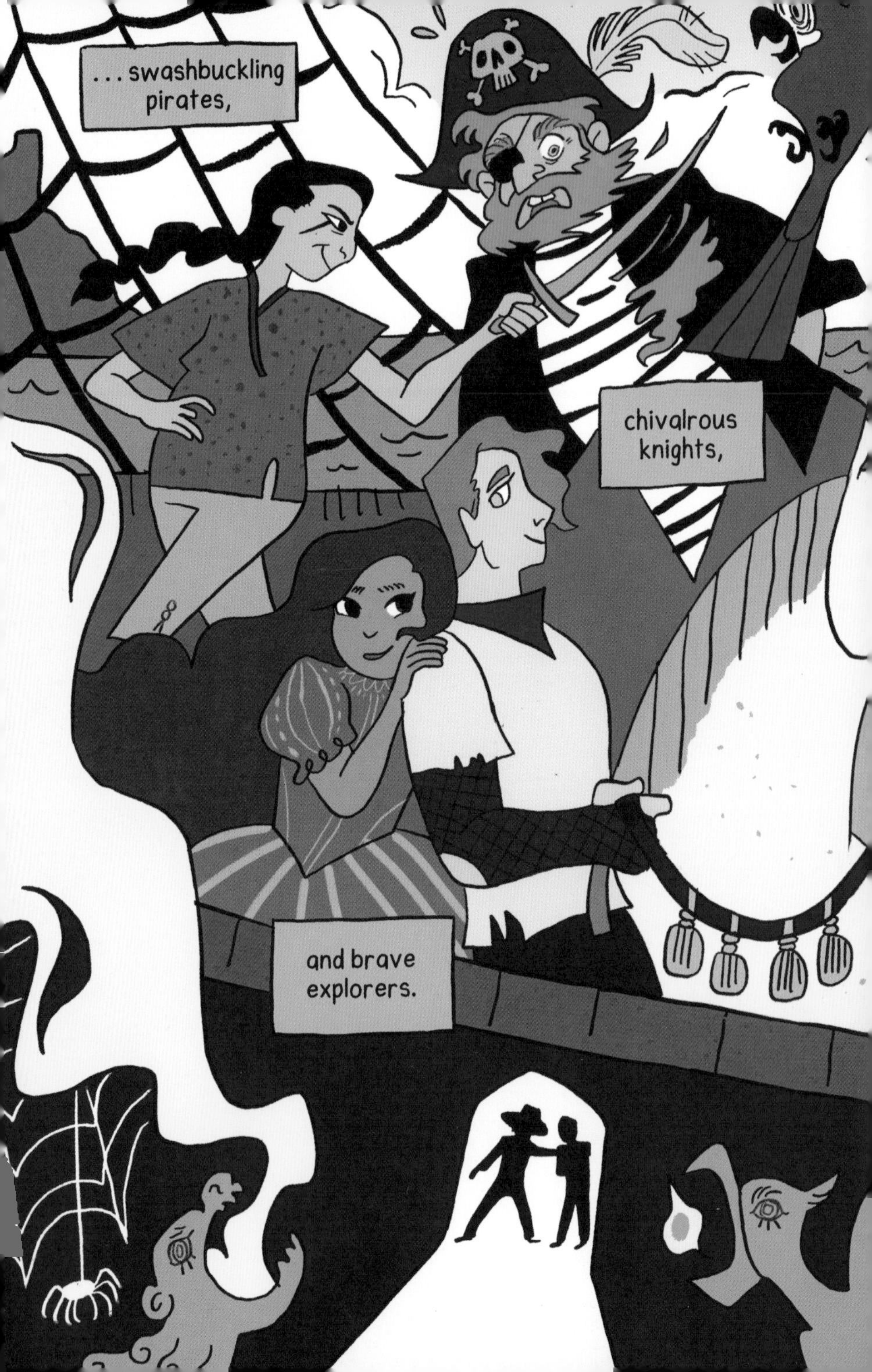
. . . swashbuckling pirates,
chivalrous knights,
and brave explorers.

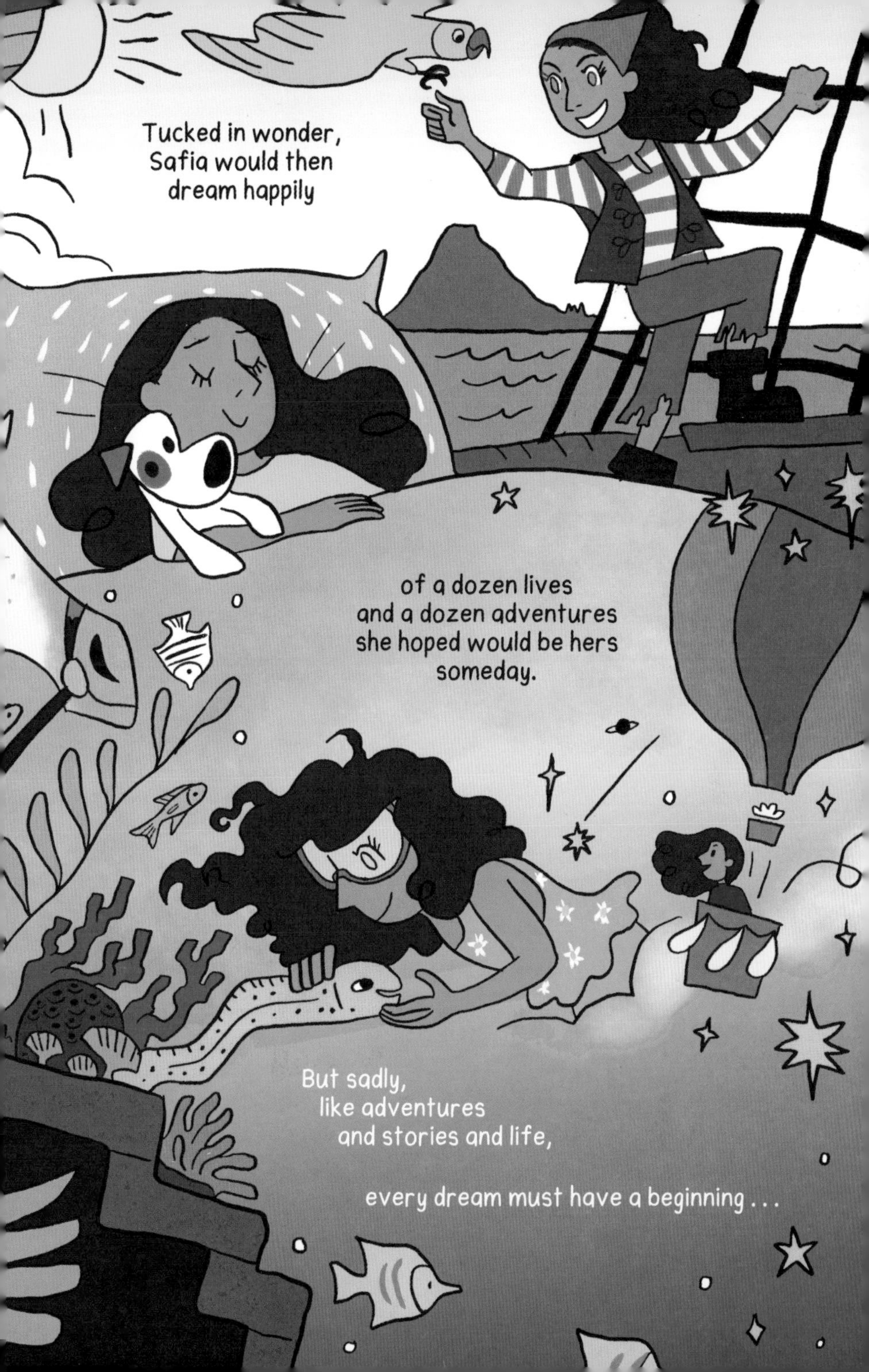
Tucked in wonder,
Safia would then
dream happily
of a dozen lives
and a dozen adventures
she hoped would be hers
someday.
But sadly,
like adventures
and stories and life,
every dream must have a beginning . . .

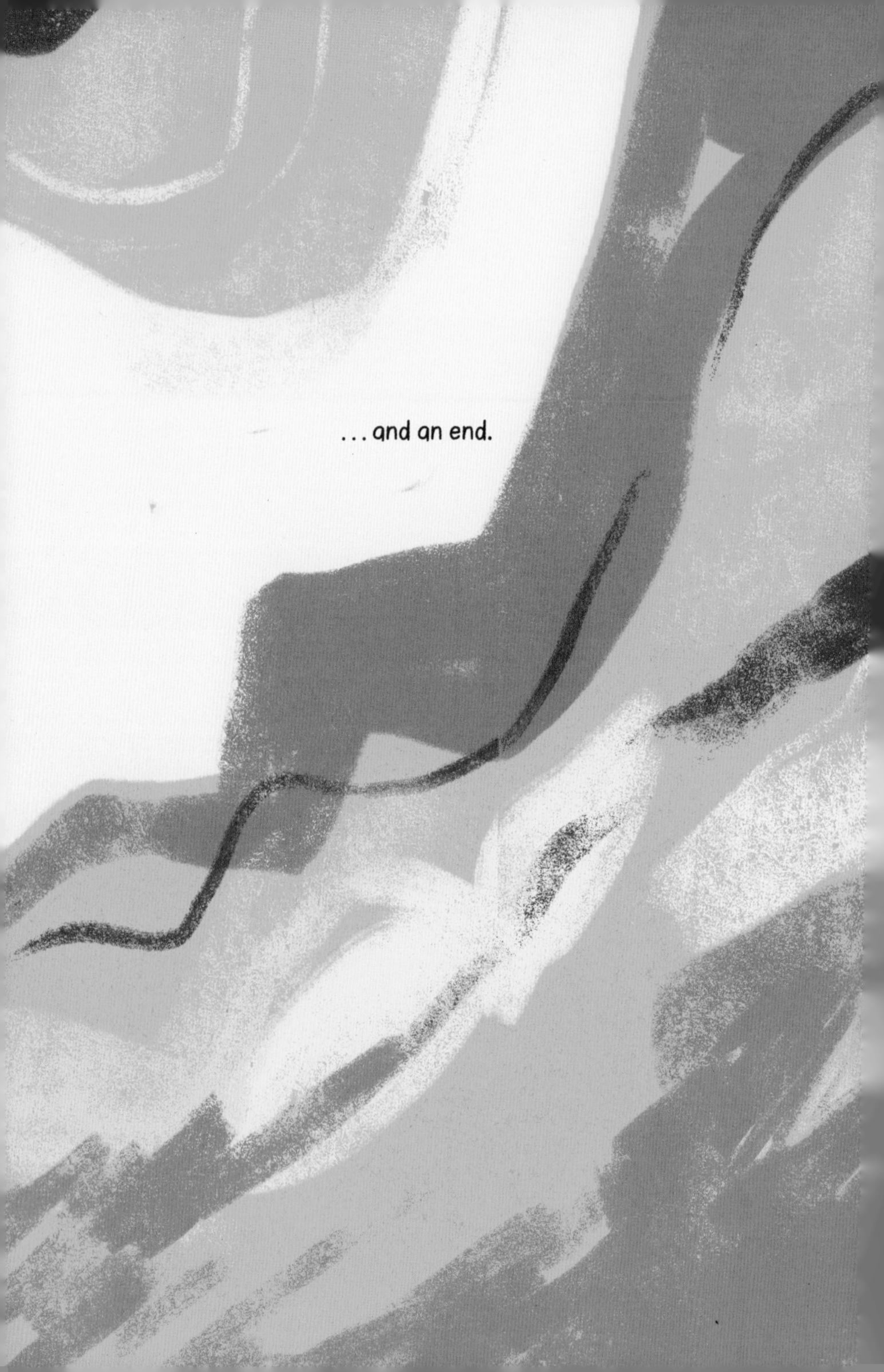
. . . and an end.

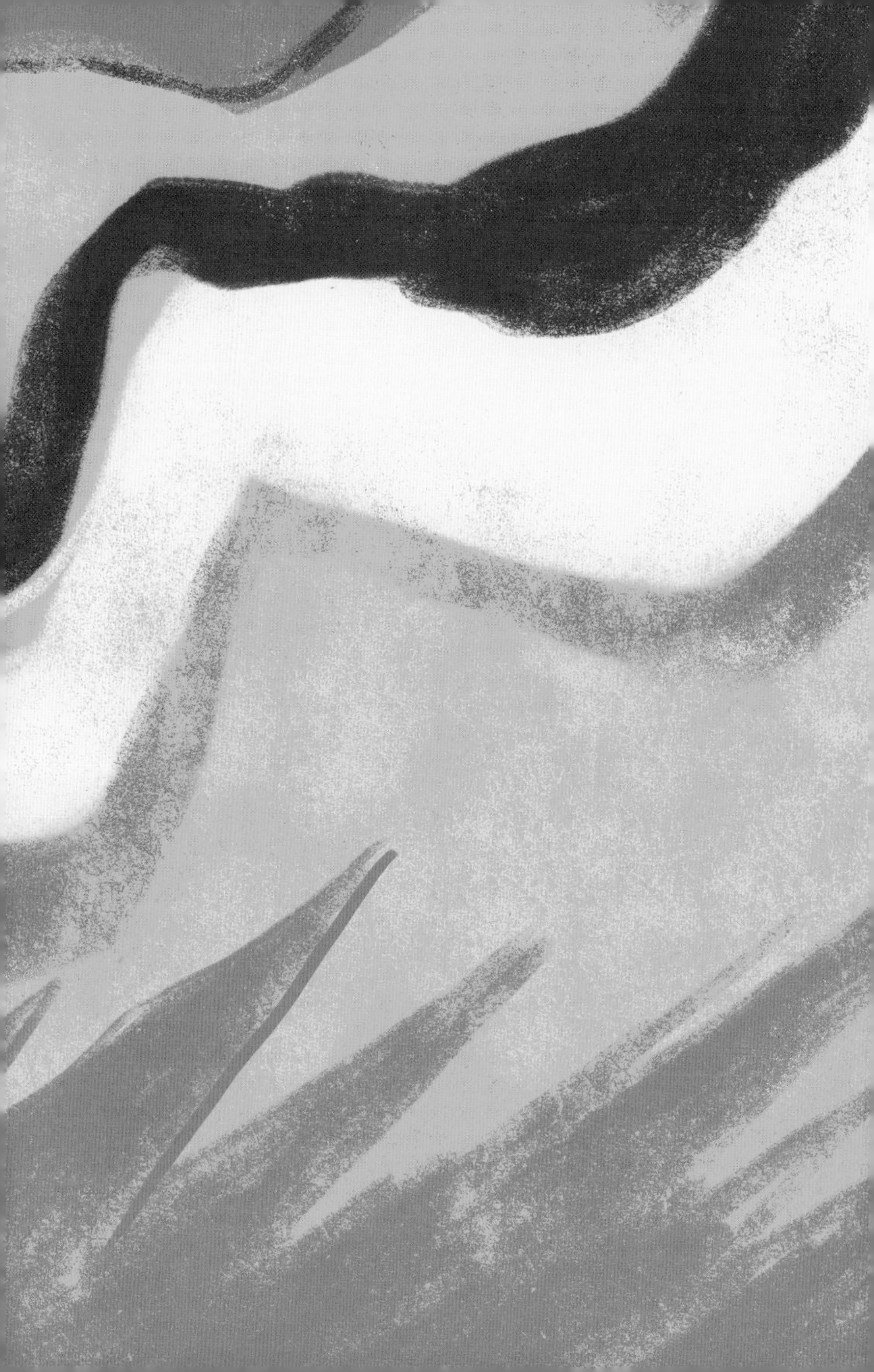

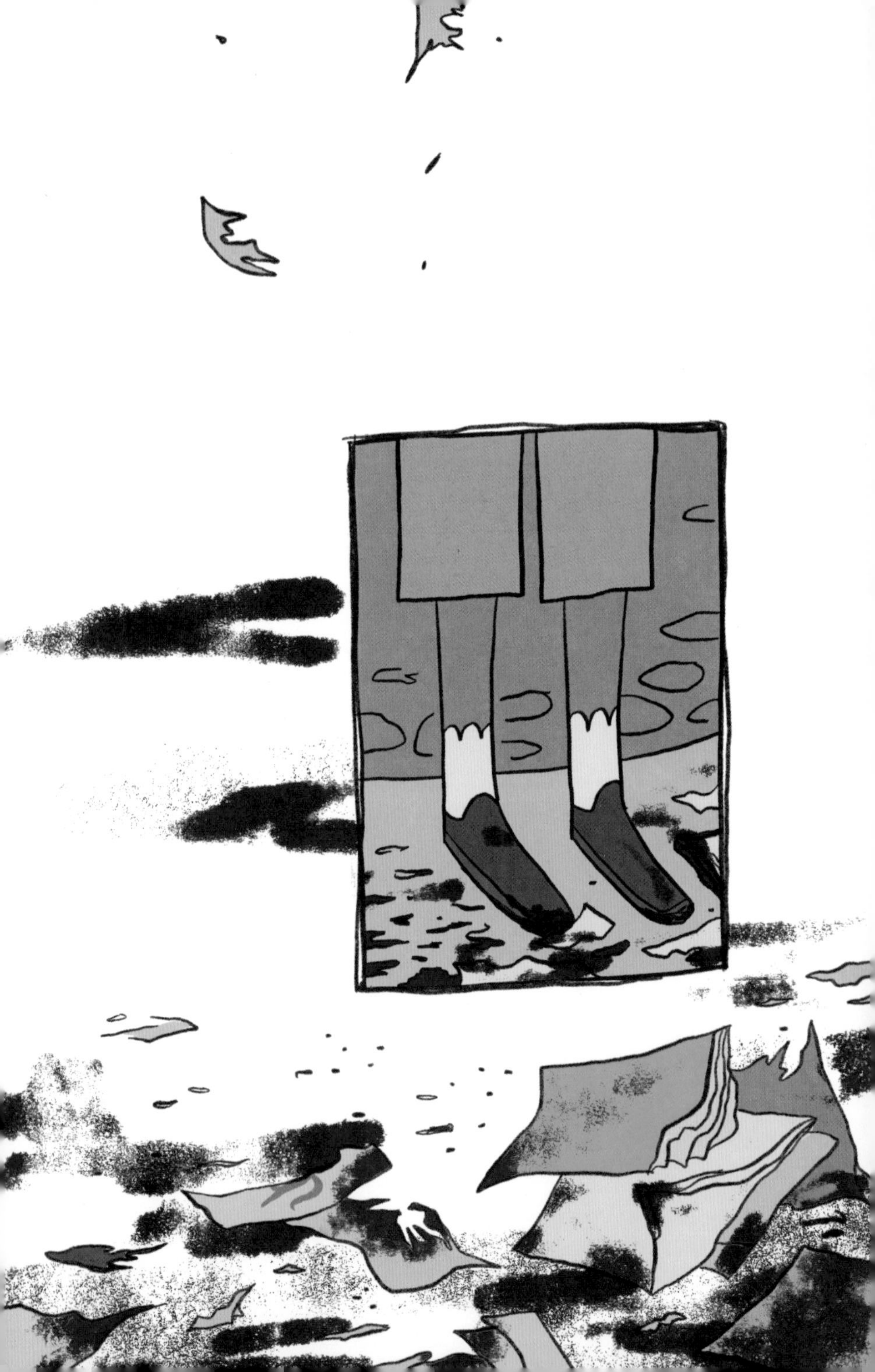

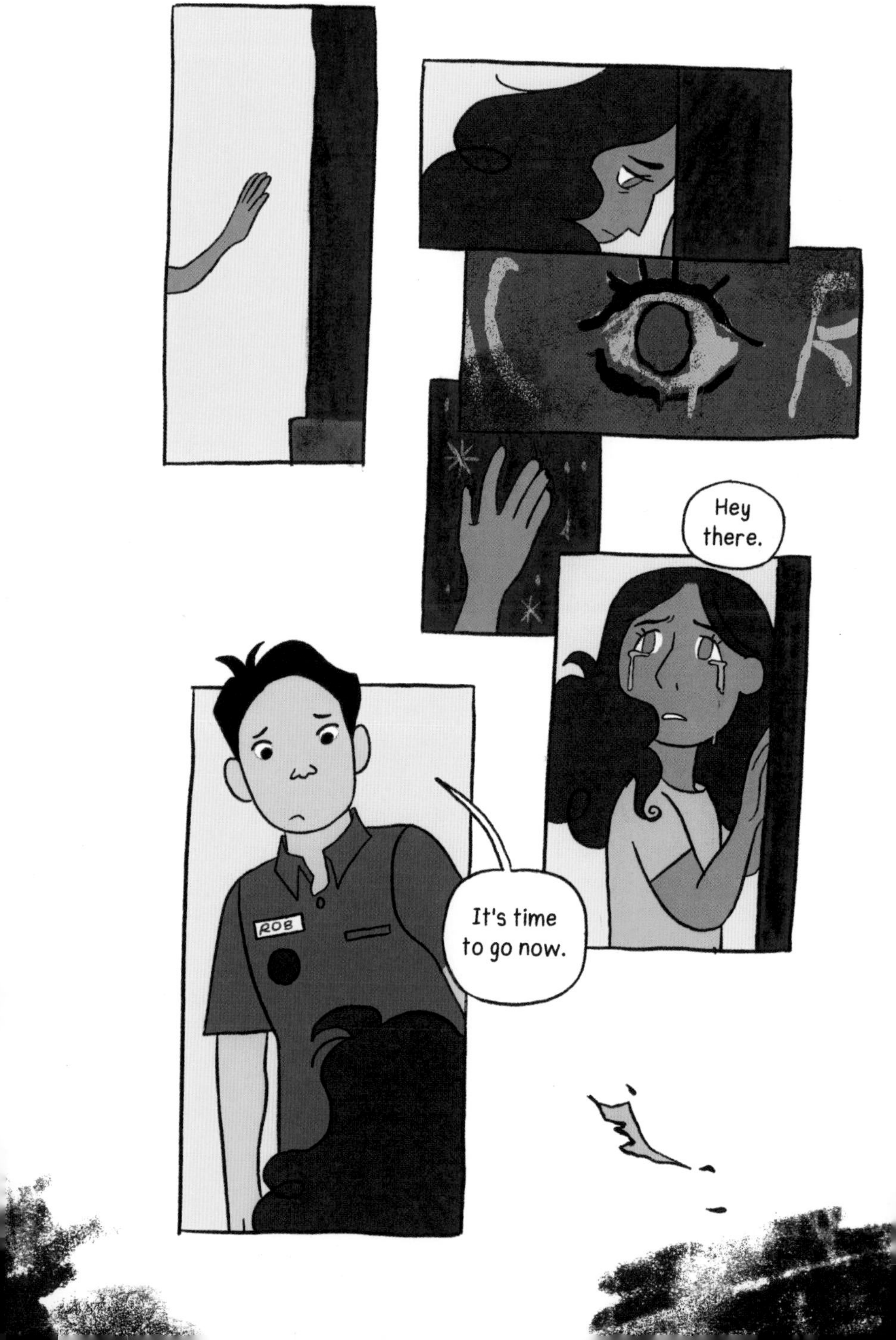
Hey there.
ROB
It's time to go now.

Once upon a time,
there was a little girl
who lived in a little bookshop
on a laneway that smelled
of roasted chestnuts
and pine leaves
opposite the lamppost
where the cobblestones
were uneven.

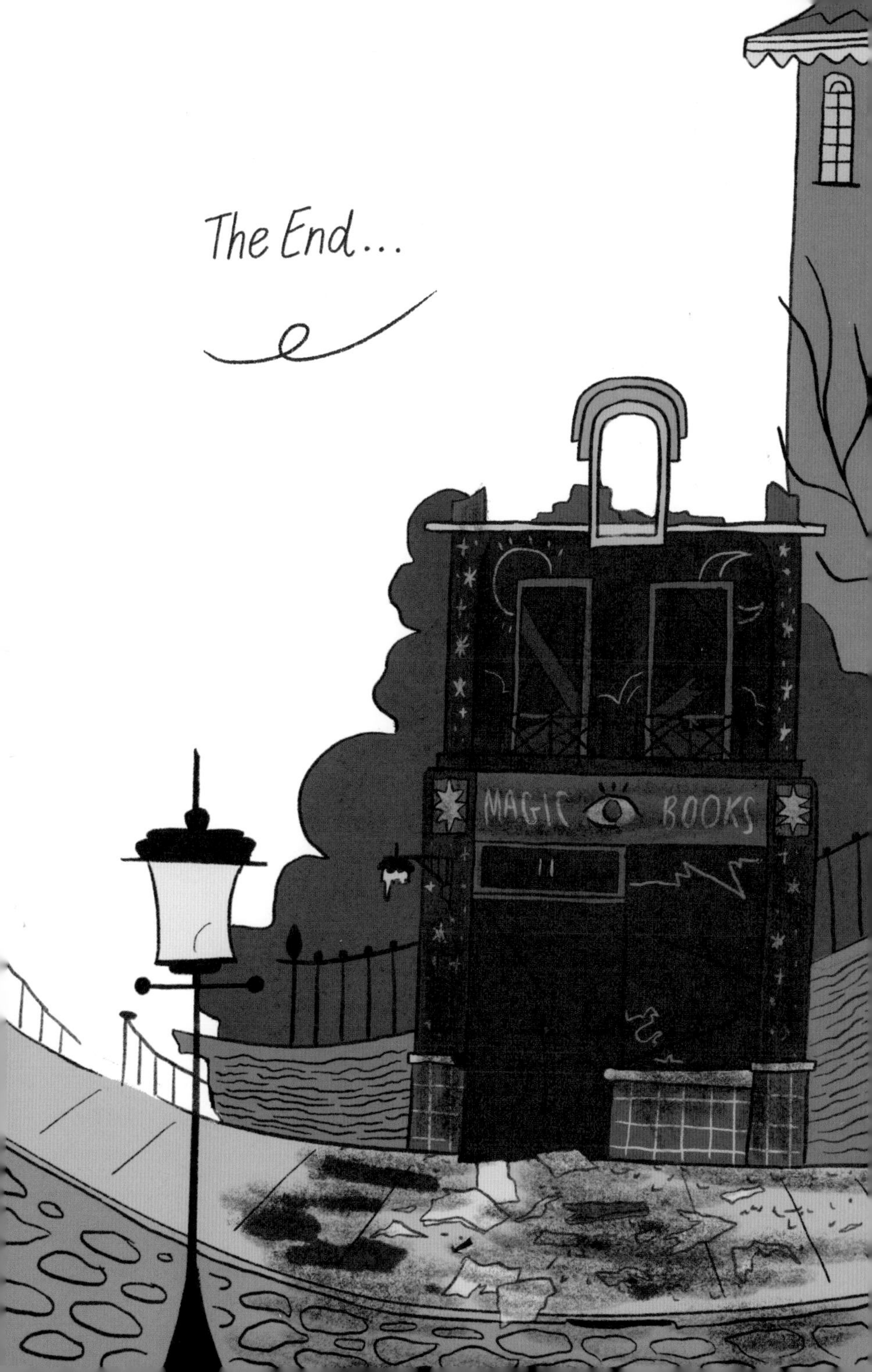
The End...
MAGIC BOOKS

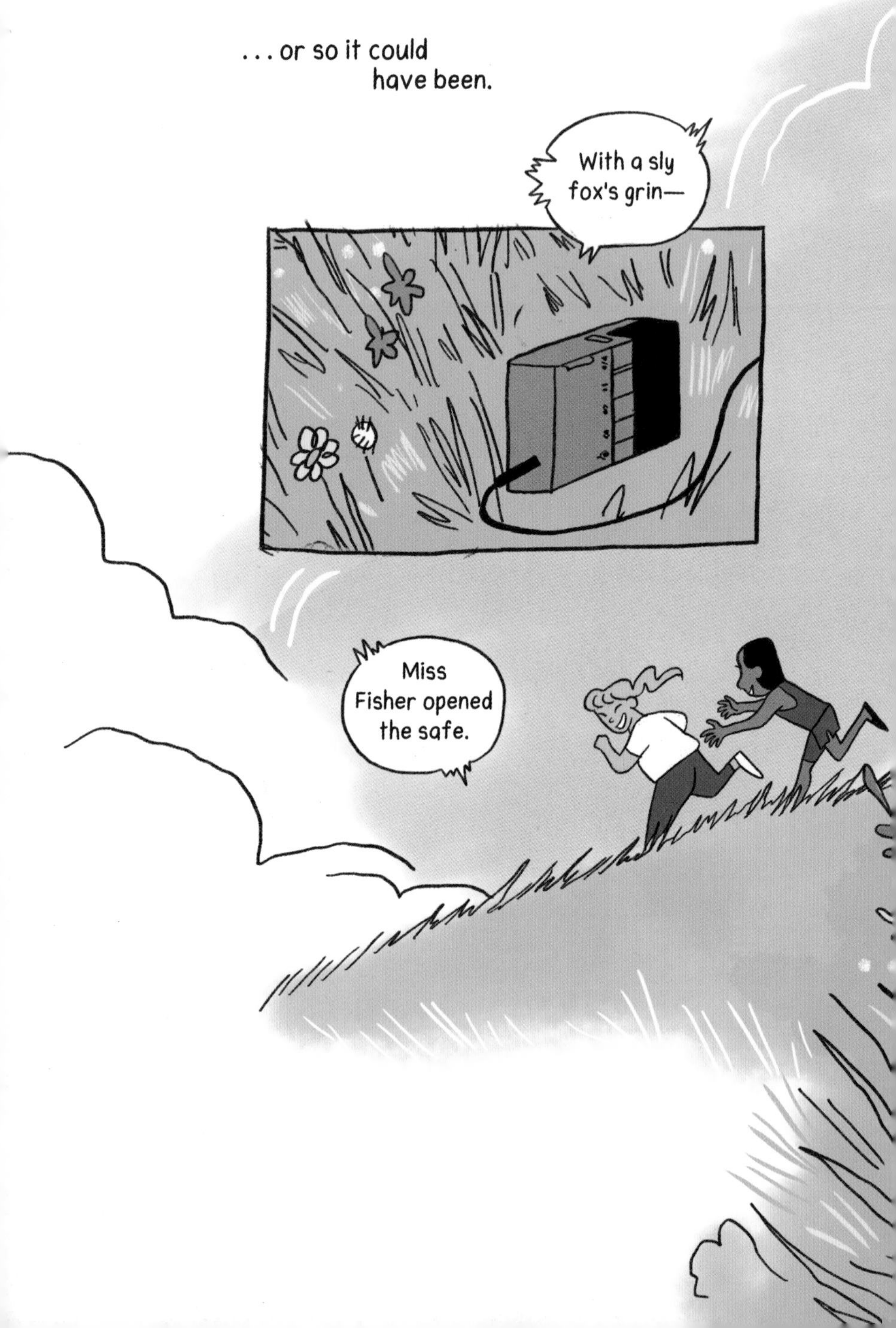
. . . or so it could have been.
With a sly fox's grin—
Miss Fisher opened the safe.

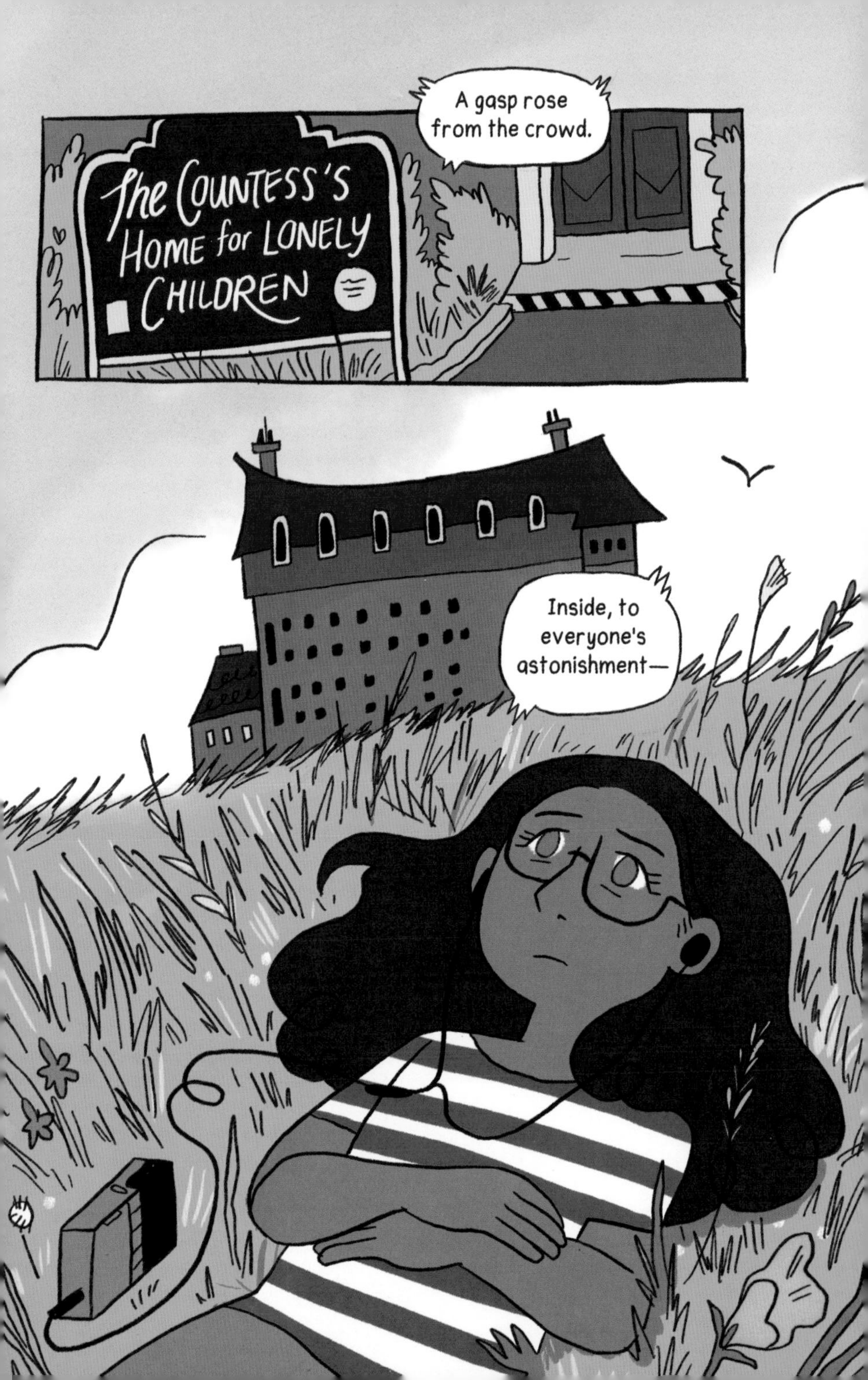
A gasp rose from the crowd.
The Countess's Home for Lonely Children
Inside, to everyone's astonishment—

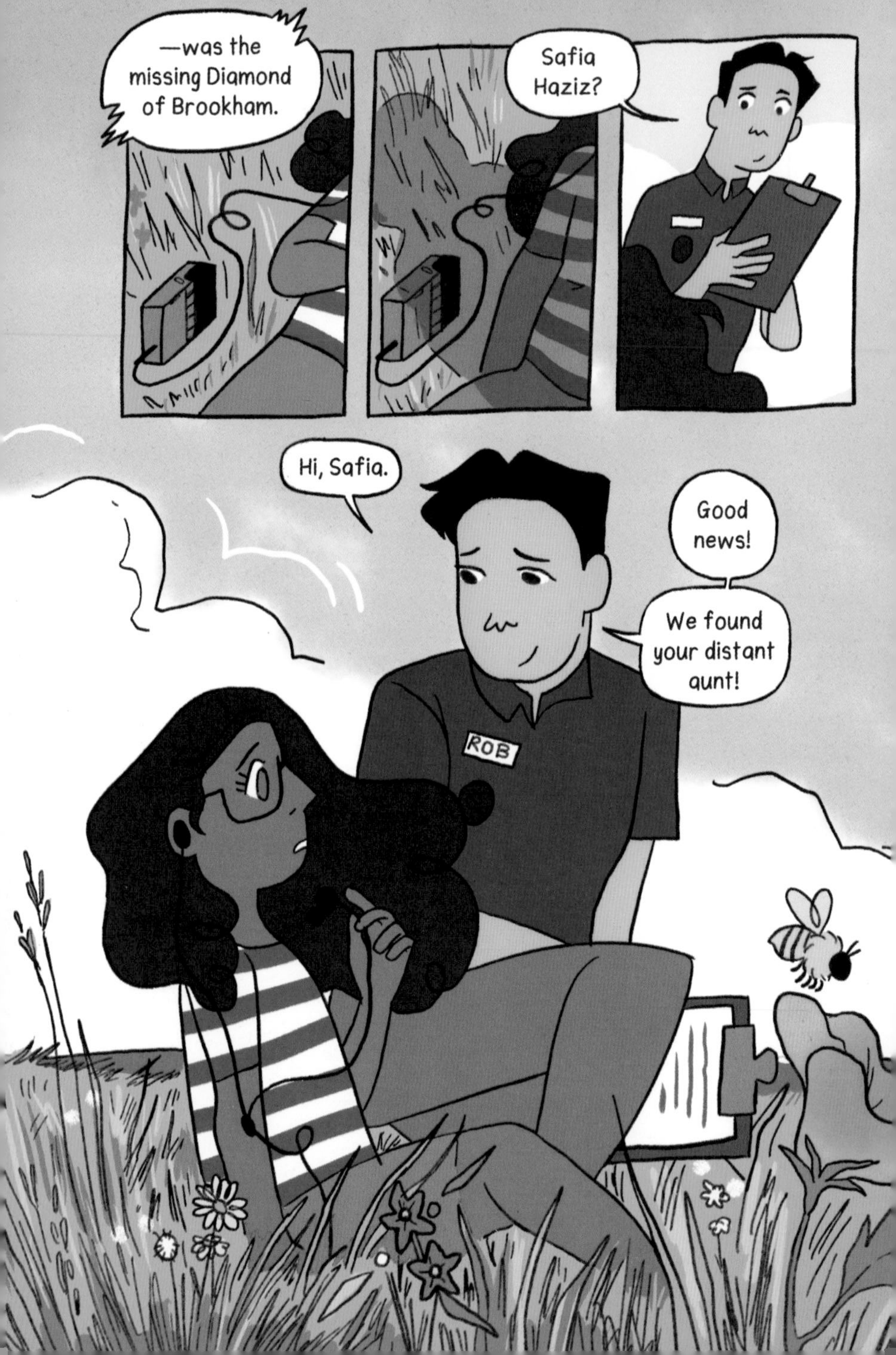
—was the missing Diamond of Brookham.
Safia Haziz?
Hi, Safia.
Good news!
We found your distant aunt!
ROB

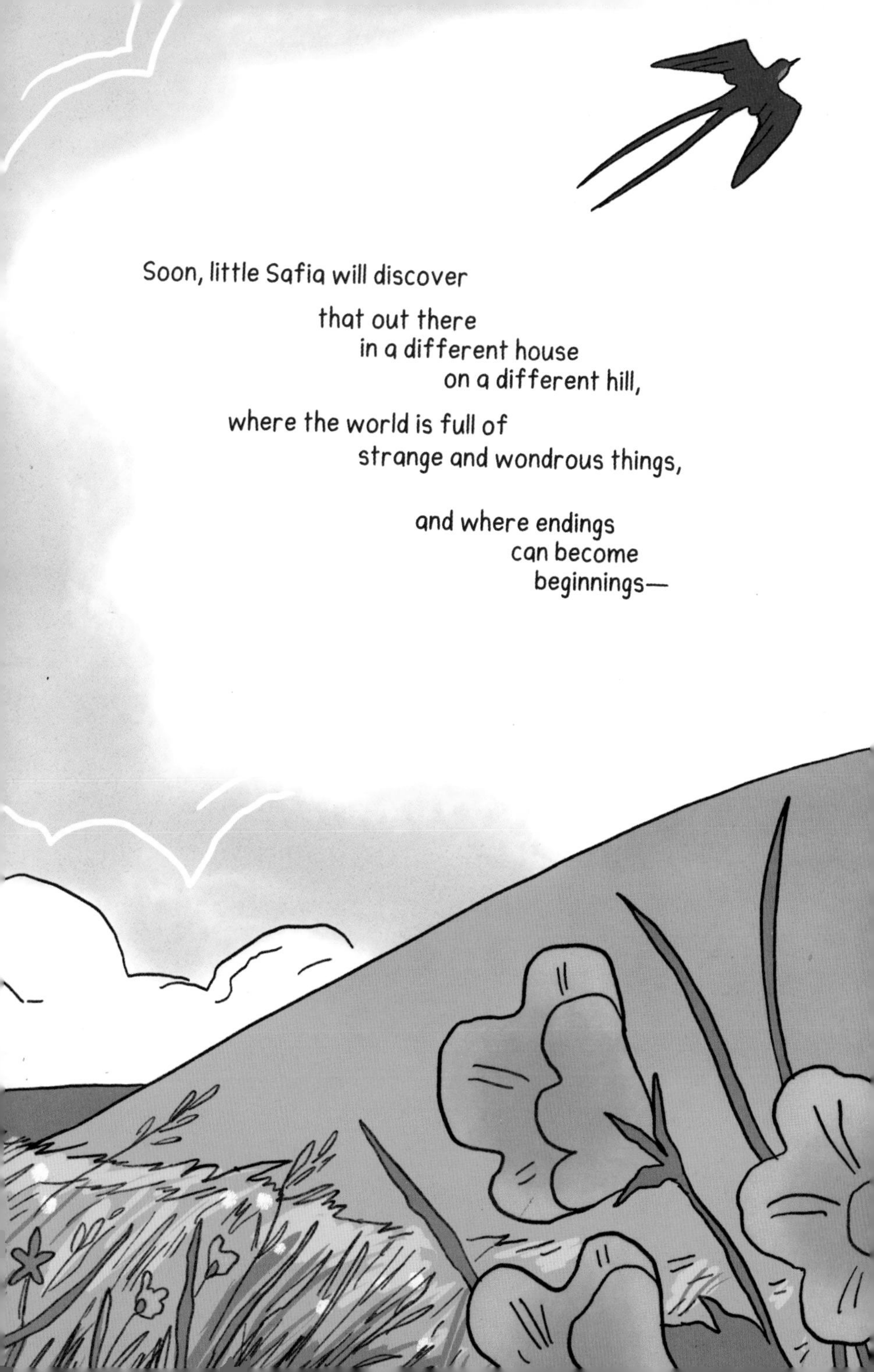

Soon, little Safia will discover
that out there
in a different house
on a different hill,
where the world is full of
strange and wondrous things,

and where endings
can become
beginnings—

—her greatest
adventure awaits.

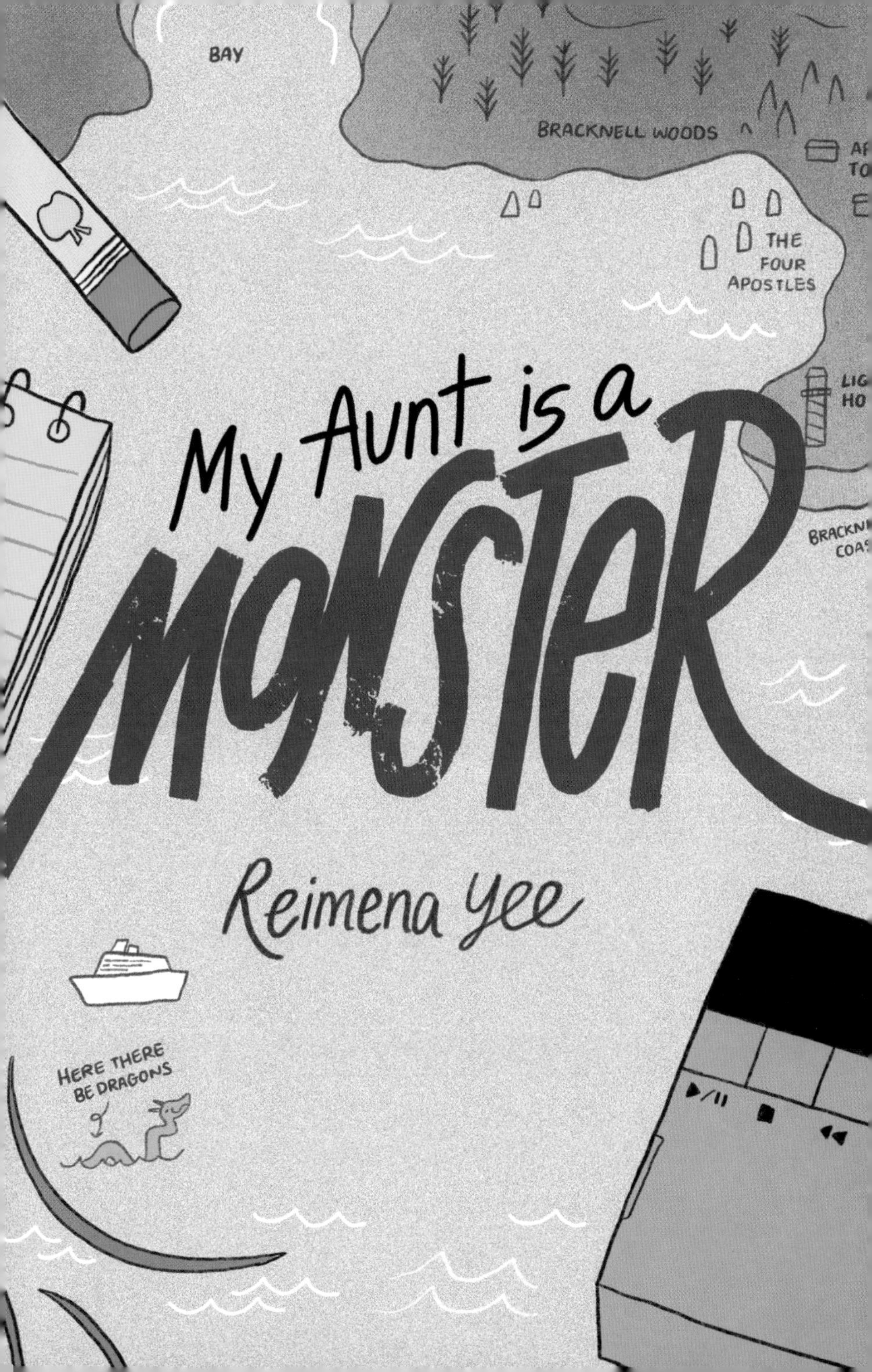
BAY
BRACKNELL WOODS
THE FOUR APOSTLES
My Aunt is a
MONSTER
Reimena Yee
HERE THERE BE DRAGONS

Chapter One

Walteranne Hakim Whimsy . . .
CHLC
Walteranne Hakim Whimsy

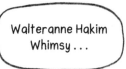

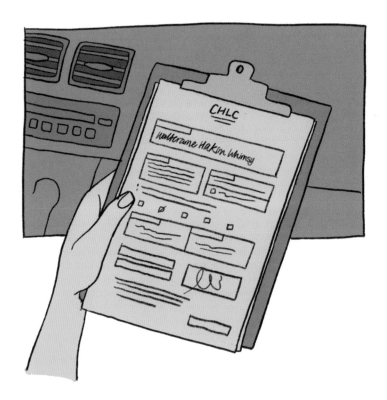

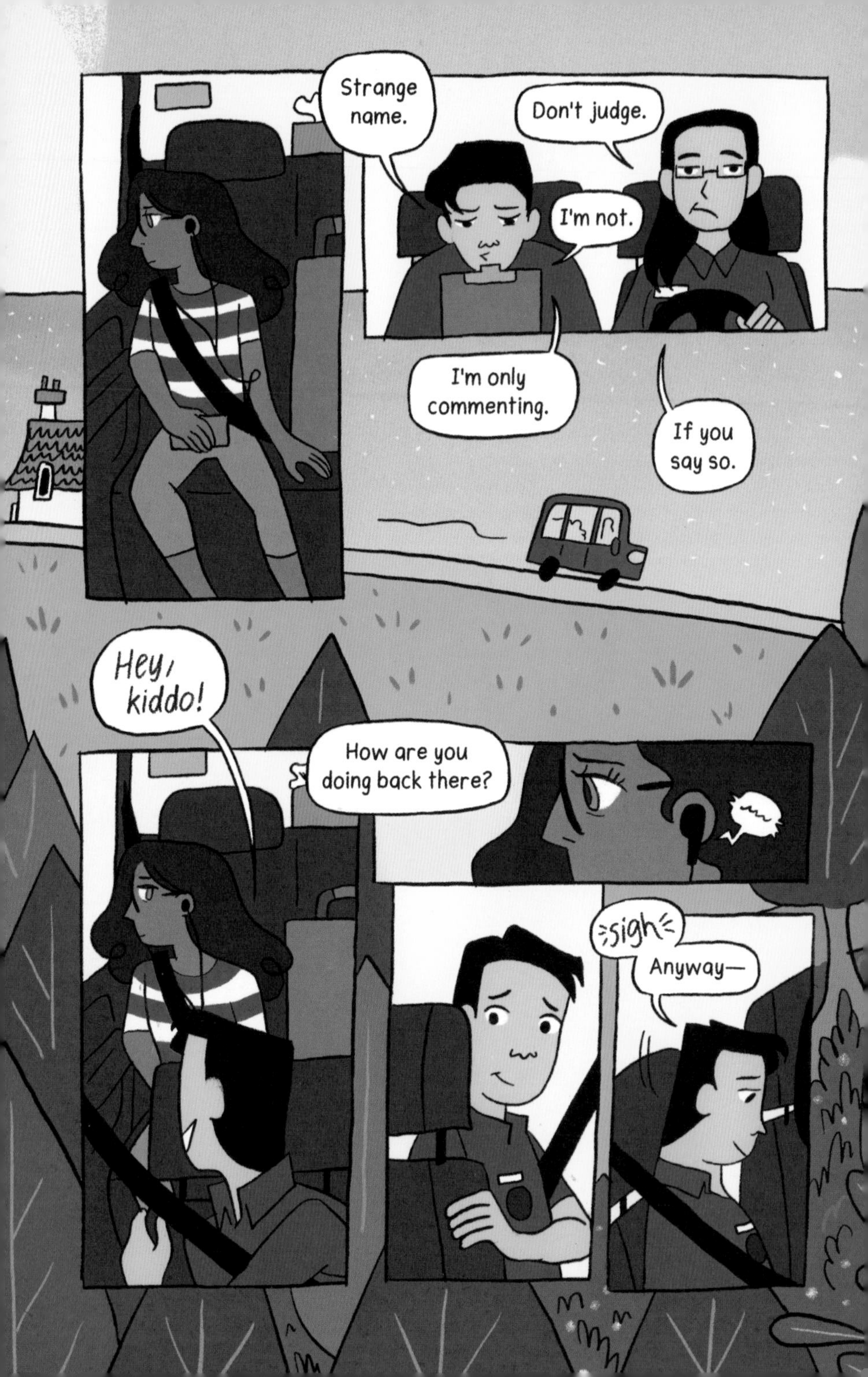
Strange name.
Don't judge.
I'm not.
I'm only commenting.
If you say so.
Hey, kiddo!
How are you doing back there?
sigh
Anyway—

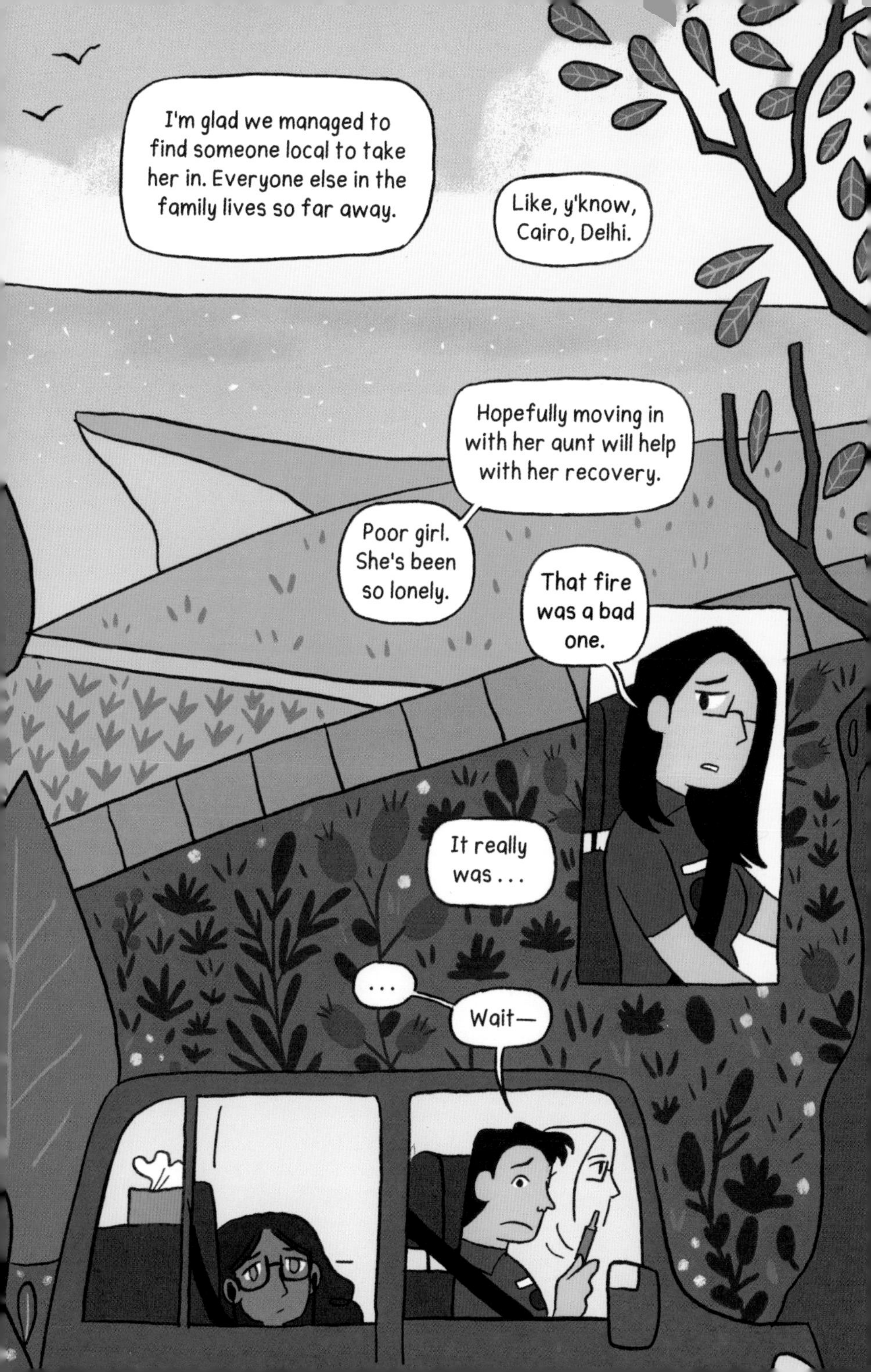
I'm glad we managed to find someone local to take her in. Everyone else in the family lives so far away.
Like, y'know, Cairo, Delhi.
Hopefully moving in with her aunt will help with her recovery.
Poor girl. She's been so lonely.
That fire was a bad one.
It really was . . .
. . .
Wait—

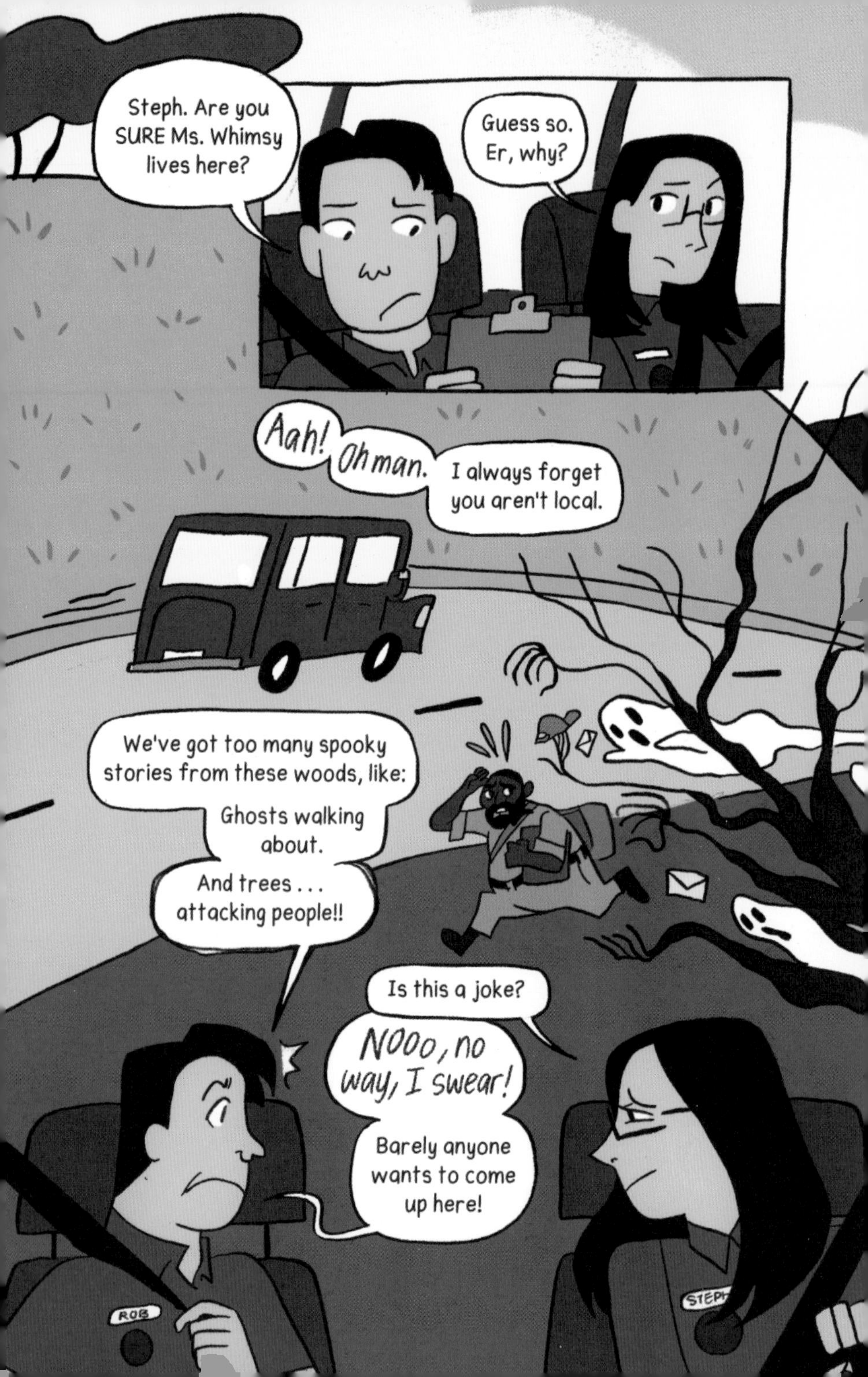

Steph. Are you SURE Ms. Whimsy lives here?
Guess so. Er, why?
Aah!
Oh man.
I always forget you aren't local.
We've got too many spooky stories from these woods, like:
Ghosts walking about.
And trees . . . attacking people!!
Is this a joke?
NOOo, no way, I swear!
Barely anyone wants to come up here!
ROB
STEPH

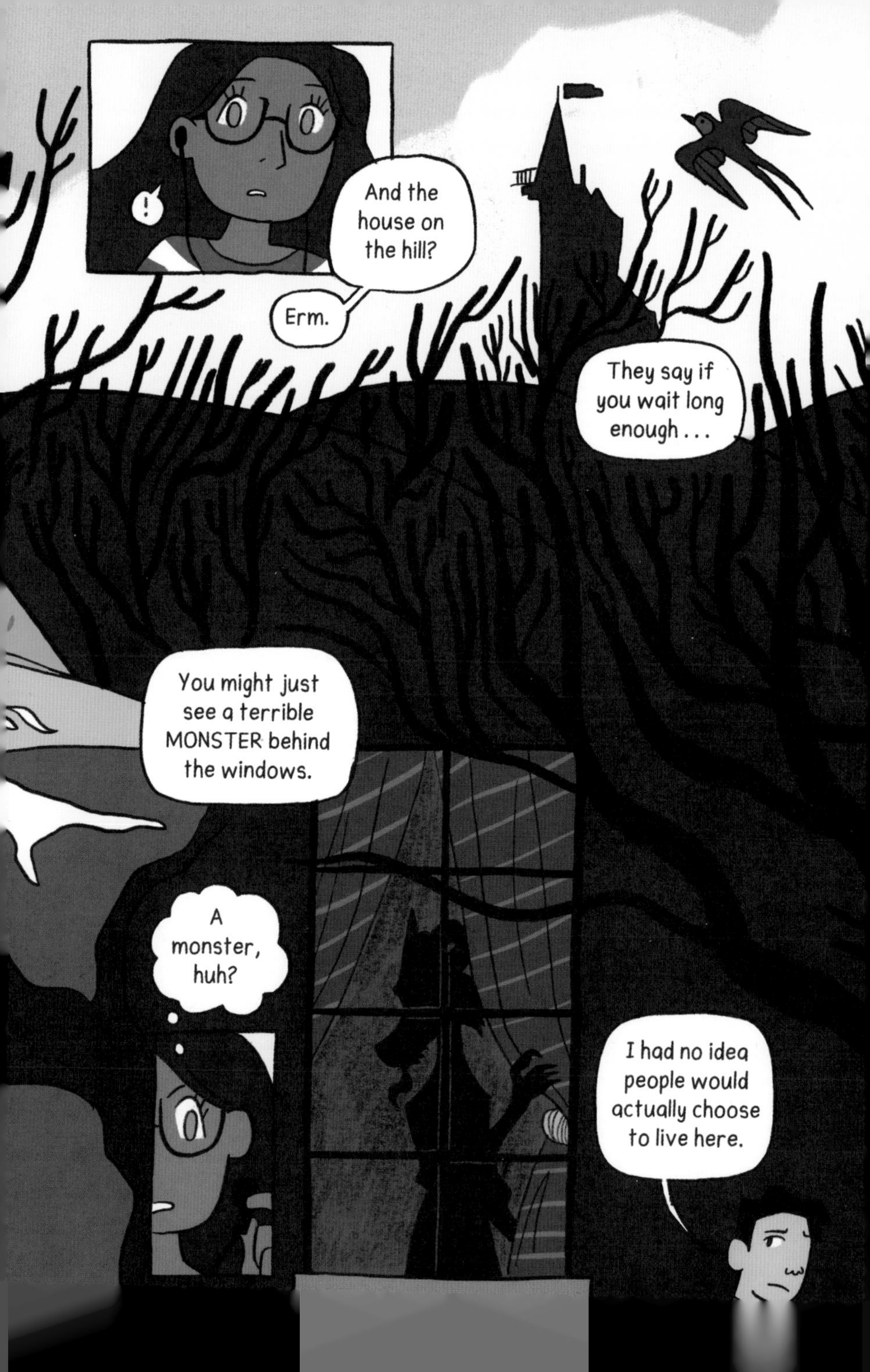
!
And the house on the hill?
Erm.
They say if you wait long enough . . .
You might just see a terrible MONSTER behind the windows.
A monster, huh?
I had no idea people would actually choose to live here.

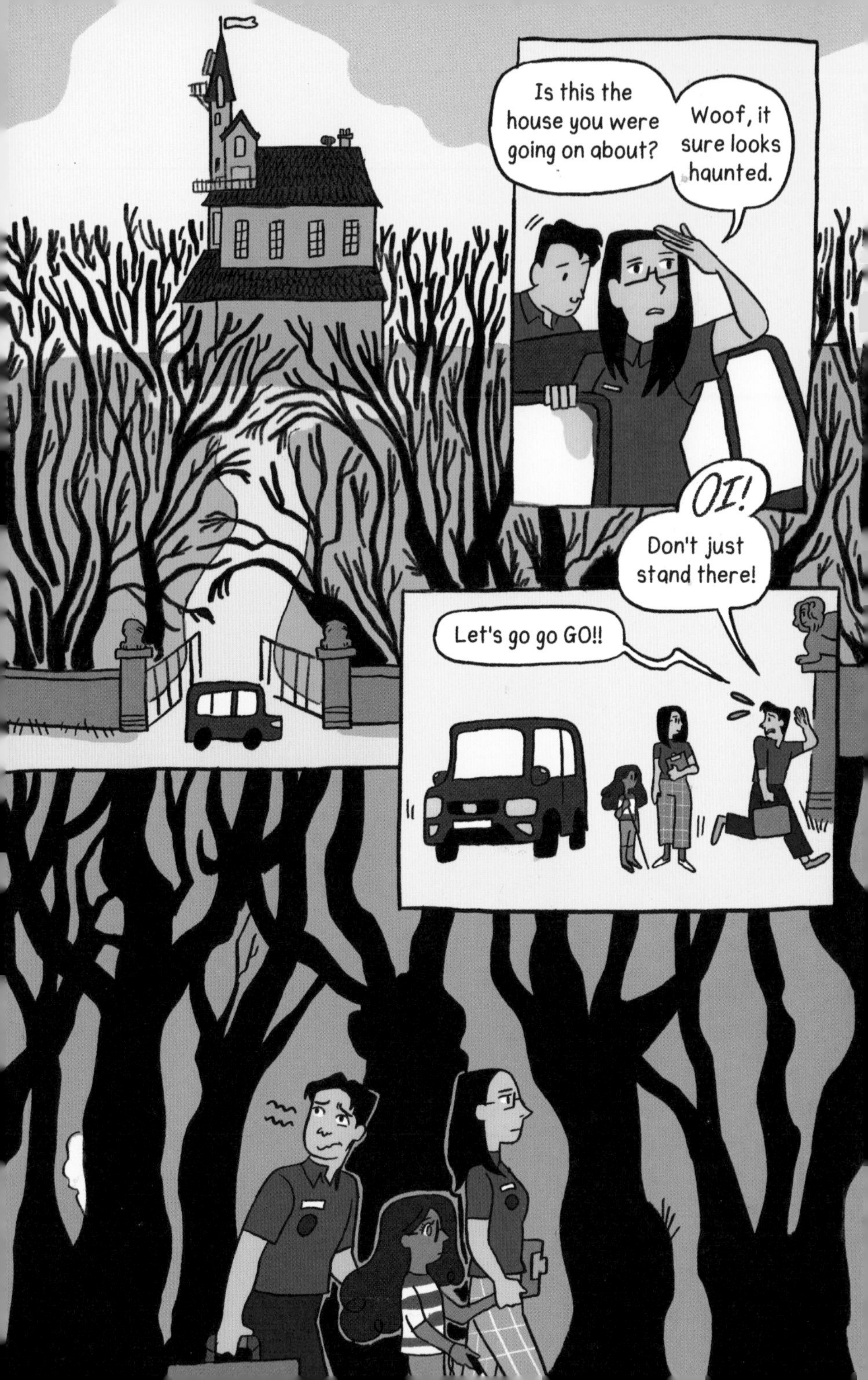
Is this the house you were going on about?
Woof, it sure looks haunted.
OI!
Don't just stand there!
Let's go go GO!!

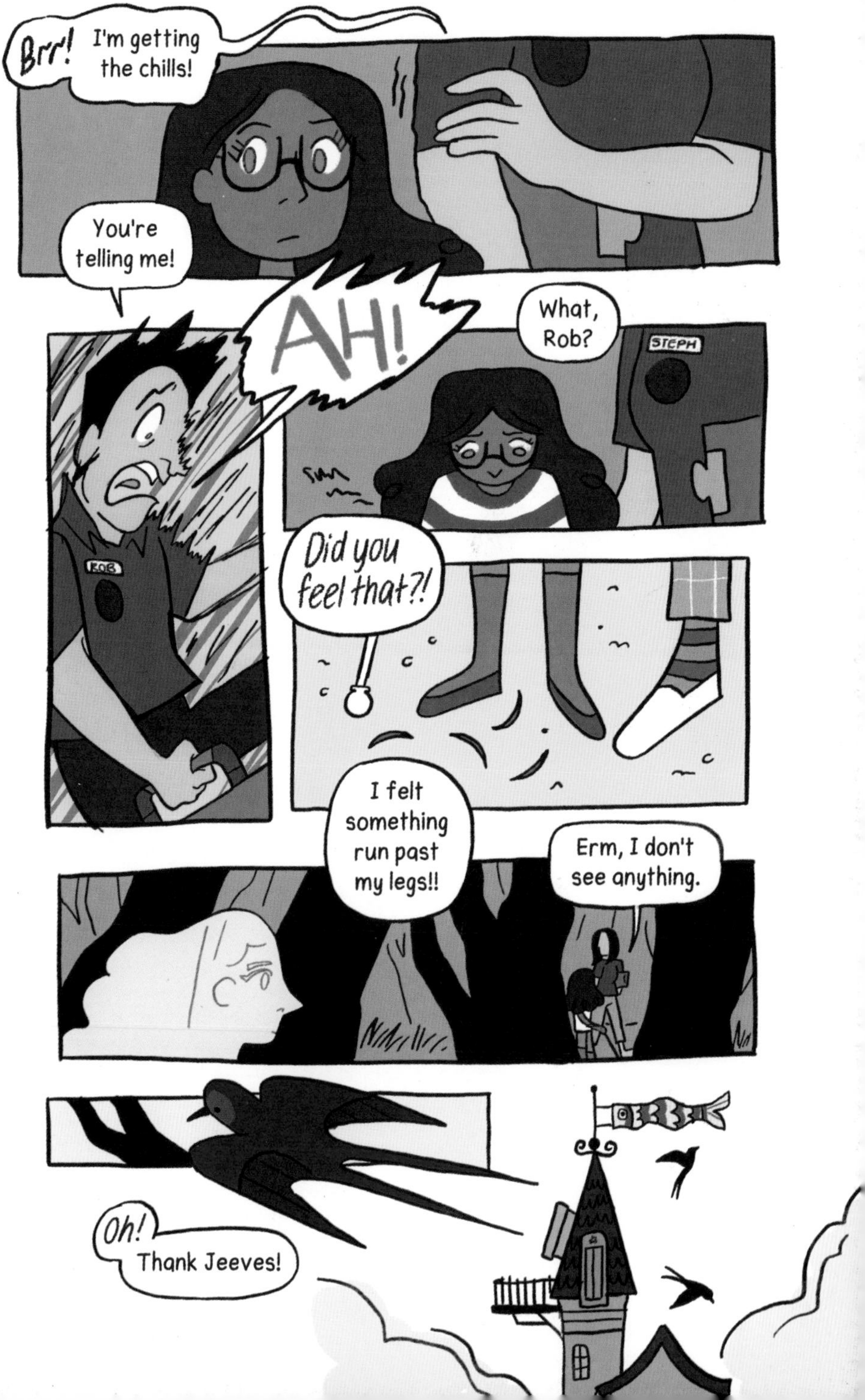
Brr! I'm getting the chills!
You're telling me!
AH!
What, Rob?
STEPH
ROB
Did you feel that?!
I felt something run past my legs!!
Erm, I don't see anything.
Oh! Thank Jeeves!

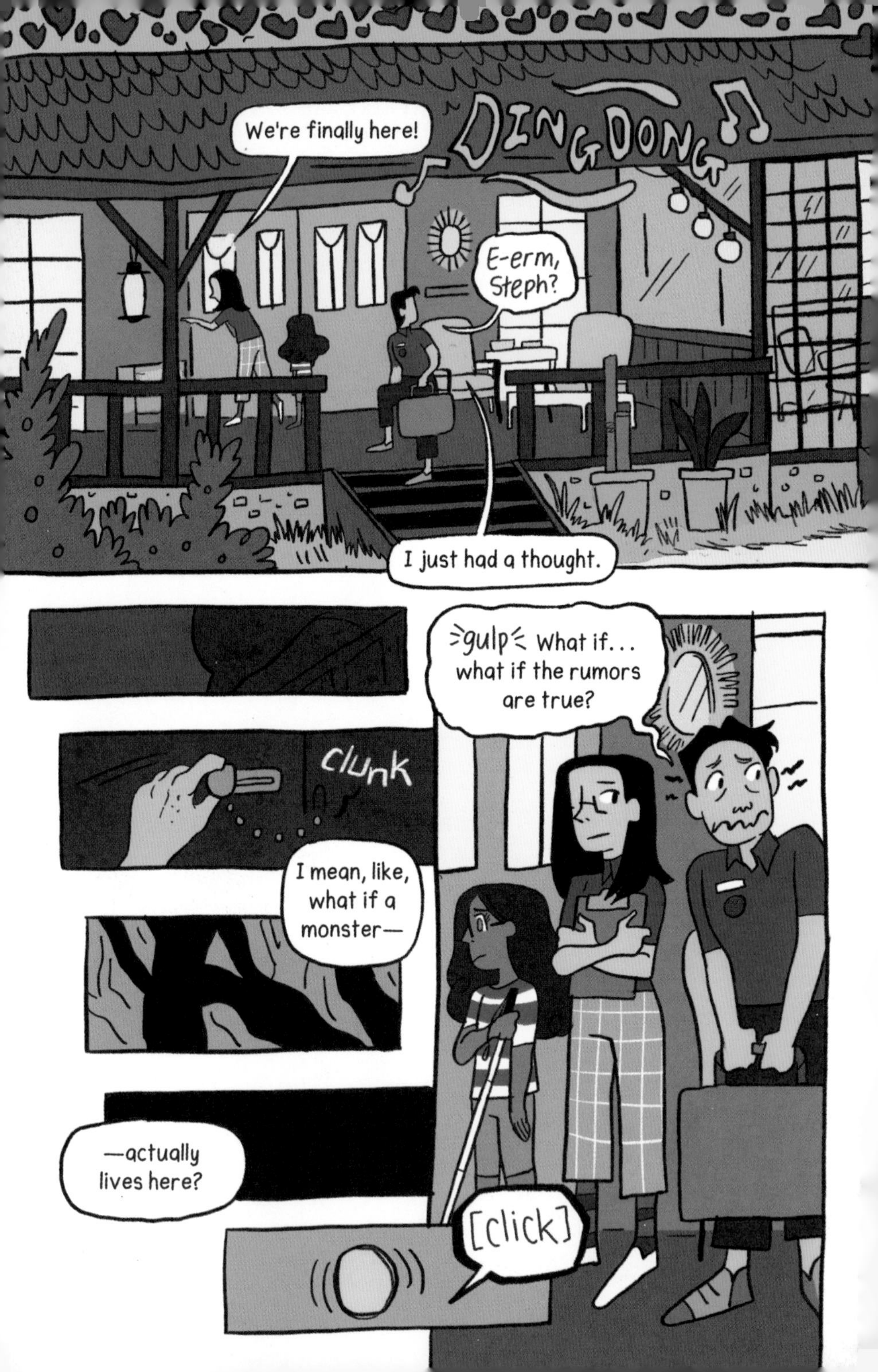

We're finally here!
DING DONG
E-erm, Steph?
I just had a thought.
gulp What if... what if the rumors are true?
clunk
I mean, like, what if a monster—
—actually lives here?
[click]

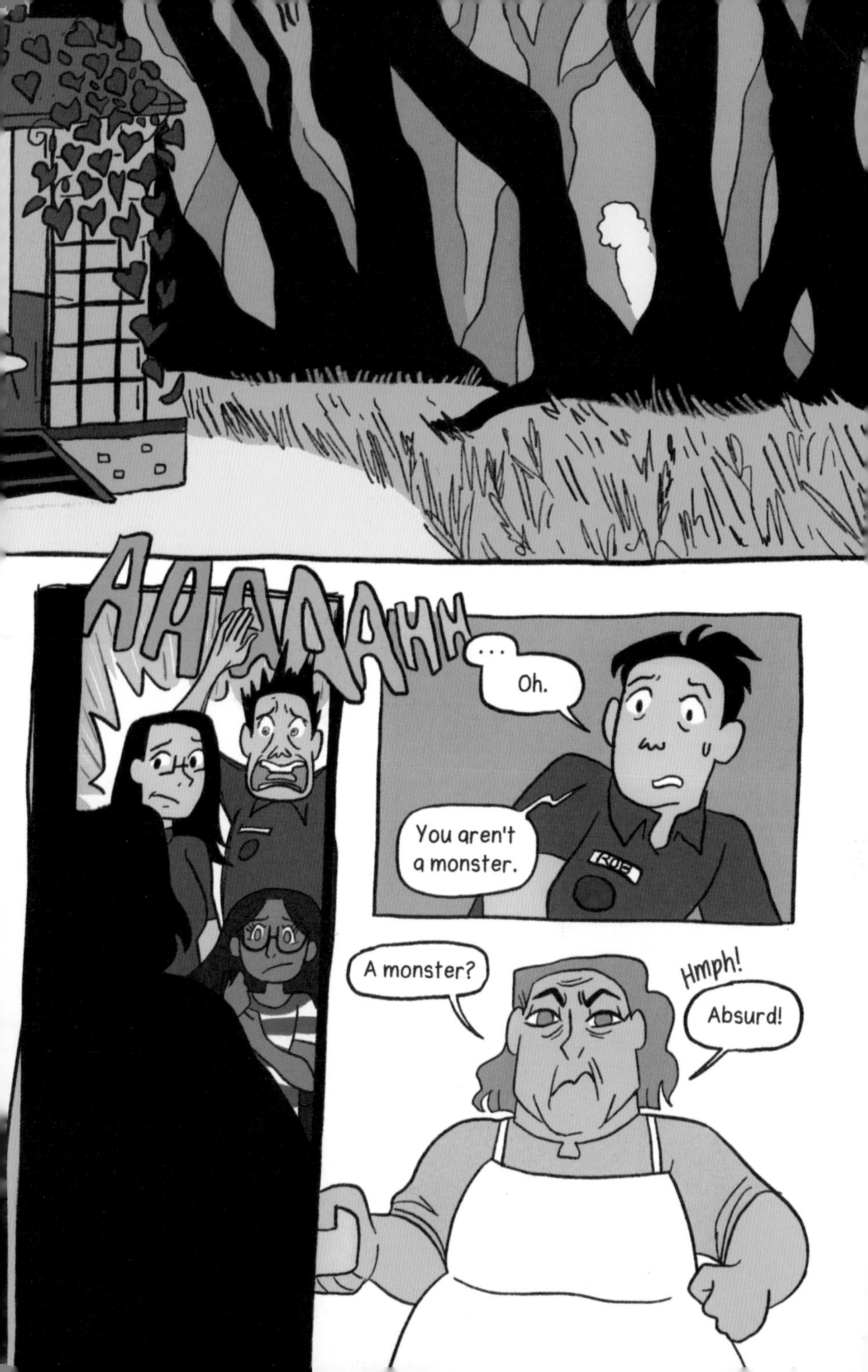
AAAAAHH
...
Oh.
You aren't a monster.
A monster?
Hmph!
Absurd!

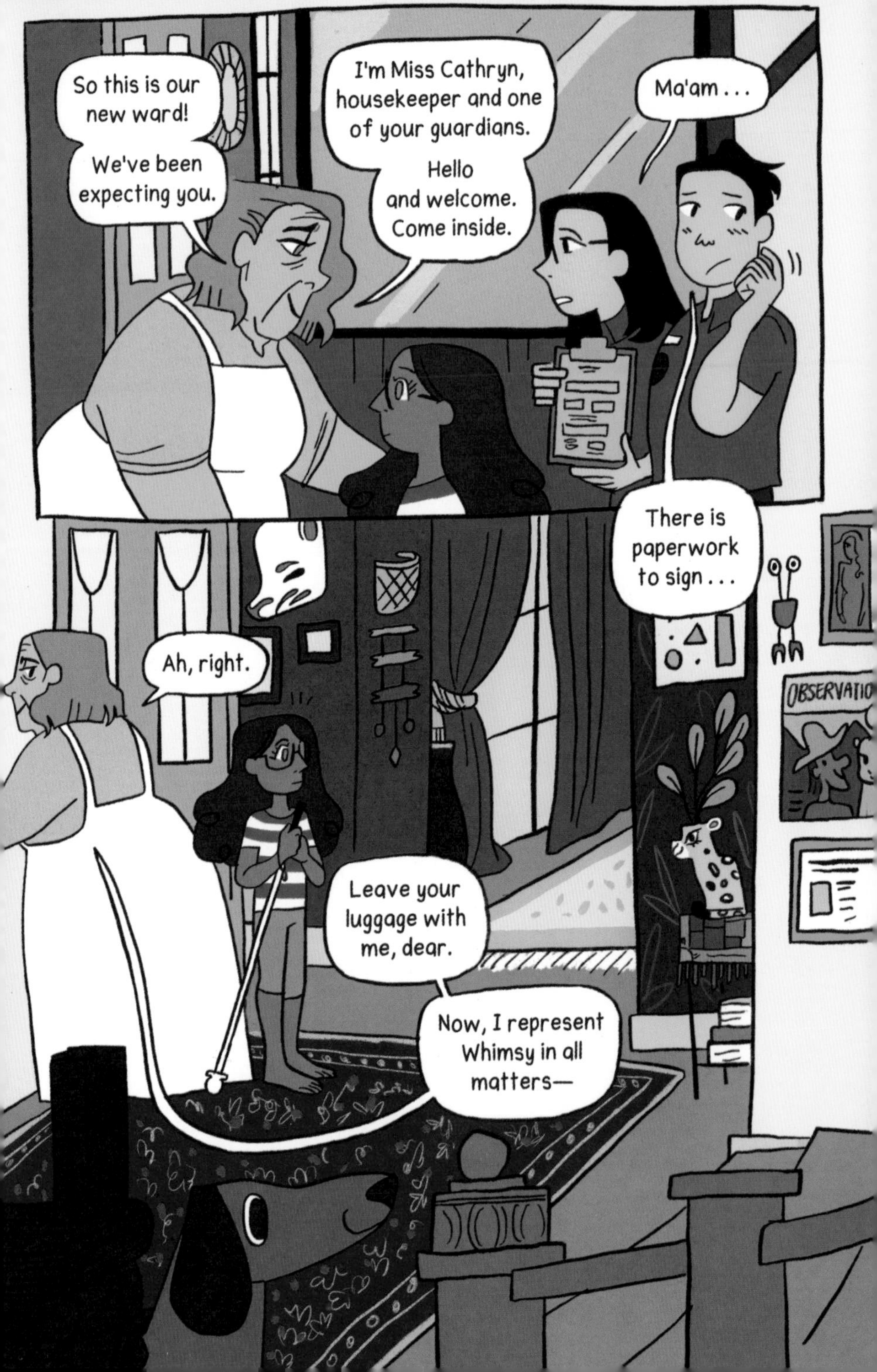
So this is our new ward!
We've been expecting you.
I'm Miss Cathryn, housekeeper and one of your guardians.
Hello and welcome. Come inside.
Ma'am . . .
There is paperwork to sign . . .
Ah, right.
OBSERVATIO
Leave your luggage with me, dear.
Now, I represent Whimsy in all matters—

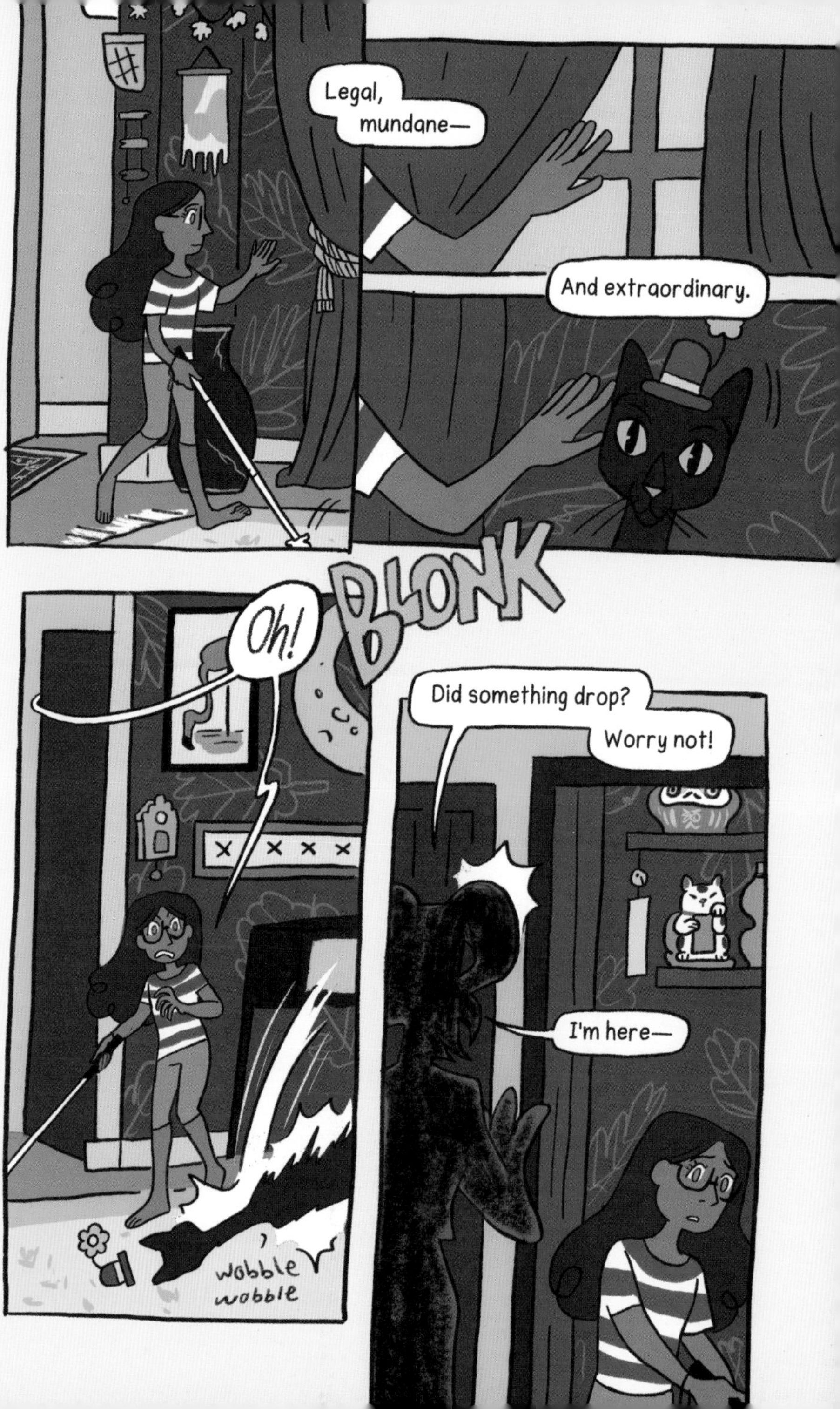
Legal, mundane—
And extraordinary.
Oh!
BLONK
wobble wobble
Did something drop?
Worry not!
I'm here—

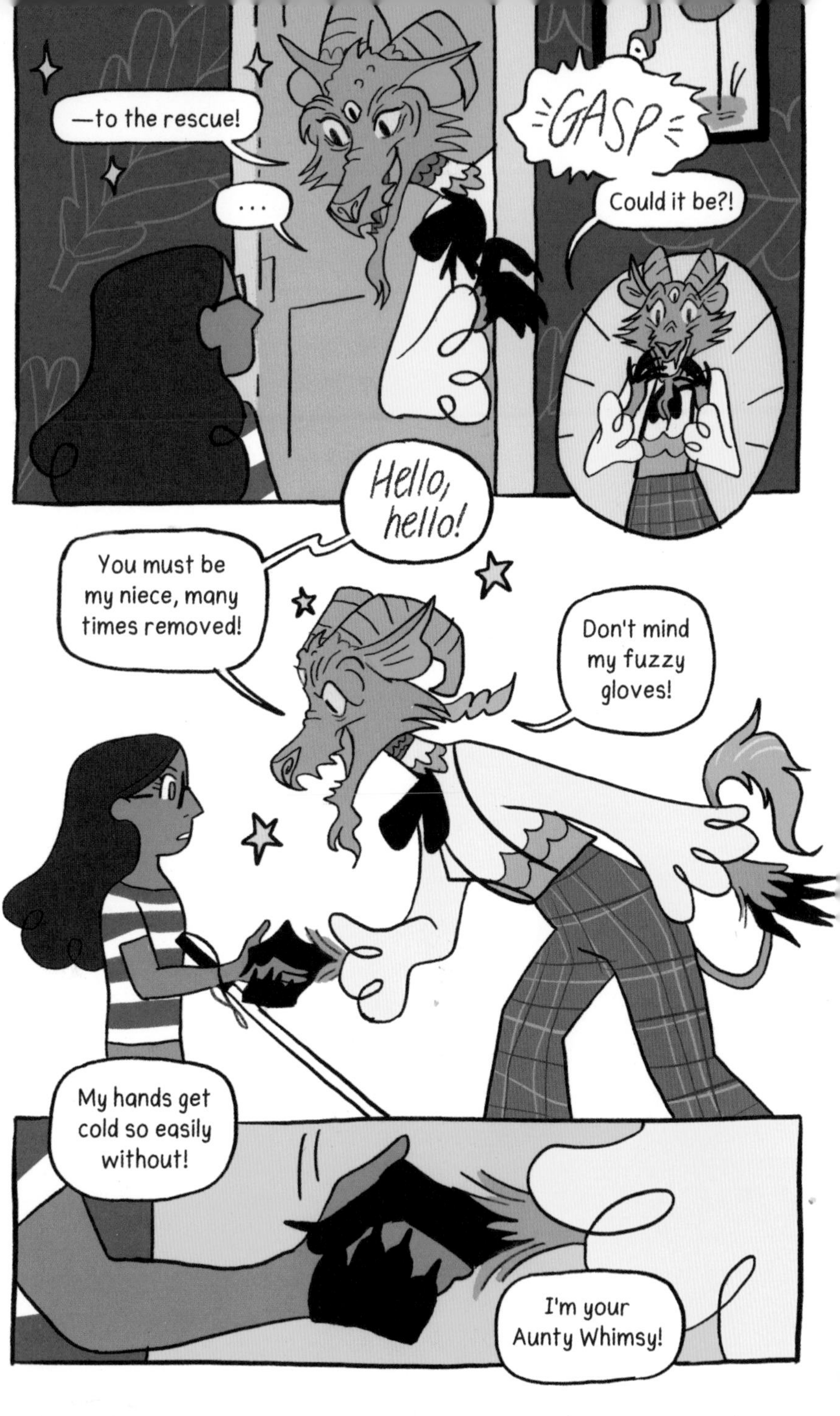
—to the rescue!
...
GASP
Could it be?!
Hello, hello!
You must be my niece, many times removed!
Don't mind my fuzzy gloves!
My hands get cold so easily without!
I'm your Aunty Whimsy!

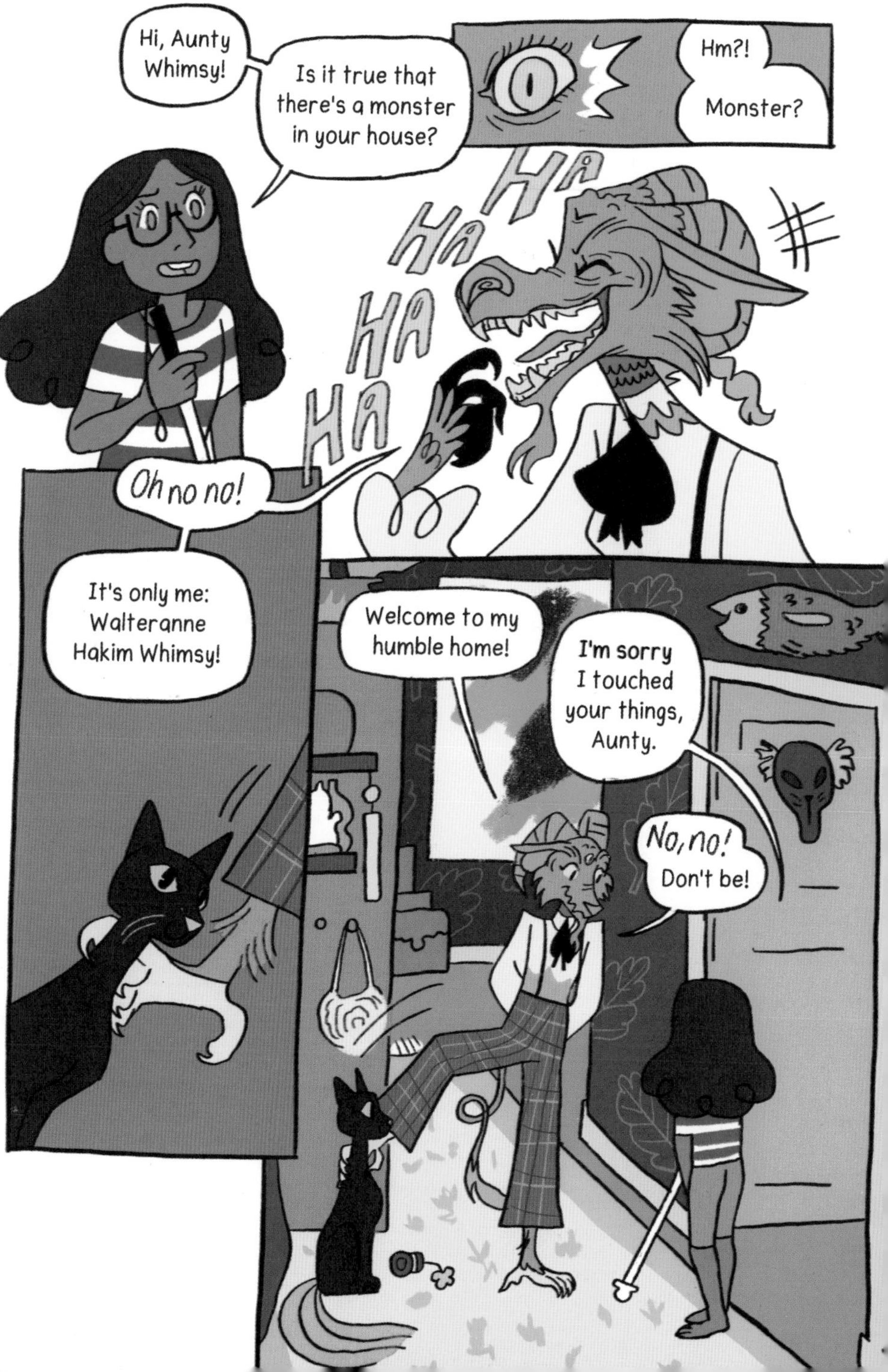
Hi, Aunty Whimsy!
Is it true that there's a monster in your house?
Hm?!
Monster?
HA HA HA HA HA
Oh no no!
It's only me: Walteranne Hakim Whimsy!
Welcome to my humble home!
I'm sorry I touched your things, Aunty.
No, no! Don't be!

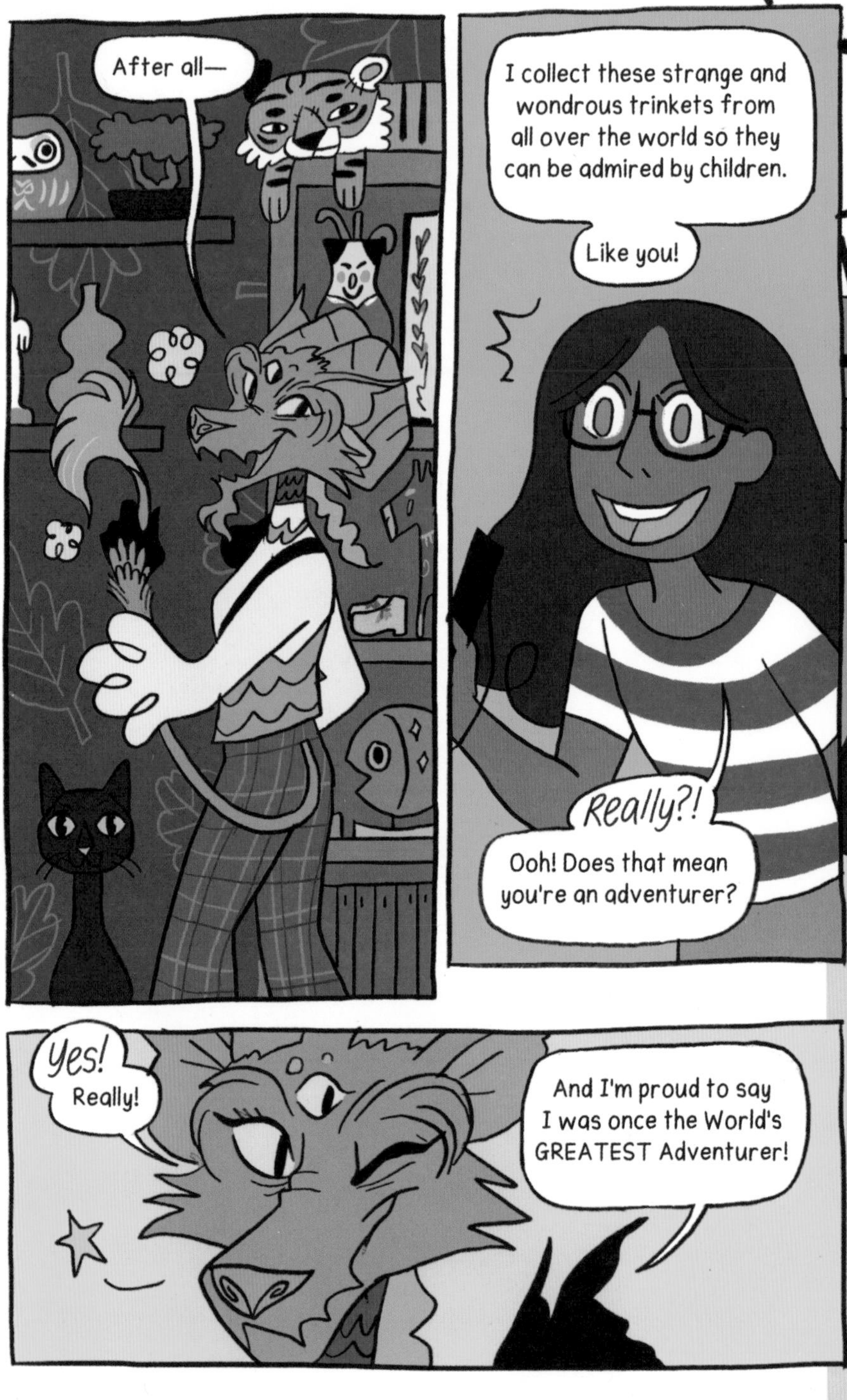
After all—
I collect these strange and wondrous trinkets from all over the world so they can be admired by children.
Like you!
Really?!
Ooh! Does that mean you're an adventurer?
Yes!
Really!
And I'm proud to say I was once the World's GREATEST Adventurer!

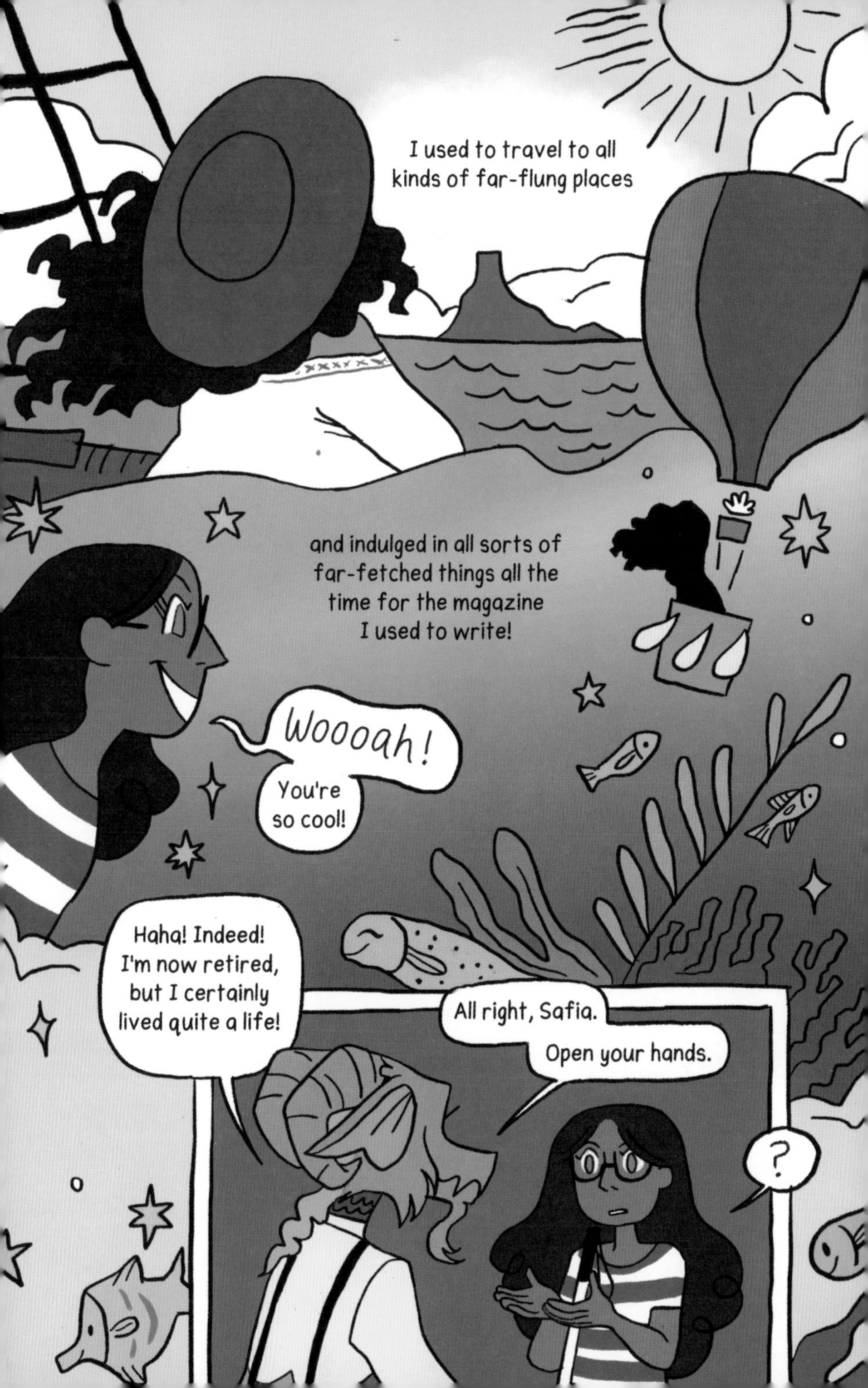
I used to travel to all kinds of far-flung places
and indulged in all sorts of far-fetched things all the time for the magazine I used to write!
Woooah!
You're so cool!
Haha! Indeed! I'm now retired, but I certainly lived quite a life!
All right, Safia.
Open your hands.
?

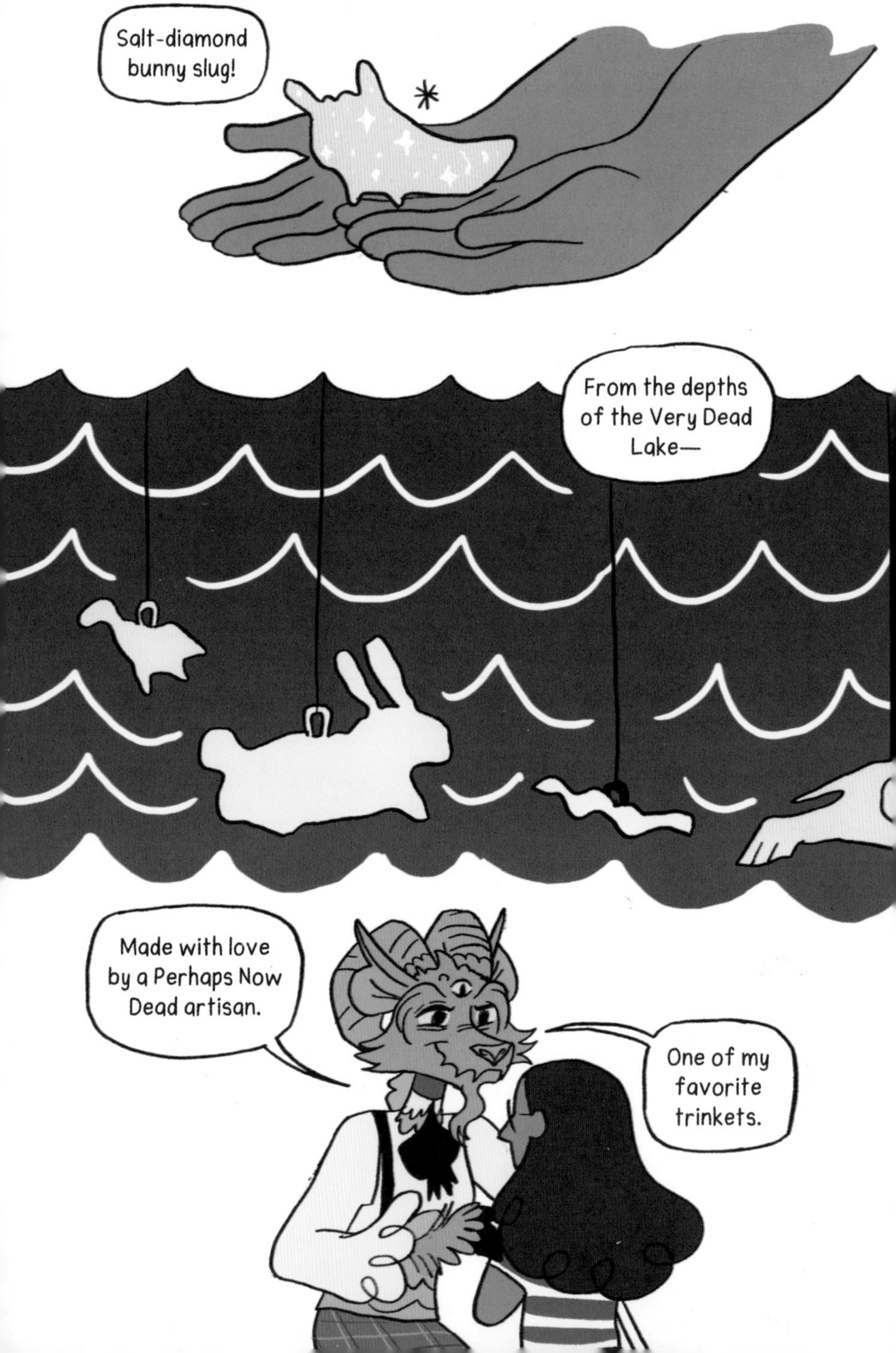
Salt-diamond bunny slug!
From the depths of the Very Dead Lake—
Made with love by a Perhaps Now Dead artisan.
One of my favorite trinkets.

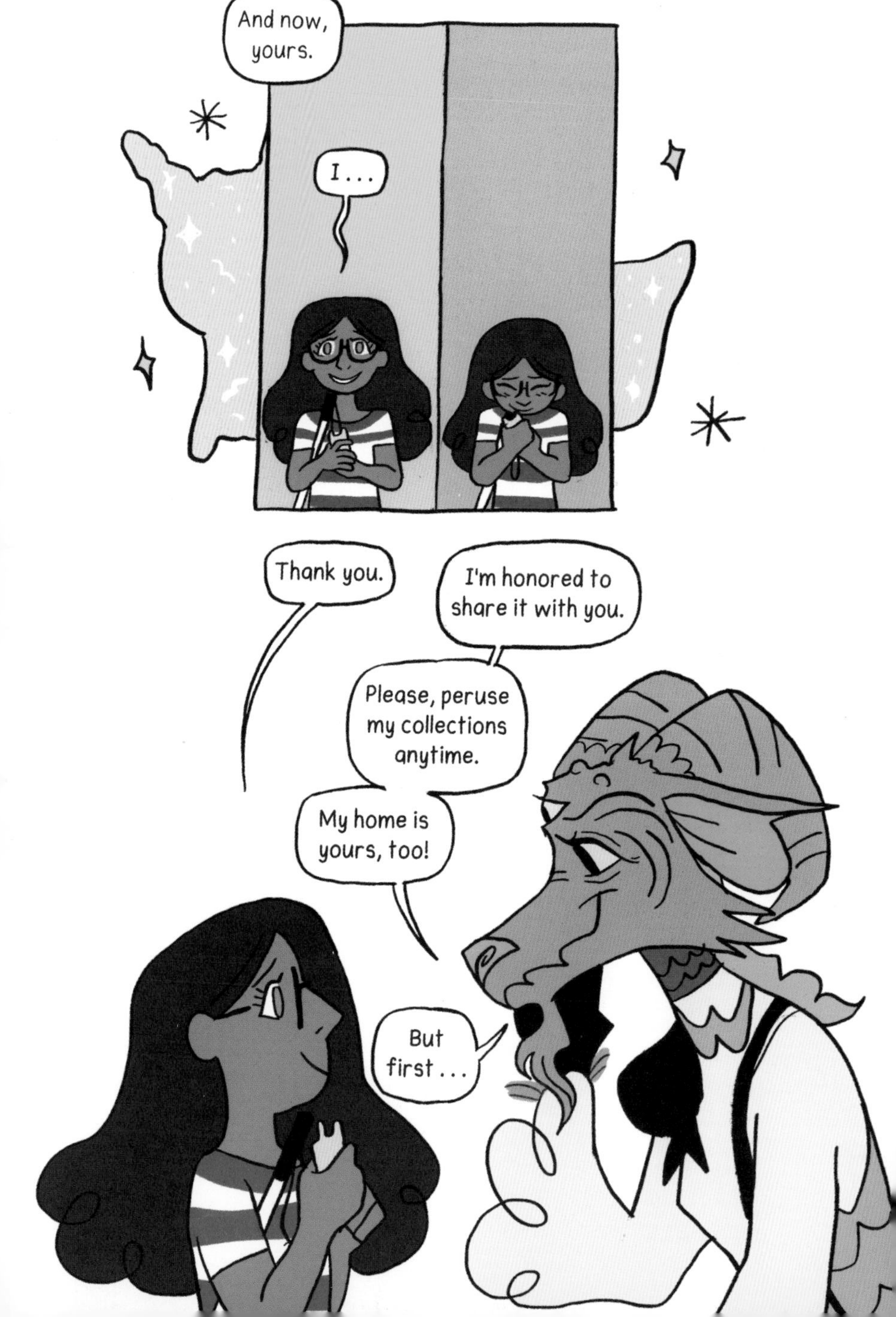
And now, yours.
I . . .
Thank you.
I'm honored to share it with you.
Please, peruse my collections anytime.
My home is yours, too!
But first . . .

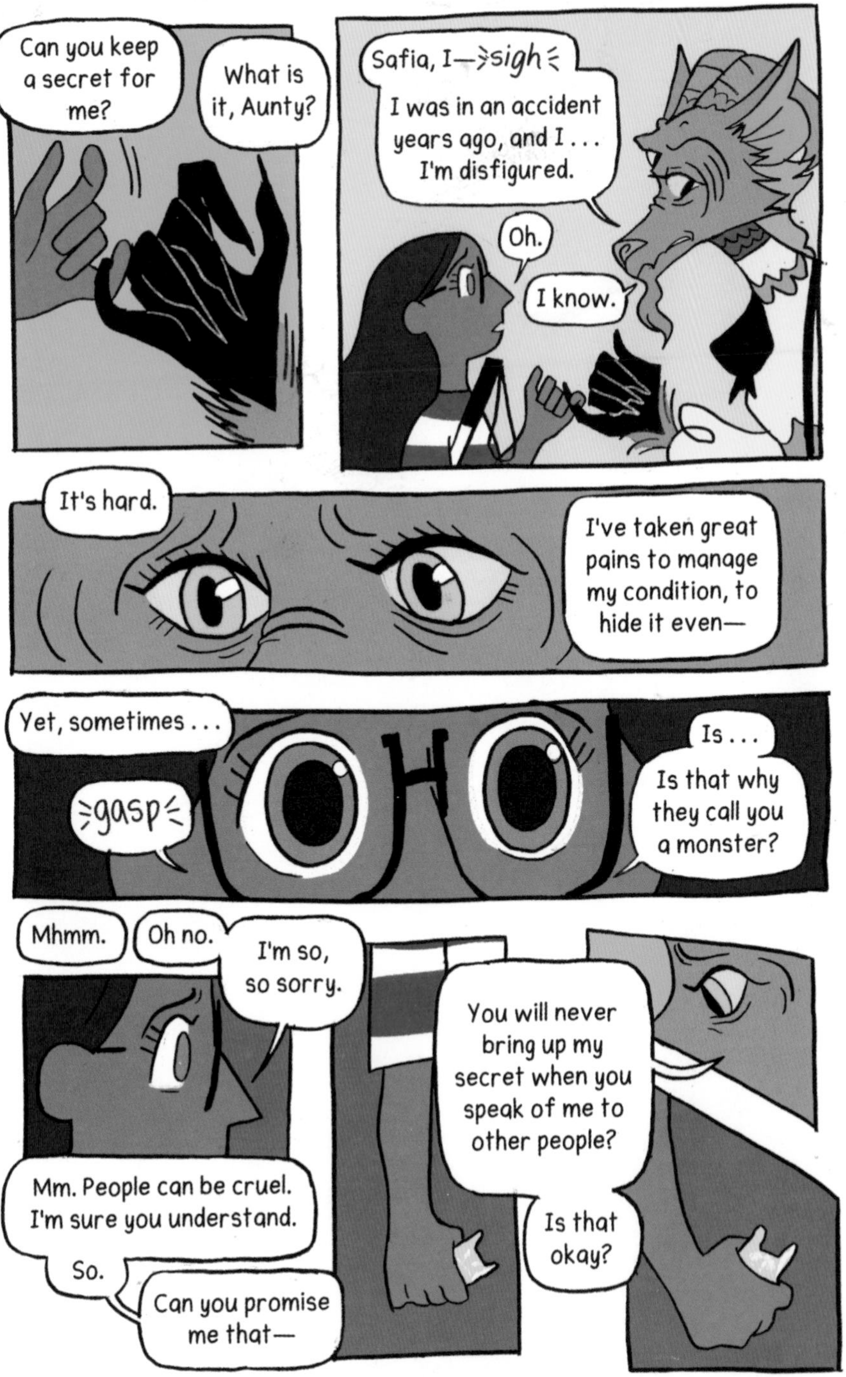
Can you keep a secret for me?
What is it, Aunty?
Safia, I—sigh
I was in an accident years ago, and I . . . I'm disfigured.
Oh.
I know.
It's hard.
I've taken great pains to manage my condition, to hide it even—
Yet, sometimes . . .
gasp
Is . . .
Is that why they call you a monster?
Mhmm.
Oh no.
I'm so, so sorry.
Mm. People can be cruel. I'm sure you understand.
So.
Can you promise me that—
You will never bring up my secret when you speak of me to other people?
Is that okay?

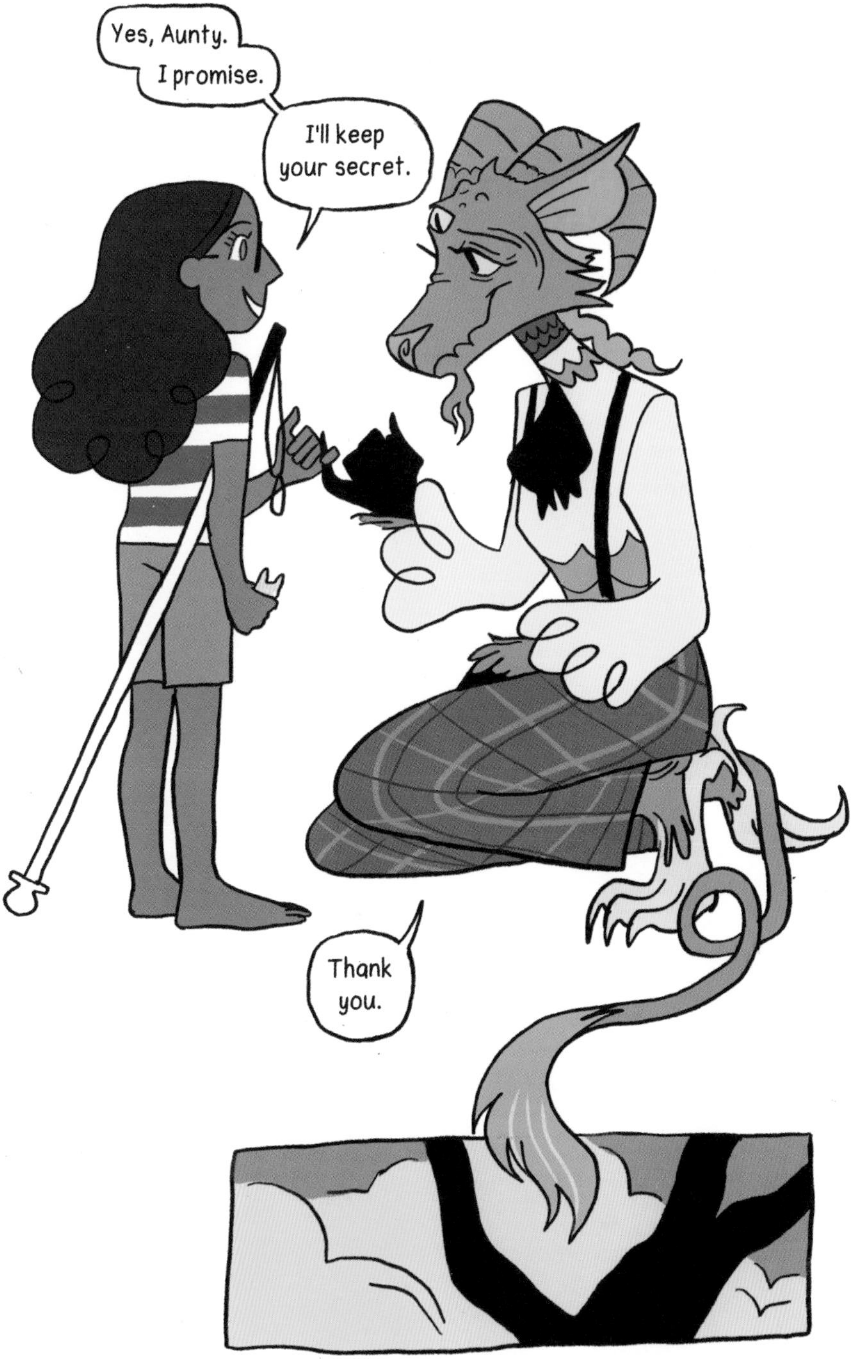
Yes, Aunty.
I promise.
I'll keep your secret.
Thank you.

A Strange and Wondrous Tale

Prof. Walter Hakim

Prof. Anne Haziz

Once upon a time, a strange and wondrous thing happened:

Aunty Whimsy was born.

This greatly pleased her parents, who taught in the Department of Understudied Subjects at the local university, specializing in the world's odds and ends.

They loved their jobs but their true passion in life, other than their only daughter, was their quarterly magazine:

Walteranne Hakim

OBSERVATIONS
of the Strange and Wondrous

ISSUE 40 $10

Edited by
WALTER HAKIM & ANNE HAZIZ

or OBSERVATIONS,
for short.

Some Highlights of the Magazine

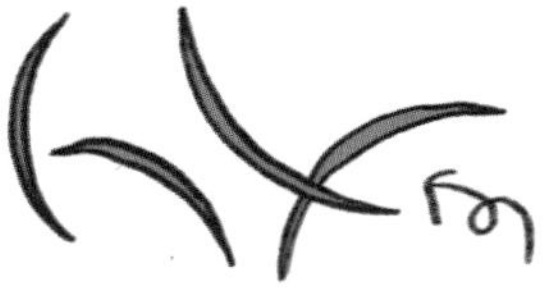

Mysterious animal. Issue 15.

Still unidentified. A creature that is invisible but leaves behind hair and the victim of its mischief—usually a household object.

Salt-diamond sea urchin. Issue 6.

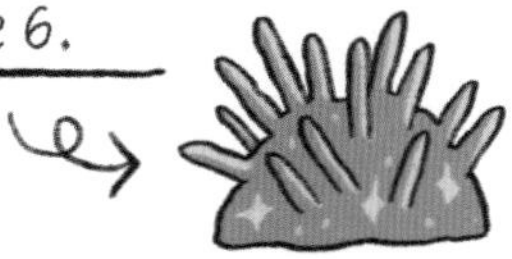

A long-gone sea urchin from the Very Dead Lake. Anything that is immersed in the lake becomes encased in layers of sparkling salt. An annual festival encourages local and international artists to design the most beautiful and unusual salt-encased objects.

The Man with a Very Long and Strong Mustache. Issue 1.

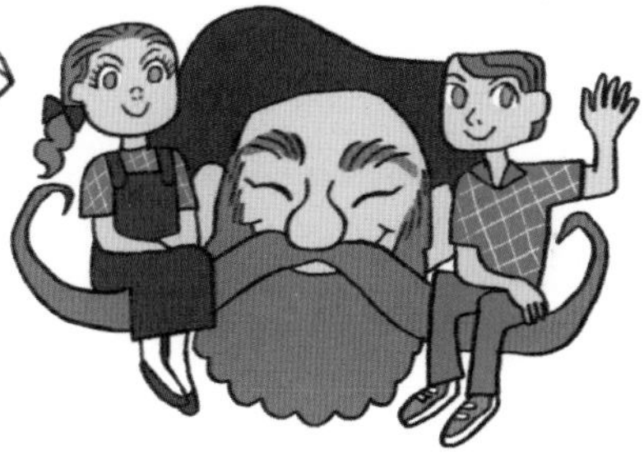

One man from the Southern Seas spent years and much money on hair products to groom one amazing mustache. It is apparently stiff and strong enough to carry his children on each side.

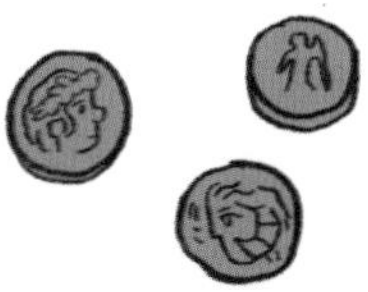

Tiny ancient coins. Issue 11.

It is a wonder how these coins were not lost, either by the ravages of time or butterfingers.

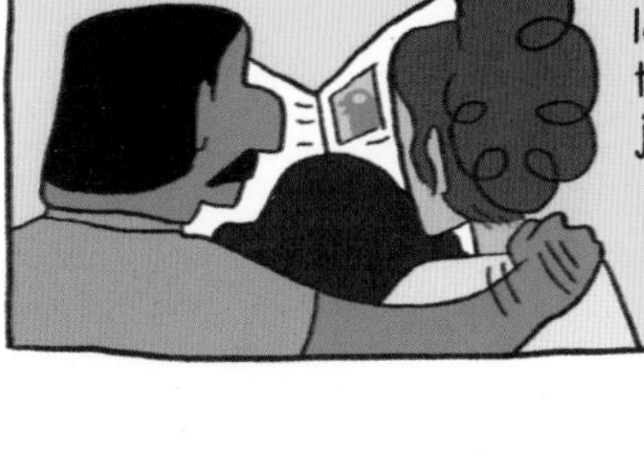

The magazine did not earn them a lot of money or fame, but it gave the professors and their friends joy. And that was enough.

Then another strange and wondrous thing happened . . .

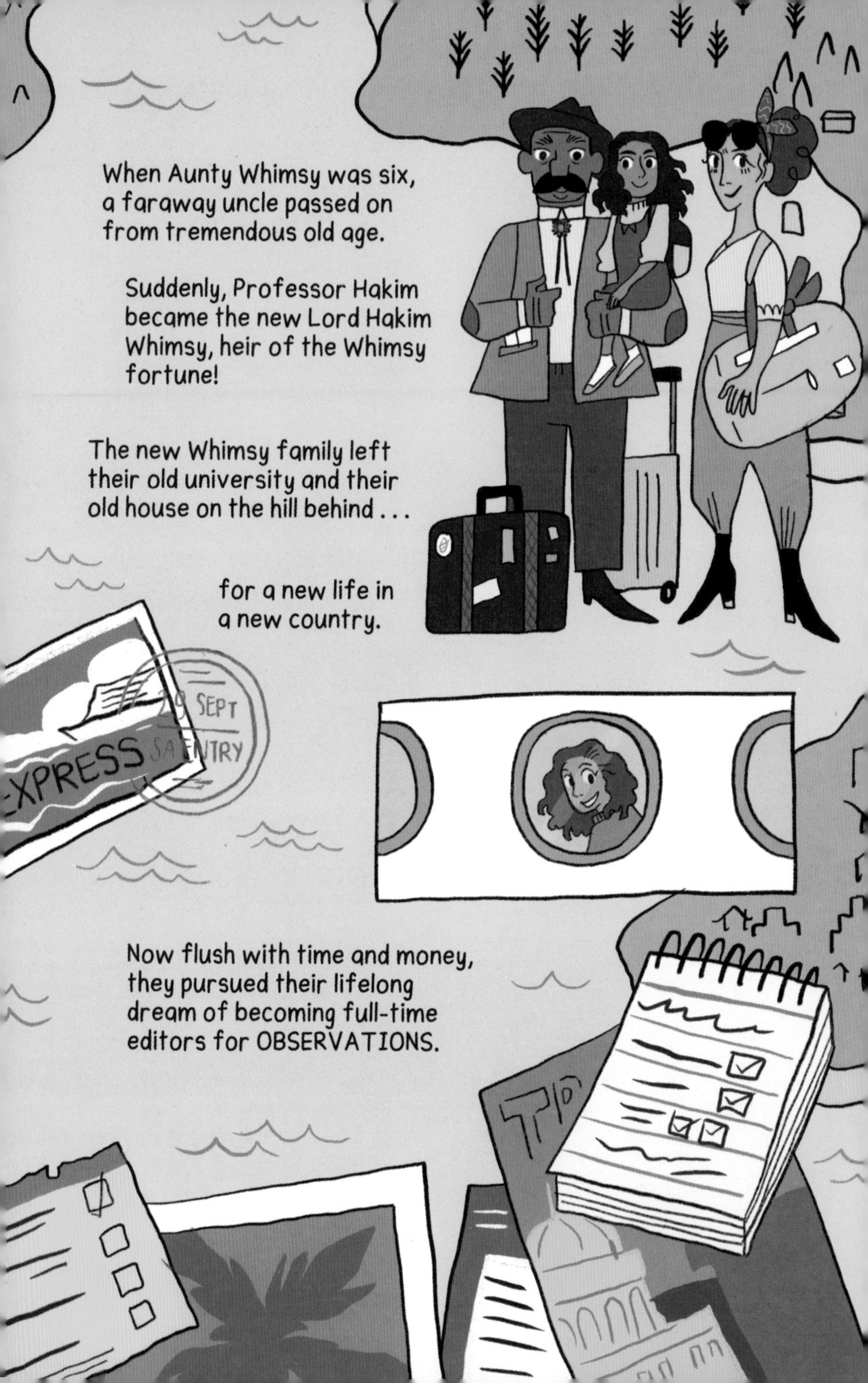
When Aunty Whimsy was six, a faraway uncle passed on from tremendous old age.
Suddenly, Professor Hakim became the new Lord Hakim Whimsy, heir of the Whimsy fortune!
The new Whimsy family left their old university and their old house on the hill behind . . .
for a new life in a new country.
EXPRESS
SEPT
Now flush with time and money, they pursued their lifelong dream of becoming full-time editors for OBSERVATIONS.

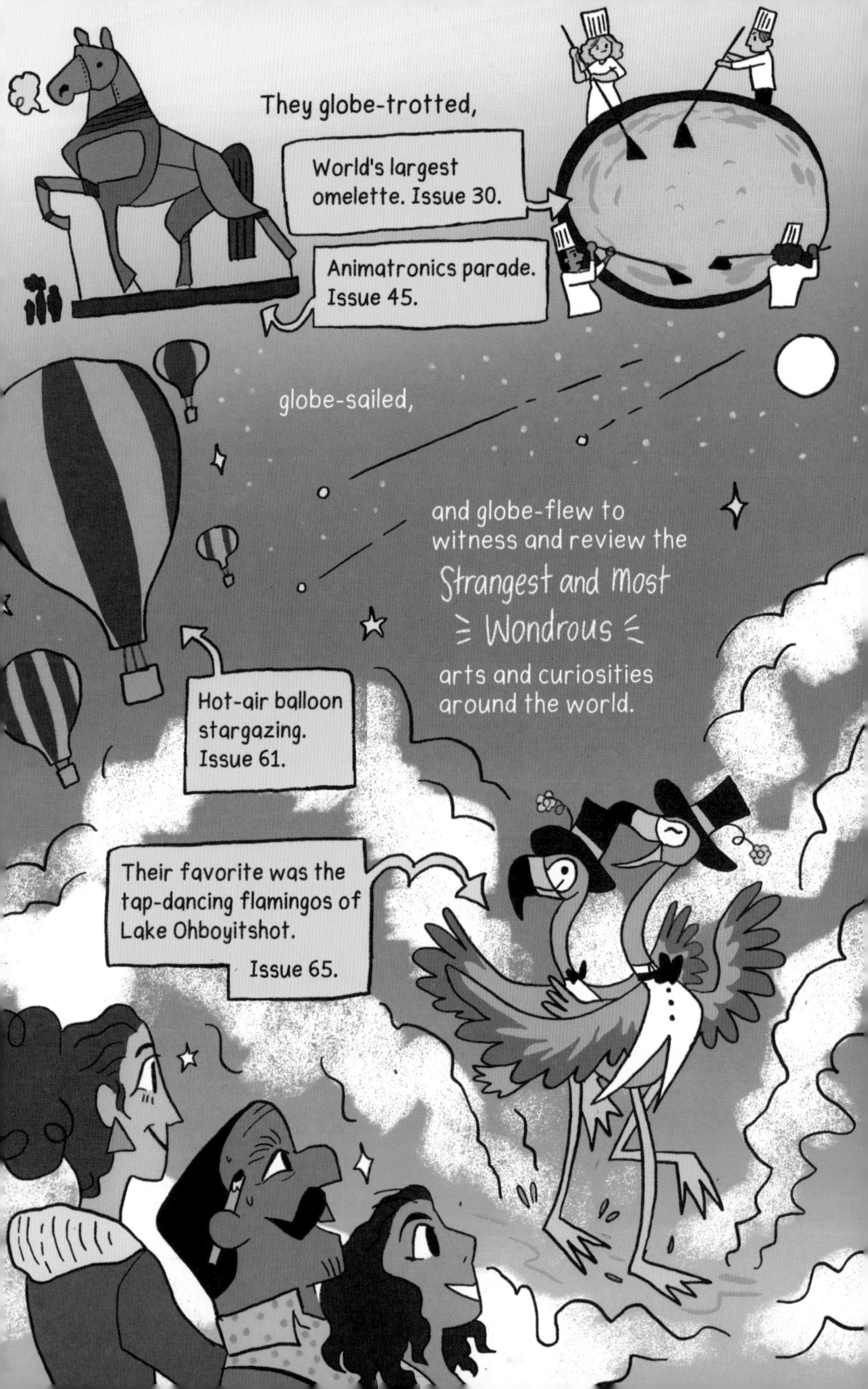
They globe-trotted,
World's largest omelette. Issue 30.
Animatronics parade. Issue 45.
globe-sailed,
and globe-flew to witness and review the Strangest and Most Wondrous arts and curiosities around the world.
Hot-air balloon stargazing. Issue 61.
Their favorite was the tap-dancing flamingos of Lake Ohboyitshot.
Issue 65.

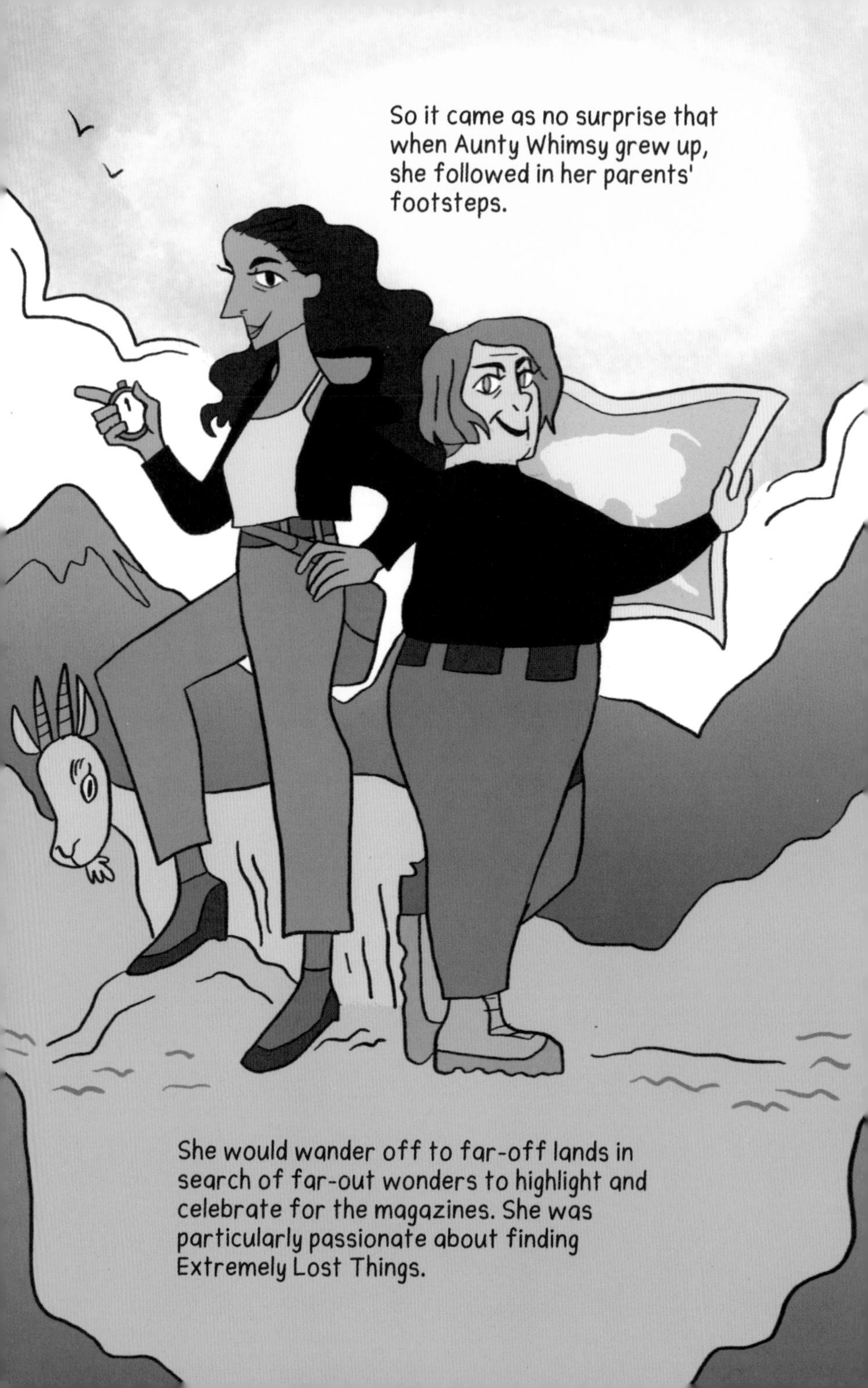
So it came as no surprise that when Aunty Whimsy grew up, she followed in her parents' footsteps.
She would wander off to far-off lands in search of far-out wonders to highlight and celebrate for the magazines. She was particularly passionate about finding Extremely Lost Things.

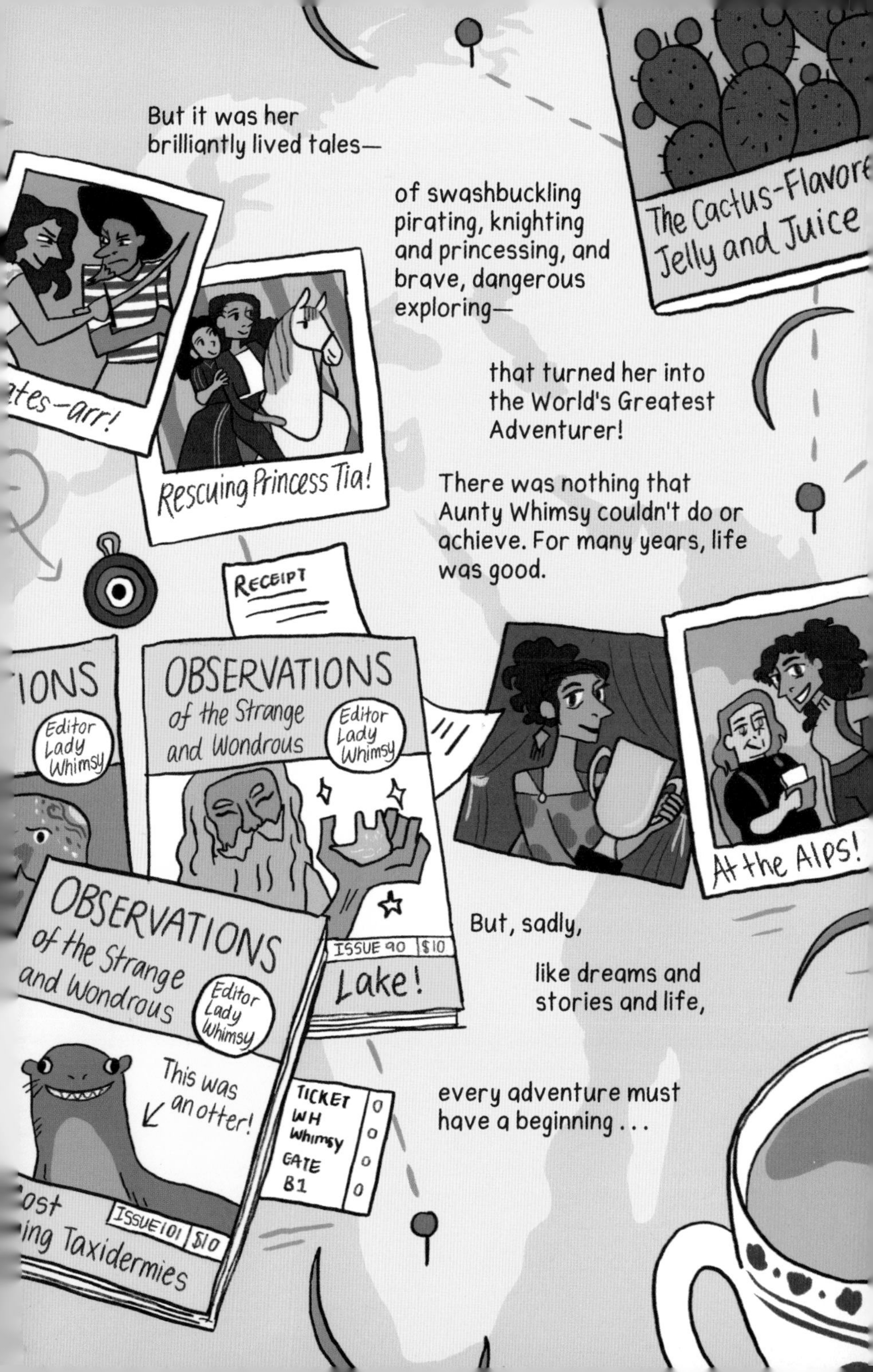
But it was her brilliantly lived tales—
of swashbuckling pirating, knighting and princessing, and brave, dangerous exploring—
that turned her into the World's Greatest Adventurer!
There was nothing that Aunty Whimsy couldn't do or achieve. For many years, life was good.
But, sadly,
like dreams and stories and life,
every adventure must have a beginning . . .
The Cactus-Flavore
Jelly and Juice
ates—arr!
Rescuing Princess Tia!
RECEIPT
IONS
Editor Lady Whimsy
OBSERVATIONS of the Strange and Wondrous
Editor Lady Whimsy
ISSUE 90 $10
Lake!
At the Alps!
OBSERVATIONS of the Strange and Wondrous
Editor Lady Whimsy
This was an otter!
ISSUE 101 $10
ing Taxidermies
TICKET
WH Whimsy
GATE B1

... and an end.

One fateful journey, a peculiarly
strange and wondrous thing happened,
though not in the way anyone expected.

BEYU

THE EARFUL

News from Brookham & Elsewhere

RENOWNED EDITOR-ADVENTURER DECLARED EXTREMELY LOST

*Lady Whimsy poses with Blanca
in front of a Northern Isles Flower
Show exhibit.*
Photo credit: Bronx Jotunn.

The Institute of Extremely Found Things in Lost History regrets to report the sudden mysterious disappearance of prolific adventurer and editor of OBSERVATIONS, Lady Walteranne H. Whimsy, and her assistant, Cathryn Blanca, following an ambitious solo expedition to the mountains of the Subcontinent.

>Continued on Page 5

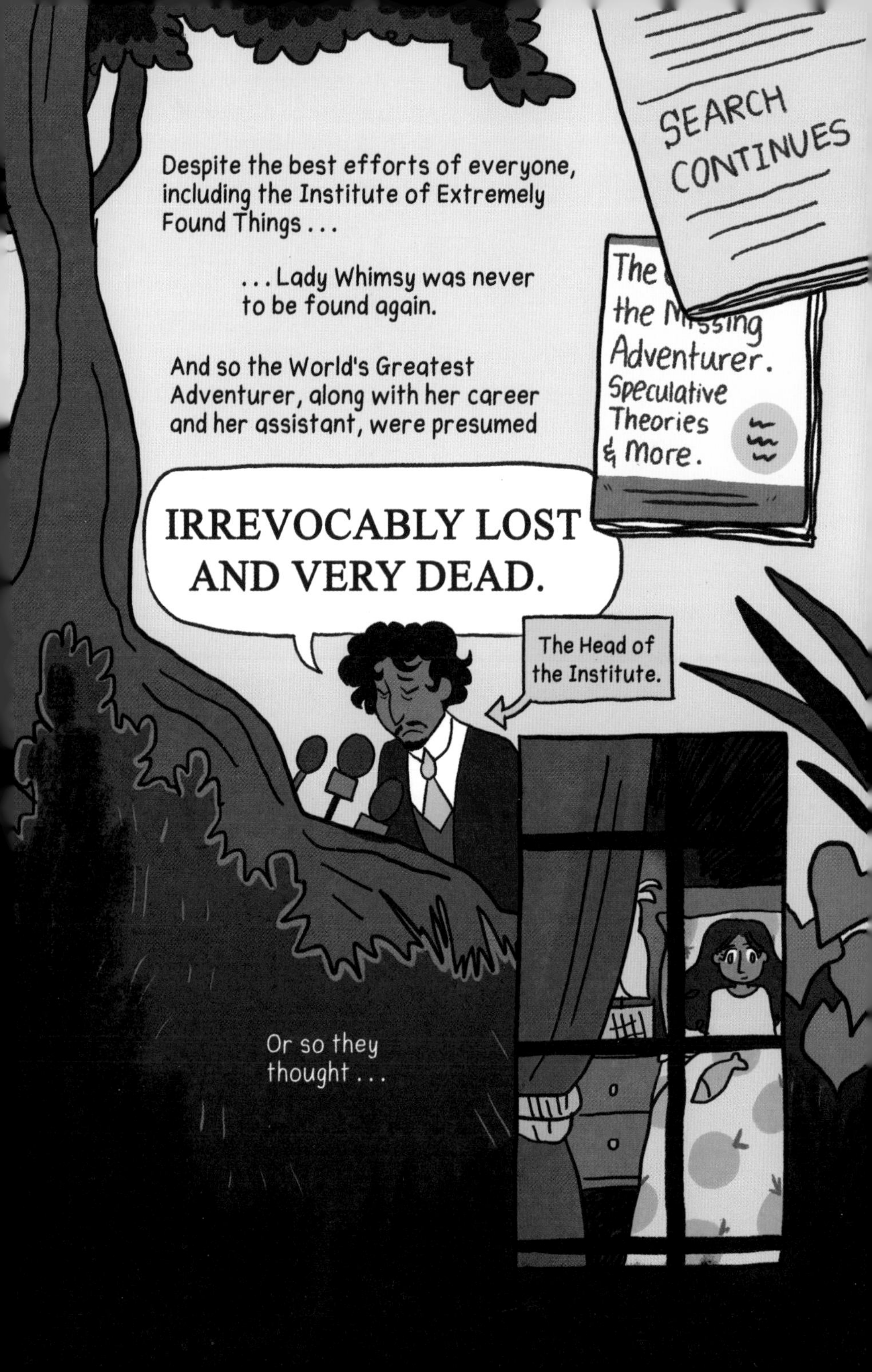
SEARCH CONTINUES
Despite the best efforts of everyone, including the Institute of Extremely Found Things . . .
. . . Lady Whimsy was never to be found again.
Adventurer. Speculative Theories & More.
And so the World's Greatest Adventurer, along with her career and her assistant, were presumed
IRREVOCABLY LOST AND VERY DEAD.
The Head of the Institute.
Or so they thought . . .

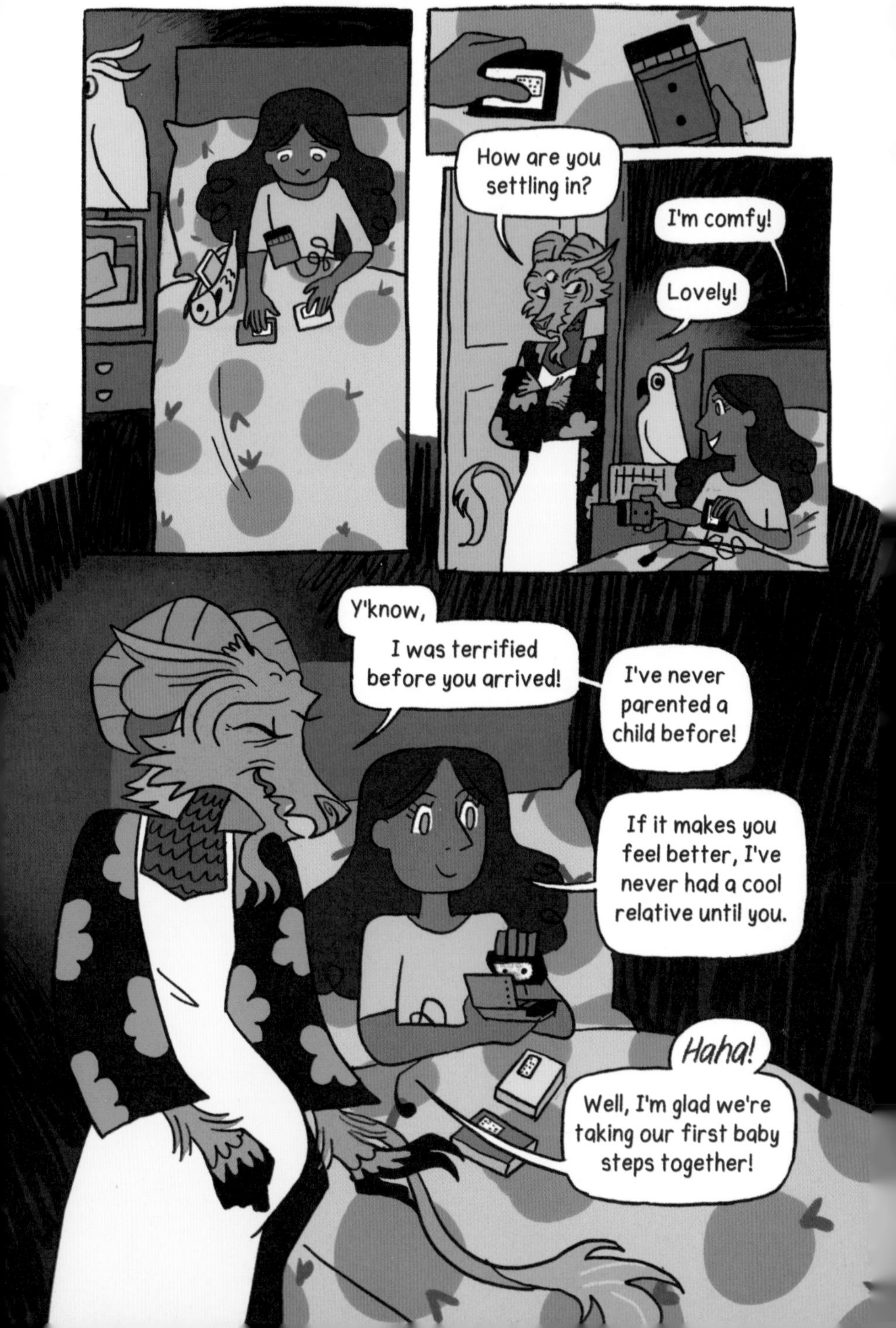
How are you settling in?
I'm comfy!
Lovely!
Y'know,
I was terrified before you arrived!
I've never parented a child before!
If it makes you feel better, I've never had a cool relative until you.
Haha!
Well, I'm glad we're taking our first baby steps together!

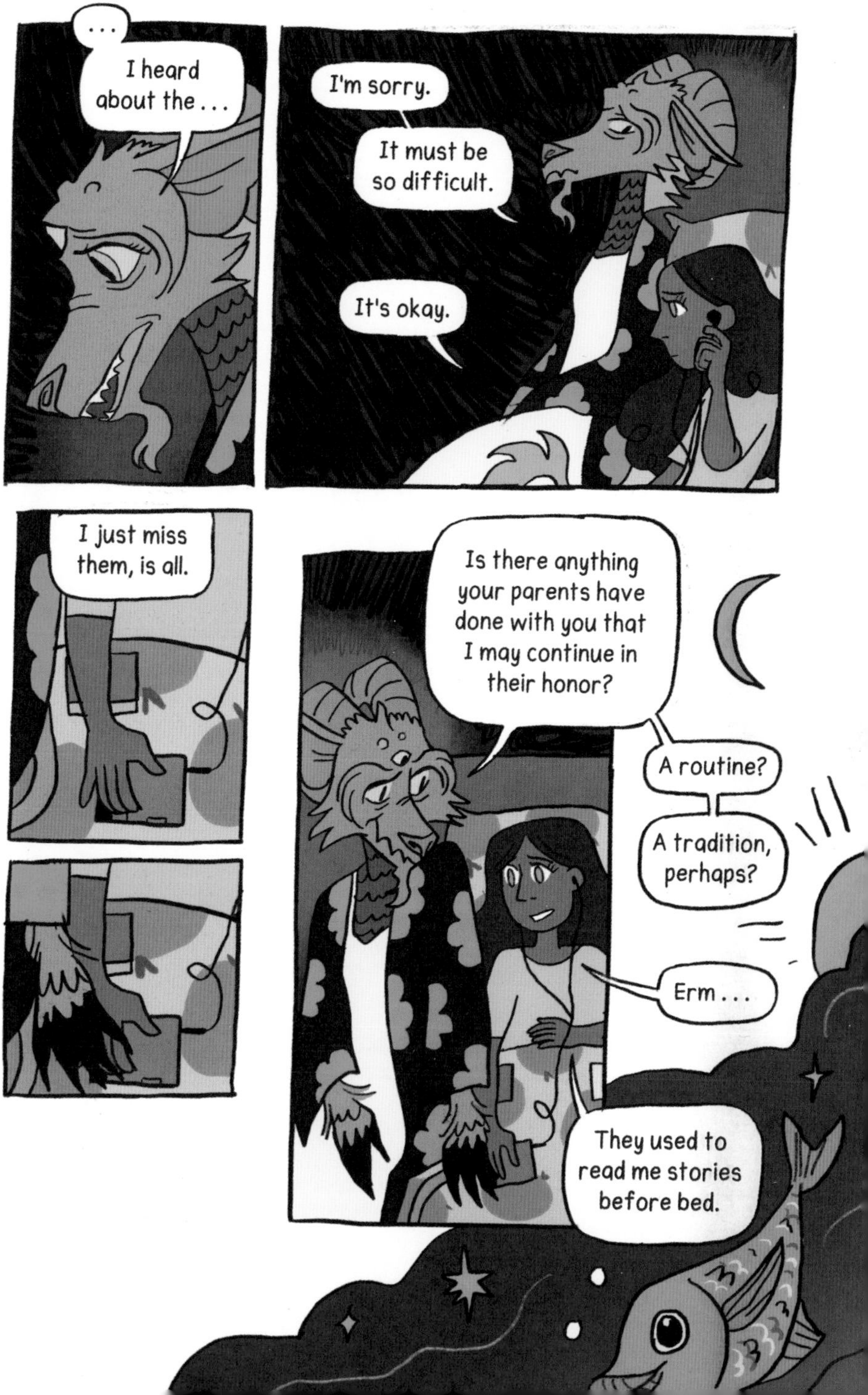

...
I heard about the...
I'm sorry.
It must be so difficult.
It's okay.
I just miss them, is all.
Is there anything your parents have done with you that I may continue in their honor?
A routine?
A tradition, perhaps?
Erm...
They used to read me stories before bed.

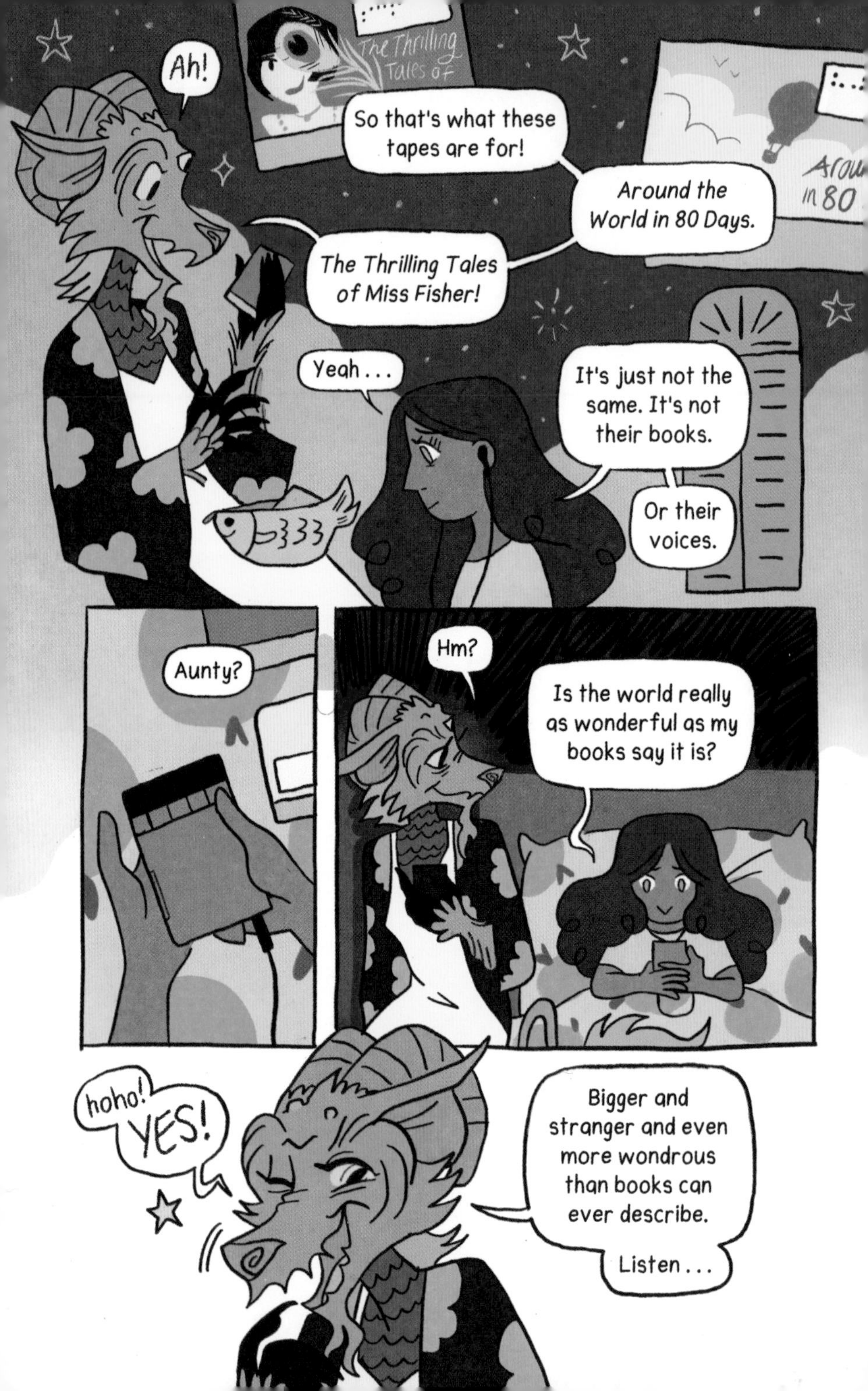
The Thrilling Tales of
Ah!
So that's what these tapes are for!
Around the World in 80 Days.
The Thrilling Tales of Miss Fisher!
Arou
in 80
Yeah . . .
It's just not the same. It's not their books.
Or their voices.
Aunty?
Hm?
Is the world really as wonderful as my books say it is?
hoho! YES!
Bigger and stranger and even more wondrous than books can ever describe.
Listen . . .

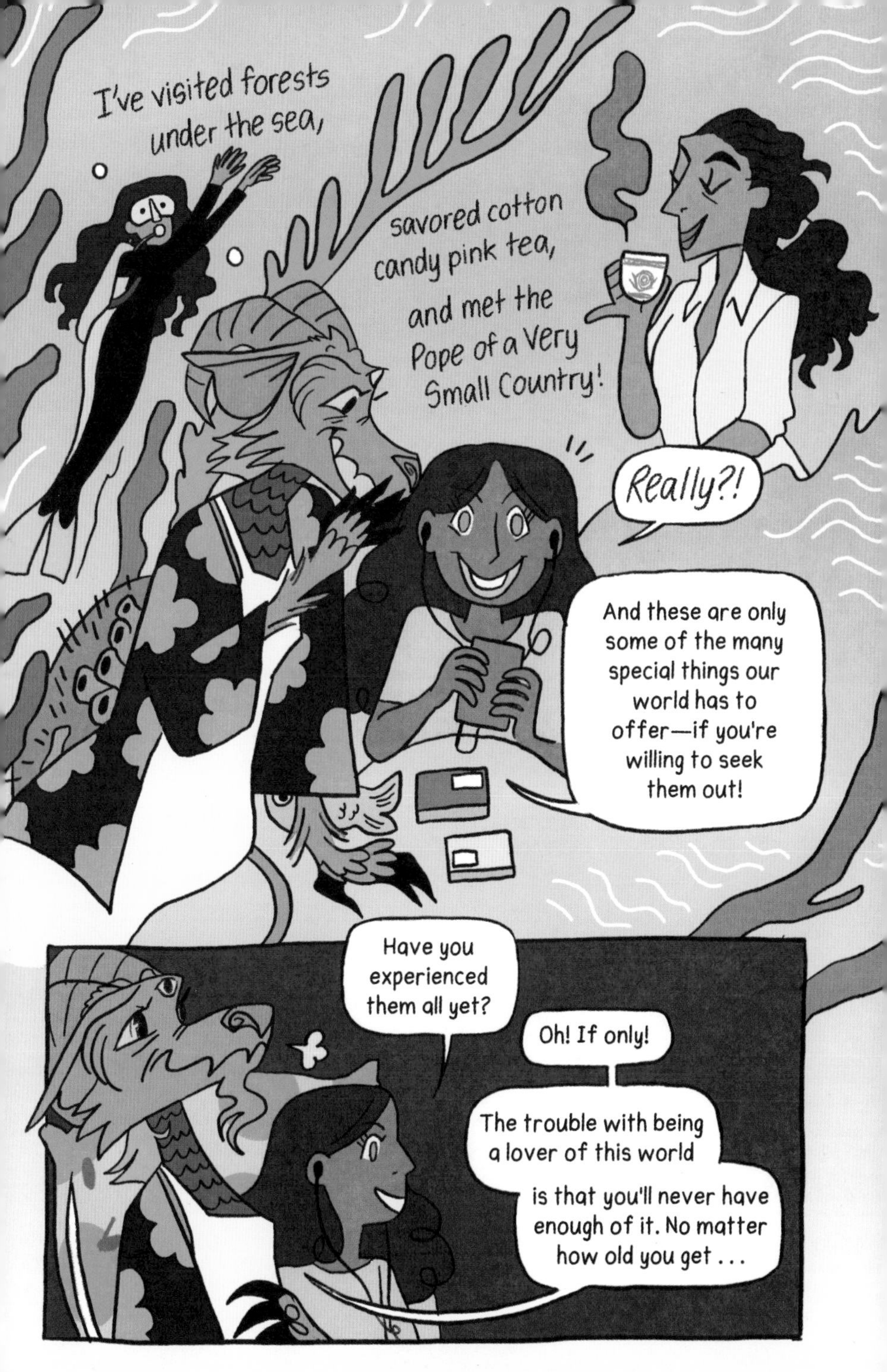
I've visited forests under the sea,
savored cotton candy pink tea,
and met the Pope of a Very Small Country!
Really?!
And these are only some of the many special things our world has to offer—if you're willing to seek them out!
Have you experienced them all yet?
Oh! If only!
The trouble with being a lover of this world
is that you'll never have enough of it. No matter how old you get . . .

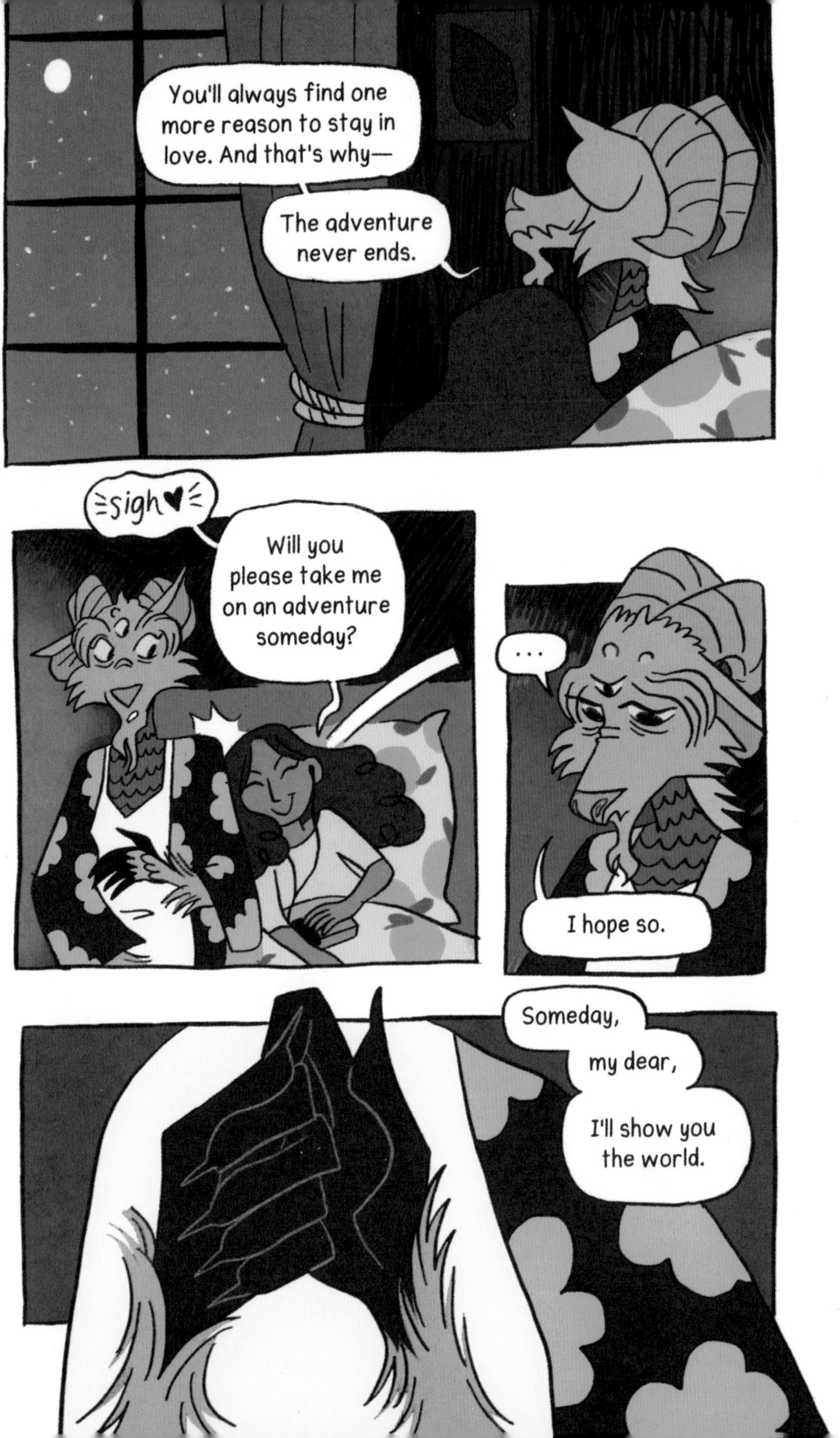
You'll always find one more reason to stay in love. And that's why—
The adventure never ends.
sigh♥
Will you please take me on an adventure someday?
. . .
I hope so.
Someday,
my dear,
I'll show you the world.

I promise.

Chapter Two

Eight years, four months, and twenty-three days since that fateful journey.

Or.

Two months since Safia's adoption.

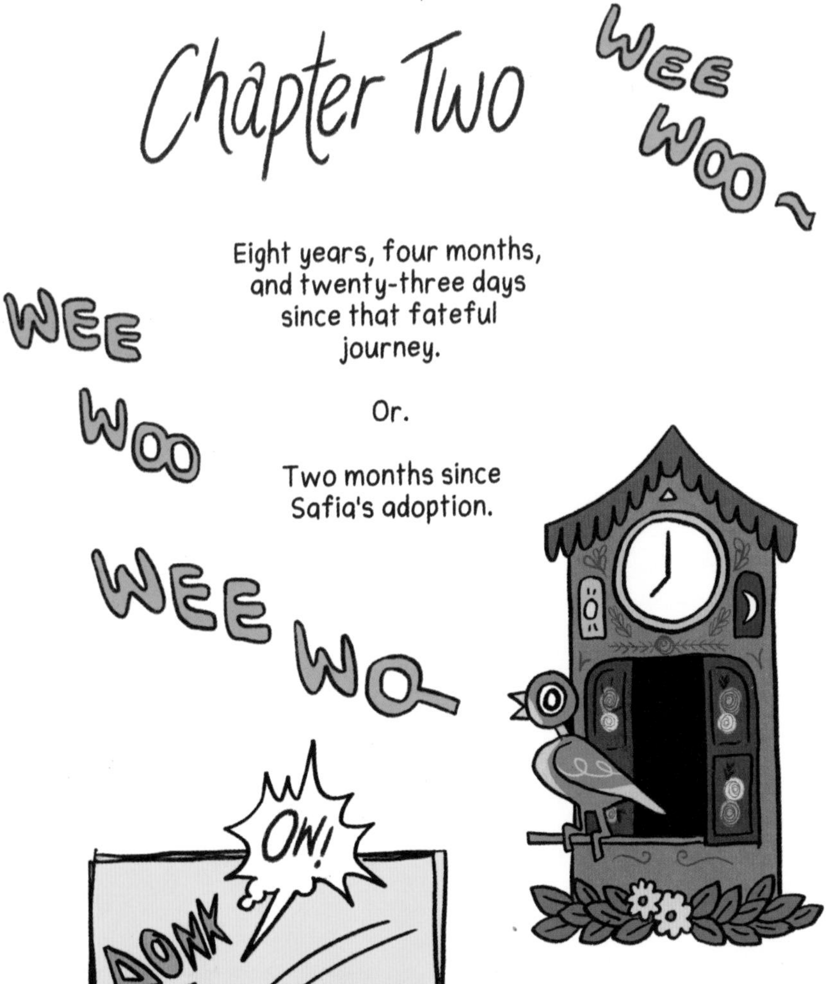
WEE WOO ~
WEE WOO
WEE WO

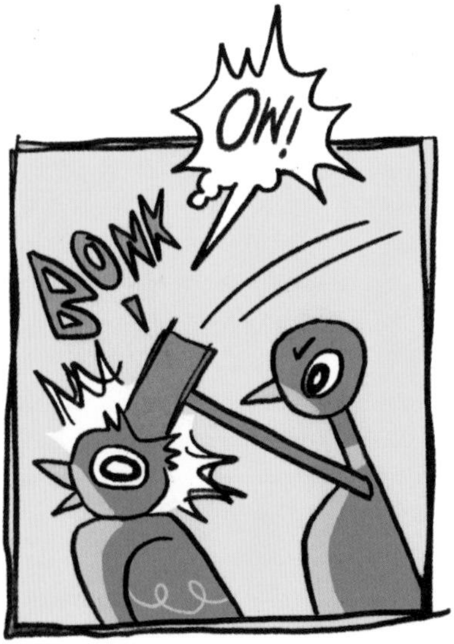
OW!
BONK

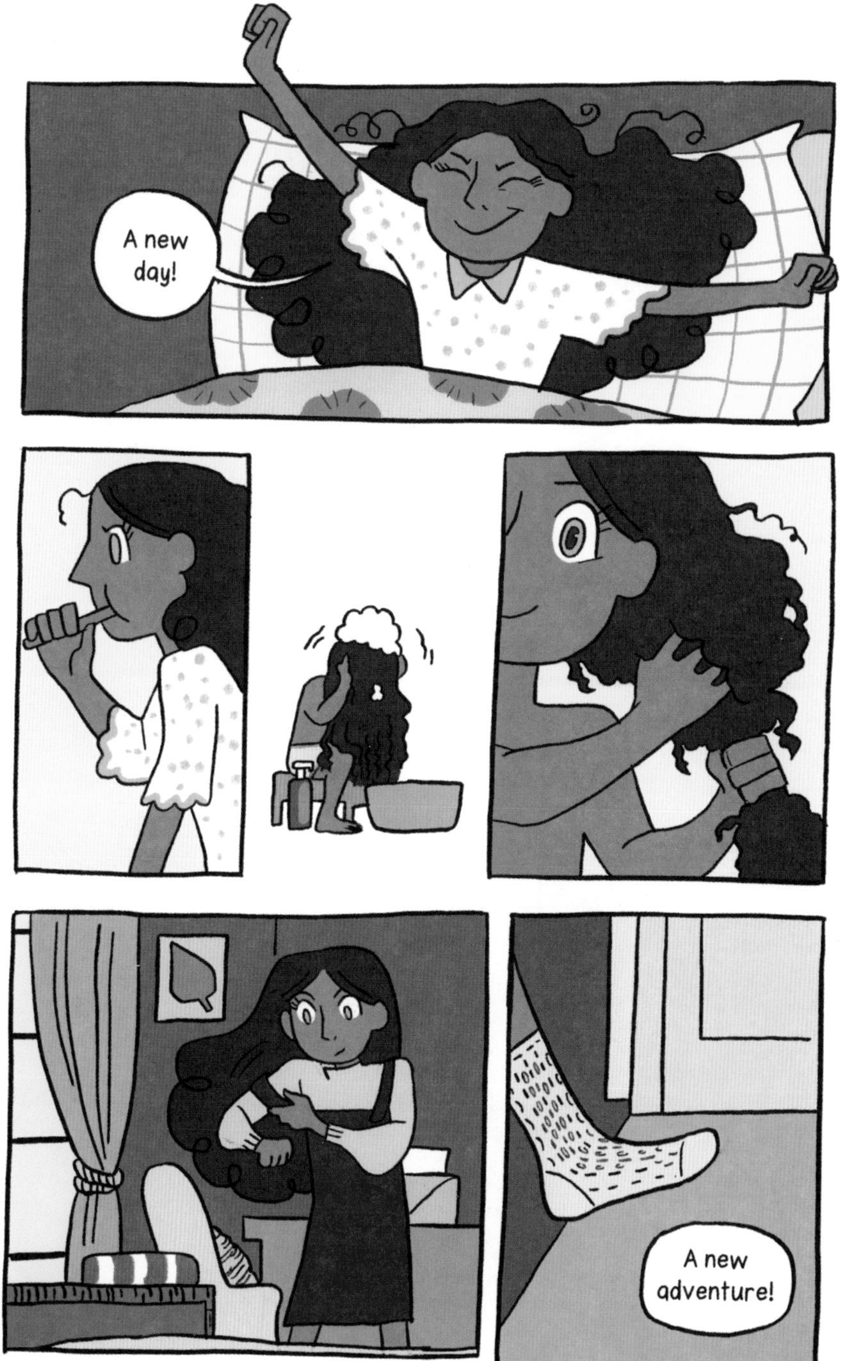
A new day!
A new adventure!

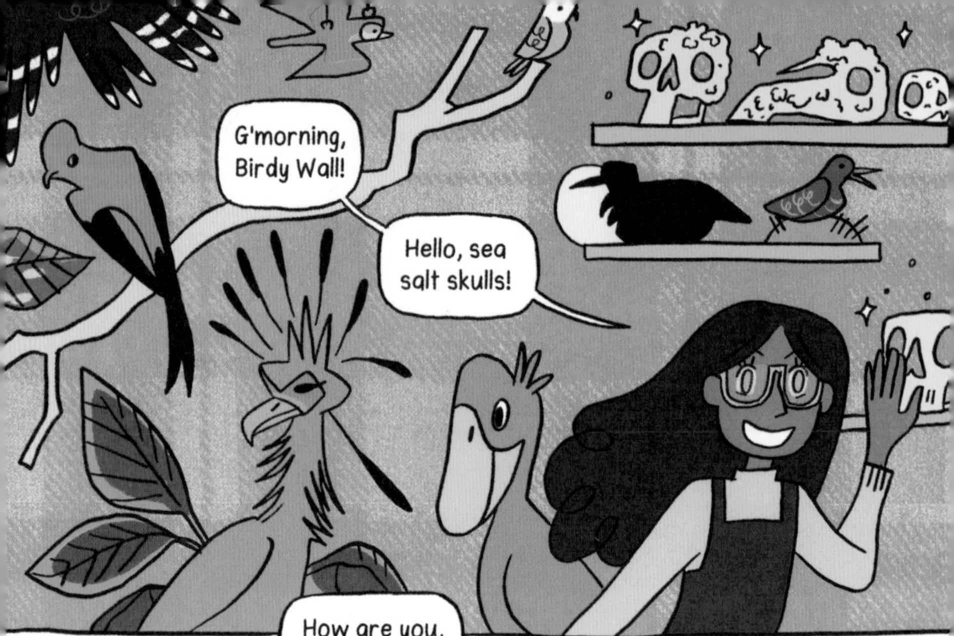
G'morning, Birdy Wall!
Hello, sea salt skulls!

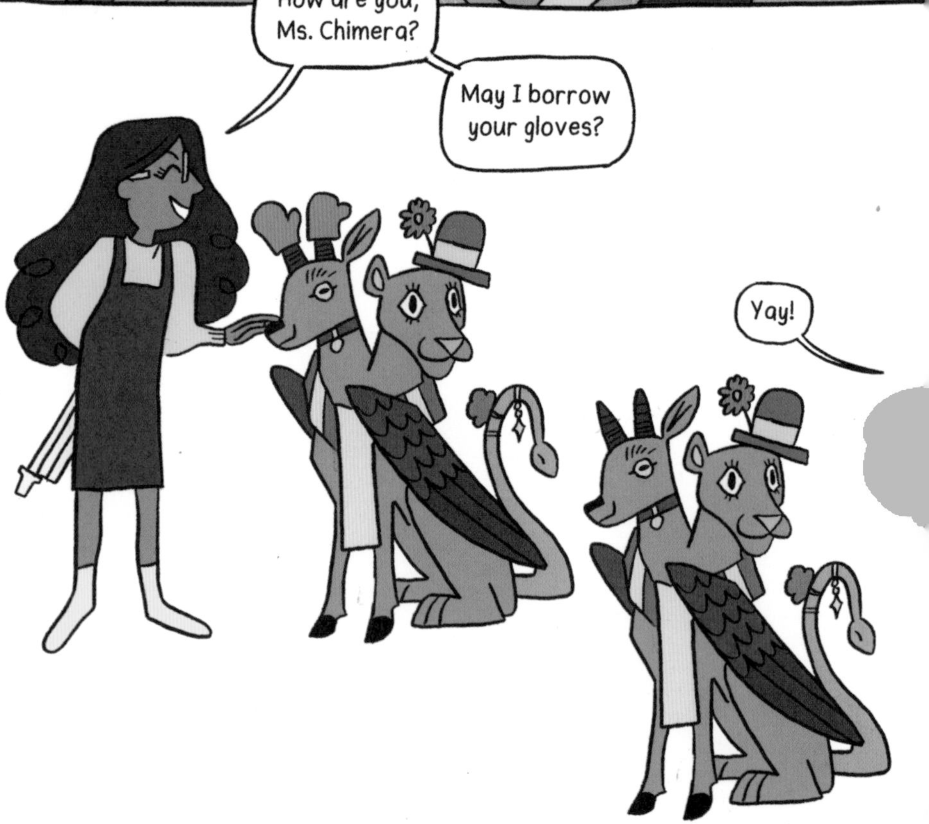
How are you, Ms. Chimera?
May I borrow your gloves?
Yay!

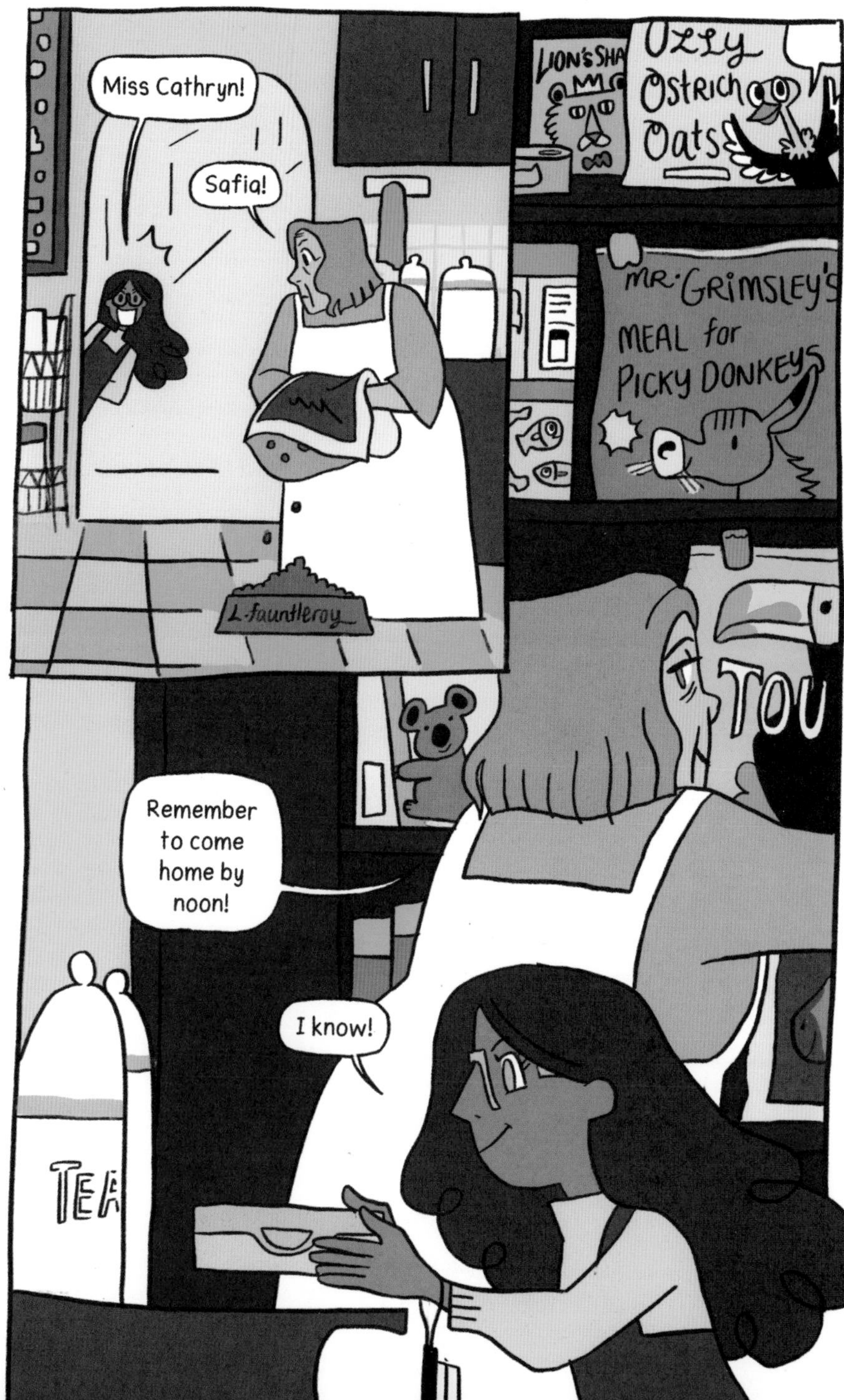
Miss Cathryn!
Safia!
LION'S SHA
OZZY Ostrich Oats
MR. GRIMSLEY'S MEAL for PICKY DONKEYS
L. fauntleroy
TOU
Remember to come home by noon!
I know!
TEA

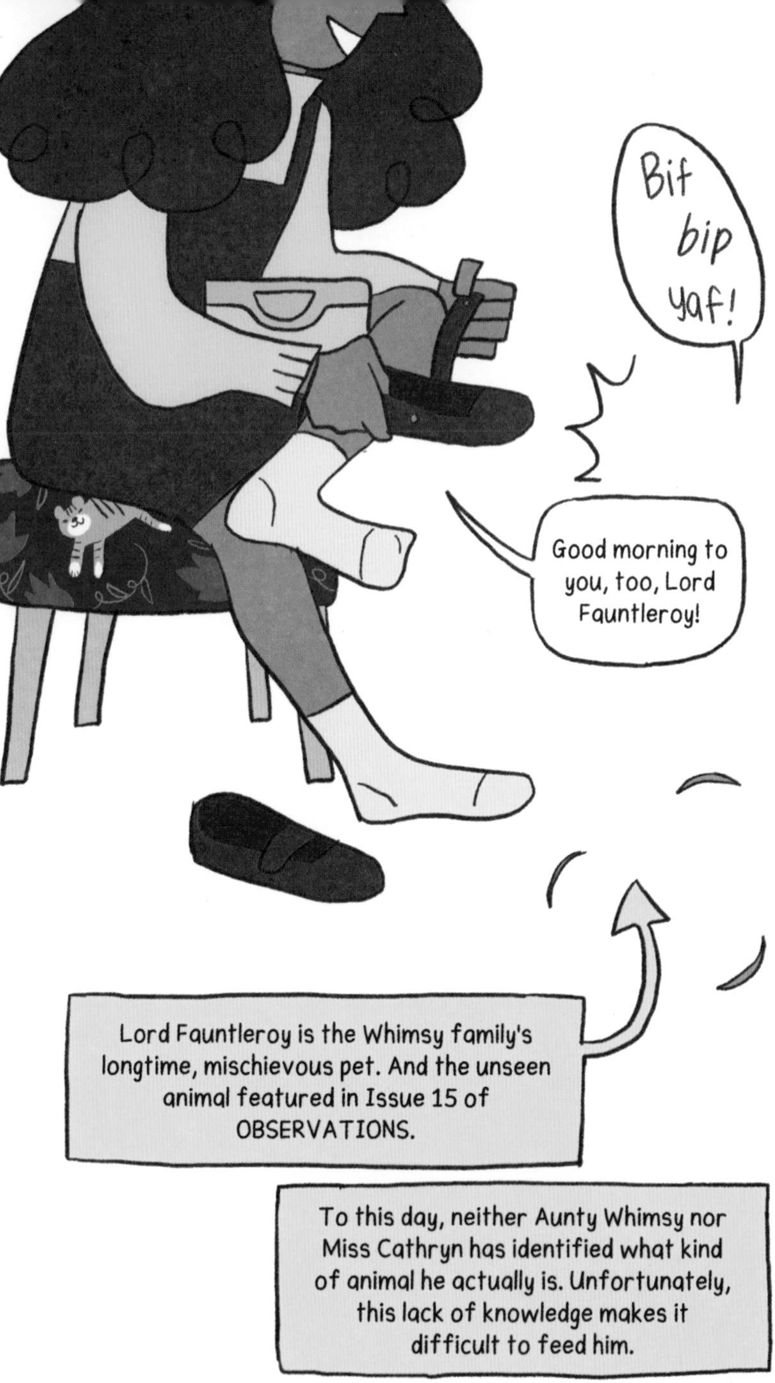
Bif bip yaf!
Good morning to you, too, Lord Fauntleroy!
Lord Fauntleroy is the Whimsy family's longtime, mischievous pet. And the unseen animal featured in Issue 15 of OBSERVATIONS.
To this day, neither Aunty Whimsy nor Miss Cathryn has identified what kind of animal he actually is. Unfortunately, this lack of knowledge makes it difficult to feed him.

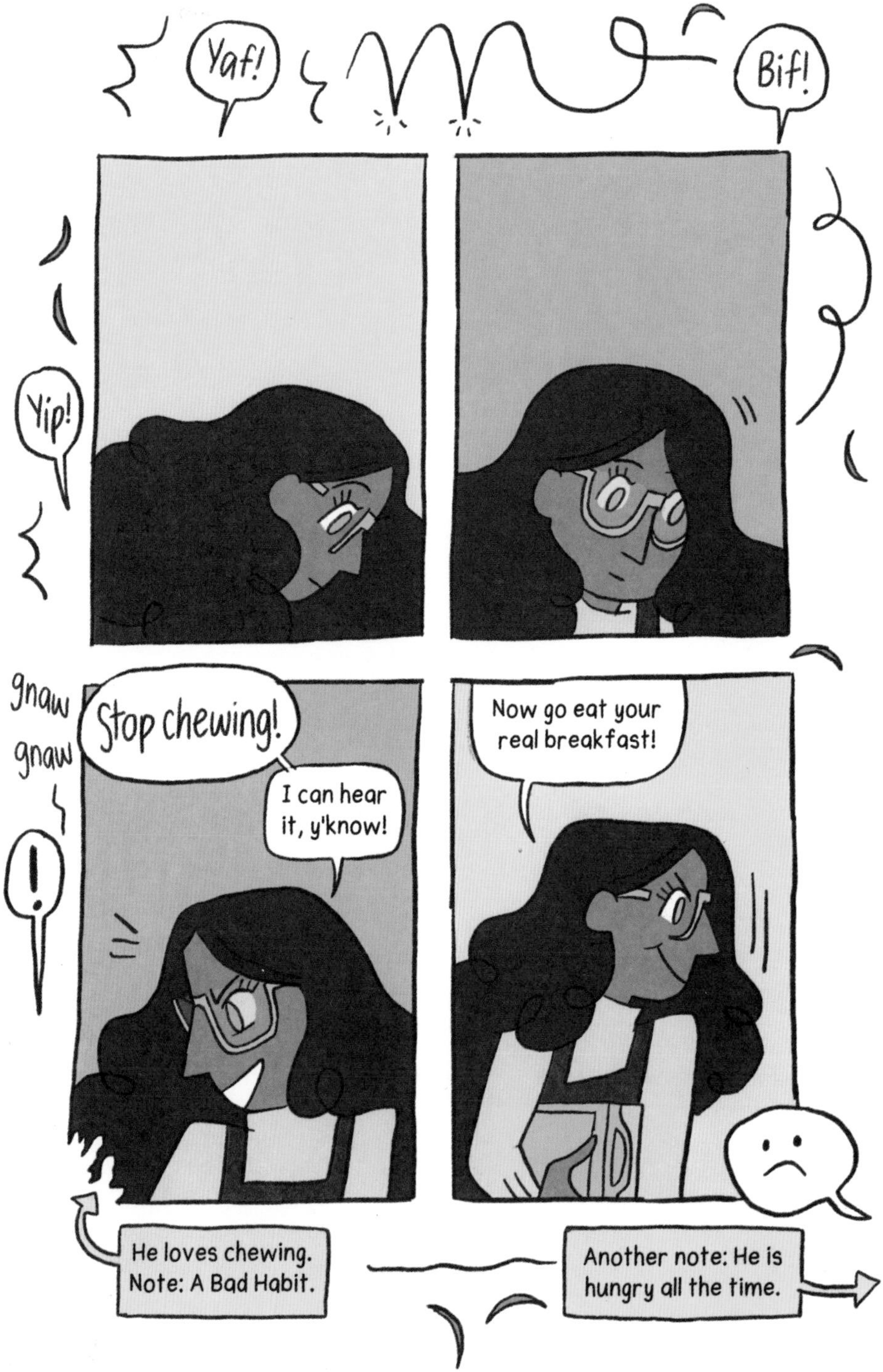
Yaf!
Bif!
Yip!
gnaw
gnaw
!
Stop chewing!
I can hear it, y'know!
Now go eat your real breakfast!
He loves chewing. Note: A Bad Habit.
Another note: He is hungry all the time.

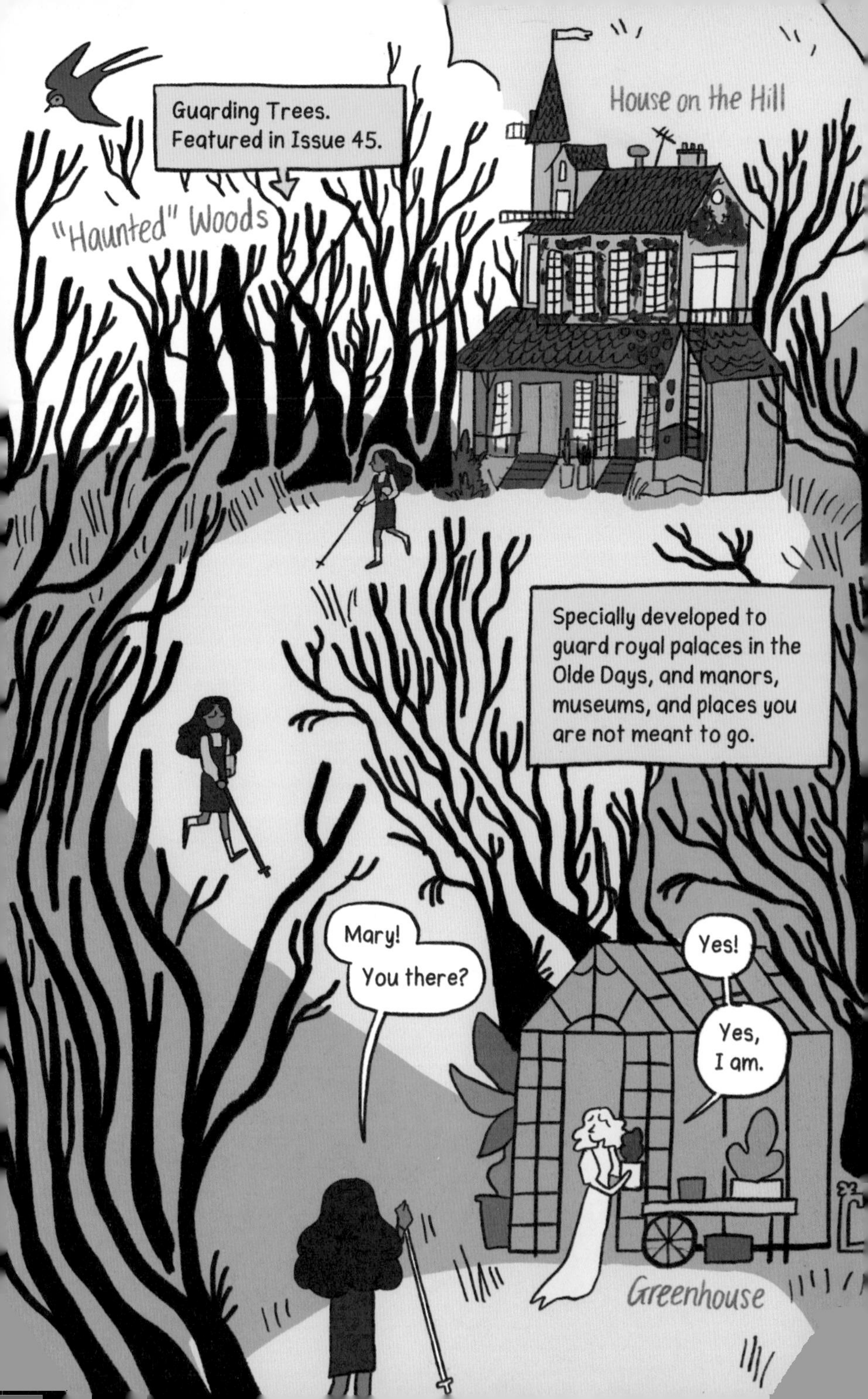
Guarding Trees. Featured in Issue 45.
House on the Hill
"Haunted" Woods
Specially developed to guard royal palaces in the Olde Days, and manors, museums, and places you are not meant to go.
Mary!
You there?
Yes!
Yes, I am.
Greenhouse

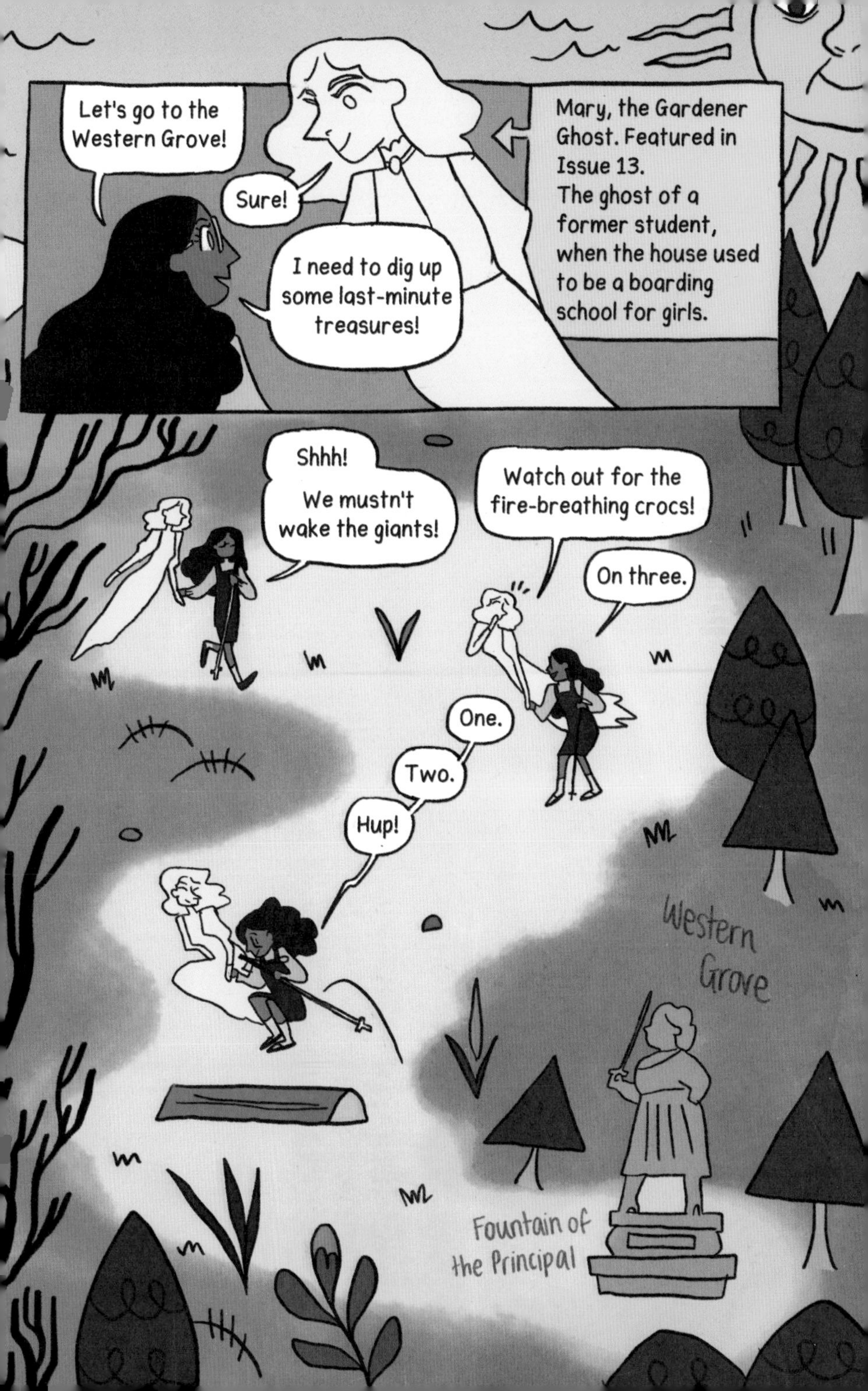
Let's go to the Western Grove!
Sure!
I need to dig up some last-minute treasures!
Mary, the Gardener Ghost. Featured in Issue 13. The ghost of a former student, when the house used to be a boarding school for girls.
Shhh! We mustn't wake the giants!
Watch out for the fire-breathing crocs!
On three.
One.
Two.
Hup!
Western Grove
Fountain of the Principal

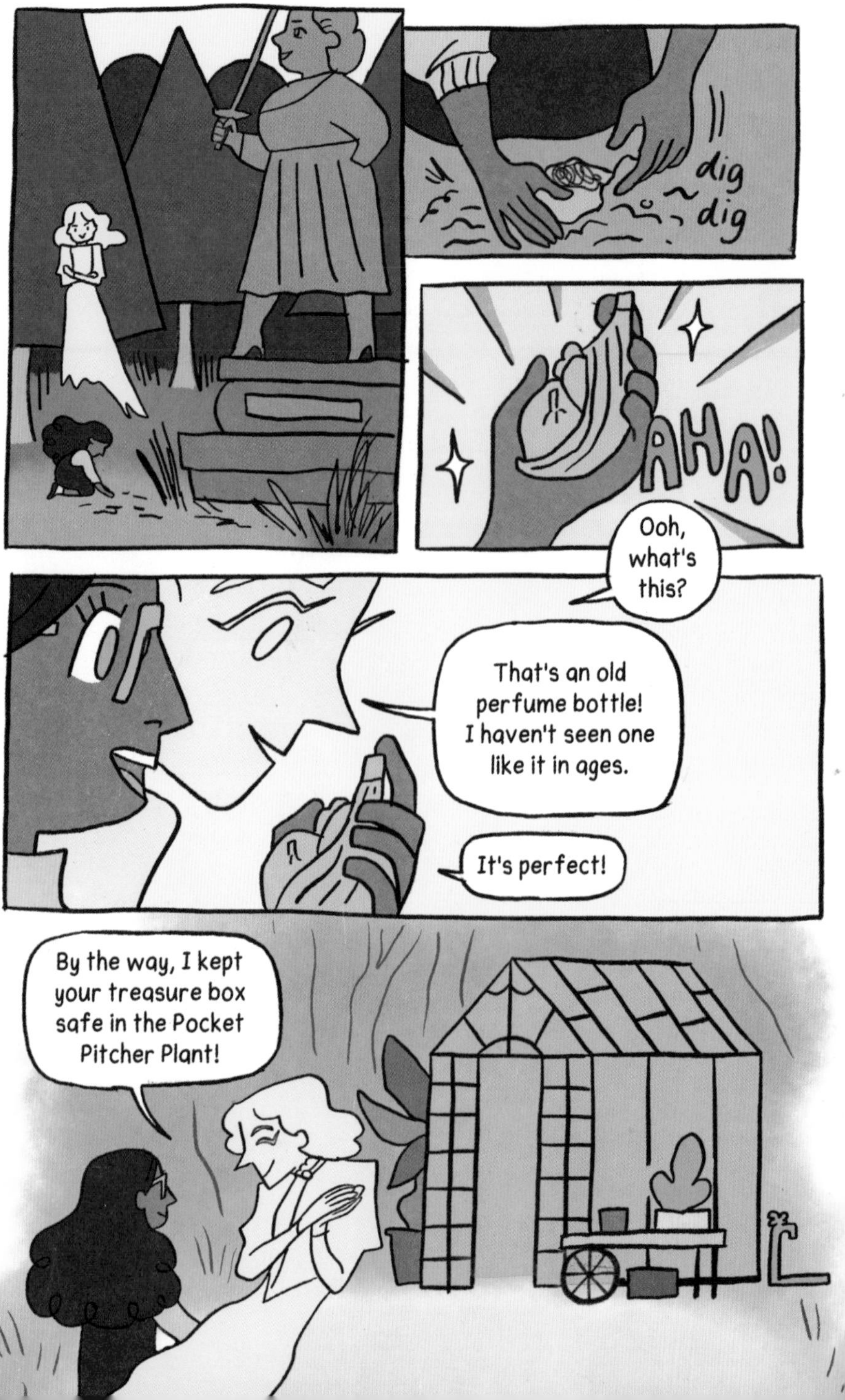
dig
dig
AHA!
Ooh, what's this?
That's an old perfume bottle! I haven't seen one like it in ages.
It's perfect!
By the way, I kept your treasure box safe in the Pocket Pitcher Plant!

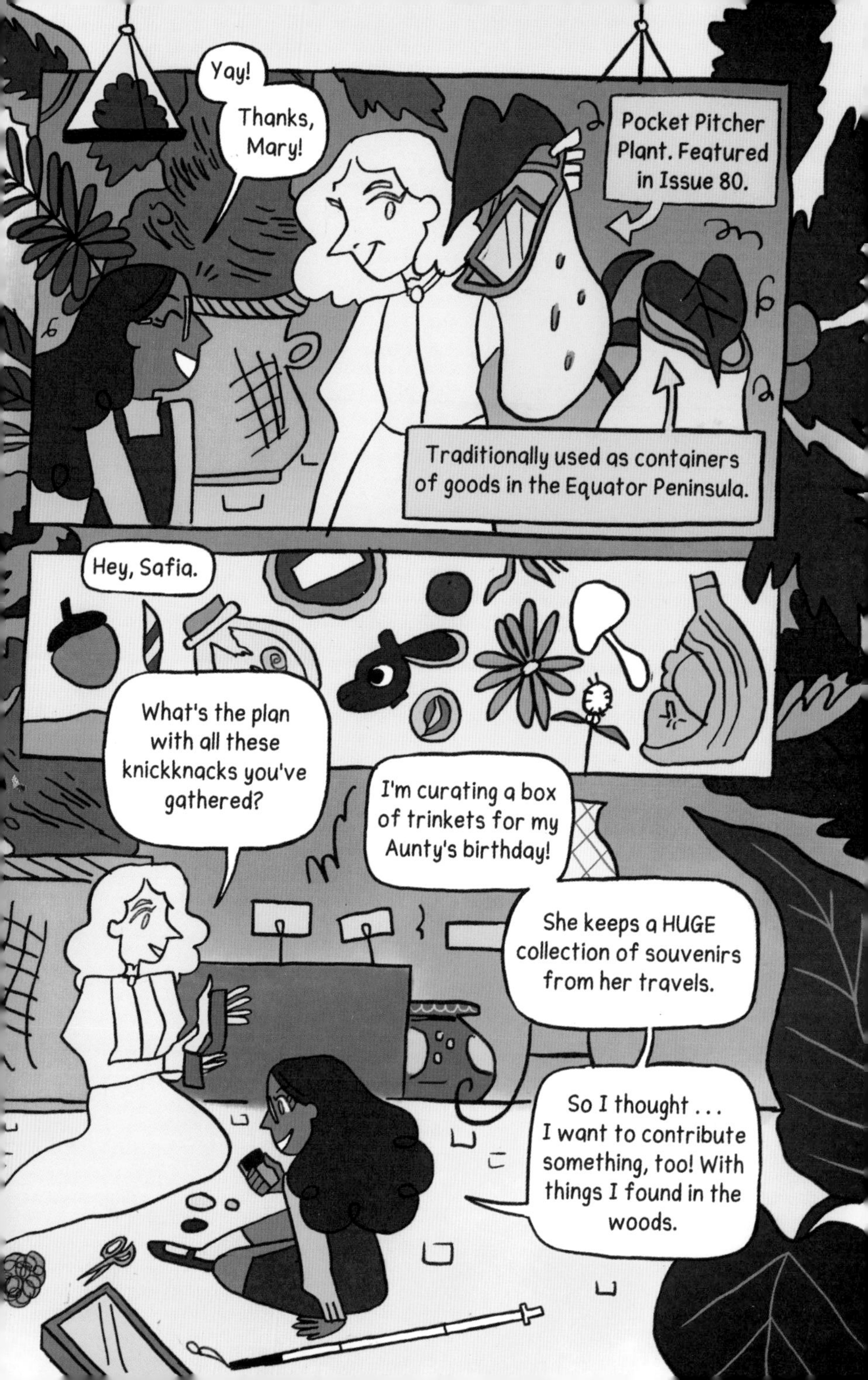
Yay!
Thanks, Mary!
Pocket Pitcher Plant. Featured in Issue 80.
Traditionally used as containers of goods in the Equator Peninsula.
Hey, Safia.
What's the plan with all these knickknacks you've gathered?
I'm curating a box of trinkets for my Aunty's birthday!
She keeps a HUGE collection of souvenirs from her travels.
So I thought . . . I want to contribute something, too! With things I found in the woods.

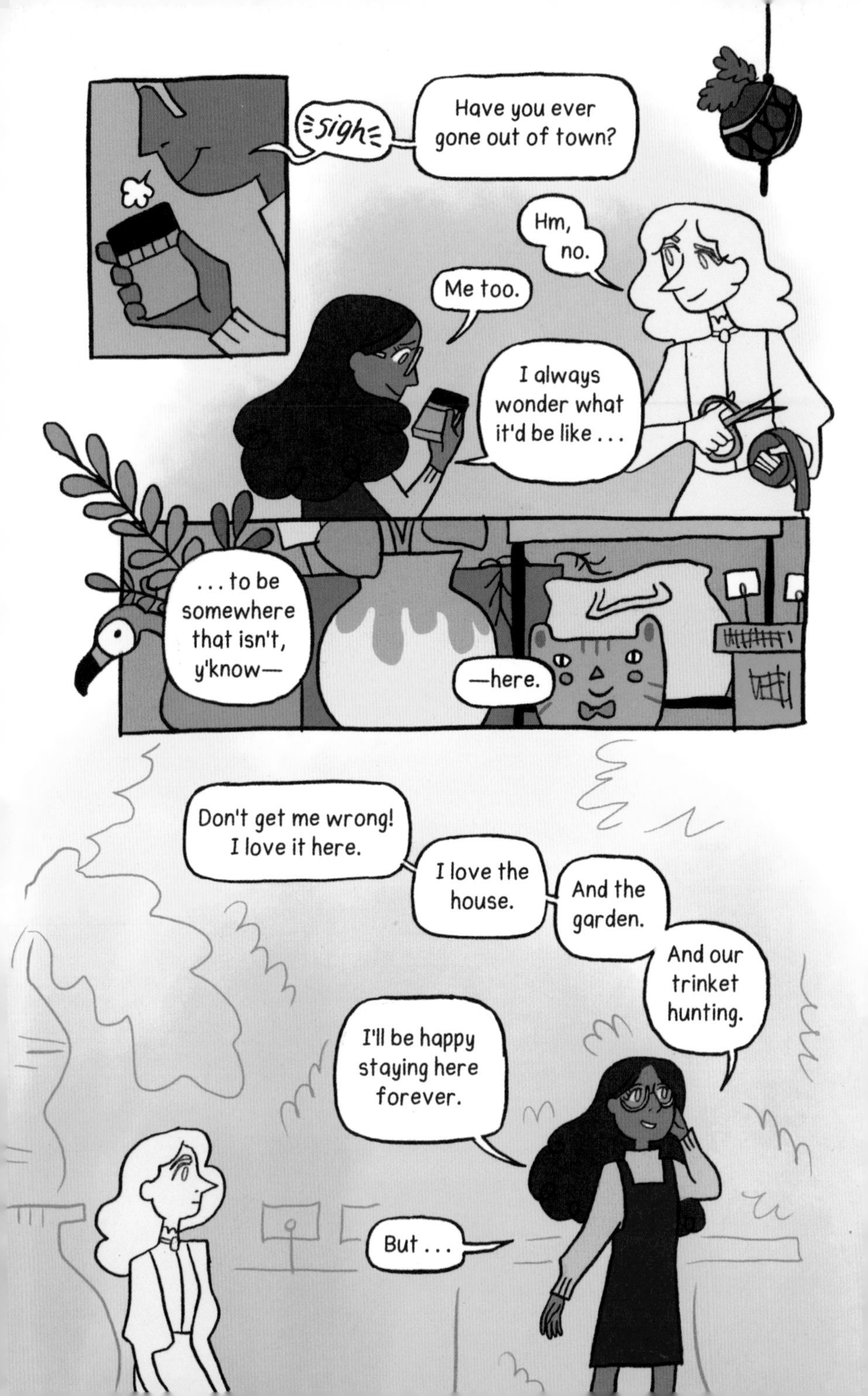

sigh
Have you ever gone out of town?
Hm, no.
Me too.
I always wonder what it'd be like . . .
. . . to be somewhere that isn't, y'know—
—here.
Don't get me wrong! I love it here.
I love the house.
And the garden.
And our trinket hunting.
I'll be happy staying here forever.
But . . .

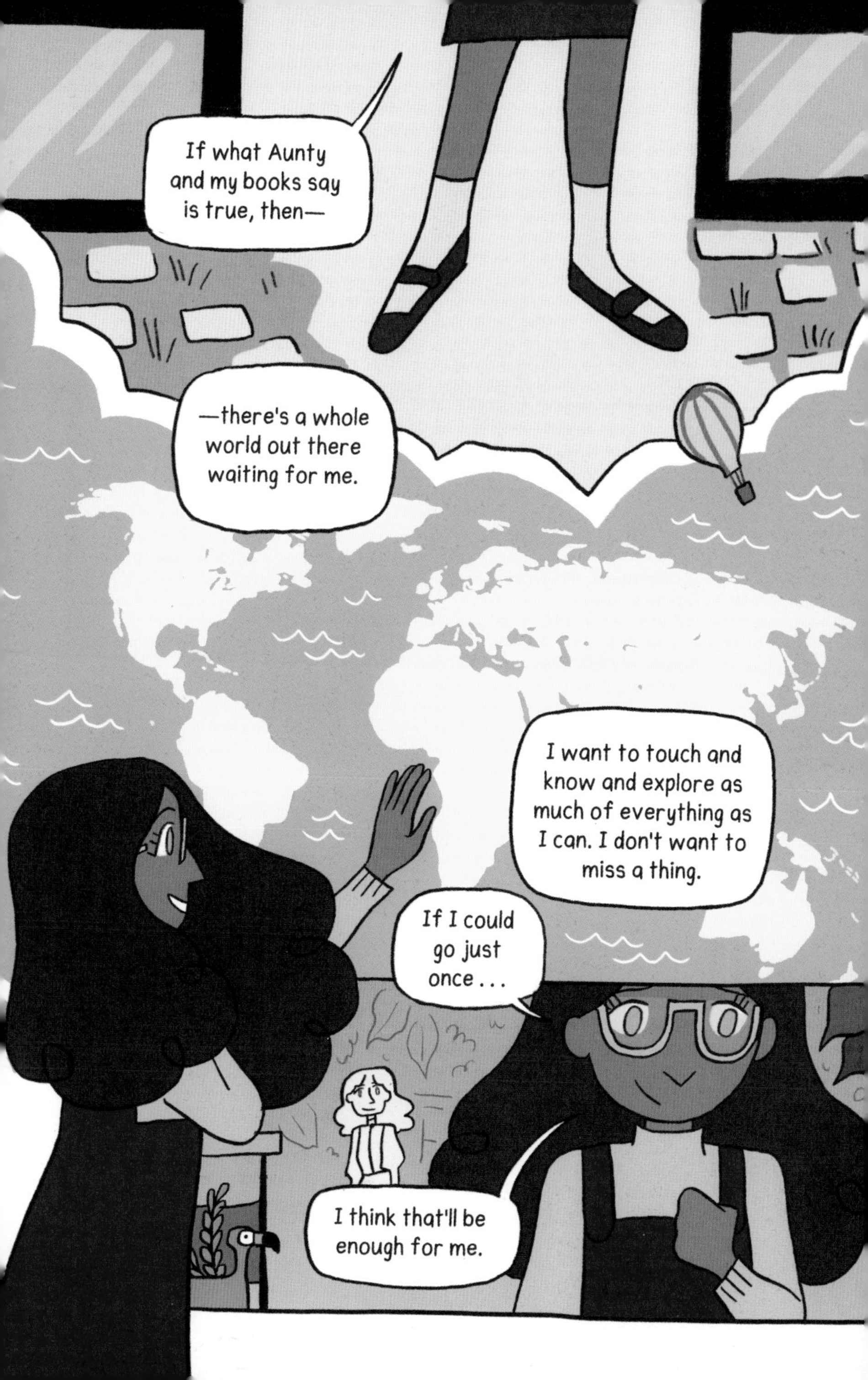
If what Aunty and my books say is true, then—
—there's a whole world out there waiting for me.
I want to touch and know and explore as much of everything as I can. I don't want to miss a thing.
If I could go just once . . .
I think that'll be enough for me.

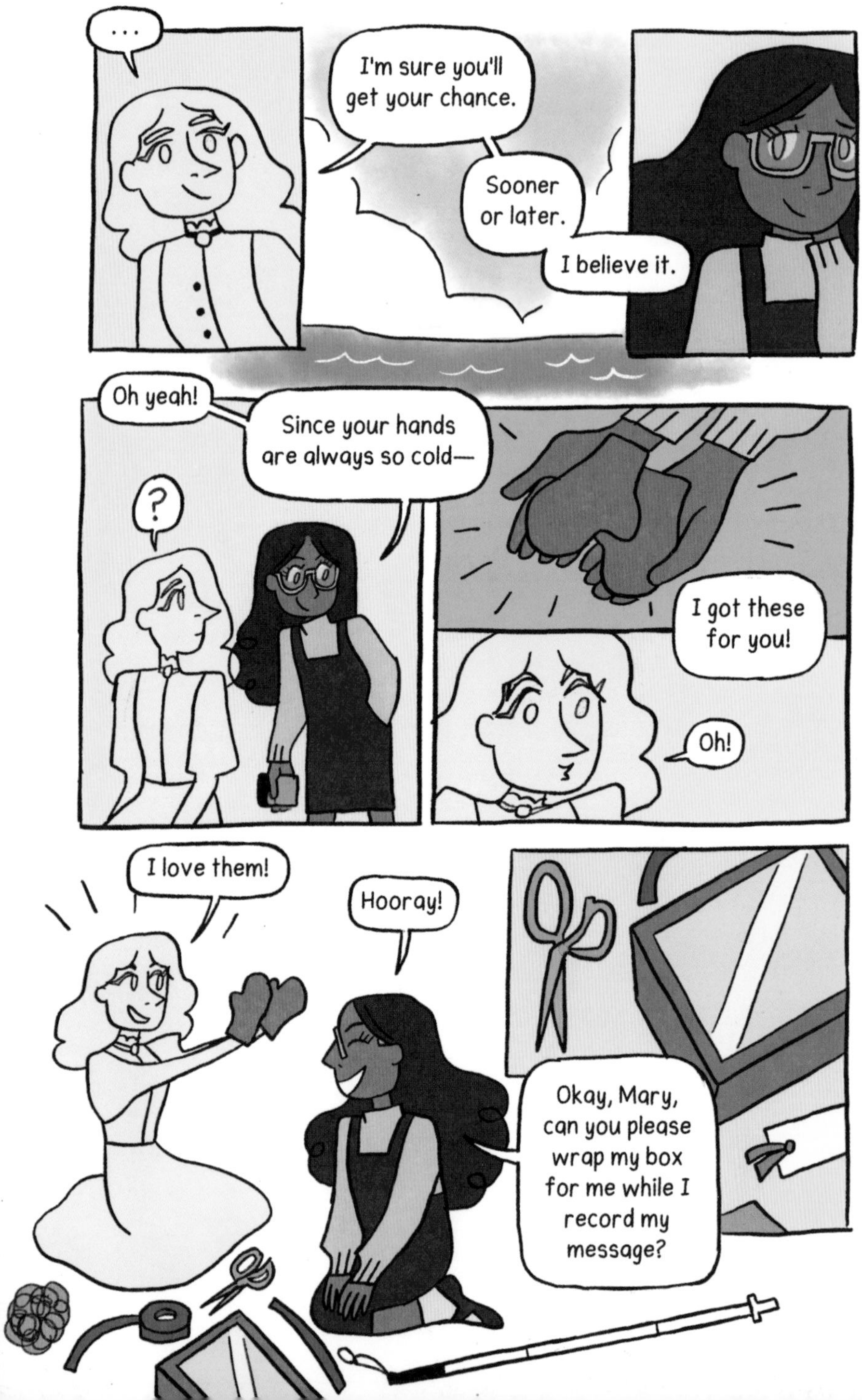
...
I'm sure you'll get your chance.
Sooner or later.
I believe it.
Oh yeah!
Since your hands are always so cold—
?
I got these for you!
Oh!
I love them!
Hooray!
Okay, Mary, can you please wrap my box for me while I record my message?

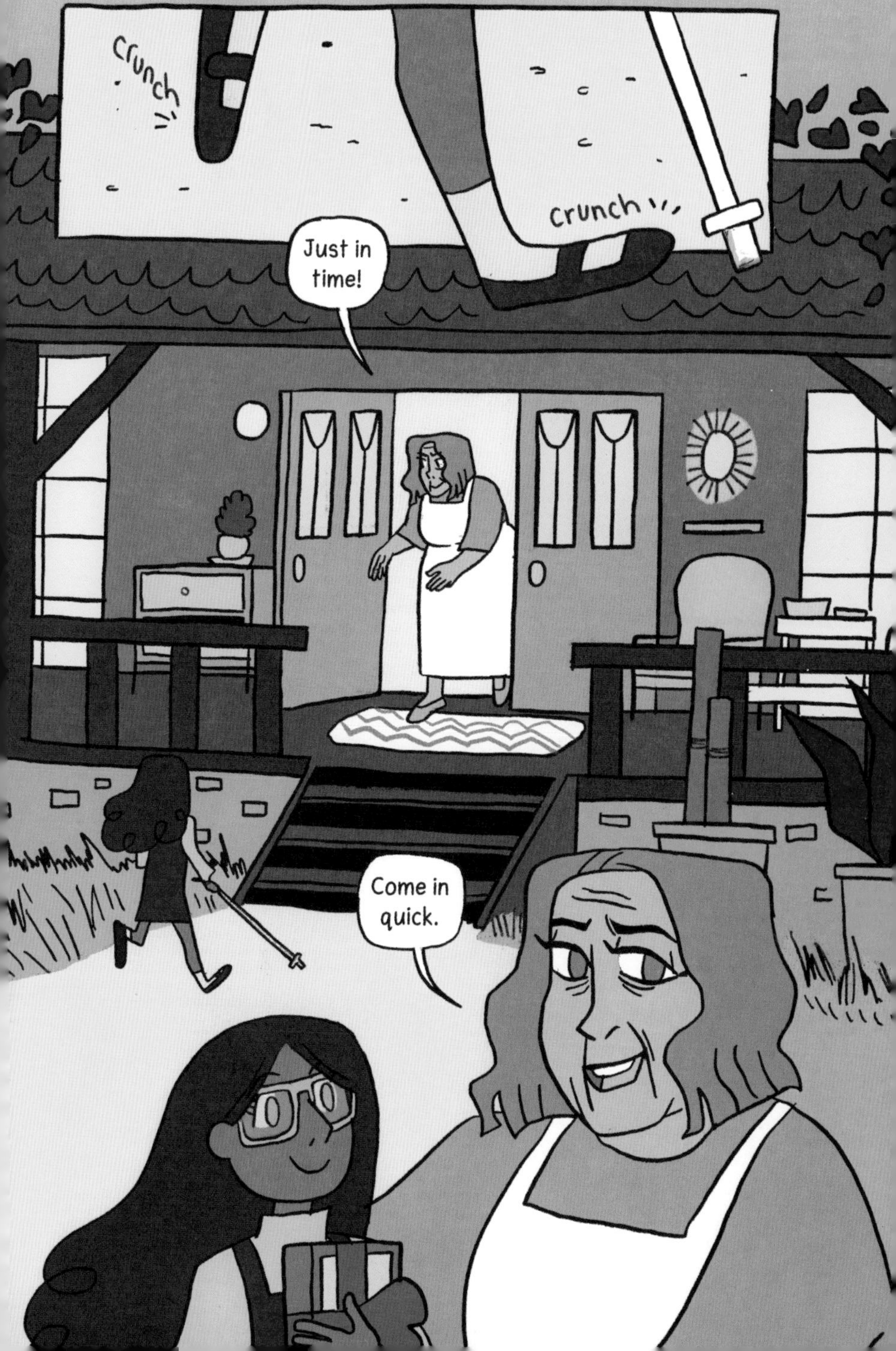
crunch
crunch
Just in time!
Come in quick.

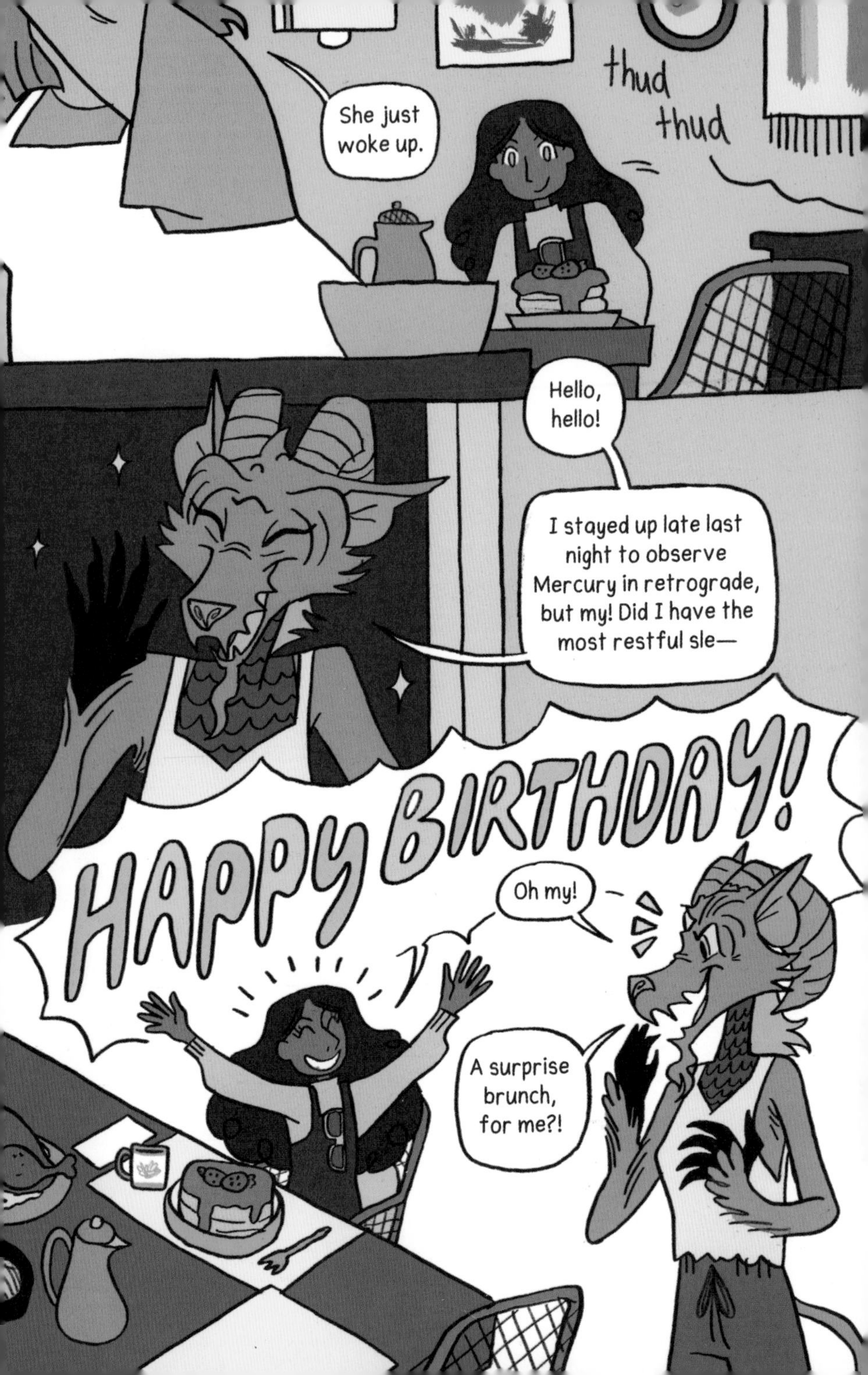
She just woke up.
thud
thud
Hello, hello!
I stayed up late last night to observe Mercury in retrograde, but my! Did I have the most restful sle—
HAPPY BIRTHDAY!
Oh my!
A surprise brunch, for me?!

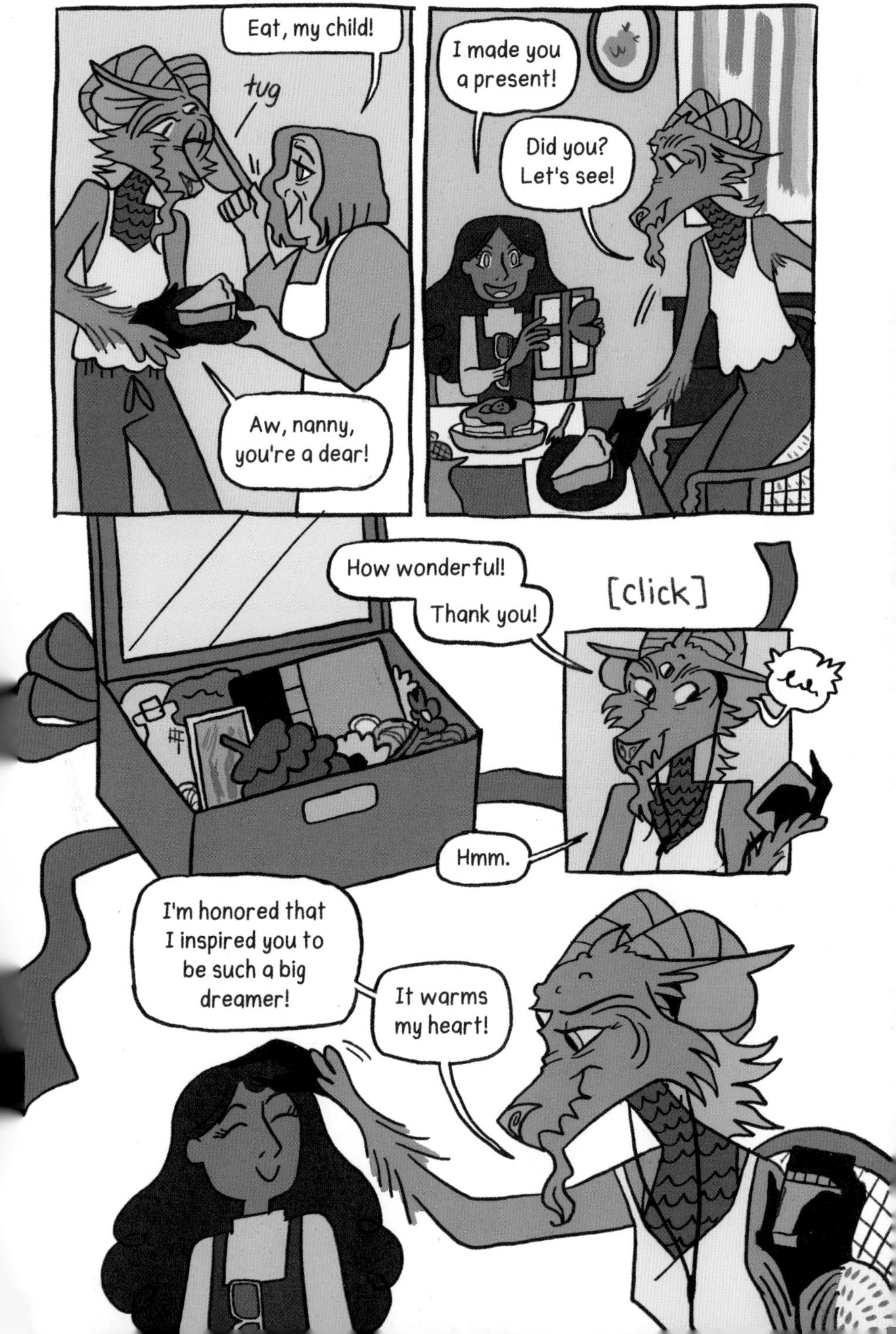
Eat, my child!
tug
Aw, nanny, you're a dear!
I made you a present!
Did you? Let's see!
How wonderful!
Thank you!
[click]
Hmm.
I'm honored that I inspired you to be such a big dreamer!
It warms my heart!

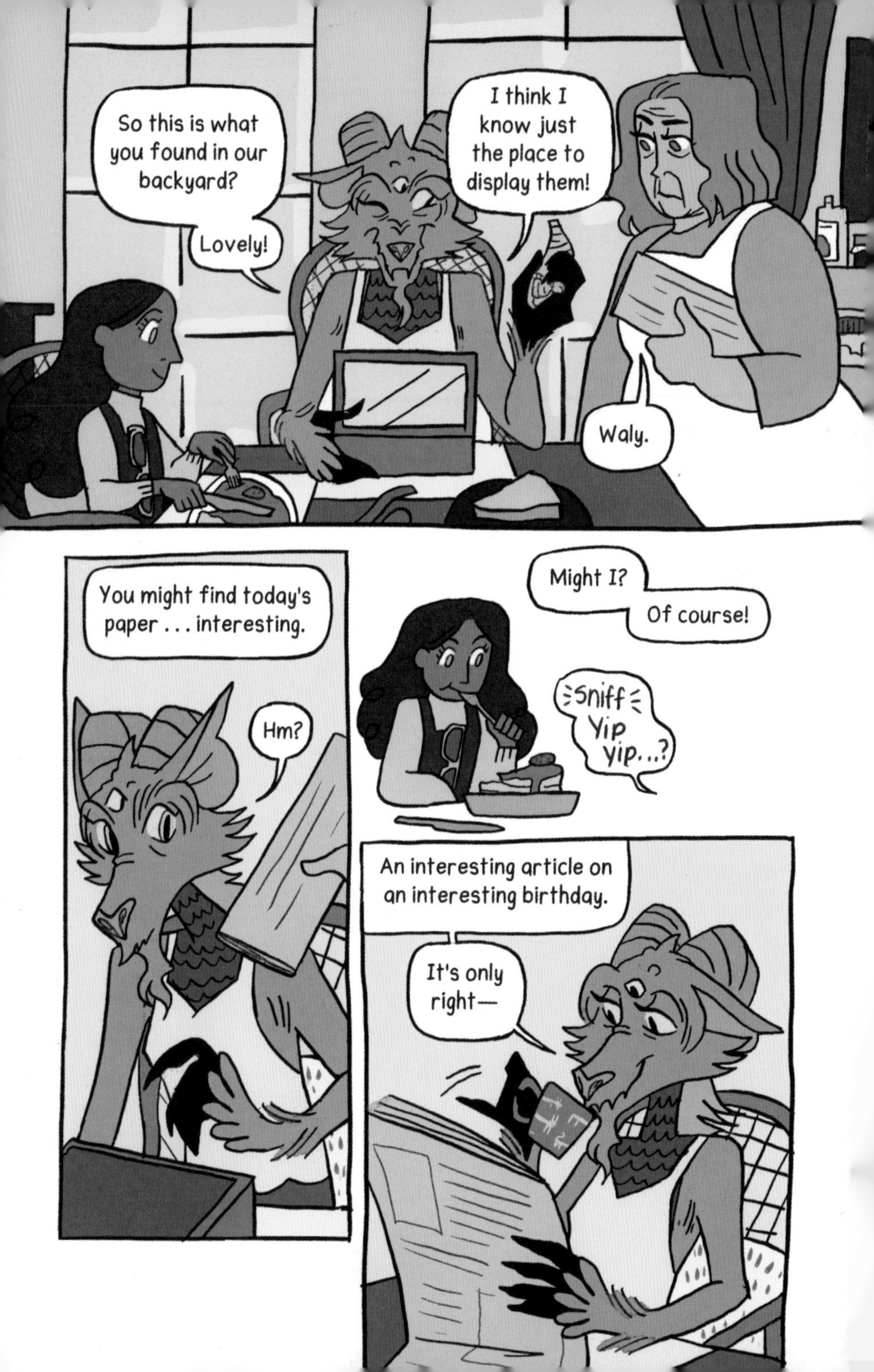
So this is what you found in our backyard?
Lovely!
I think I know just the place to display them!
Waly.
You might find today's paper . . . interesting.
Hm?
Might I?
Of course!
Sniff
Yip yip...?
An interesting article on an interesting birthday.
It's only right—

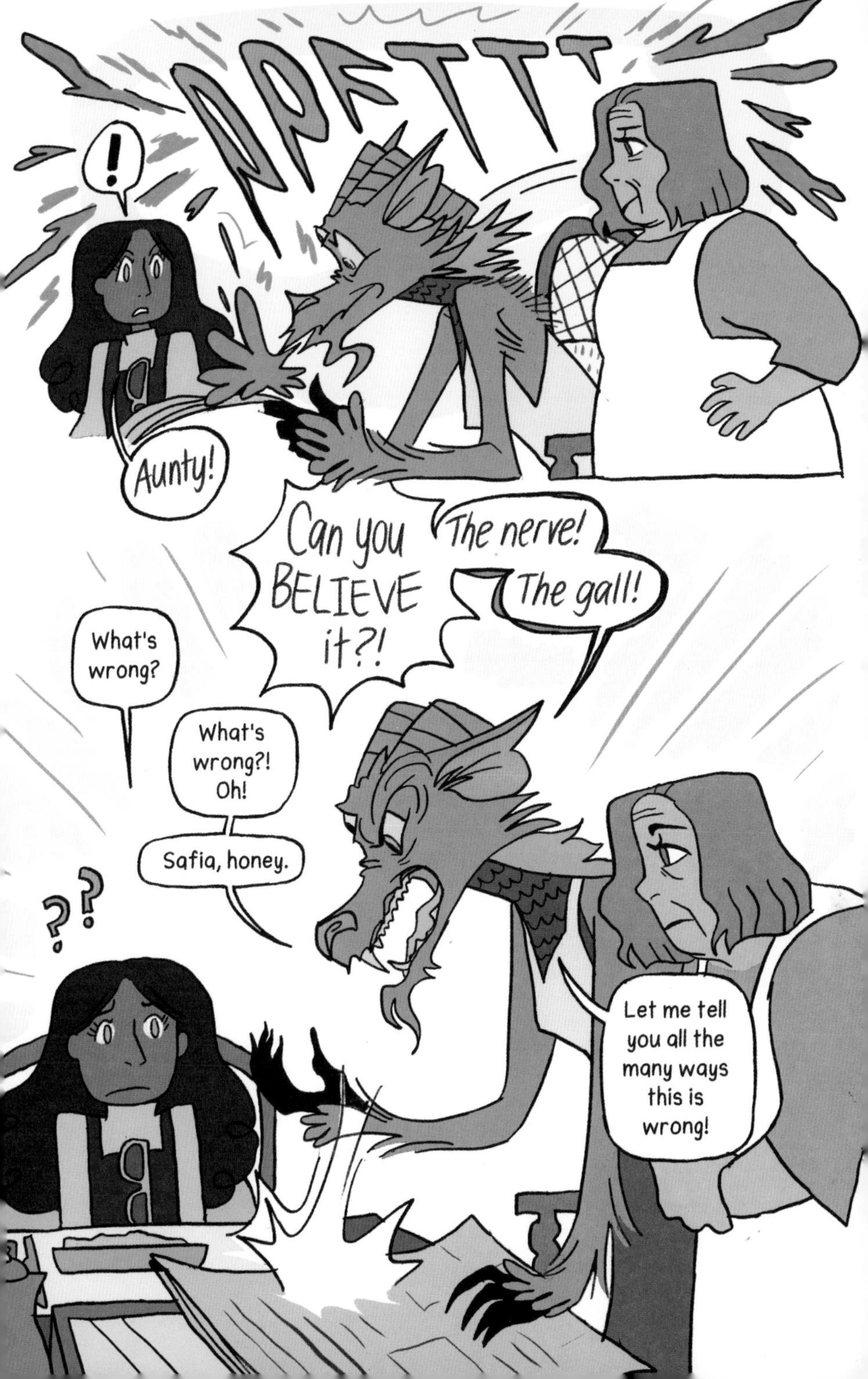
PPFTTT
!
Aunty!
Can you BELIEVE it?!
The nerve!
The gall!
What's wrong?
What's wrong?! Oh!
Safia, honey.
??
Let me tell you all the many ways this is wrong!

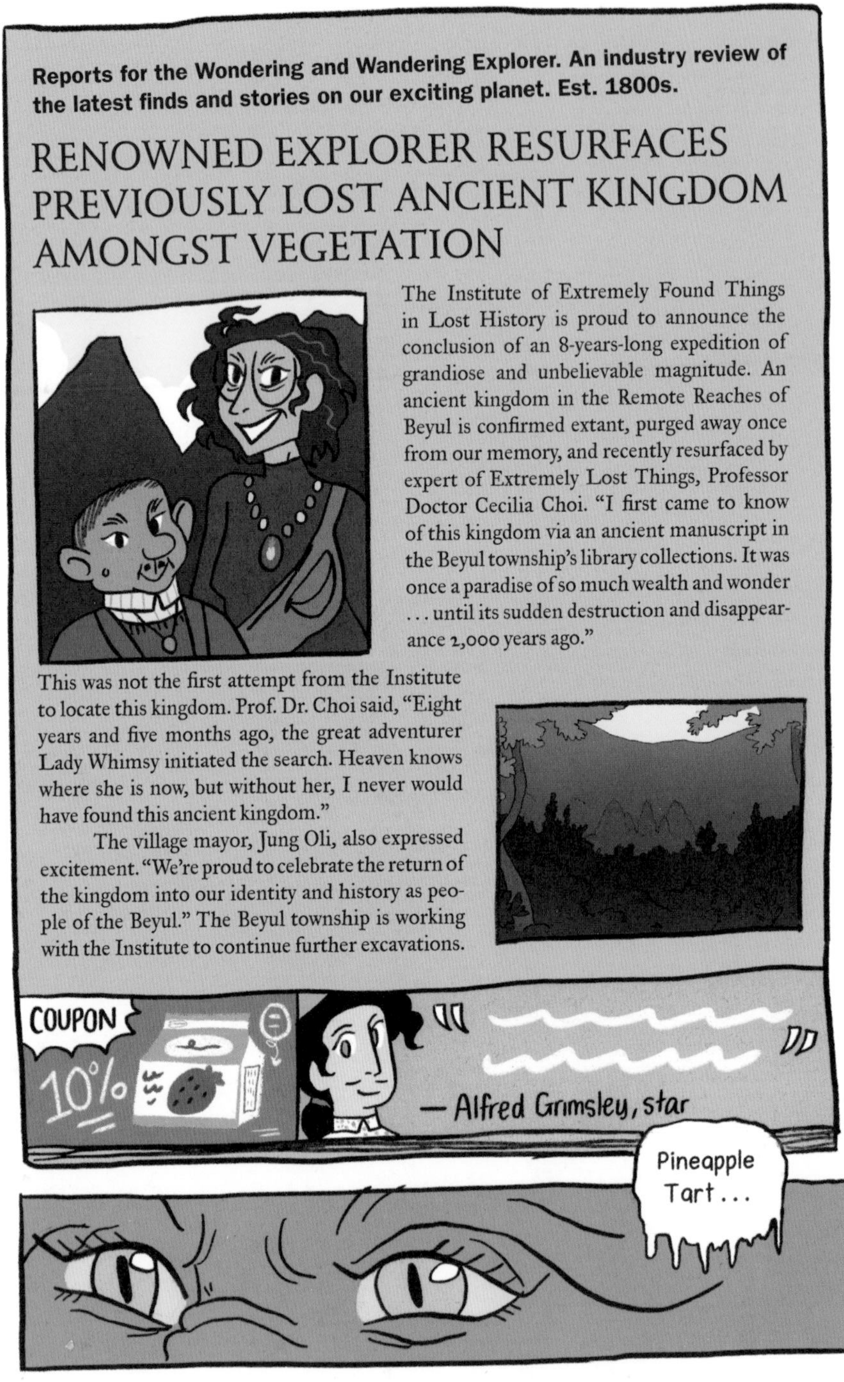
Reports for the Wondering and Wandering Explorer. An industry review of the latest finds and stories on our exciting planet. Est. 1800s.

RENOWNED EXPLORER RESURFACES PREVIOUSLY LOST ANCIENT KINGDOM AMONGST VEGETATION

The Institute of Extremely Found Things in Lost History is proud to announce the conclusion of an 8-years-long expedition of grandiose and unbelievable magnitude. An ancient kingdom in the Remote Reaches of Beyul is confirmed extant, purged away once from our memory, and recently resurfaced by expert of Extremely Lost Things, Professor Doctor Cecilia Choi. "I first came to know of this kingdom via an ancient manuscript in the Beyul township's library collections. It was once a paradise of so much wealth and wonder . . . until its sudden destruction and disappearance 2,000 years ago."

This was not the first attempt from the Institute to locate this kingdom. Prof. Dr. Choi said, "Eight years and five months ago, the great adventurer Lady Whimsy initiated the search. Heaven knows where she is now, but without her, I never would have found this ancient kingdom."

The village mayor, Jung Oli, also expressed excitement. "We're proud to celebrate the return of the kingdom into our identity and history as people of the Beyul." The Beyul township is working with the Institute to continue further excavations.

COUPON
10%
— Alfred Grimsley, star
Pineapple Tart . . .

An Endless Game of Tag

When Aunty Whimsy was six and moved to a new country,

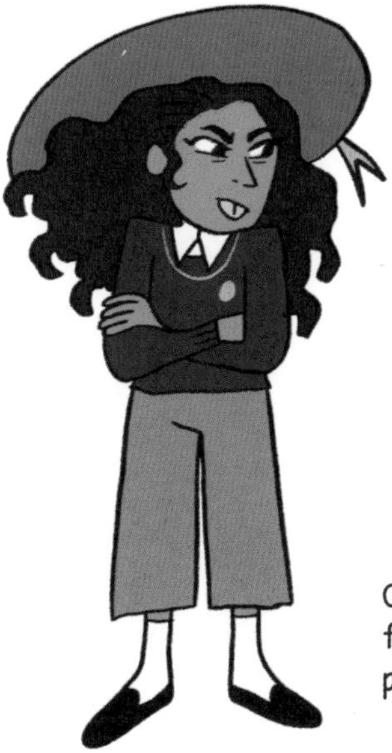

she regrettably became neighbors with an Annoying Child of Not Much Interest.

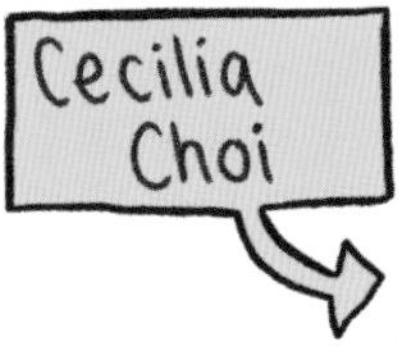
Cecilia Choi

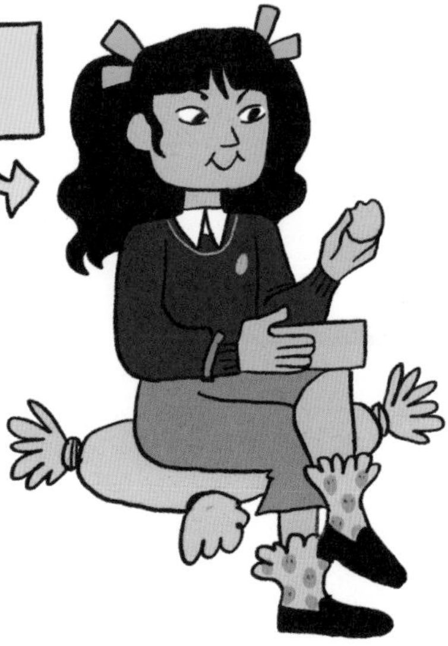

Cecilia had a great fondness for pineapple tarts—

which was the origin of Aunty Whimsy's nickname for them.

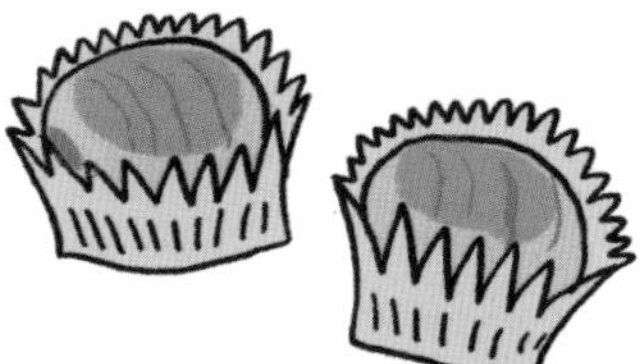

Aunty Whimsy and Pineapple Tart shared an enduring rivalry that began from a childhood game of tag.

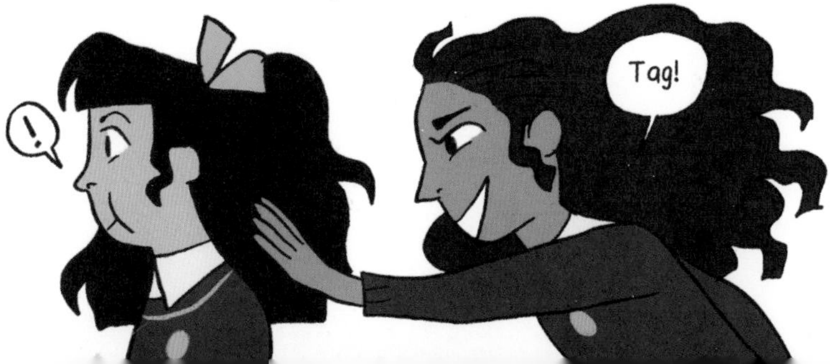
!
Tag!

Since then, they had competed in everything,

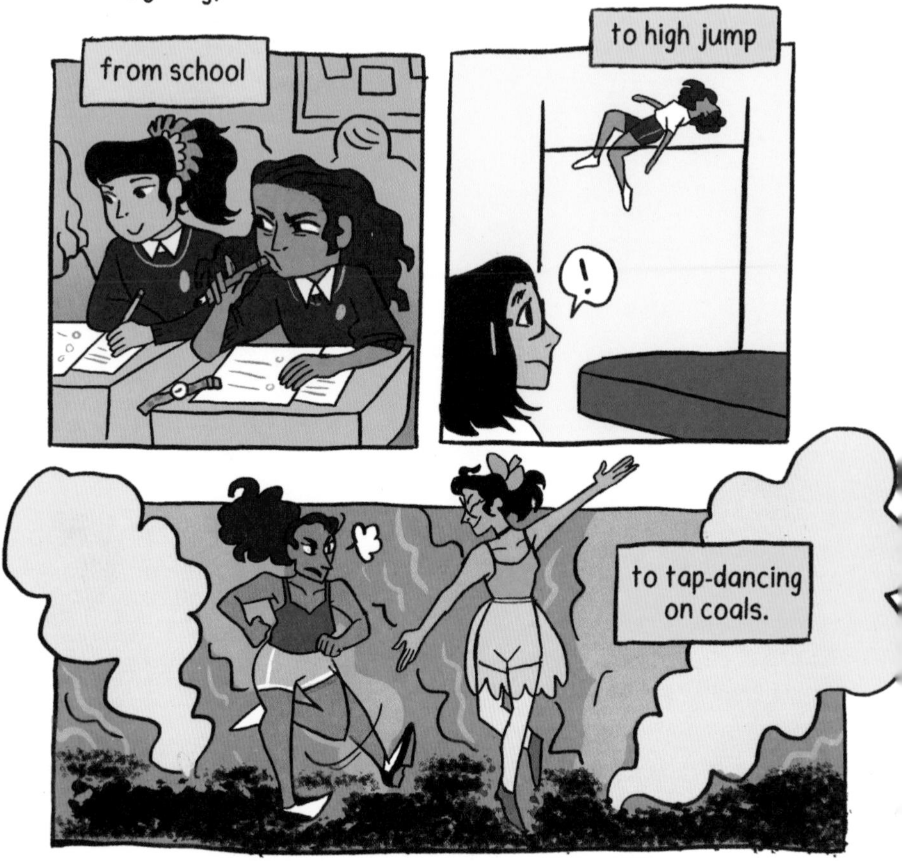
from school
to high jump
!
to tap-dancing on coals.

Luckily, Pineapple Tart was never as competent as Aunty Whimsy.

They also never had a passion for adventuring, swashbuckling, or far-flinging, so Aunty Whimsy never worried about them catching up in these areas and stealing the spotlight.

Or so she thought...

Today, on Aunty Whimsy's birthday,
they had the guts to finally catch up to her
and shamelessly use the term
"RENOWNED EXPLORER"
and boldly brag in the newspaper:

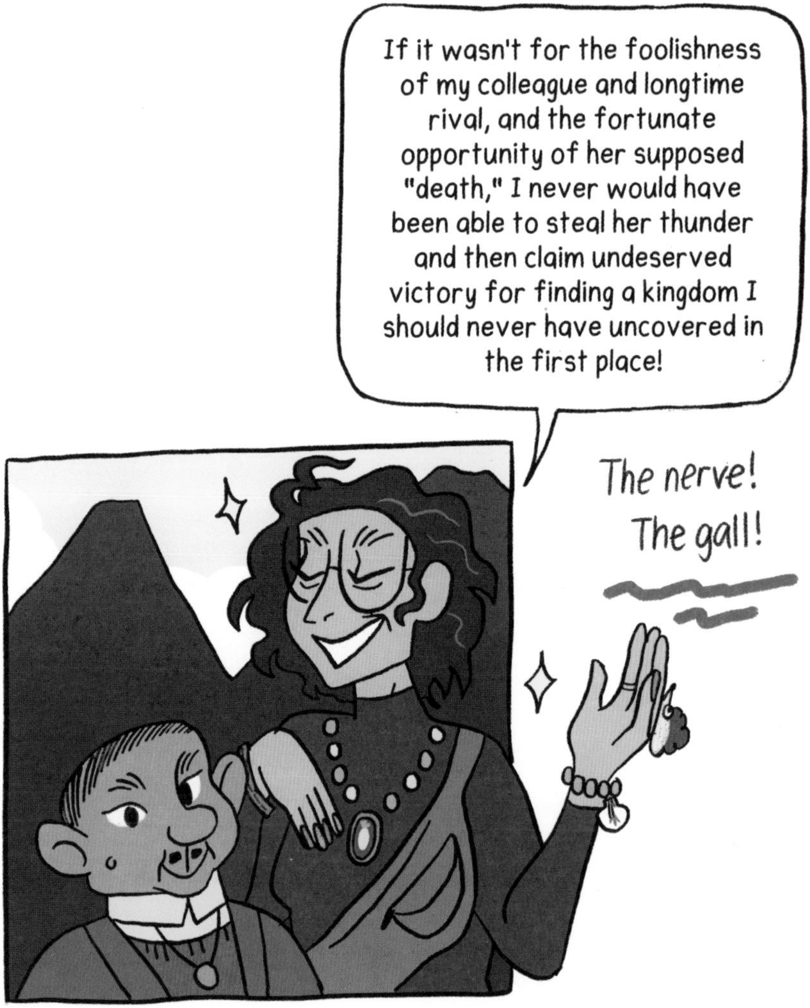
If it wasn't for the foolishness of my colleague and longtime rival, and the fortunate opportunity of her supposed "death," I never would have been able to steal her thunder and then claim undeserved victory for finding a kingdom I should never have uncovered in the first place!
The nerve!
The gall!

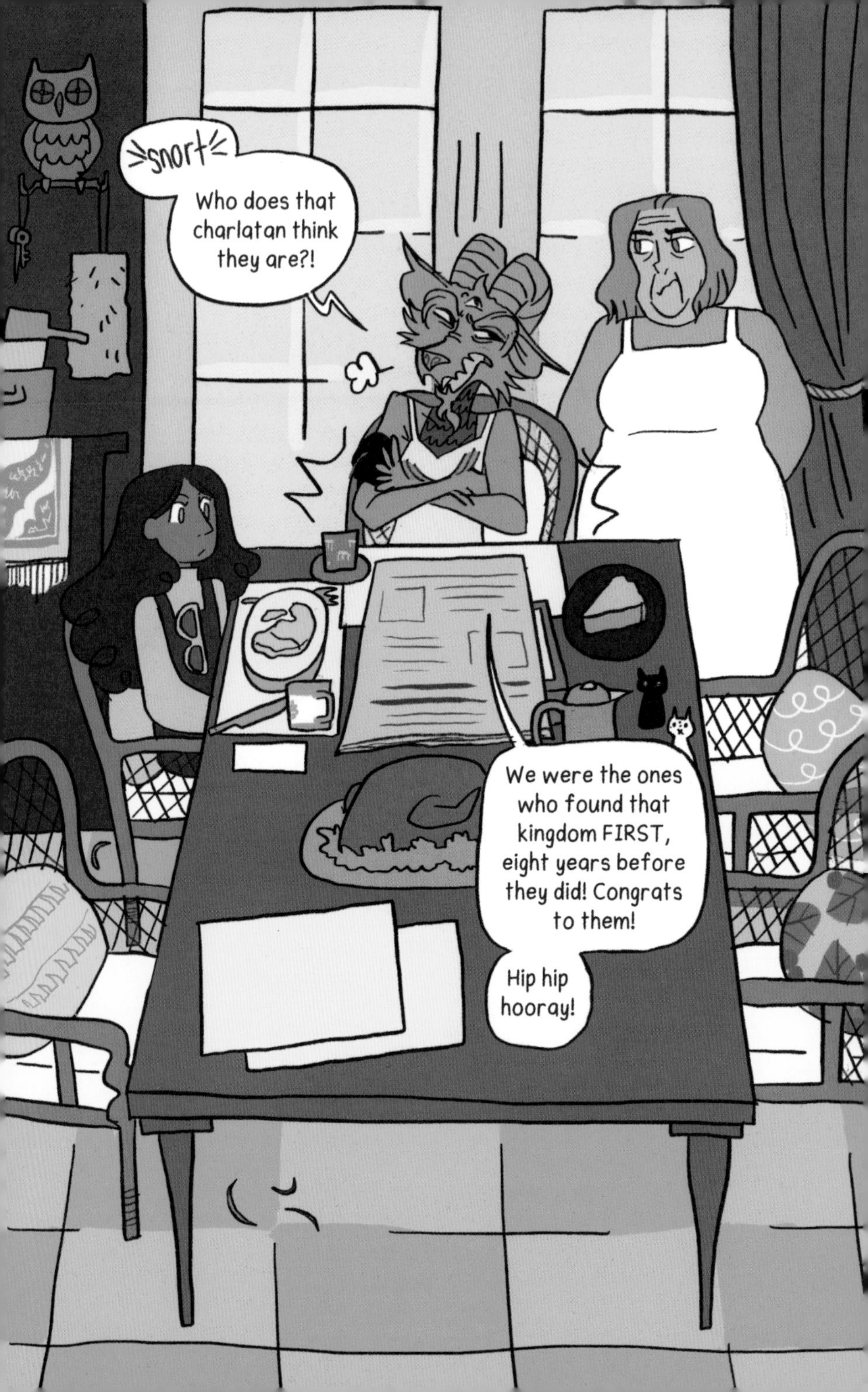
snort
Who does that charlatan think they are?!
We were the ones who found that kingdom FIRST, eight years before they did! Congrats to them!
Hip hip hooray!

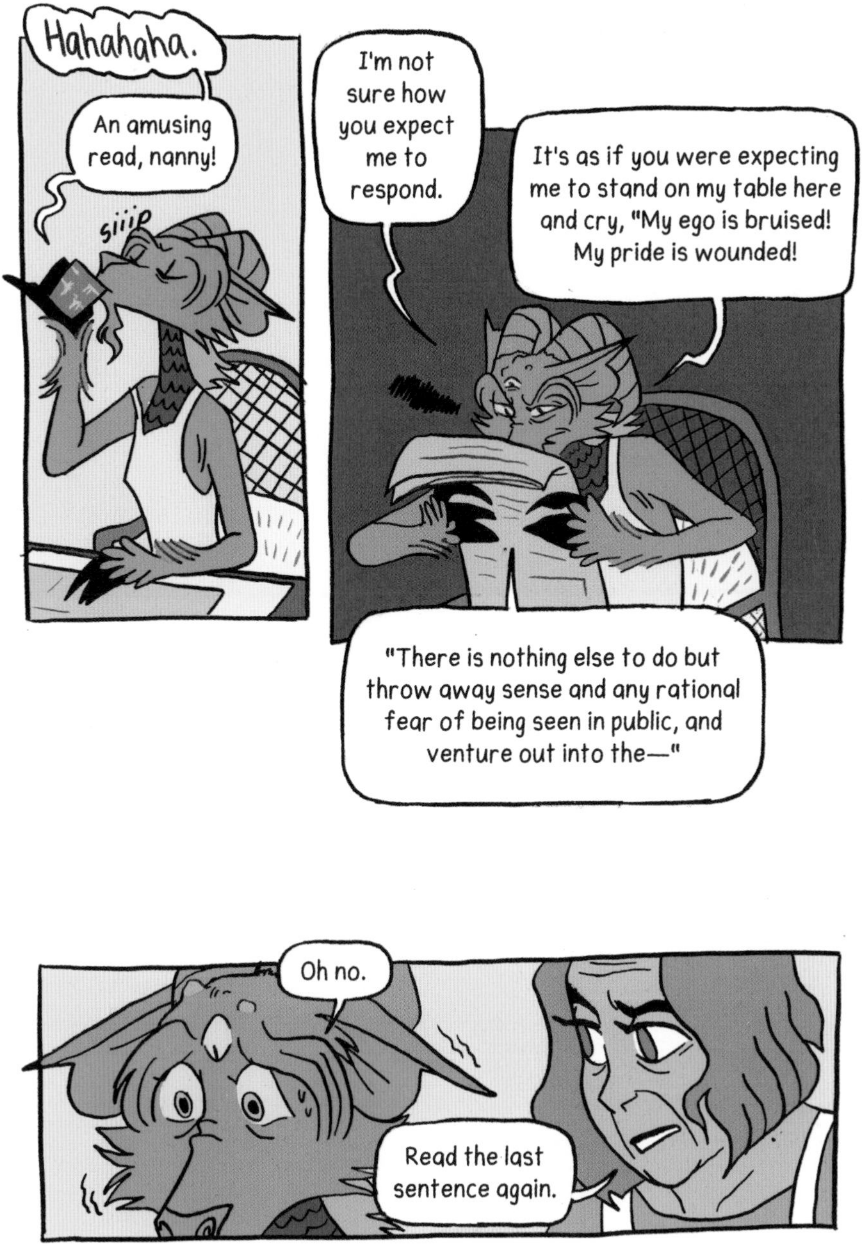
Hahahaha.
An amusing read, nanny!
siiip
I'm not sure how you expect me to respond.
It's as if you were expecting me to stand on my table here and cry, "My ego is bruised! My pride is wounded!
"There is nothing else to do but throw away sense and any rational fear of being seen in public, and venture out into the—"
Oh no.
Read the last sentence again.

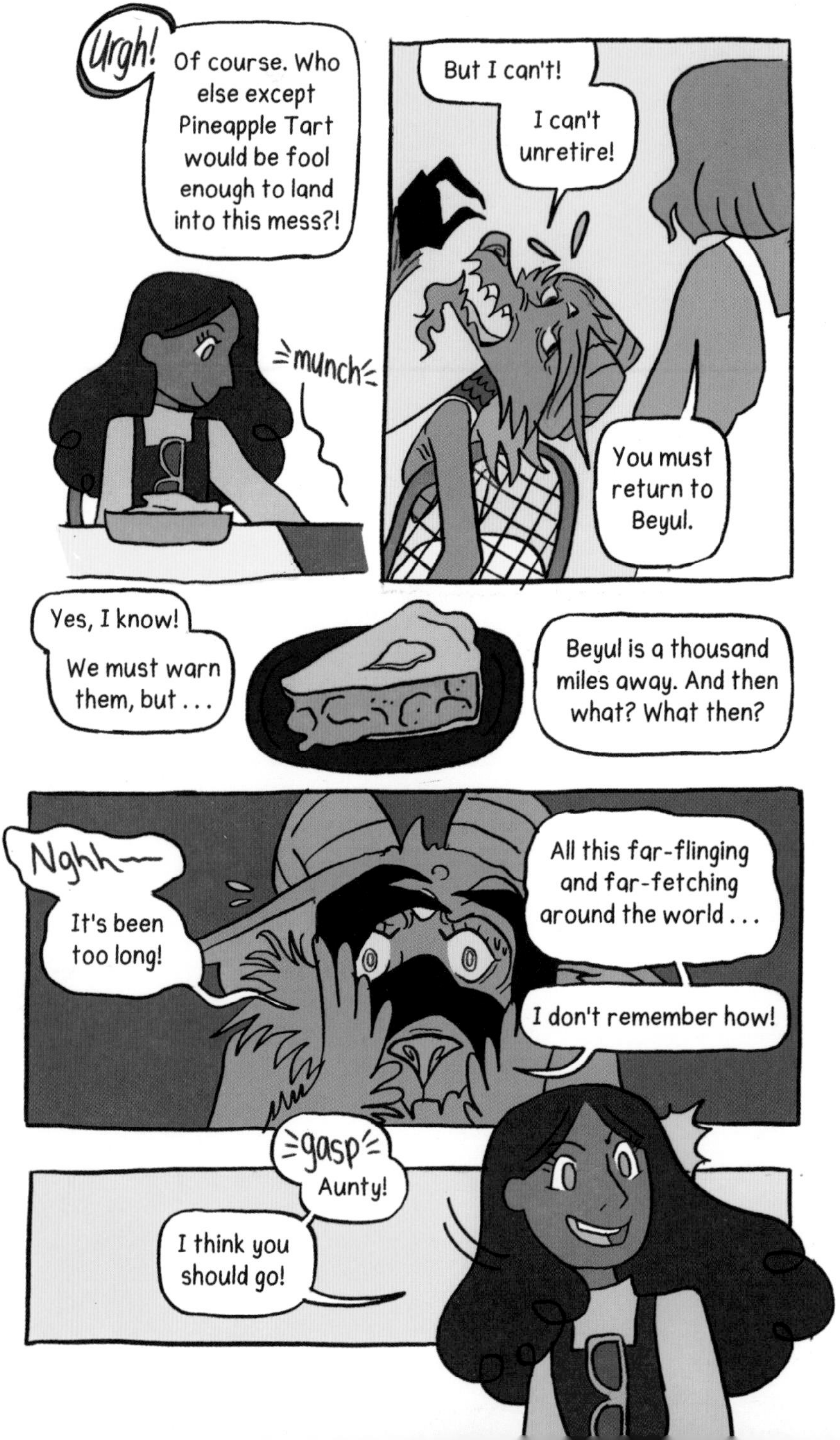
Urgh!
Of course. Who else except Pineapple Tart would be fool enough to land into this mess?!
munch
But I can't!
I can't unretire!
You must return to Beyul.
Yes, I know!
We must warn them, but . . .
Beyul is a thousand miles away. And then what? What then?
Nghh—
It's been too long!
All this far-flinging and far-fetching around the world . . .
I don't remember how!
gasp
Aunty!
I think you should go!

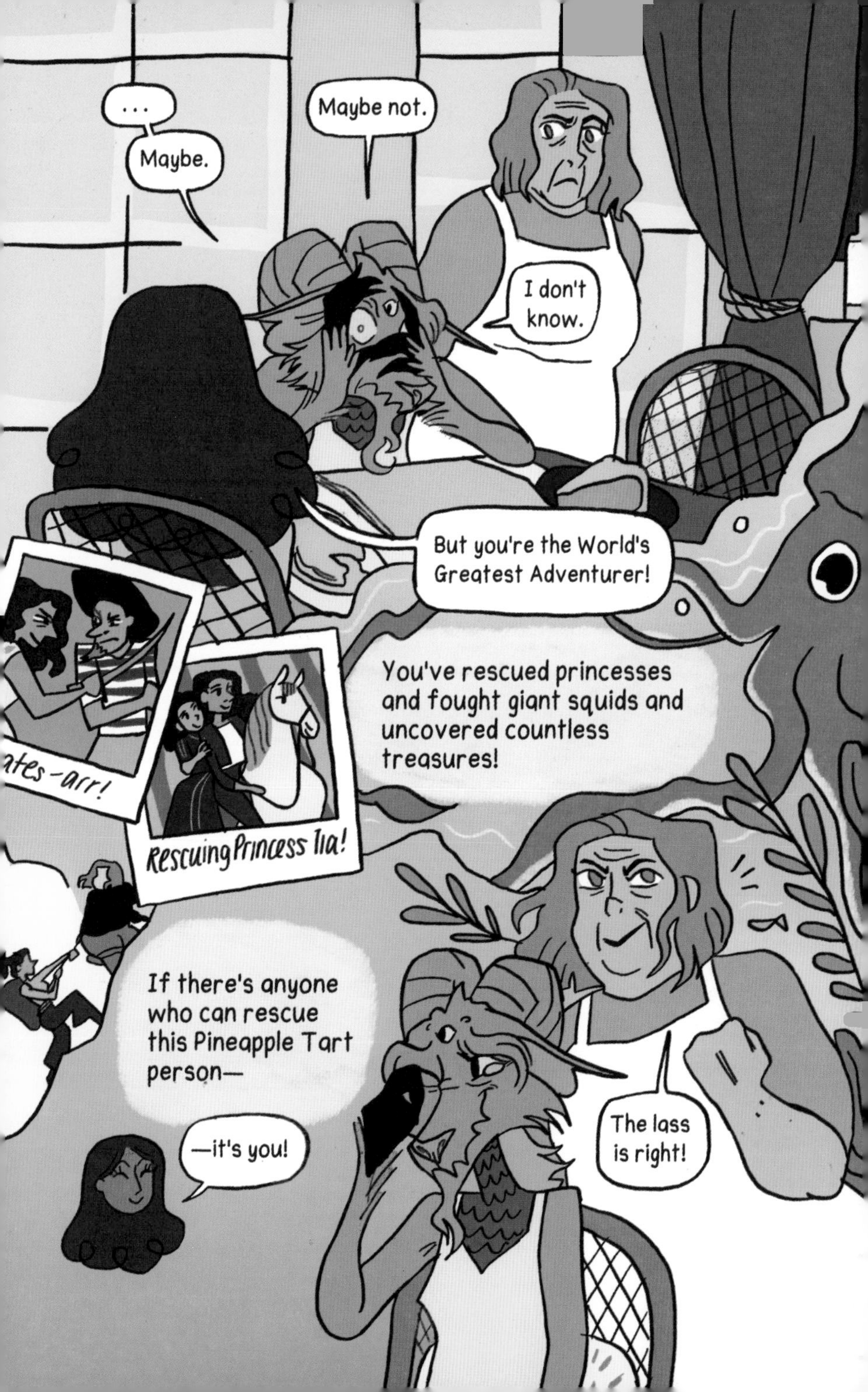
...
Maybe.
Maybe not.
I don't know.
But you're the World's Greatest Adventurer!
You've rescued princesses and fought giant squids and uncovered countless treasures!
ates—arr!
Rescuing Princess Lia!
If there's anyone who can rescue this Pineapple Tart person—
—it's you!
The lass is right!

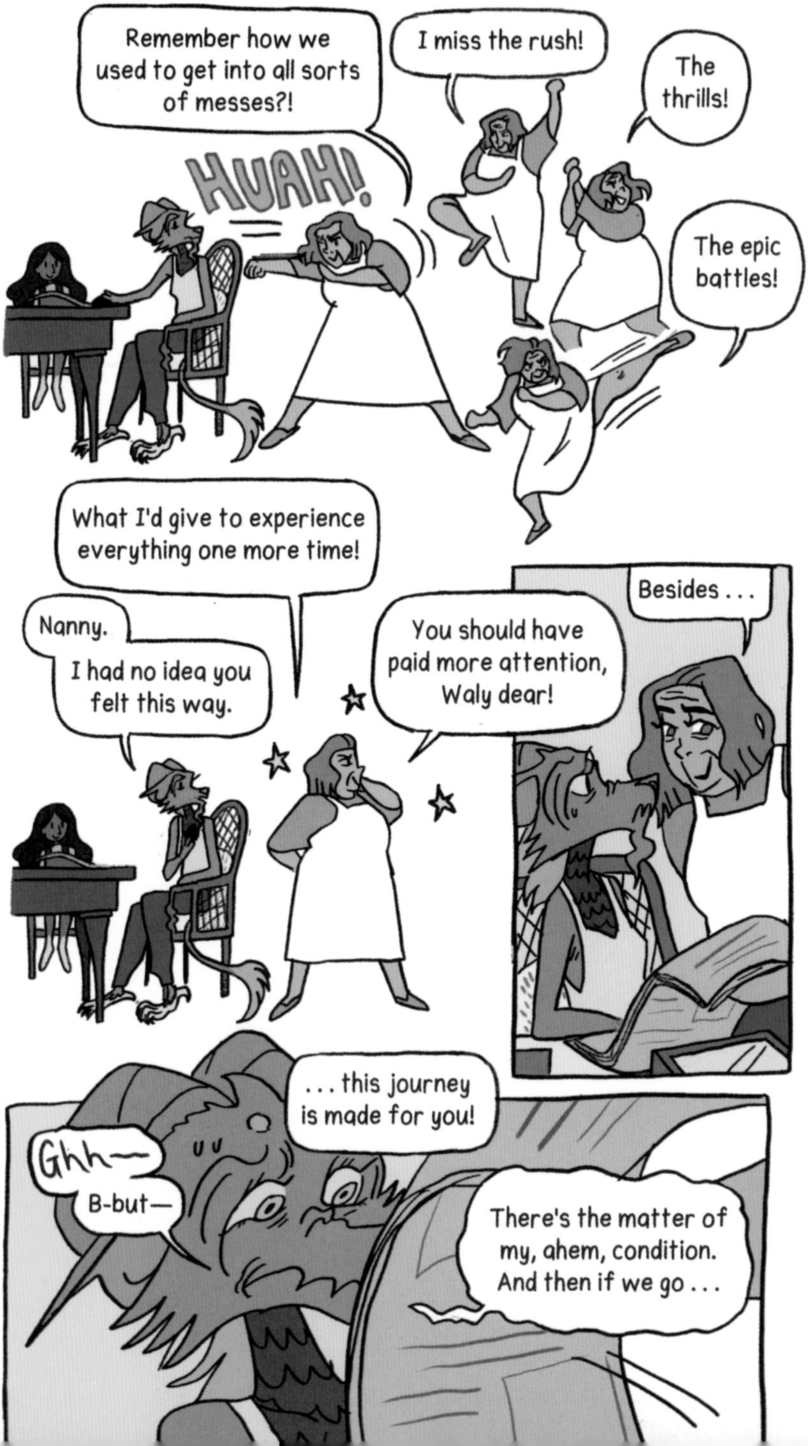
Remember how we used to get into all sorts of messes?!
I miss the rush!
The thrills!
HUAH!
The epic battles!
What I'd give to experience everything one more time!
Nanny.
I had no idea you felt this way.
You should have paid more attention, Waly dear!
Besides . . .
. . . this journey is made for you!
Ghh—
B-but—
There's the matter of my, ahem, condition. And then if we go . . .

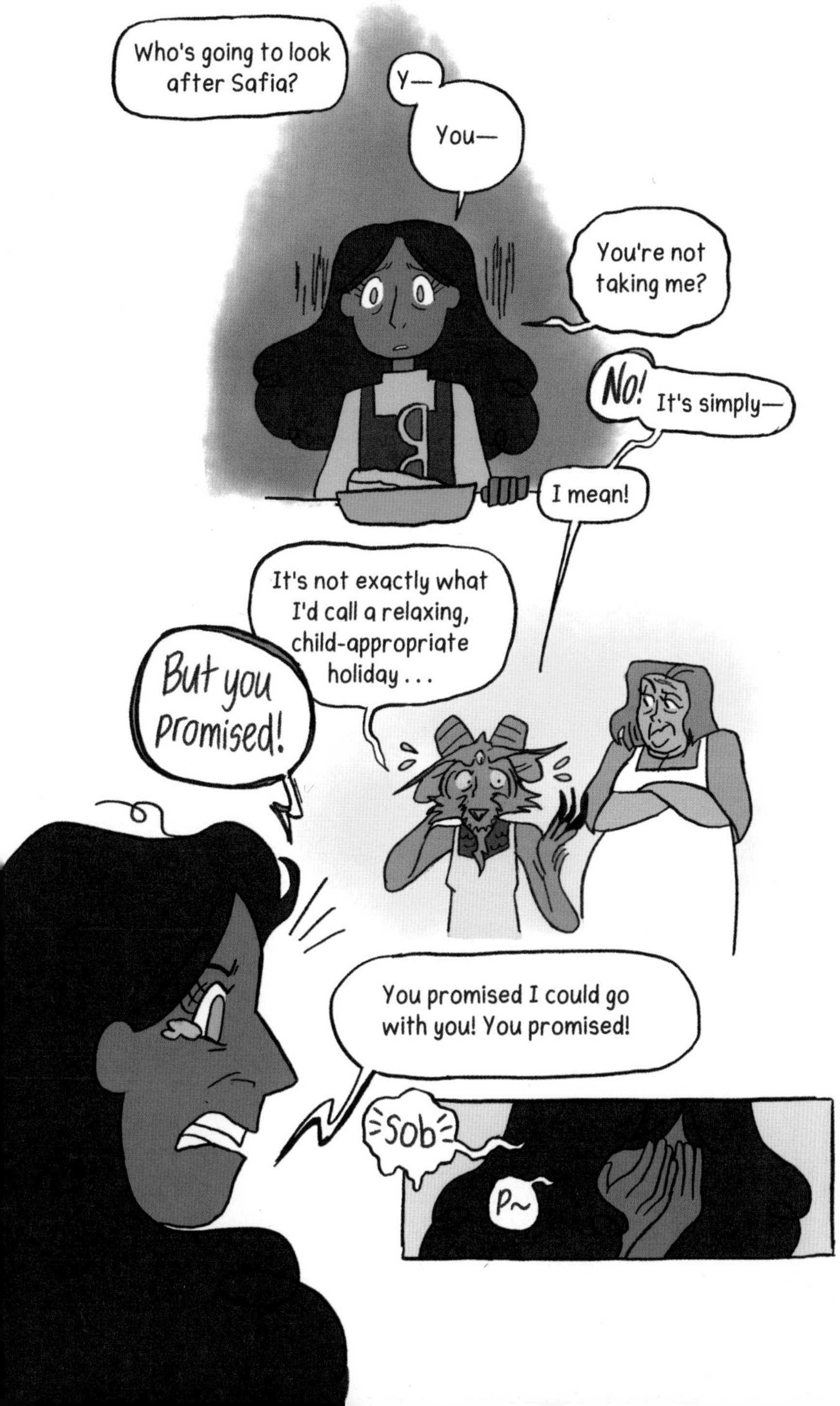
Who's going to look after Safia?
Y—
You—
You're not taking me?
No! It's simply—
I mean!
It's not exactly what I'd call a relaxing, child-appropriate holiday . . .
But you promised!
You promised I could go with you! You promised!
Sob
P~

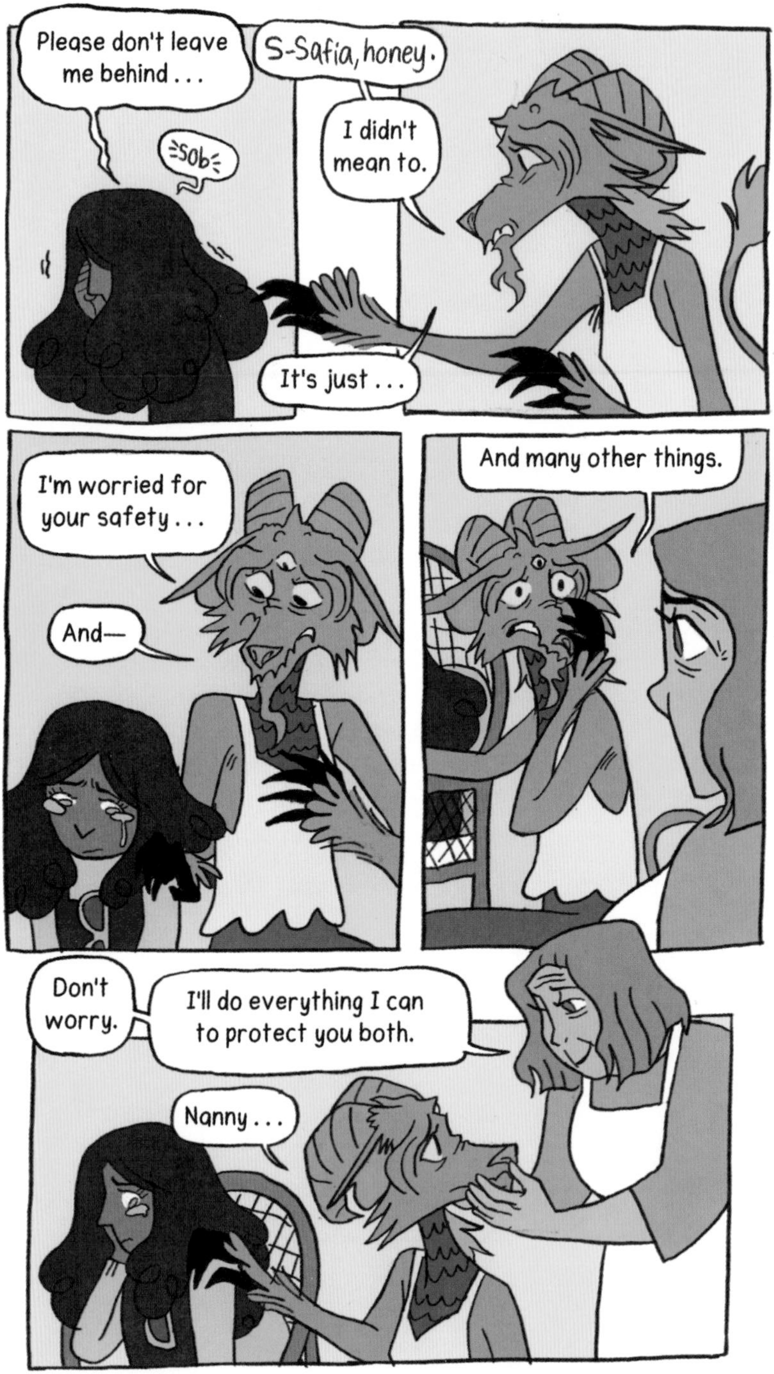
Please don't leave me behind . . .
Sob
S-Safia, honey.
I didn't mean to.
It's just . . .
I'm worried for your safety . . .
And—
And many other things.
Don't worry.
I'll do everything I can to protect you both.
Nanny . . .

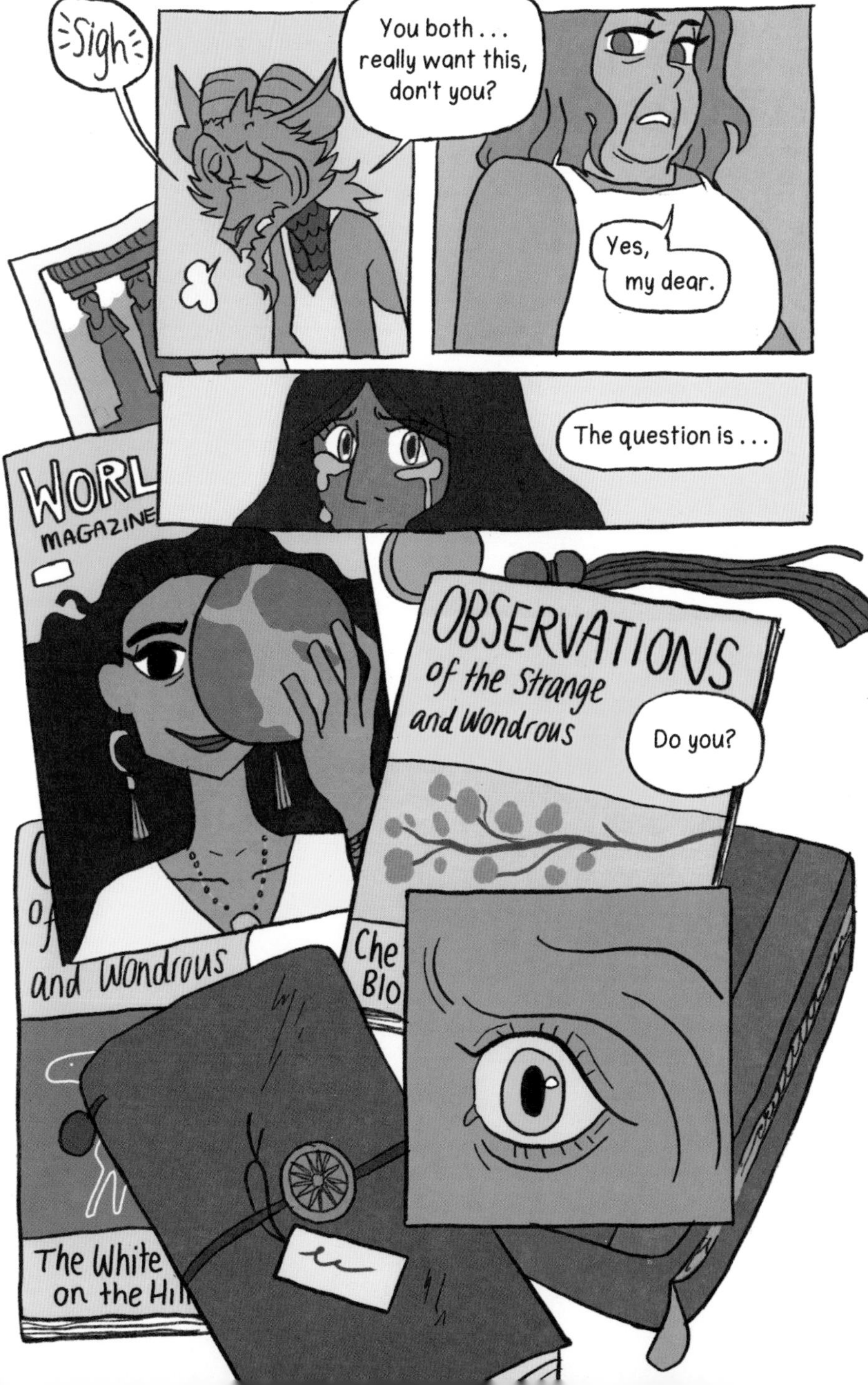
Sigh
You both . . . really want this, don't you?
Yes, my dear.
WORL
MAGAZINE
The question is . . .
OBSERVATIONS of the Strange and Wondrous
Do you?
and Wondrous
The White
on the Hi

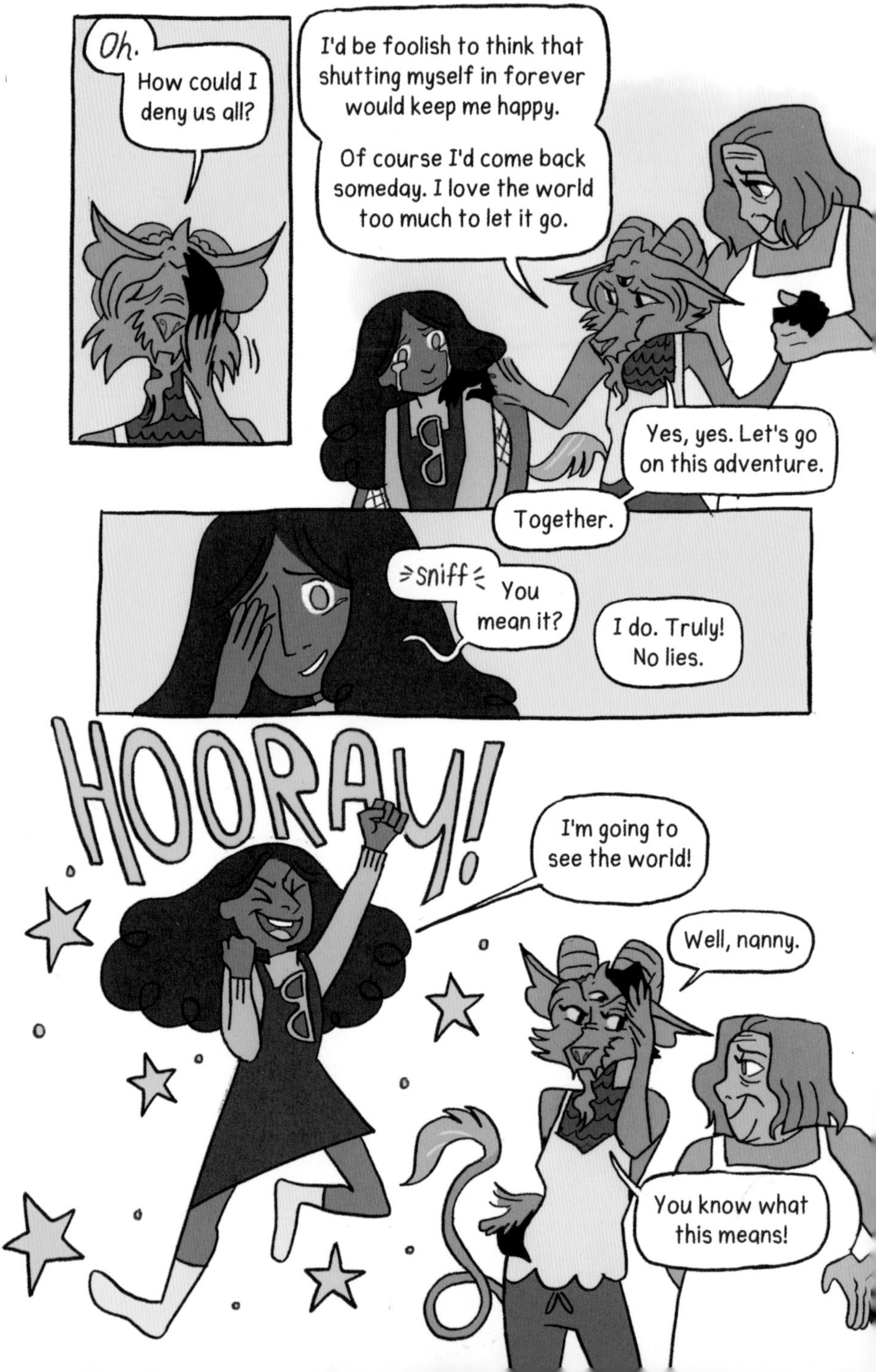
Oh.
How could I deny us all?
I'd be foolish to think that shutting myself in forever would keep me happy.
Of course I'd come back someday. I love the world too much to let it go.
Yes, yes. Let's go on this adventure.
Together.
sniff You mean it?
I do. Truly! No lies.
HOORAY!
I'm going to see the world!
Well, nanny.
You know what this means!

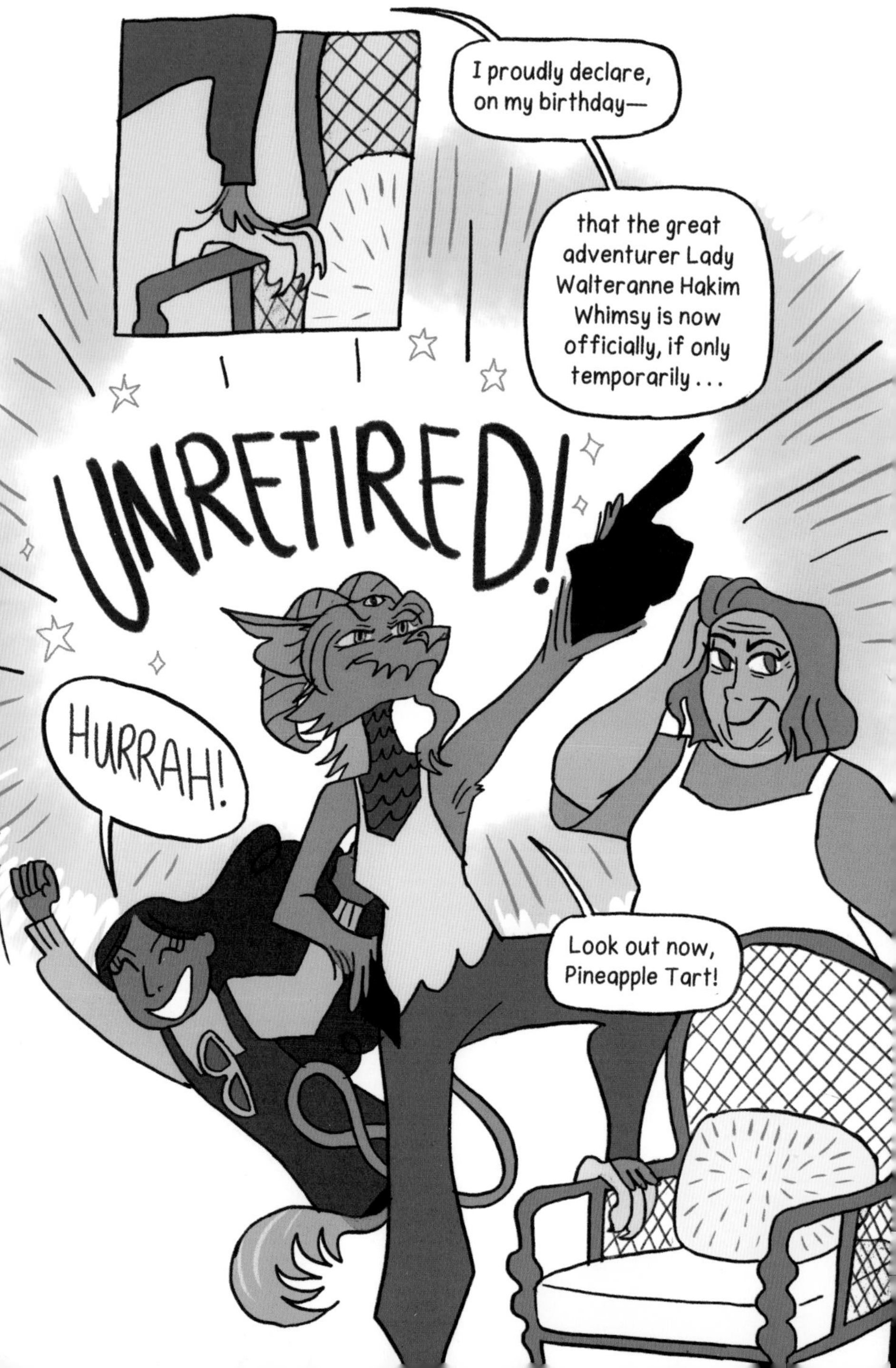
I proudly declare, on my birthday—
that the great adventurer Lady Walteranne Hakim Whimsy is now officially, if only temporarily . . .
UNRETIRED!
HURRAH!
Look out now, Pineapple Tart!

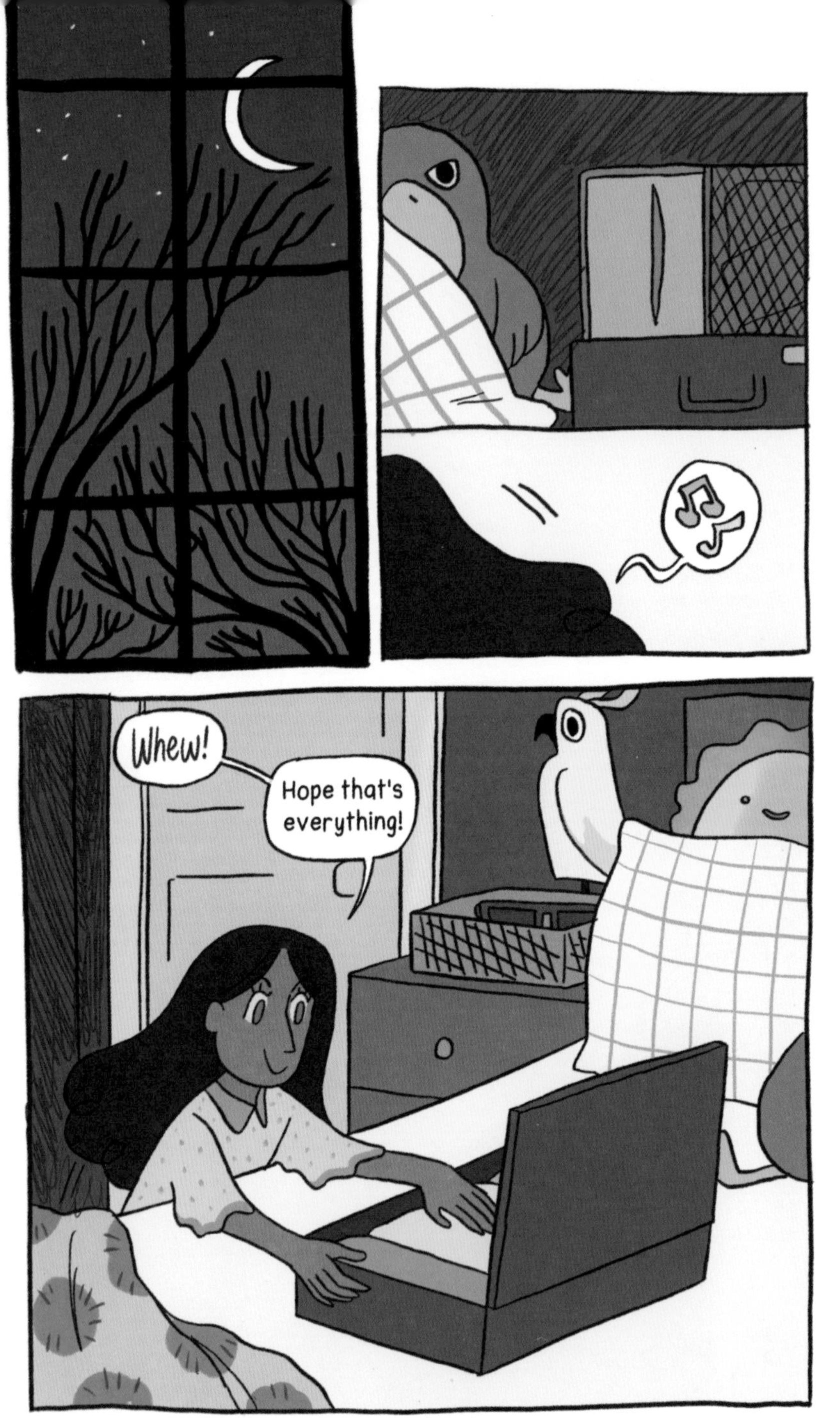
Whew!
Hope that's everything!

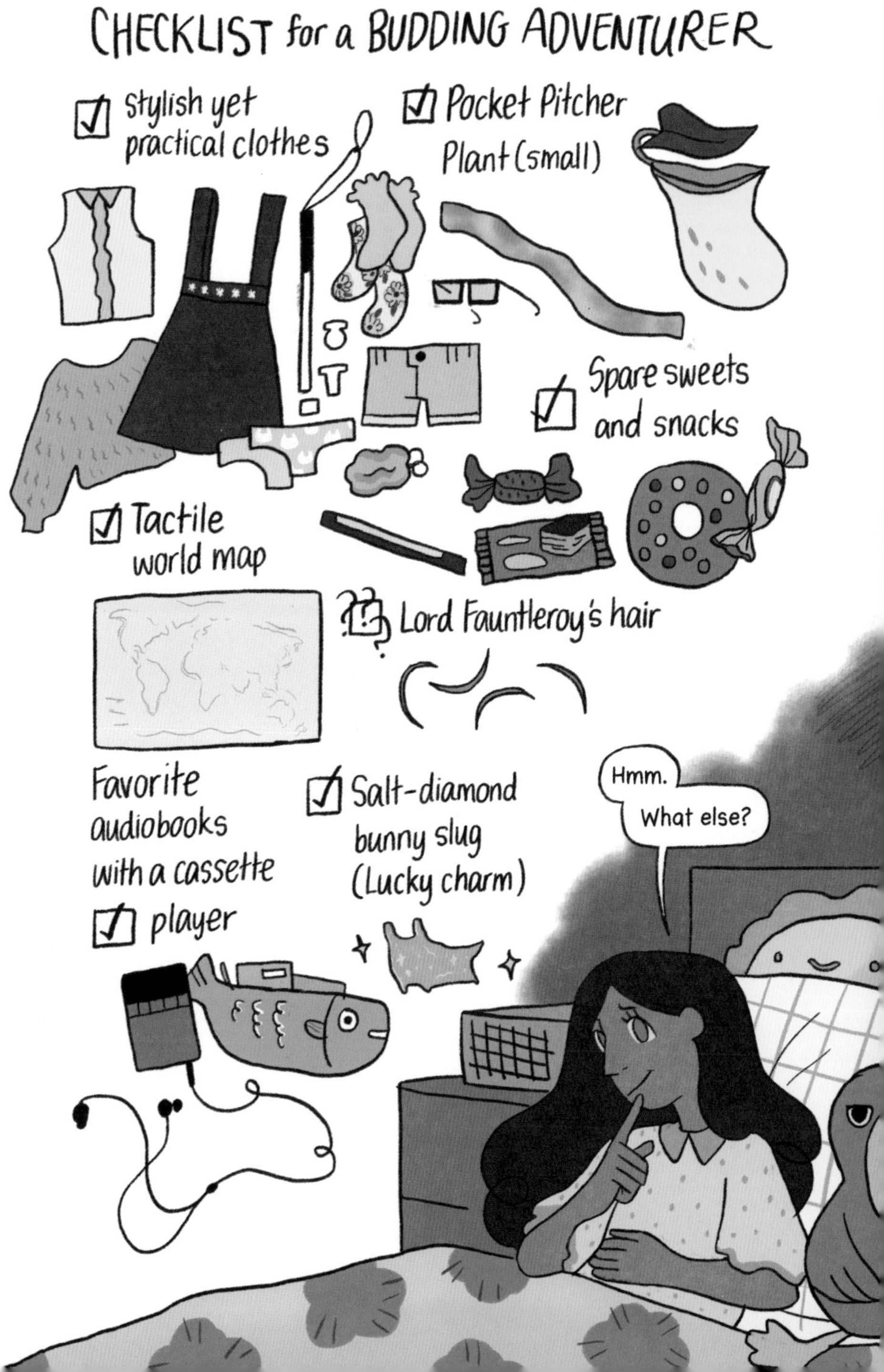
CHECKLIST for a BUDDING ADVENTURER
stylish yet practical clothes
Pocket Pitcher Plant (small)
Spare sweets and snacks
Tactile world map
Lord Fauntleroy's hair
Favorite audiobooks with a cassette player
Salt-diamond bunny slug (Lucky charm)
Hmm.
What else?

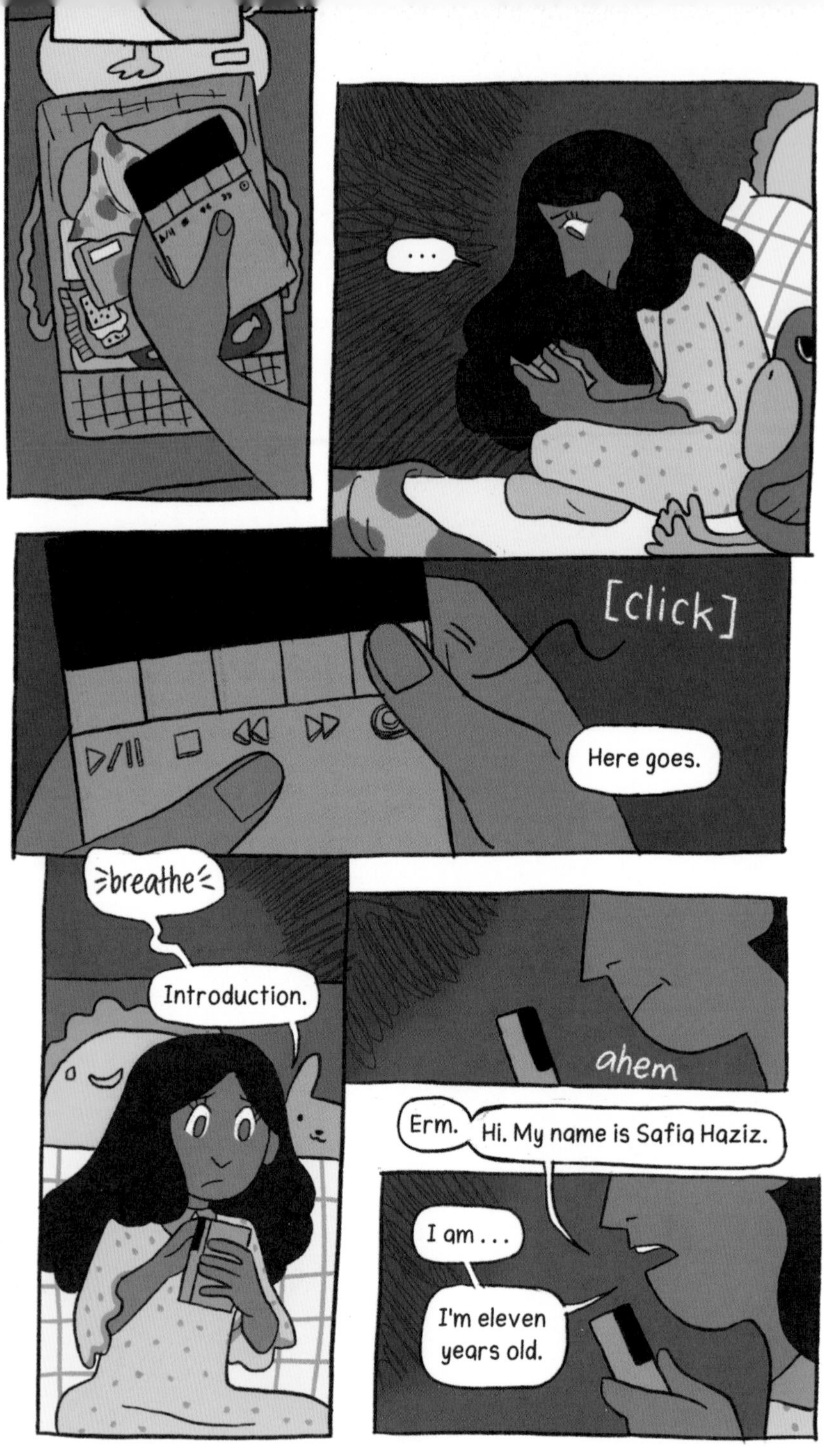
. . .
[click]
Here goes.
breathe
Introduction.
ahem
Erm.
Hi. My name is Safia Haziz.
I am . . .
I'm eleven
years old.

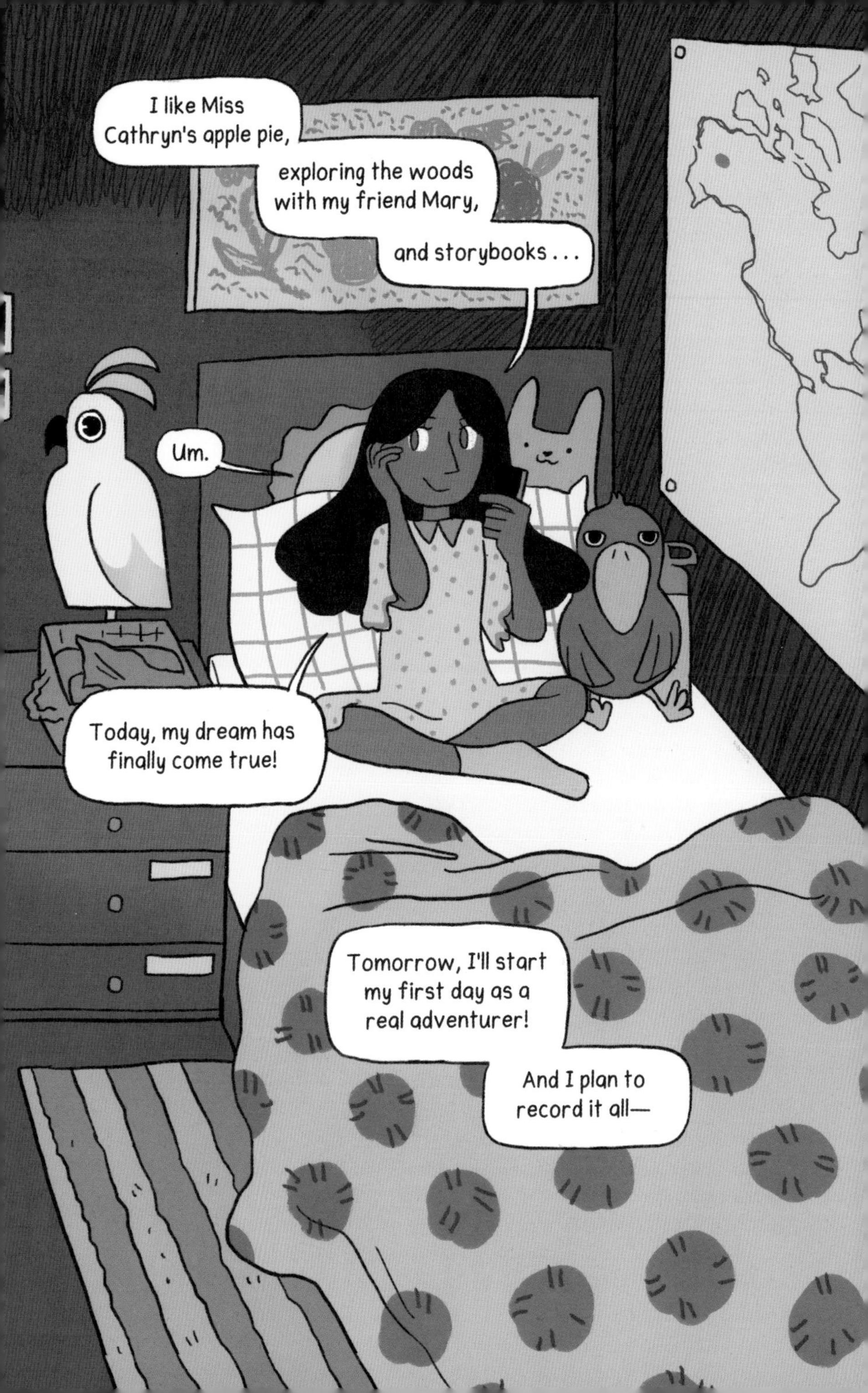
I like Miss Cathryn's apple pie,
exploring the woods with my friend Mary,
and storybooks . . .
Um.
Today, my dream has finally come true!
Tomorrow, I'll start my first day as a real adventurer!
And I plan to record it all—

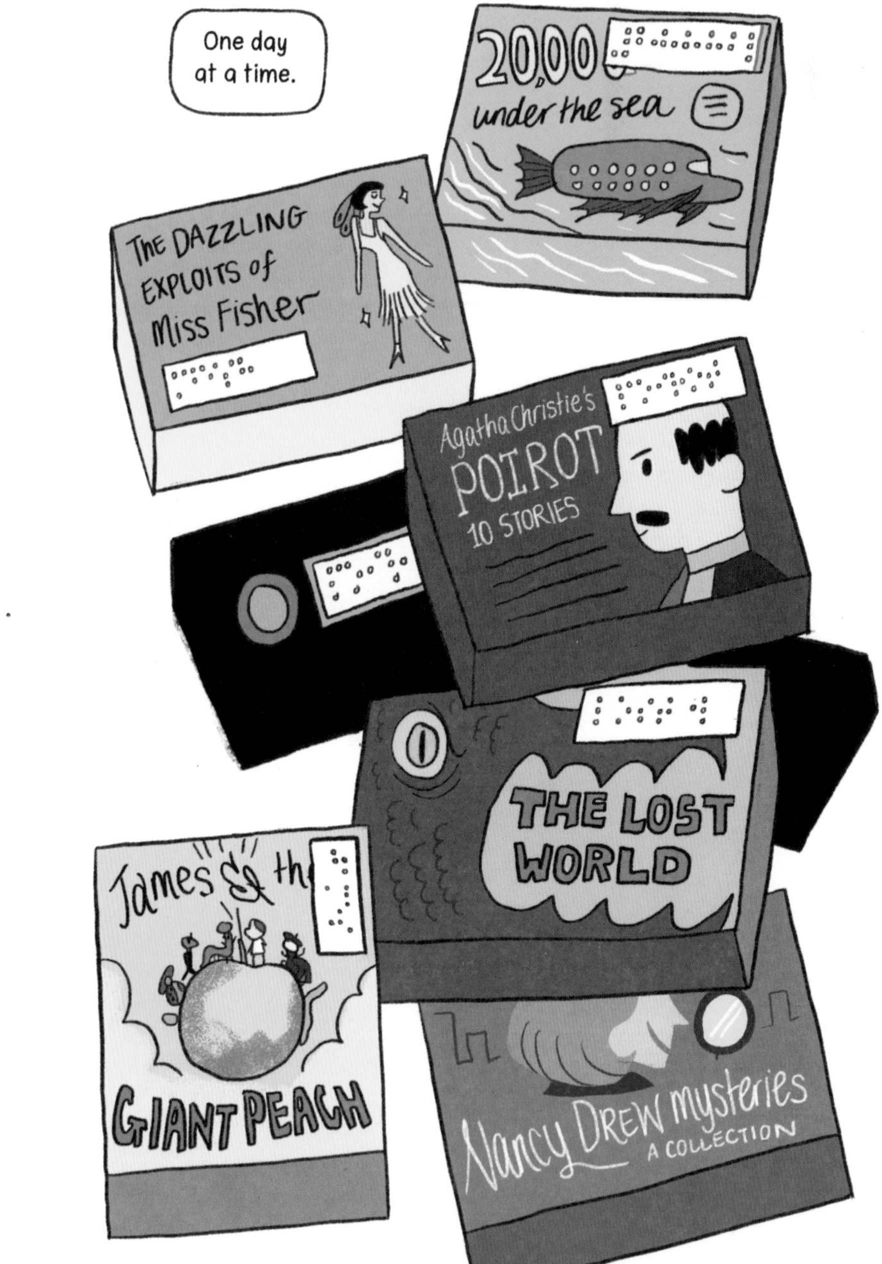
One day at a time.
20,000 under the sea
THE DAZZLING EXPLOITS of Miss Fisher
Agatha Christie's POIROT 10 STORIES
THE LOST WORLD
James & the GIANT PEACH
Nancy Drew mysteries A COLLECTION

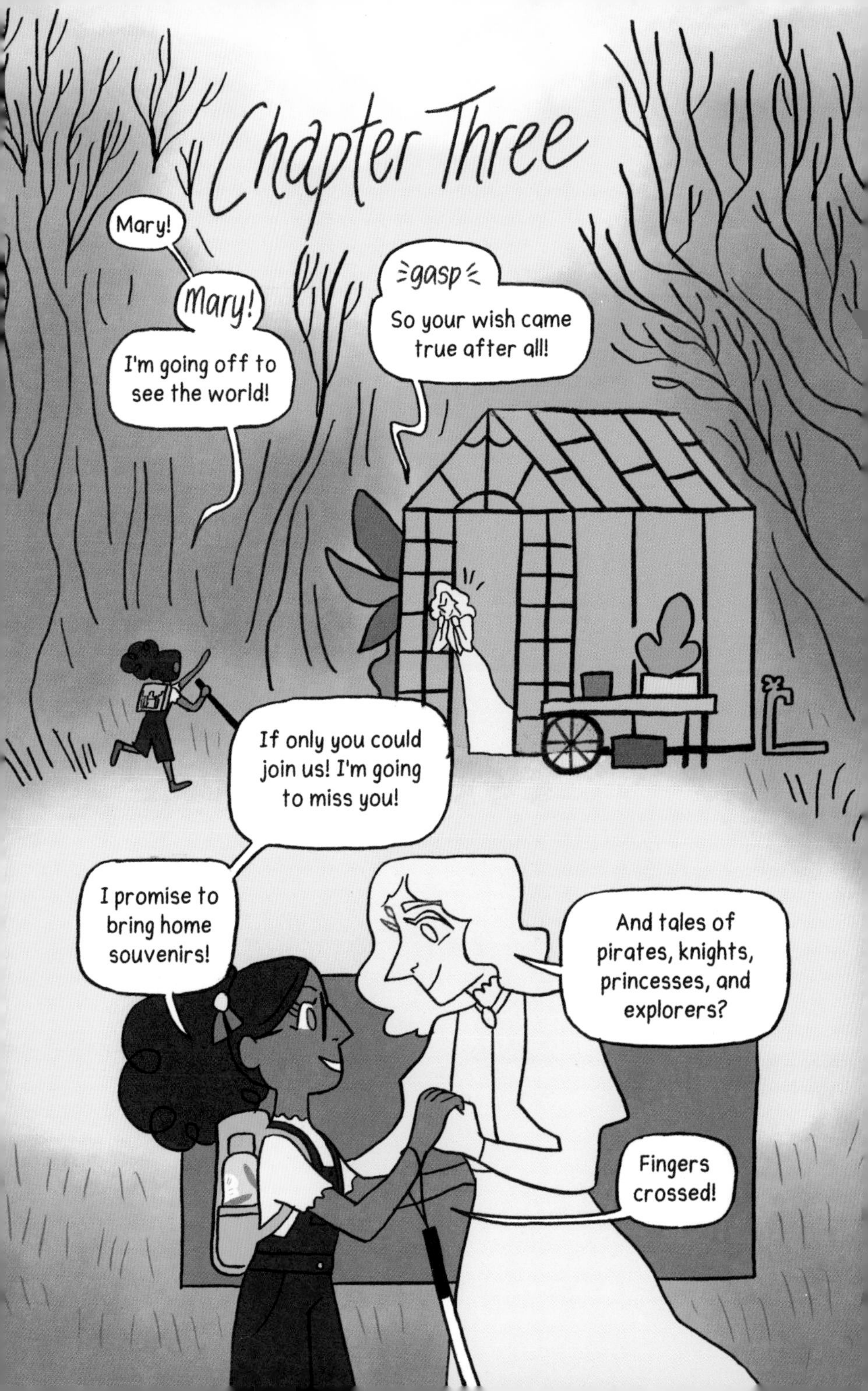
Chapter Three
Mary!
Mary!
I'm going off to see the world!
gasp
So your wish came true after all!
If only you could join us! I'm going to miss you!
I promise to bring home souvenirs!
And tales of pirates, knights, princesses, and explorers?
Fingers crossed!

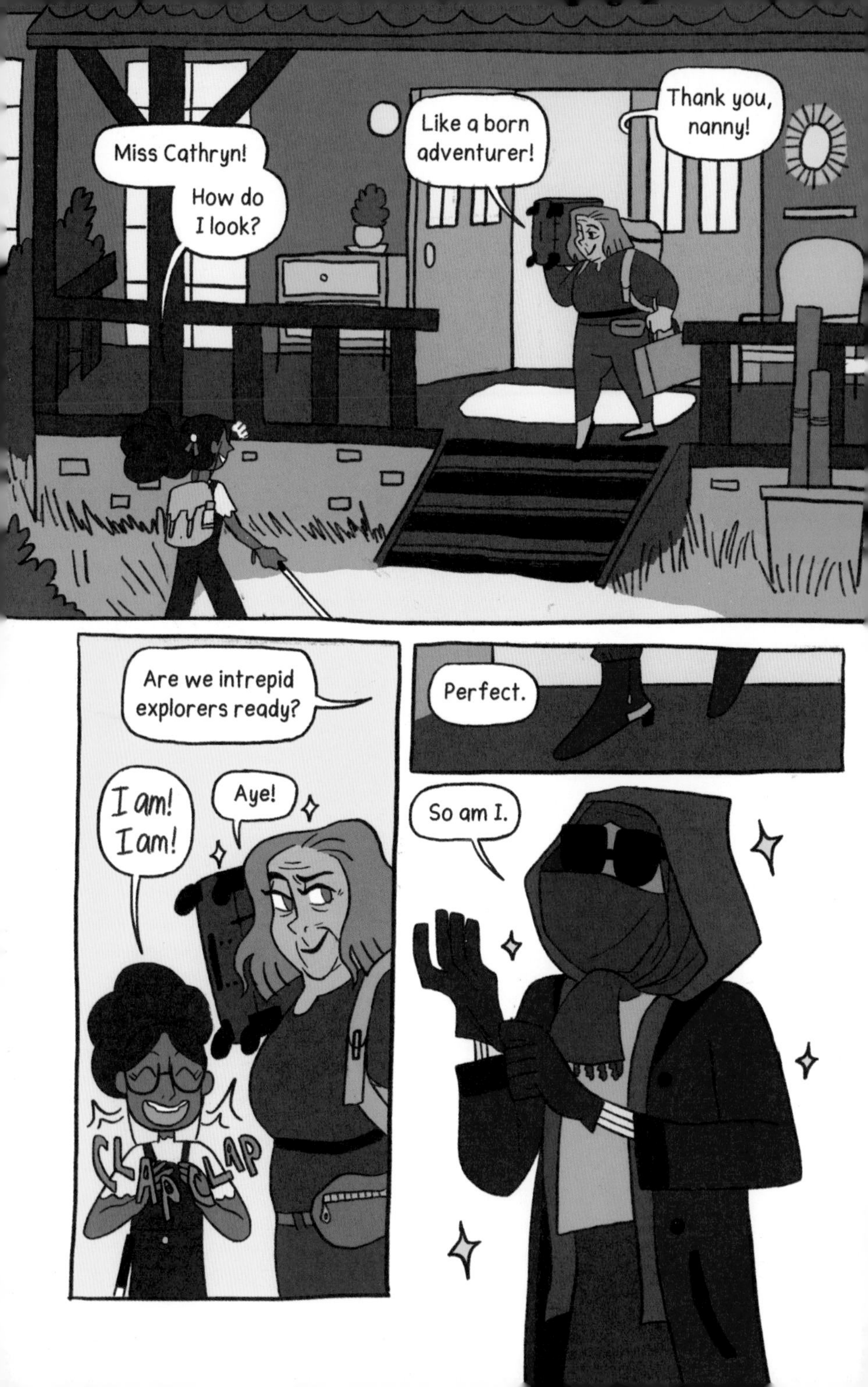
Miss Cathryn!
How do I look?
Like a born adventurer!
Thank you, nanny!
Are we intrepid explorers ready?
Perfect.
I am! I am!
Aye!
So am I.
CLAP CLAP CLAP

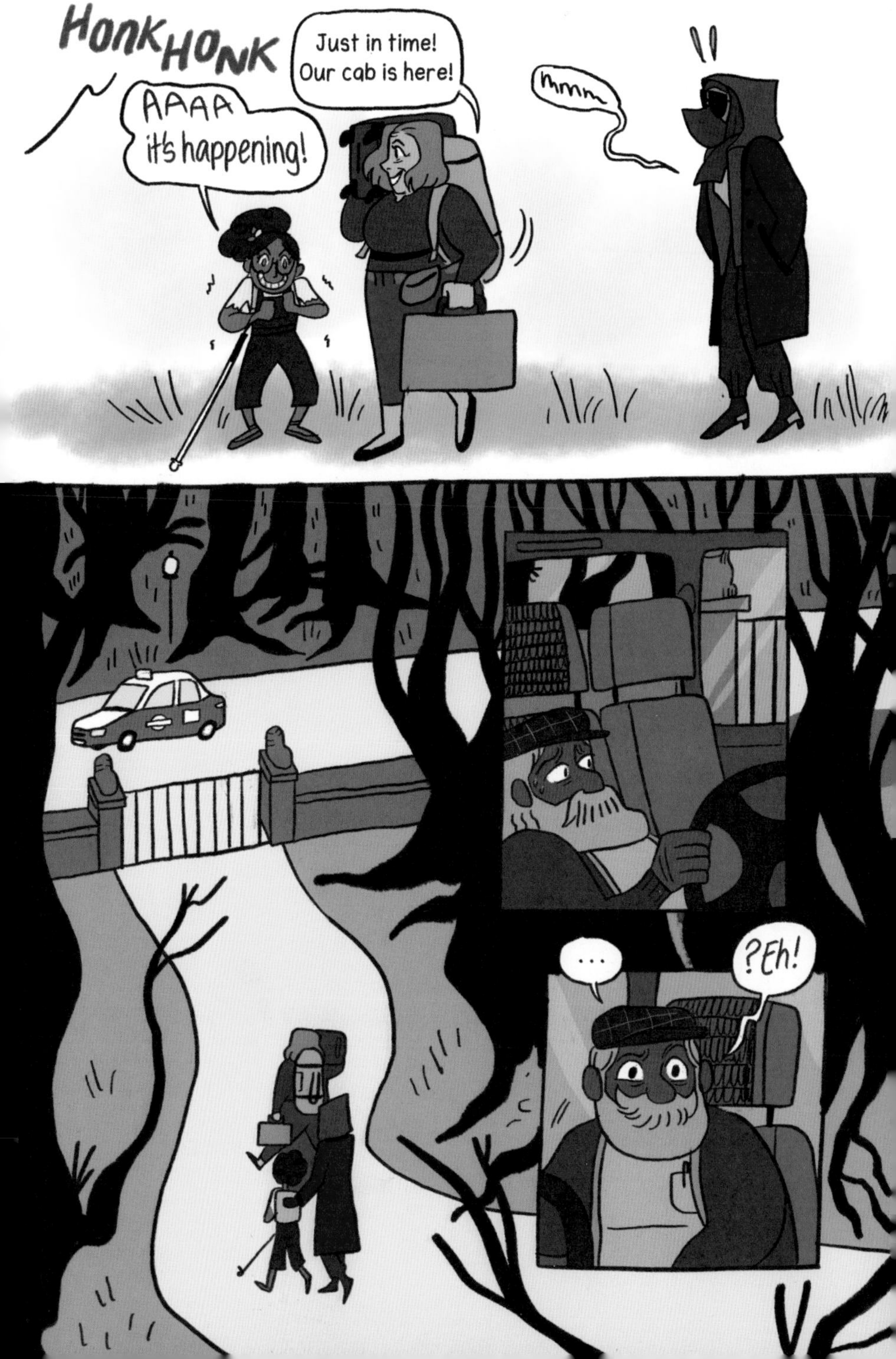
HONK HONK
AAAA it's happening!
Just in time! Our cab is here!
mmm
...
?Eh!

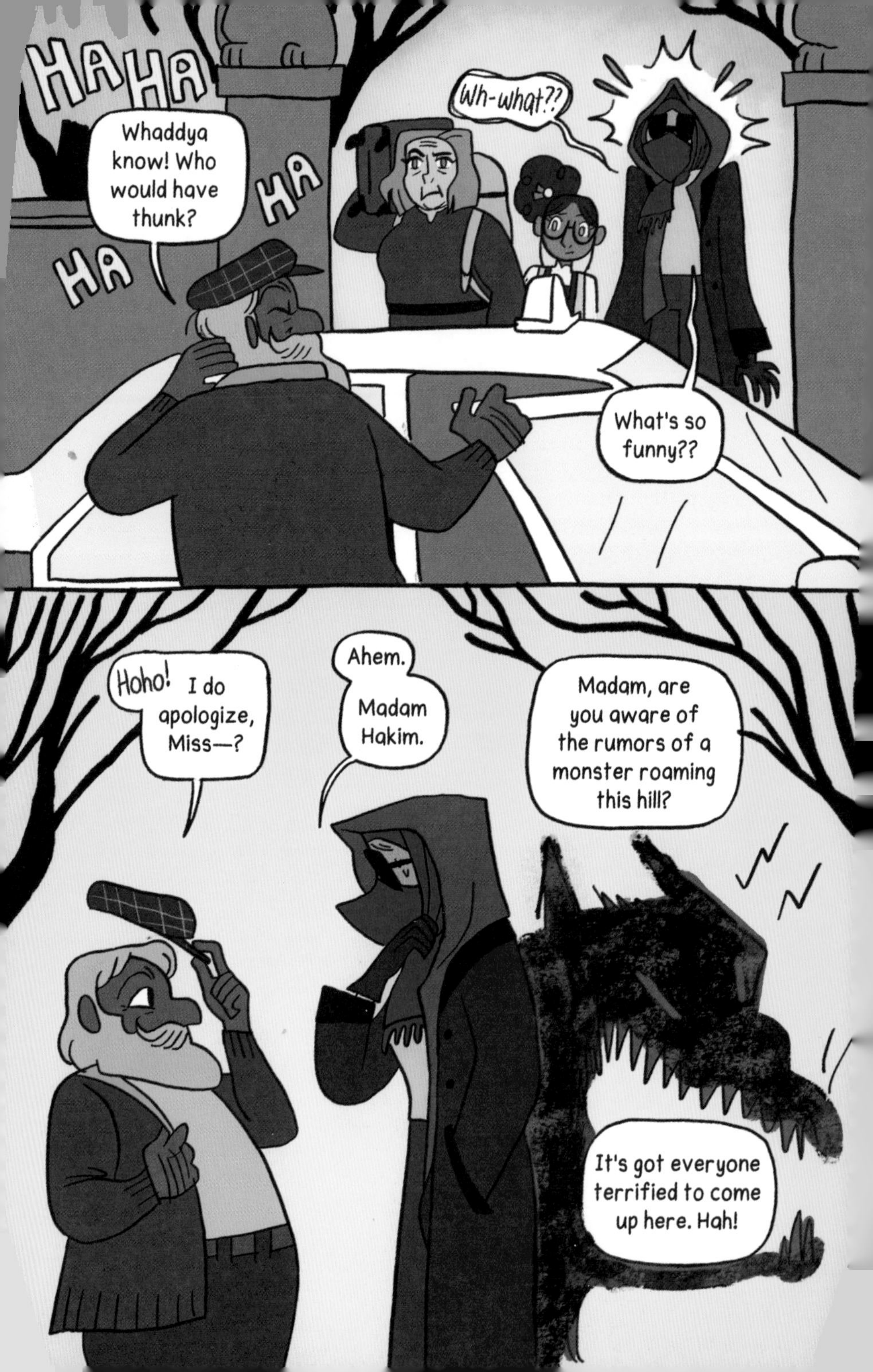

HAHAHA
Whaddya know! Who would have thunk?
HA
HA
Wh-what??
What's so funny??
Hoho! I do apologize, Miss—?
Ahem.
Madam Hakim.
Madam, are you aware of the rumors of a monster roaming this hill?
It's got everyone terrified to come up here. Hah!

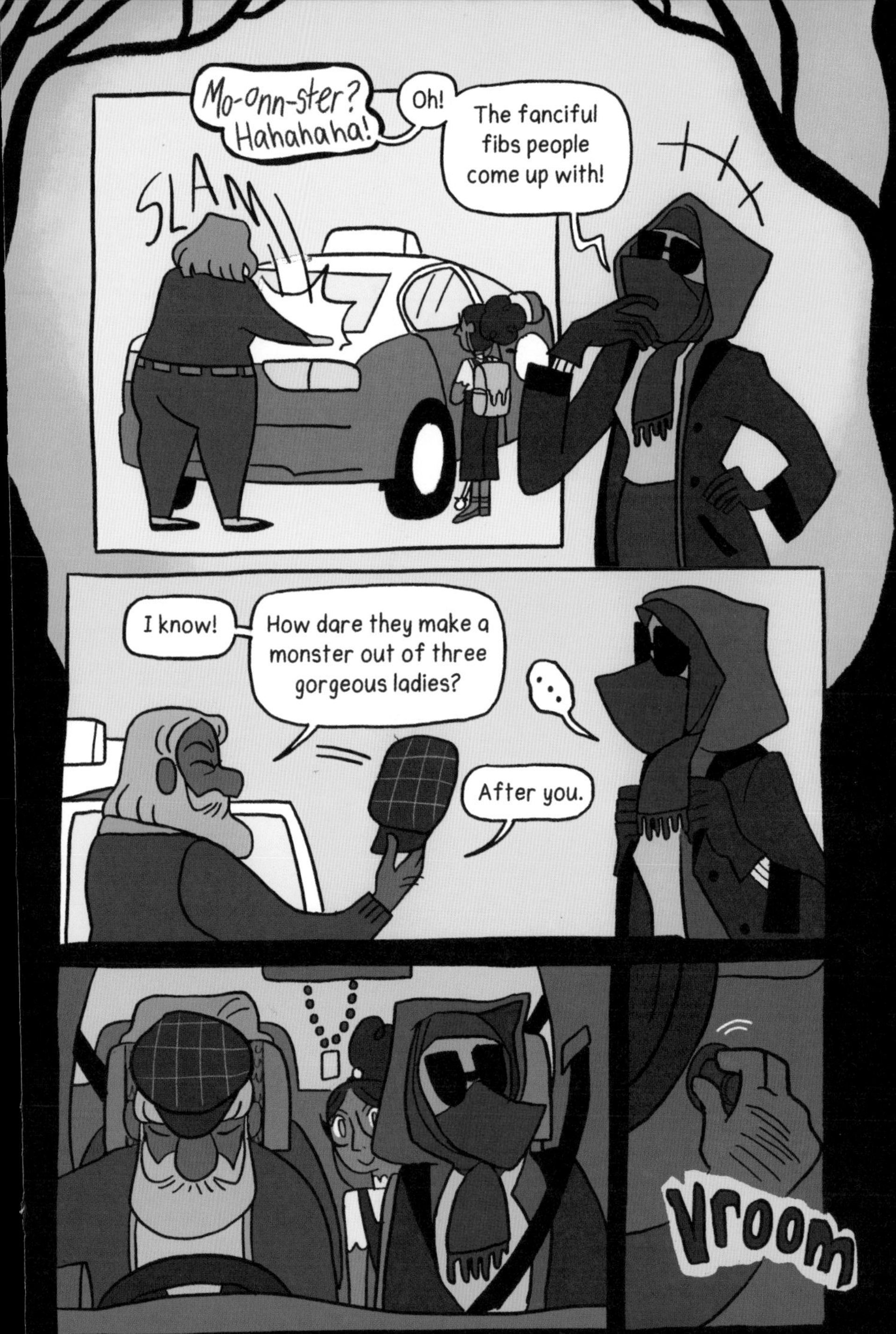

Mo-onn-ster? Hahahaha!
Oh!
The fanciful fibs people come up with!
SLAM
I know!
How dare they make a monster out of three gorgeous ladies?
...
After you.
Vroom

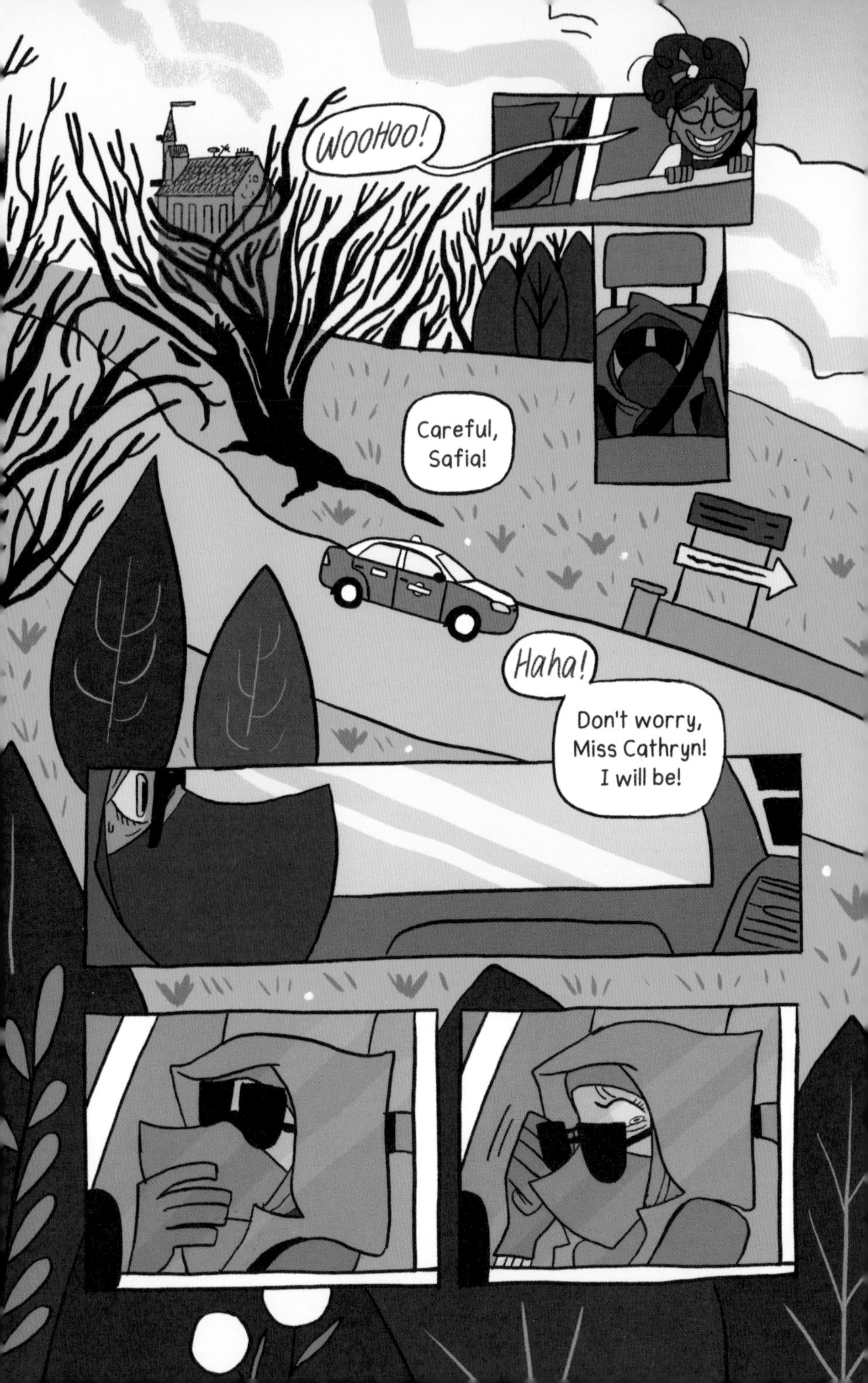
WOOHOO!
Careful, Safia!
Haha!
Don't worry, Miss Cathryn! I will be!

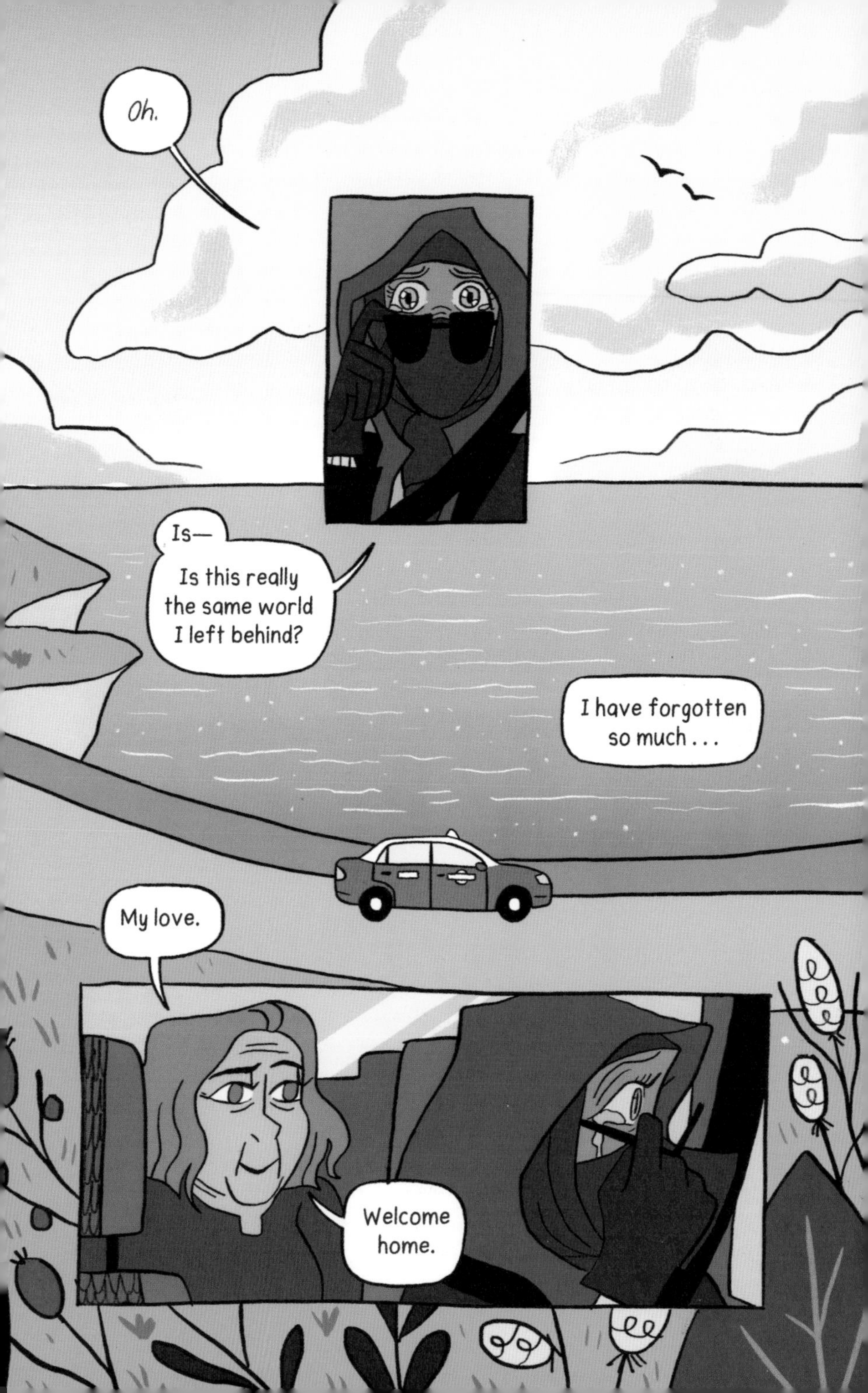
Oh.
Is—
Is this really the same world I left behind?
I have forgotten so much . . .
My love.
Welcome home.

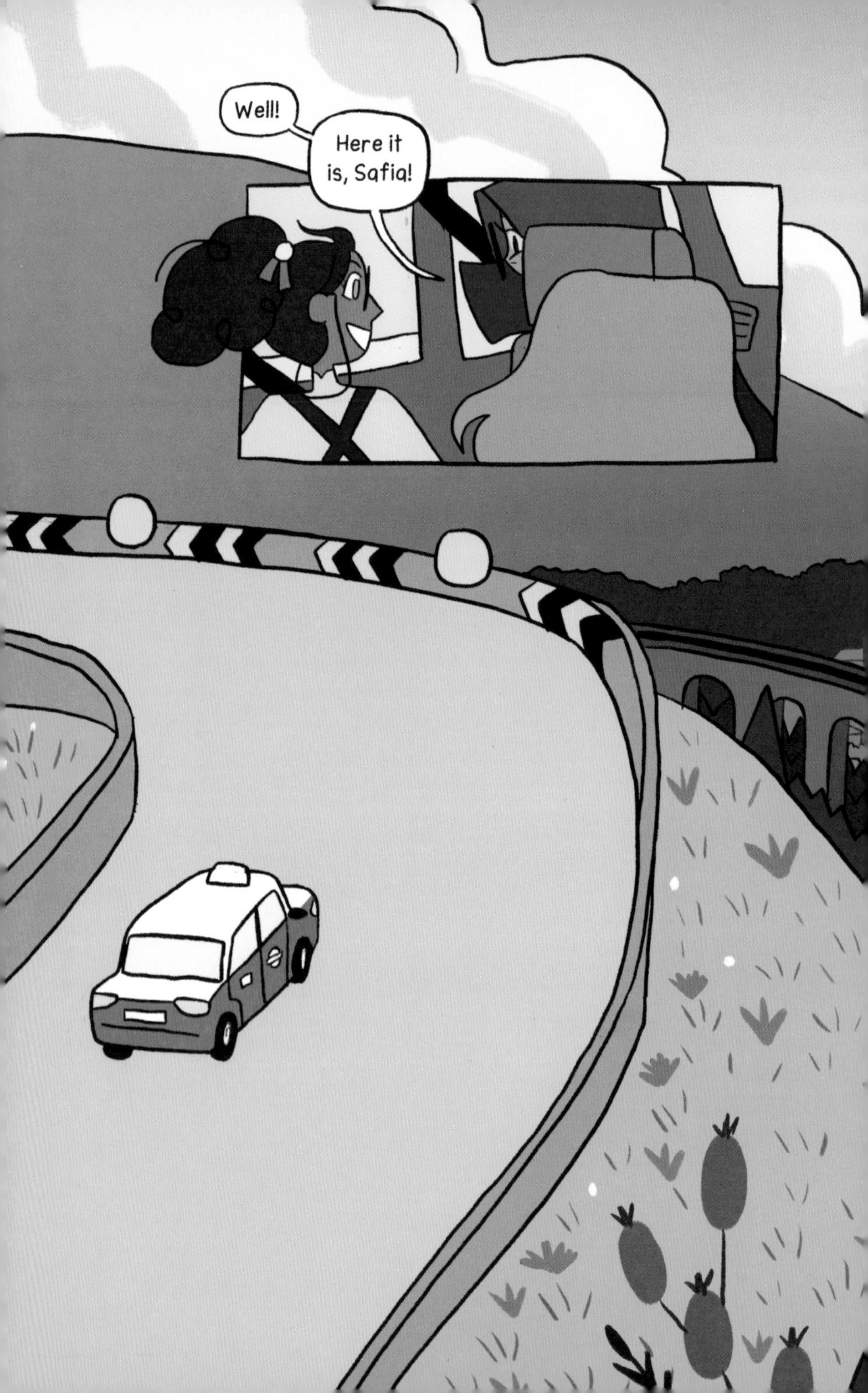
Well!
Here it is, Safia!

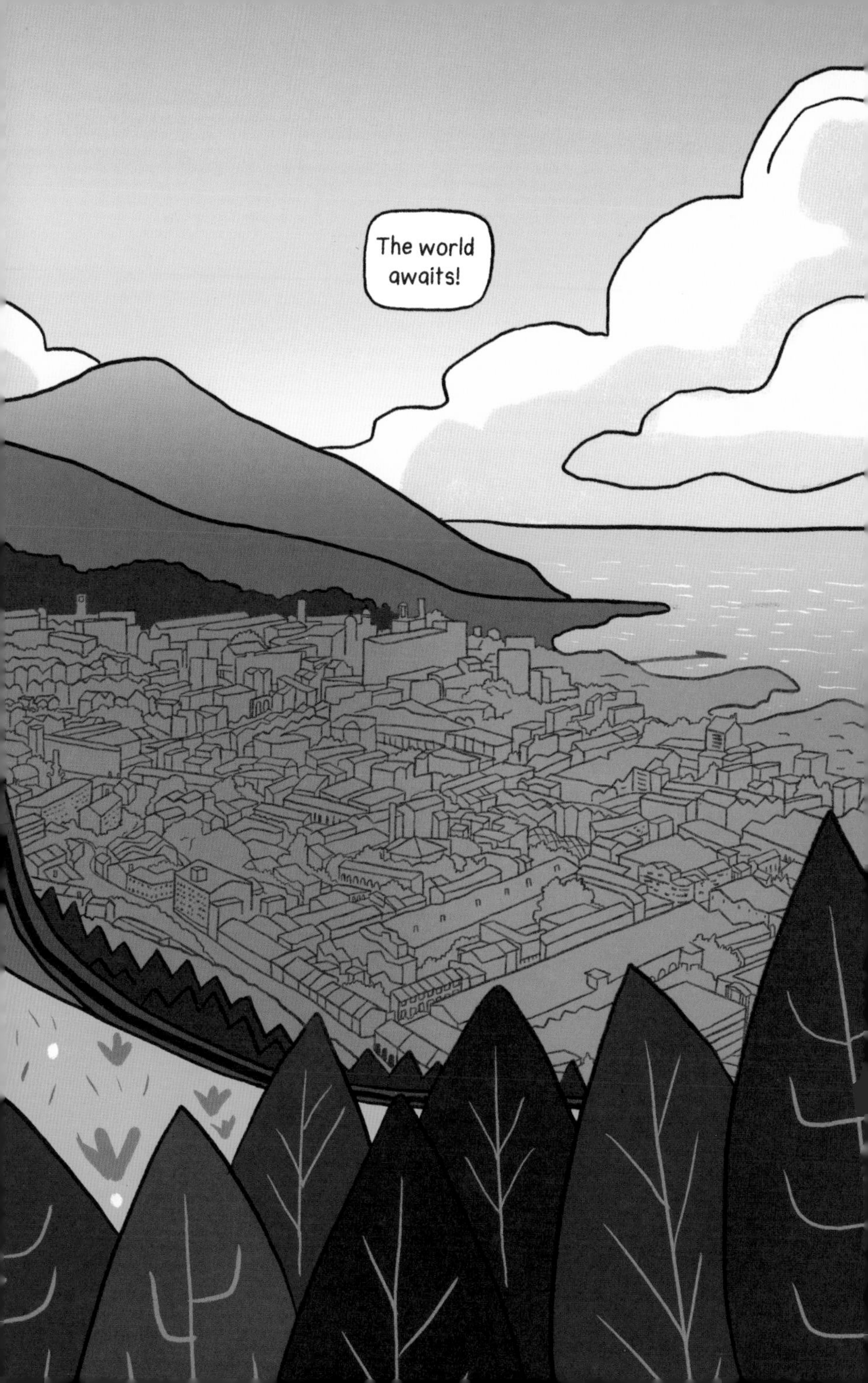
The world awaits!

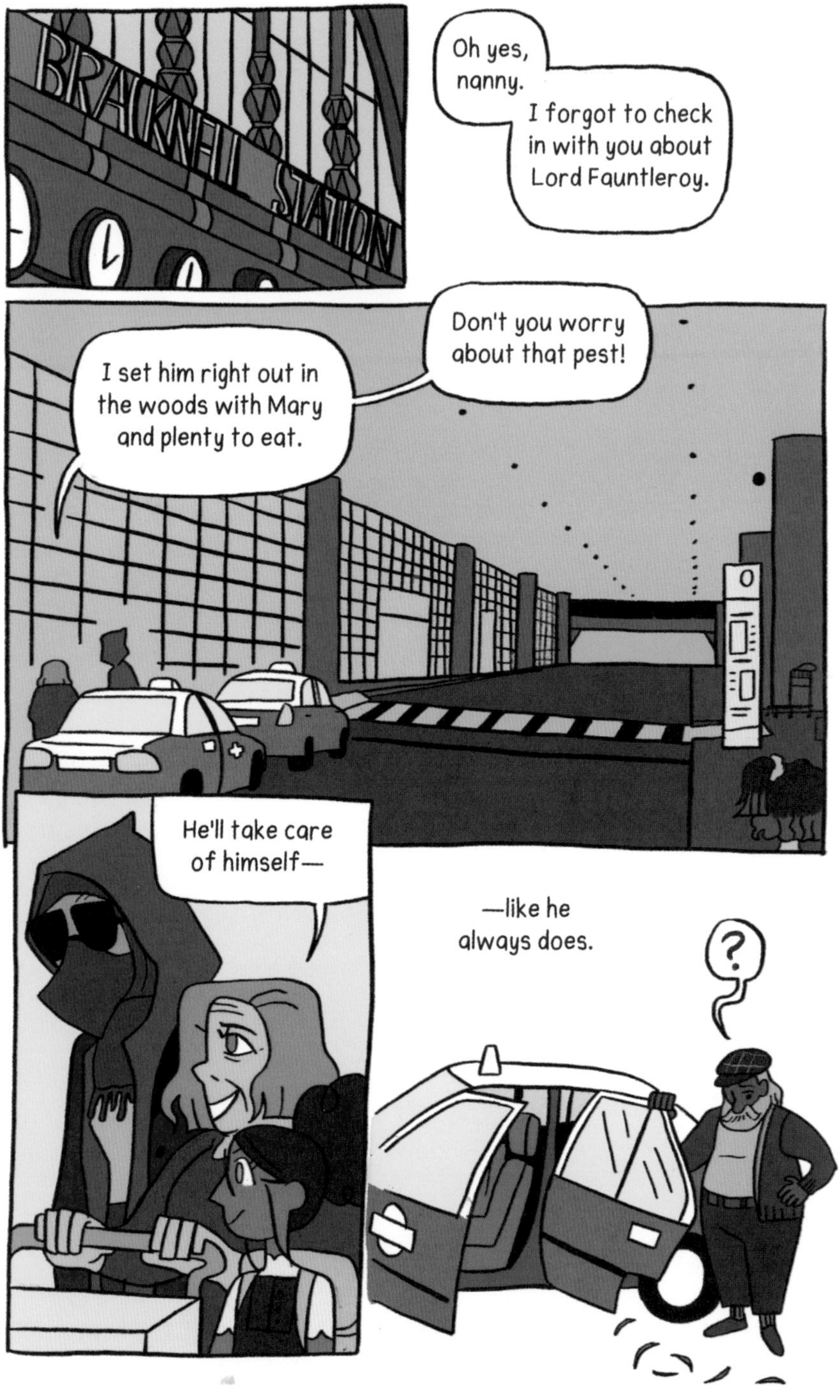
BRACKNELL STATION
Oh yes, nanny.
I forgot to check in with you about Lord Fauntleroy.
Don't you worry about that pest!
I set him right out in the woods with Mary and plenty to eat.
He'll take care of himself—
—like he always does.
?

An Adventure of a Lifetime

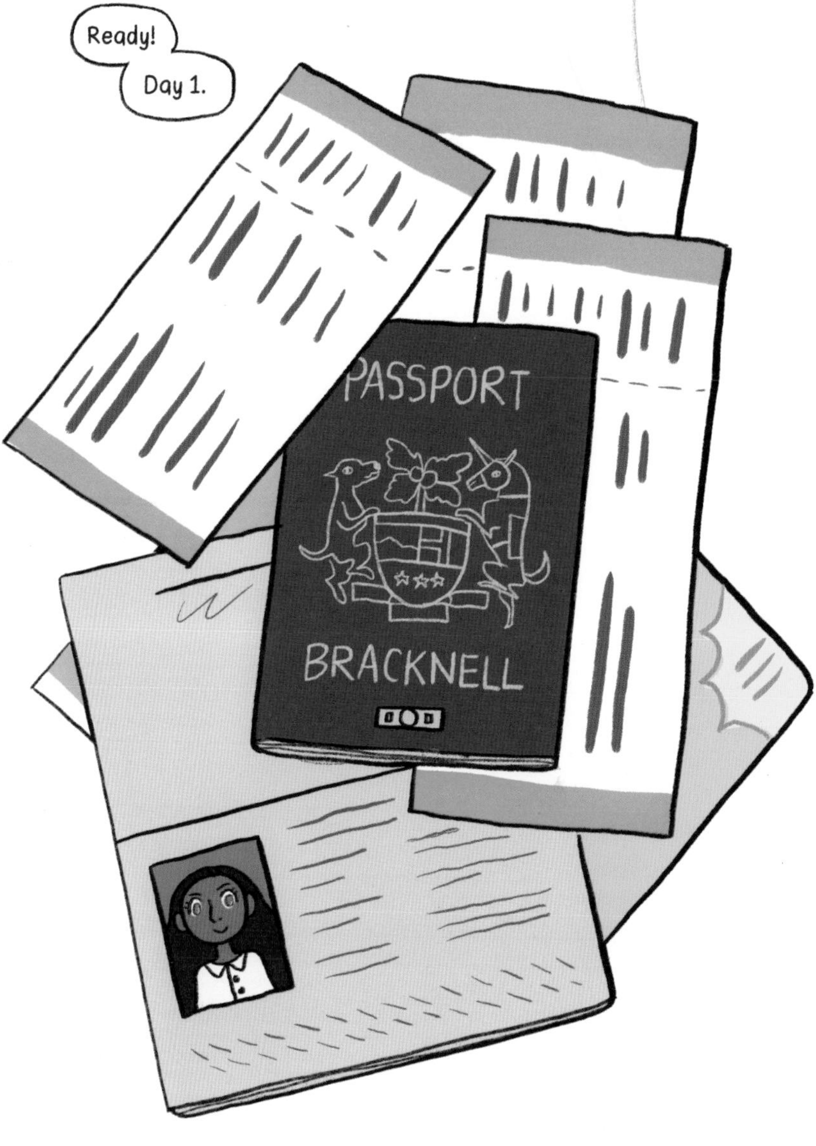
Ready!
Day 1.
PASSPORT
BRACKNELL

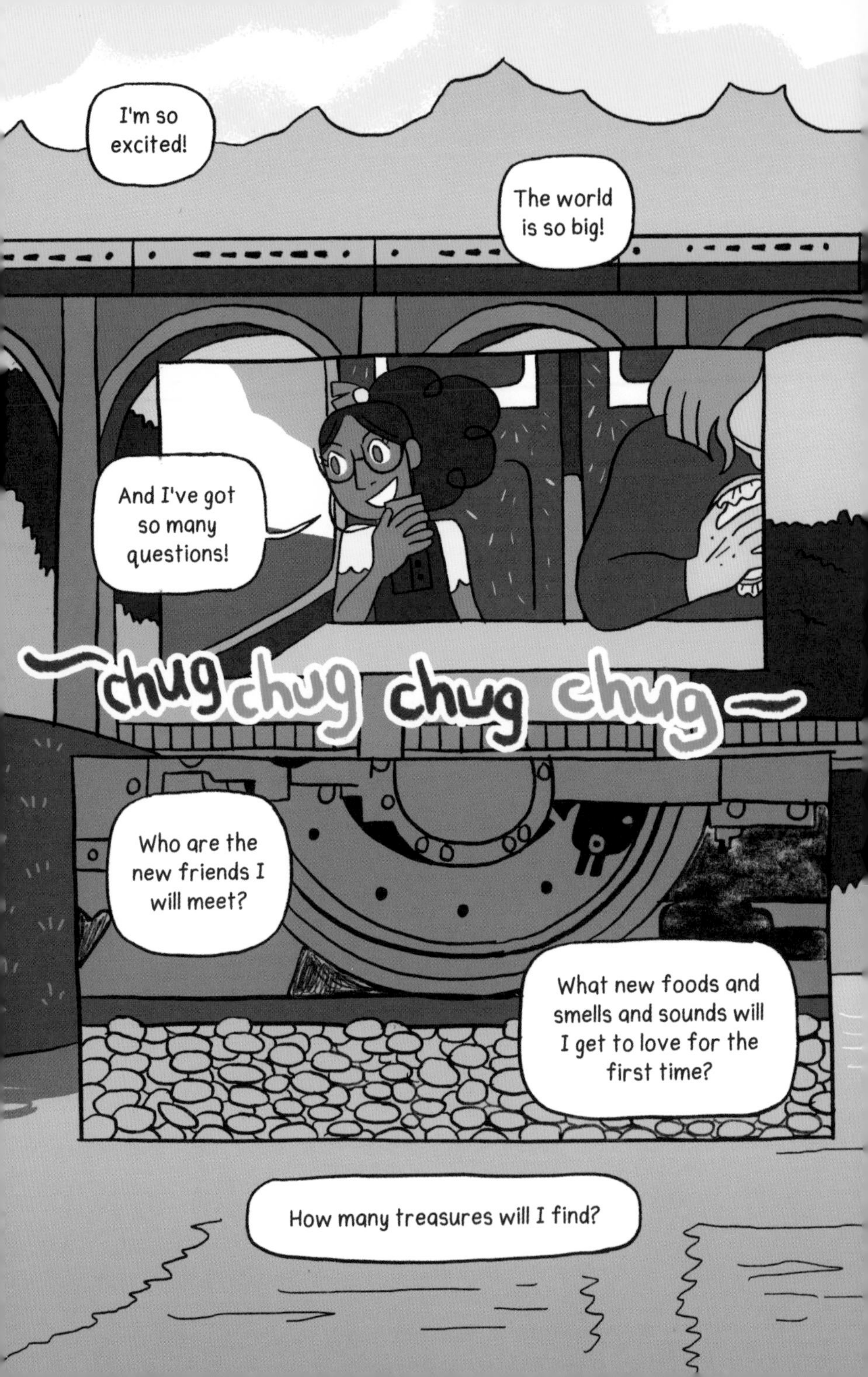
I'm so excited!
The world is so big!
And I've got so many questions!
chug chug chug chug
Who are the new friends I will meet?
What new foods and smells and sounds will I get to love for the first time?
How many treasures will I find?

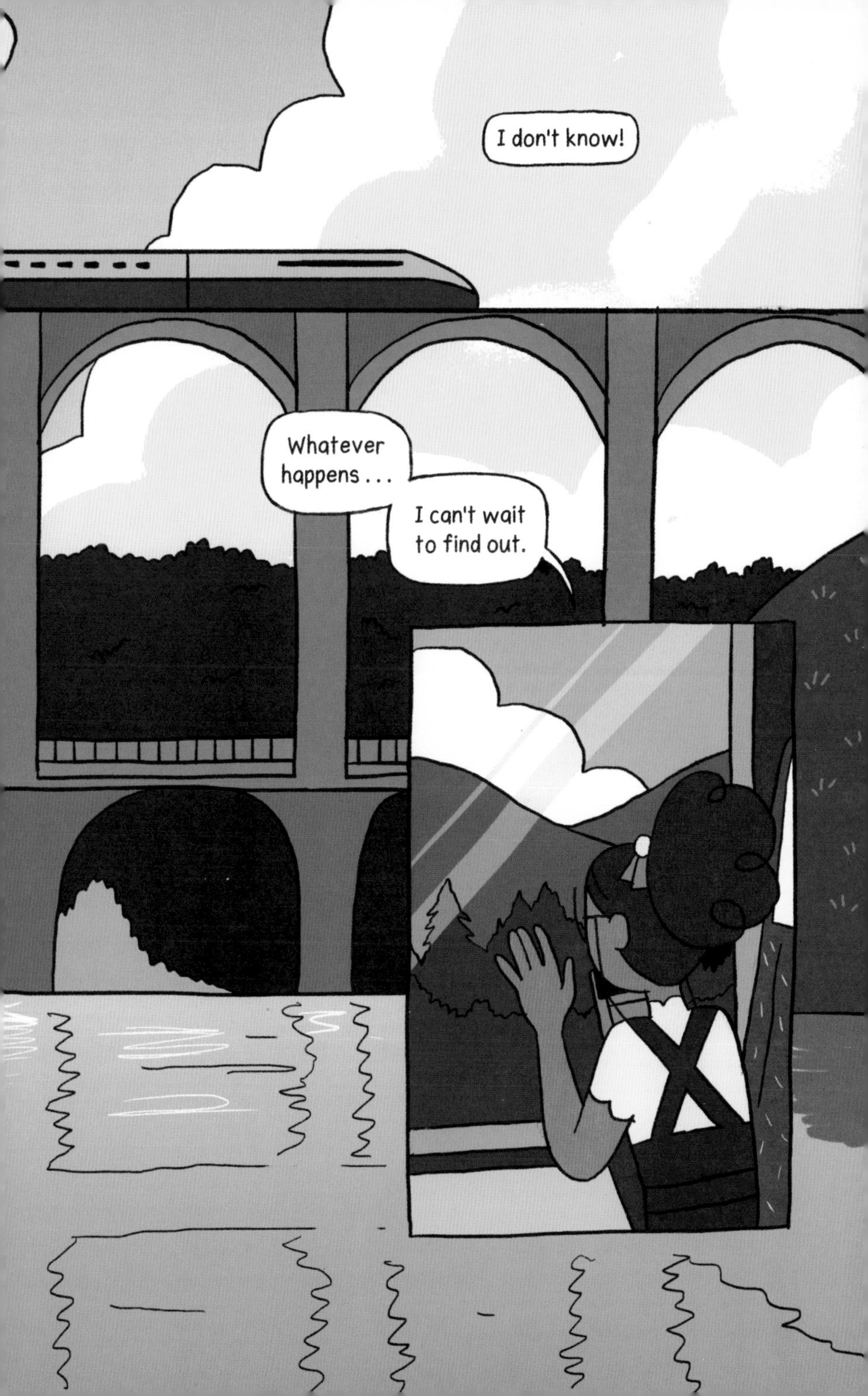
I don't know!
Whatever happens . . .
I can't wait to find out.

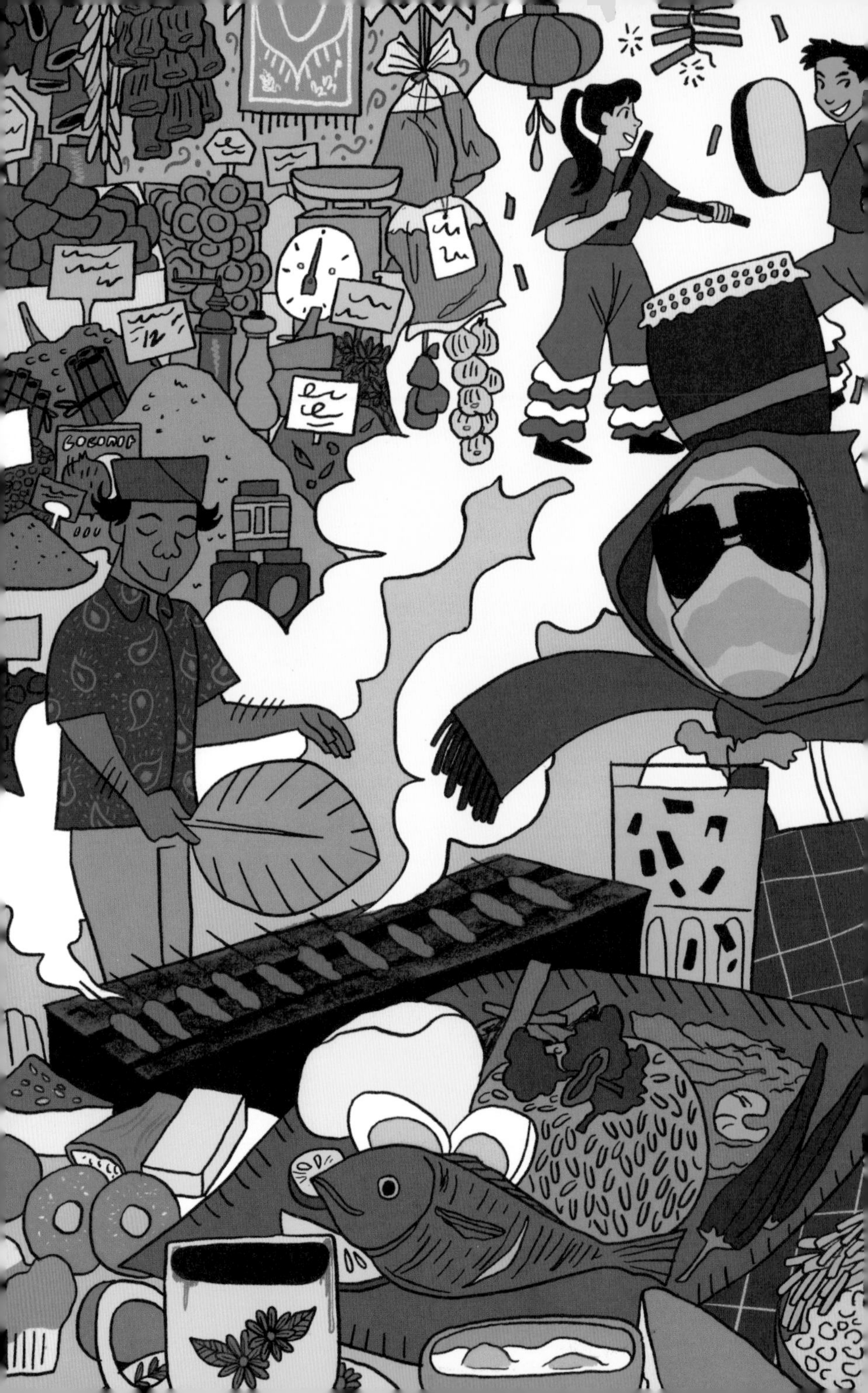
12

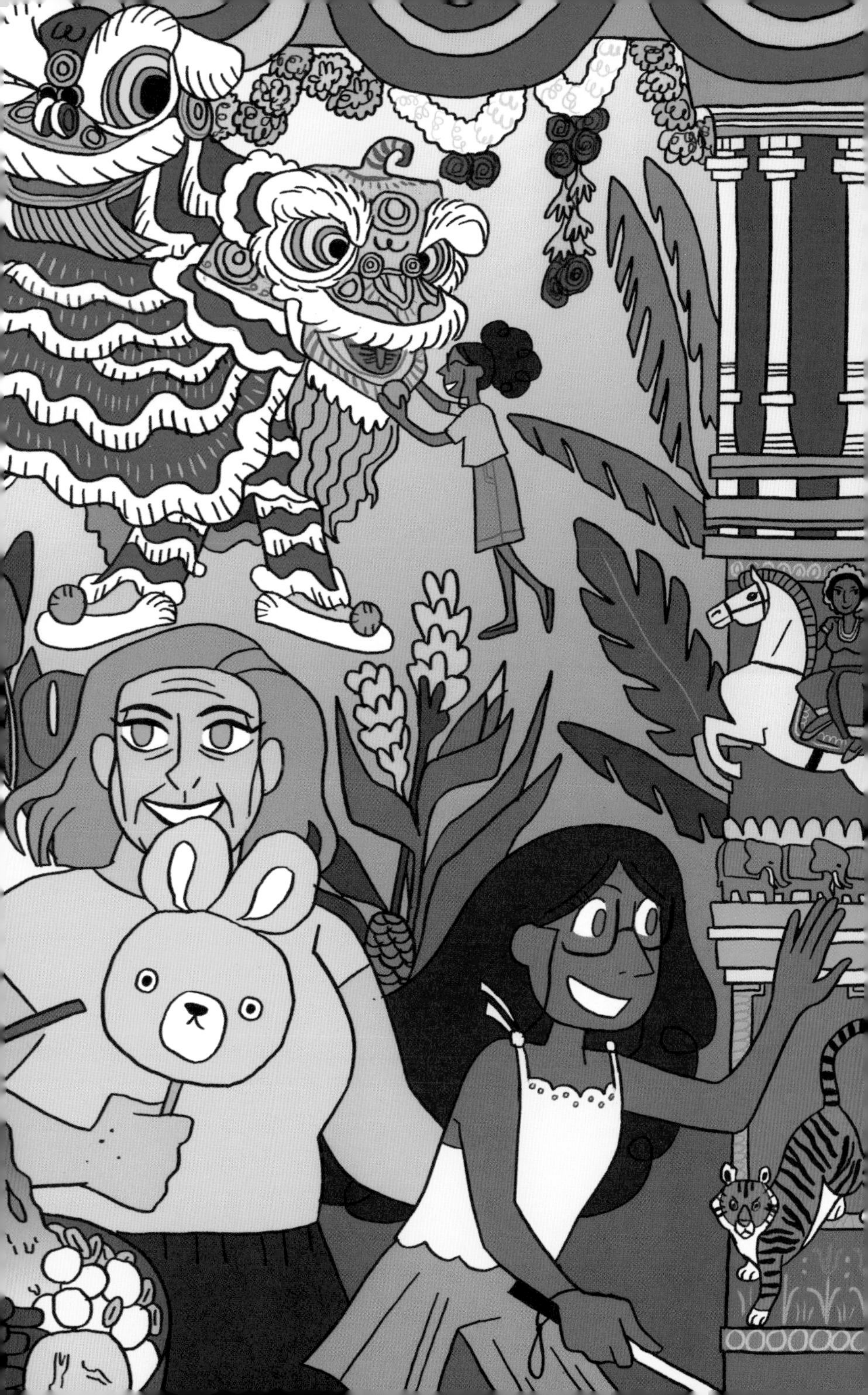

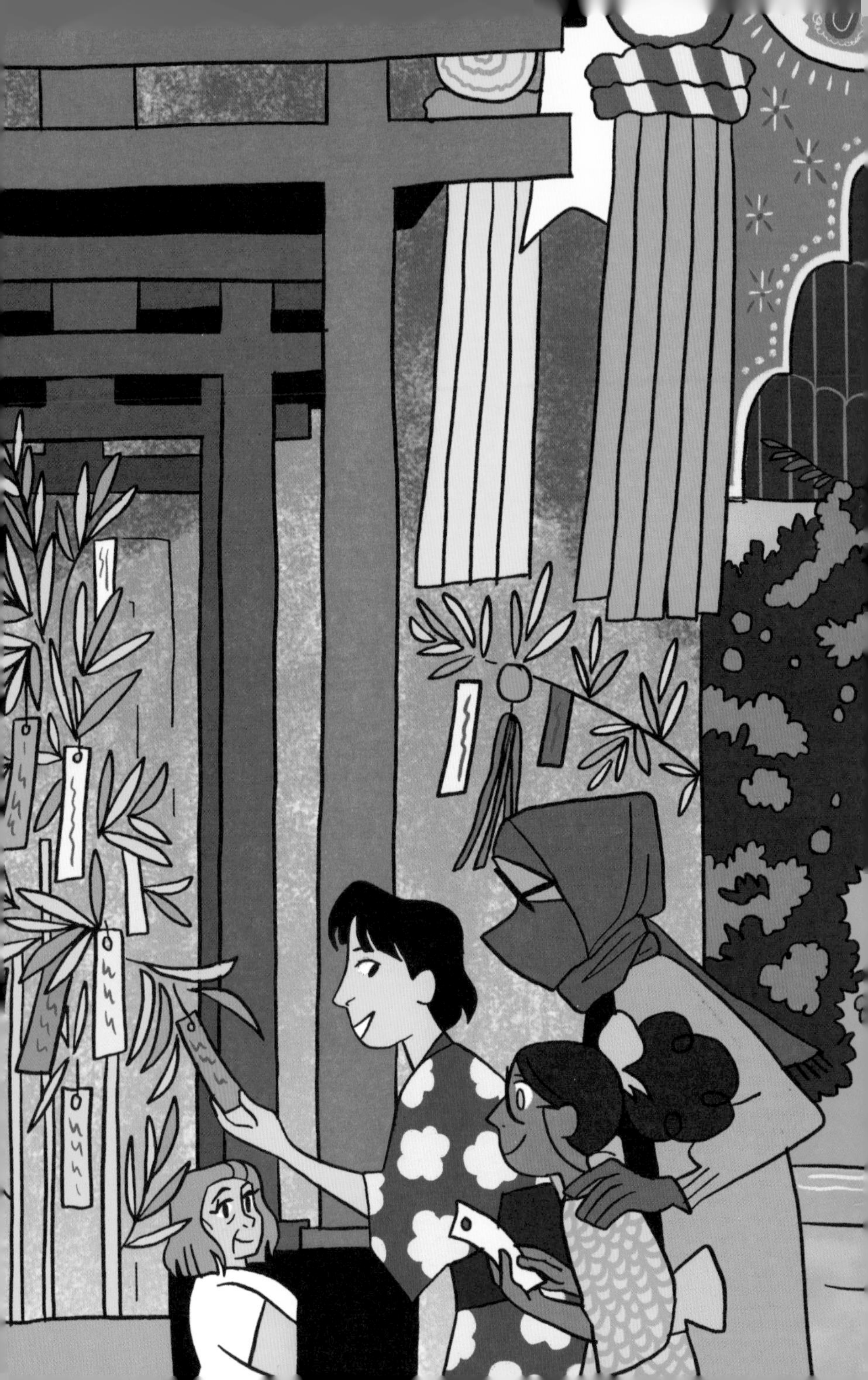

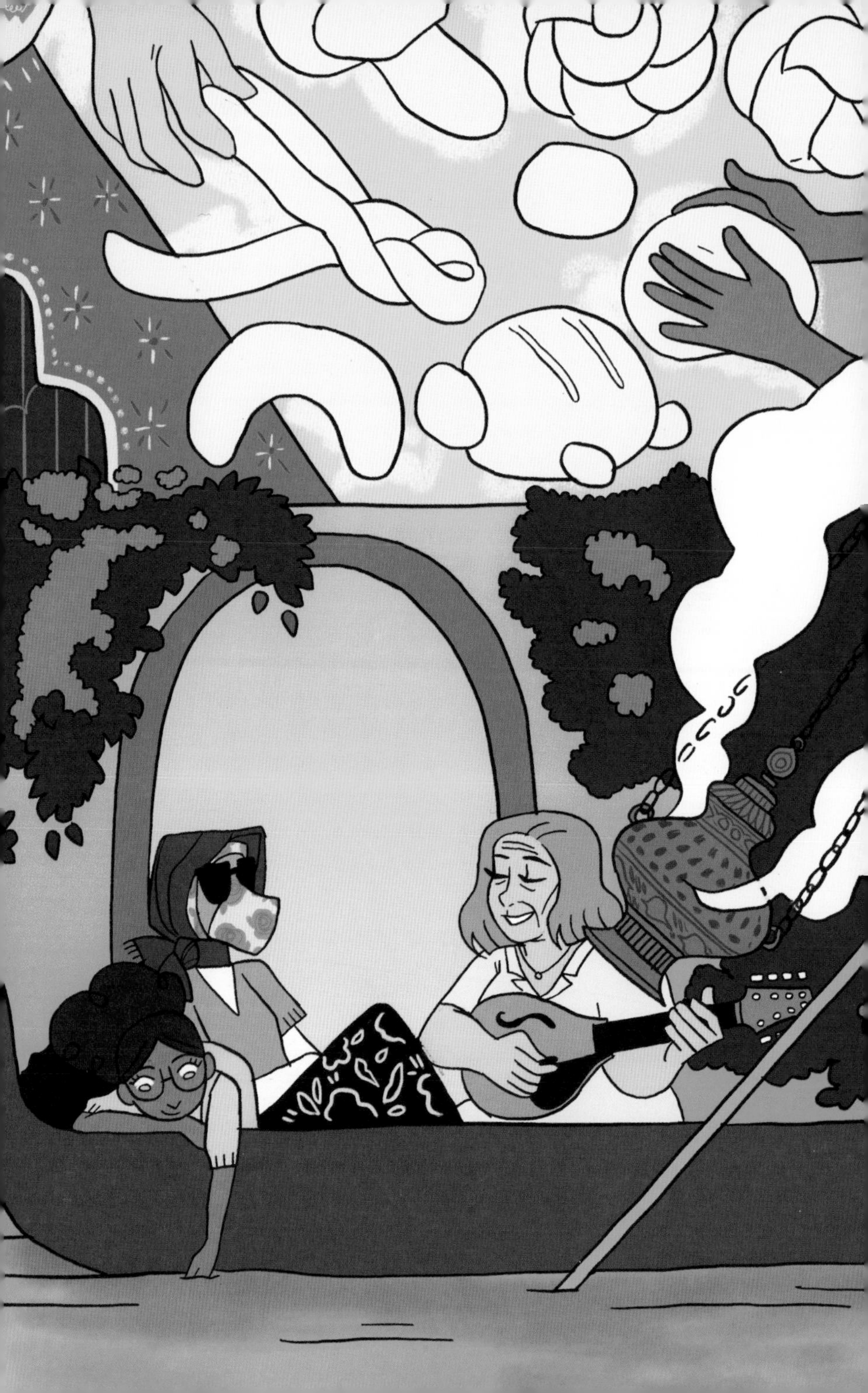

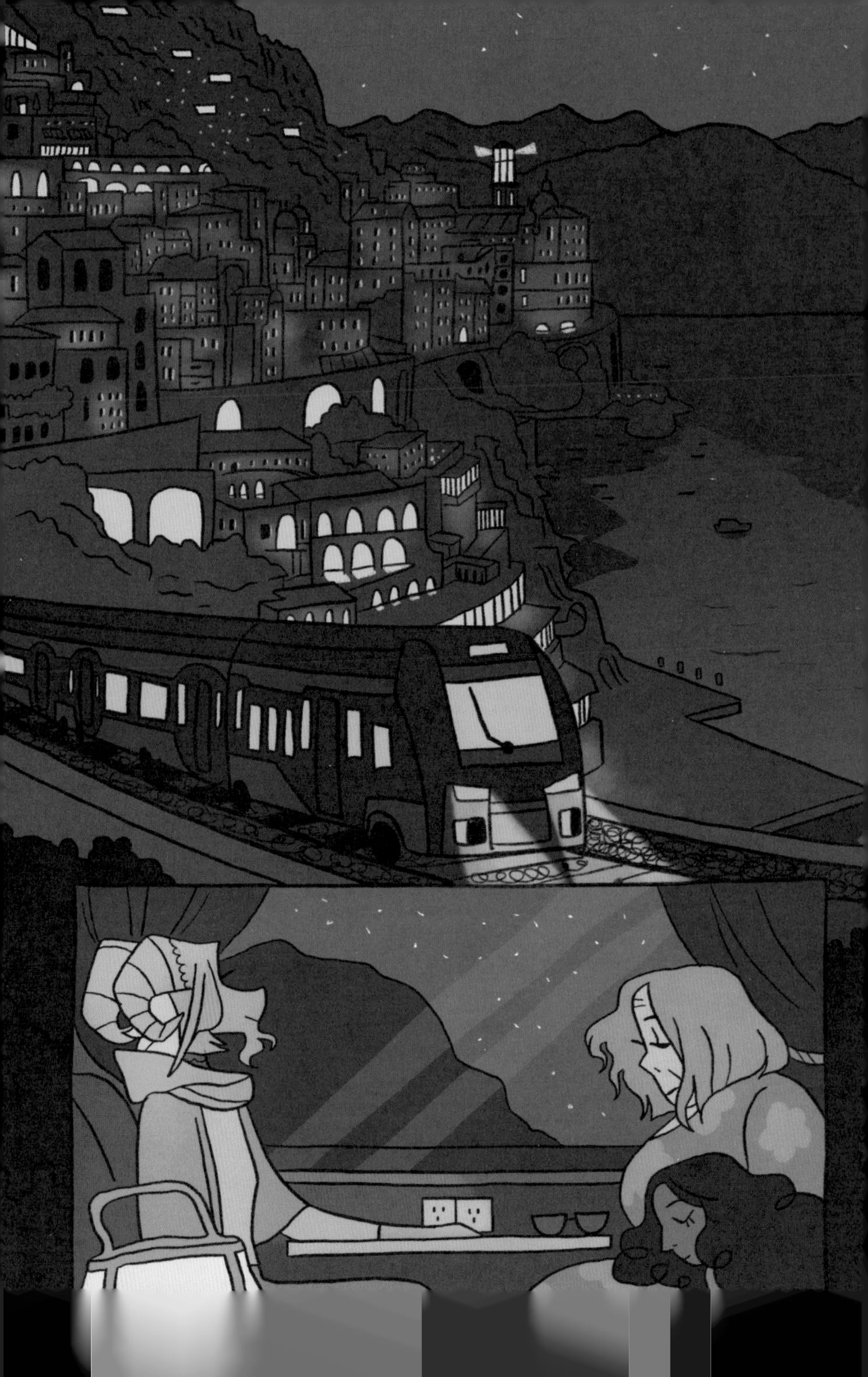

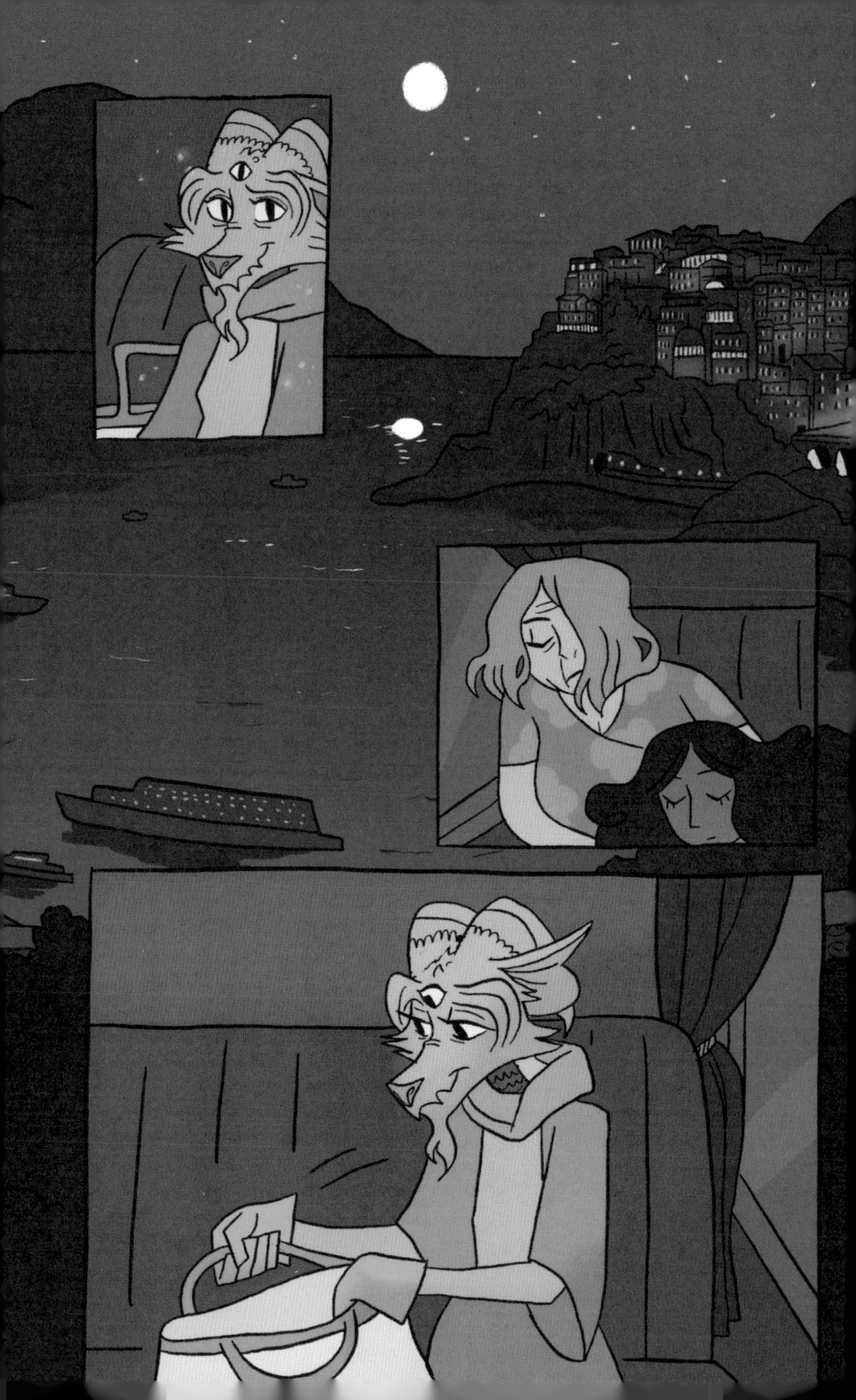

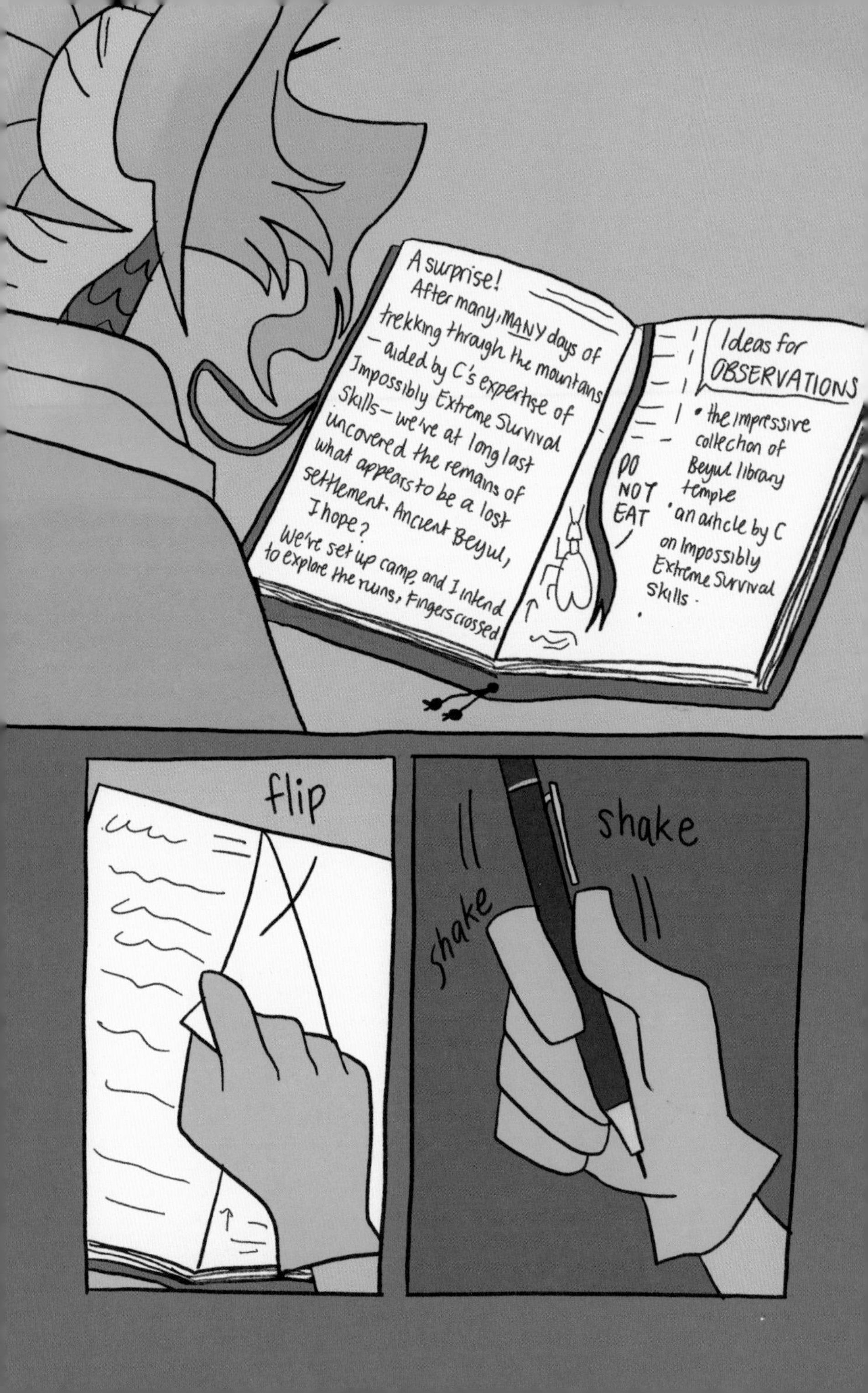

A surprise!
After many, MANY days of trekking through the mountains – aided by C's expertise of Impossibly Extreme Survival Skills – we're at long last uncovered the remains of what appears to be a lost settlement. Ancient Beyul, I hope?
We're set up camp, and I intend to explore the ruins, fingers crossed
Ideas for OBSERVATIONS
• the impressive collection of Beyul library temple
• an article by C on Impossibly Extreme Survival Skills
DO NOT EAT
flip
shake
shake

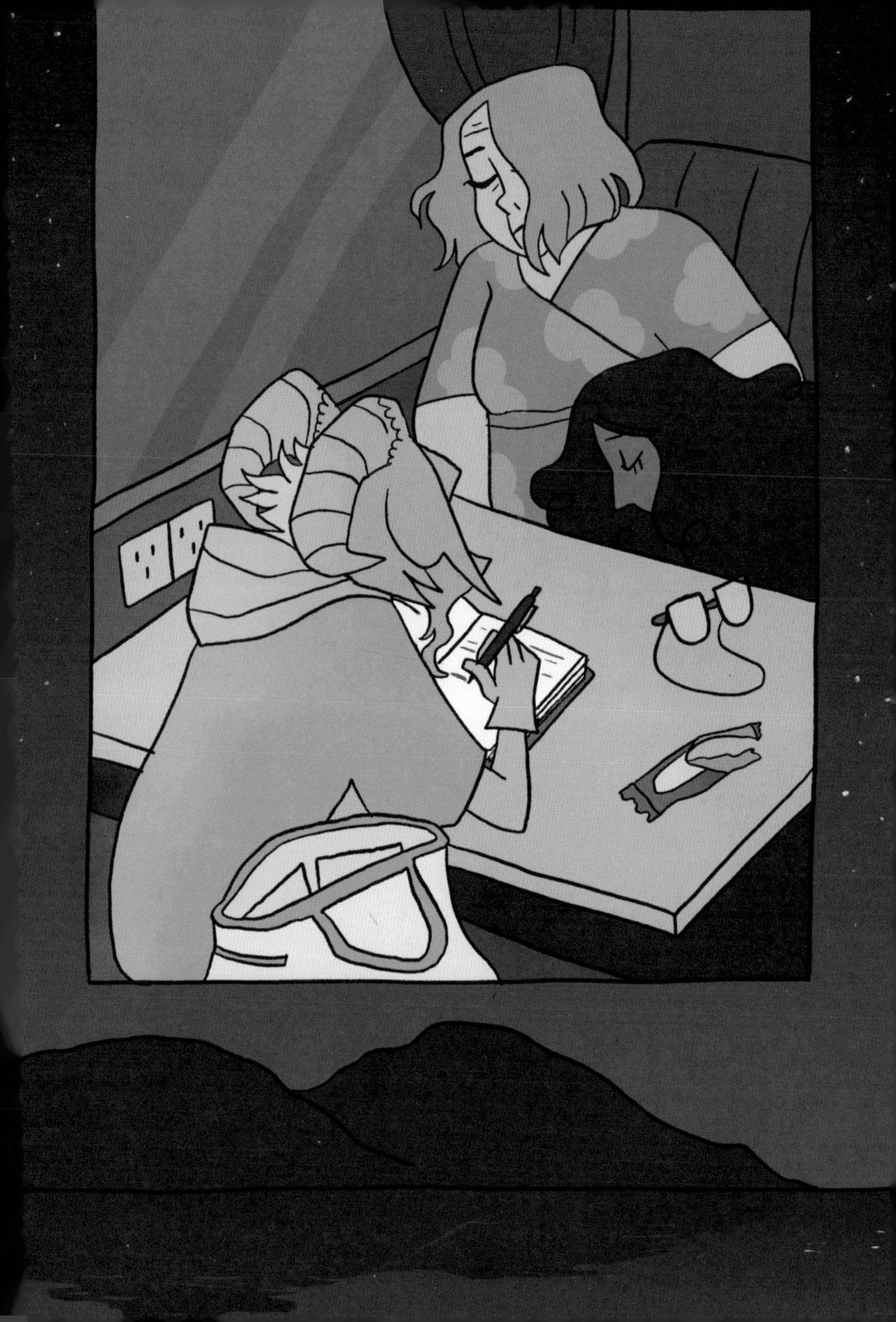

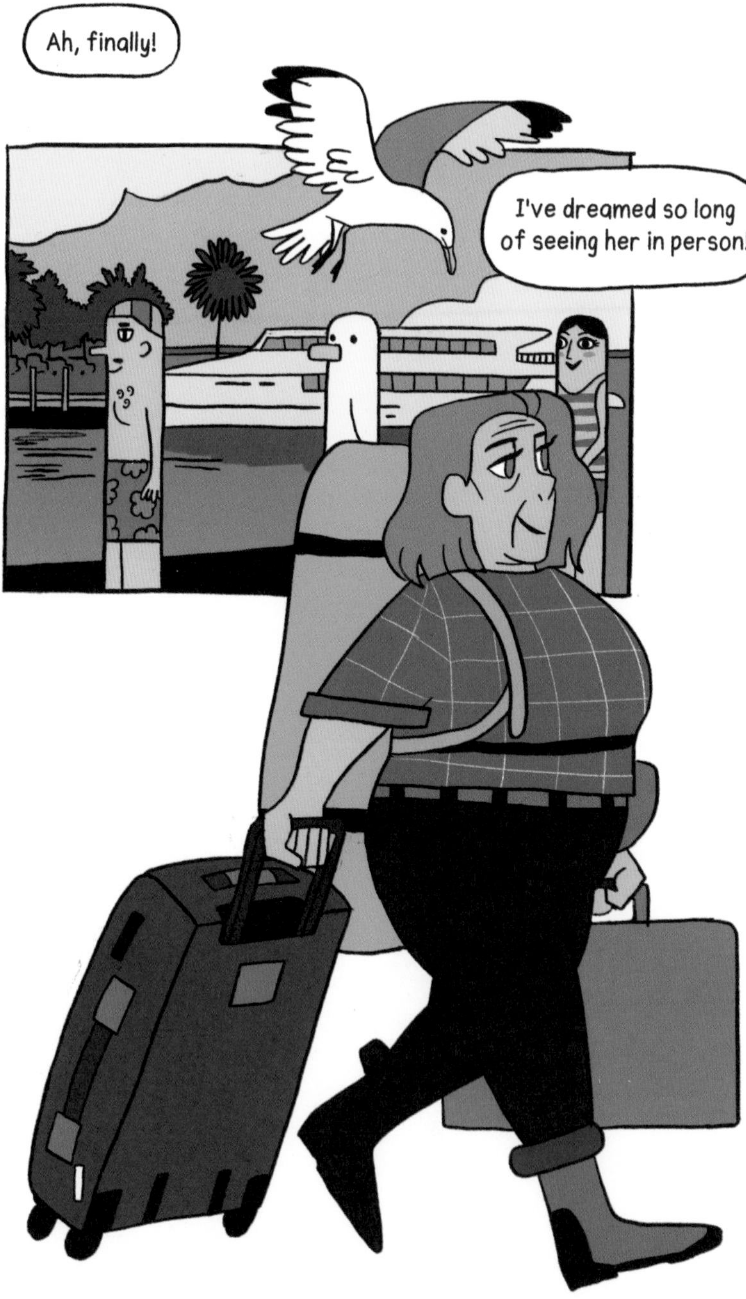
Ah, finally!
I've dreamed so long of seeing her in person!

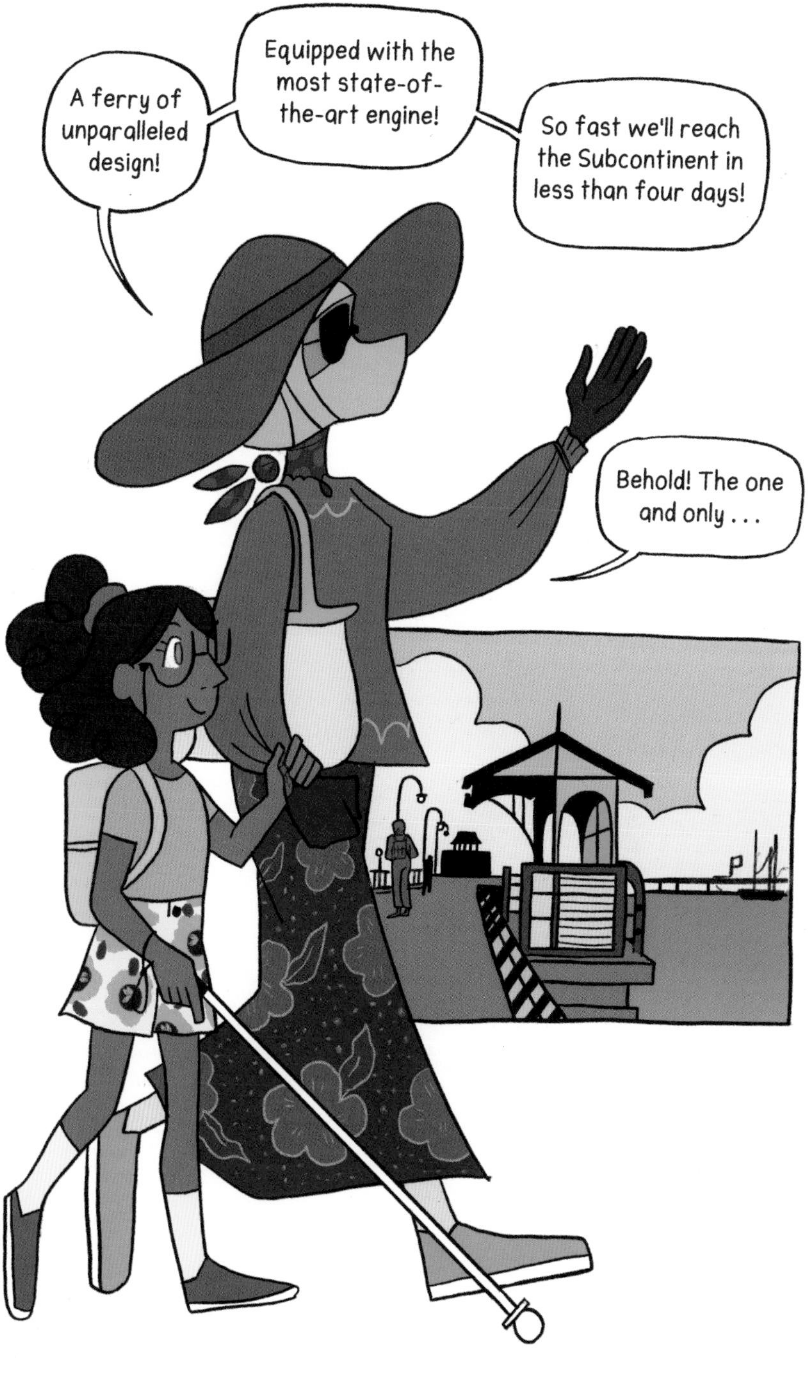
A ferry of unparalleled design!
Equipped with the most state-of-the-art engine!
So fast we'll reach the Subcontinent in less than four days!
Behold! The one and only . . .

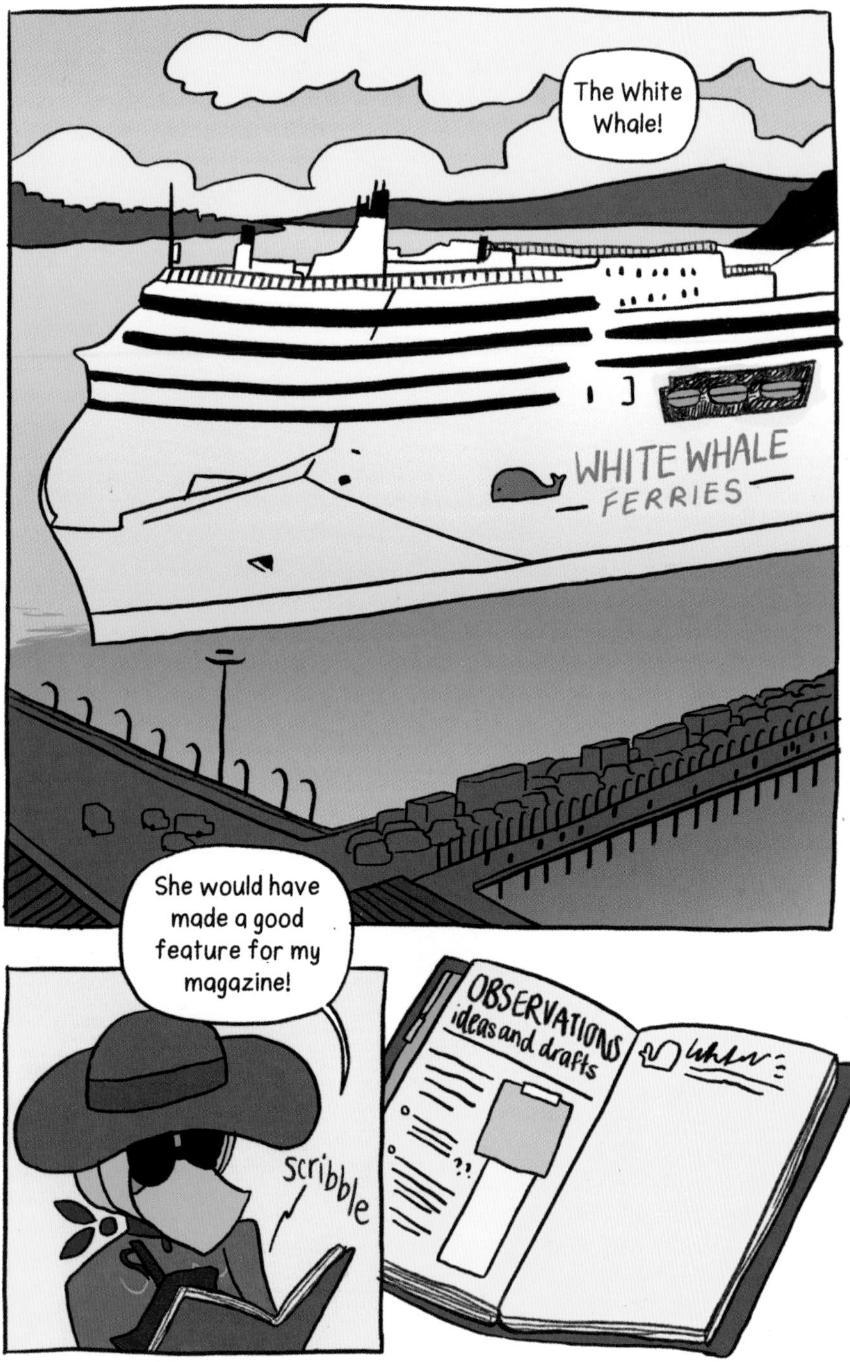
The White Whale!
WHITE WHALE FERRIES
She would have made a good feature for my magazine!
scribble
OBSERVATIONS ideas and drafts

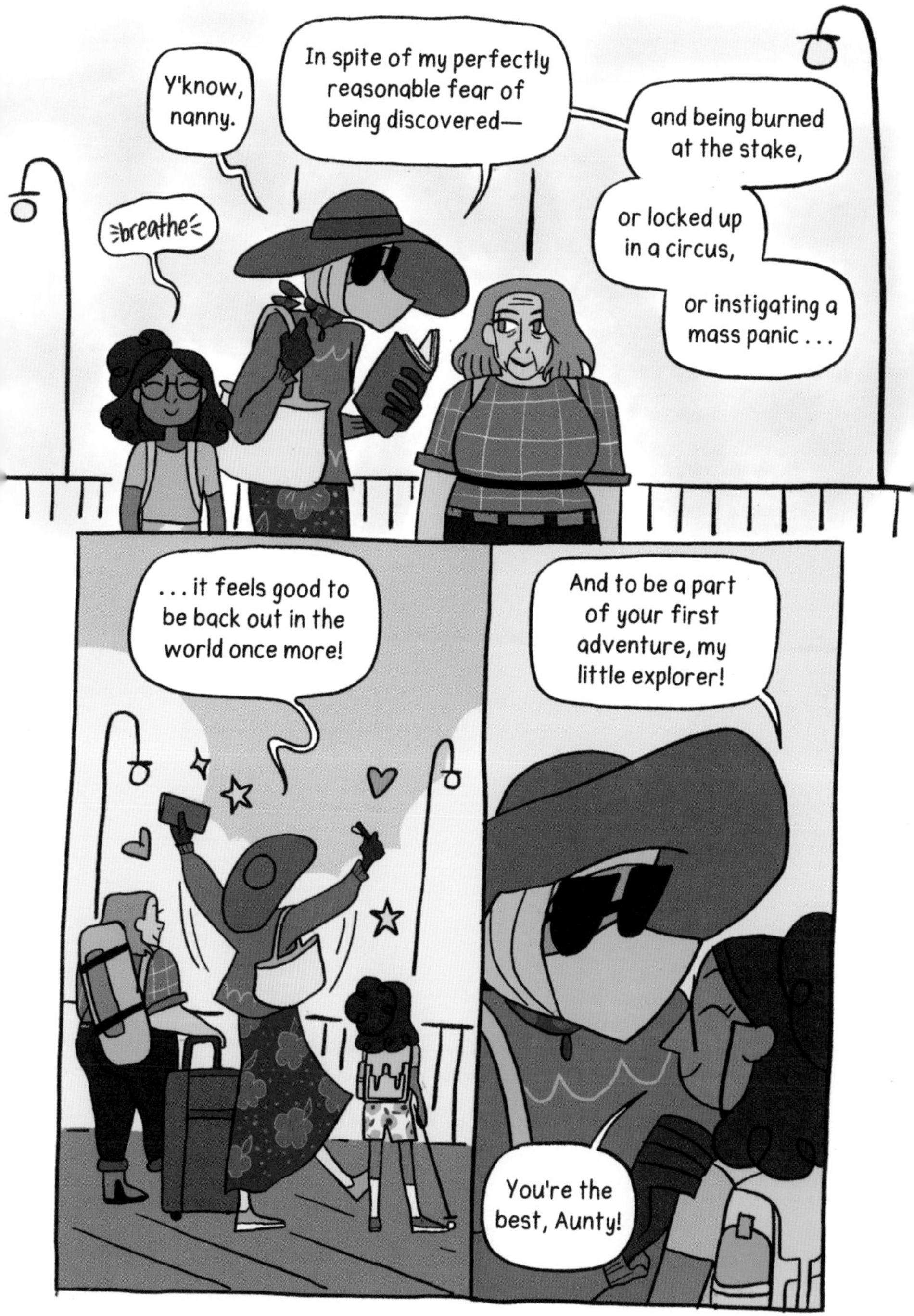

Y'know, nanny.
In spite of my perfectly reasonable fear of being discovered—
and being burned at the stake,
or locked up in a circus,
or instigating a mass panic . . .
breathe
. . . it feels good to be back out in the world once more!
And to be a part of your first adventure, my little explorer!
You're the best, Aunty!

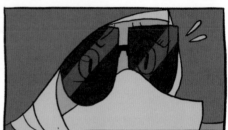

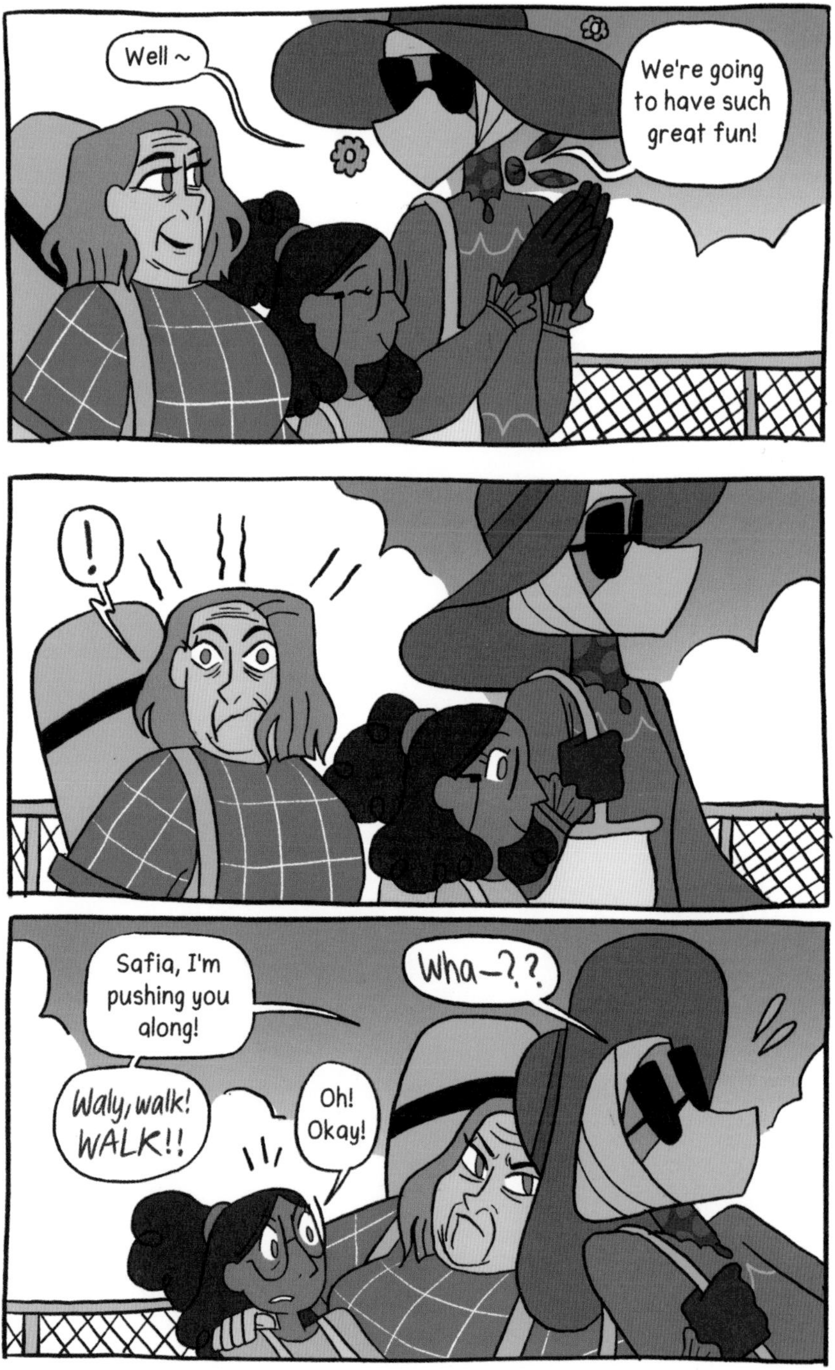
Well ~
We're going to have such great fun!
!
Safia, I'm pushing you along!
Wha—?.?.
Waly, walk! WALK!!
Oh! Okay!

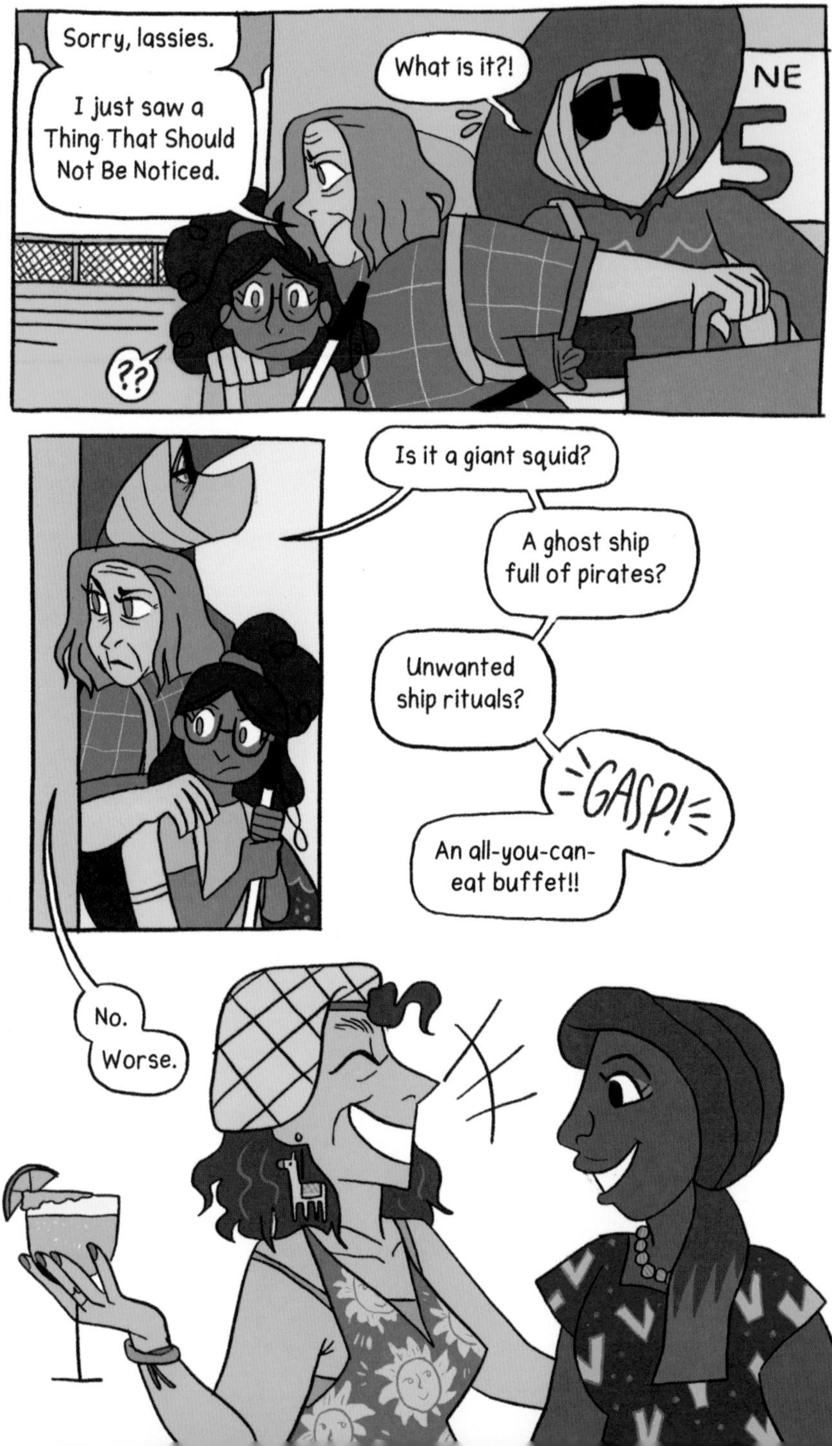

Sorry, lassies.
I just saw a Thing That Should Not Be Noticed.
What is it?!
NE
??
Is it a giant squid?
A ghost ship full of pirates?
Unwanted ship rituals?
GASP!
An all-you-can-eat buffet!!
No.
Worse.

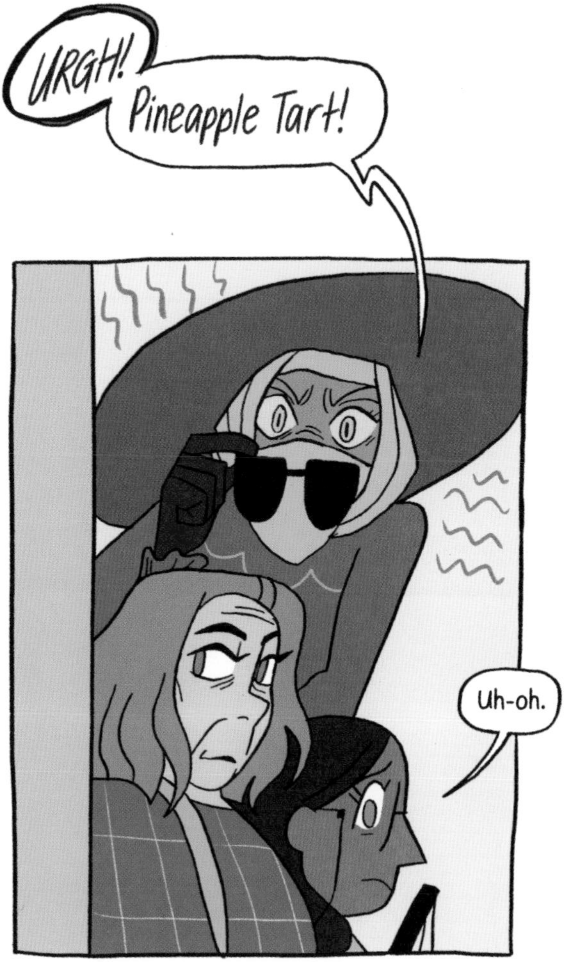
URGH!
Pineapple Tart!
Uh-oh.

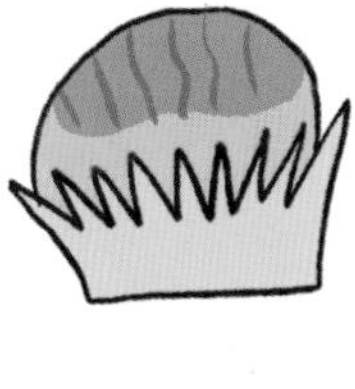

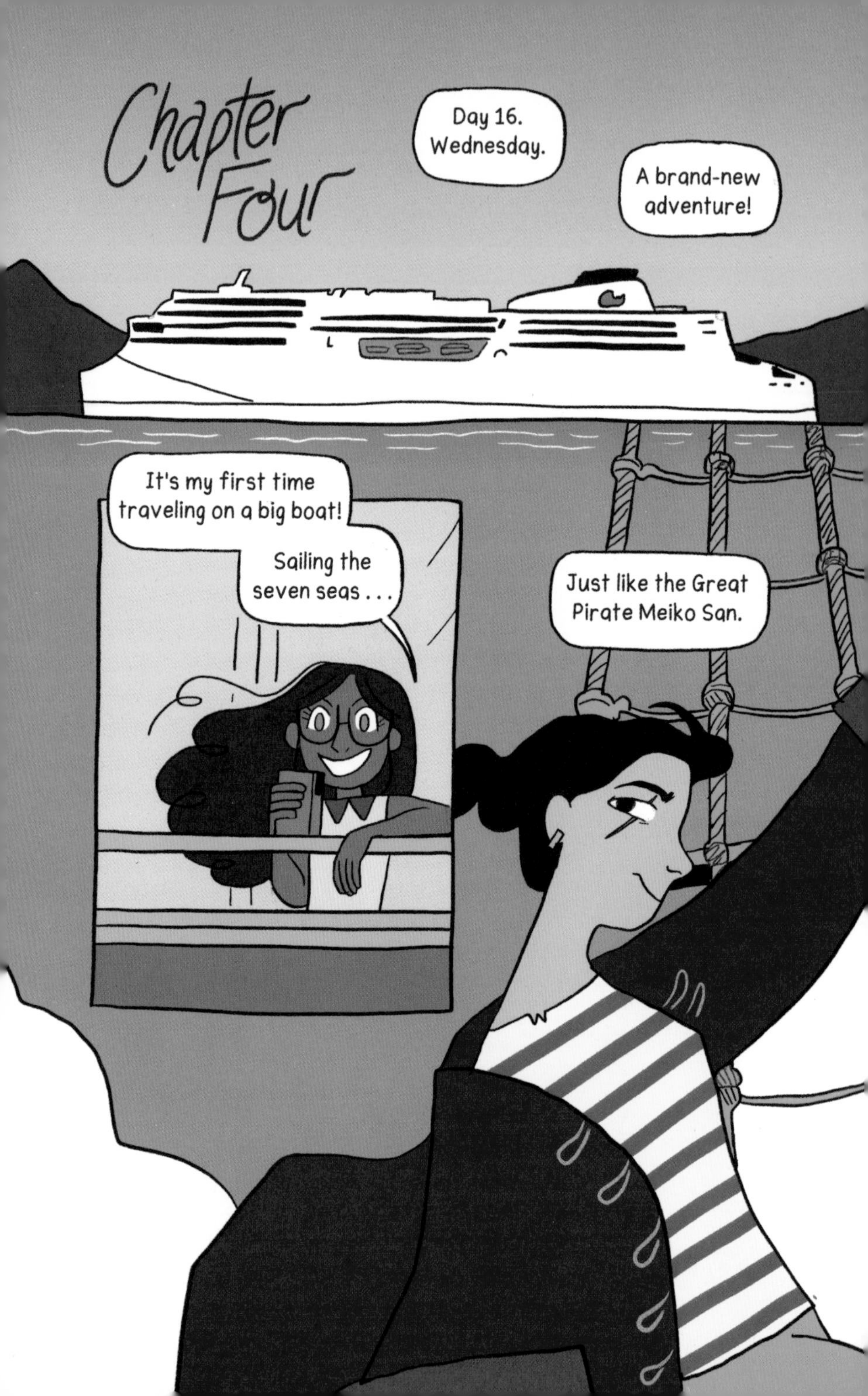
Chapter Four
Day 16. Wednesday.
A brand-new adventure!
It's my first time traveling on a big boat!
Sailing the seven seas . . .
Just like the Great Pirate Meiko San.

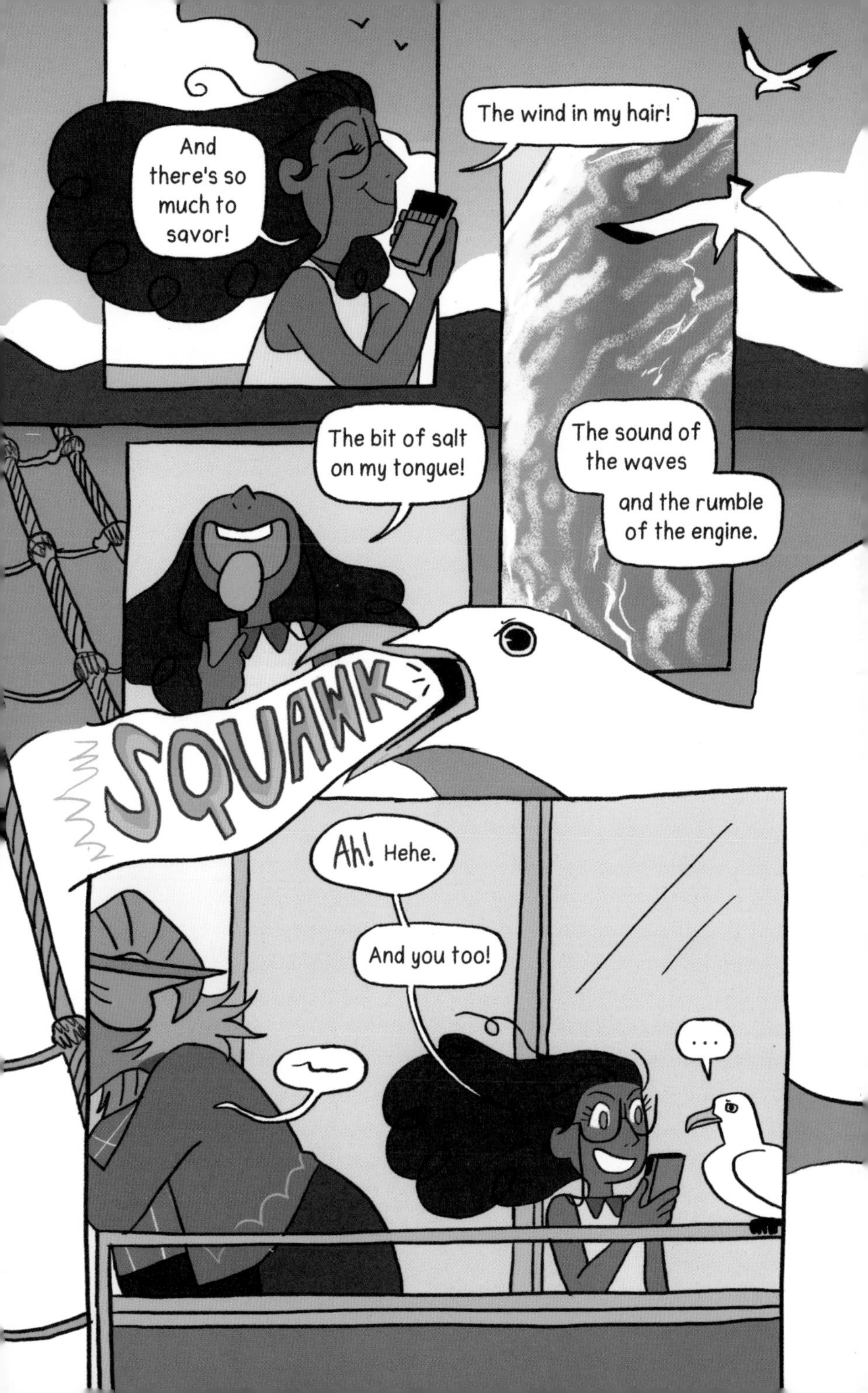
And there's so much to savor!
The wind in my hair!
The bit of salt on my tongue!
The sound of the waves
and the rumble of the engine.
SQUAWK
Ah! Hehe.
And you too!
...

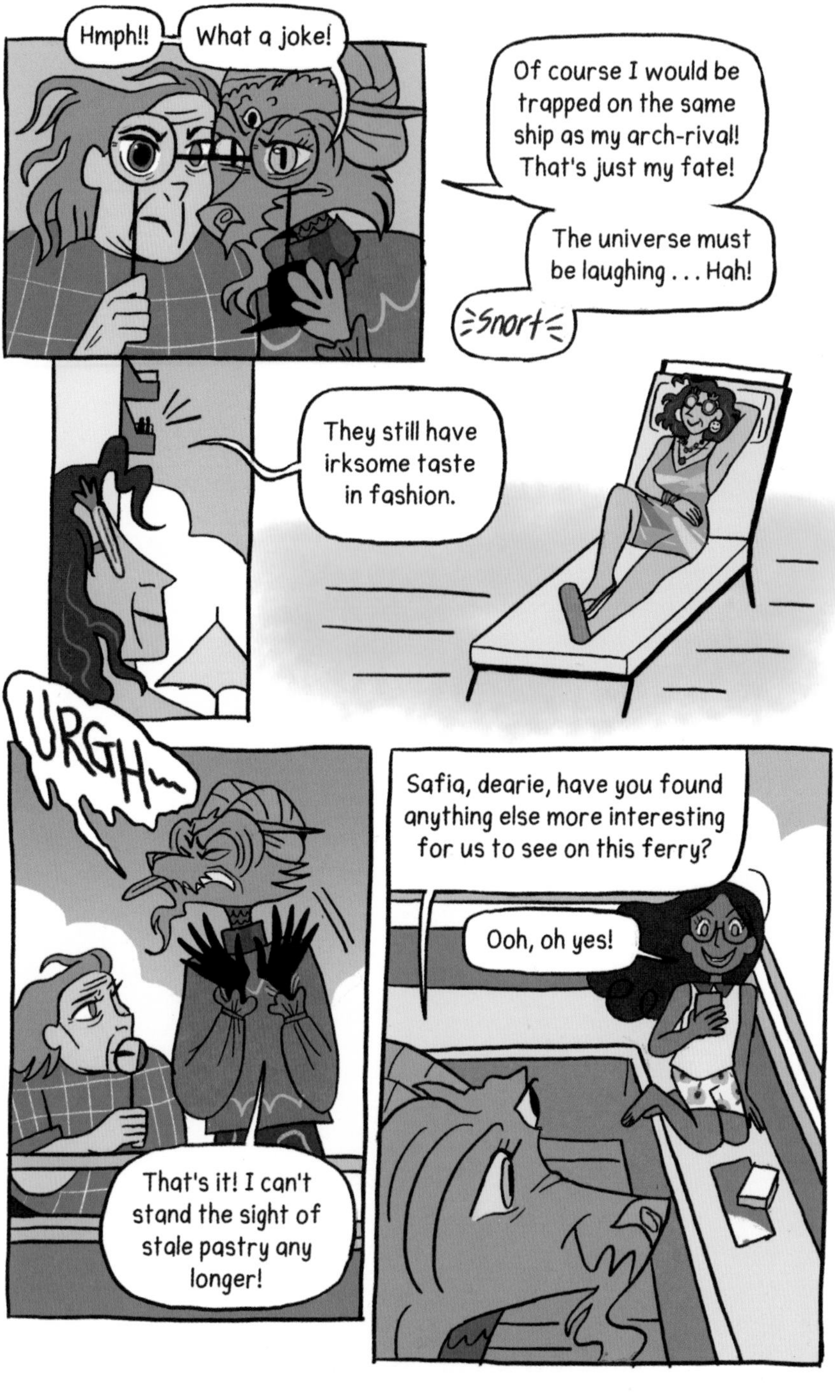
Hmph!!
What a joke!
Of course I would be trapped on the same ship as my arch-rival! That's just my fate!
The universe must be laughing . . . Hah!
Snort
They still have irksome taste in fashion.
URGH
That's it! I can't stand the sight of stale pastry any longer!
Safia, dearie, have you found anything else more interesting for us to see on this ferry?
Ooh, oh yes!

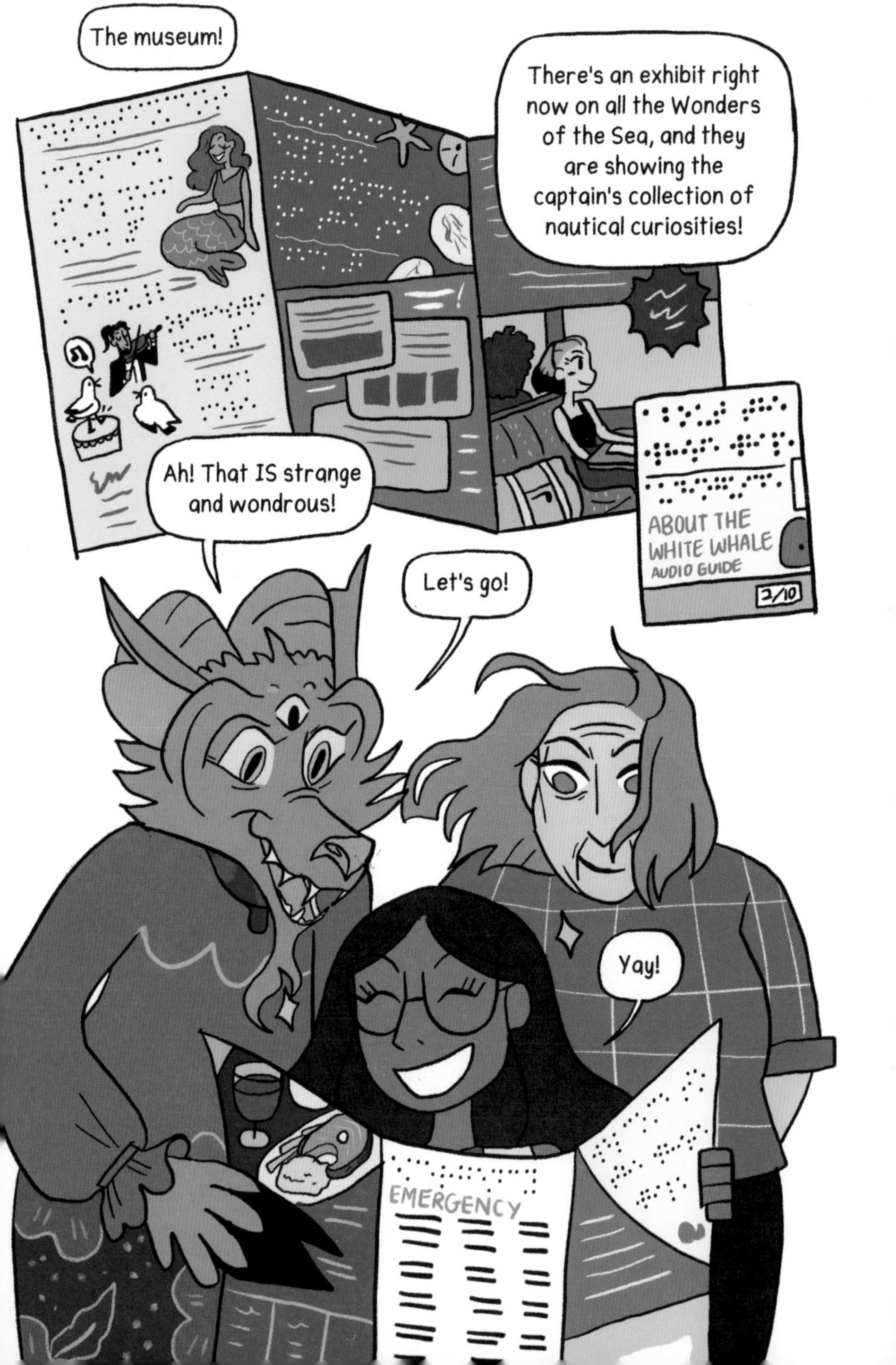
The museum!
There's an exhibit right now on all the Wonders of the Sea, and they are showing the captain's collection of nautical curiosities!
ABOUT THE WHITE WHALE
AUDIO GUIDE
2/10
Ah! That IS strange and wondrous!
Let's go!
Yay!
EMERGENCY

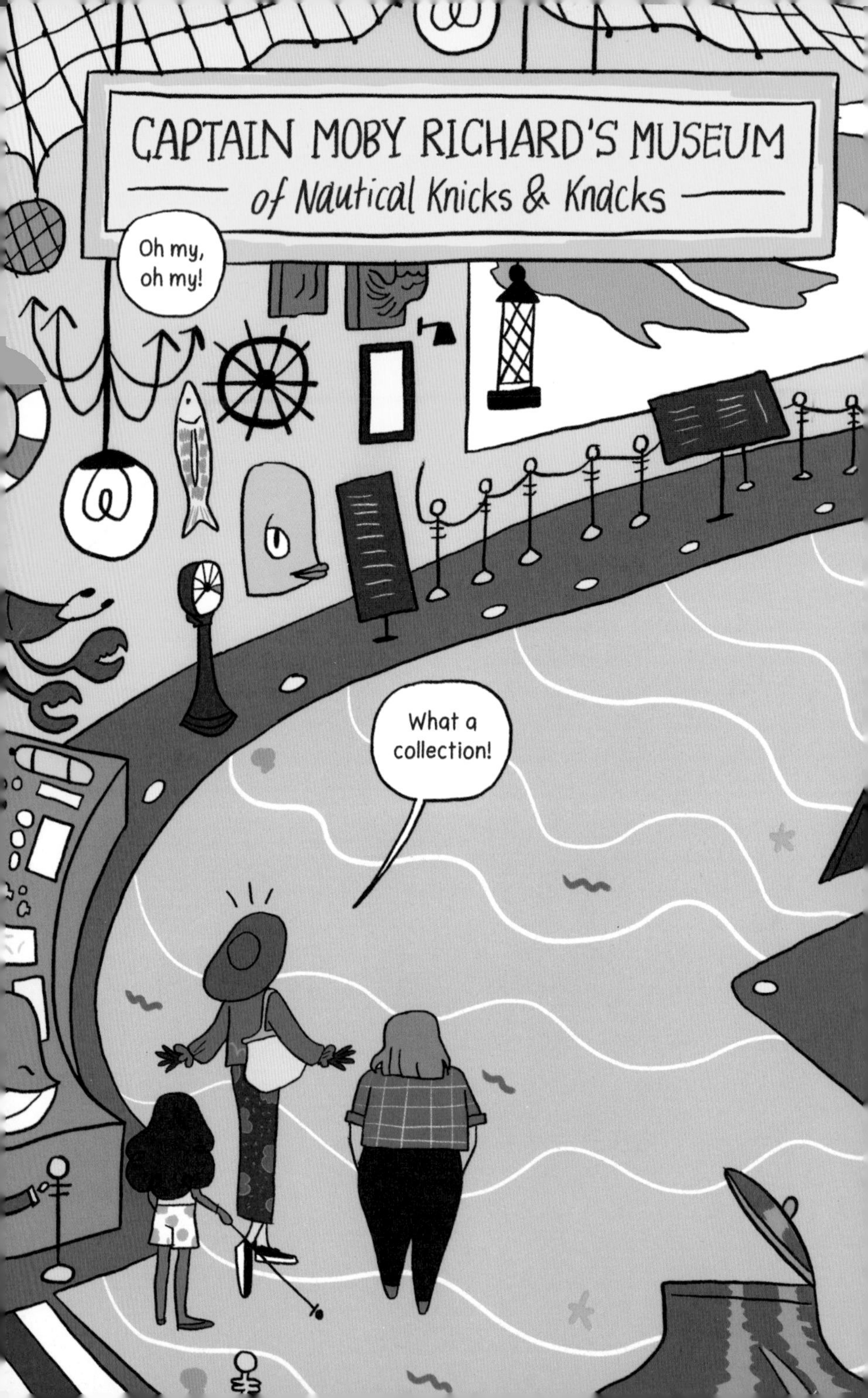
CAPTAIN MOBY RICHARD'S MUSEUM
of Nautical Knicks & Knacks
Oh my, oh my!
What a collection!

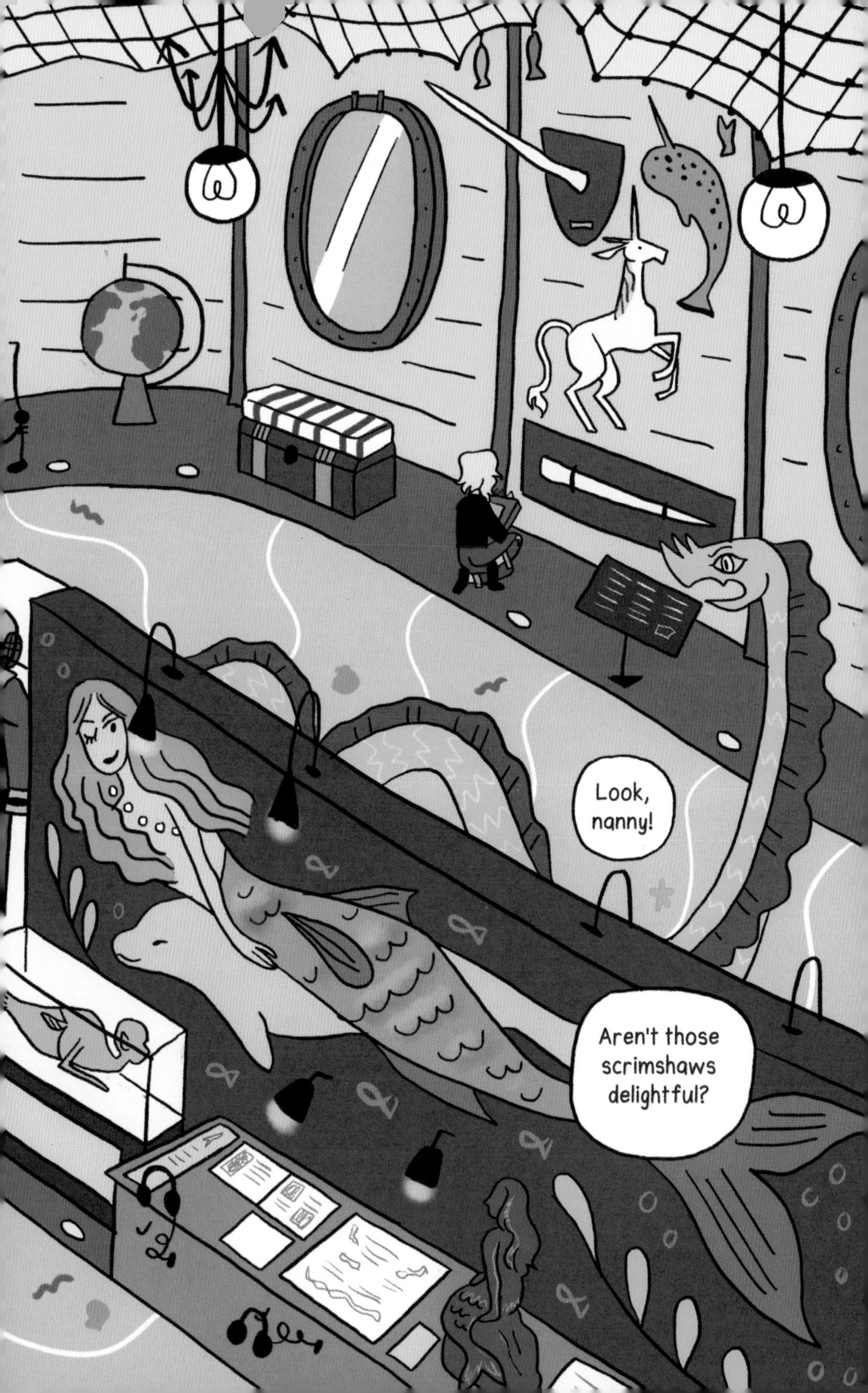
Look, nanny!
Aren't those scrimshaws delightful?

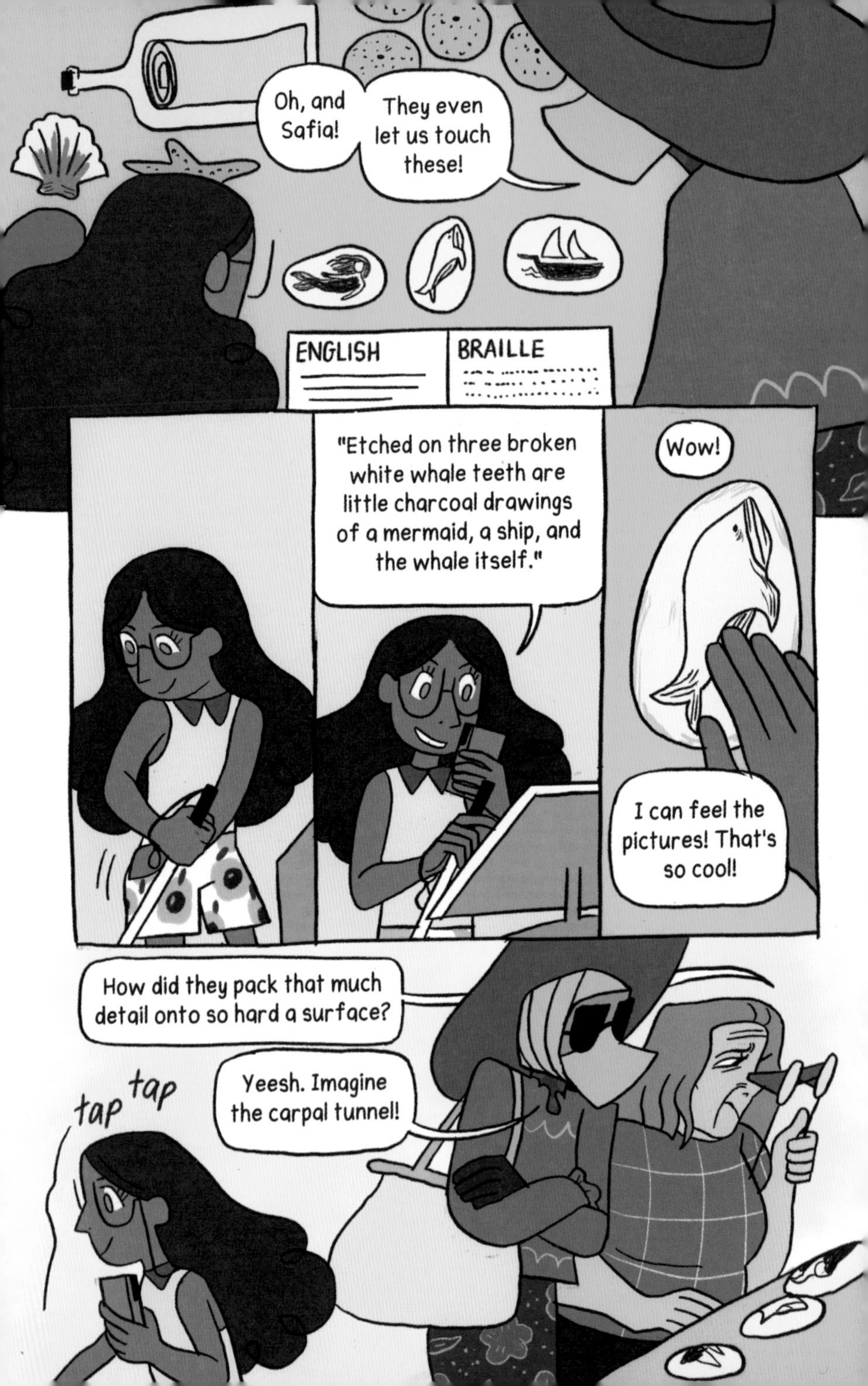
Oh, and Safia!
They even let us touch these!
ENGLISH
BRAILLE
"Etched on three broken white whale teeth are little charcoal drawings of a mermaid, a ship, and the whale itself."
Wow!
I can feel the pictures! That's so cool!
How did they pack that much detail onto so hard a surface?
Yeesh. Imagine the carpal tunnel!
tap tap

"Shorn-off skin of a white whale. Some whales will travel great distances for the perfect boulder to scratch off old skin."
"Ambergris is made from whale vomit or poop. It is a special ingredient, used to enhance the quality of perfume."
sniff
YUCK!
Is that REALLY perfume?!
Who would want to put that on—?

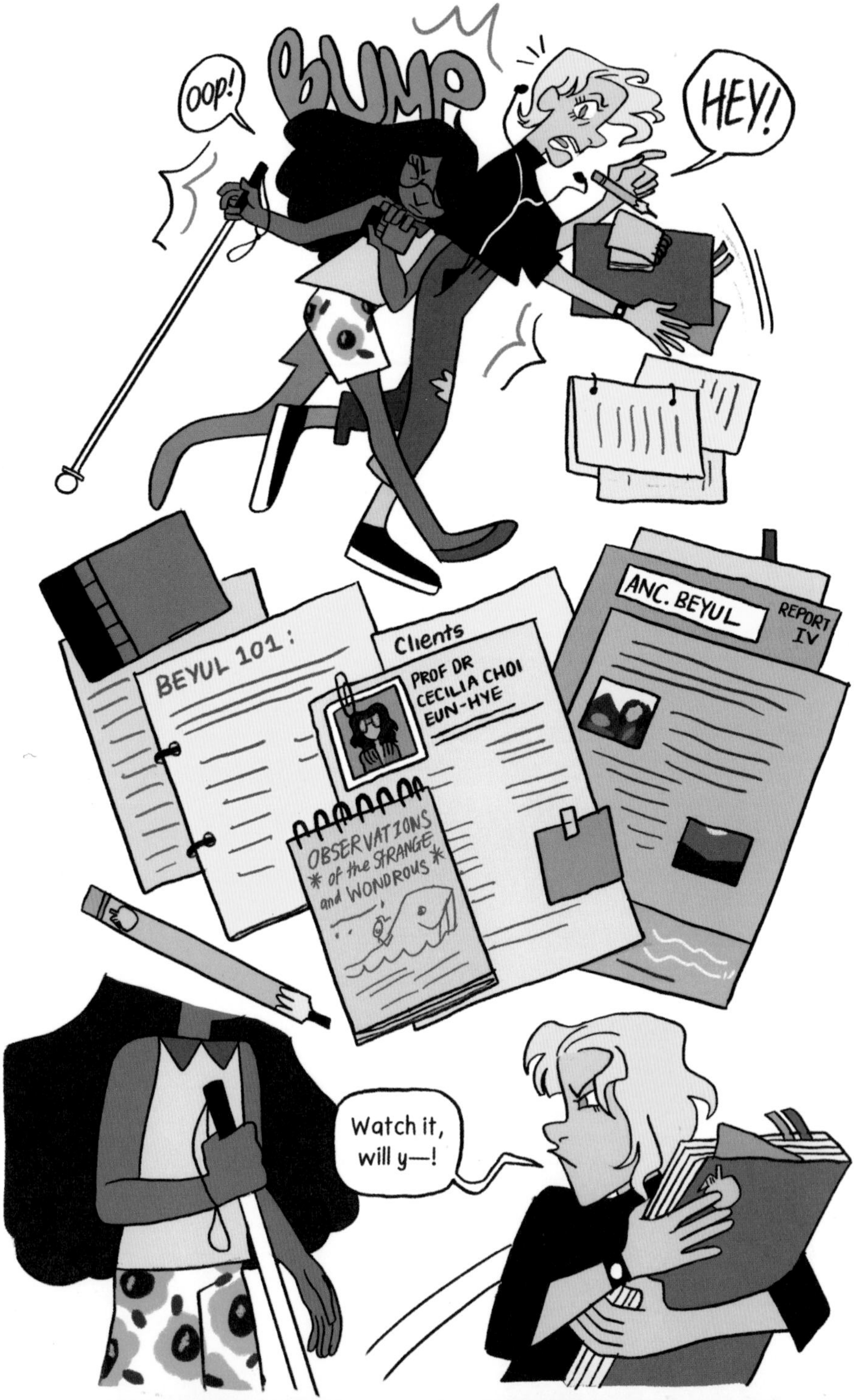

OOP!
BUMP
HEY!
BEYUL 101:
Clients
PROF DR CECILIA CHOI EUN-HYE
ANC. BEYUL
REPORT IV
OBSERVATIONS * of the STRANGE * and WONDROUS
Watch it, will y—!

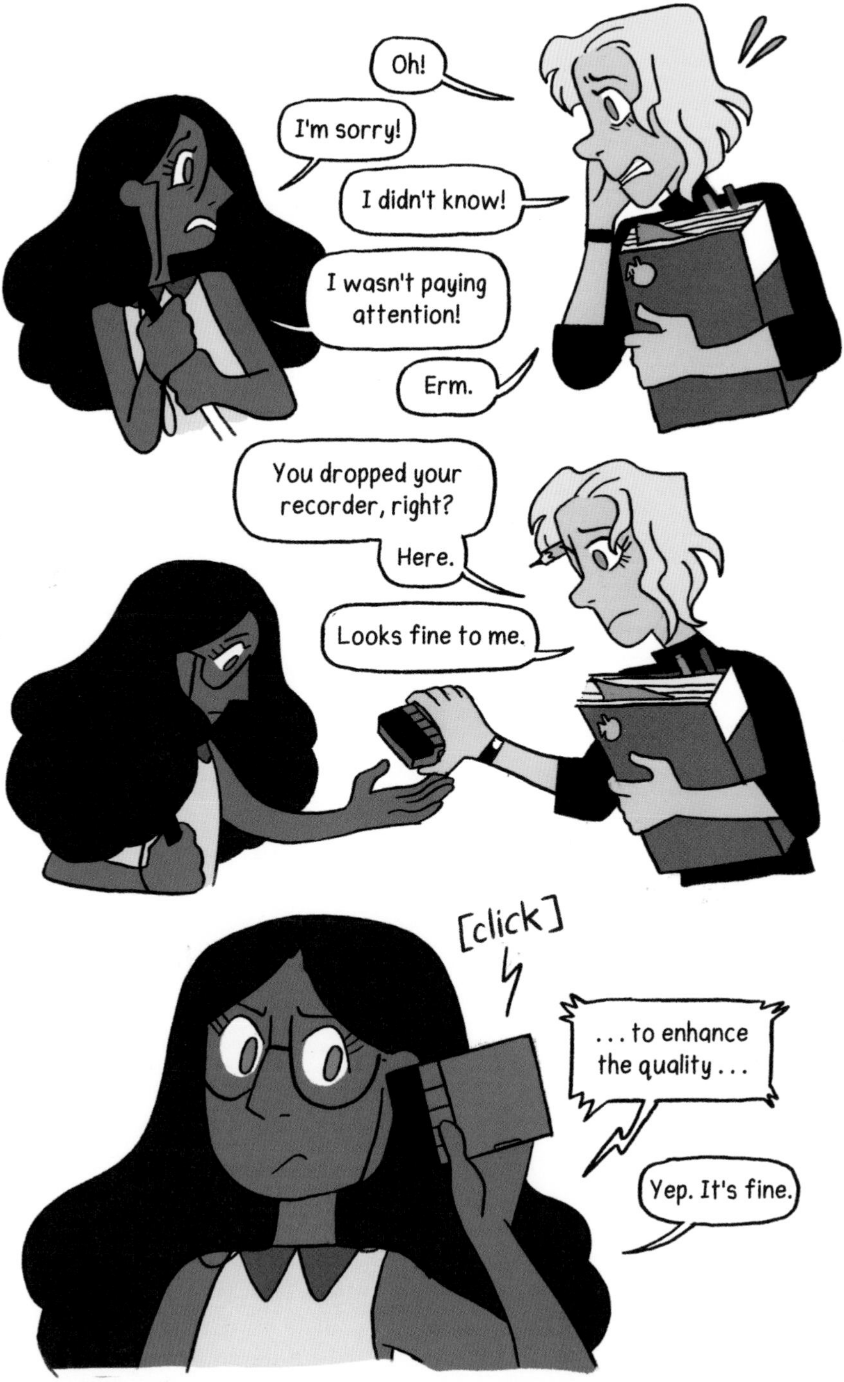
Oh!
I'm sorry!
I didn't know!
I wasn't paying attention!
Erm.
You dropped your recorder, right?
Here.
Looks fine to me.
[click]
. . . to enhance the quality . . .
Yep. It's fine.

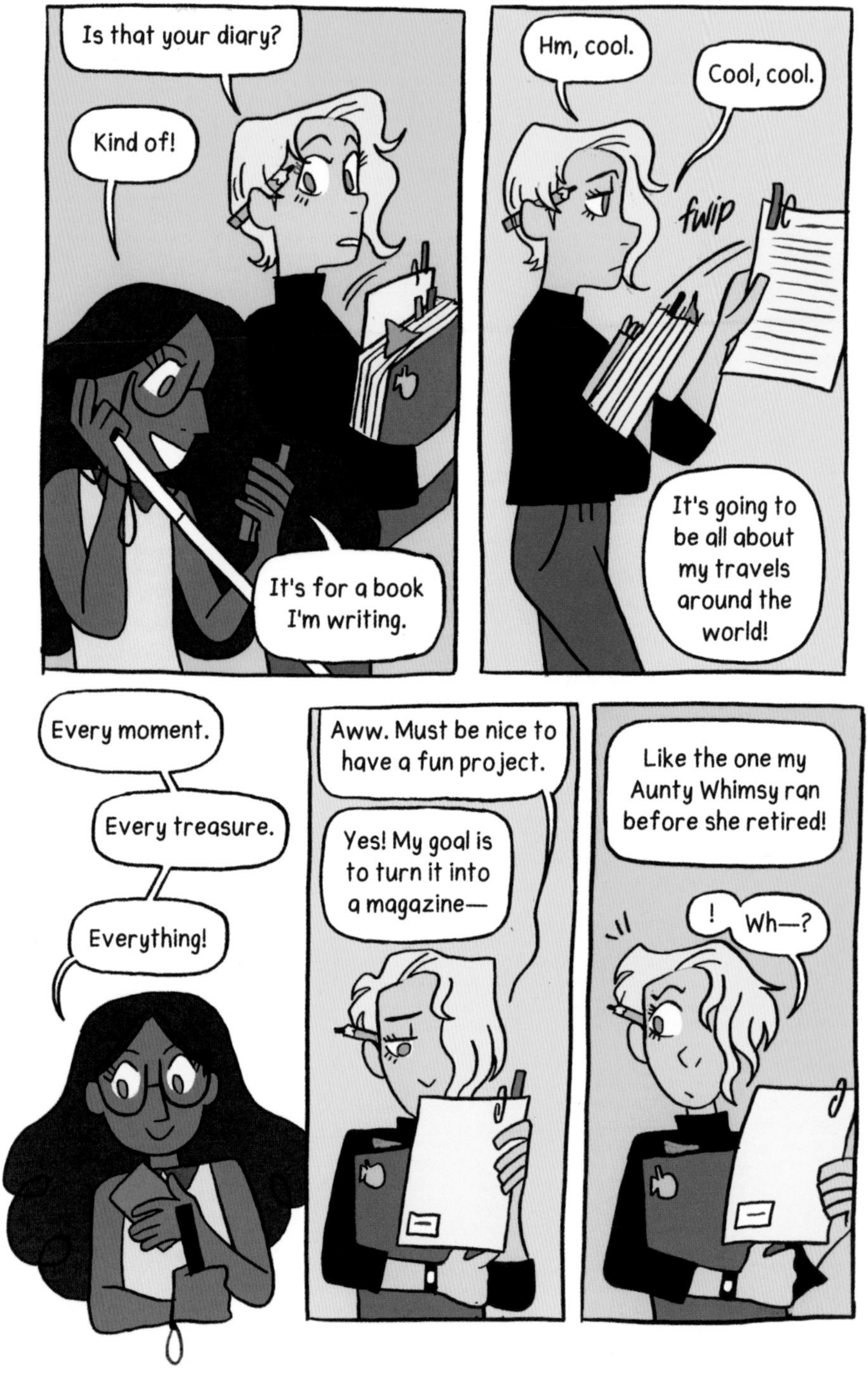
Is that your diary?
Kind of!
It's for a book I'm writing.
Hm, cool.
Cool, cool.
fwip
It's going to be all about my travels around the world!
Every moment.
Every treasure.
Everything!
Aww. Must be nice to have a fun project.
Yes! My goal is to turn it into a magazine—
Like the one my Aunty Whimsy ran before she retired!
!
Wh—?

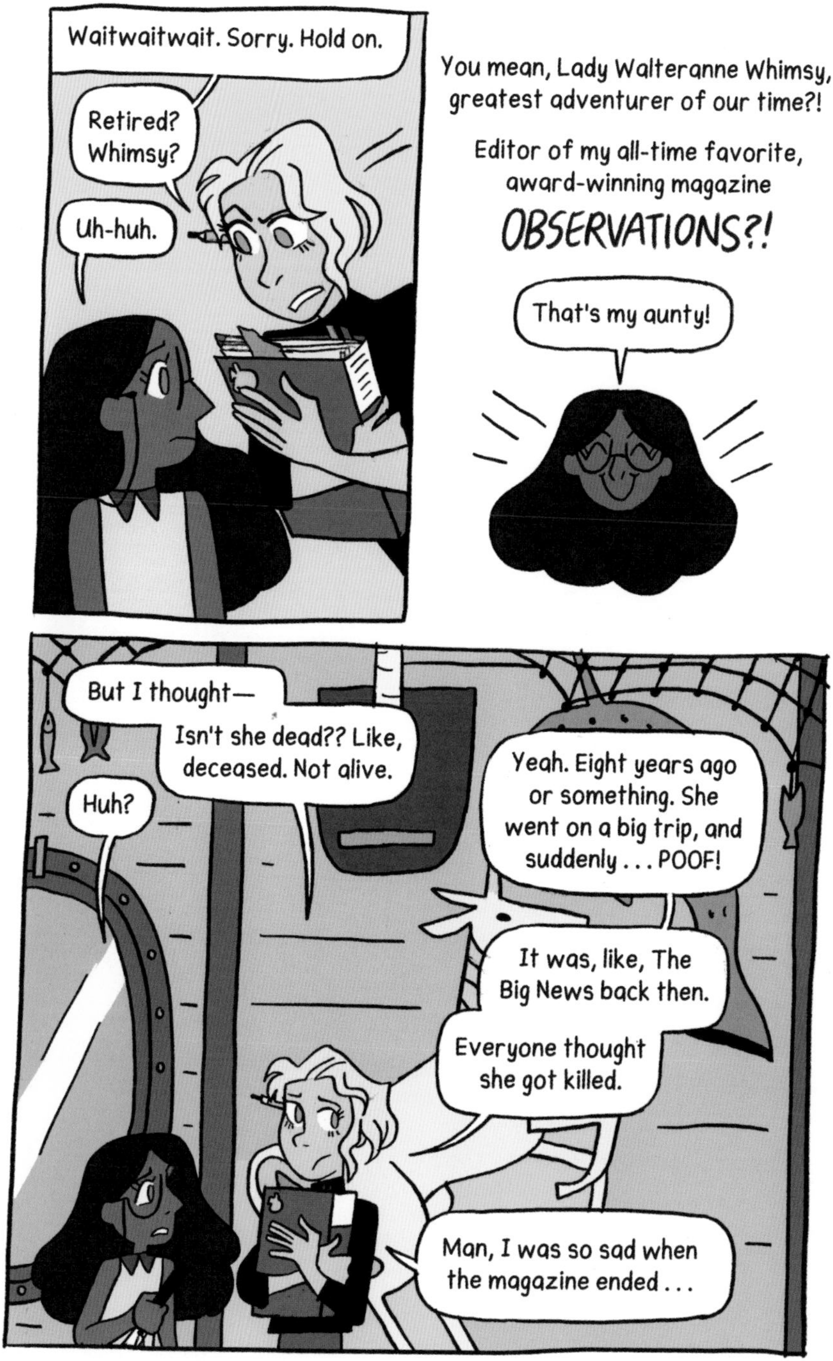

Waitwaitwait. Sorry. Hold on.
Retired? Whimsy?
Uh-huh.
You mean, Lady Walteranne Whimsy, greatest adventurer of our time?!
Editor of my all-time favorite, award-winning magazine
OBSERVATIONS?!
That's my aunty!
But I thought—
Isn't she dead?? Like, deceased. Not alive.
Huh?
Yeah. Eight years ago or something. She went on a big trip, and suddenly . . . POOF!
It was, like, The Big News back then.
Everyone thought she got killed.
Man, I was so sad when the magazine ended . . .

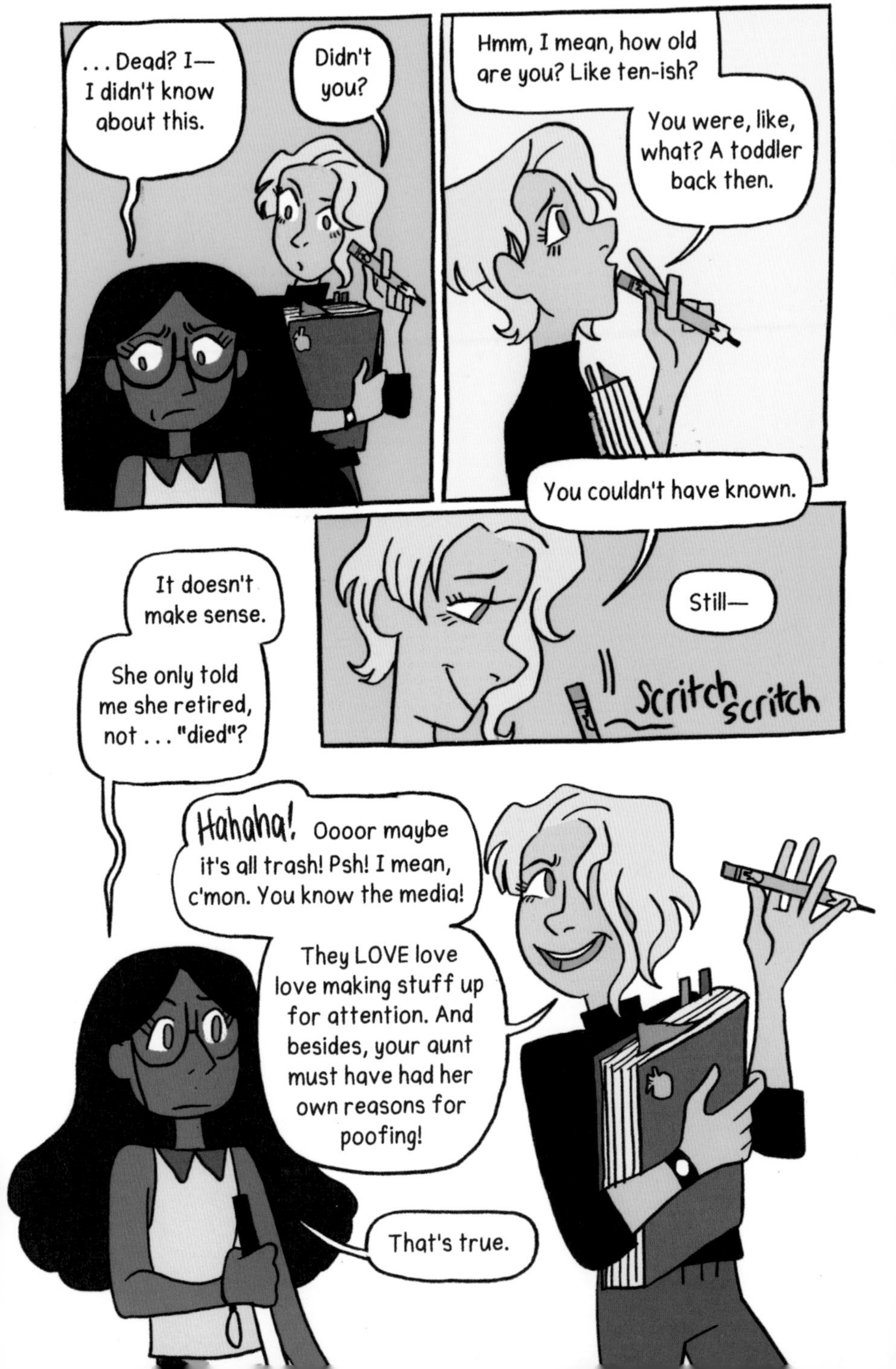

. . . Dead? I— I didn't know about this.
Didn't you?
Hmm, I mean, how old are you? Like ten-ish?
You were, like, what? A toddler back then.
You couldn't have known.
Still—
Scritch scritch
It doesn't make sense.
She only told me she retired, not . . . "died"?
Hahaha! Oooor maybe it's all trash! Psh! I mean, c'mon. You know the media!
They LOVE love love making stuff up for attention. And besides, your aunt must have had her own reasons for poofing!
That's true.

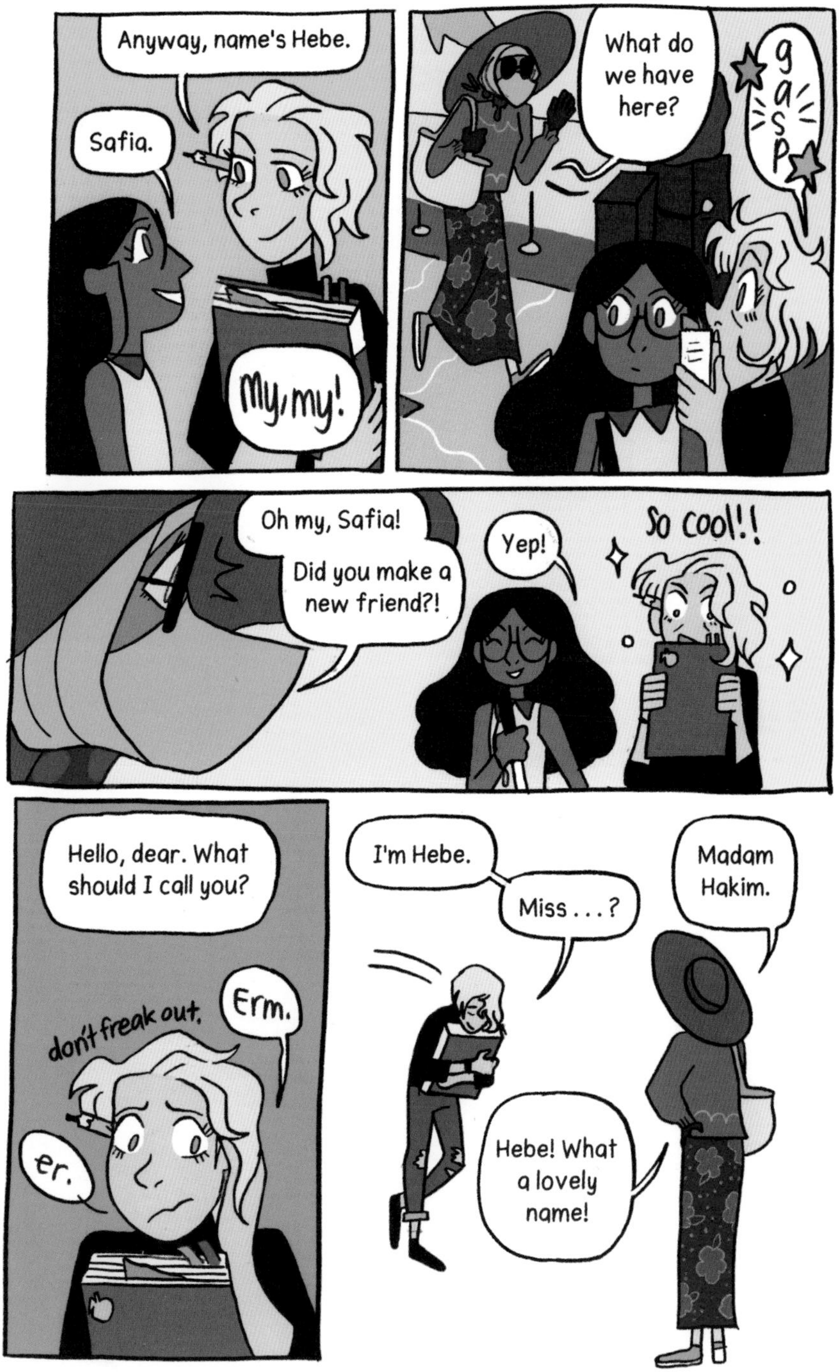
Anyway, name's Hebe.
Safia.
My, my!
What do we have here?
gasp
Oh my, Safia!
Did you make a new friend?!
Yep!
So cool!!
Hello, dear. What should I call you?
Erm.
don't freak out.
er.
I'm Hebe.
Miss . . . ?
Madam Hakim.
Hebe! What a lovely name!

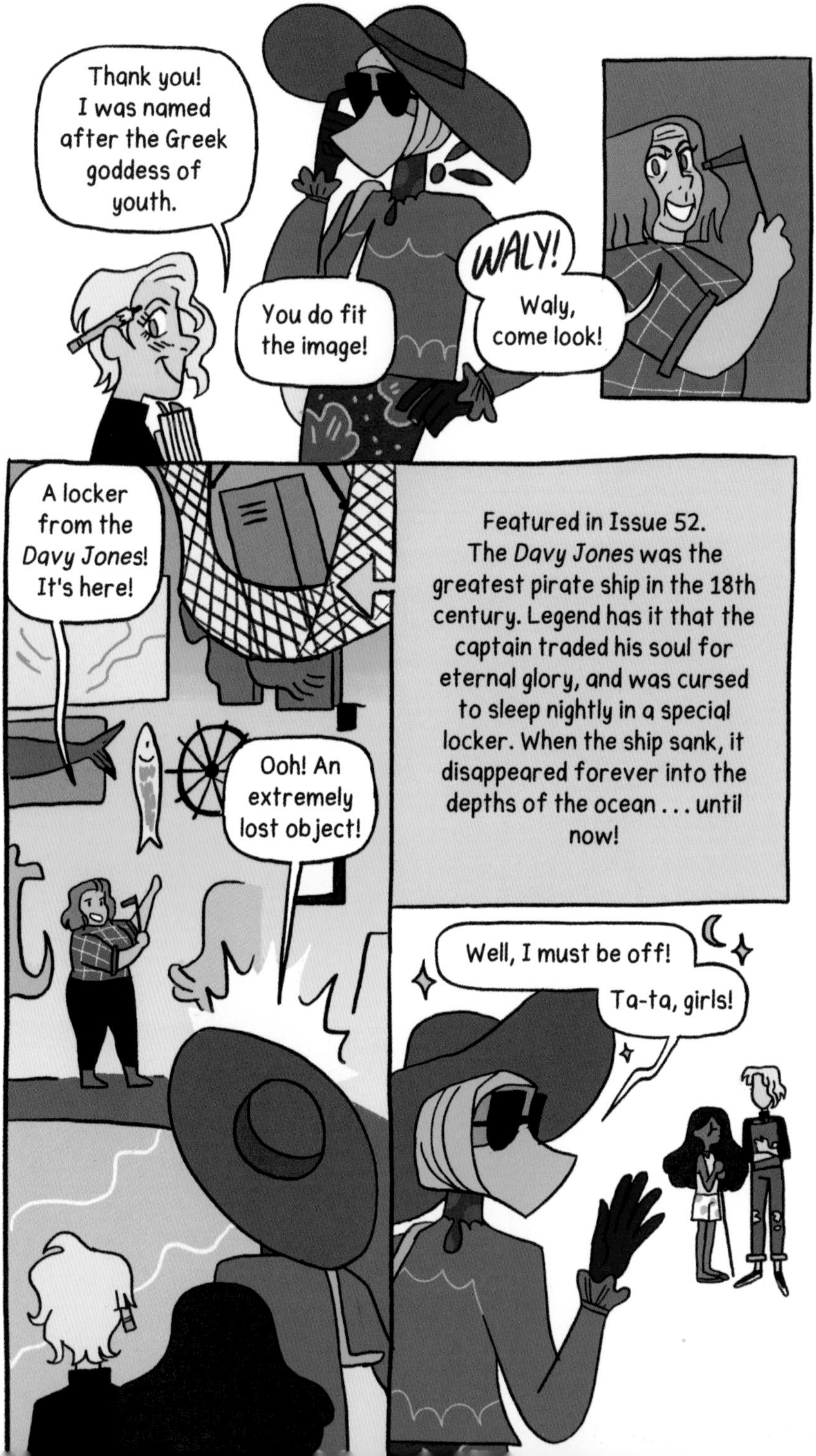
Thank you! I was named after the Greek goddess of youth.
You do fit the image!
WALY!
Waly, come look!
A locker from the *Davy Jones*! It's here!
Ooh! An extremely lost object!
Featured in Issue 52. The *Davy Jones* was the greatest pirate ship in the 18th century. Legend has it that the captain traded his soul for eternal glory, and was cursed to sleep nightly in a special locker. When the ship sank, it disappeared forever into the depths of the ocean . . . until now!
Well, I must be off!
Ta-ta, girls!

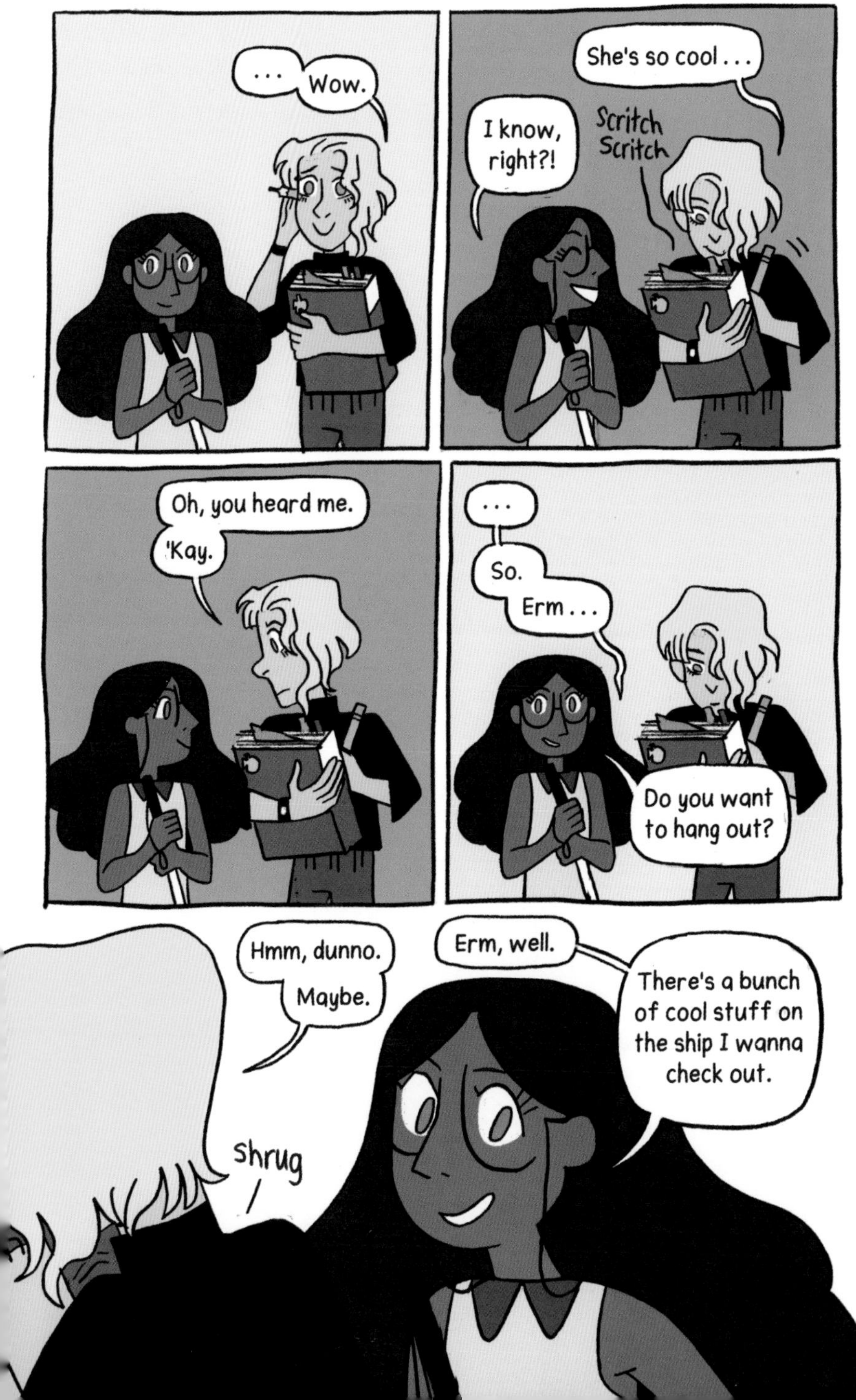
. . .
Wow.
She's so cool . . .
I know, right?!
Scritch Scritch
Oh, you heard me.
'Kay.
. . .
So.
Erm . . .
Do you want to hang out?
Hmm, dunno.
Maybe.
Shrug
Erm, well.
There's a bunch of cool stuff on the ship I wanna check out.

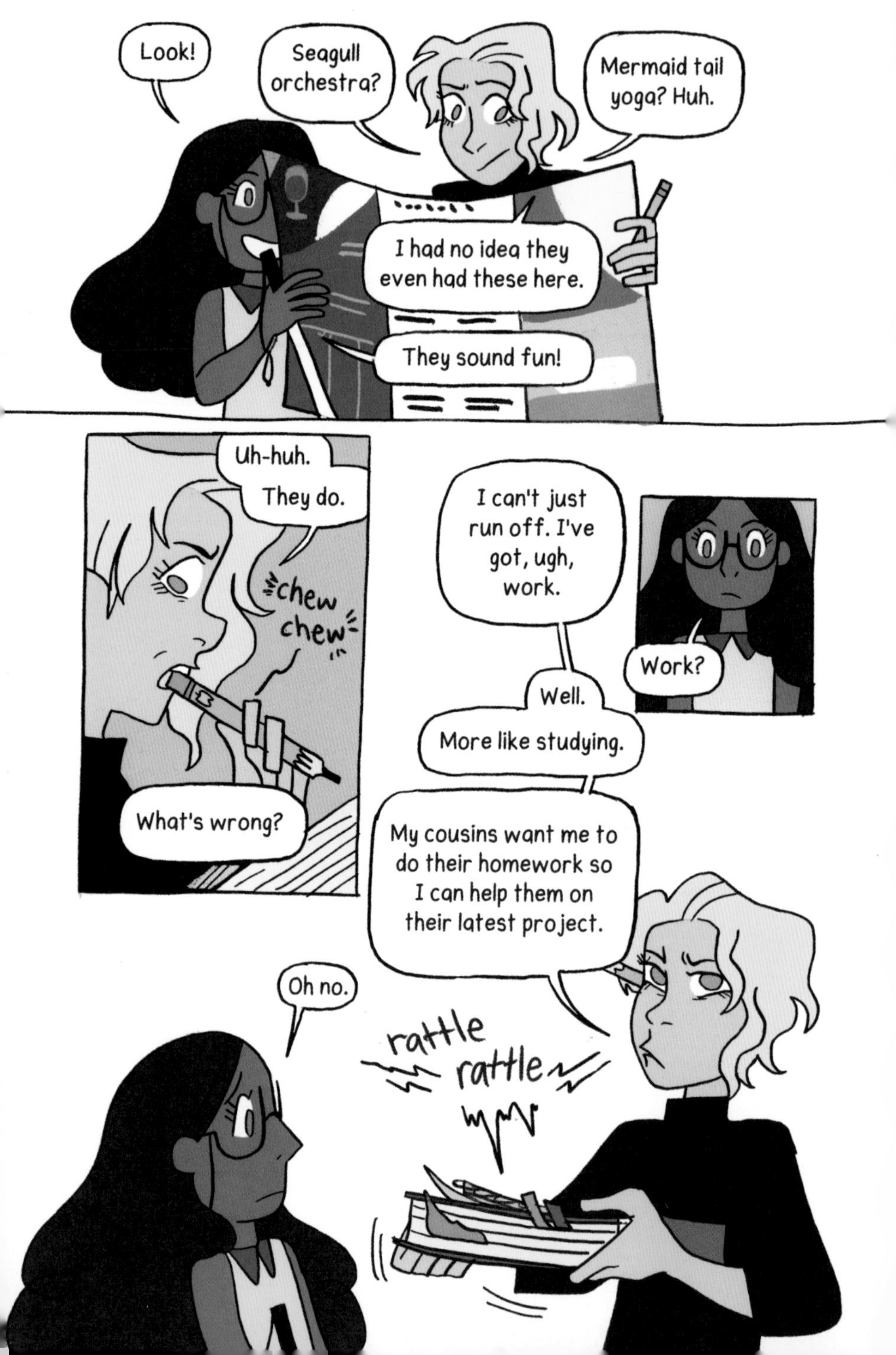

Look!
Seagull orchestra?
Mermaid tail yoga? Huh.
I had no idea they even had these here.
They sound fun!
Uh-huh.
They do.
chew chew
What's wrong?
I can't just run off. I've got, ugh, work.
Work?
Well.
More like studying.
My cousins want me to do their homework so I can help them on their latest project.
Oh no.
rattle rattle

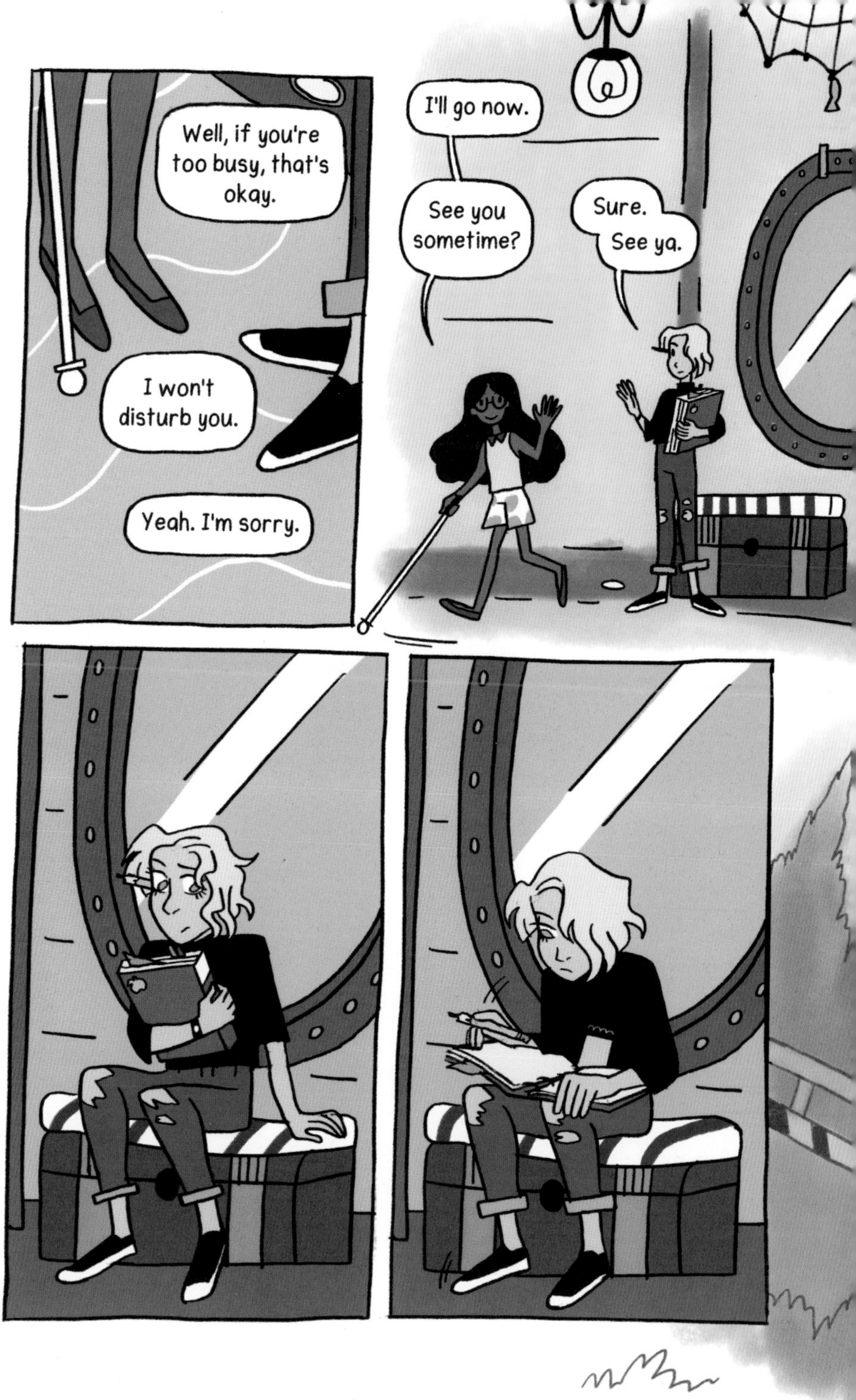
Well, if you're too busy, that's okay.
I won't disturb you.
Yeah. I'm sorry.
I'll go now.
See you sometime?
Sure.
See ya.

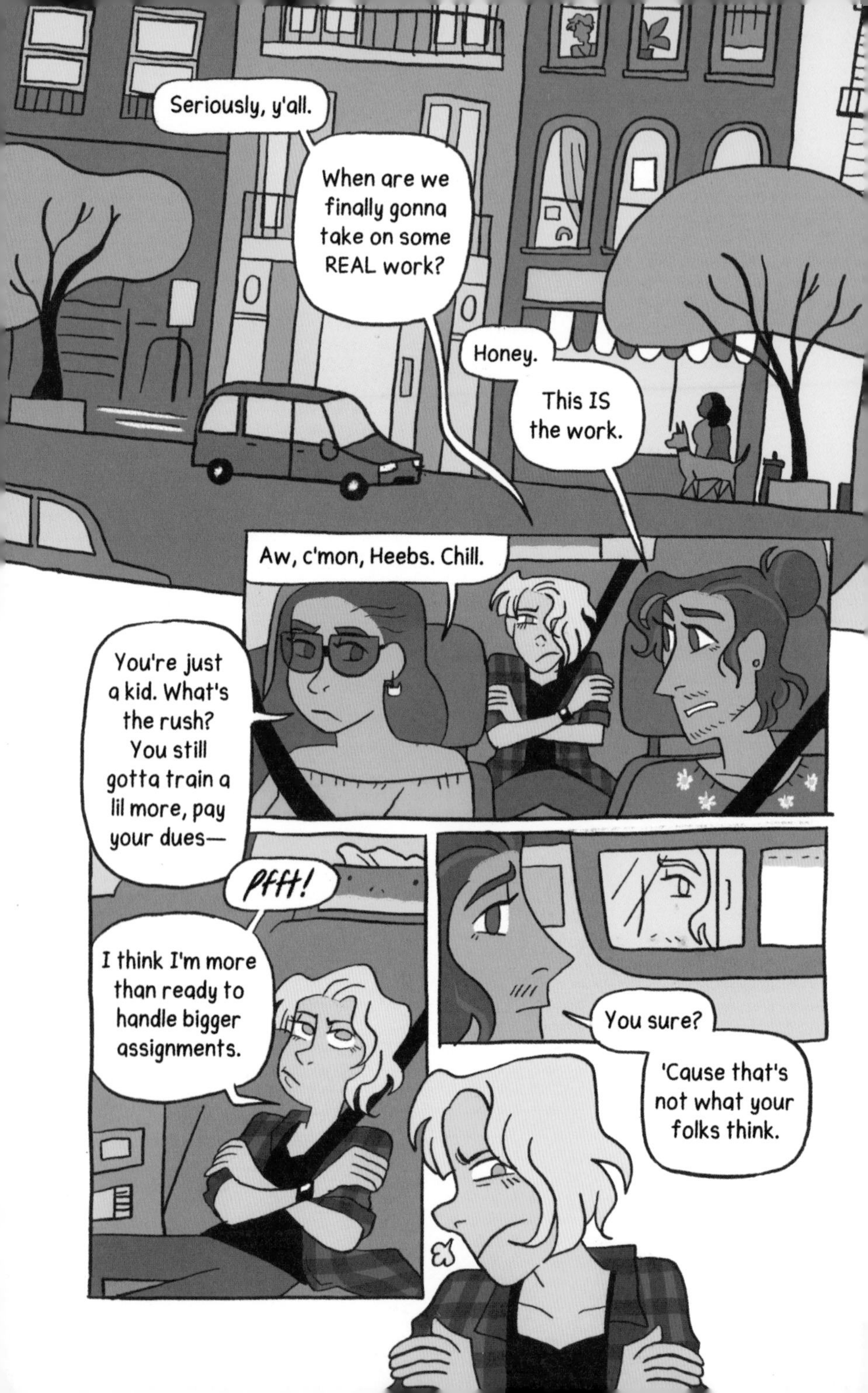
Seriously, y'all.
When are we finally gonna take on some REAL work?
Honey.
This IS the work.
Aw, c'mon, Heebs. Chill.
You're just a kid. What's the rush? You still gotta train a lil more, pay your dues—
Pfft!
I think I'm more than ready to handle bigger assignments.
You sure?
'Cause that's not what your folks think.

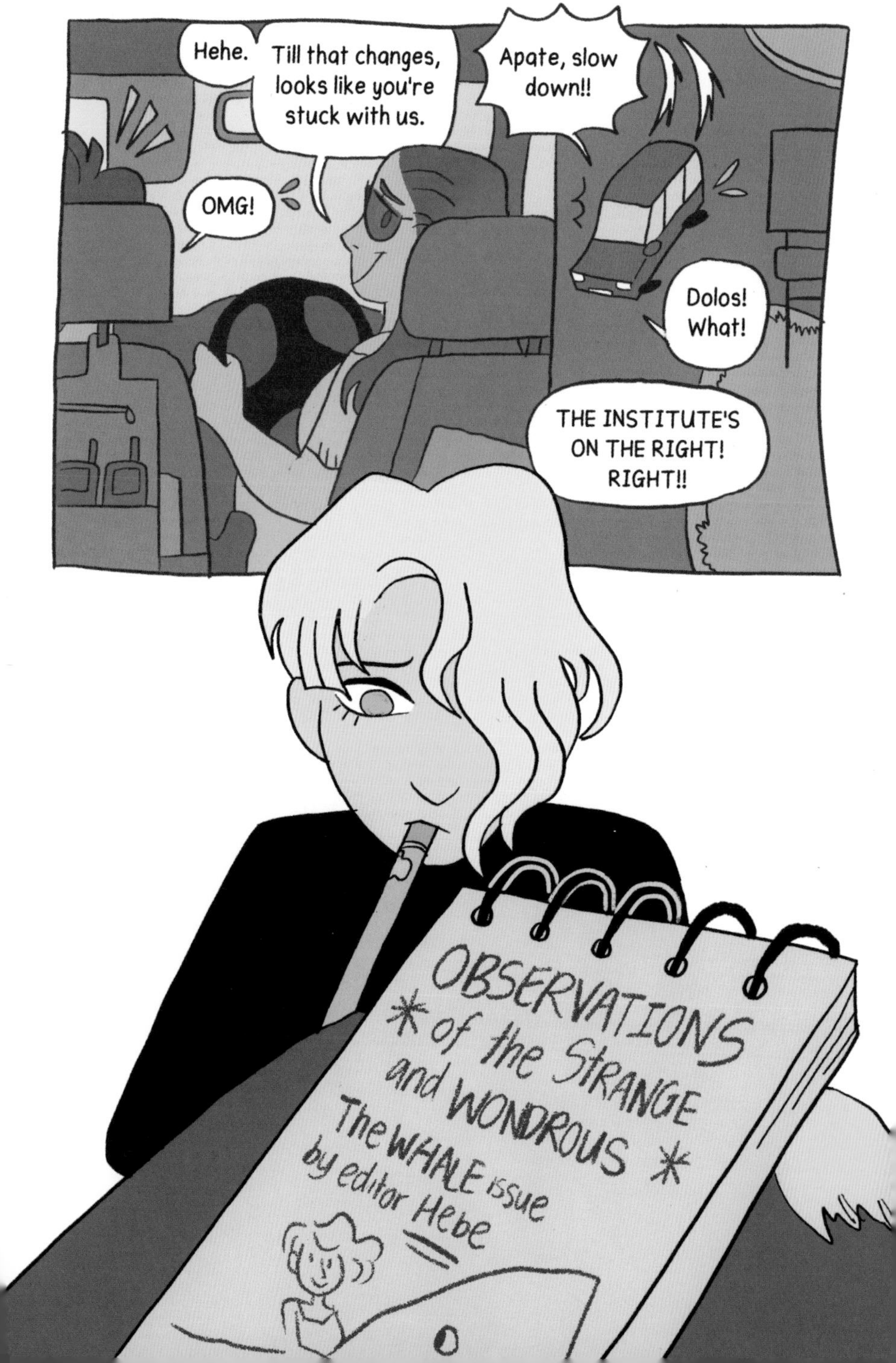
Hehe.
Till that changes, looks like you're stuck with us.
Apate, slow down!!
OMG!
Dolos! What!
THE INSTITUTE'S ON THE RIGHT! RIGHT!!
OBSERVATIONS of the STRANGE and WONDROUS
The WHALE issue
by editor Hebe

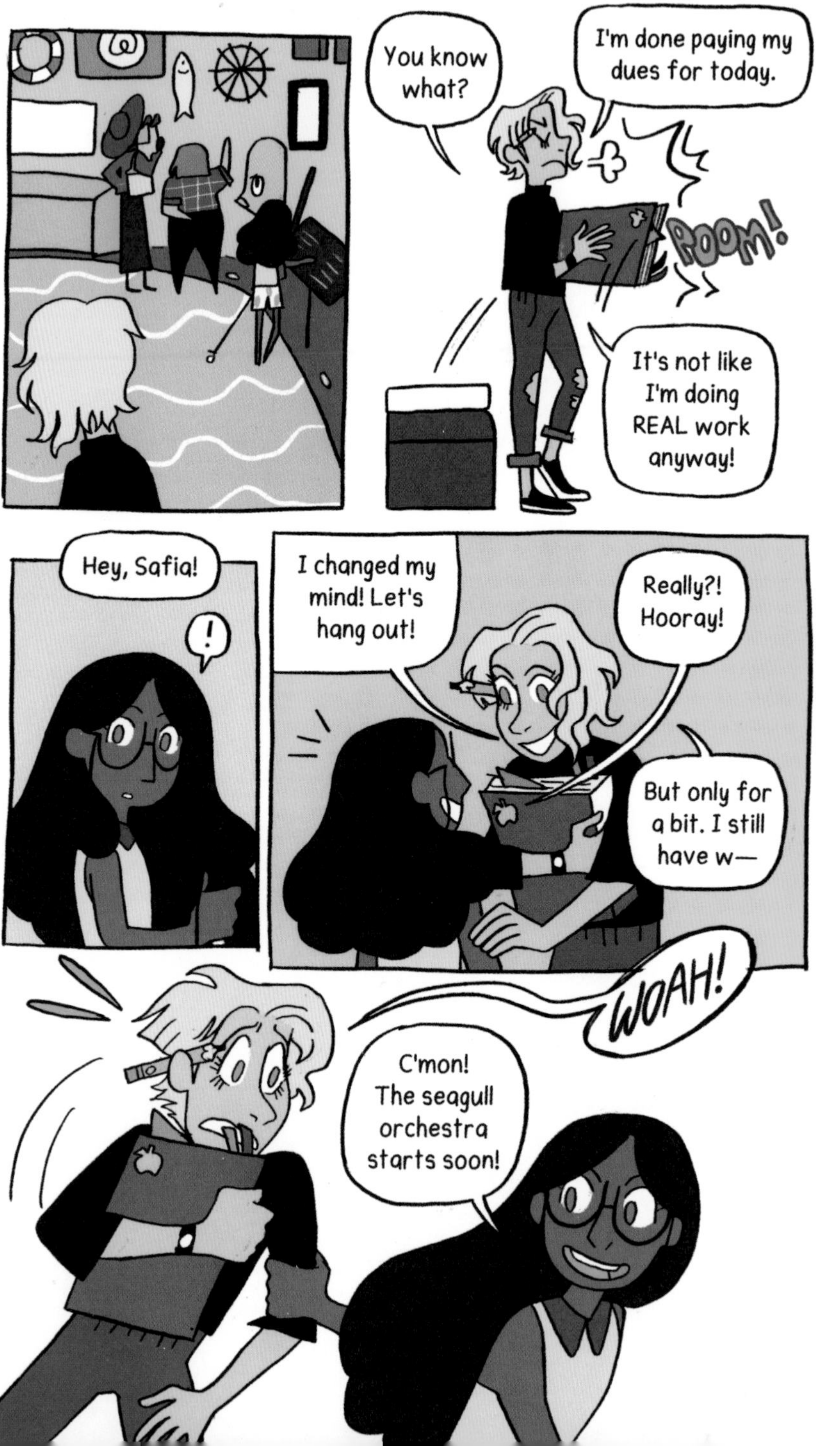
You know what?
I'm done paying my dues for today.
BOOM!
It's not like I'm doing REAL work anyway!
Hey, Safia!
!
I changed my mind! Let's hang out!
Really?! Hooray!
But only for a bit. I still have w—
WOAH!
C'mon! The seagull orchestra starts soon!

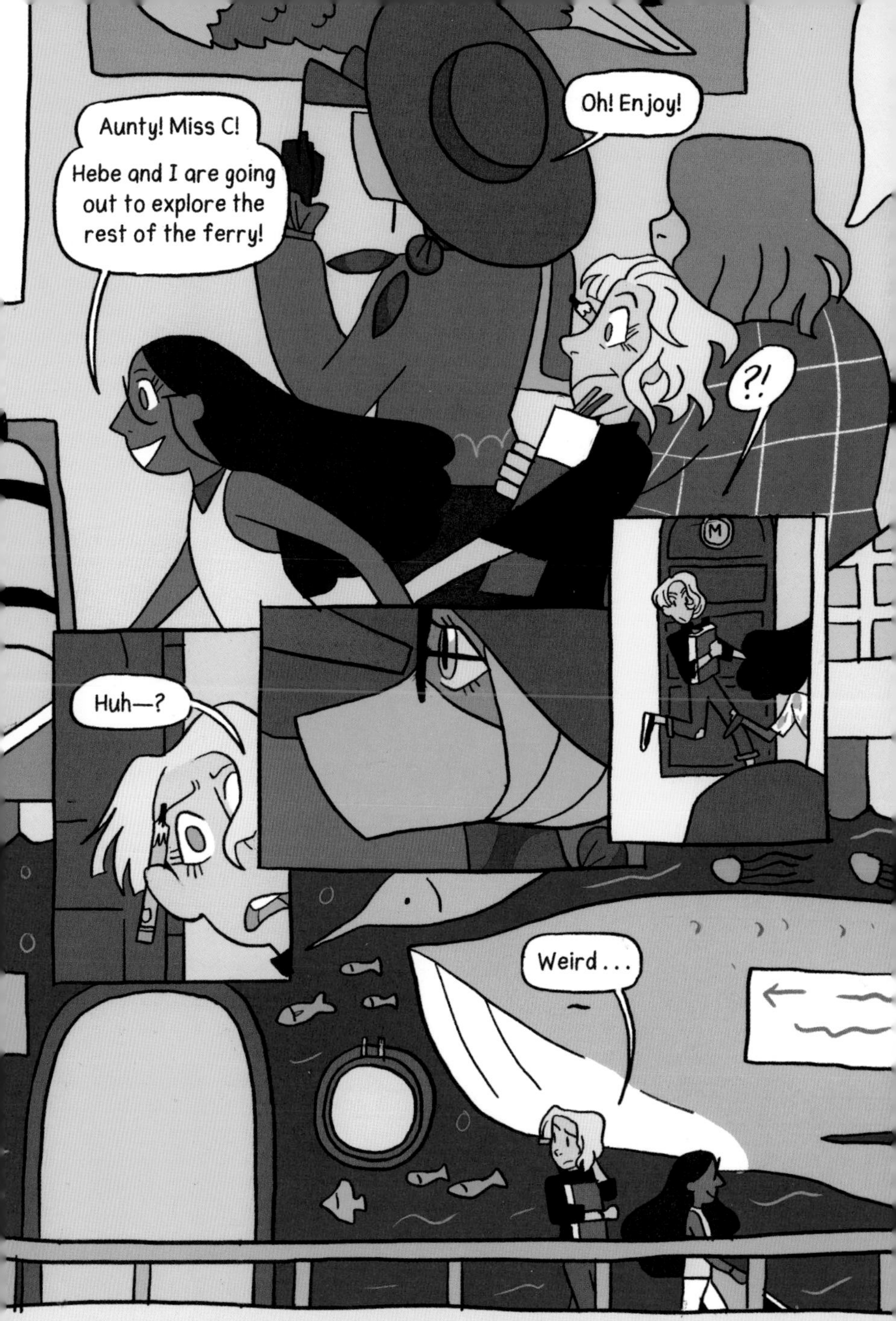

Aunty! Miss C!
Hebe and I are going out to explore the rest of the ferry!
Oh! Enjoy!
?!
Huh—?
Weird . . .

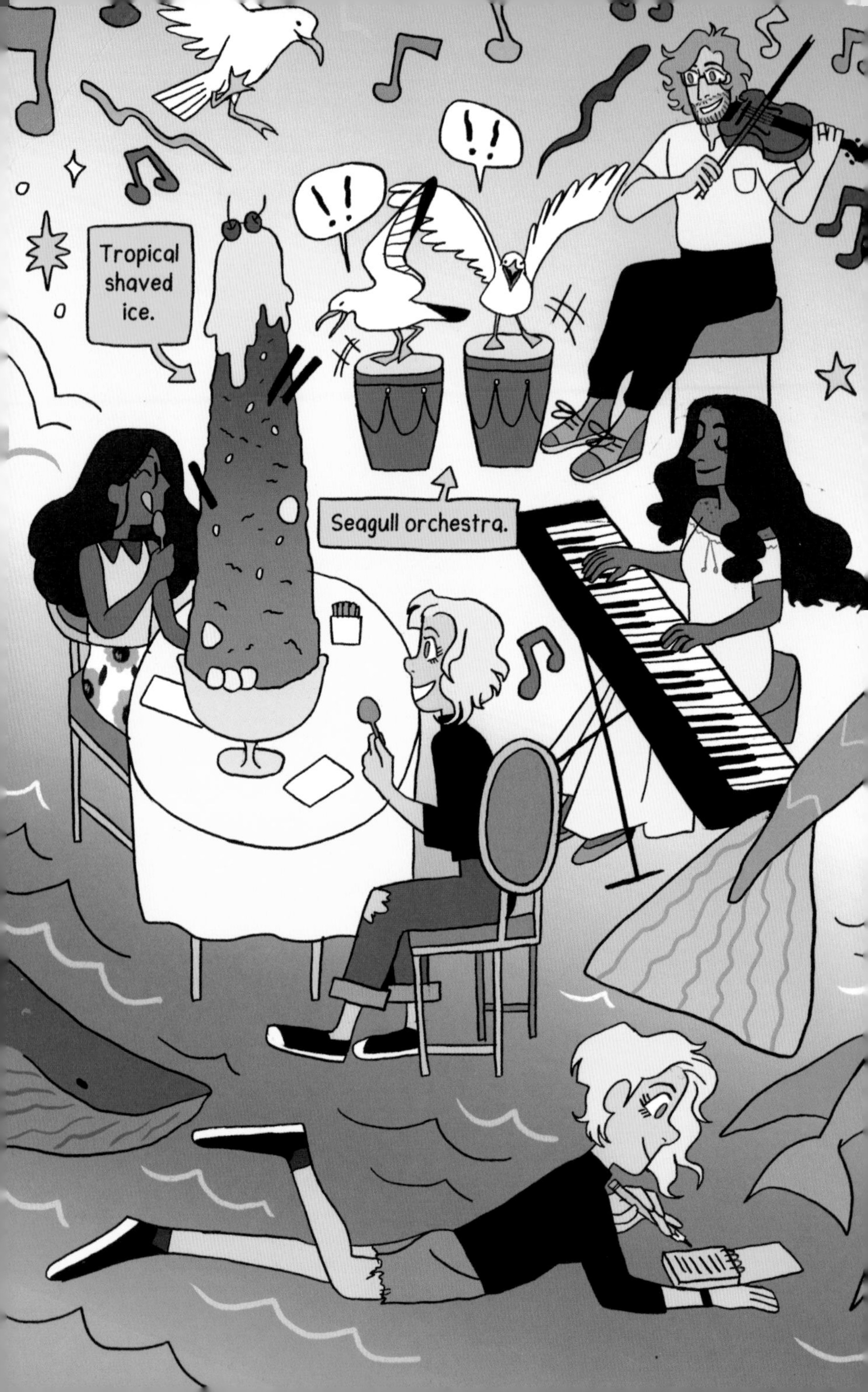

Tropical shaved ice.
!!
!!
Seagull orchestra.

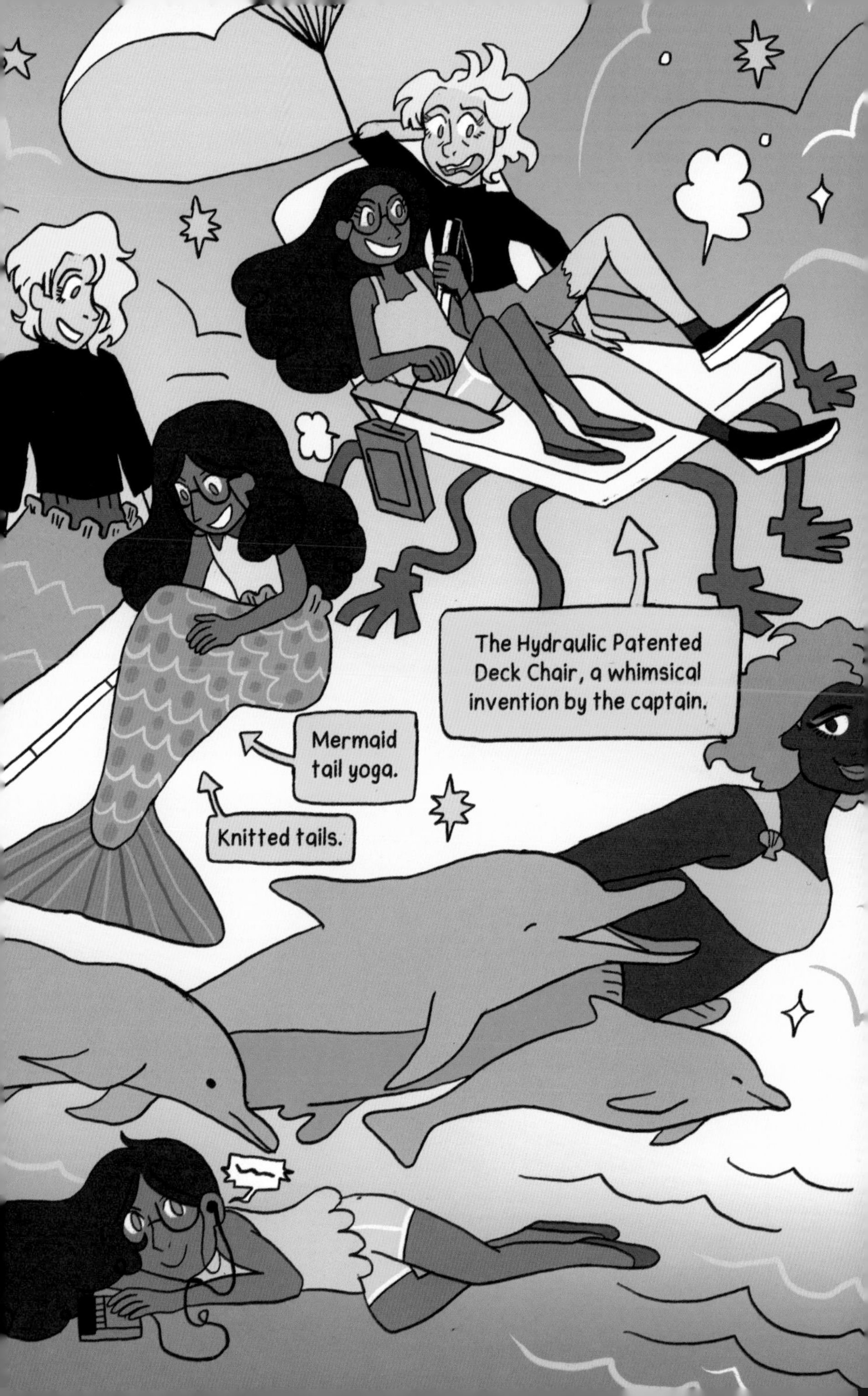
The Hydraulic Patented Deck Chair, a whimsical invention by the captain.
Mermaid tail yoga.
Knitted tails.

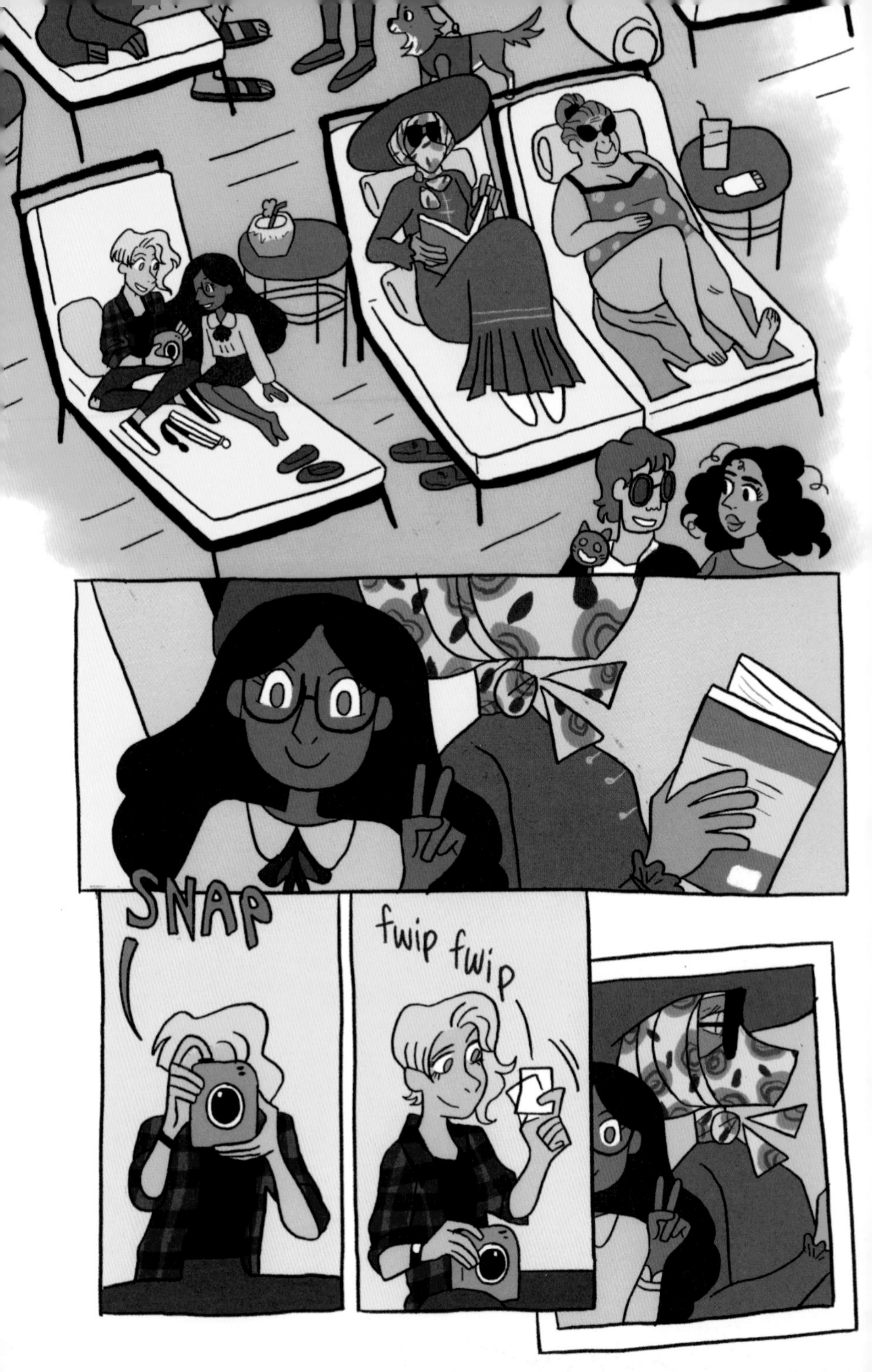
SNAP
fwip fwip

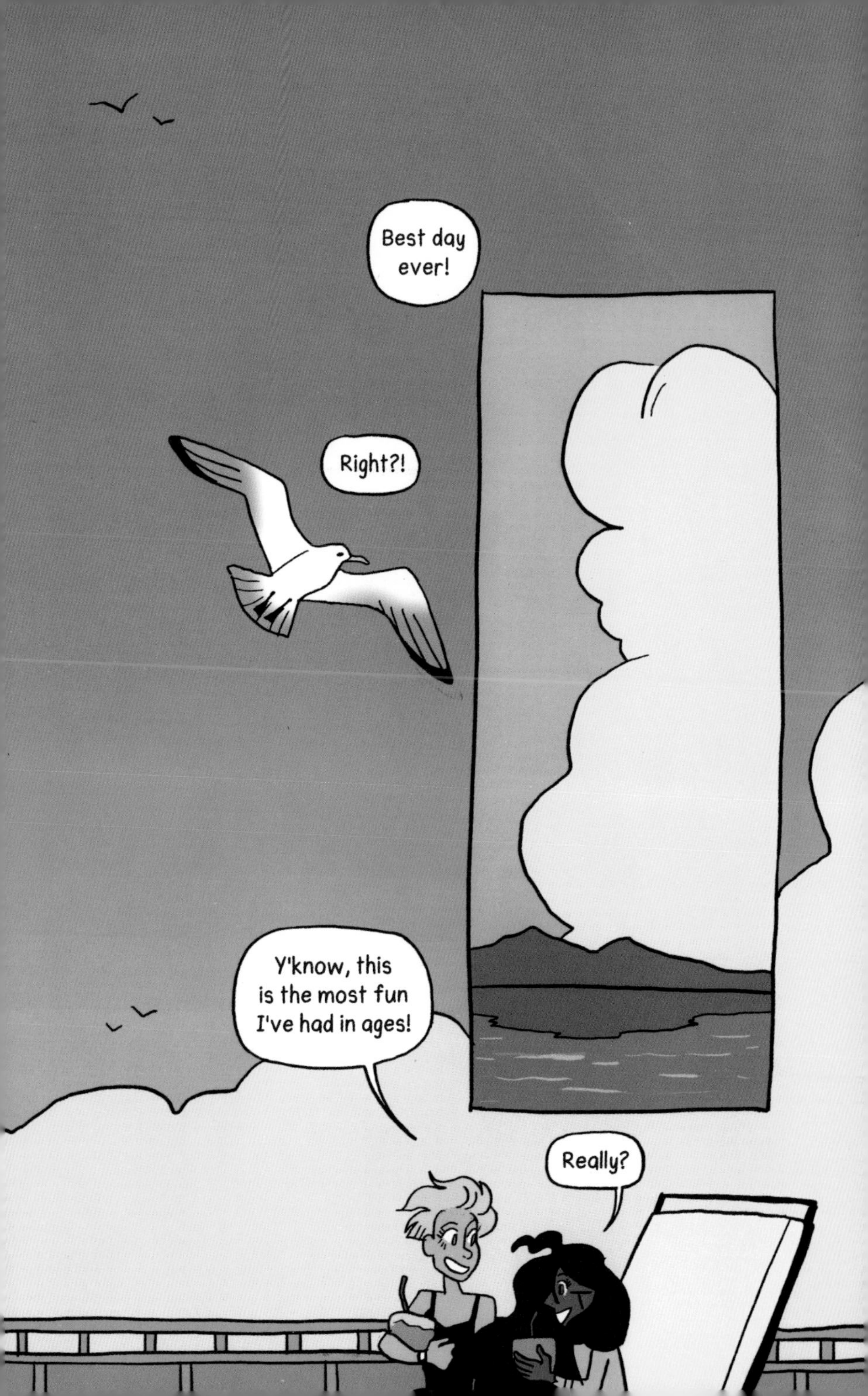
Best day ever!
Right?!
Y'know, this is the most fun I've had in ages!
Really?

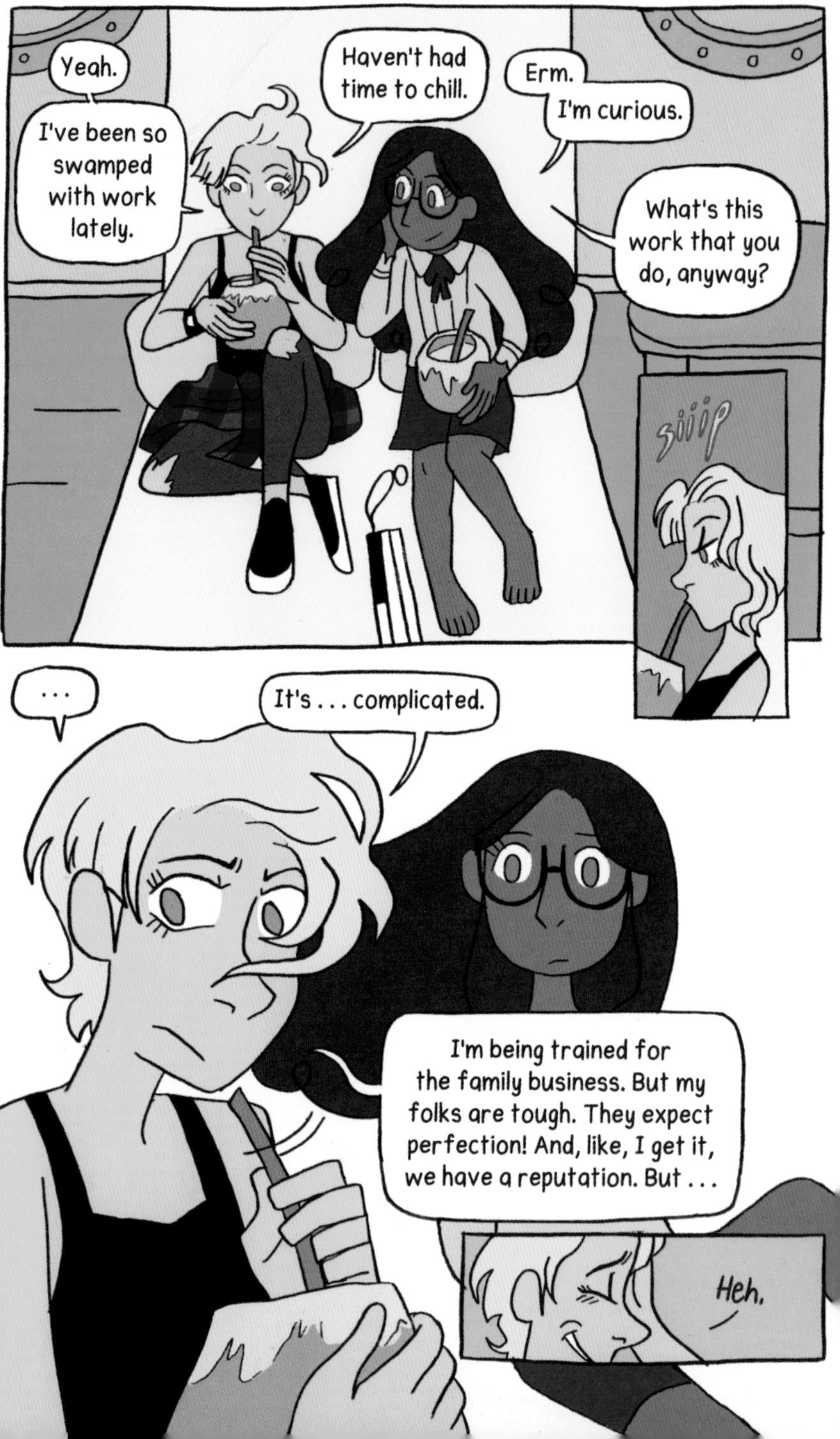
Yeah.
I've been so swamped with work lately.
Haven't had time to chill.
Erm.
I'm curious.
What's this work that you do, anyway?
siiip
. . .
It's . . . complicated.
I'm being trained for the family business. But my folks are tough. They expect perfection! And, like, I get it, we have a reputation. But . . .
Heh.

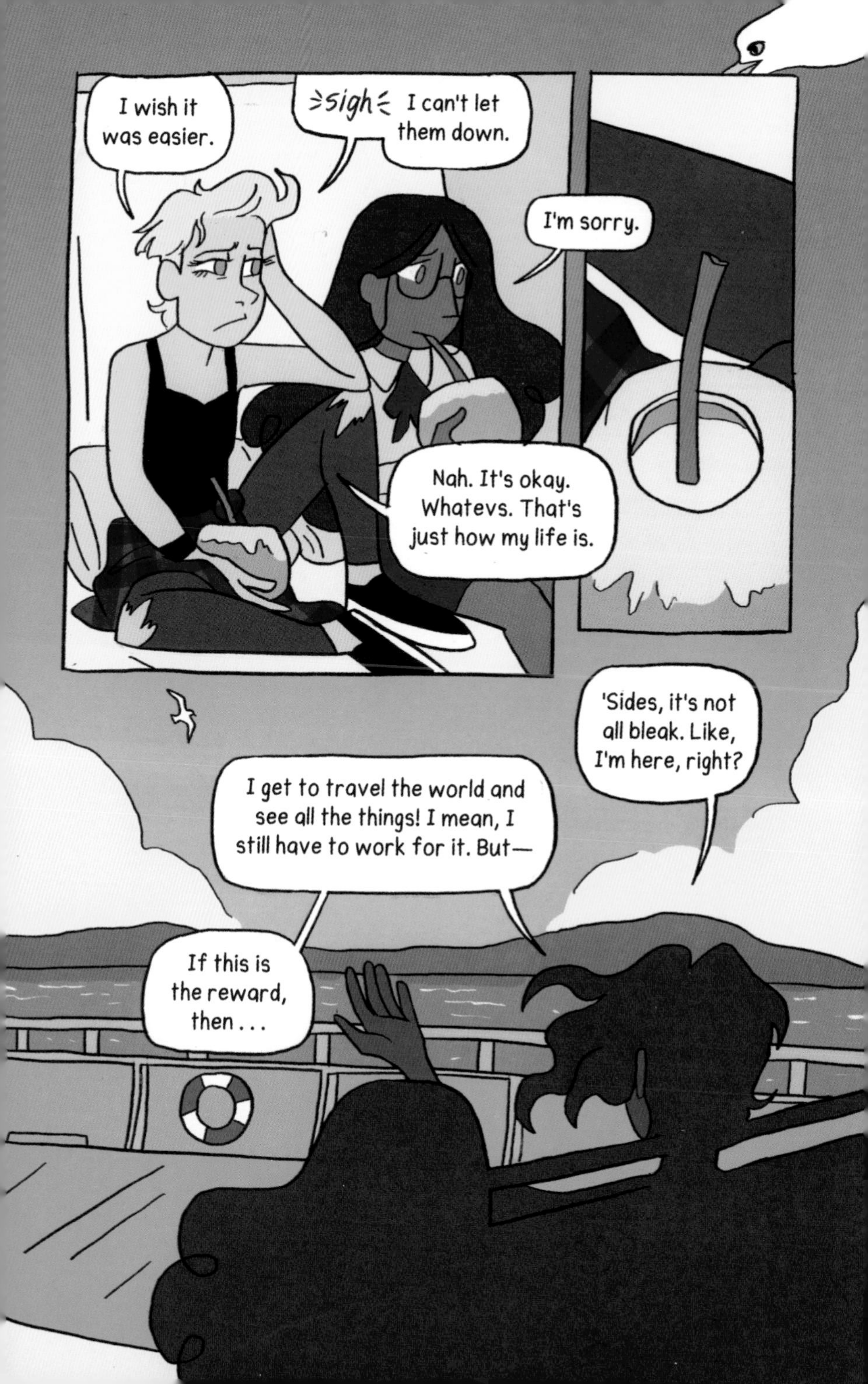
I wish it was easier.
≥sigh≤ I can't let them down.
I'm sorry.
Nah. It's okay. Whatevs. That's just how my life is.
'Sides, it's not all bleak. Like, I'm here, right?
I get to travel the world and see all the things! I mean, I still have to work for it. But—
If this is the reward, then . . .

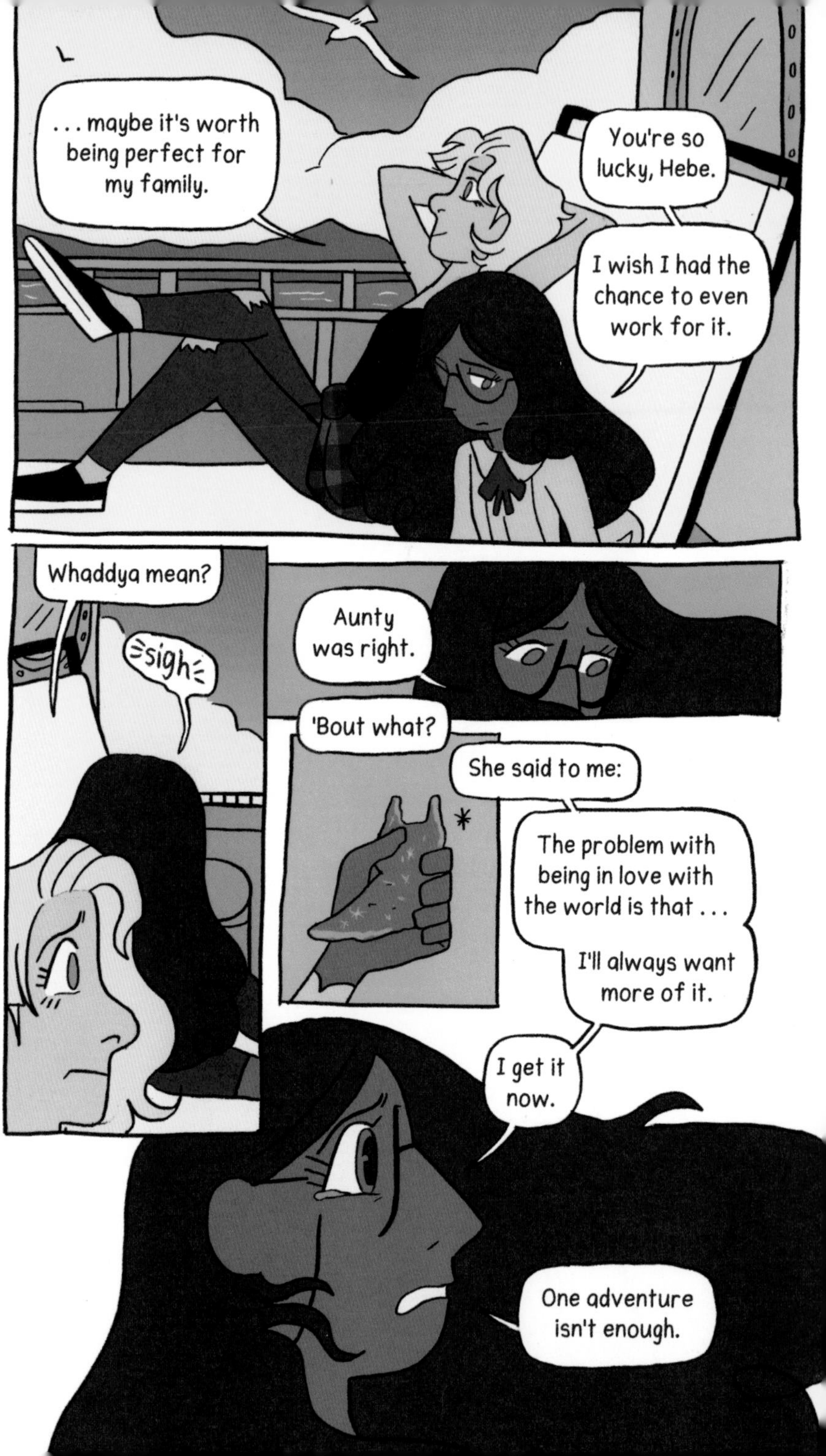

. . . maybe it's worth being perfect for my family.
You're so lucky, Hebe.
I wish I had the chance to even work for it.
Whaddya mean?
sigh
Aunty was right.
'Bout what?
She said to me:
The problem with being in love with the world is that . . .
I'll always want more of it.
I get it now.
One adventure isn't enough.

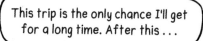

This trip is the only chance I'll get for a long time. After this . . .

Aunty will re-retire.

And I'll have to stay home.

For another nine or ten years or who knows how long . . .

Till I'm old enough to move out and travel on my own.

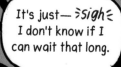

It's just— ≷sigh≷ I don't know if I can wait that long.

And I don't know if I'll be satisfied ever again—

—living vicariously through my books. ≷Sniff≷

I just know . . .

Hebe. I don't want to go home yet.

I'm not ready.

Hey. Look.

Erm.

≋Sniff≋

We're pals, right?

... I hope so?

Huh! Yeah! Hahahaha!

We are! Cool, cool. I wanted to say . . .

What if I bring the world to you while you wait?

You know, postcards, prezzies, that kinda thing.

Like pen pals?

Yep! Hopefully that will help ease the pain of being stuck at home.

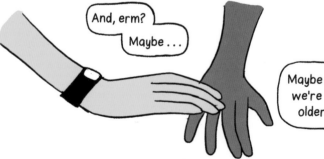

And, erm?

Maybe . . .

Maybe when we're both older . . .

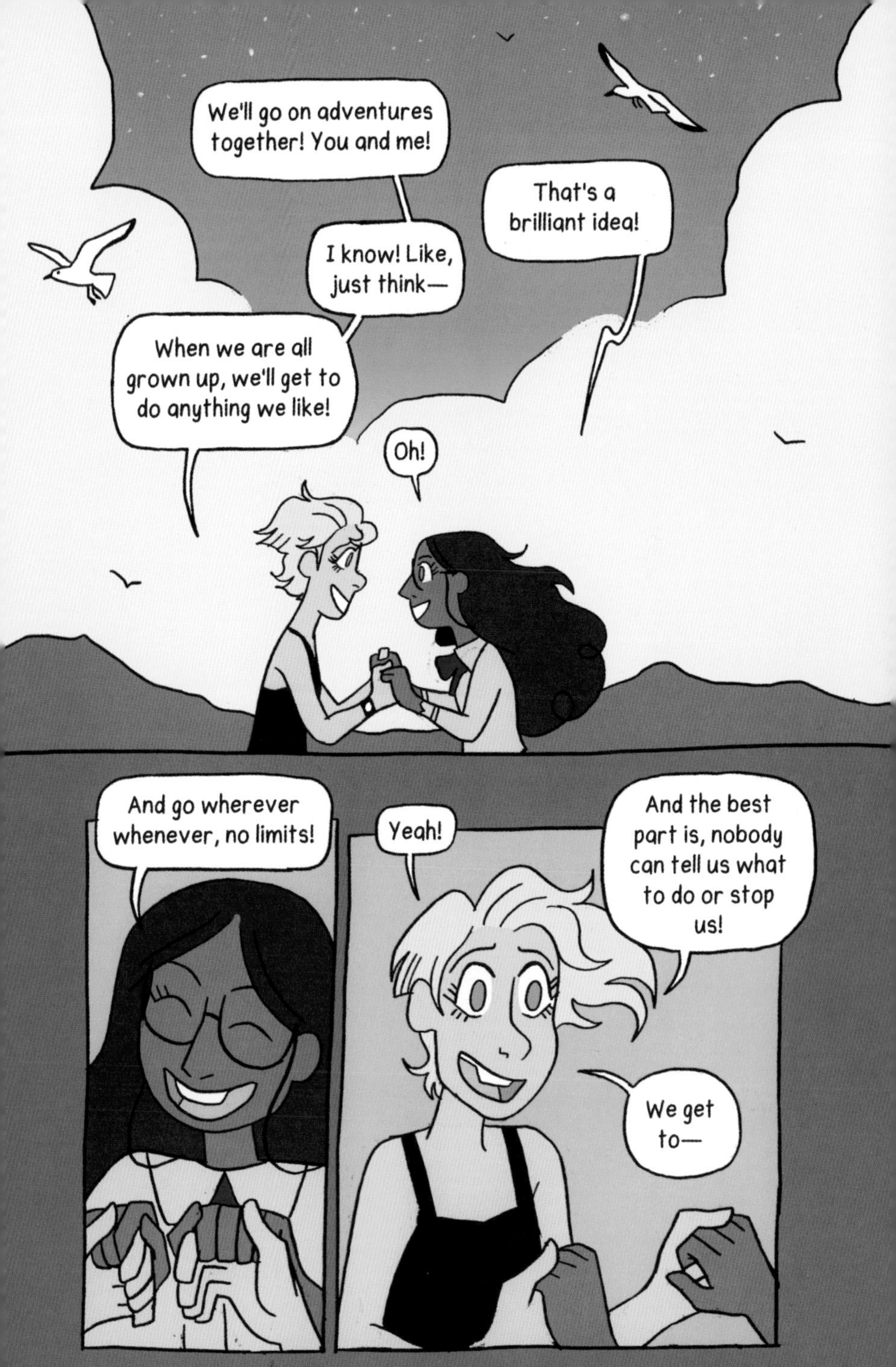
We'll go on adventures together! You and me!
That's a brilliant idea!
I know! Like, just think—
When we are all grown up, we'll get to do anything we like!
Oh!
And go wherever whenever, no limits!
Yeah!
And the best part is, nobody can tell us what to do or stop us!
We get to—

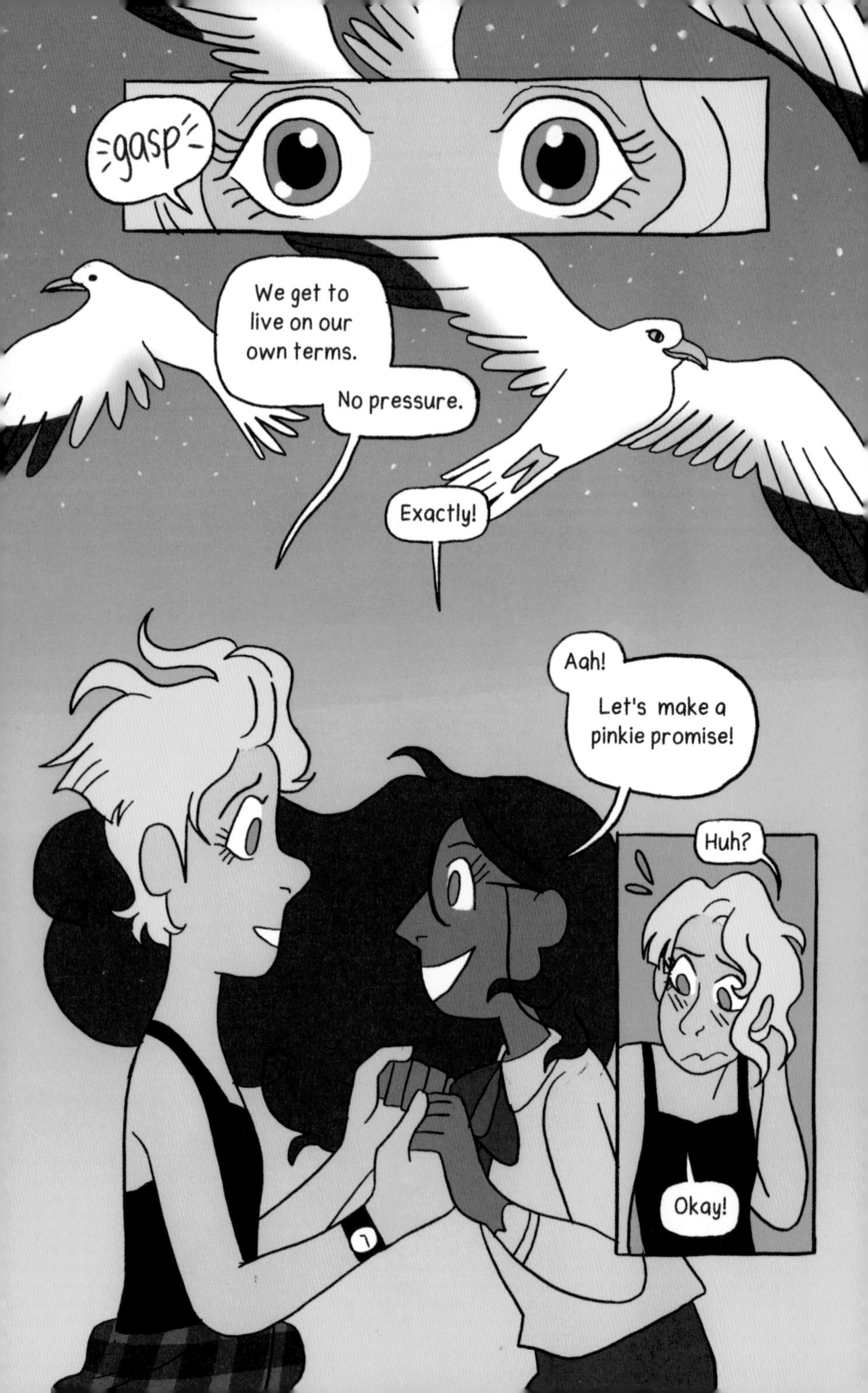
gasp
We get to live on our own terms.
No pressure.
Exactly!
Aah!
Let's make a pinkie promise!
Huh?
Okay!

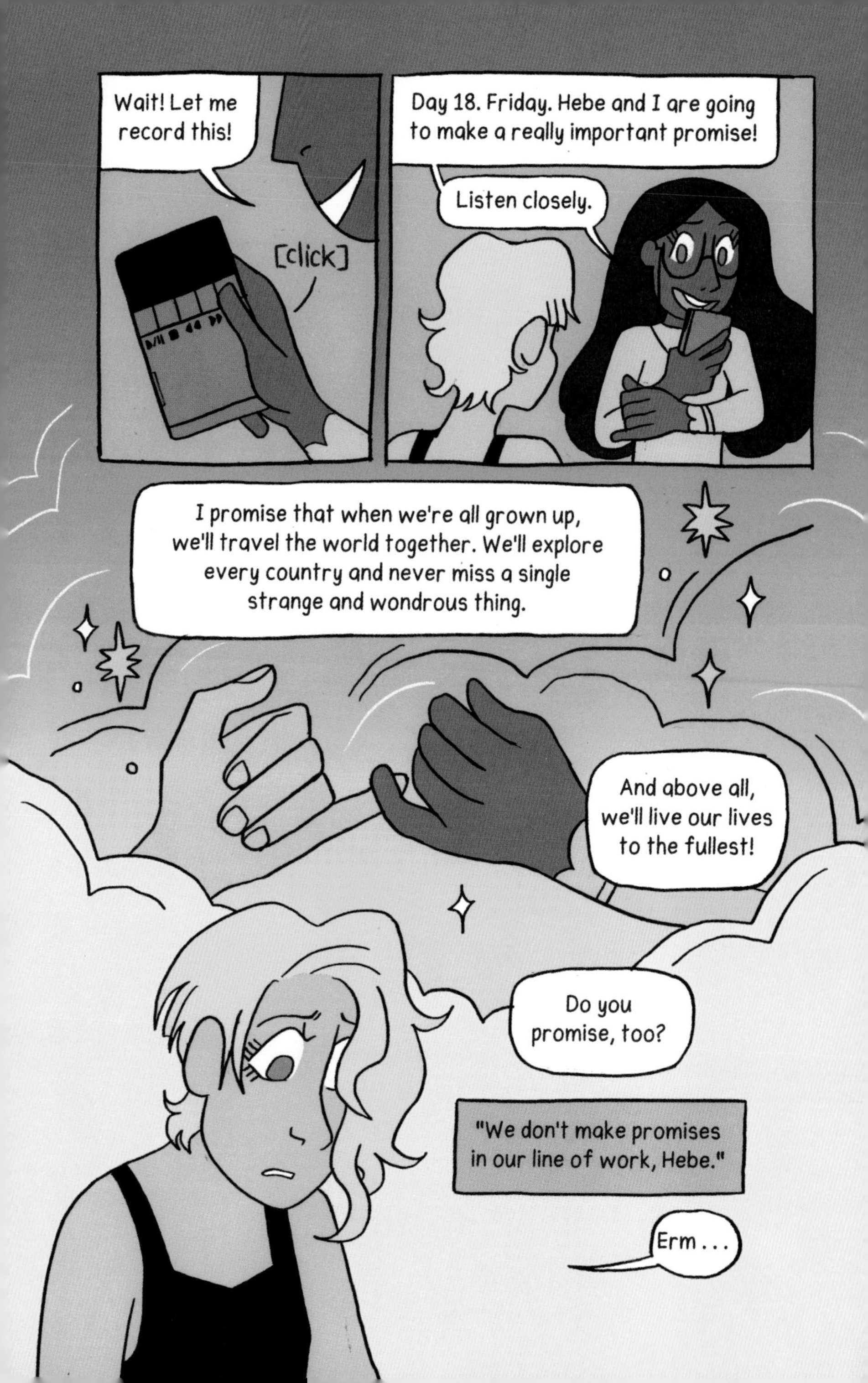

Wait! Let me record this!
[click]
Day 18. Friday. Hebe and I are going to make a really important promise!
Listen closely.
I promise that when we're all grown up, we'll travel the world together. We'll explore every country and never miss a single strange and wondrous thing.
And above all, we'll live our lives to the fullest!
Do you promise, too?
"We don't make promises in our line of work, Hebe."
Erm . . .

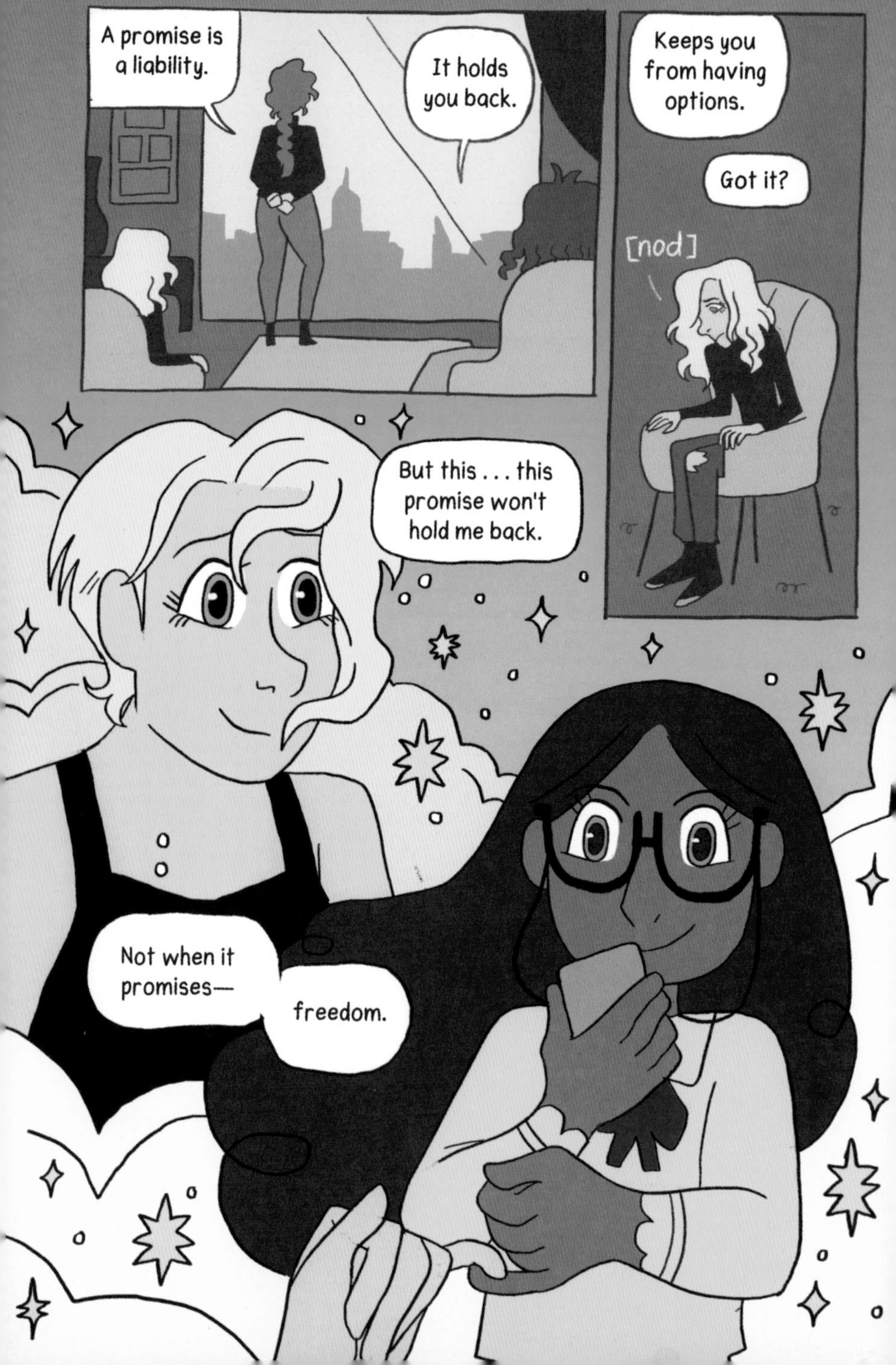
A promise is a liability.
It holds you back.
Keeps you from having options.
Got it?
[nod]
But this . . . this promise won't hold me back.
Not when it promises—
freedom.

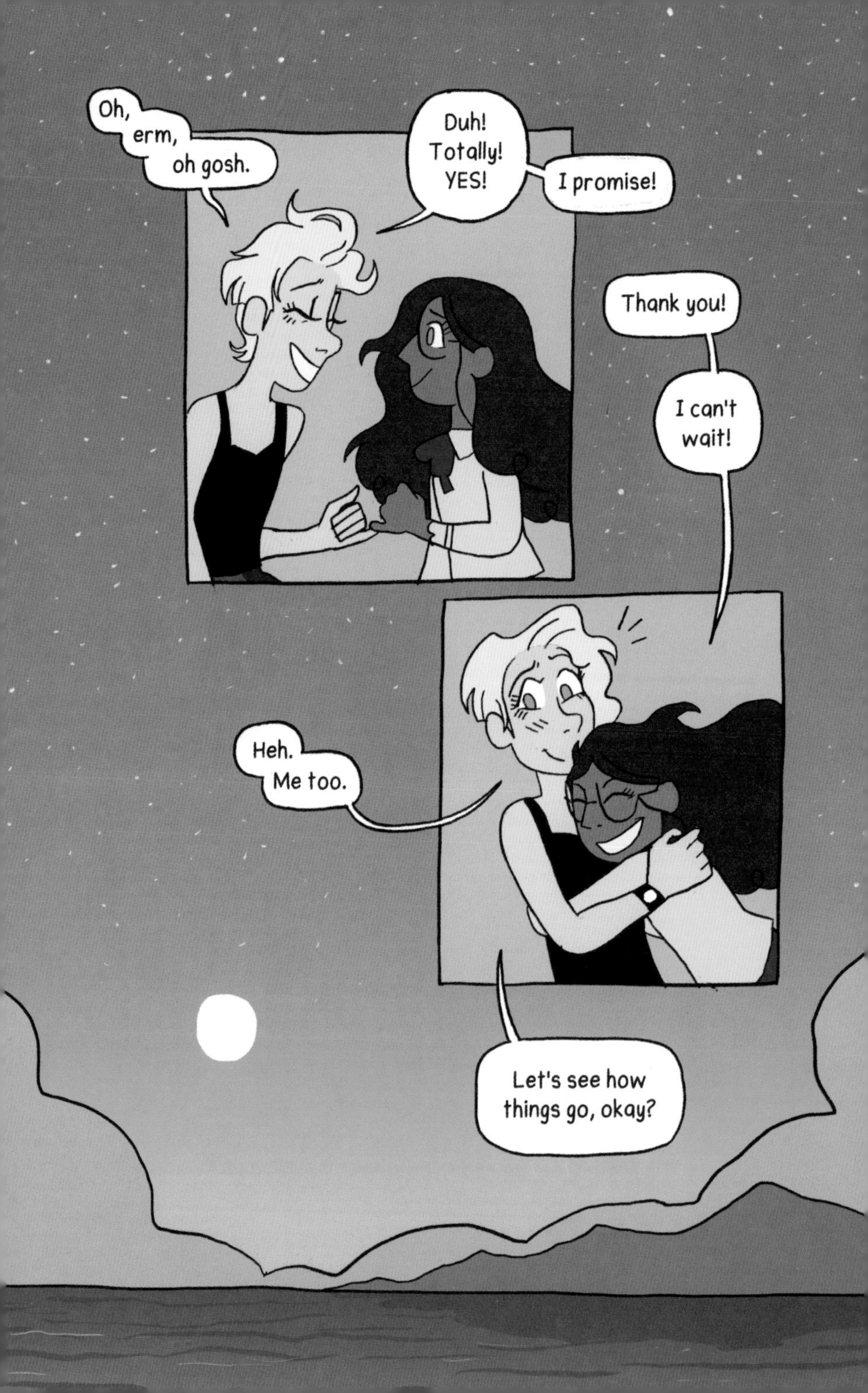
Oh, erm, oh gosh.
Duh! Totally! YES!
I promise!
Thank you!
I can't wait!
Heh. Me too.
Let's see how things go, okay?

How Miss Cathryn Became an Adventurer's Assistant

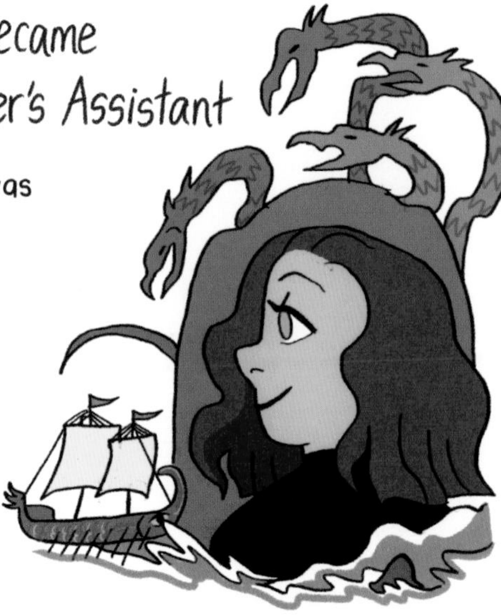

Many decades ago, there was a young lady who had it all:

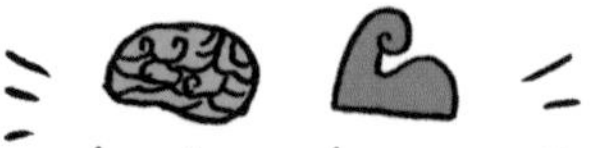

brains, brawn,

and a budding career at the Bureau of Suspicious Intent.

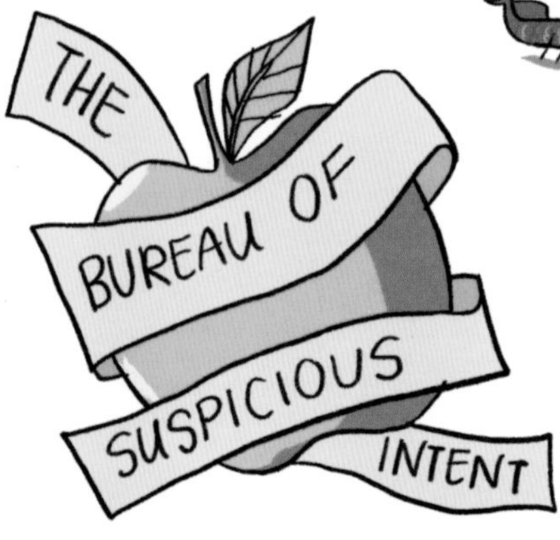
THE
BUREAU OF
SUSPICIOUS
INTENT

Scylla wasn't like most young people. Young people often dreamed of using their talents to do good.

For example:

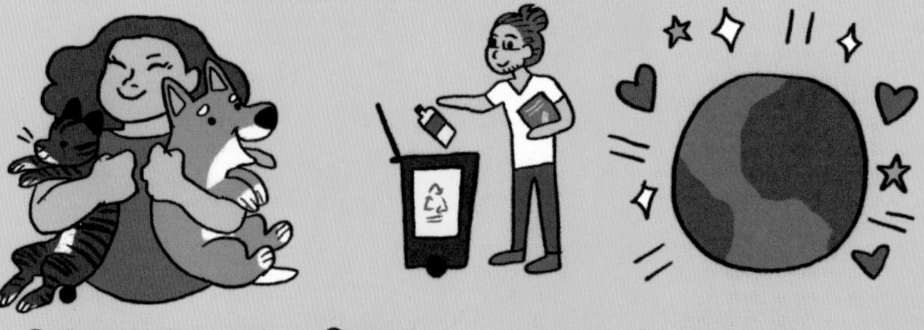

① Opening animal shelters.

② Reducing plastic usage.

③ Generally building a better world.

Not Scylla. Her true passion was chaos.

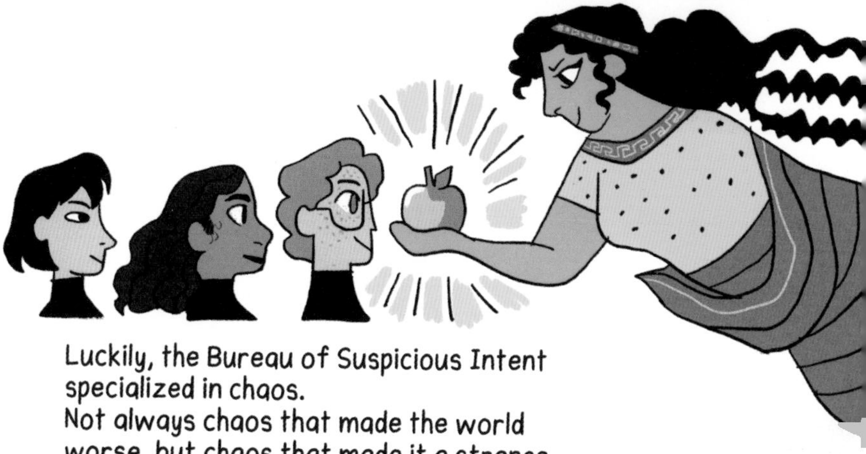

Luckily, the Bureau of Suspicious Intent specialized in chaos.
Not always chaos that made the world worse, but chaos that made it a strange and terrible place to be.

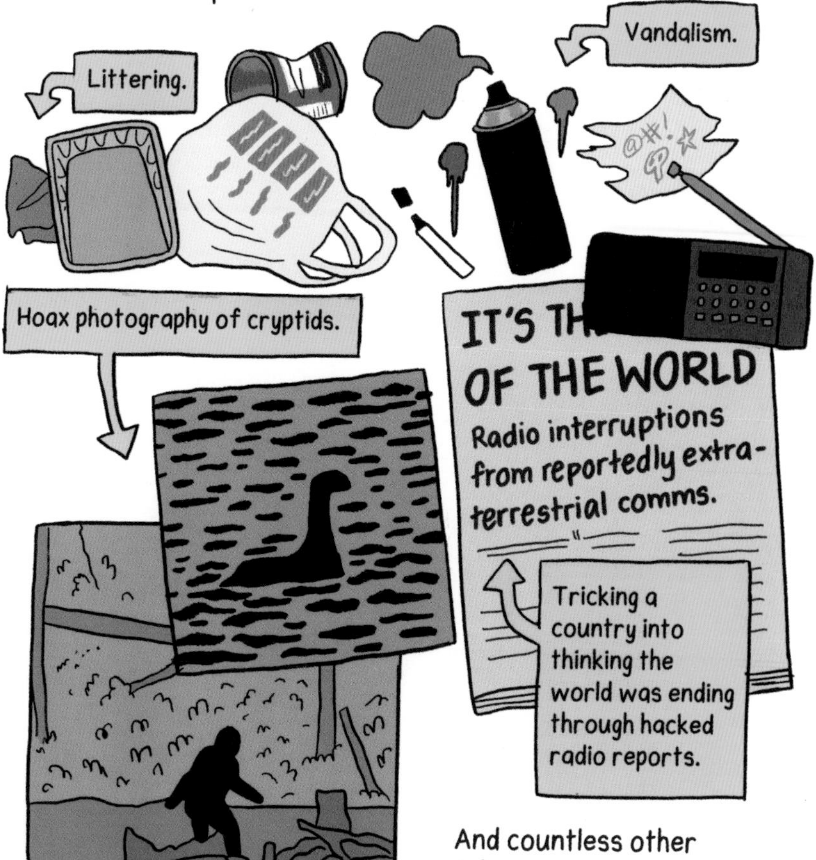

Littering.
Vandalism.
Hoax photography of cryptids.
IT'S TH
OF THE WORLD
Radio interruptions from reportedly extra-terrestrial comms.
Tricking a country into thinking the world was ending through hacked radio reports.

And countless other crimes . . .

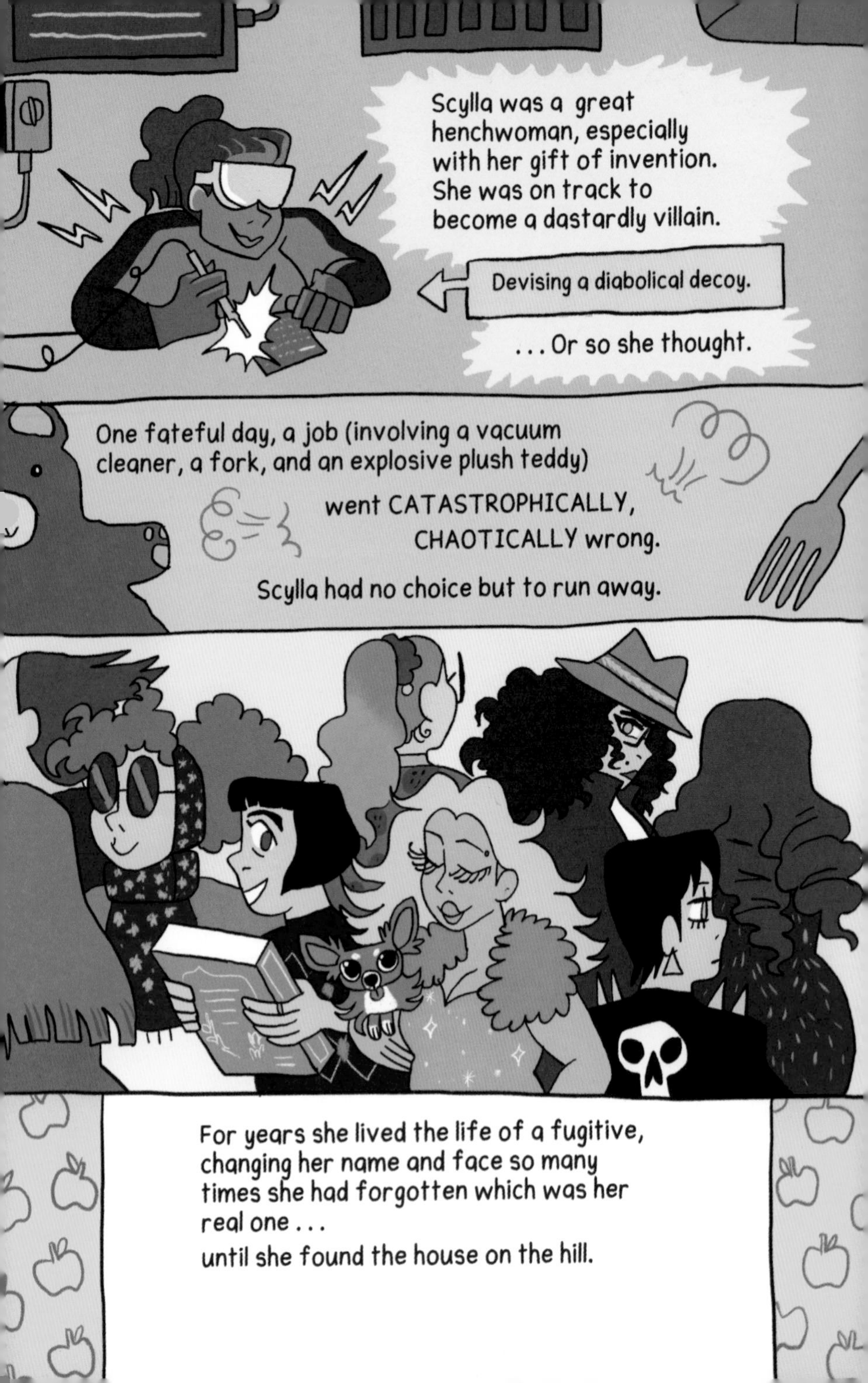
Scylla was a great henchwoman, especially with her gift of invention. She was on track to become a dastardly villain.
Devising a diabolical decoy.
. . . Or so she thought.
One fateful day, a job (involving a vacuum cleaner, a fork, and an explosive plush teddy)
went CATASTROPHICALLY, CHAOTICALLY wrong.
Scylla had no choice but to run away.
For years she lived the life of a fugitive, changing her name and face so many times she had forgotten which was her real one . . .
until she found the house on the hill.

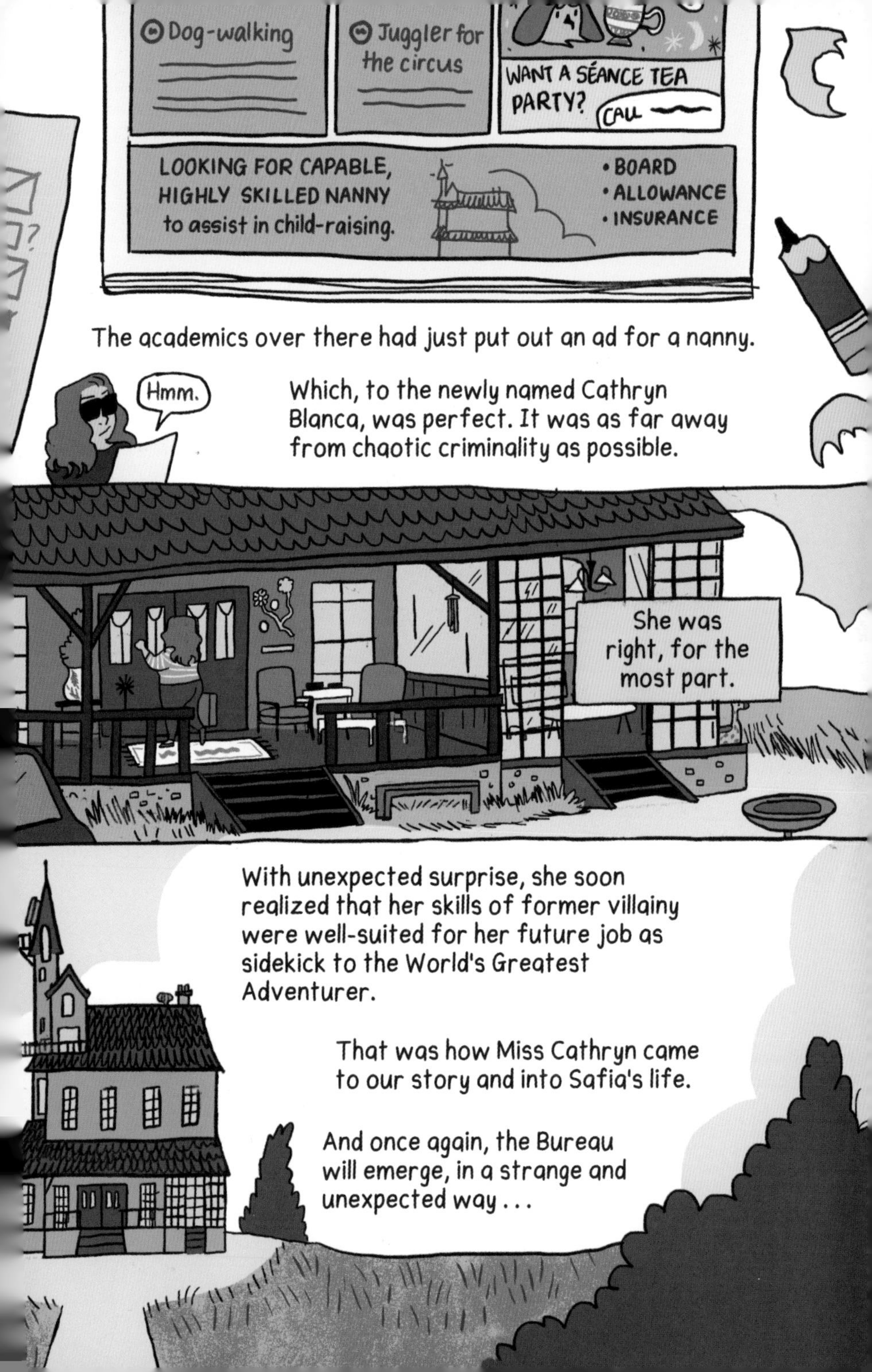
Dog-walking
Juggler for the circus
WANT A SÉANCE TEA PARTY? CALL
LOOKING FOR CAPABLE, HIGHLY SKILLED NANNY to assist in child-raising.
• BOARD
• ALLOWANCE
• INSURANCE
The academics over there had just put out an ad for a nanny.
Hmm.
Which, to the newly named Cathryn Blanca, was perfect. It was as far away from chaotic criminality as possible.
She was right, for the most part.
With unexpected surprise, she soon realized that her skills of former villainy were well-suited for her future job as sidekick to the World's Greatest Adventurer.
That was how Miss Cathryn came to our story and into Safia's life.
And once again, the Bureau will emerge, in a strange and unexpected way . . .

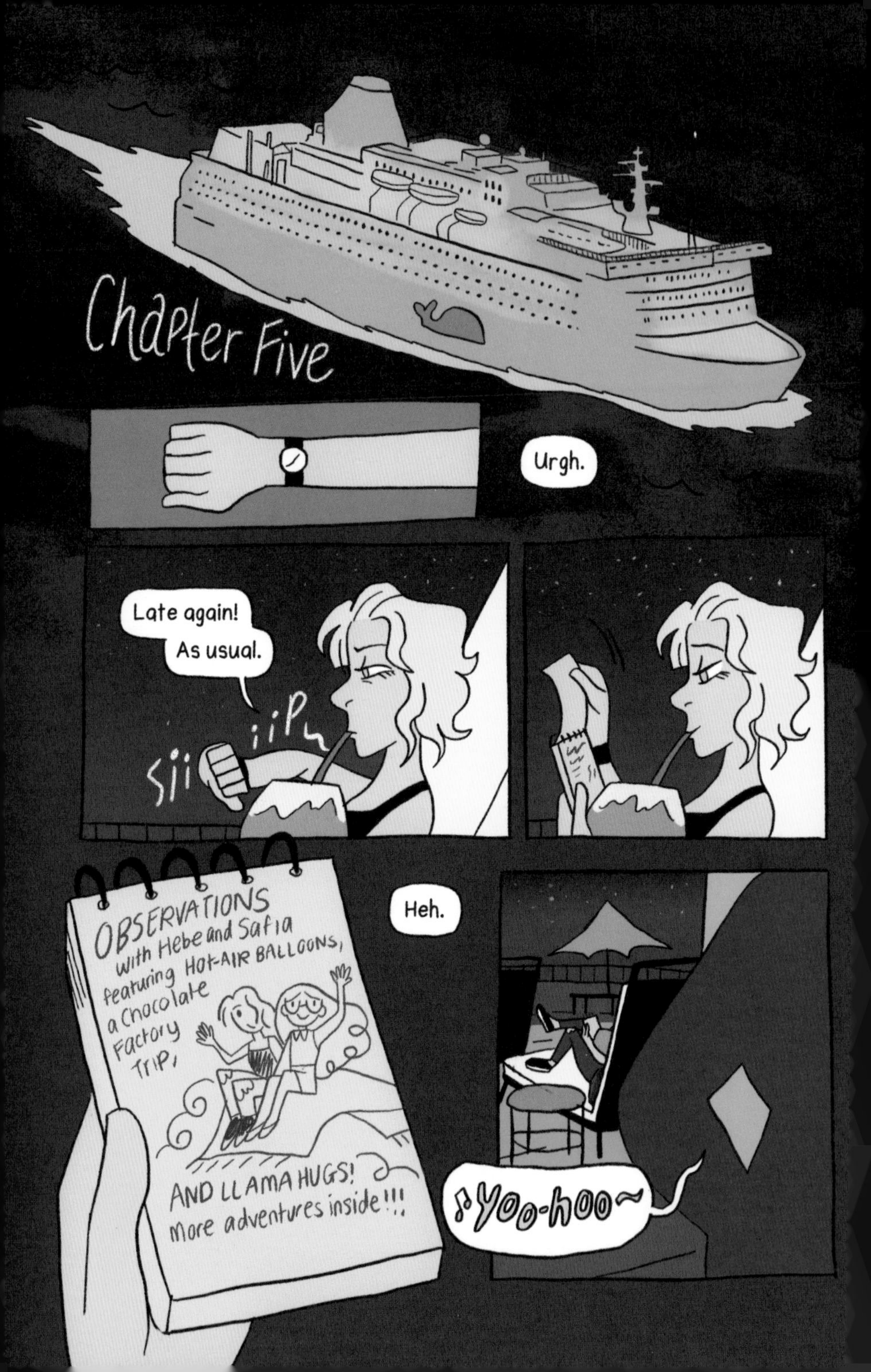

Chapter Five
Urgh.
Late again!
As usual.
Siiiip
Heh.
OBSERVATIONS
with Hebe and Safia
featuring HOT-AIR BALLOONS,
a Chocolate Factory Trip,
AND LLAMA HUGS!
More adventures inside!!!
♪Yoo-hoo~

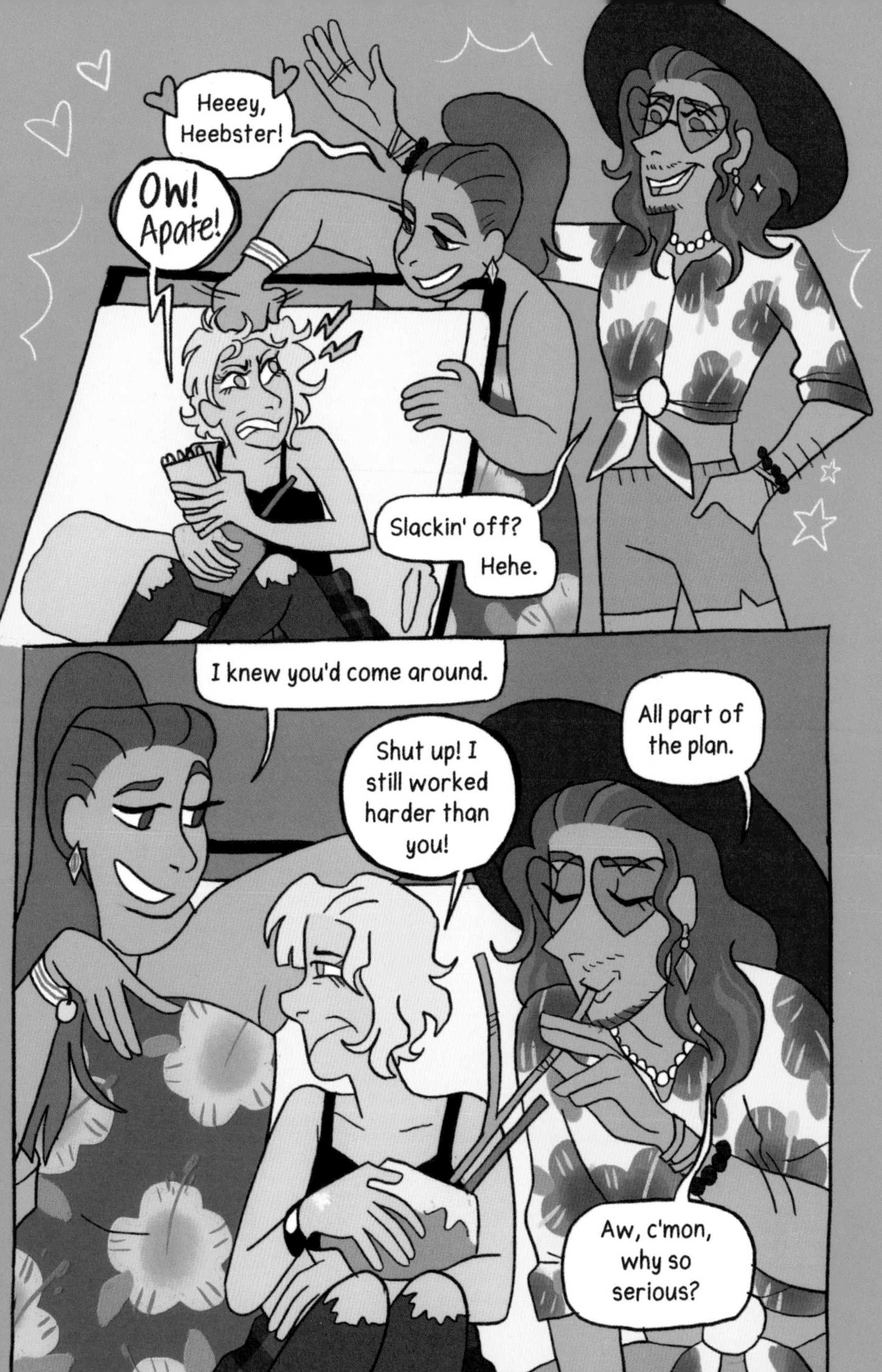
Heeey, Heebster!
OW! Apate!
Slackin' off?
Hehe.
I knew you'd come around.
Shut up! I still worked harder than you!
All part of the plan.
Aw, c'mon, why so serious?

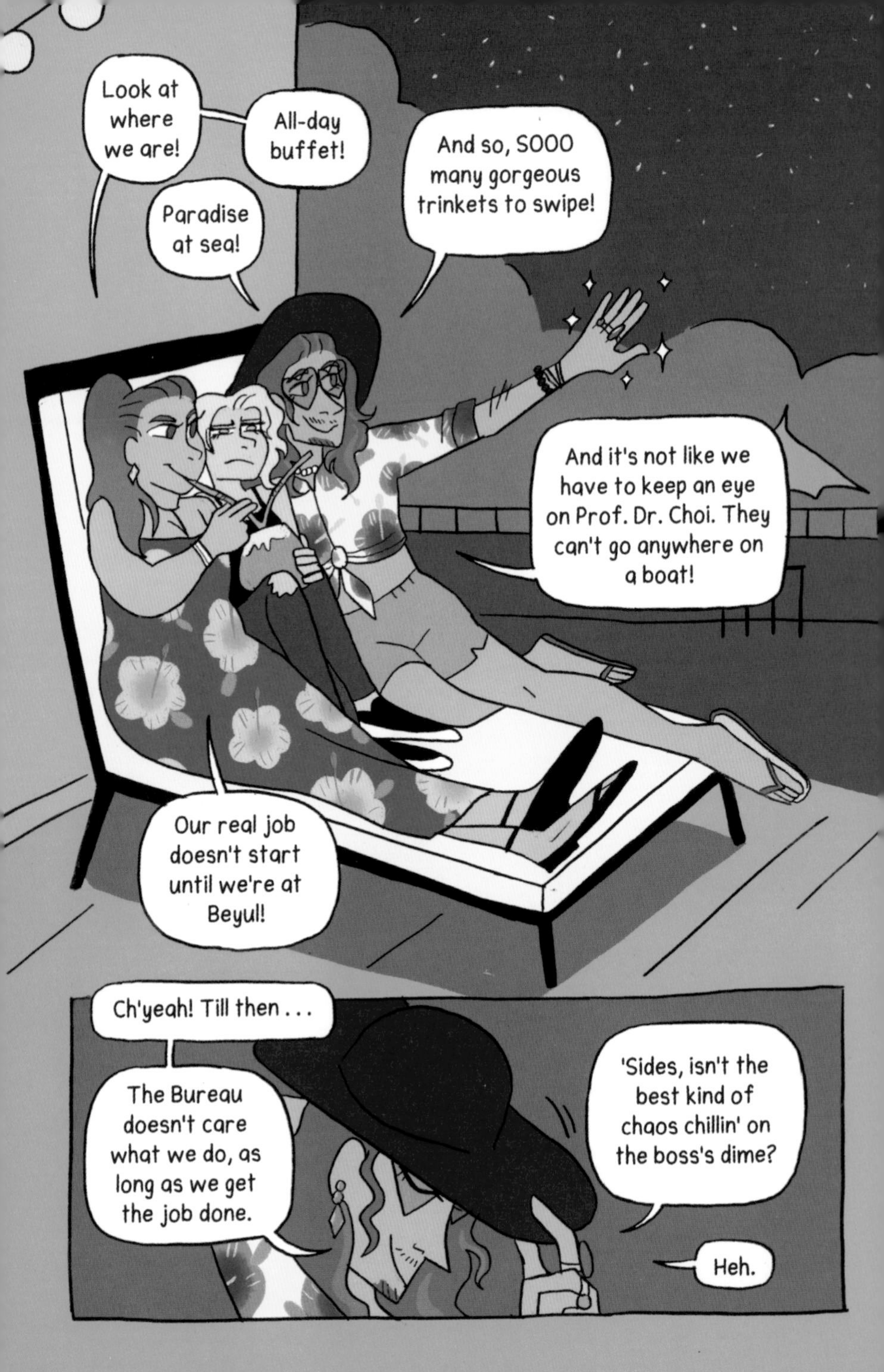
Look at where we are!
All-day buffet!
Paradise at sea!
And so, SOOO many gorgeous trinkets to swipe!
And it's not like we have to keep an eye on Prof. Dr. Choi. They can't go anywhere on a boat!
Our real job doesn't start until we're at Beyul!
Ch'yeah! Till then . . .
The Bureau doesn't care what we do, as long as we get the job done.
'Sides, isn't the best kind of chaos chillin' on the boss's dime?
Heh.

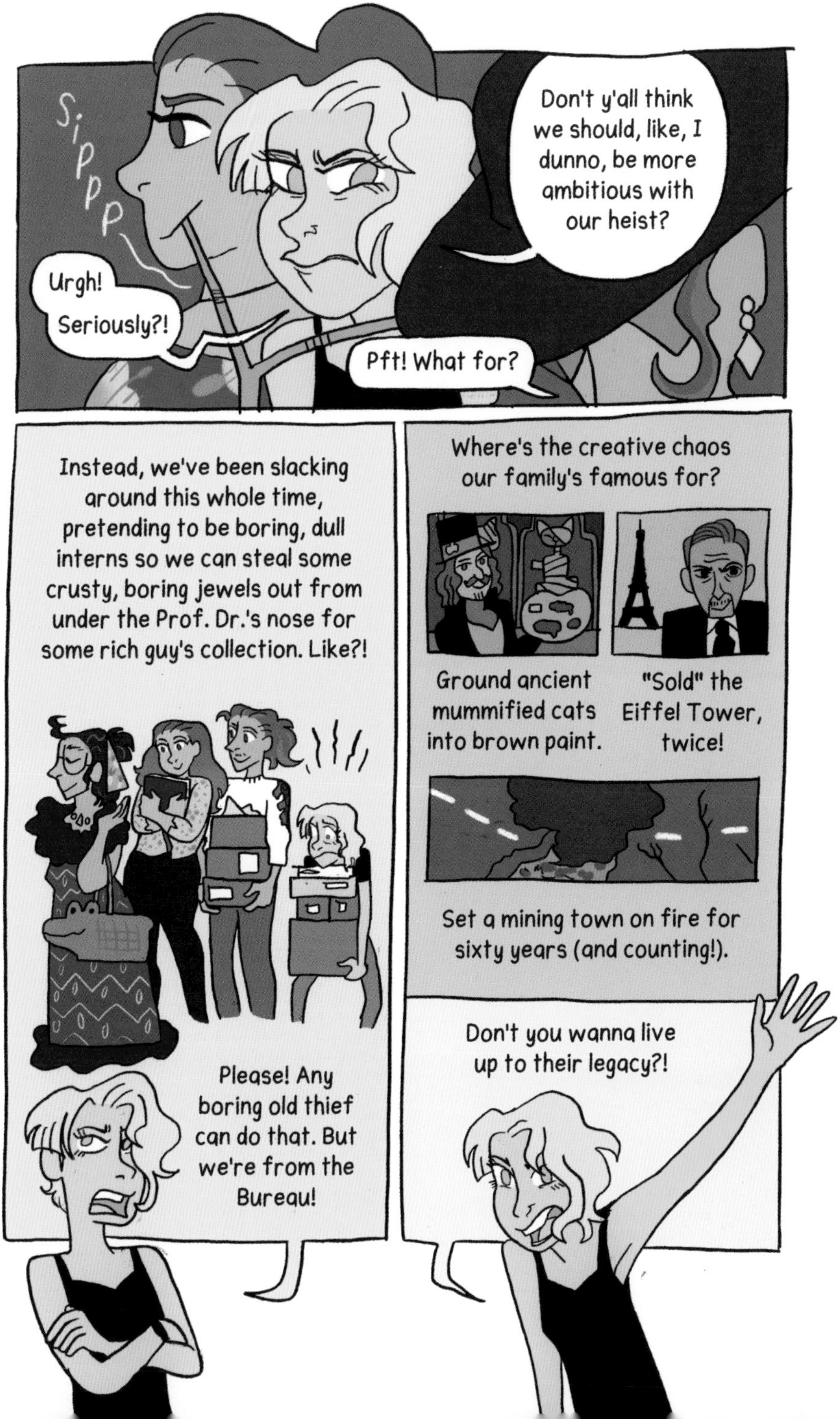

Sippp
Don't y'all think we should, like, I dunno, be more ambitious with our heist?
Urgh! Seriously?!
Pft! What for?
Instead, we've been slacking around this whole time, pretending to be boring, dull interns so we can steal some crusty, boring jewels out from under the Prof. Dr.'s nose for some rich guy's collection. Like?!
Where's the creative chaos our family's famous for?
Ground ancient mummified cats into brown paint.
"Sold" the Eiffel Tower, twice!
Set a mining town on fire for sixty years (and counting!).
Please! Any boring old thief can do that. But we're from the Bureau!
Don't you wanna live up to their legacy?!

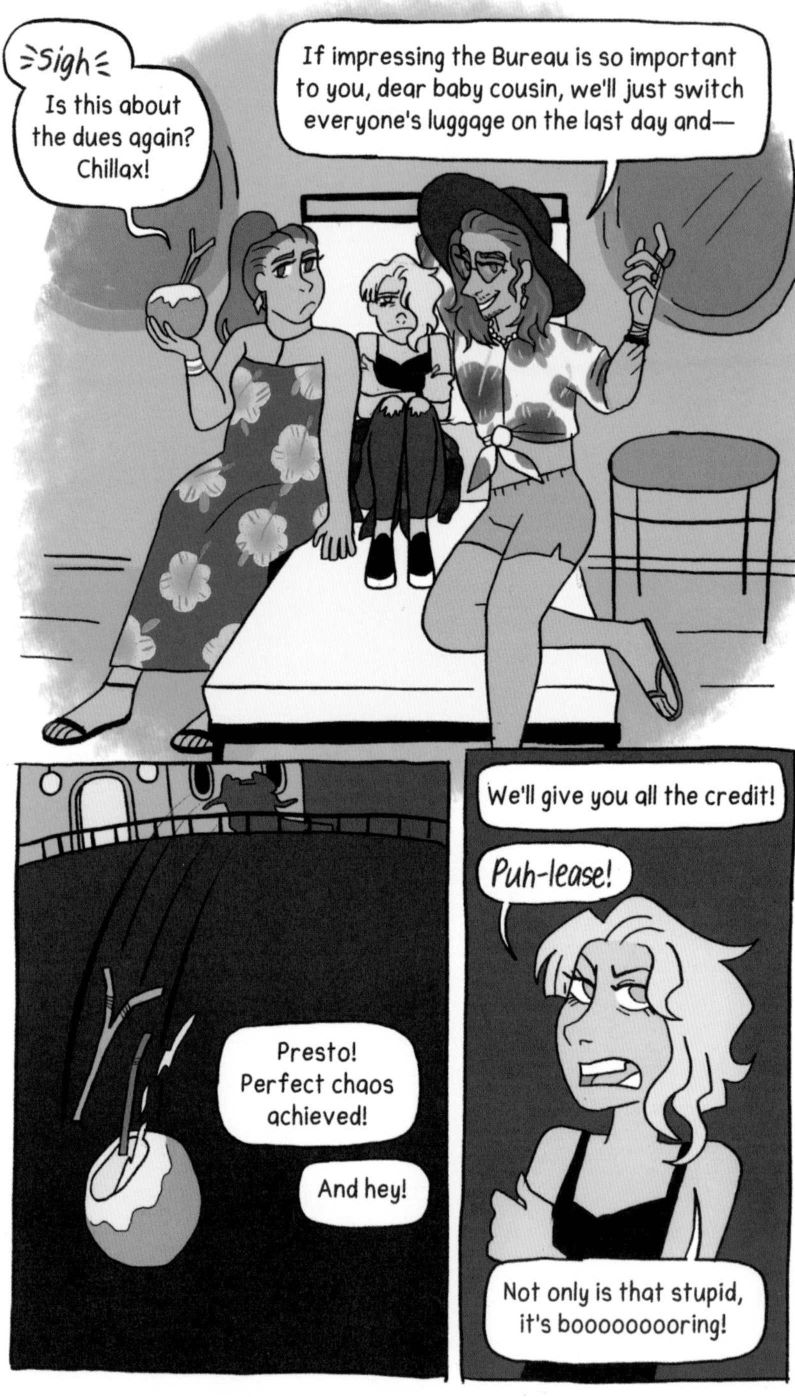
Sigh
Is this about the dues again? Chillax!
If impressing the Bureau is so important to you, dear baby cousin, we'll just switch everyone's luggage on the last day and—
Presto! Perfect chaos achieved!
And hey!
We'll give you all the credit!
Puh-lease!
Not only is that stupid, it's booooooooring!

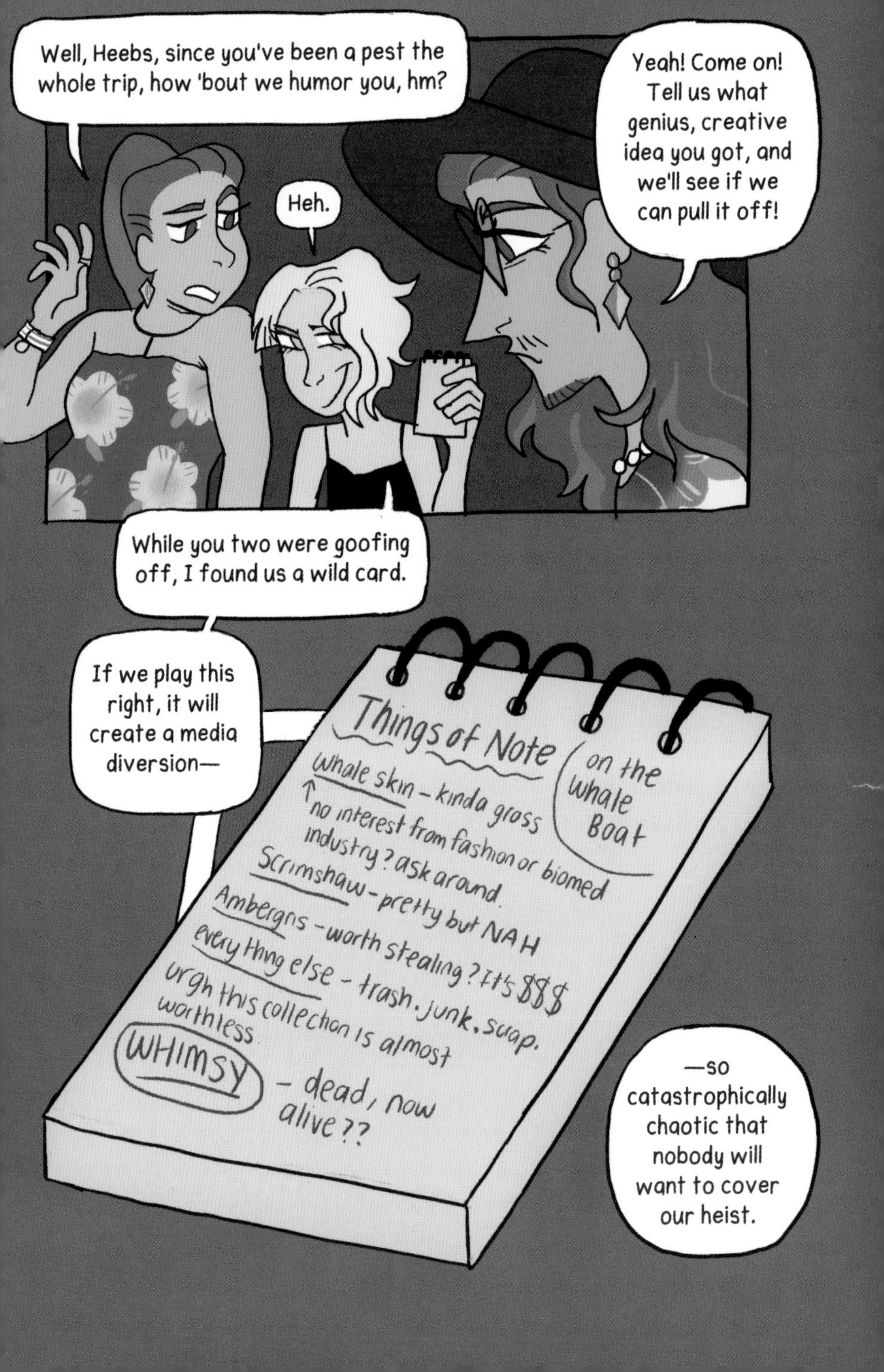
Well, Heebs, since you've been a pest the whole trip, how 'bout we humor you, hm?
Heh.
Yeah! Come on! Tell us what genius, creative idea you got, and we'll see if we can pull it off!
While you two were goofing off, I found us a wild card.
If we play this right, it will create a media diversion—
Things of Note
on the whale Boat
whale skin - kinda gross
↑ no interest from fashion or biomed industry? ask around.
Scrimshaw - pretty but NAH
Ambergris - worth stealing? It's $$$
every thing else - trash. junk. soap.
urgh this collection is almost worthless.
WHIMSY - dead, now alive??
—so catastrophically chaotic that nobody will want to cover our heist.

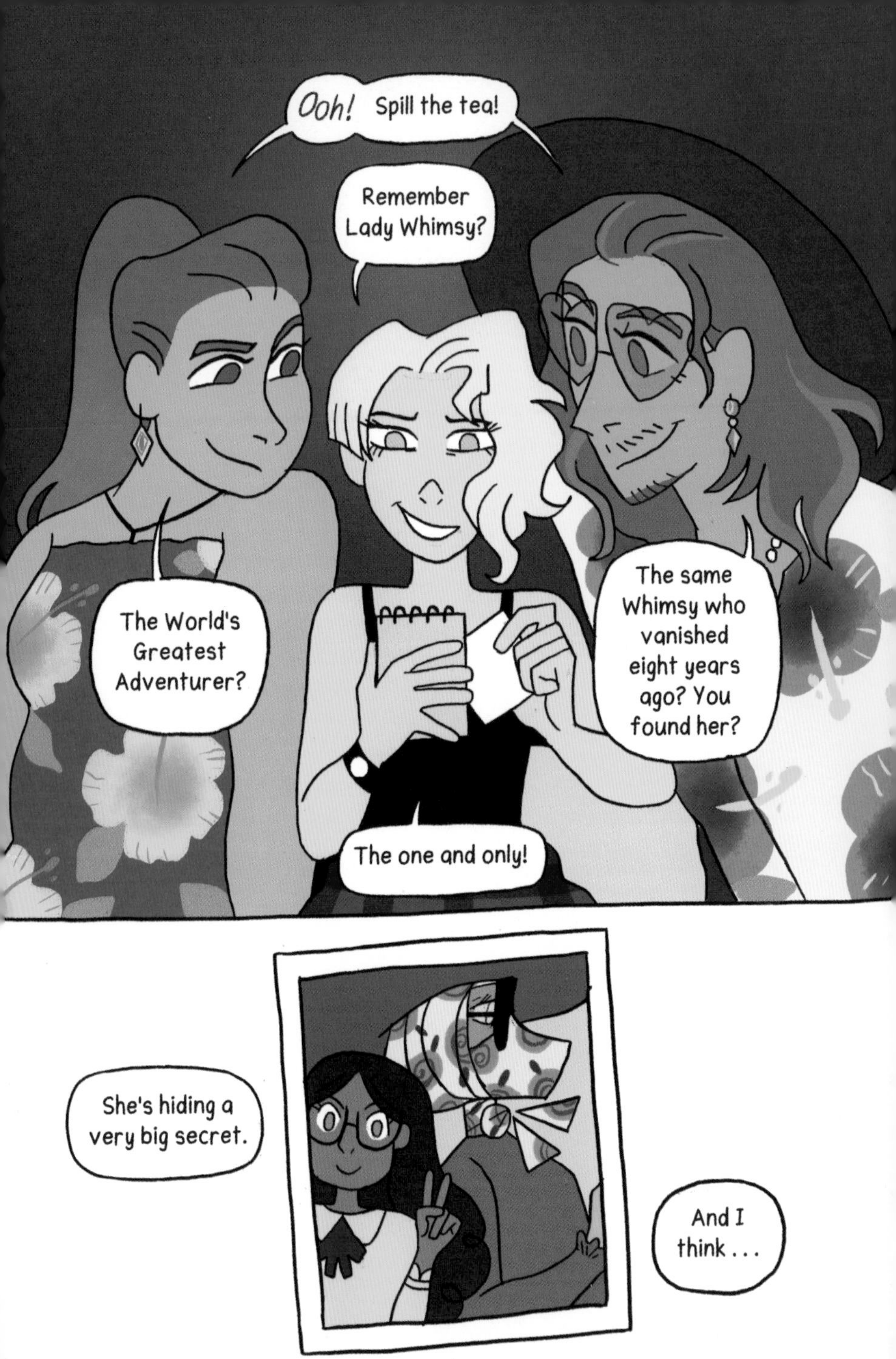
Ooh! Spill the tea!
Remember Lady Whimsy?
The World's Greatest Adventurer?
The same Whimsy who vanished eight years ago? You found her?
The one and only!
She's hiding a very big secret.
And I think . . .

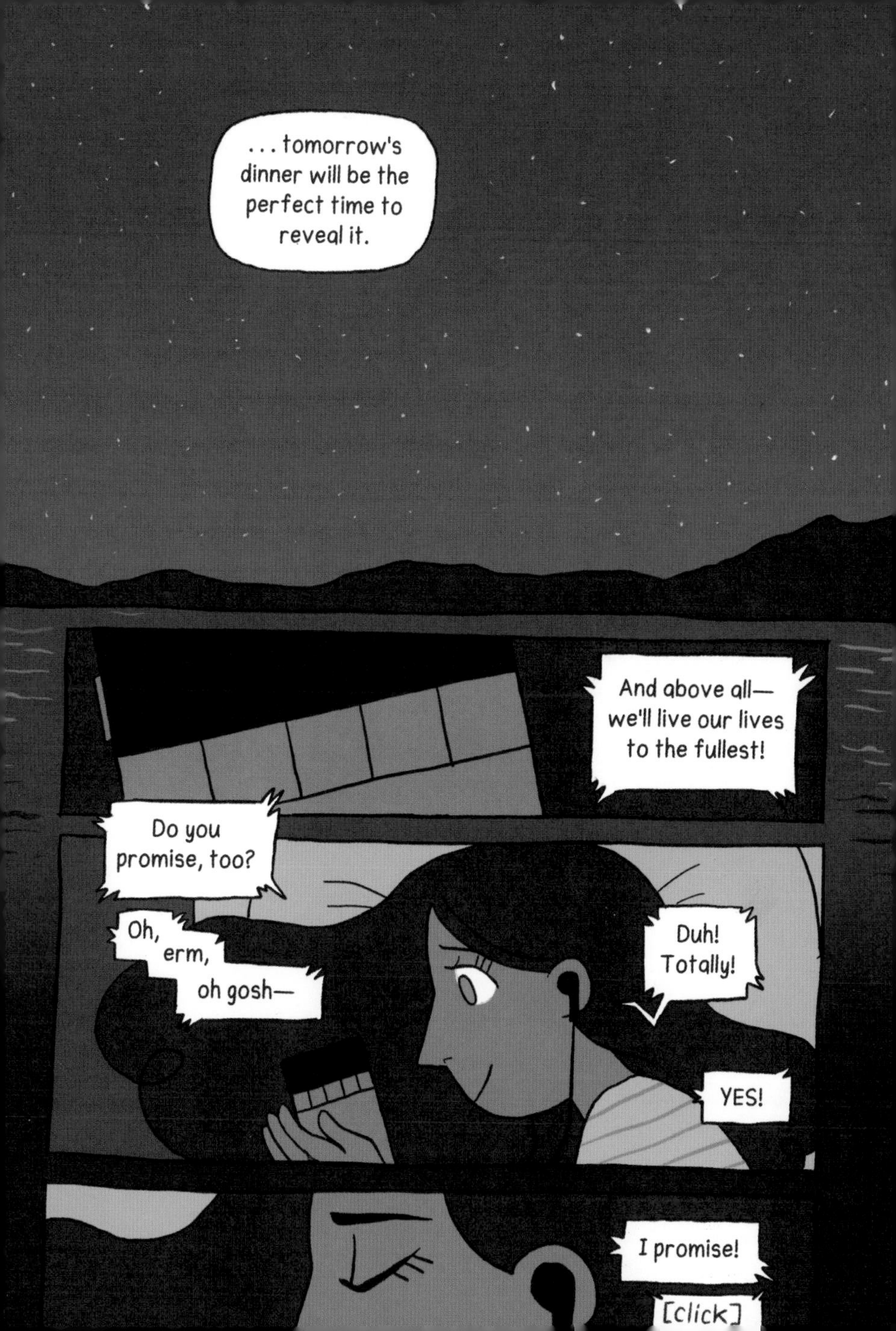
. . . tomorrow's dinner will be the perfect time to reveal it.
And above all—we'll live our lives to the fullest!
Do you promise, too?
Oh,
erm,
oh gosh—
Duh! Totally!
YES!
I promise!
[click]

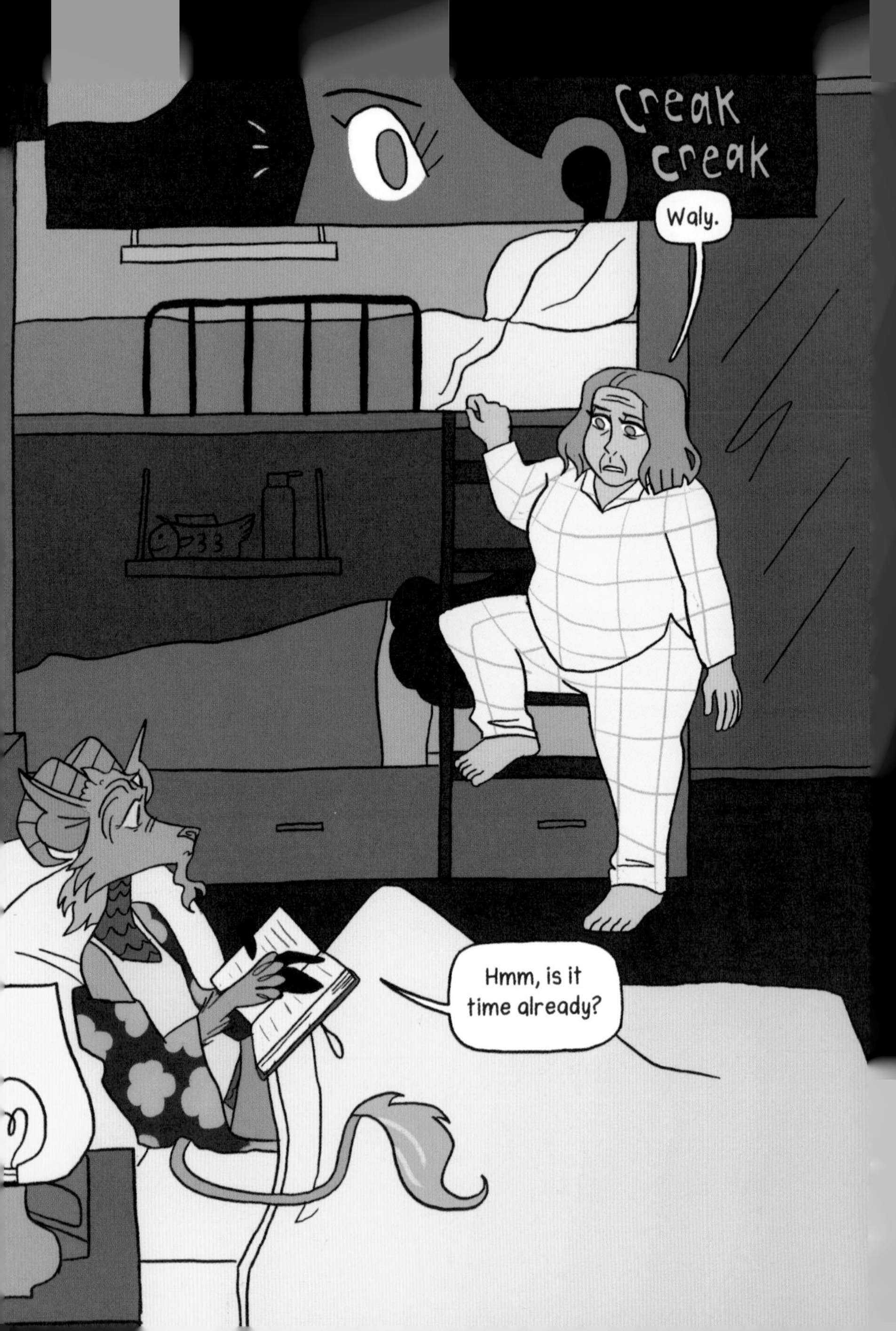
Creak
creak
Waly.
Hmm, is it time already?

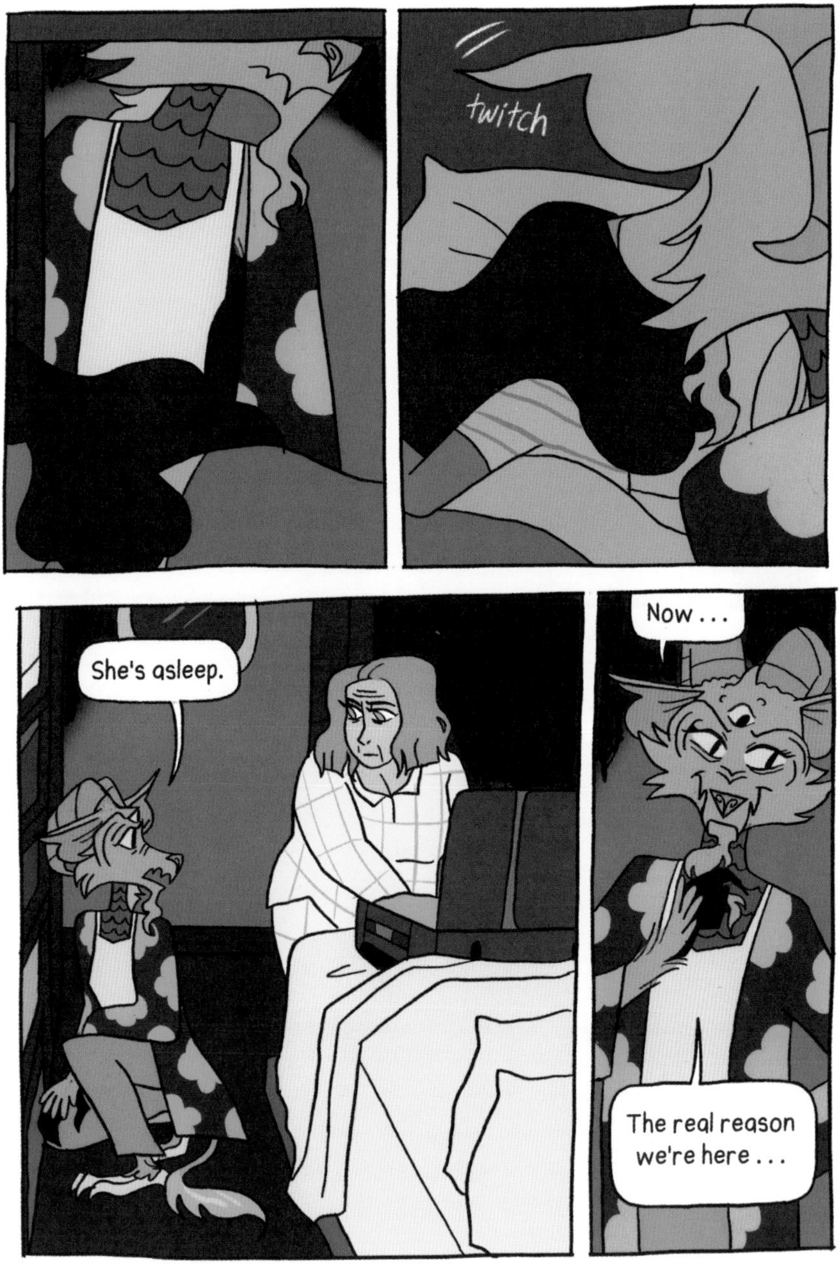
twitch
She's asleep.
Now . . .
The real reason we're here . . .

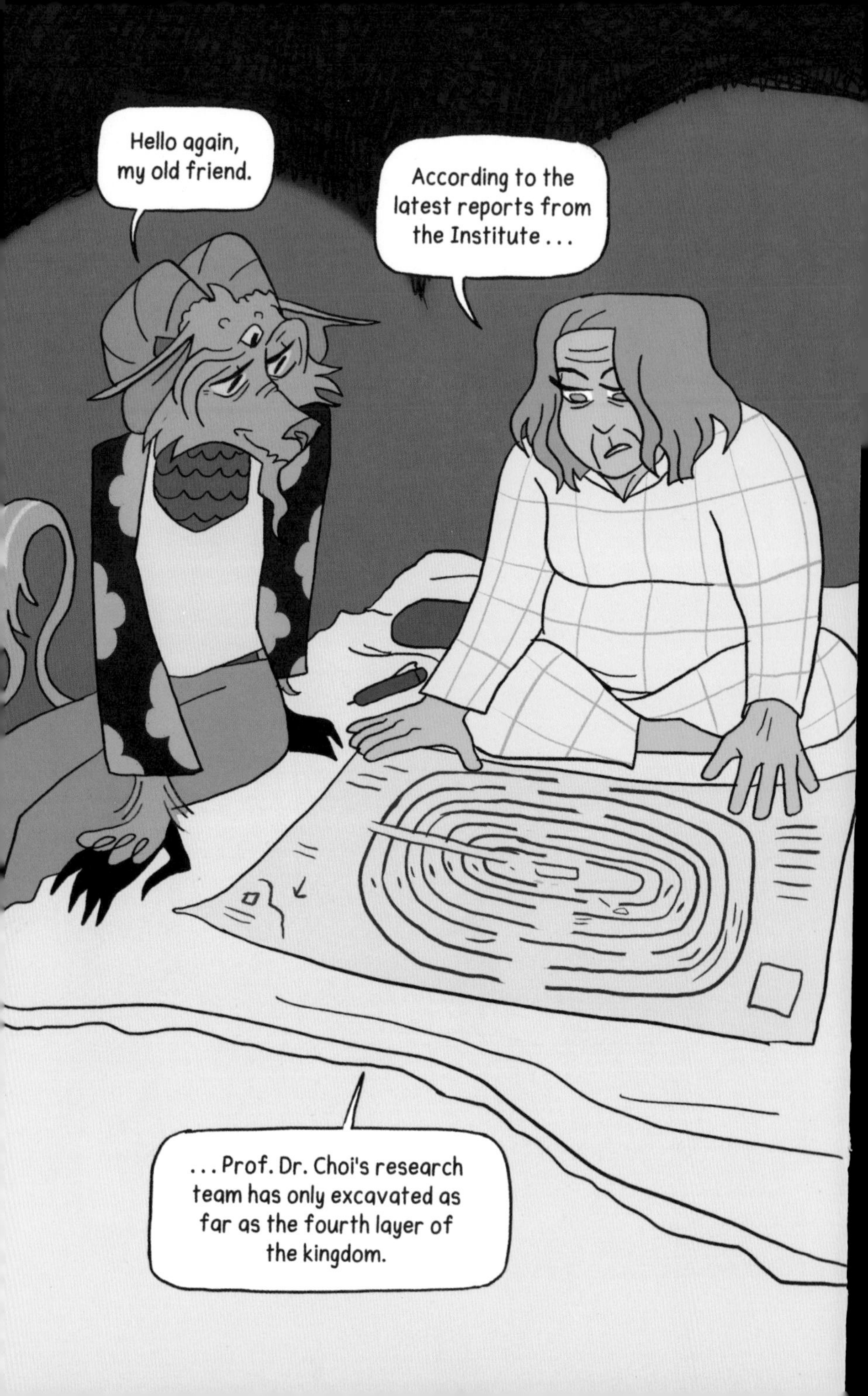
Hello again, my old friend.
According to the latest reports from the Institute . . .
. . . Prof. Dr. Choi's research team has only excavated as far as the fourth layer of the kingdom.

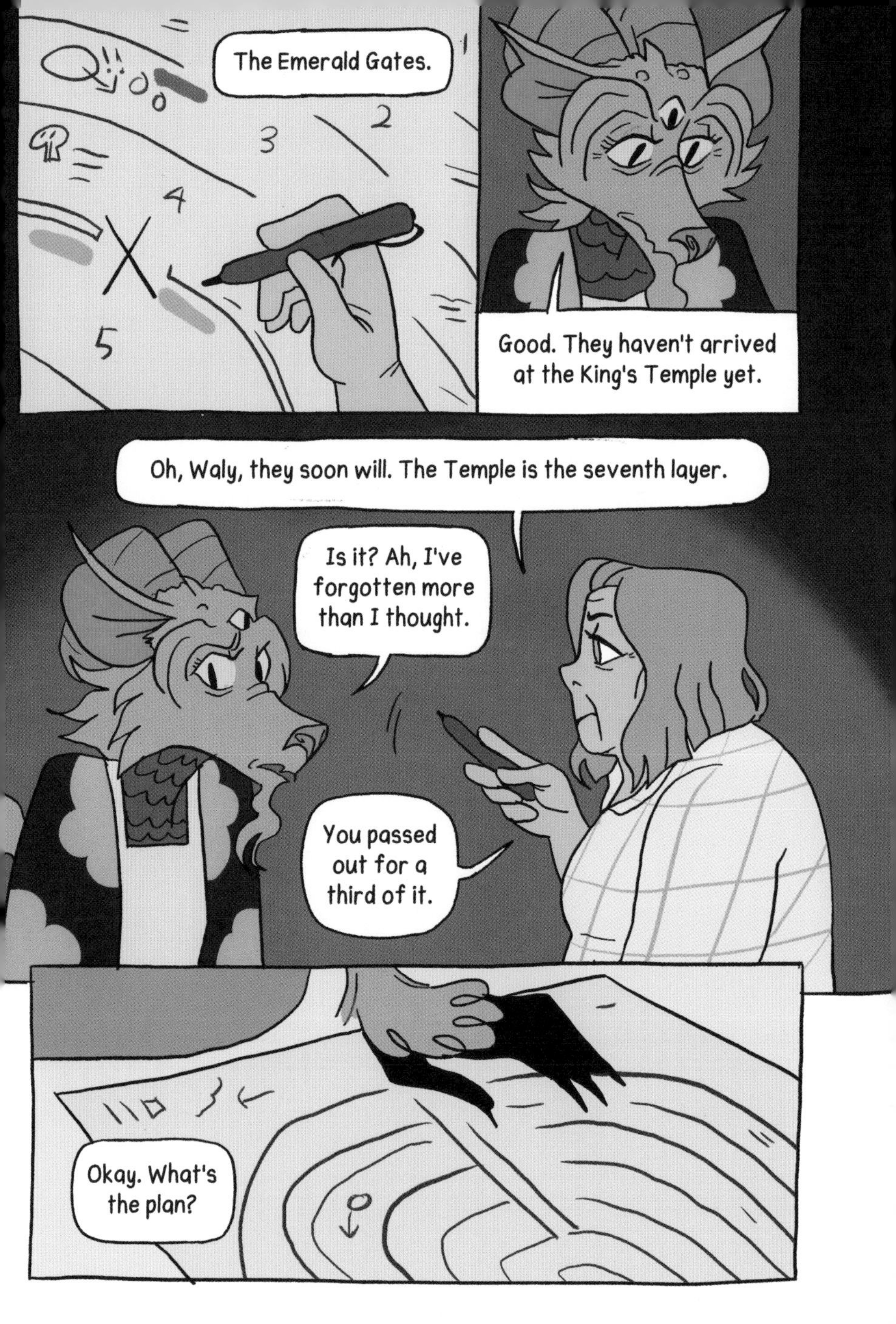
The Emerald Gates.
1
2
3
4
5
Good. They haven't arrived at the King's Temple yet.
Oh, Waly, they soon will. The Temple is the seventh layer.
Is it? Ah, I've forgotten more than I thought.
You passed out for a third of it.
Okay. What's the plan?

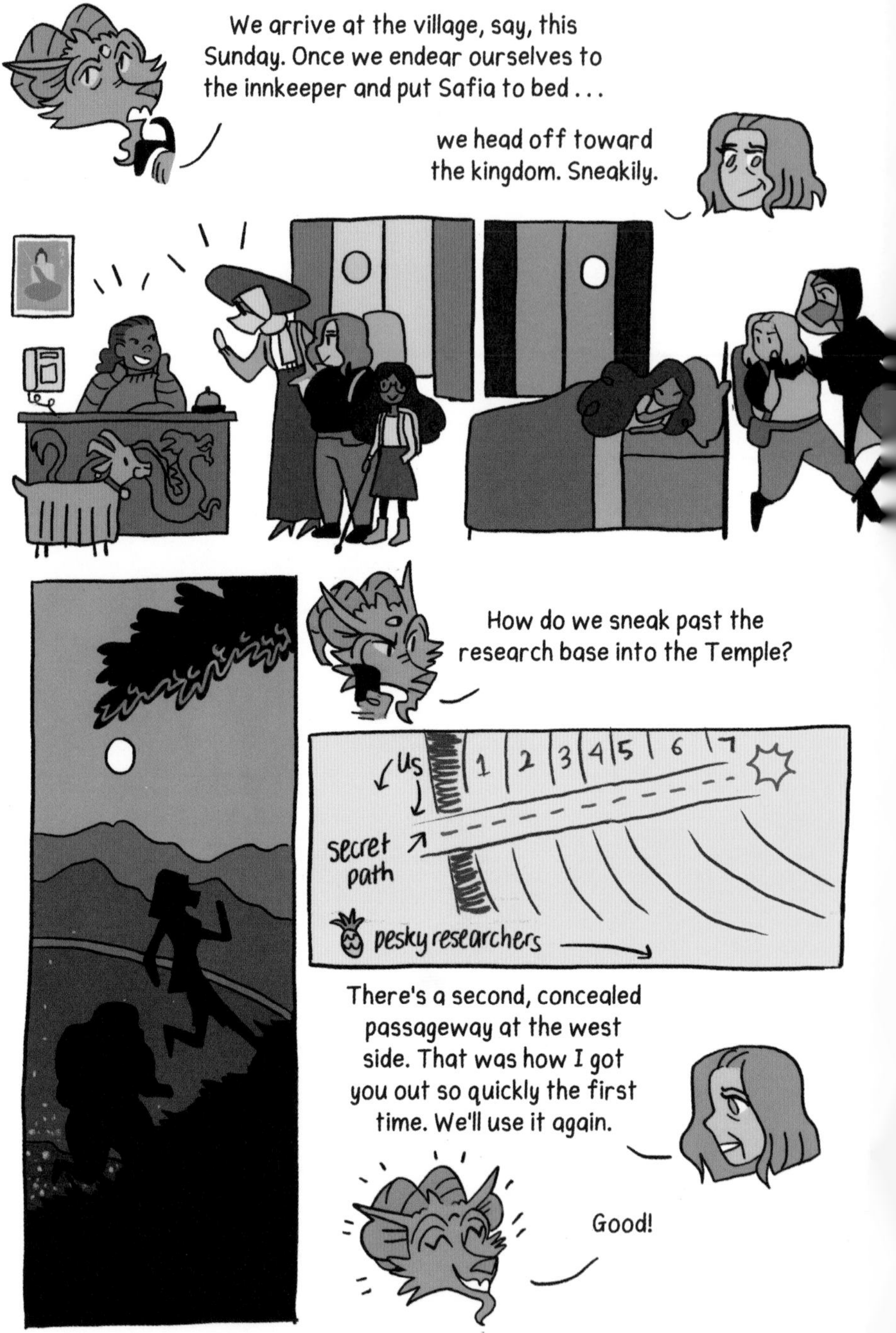
We arrive at the village, say, this Sunday. Once we endear ourselves to the innkeeper and put Safia to bed . . .
we head off toward the kingdom. Sneakily.
How do we sneak past the research base into the Temple?
Us
1
2
3
4
5
6
7
secret path
pesky researchers
There's a second, concealed passageway at the west side. That was how I got you out so quickly the first time. We'll use it again.
Good!

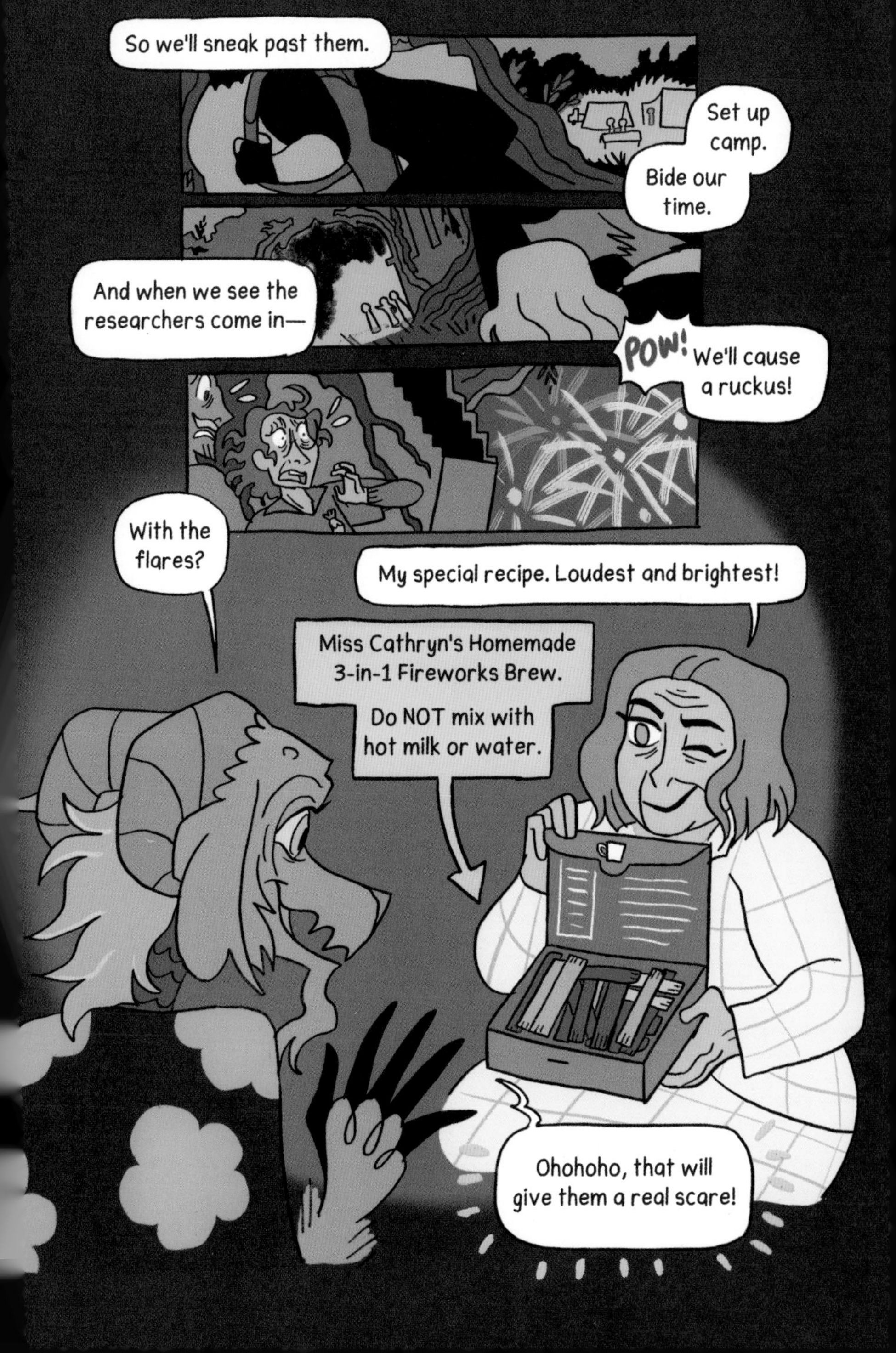
So we'll sneak past them.
Set up camp.
Bide our time.
And when we see the researchers come in—
POW!
We'll cause a ruckus!
With the flares?
My special recipe. Loudest and brightest!
Miss Cathryn's Homemade 3-in-1 Fireworks Brew.
Do NOT mix with hot milk or water.
Ohohoho, that will give them a real scare!

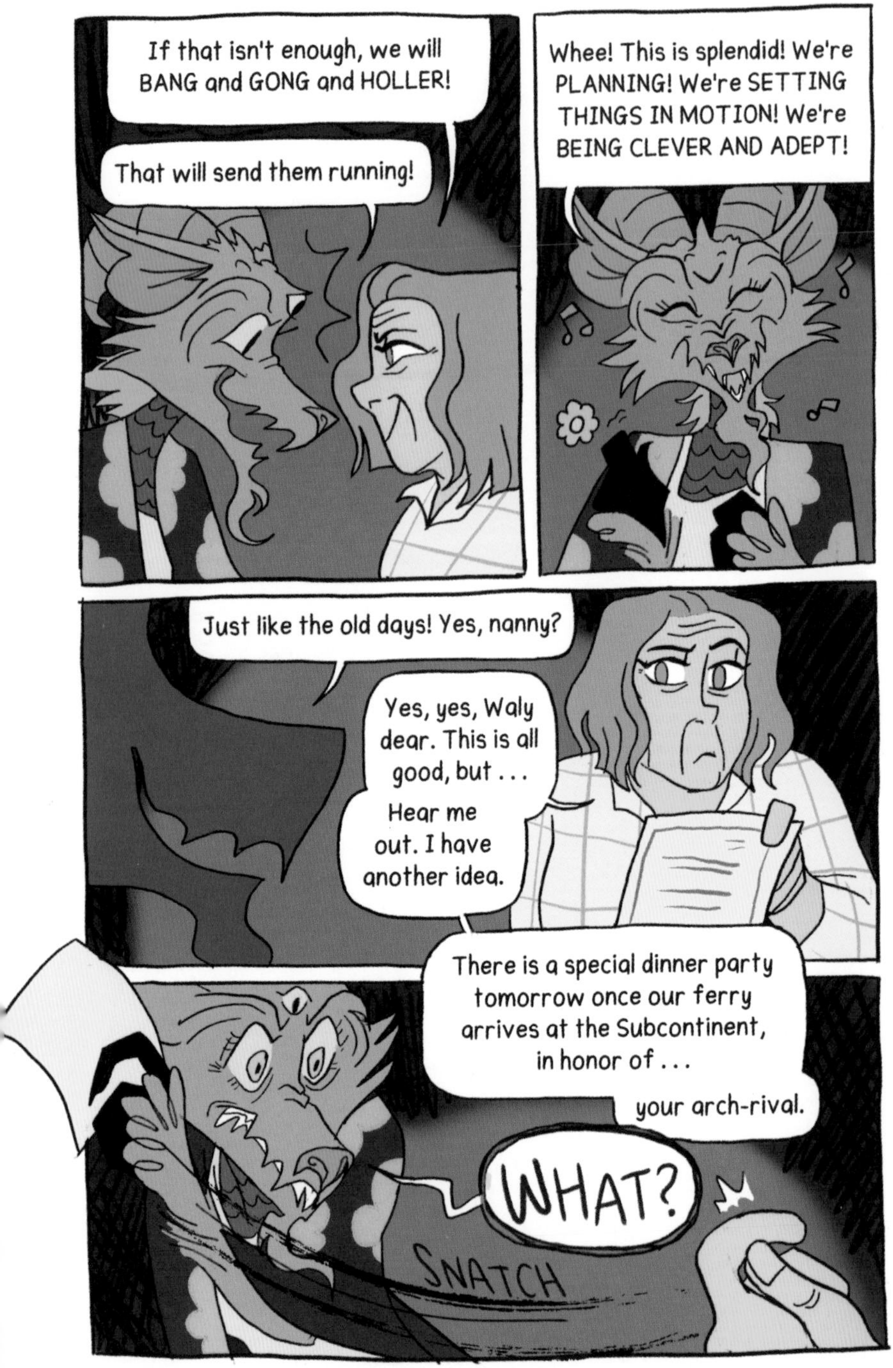
If that isn't enough, we will BANG and GONG and HOLLER!
That will send them running!
Whee! This is splendid! We're PLANNING! We're SETTING THINGS IN MOTION! We're BEING CLEVER AND ADEPT!
Just like the old days! Yes, nanny?
Yes, yes, Waly dear. This is all good, but . . .
Hear me out. I have another idea.
There is a special dinner party tomorrow once our ferry arrives at the Subcontinent, in honor of . . .
your arch-rival.
WHAT?
SNATCH

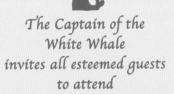

The Captain of the
White Whale
invites all esteemed guests
to attend

**A VERY SPECIAL
DINNER CELEBRATING
THE RENOWNED VERY
SPECIAL EXPLORER**

Prof. Dr. Cecilia Choi

**CONGRATULATING
THEIR SUCCESS.**

We're honored for their
friendship and patronage.

ONE unearned success, and the Tart has the public fawning at their knees!

Oh! Saint Jude of the lost cause! Have world standards fallen since my retirement?

. . . I think we should attend.

HAH! Attend? What for?!

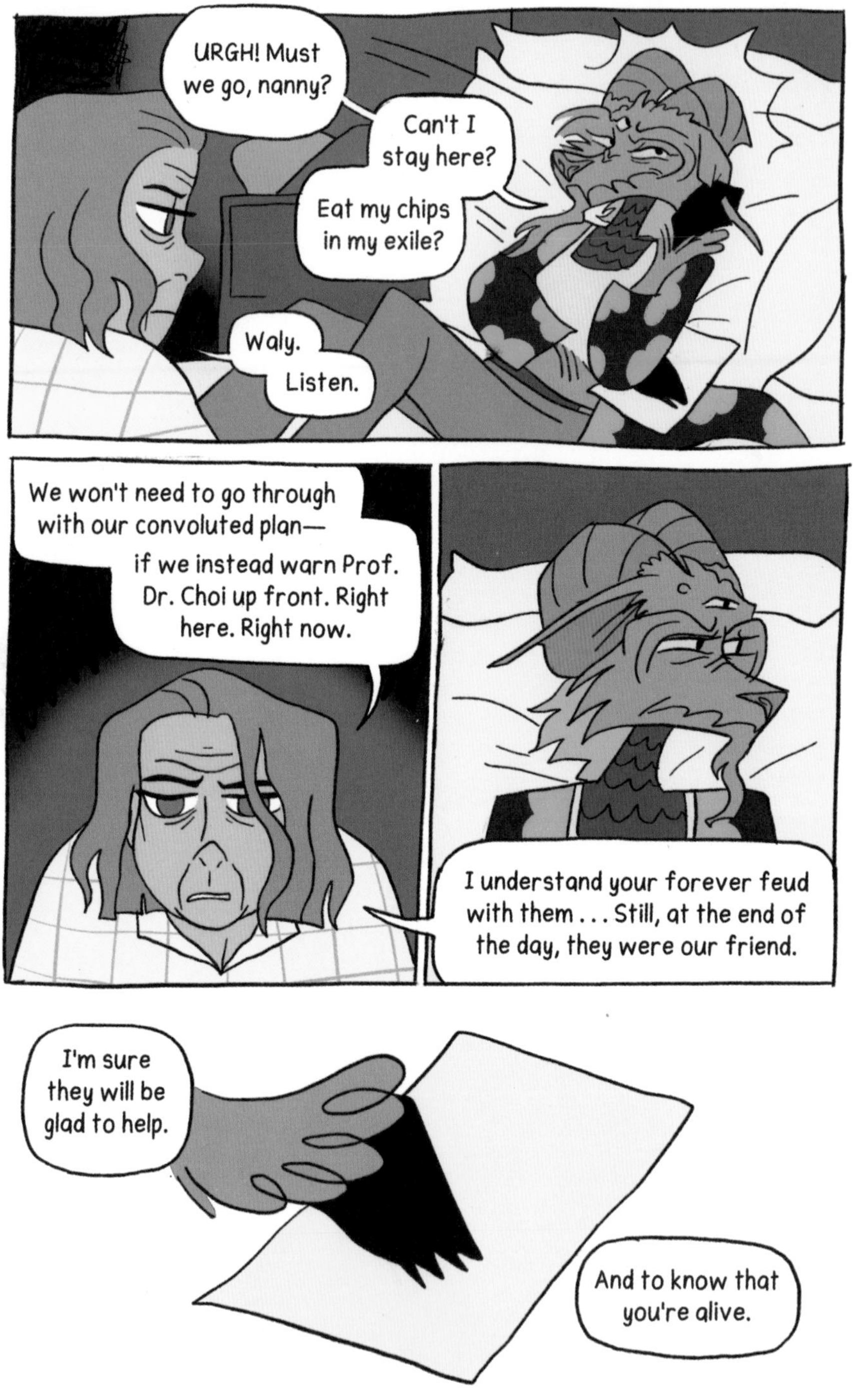
URGH! Must we go, nanny?
Can't I stay here?
Eat my chips in my exile?
Waly.
Listen.
We won't need to go through with our convoluted plan—
if we instead warn Prof. Dr. Choi up front. Right here. Right now.
I understand your forever feud with them . . . Still, at the end of the day, they were our friend.
I'm sure they will be glad to help.
And to know that you're alive.

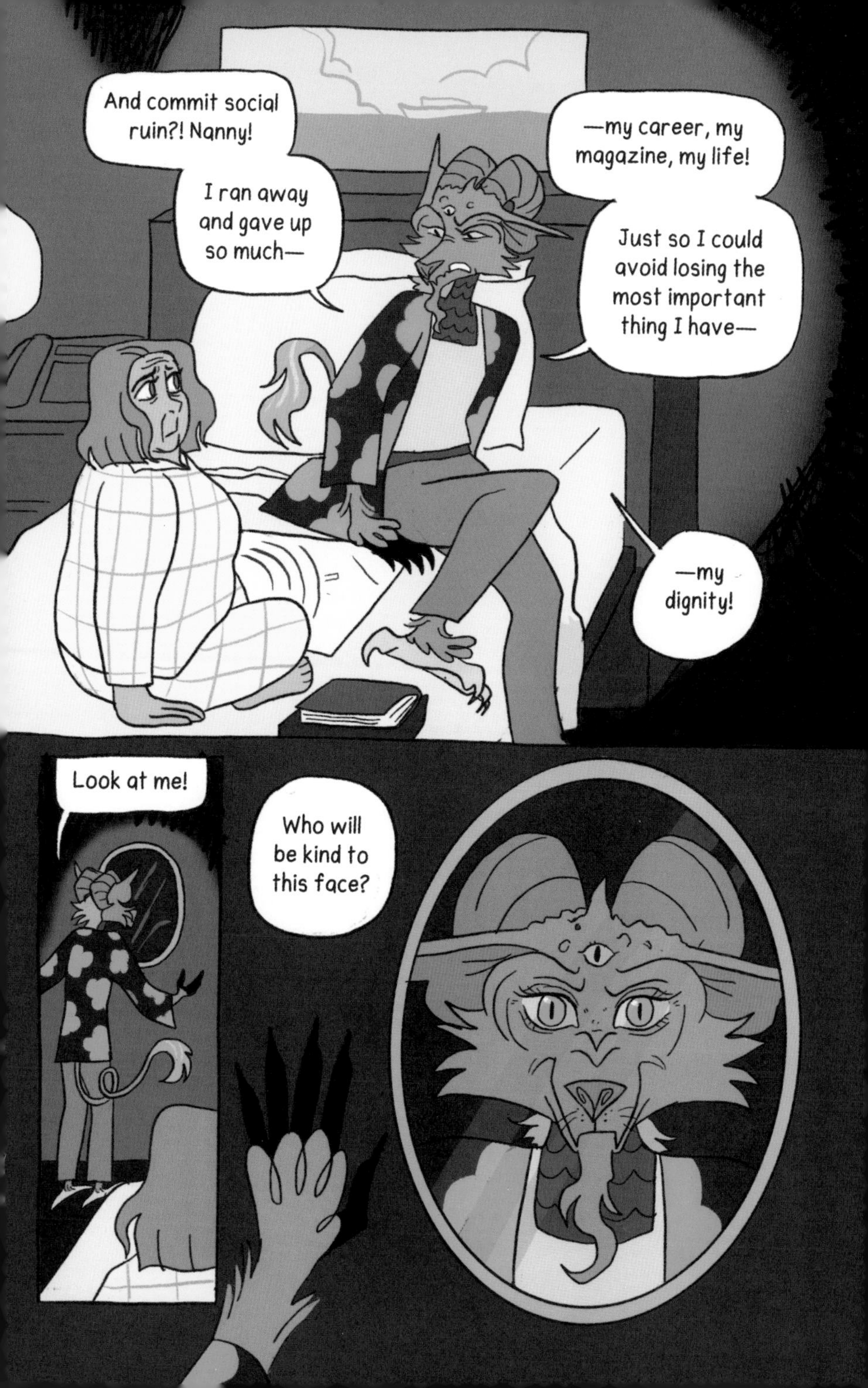
And commit social ruin?! Nanny!
I ran away and gave up so much—
—my career, my magazine, my life!
Just so I could avoid losing the most important thing I have—
—my dignity!
Look at me!
Who will be kind to this face?

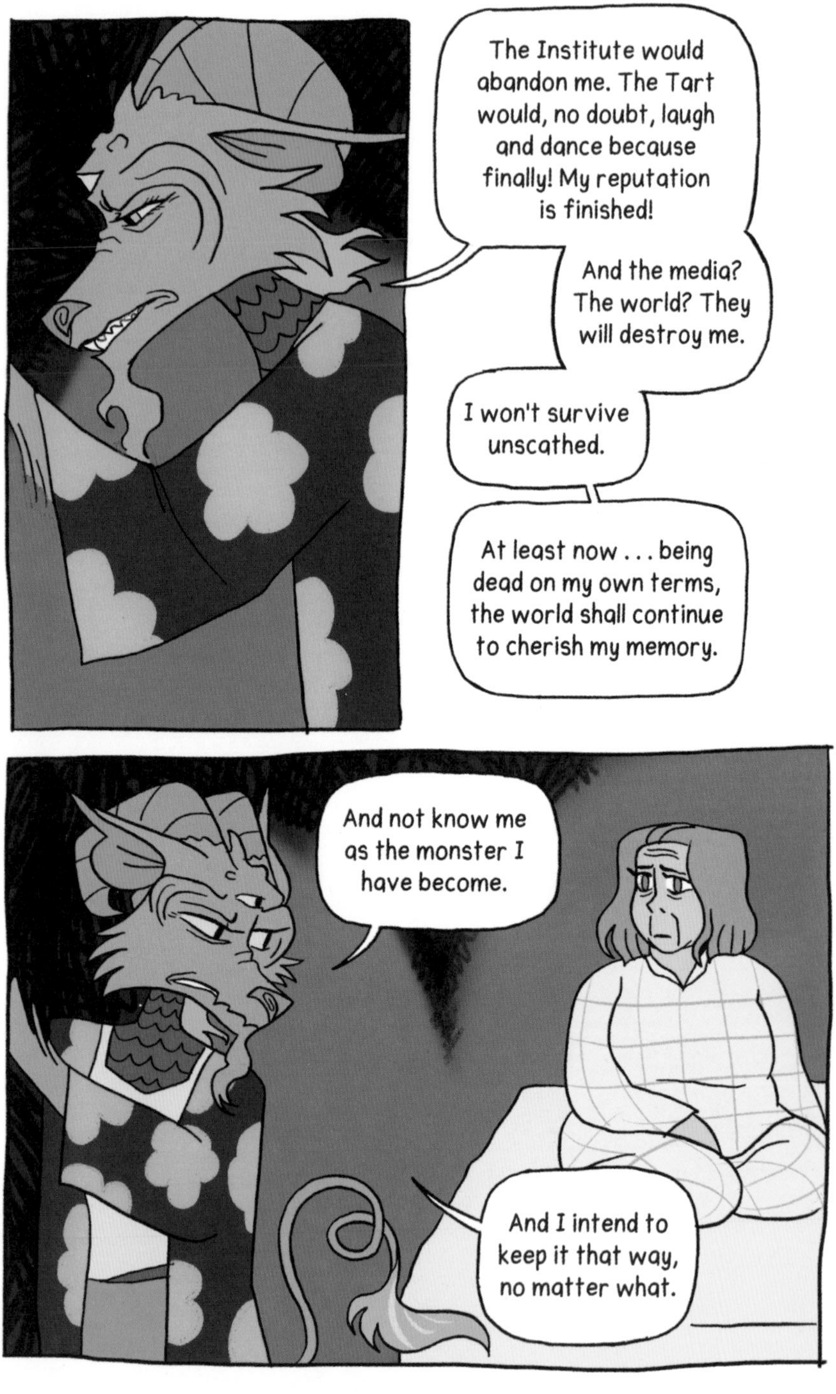
The Institute would abandon me. The Tart would, no doubt, laugh and dance because finally! My reputation is finished!
And the media? The world? They will destroy me.
I won't survive unscathed.
At least now . . . being dead on my own terms, the world shall continue to cherish my memory.
And not know me as the monster I have become.
And I intend to keep it that way, no matter what.

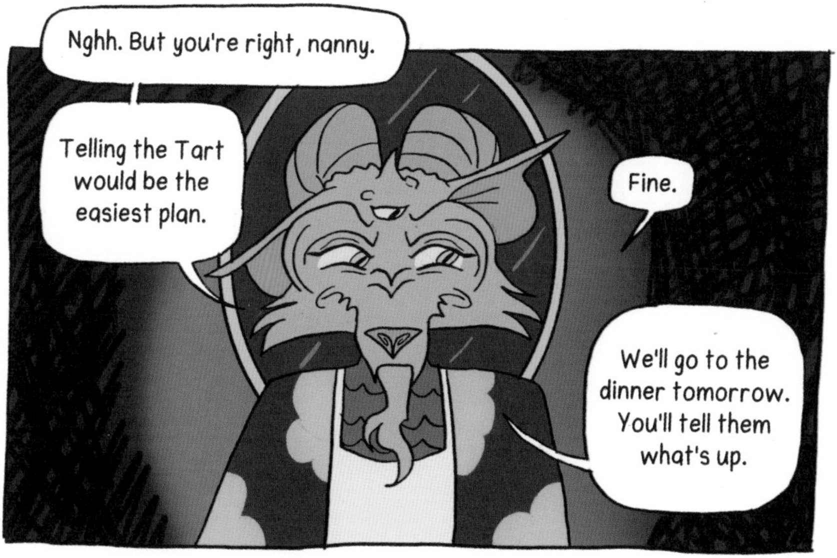
Nghh. But you're right, nanny.
Telling the Tart would be the easiest plan.
Fine.
We'll go to the dinner tomorrow. You'll tell them what's up.

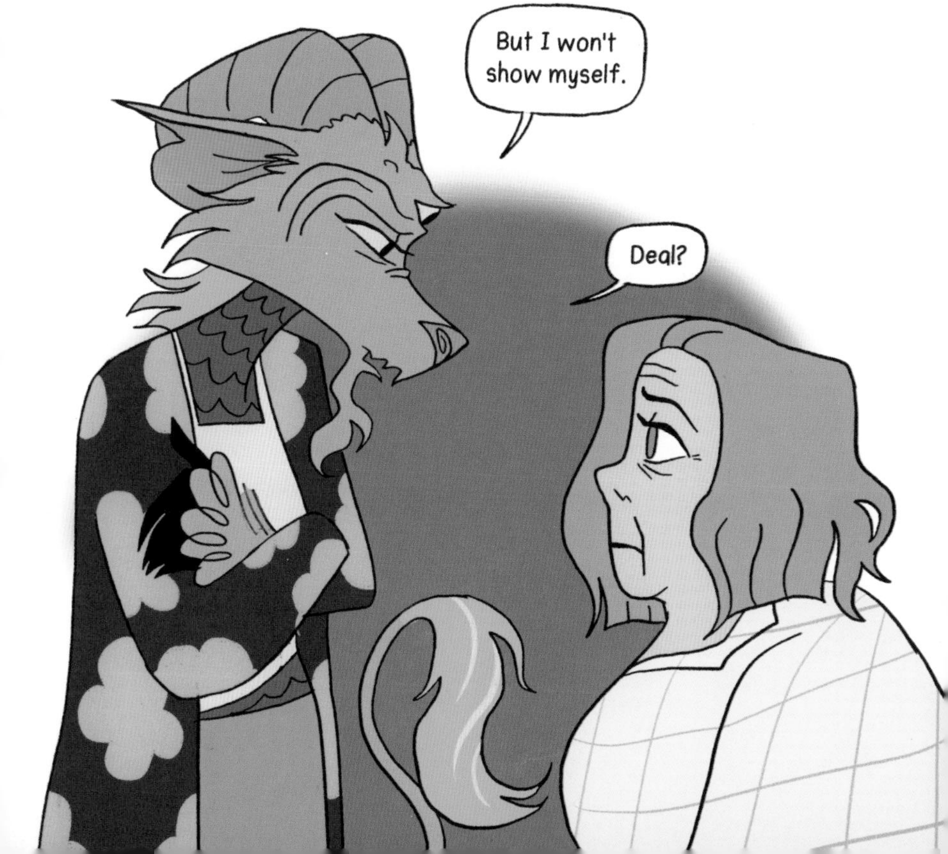
But I won't show myself.
Deal?

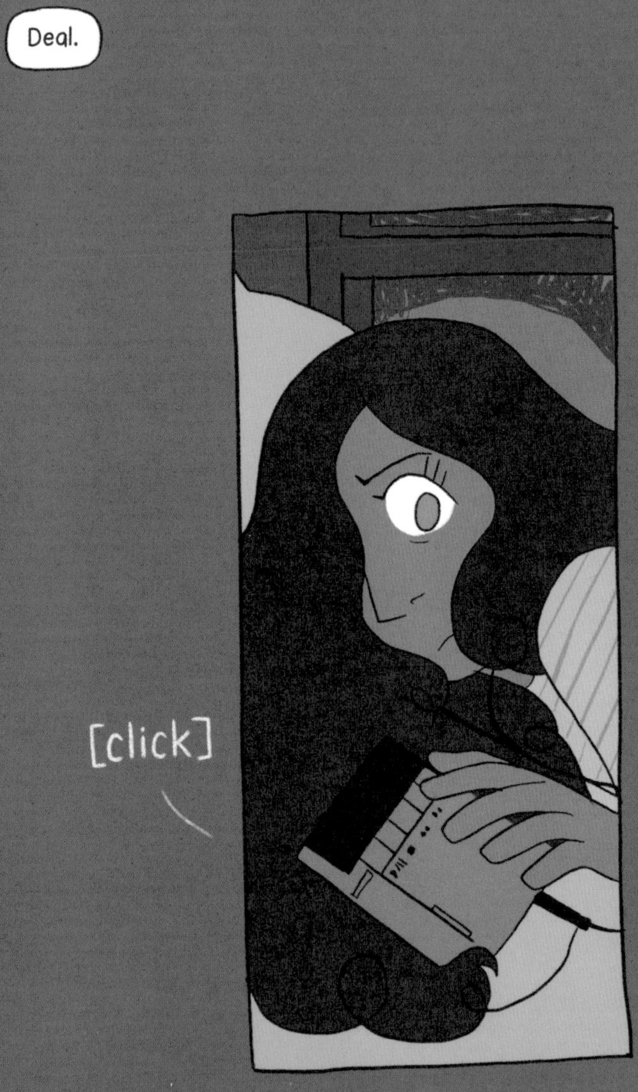
Deal.
[click]

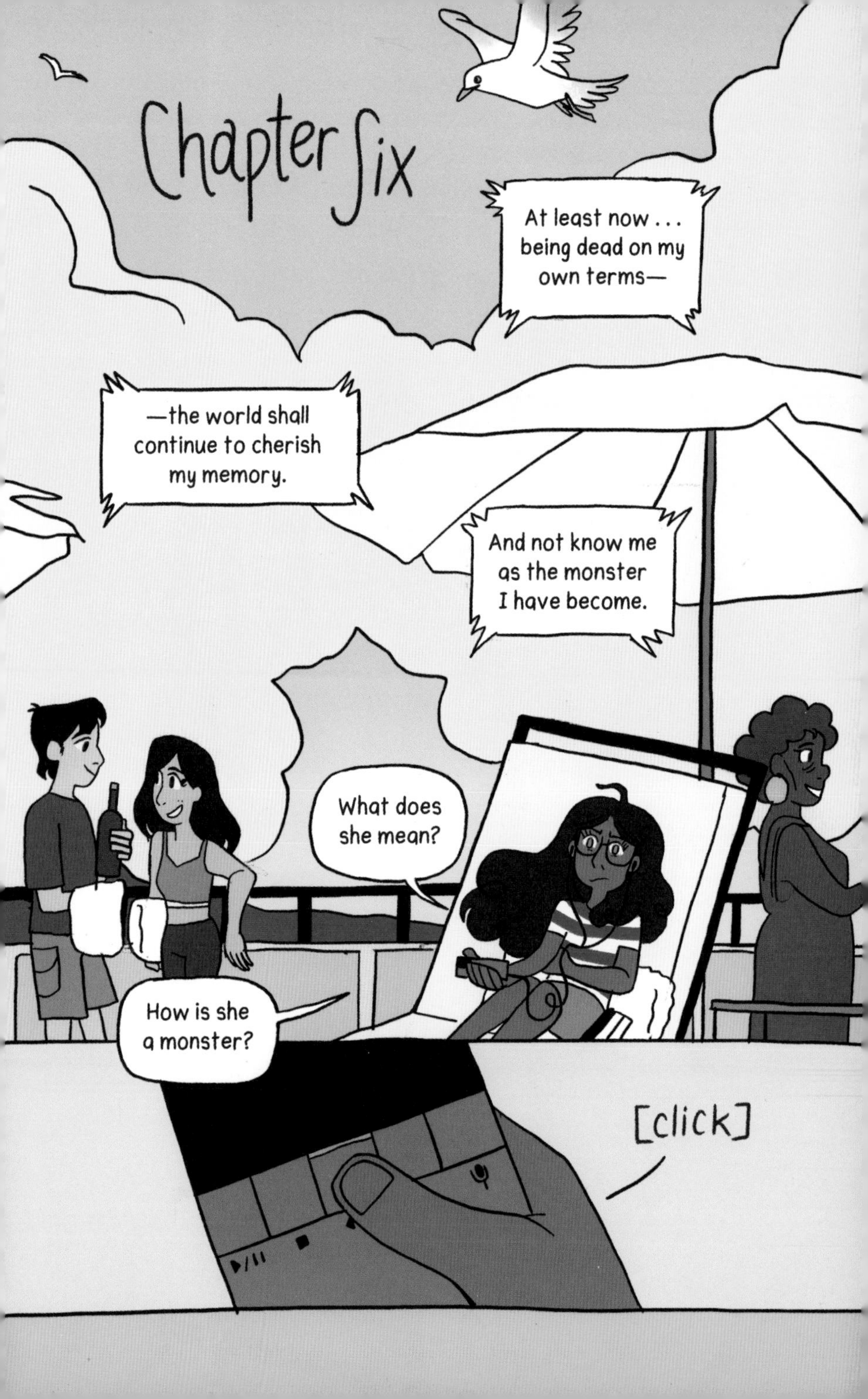
Chapter Six
At least now . . . being dead on my own terms—
—the world shall continue to cherish my memory.
And not know me as the monster I have become.
What does she mean?
How is she a monster?
[click]

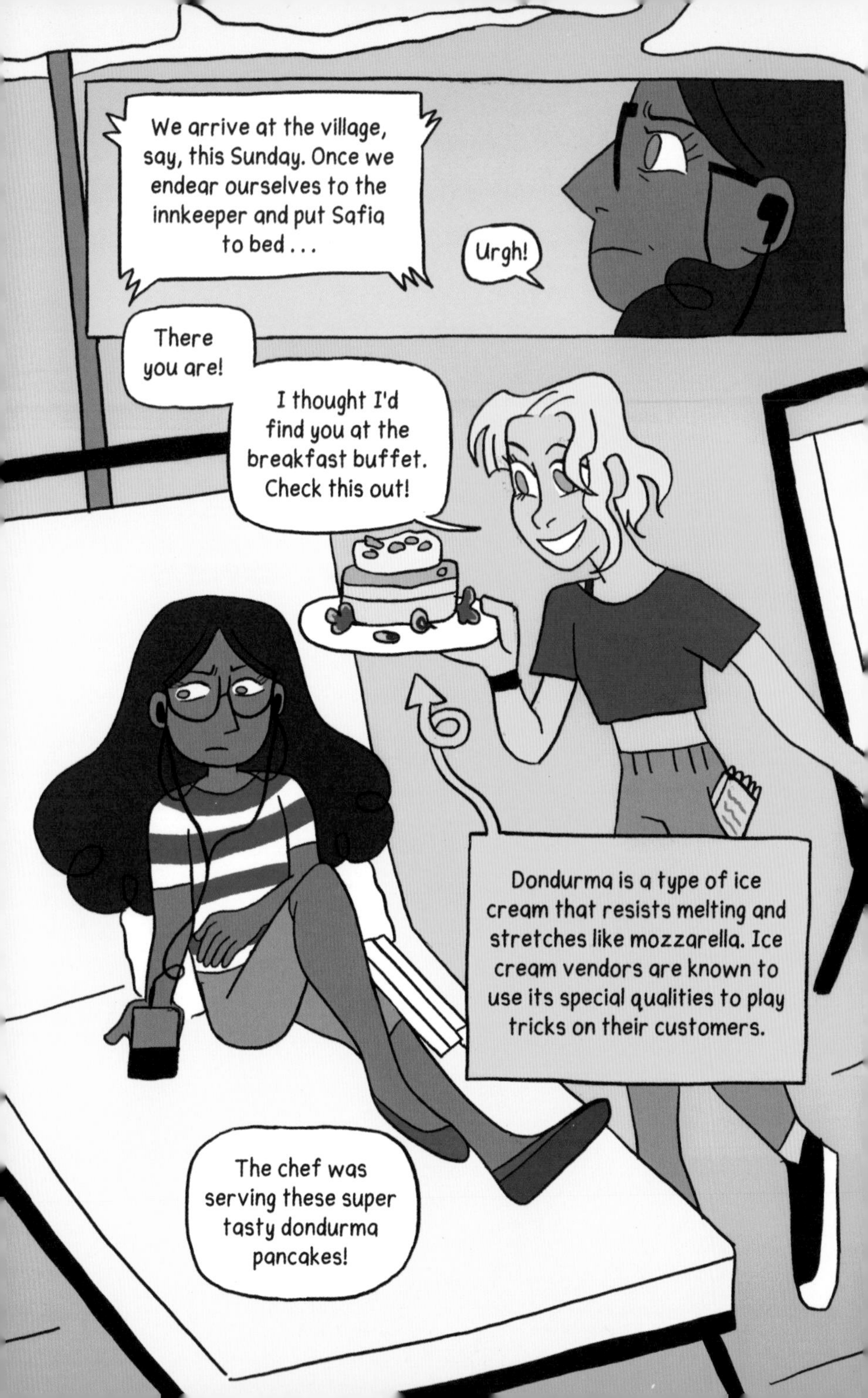
We arrive at the village, say, this Sunday. Once we endear ourselves to the innkeeper and put Safia to bed . . .
Urgh!
There you are!
I thought I'd find you at the breakfast buffet. Check this out!
Dondurma is a type of ice cream that resists melting and stretches like mozzarella. Ice cream vendors are known to use its special qualities to play tricks on their customers.
The chef was serving these super tasty dondurma pancakes!

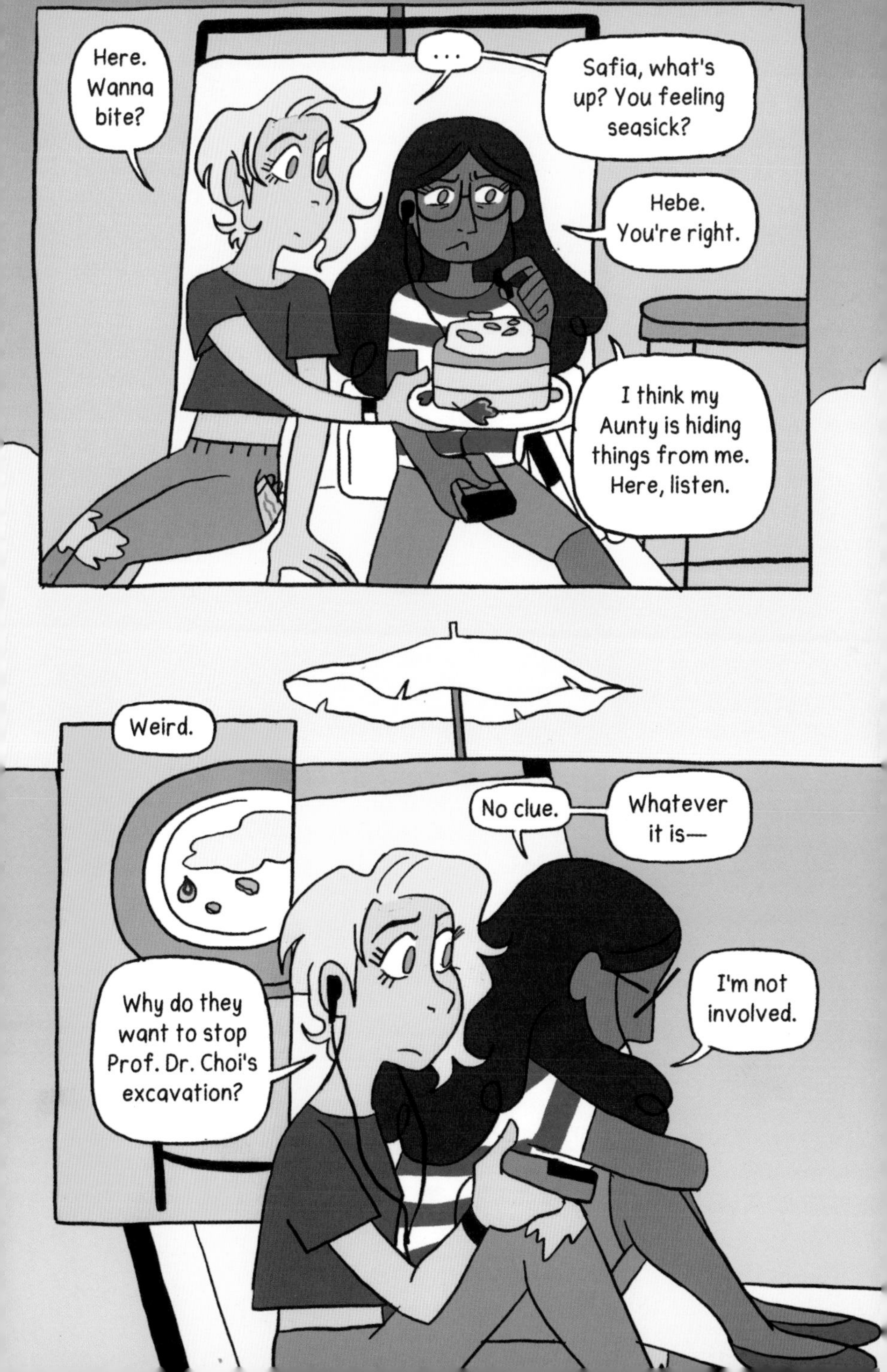
Here. Wanna bite?
...
Safia, what's up? You feeling seasick?
Hebe. You're right.
I think my Aunty is hiding things from me. Here, listen.
Weird.
Why do they want to stop Prof. Dr. Choi's excavation?
No clue.
Whatever it is—
I'm not involved.

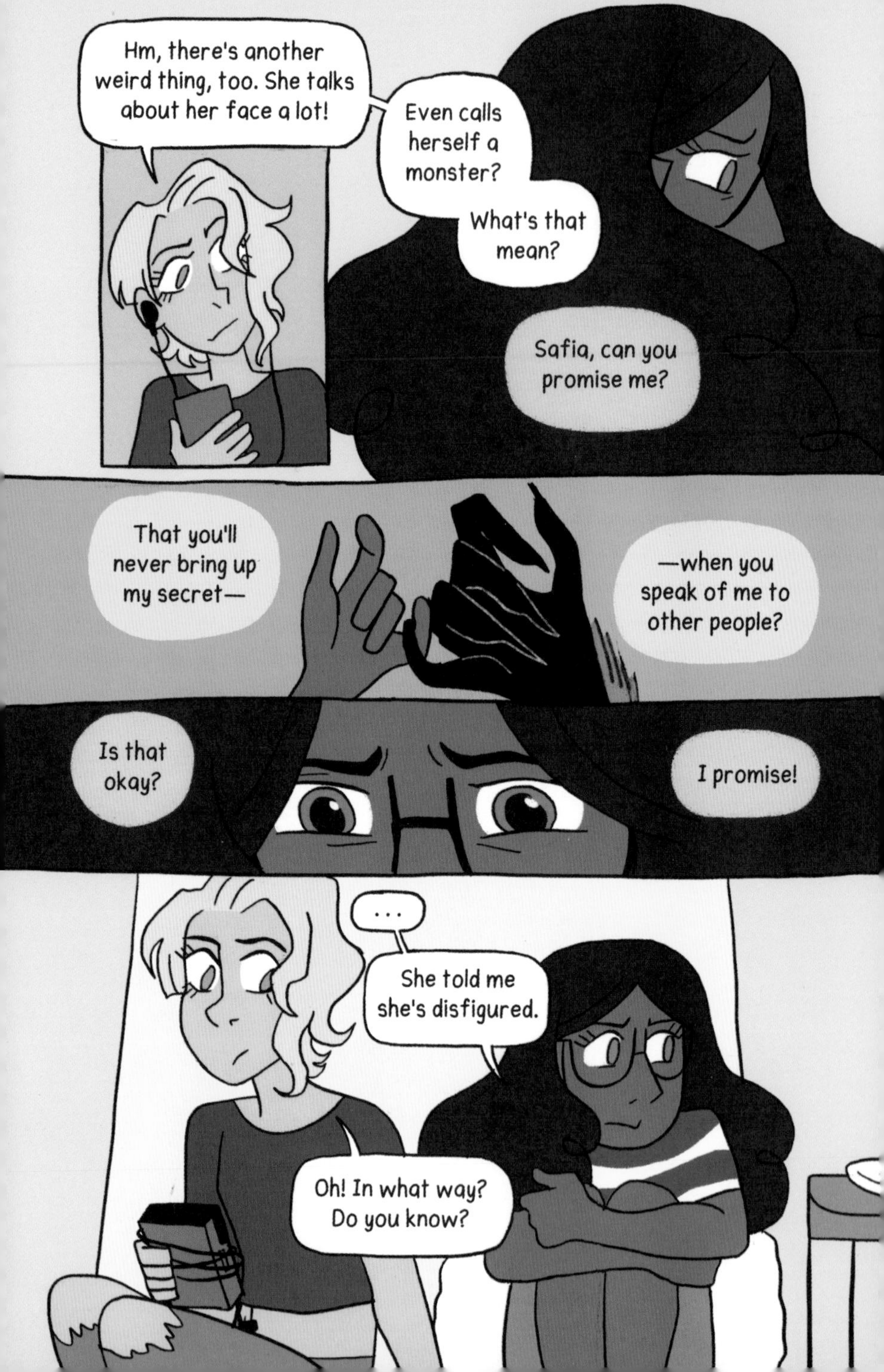
Hm, there's another weird thing, too. She talks about her face a lot!
Even calls herself a monster?
What's that mean?
Safia, can you promise me?
That you'll never bring up my secret—
—when you speak of me to other people?
Is that okay?
I promise!
...
She told me she's disfigured.
Oh! In what way? Do you know?

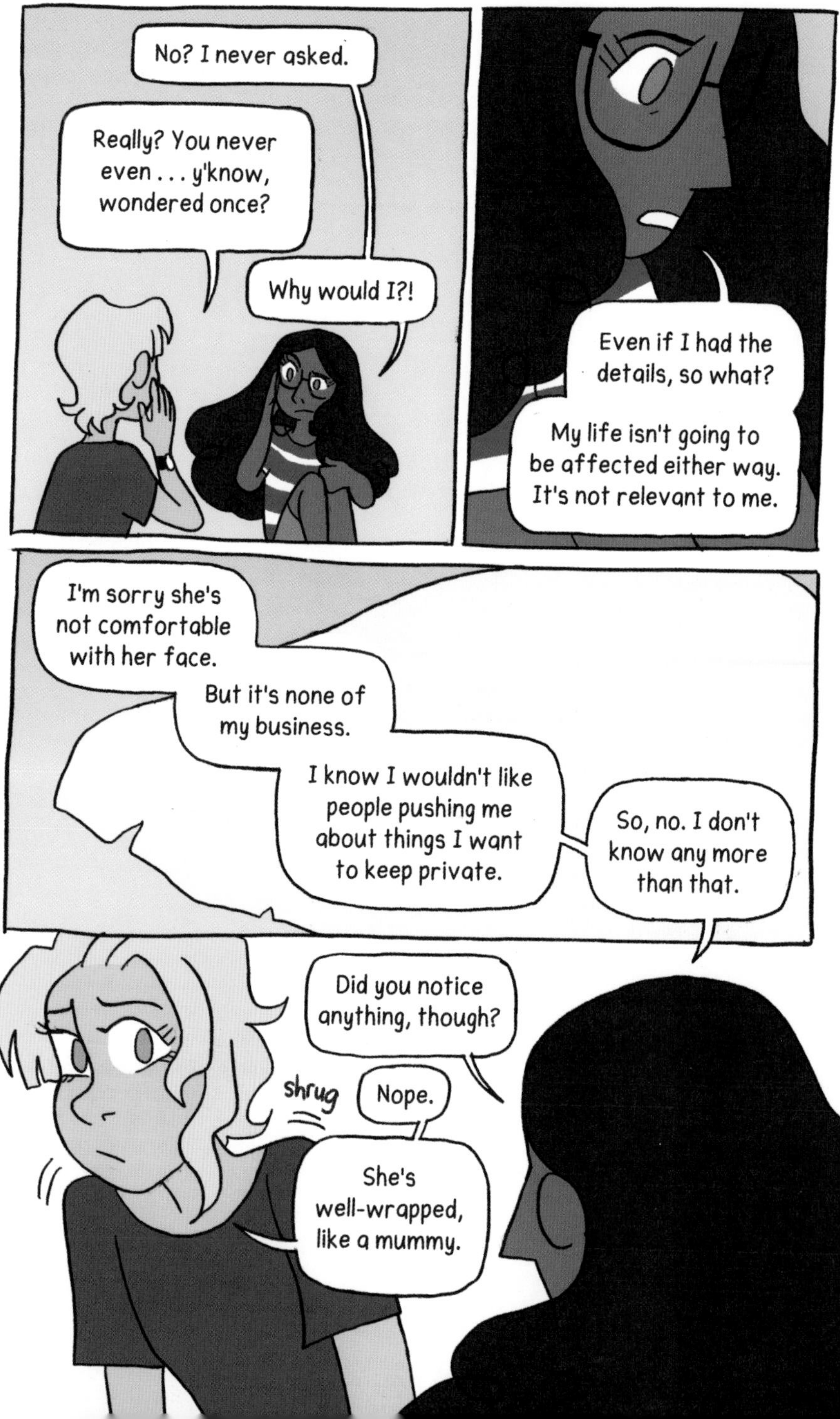
No? I never asked.
Really? You never even . . . y'know, wondered once?
Why would I?!
Even if I had the details, so what?
My life isn't going to be affected either way. It's not relevant to me.
I'm sorry she's not comfortable with her face.
But it's none of my business.
I know I wouldn't like people pushing me about things I want to keep private.
So, no. I don't know any more than that.
Did you notice anything, though?
shrug
Nope.
She's well-wrapped, like a mummy.

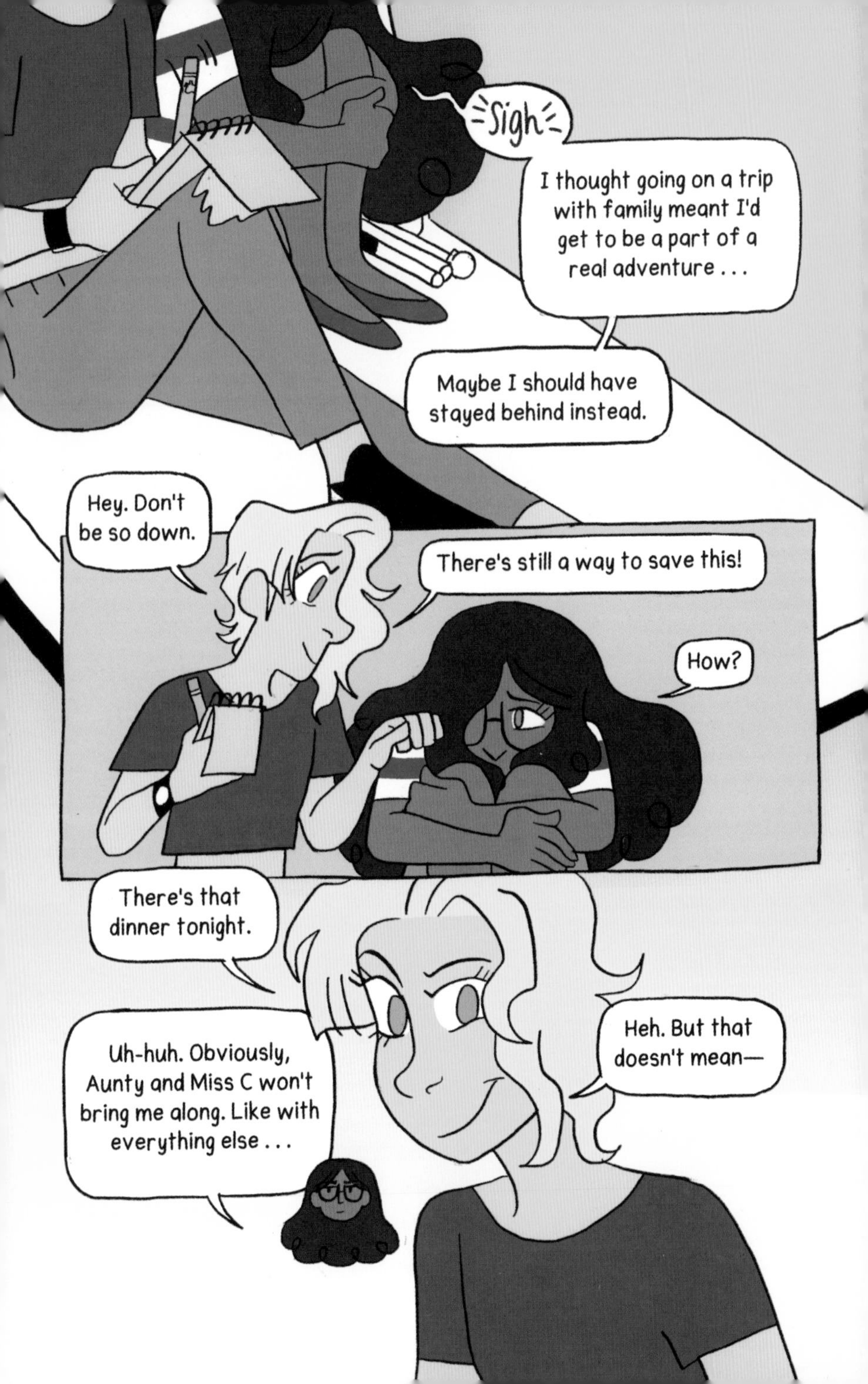
Sigh
I thought going on a trip with family meant I'd get to be a part of a real adventure . . .
Maybe I should have stayed behind instead.
Hey. Don't be so down.
There's still a way to save this!
How?
There's that dinner tonight.
Uh-huh. Obviously, Aunty and Miss C won't bring me along. Like with everything else . . .
Heh. But that doesn't mean—

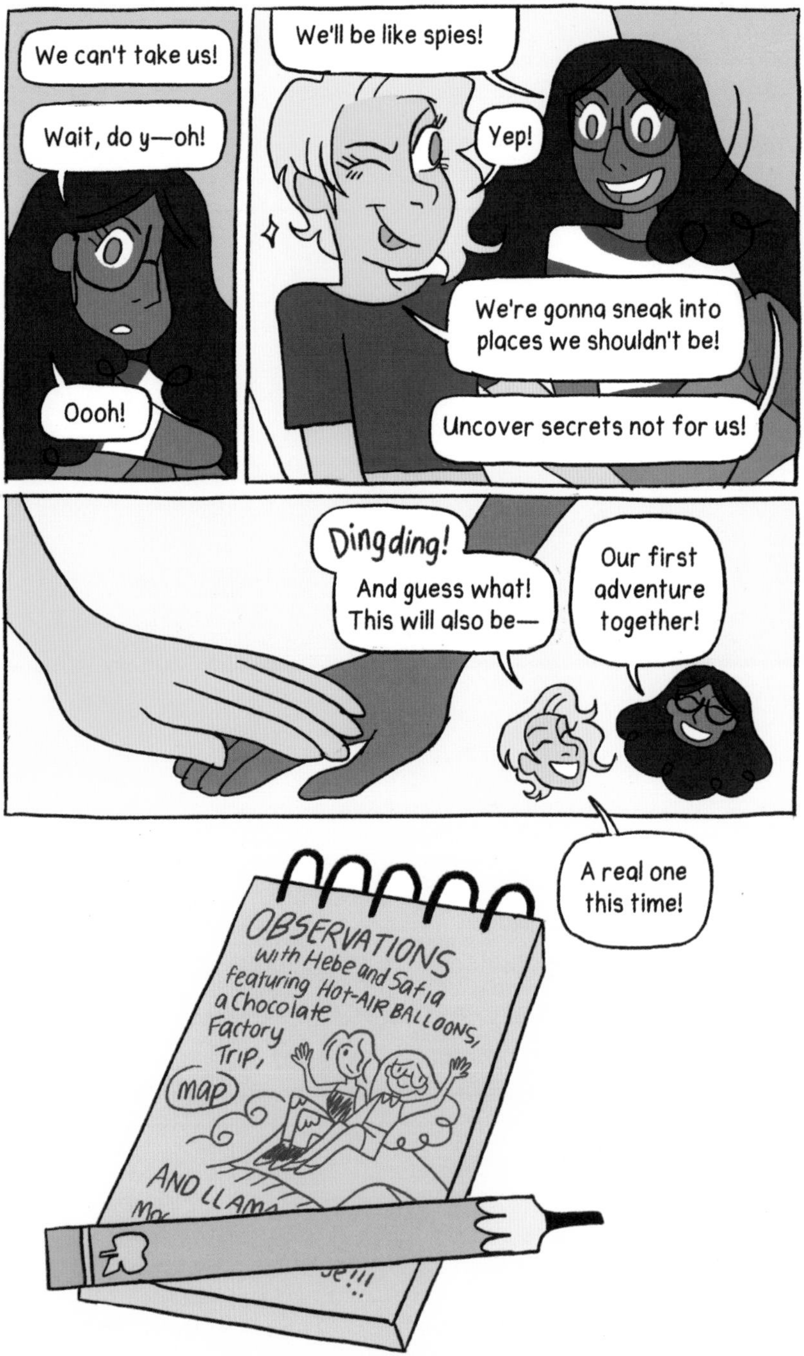
We can't take us!
Wait, do y—oh!
Oooh!
We'll be like spies!
Yep!
We're gonna sneak into places we shouldn't be!
Uncover secrets not for us!
Dingding!
And guess what! This will also be—
Our first adventure together!
A real one this time!
OBSERVATIONS
with Hebe and Safia
featuring HOT-AIR BALLOONS,
a Chocolate Factory Trip,
map

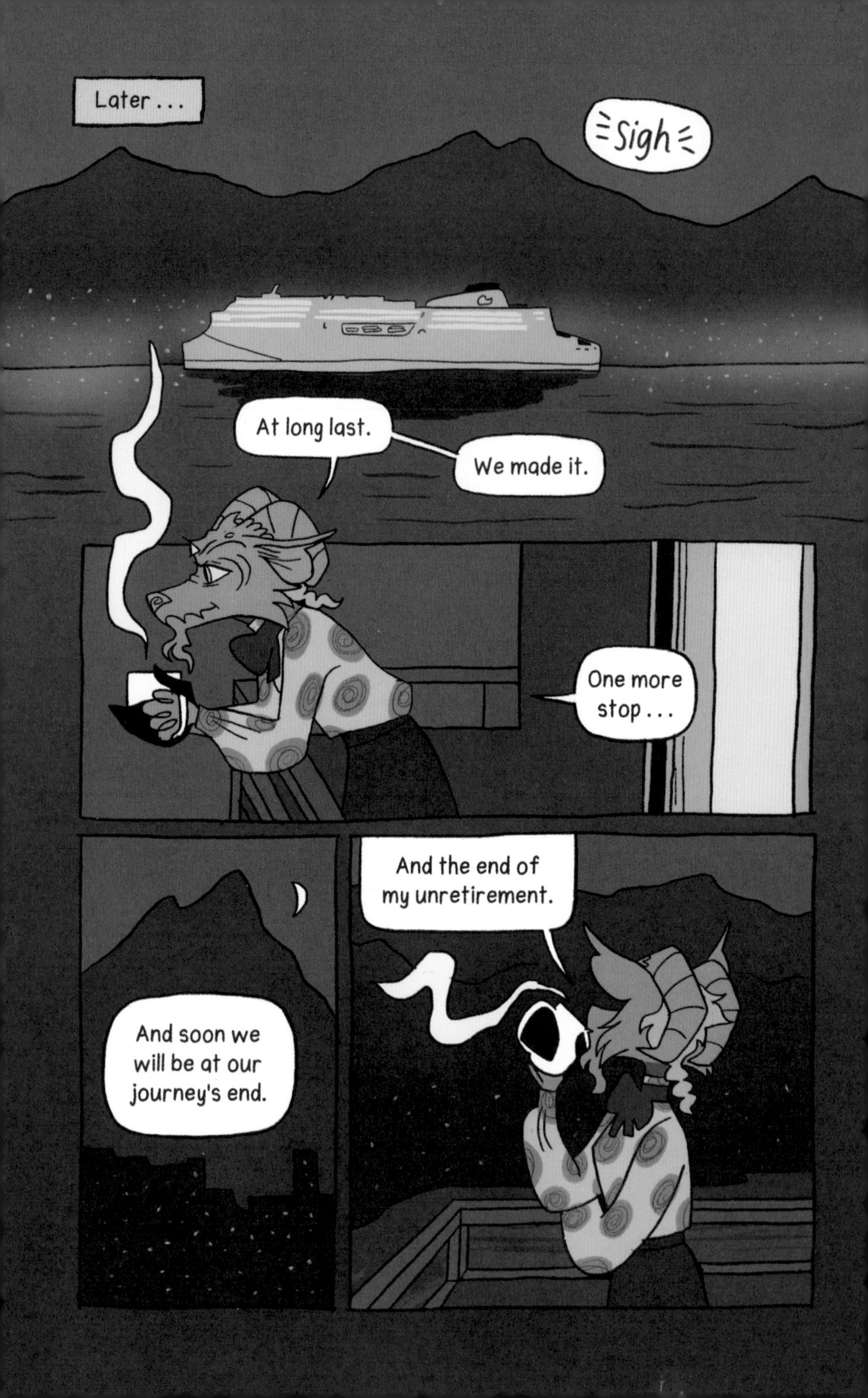
Later . . .
Sigh
At long last.
We made it.
One more stop . . .
And soon we will be at our journey's end.
And the end of my unretirement.

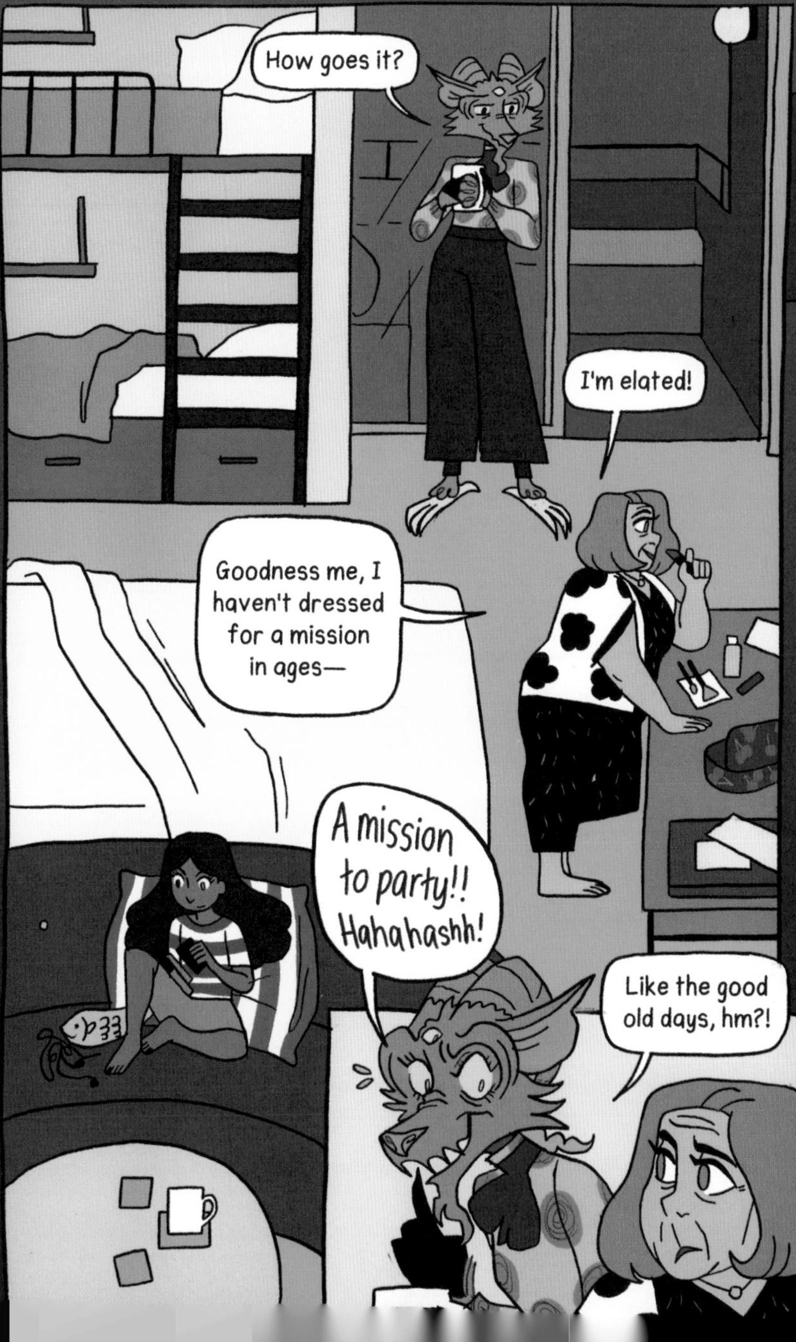
How goes it?
I'm elated!
Goodness me, I haven't dressed for a mission in ages—
A mission to party!! Hahahashh!
Like the good old days, hm?!

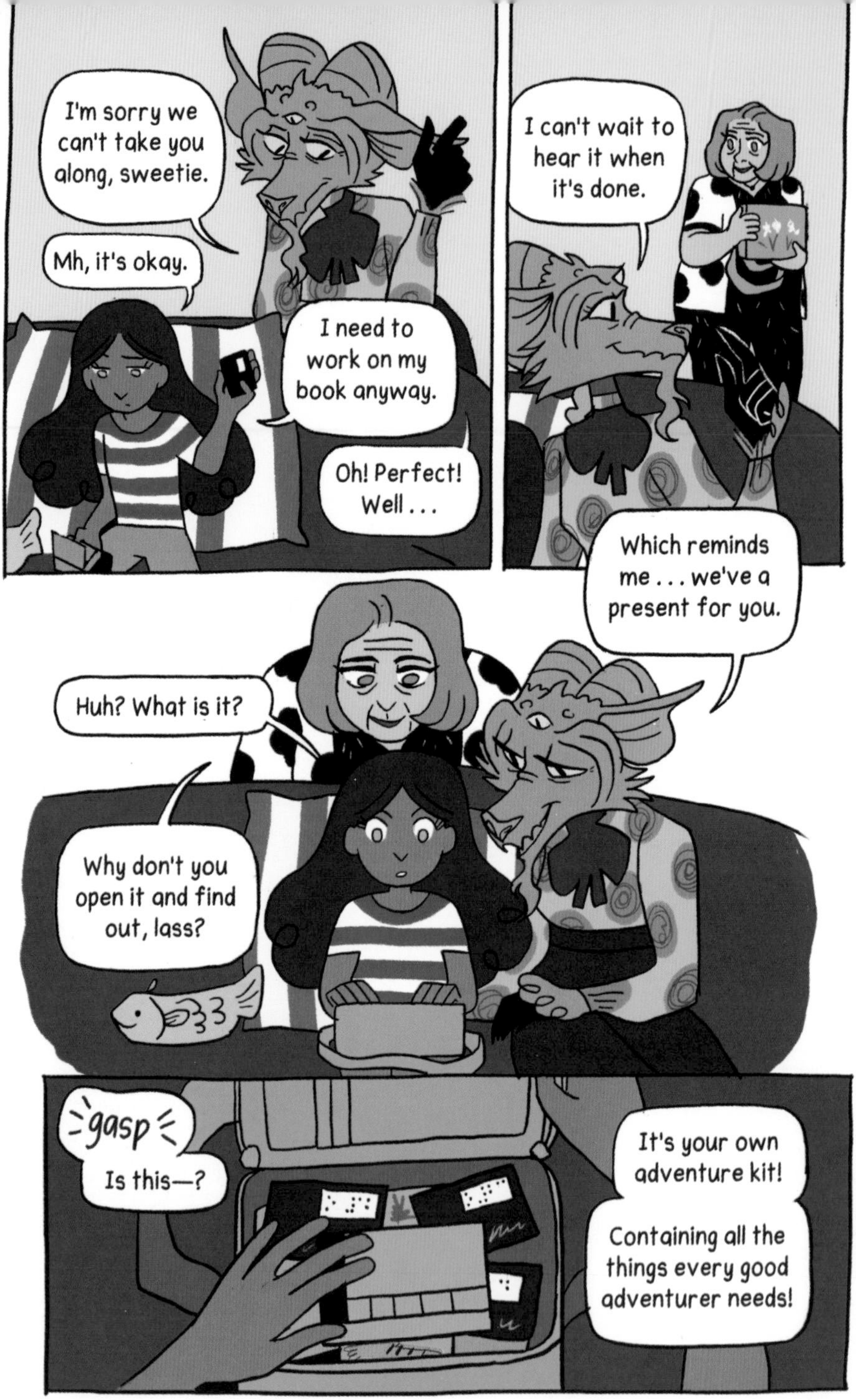
I'm sorry we can't take you along, sweetie.
Mh, it's okay.
I need to work on my book anyway.
Oh! Perfect! Well . . .
I can't wait to hear it when it's done.
Which reminds me . . . we've a present for you.
Huh? What is it?
Why don't you open it and find out, lass?
gasp
Is this—?
It's your own adventure kit!
Containing all the things every good adventurer needs!

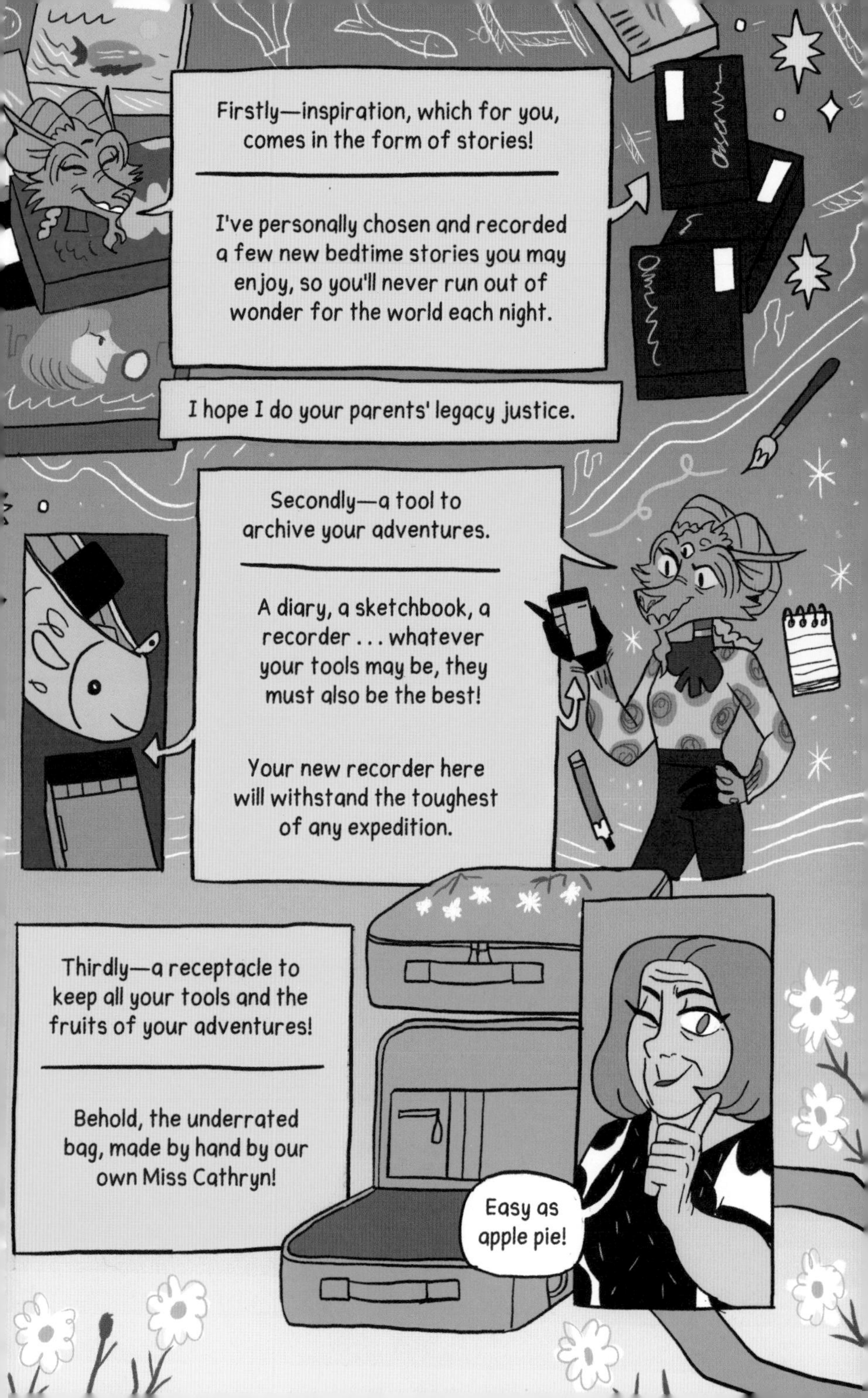
Firstly—inspiration, which for you, comes in the form of stories!
I've personally chosen and recorded a few new bedtime stories you may enjoy, so you'll never run out of wonder for the world each night.
I hope I do your parents' legacy justice.
Secondly—a tool to archive your adventures.
A diary, a sketchbook, a recorder . . . whatever your tools may be, they must also be the best!
Your new recorder here will withstand the toughest of any expedition.
Thirdly—a receptacle to keep all your tools and the fruits of your adventures!
Behold, the underrated bag, made by hand by our own Miss Cathryn!
Easy as apple pie!

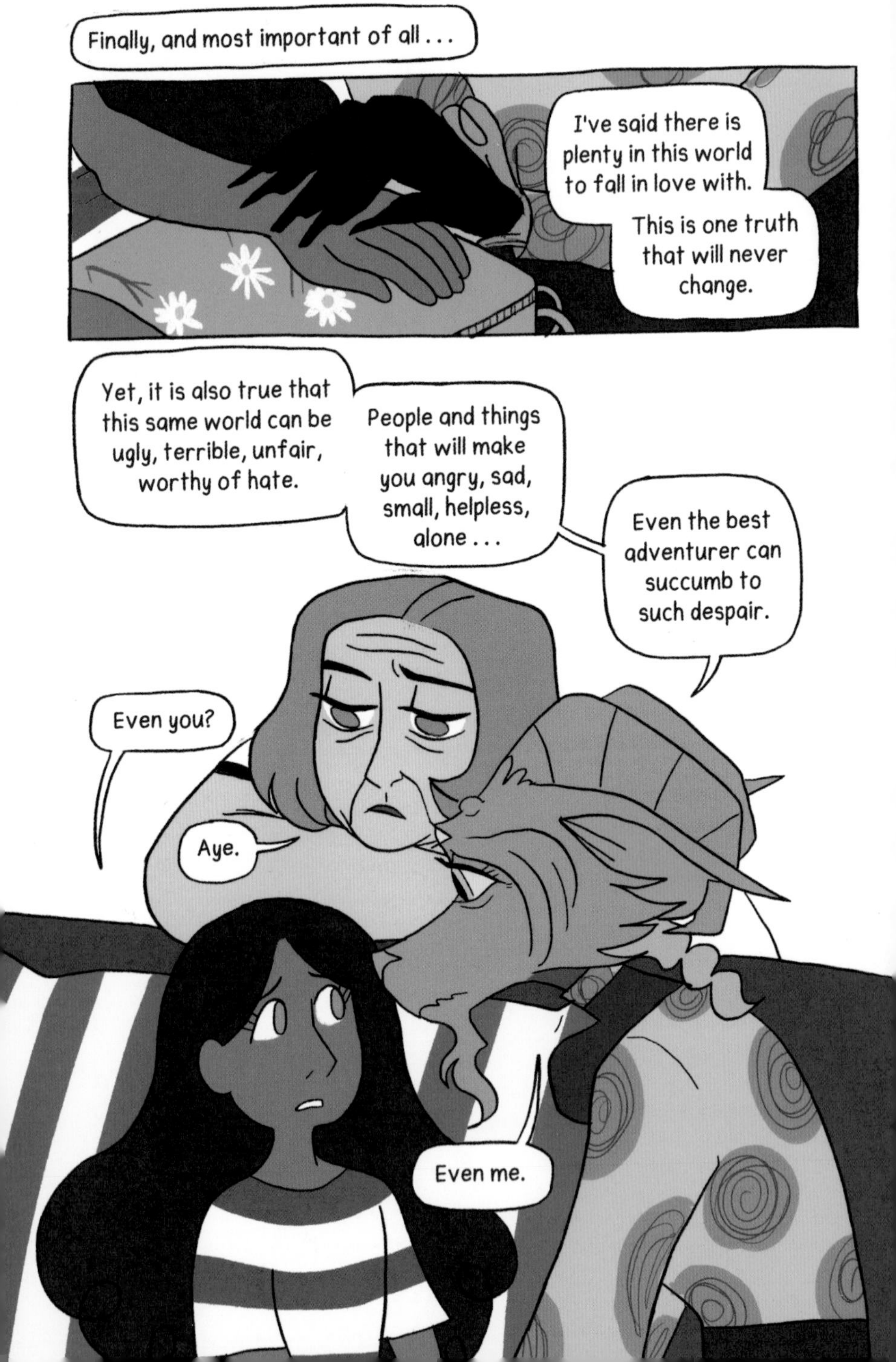
Finally, and most important of all . . .
I've said there is plenty in this world to fall in love with.
This is one truth that will never change.
Yet, it is also true that this same world can be ugly, terrible, unfair, worthy of hate.
People and things that will make you angry, sad, small, helpless, alone . . .
Even the best adventurer can succumb to such despair.
Even you?
Aye.
Even me.

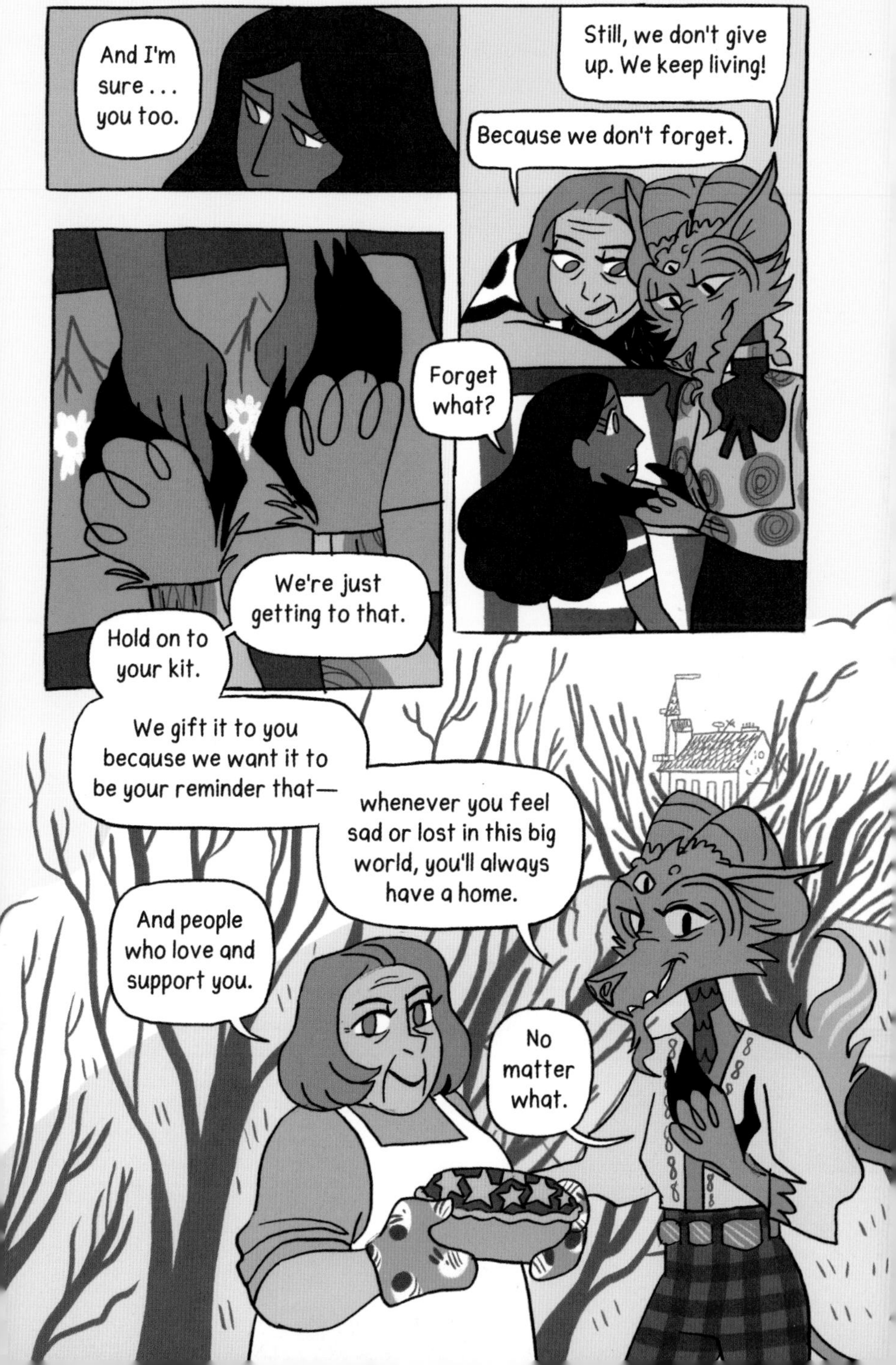
And I'm sure . . . you too.
Still, we don't give up. We keep living!
Because we don't forget.
Forget what?
We're just getting to that.
Hold on to your kit.
We gift it to you because we want it to be your reminder that—
whenever you feel sad or lost in this big world, you'll always have a home.
And people who love and support you.
No matter what.

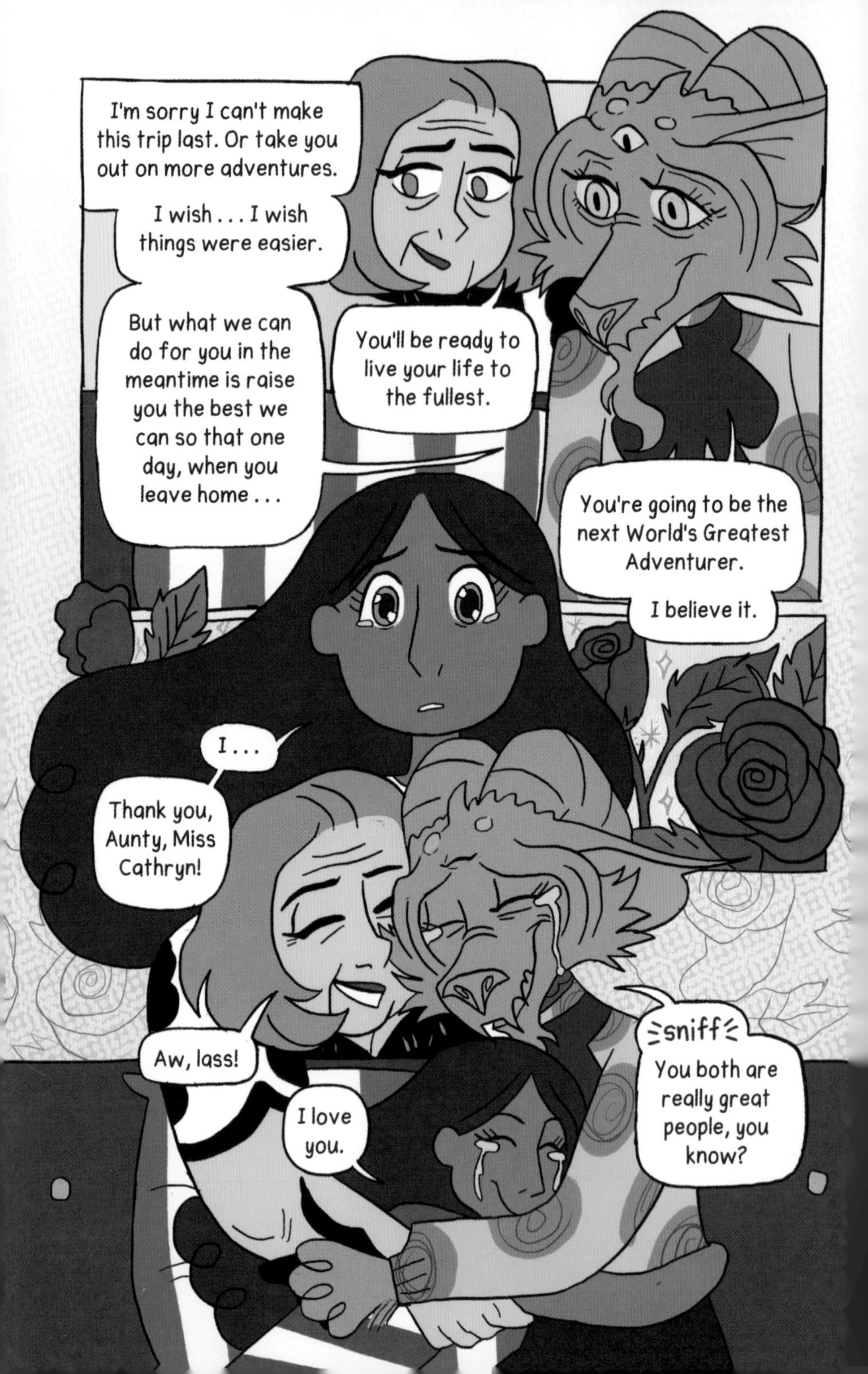
I'm sorry I can't make this trip last. Or take you out on more adventures.
I wish . . . I wish things were easier.
But what we can do for you in the meantime is raise you the best we can so that one day, when you leave home . . .
You'll be ready to live your life to the fullest.
You're going to be the next World's Greatest Adventurer.
I believe it.
I . . .
Thank you, Aunty, Miss Cathryn!
Aw, lass!
I love you.
sniff
You both are really great people, you know?

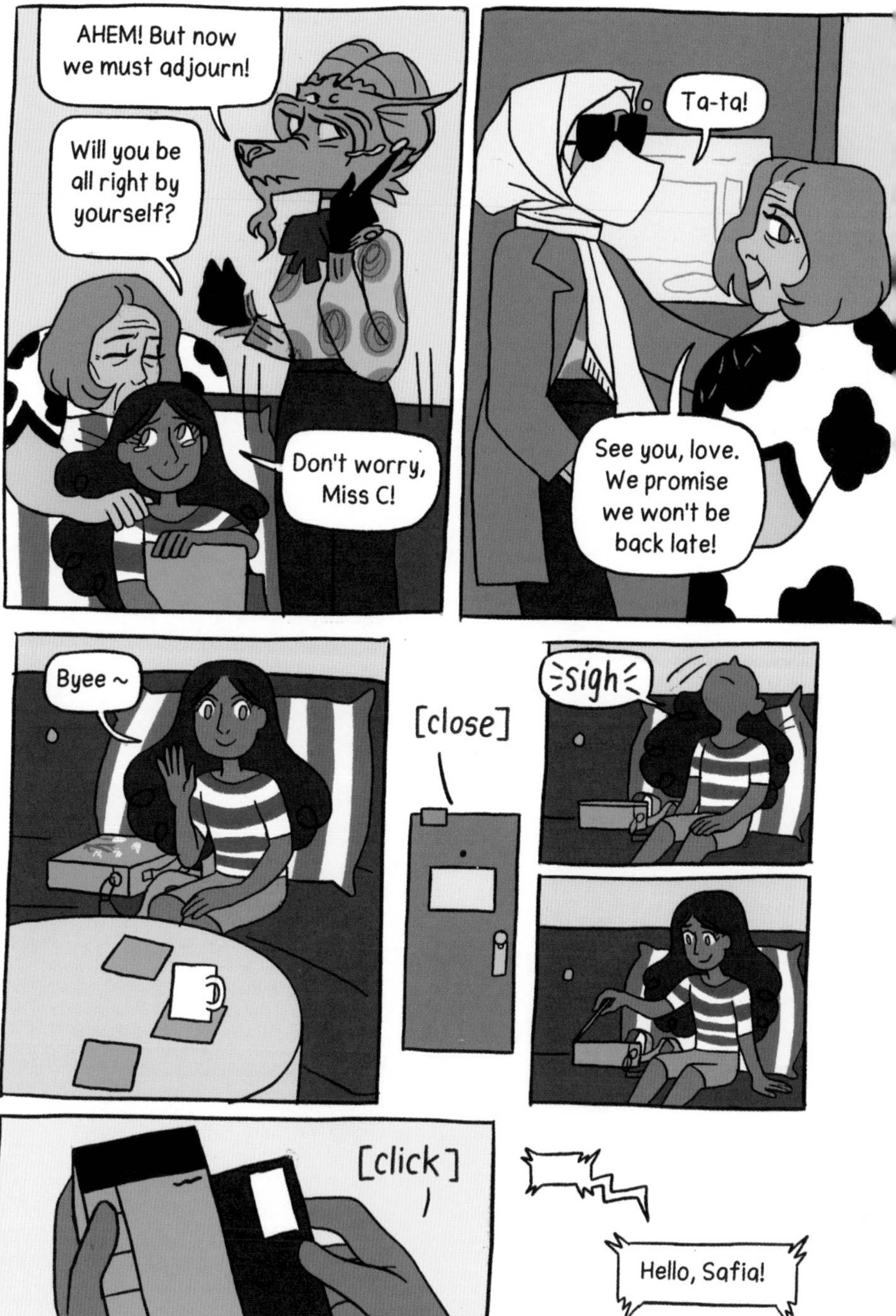
AHEM! But now we must adjourn!
Will you be all right by yourself?
Don't worry, Miss C!
Ta-ta!
See you, love. We promise we won't be back late!
Byee ~
[close]
sigh
[click]
Hello, Safia!

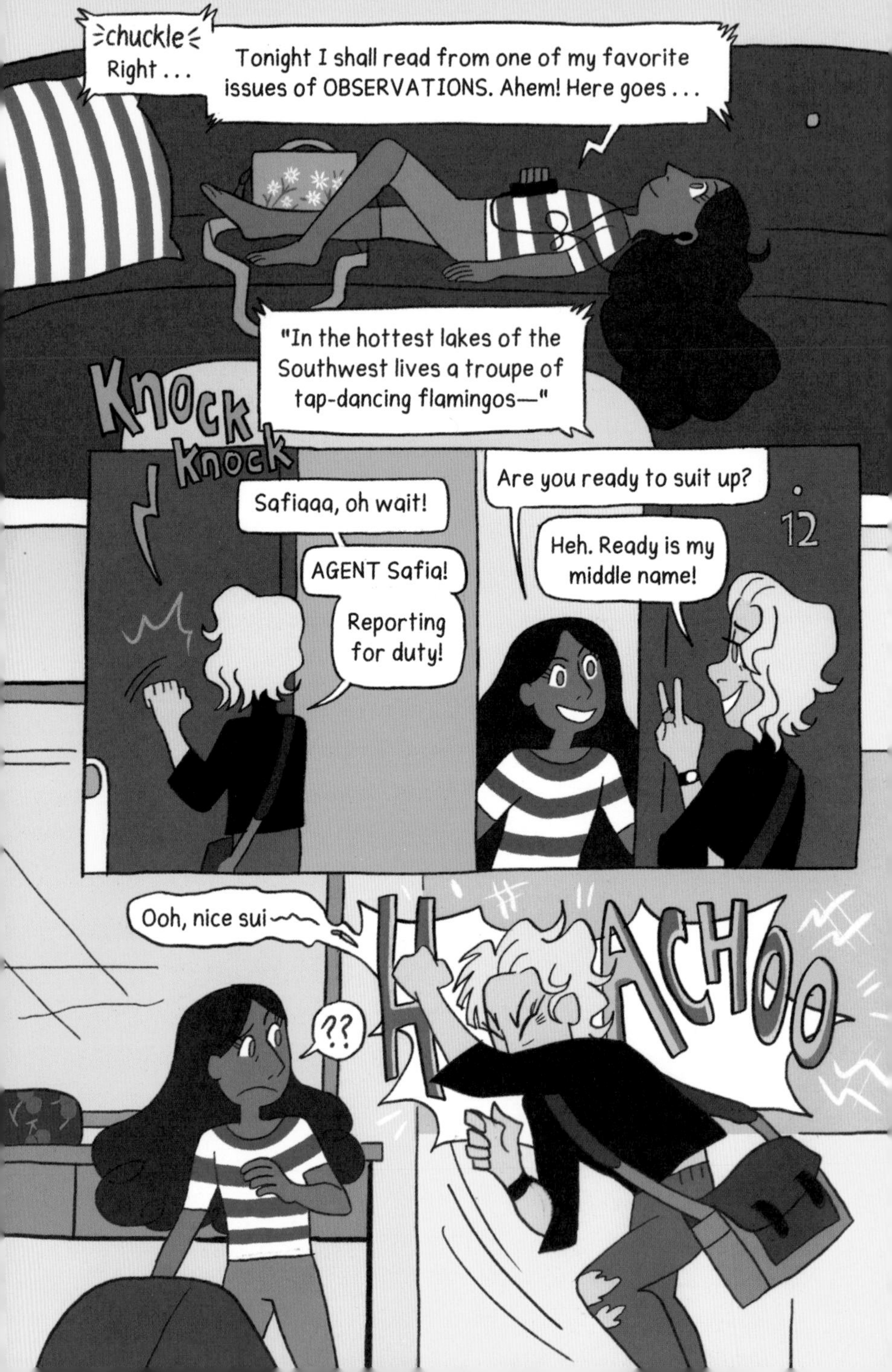

chuckle
Right . . .
Tonight I shall read from one of my favorite issues of OBSERVATIONS. Ahem! Here goes . . .
"In the hottest lakes of the Southwest lives a troupe of tap-dancing flamingos—"
KNOCK
knock
Safiaaa, oh wait!
AGENT Safia!
Reporting for duty!
Are you ready to suit up?
Heh. Ready is my middle name!
12
Ooh, nice sui~
??
HACHOO

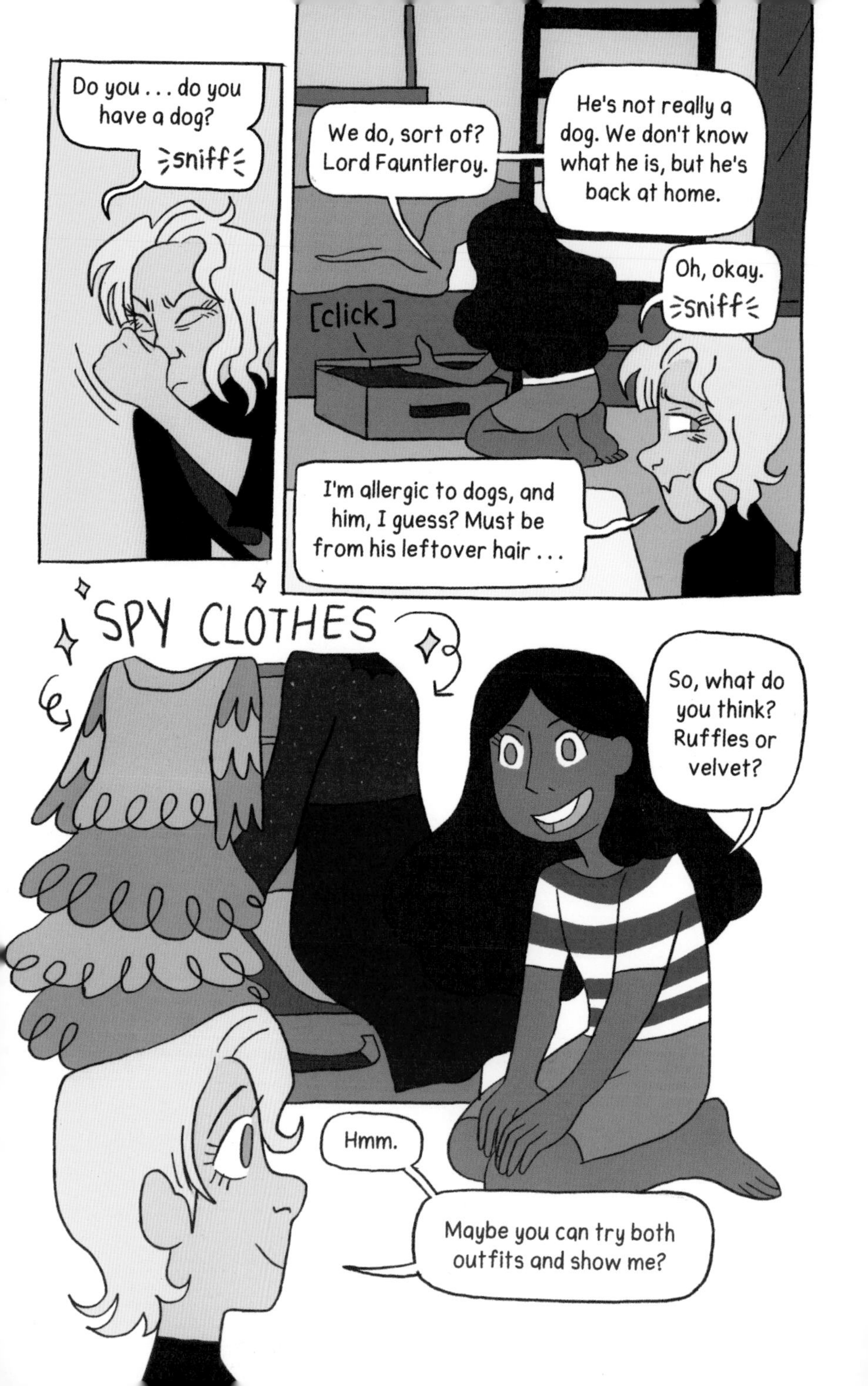
Do you . . . do you have a dog?
sniff
We do, sort of? Lord Fauntleroy.
He's not really a dog. We don't know what he is, but he's back at home.
[click]
Oh, okay.
sniff
I'm allergic to dogs, and him, I guess? Must be from his leftover hair . . .
SPY CLOTHES
So, what do you think? Ruffles or velvet?
Hmm.
Maybe you can try both outfits and show me?

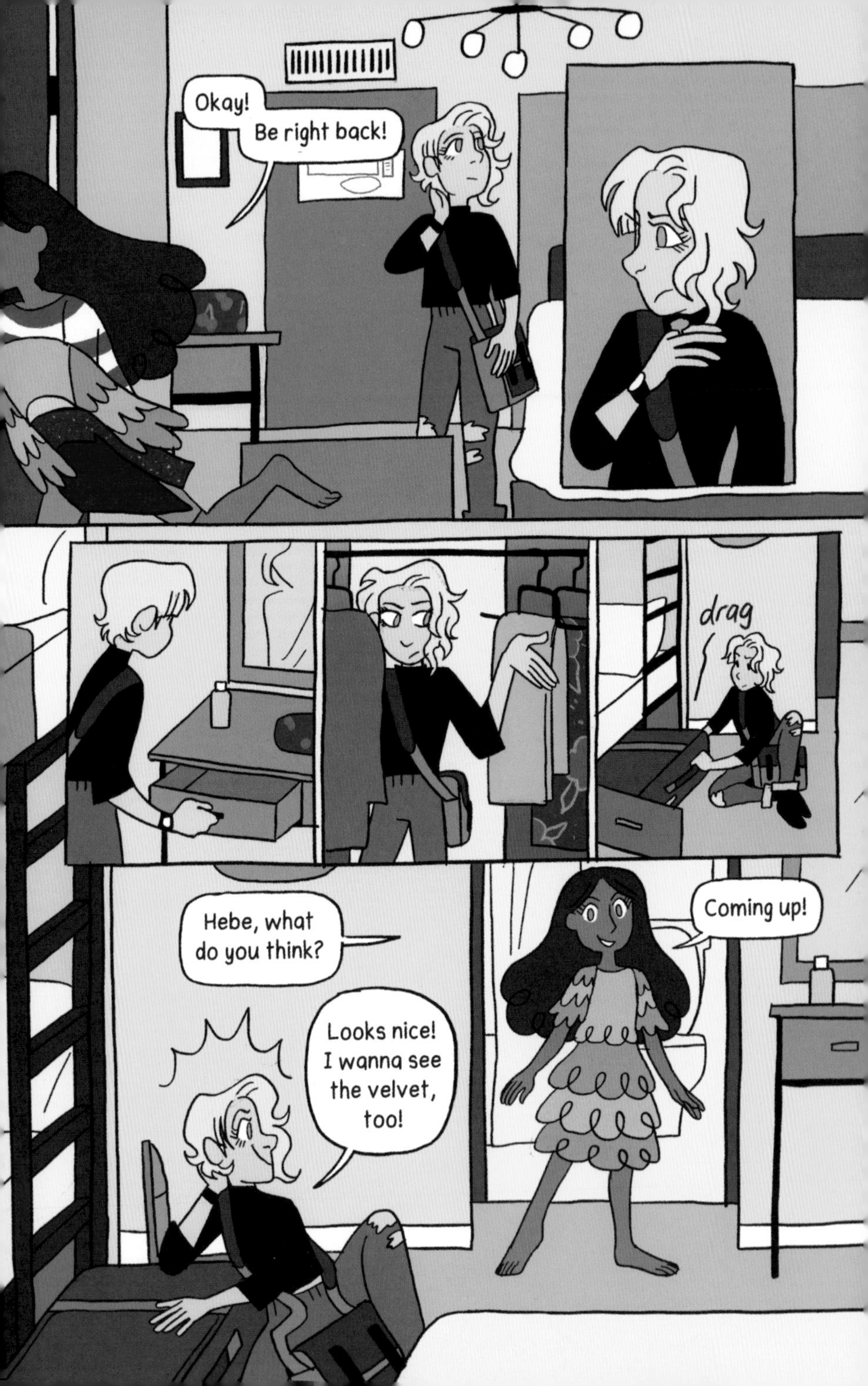
Okay!
Be right back!
drag
Hebe, what do you think?
Looks nice! I wanna see the velvet, too!
Coming up!

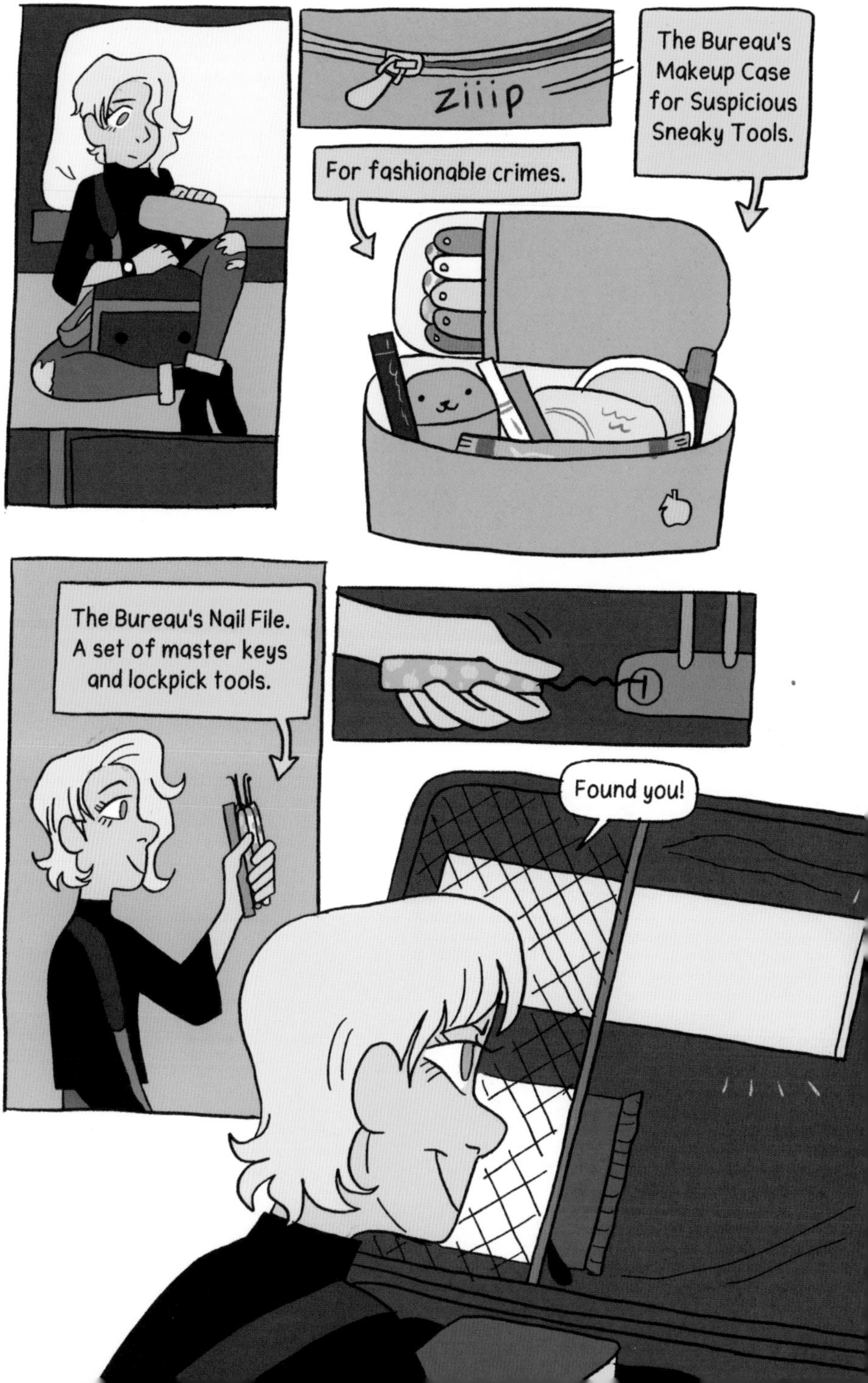
ziiip
The Bureau's Makeup Case for Suspicious Sneaky Tools.
For fashionable crimes.
The Bureau's Nail File. A set of master keys and lockpick tools.
Found you!

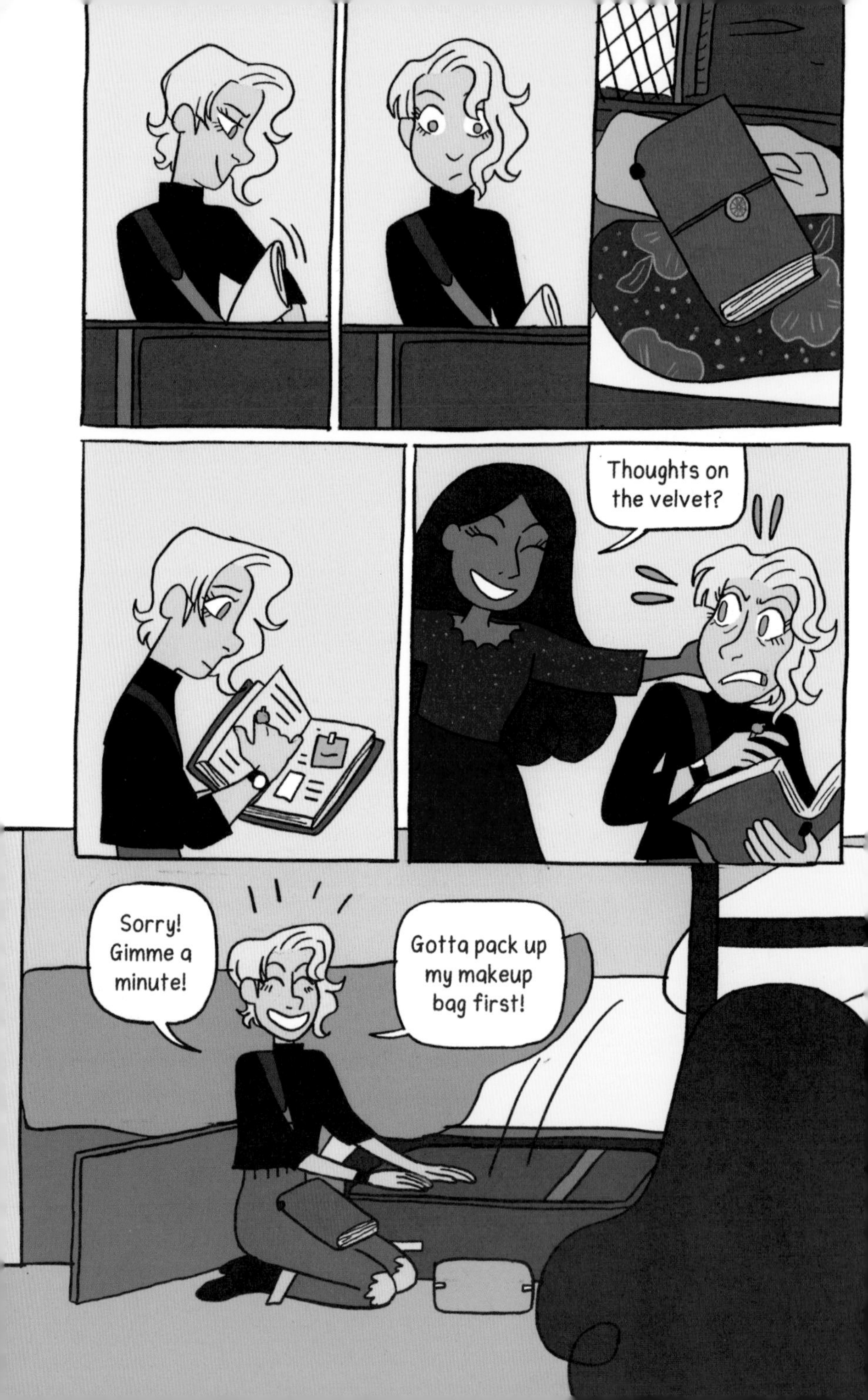
Thoughts on the velvet?
Sorry! Gimme a minute!
Gotta pack up my makeup bag first!

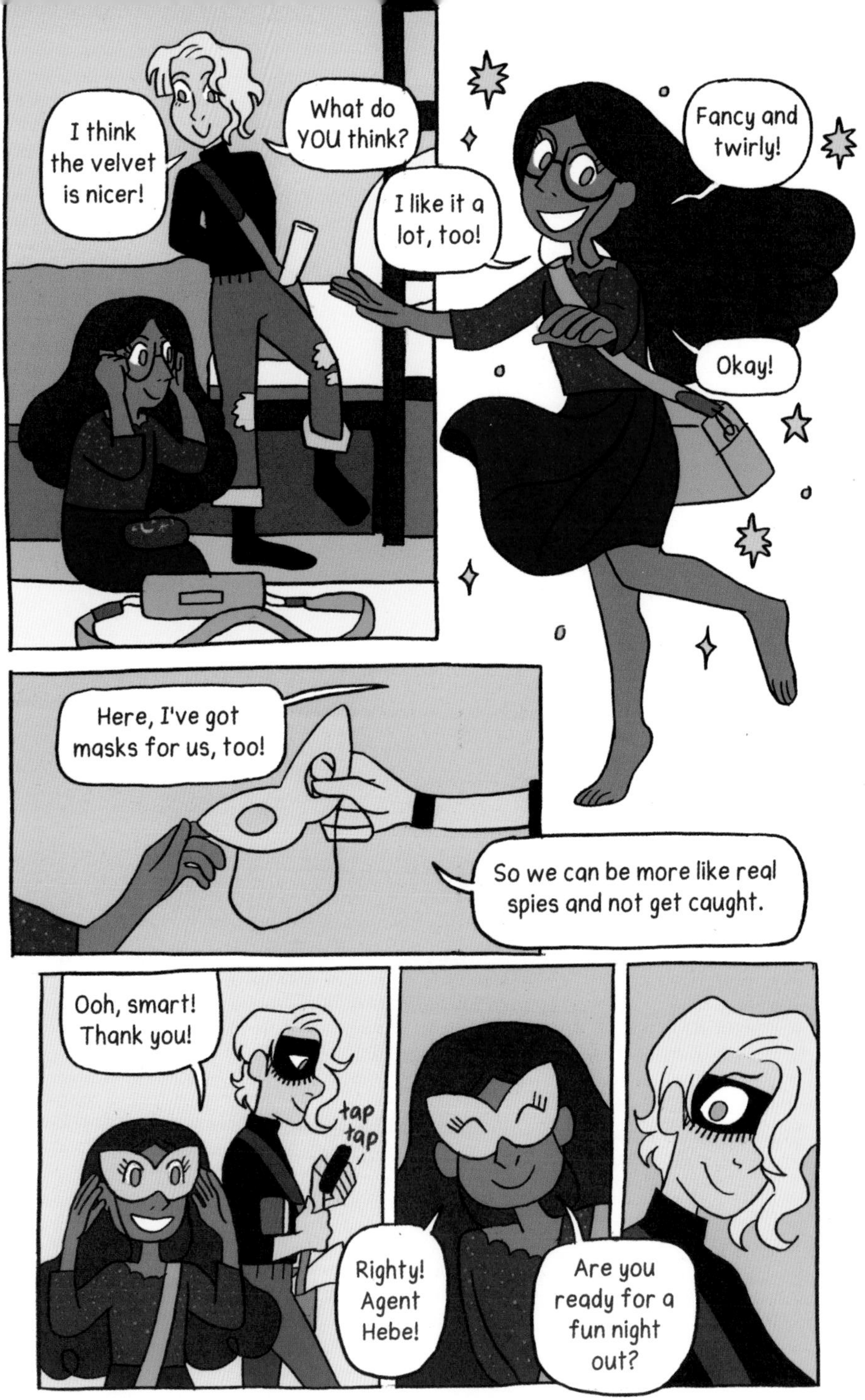
I think the velvet is nicer!
What do YOU think?
I like it a lot, too!
Fancy and twirly!
Okay!
Here, I've got masks for us, too!
So we can be more like real spies and not get caught.
Ooh, smart! Thank you!
tap tap
Righty! Agent Hebe!
Are you ready for a fun night out?

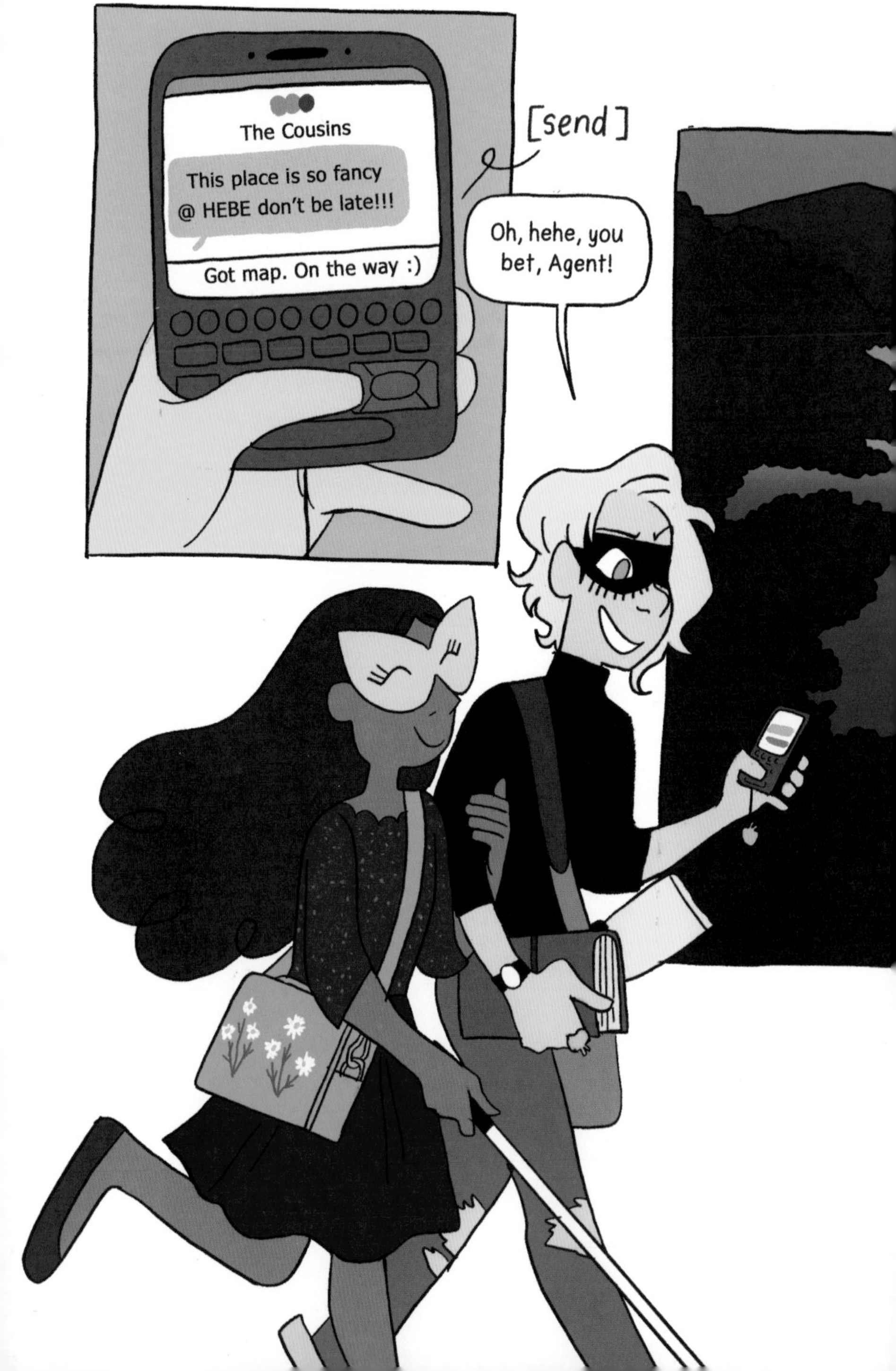
The Cousins
This place is so fancy
@ HEBE don't be late!!!
Got map. On the way :)
[send]
Oh, hehe, you bet, Agent!

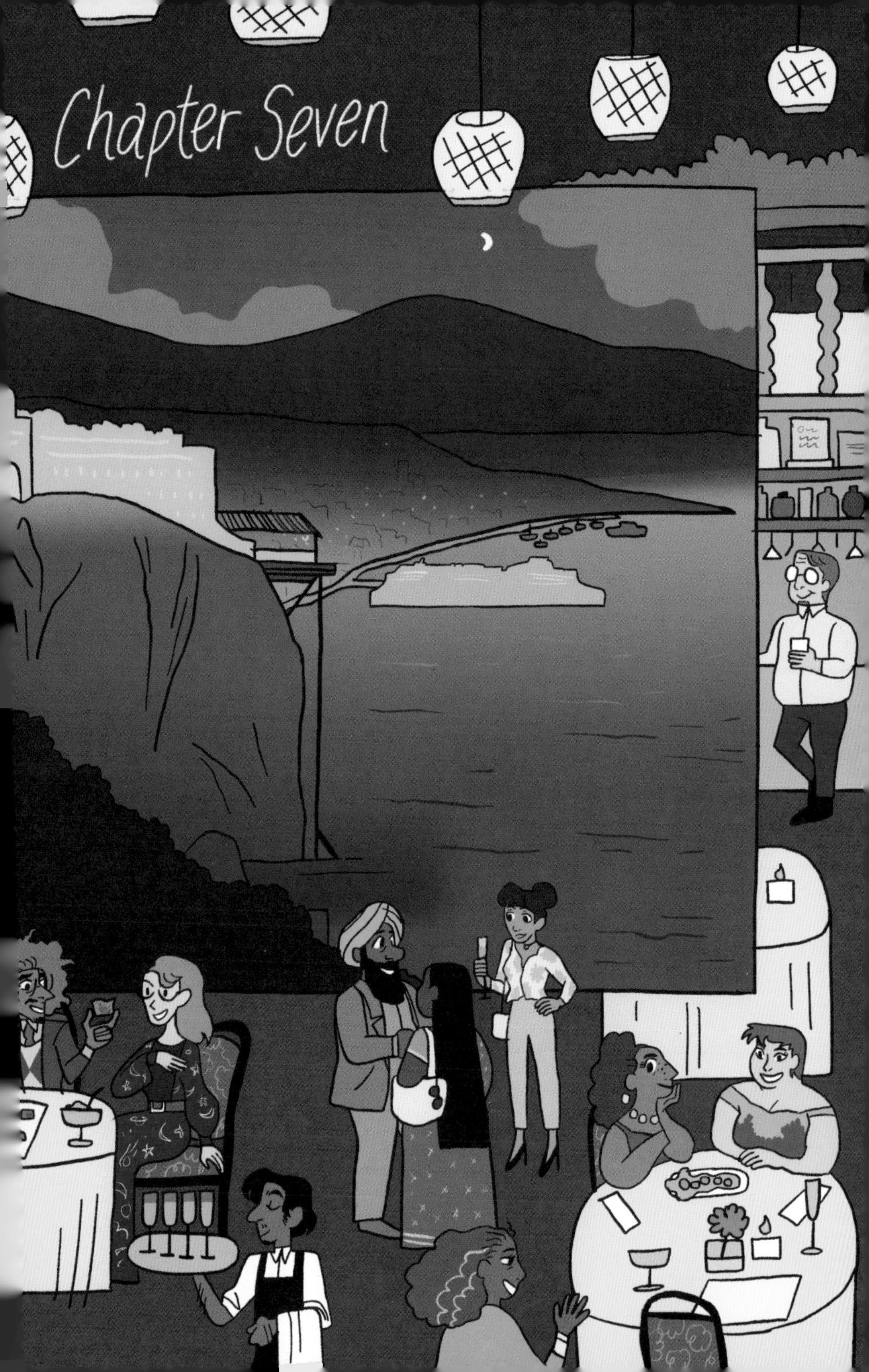
Chapter Seven

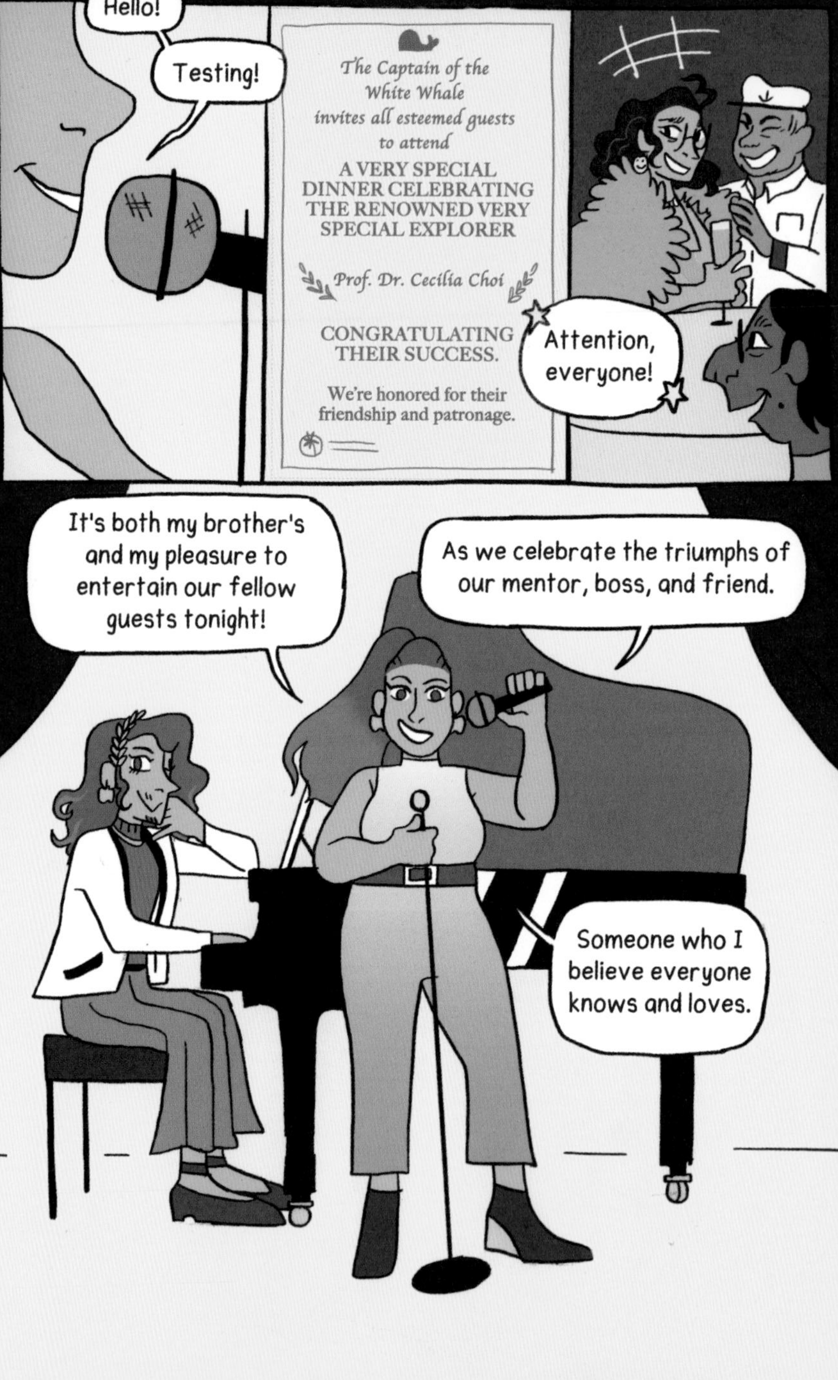
Hello!
Testing!
The Captain of the White Whale invites all esteemed guests to attend
A VERY SPECIAL DINNER CELEBRATING THE RENOWNED VERY SPECIAL EXPLORER
Prof. Dr. Cecilia Choi
CONGRATULATING THEIR SUCCESS.
We're honored for their friendship and patronage.
Attention, everyone!
It's both my brother's and my pleasure to entertain our fellow guests tonight!
As we celebrate the triumphs of our mentor, boss, and friend.
Someone who I believe everyone knows and loves.

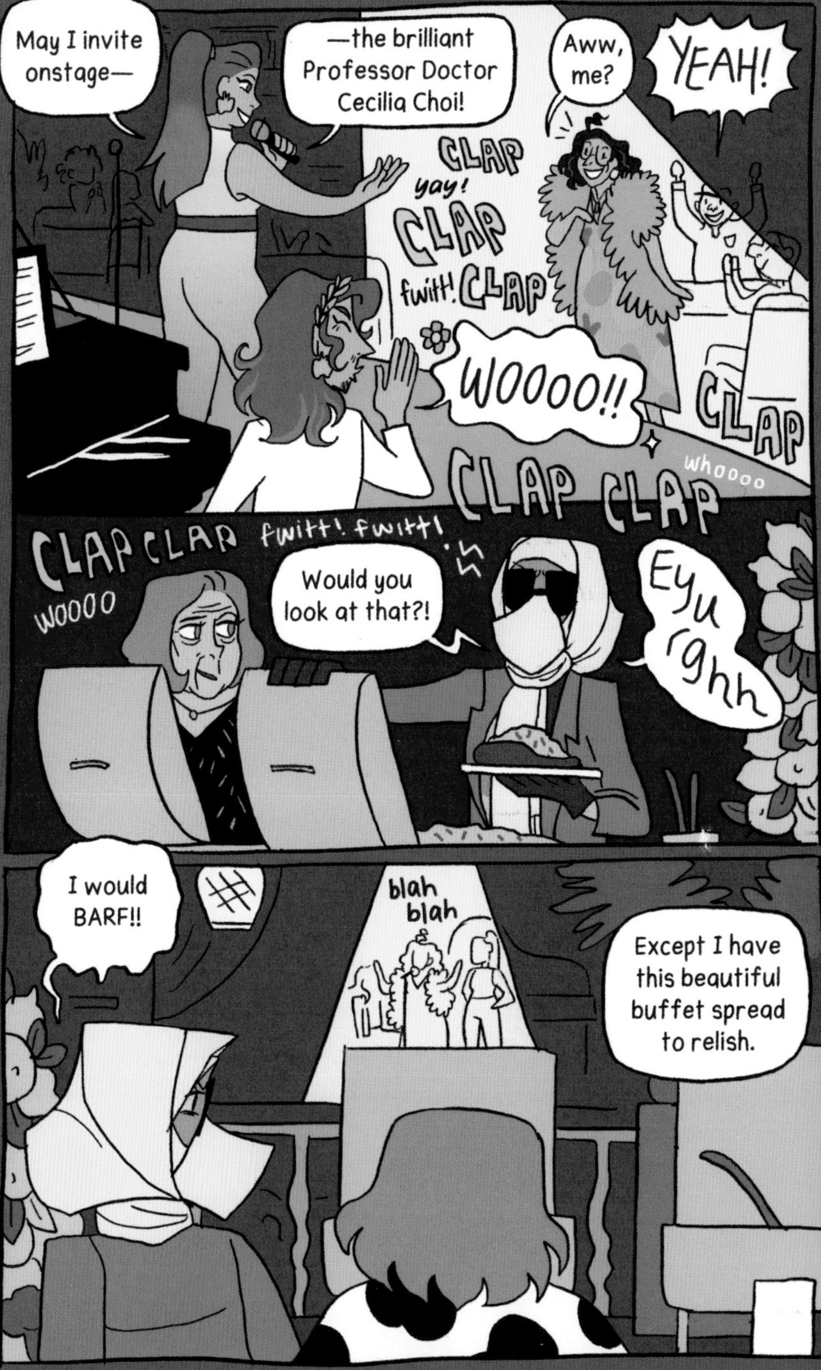
May I invite onstage—
—the brilliant Professor Doctor Cecilia Choi!
Aww, me?
YEAH!
CLAP
yay!
CLAP
fwitt! CLAP
WOOOO!!
CLAP
CLAP CLAP
whoooo
CLAP CLAP fwitt! fwitt!
WOOOO
Would you look at that?!
Eyurghh
I would BARF!!
blah blah
Except I have this beautiful buffet spread to relish.

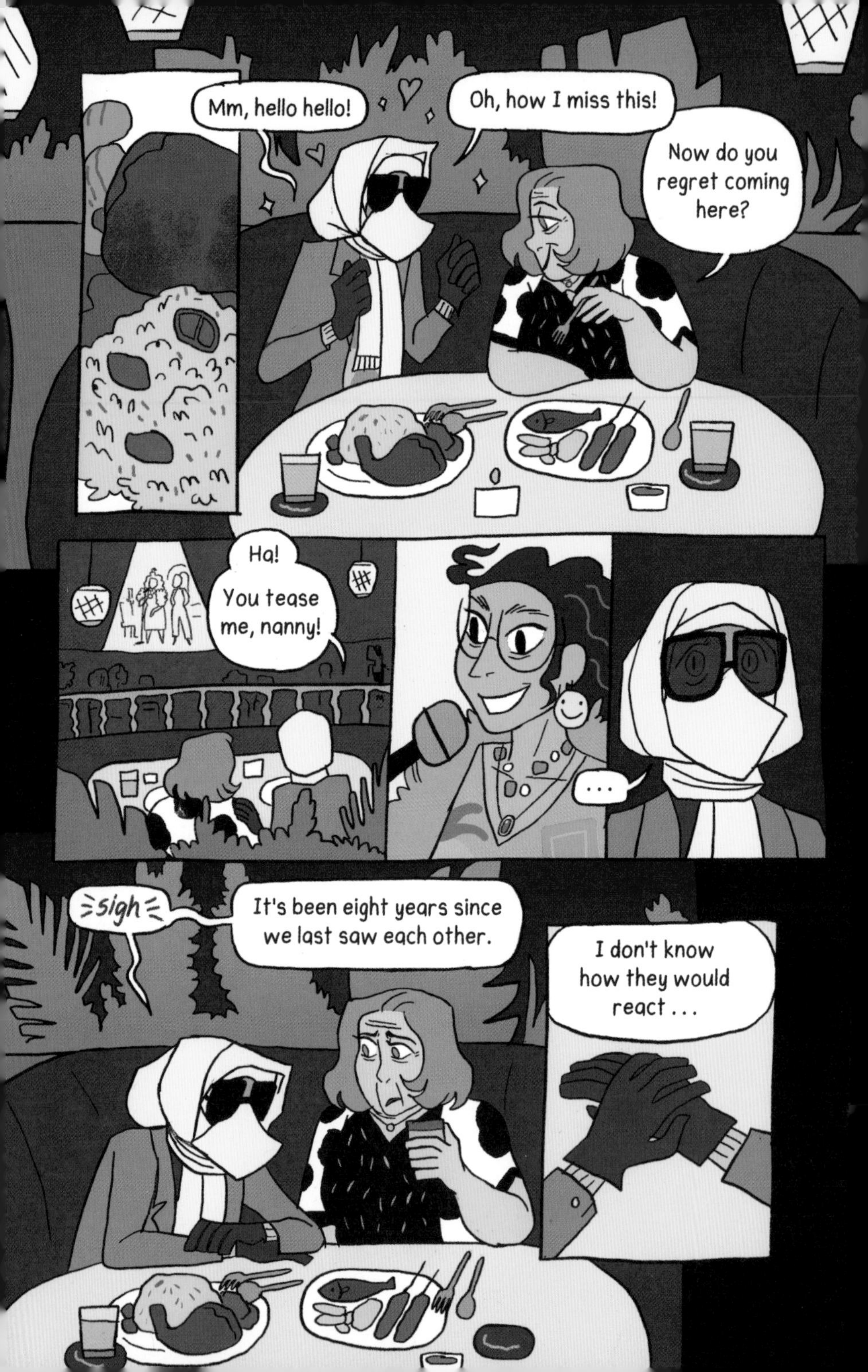

Mm, hello hello!
Oh, how I miss this!
Now do you regret coming here?
Ha!
You tease me, nanny!
...
sigh
It's been eight years since we last saw each other.
I don't know how they would react . . .

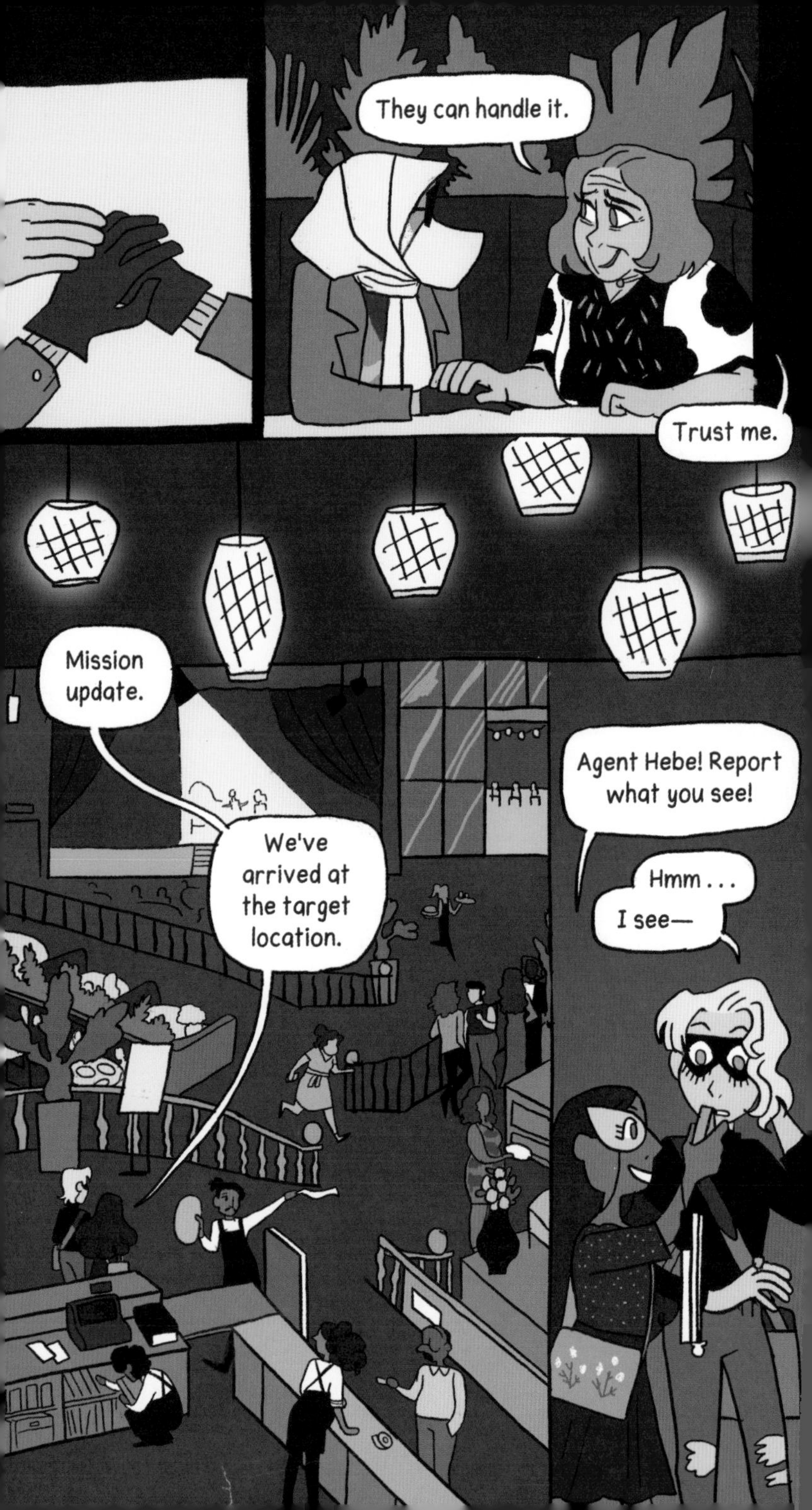
They can handle it.
Trust me.
Mission update.
We've arrived at the target location.
Agent Hebe! Report what you see!
Hmm . . .
I see—

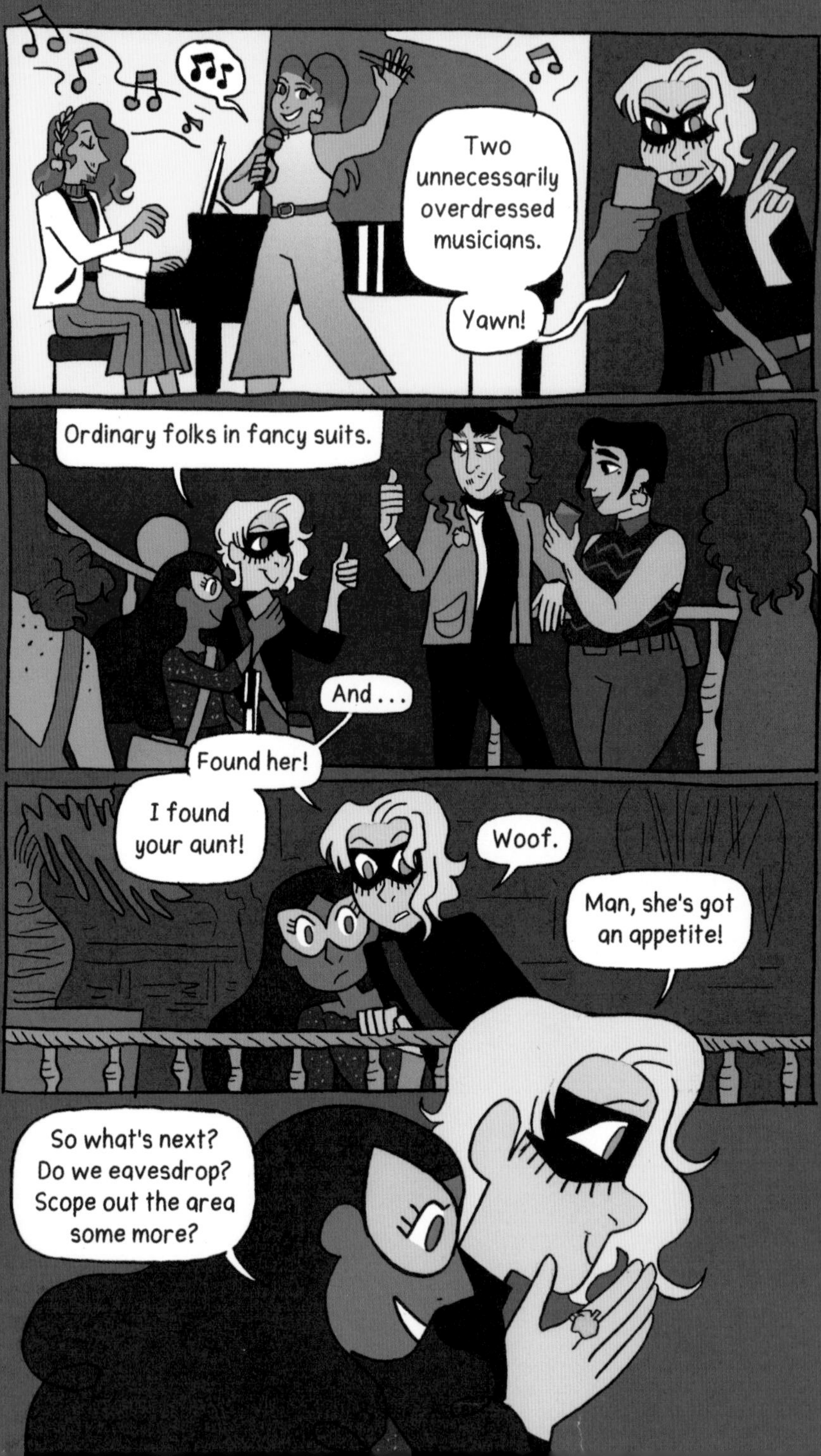
Two unnecessarily overdressed musicians.
Yawn!
Ordinary folks in fancy suits.
And . . .
Found her!
I found your aunt!
Woof.
Man, she's got an appetite!
So what's next? Do we eavesdrop? Scope out the area some more?

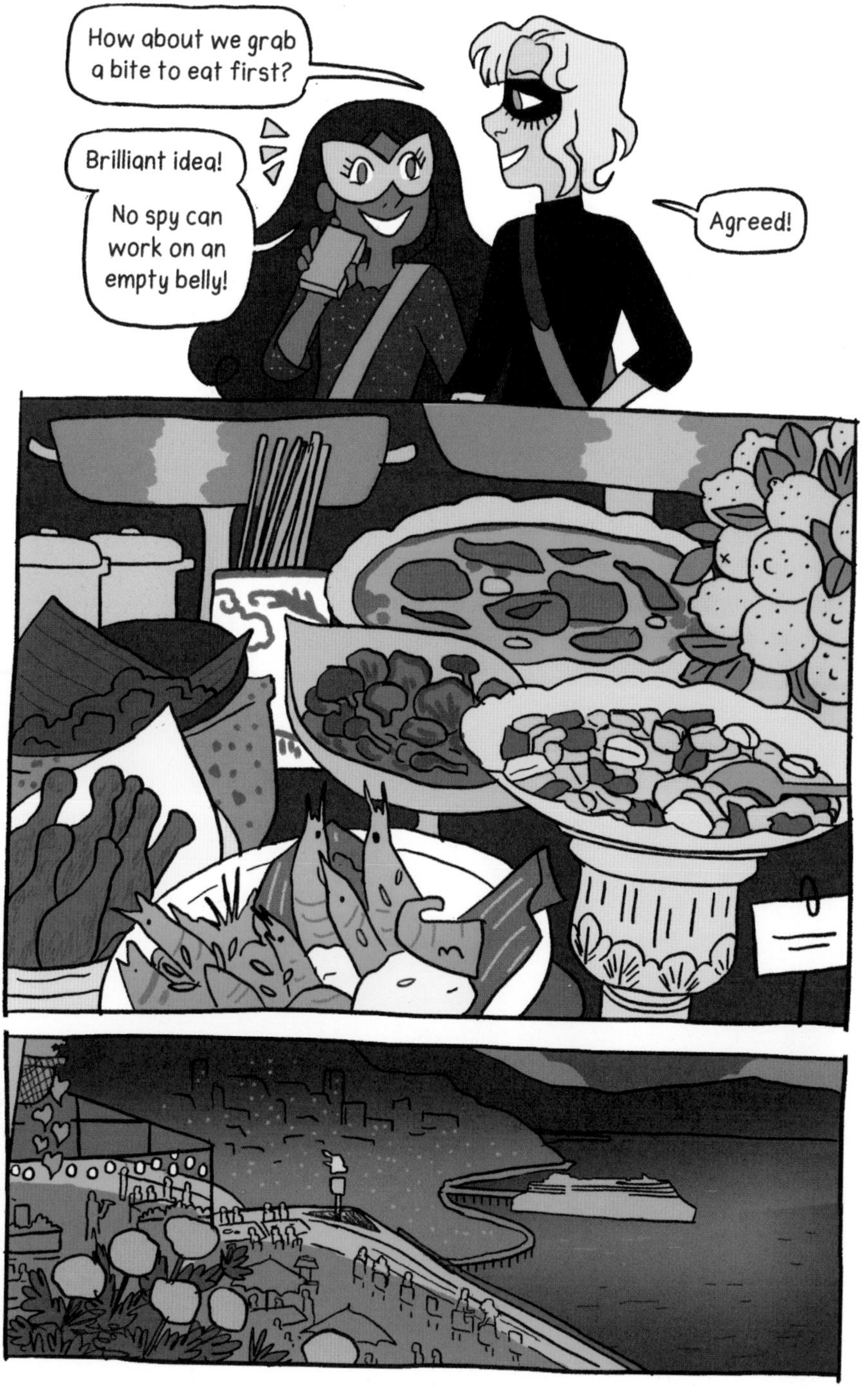
How about we grab a bite to eat first?
Brilliant idea!
No spy can work on an empty belly!
Agreed!

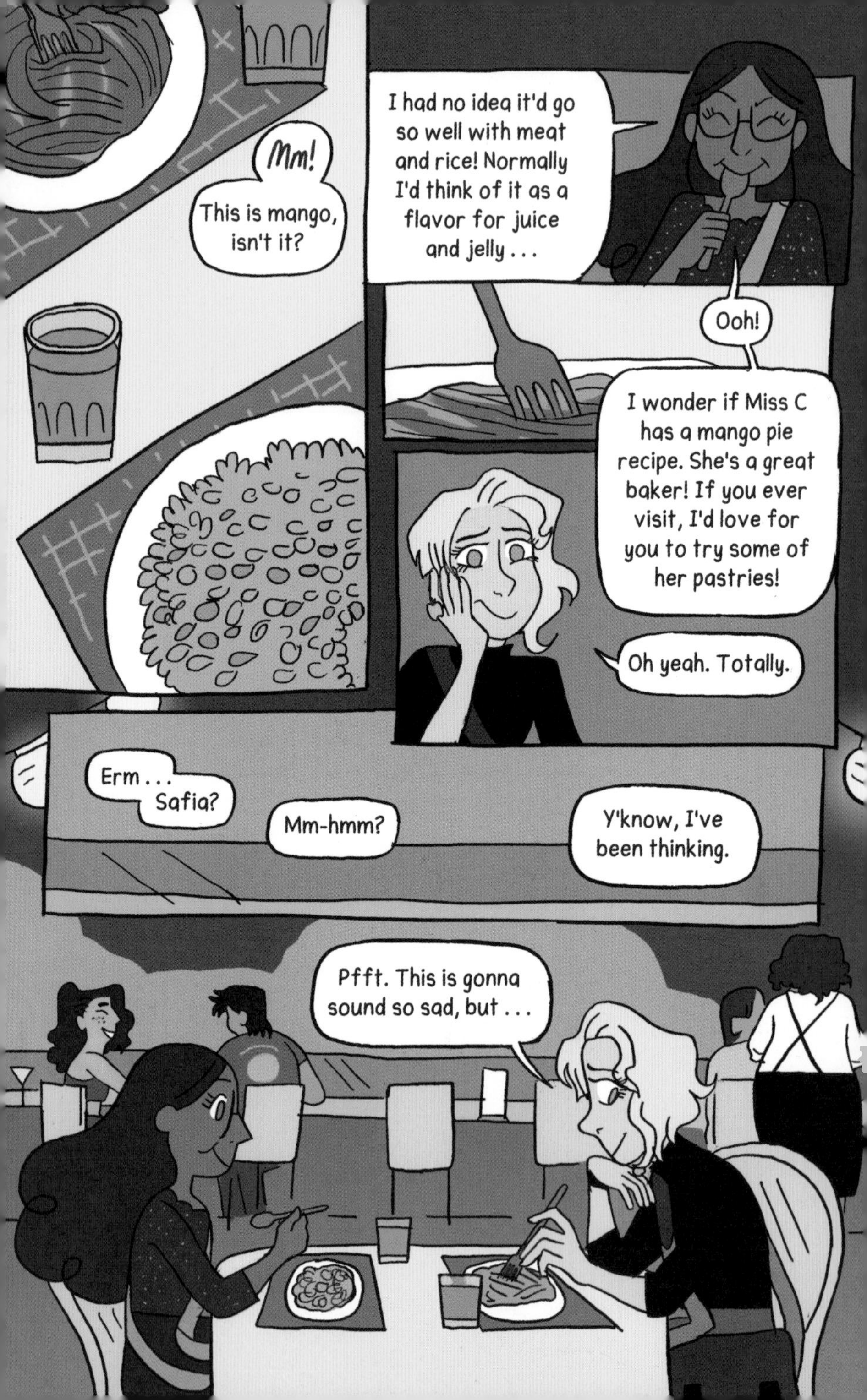
Mm!
This is mango, isn't it?
I had no idea it'd go so well with meat and rice! Normally I'd think of it as a flavor for juice and jelly . . .
Ooh!
I wonder if Miss C has a mango pie recipe. She's a great baker! If you ever visit, I'd love for you to try some of her pastries!
Oh yeah. Totally.
Erm . . . Safia?
Mm-hmm?
Y'know, I've been thinking.
Pfft. This is gonna sound so sad, but . . .

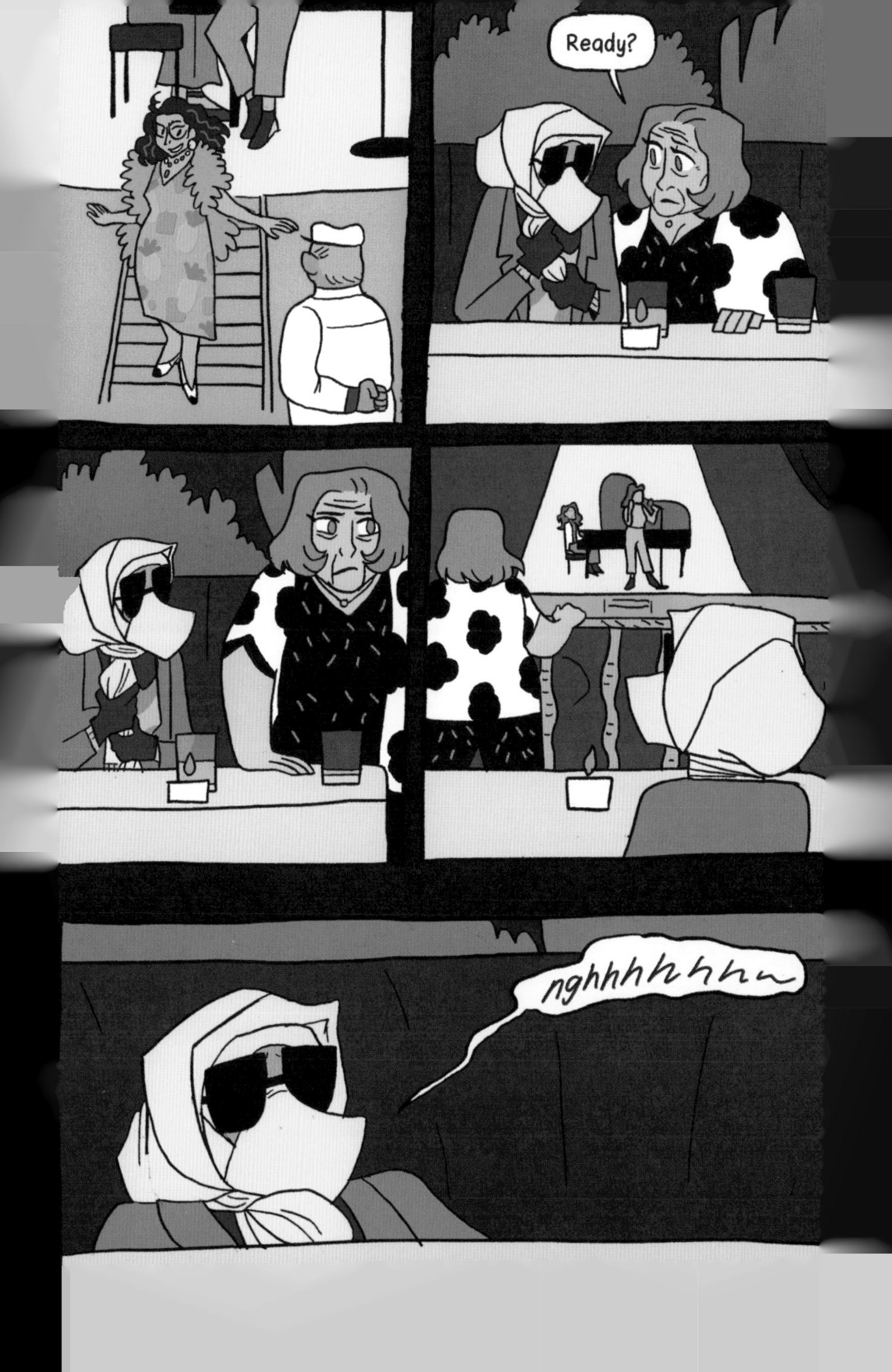
Ready?
nghhhhhhhh

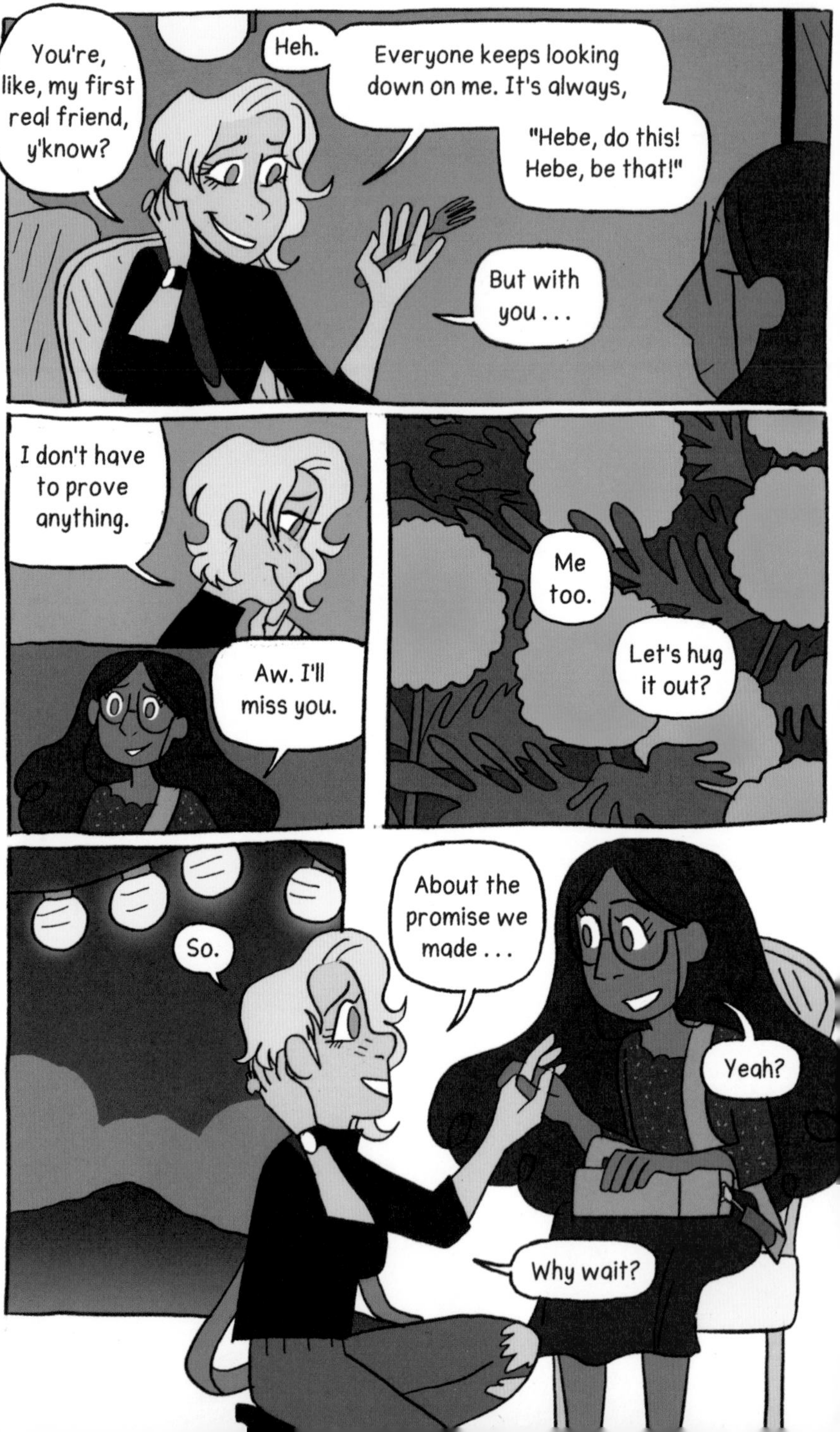
You're, like, my first real friend, y'know?
Heh.
Everyone keeps looking down on me. It's always,
"Hebe, do this! Hebe, be that!"
But with you . . .
I don't have to prove anything.
Aw. I'll miss you.
Me too.
Let's hug it out?
So.
About the promise we made . . .
Yeah?
Why wait?

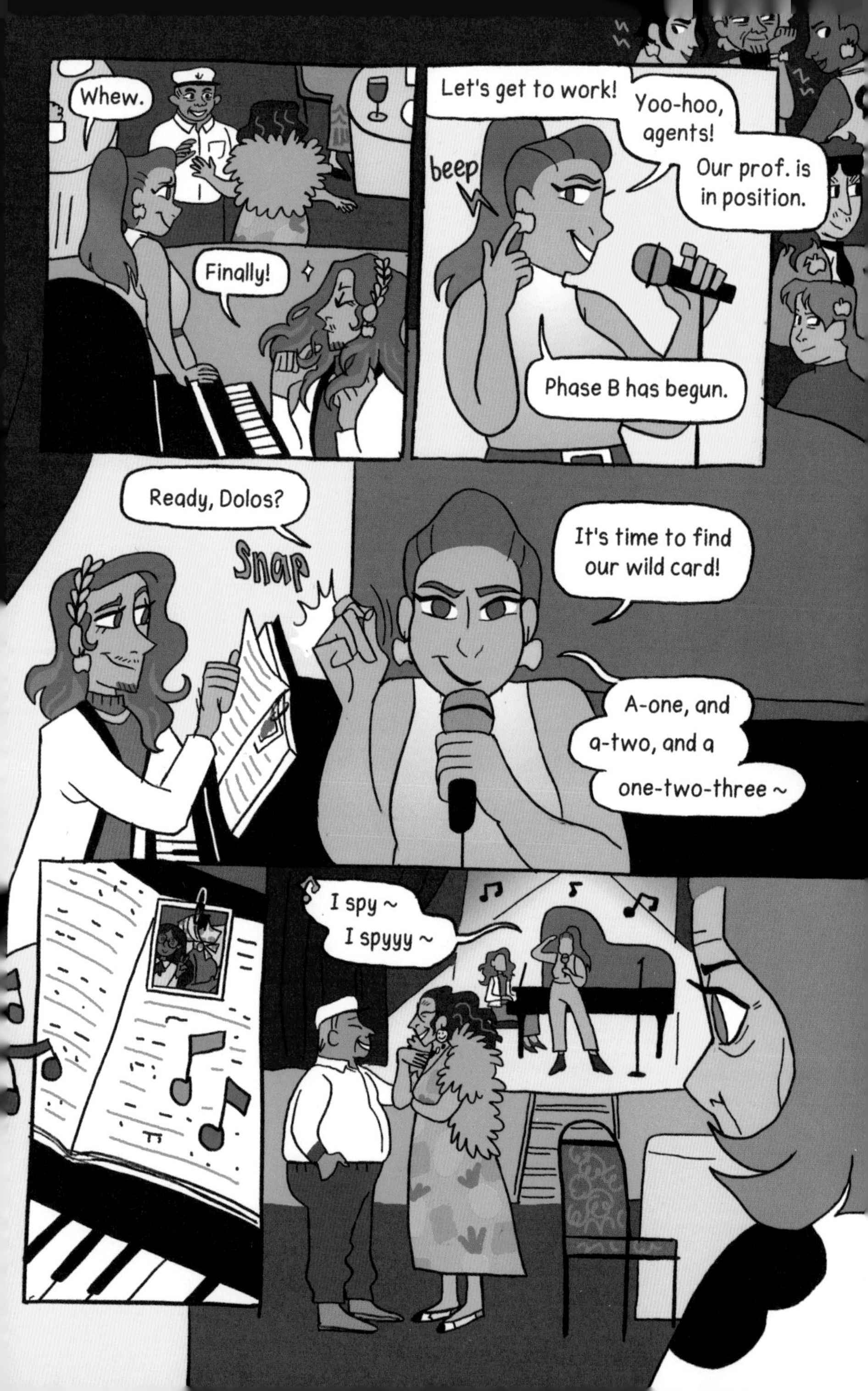

Whew.
Finally!
Let's get to work!
beep
Yoo-hoo, agents!
Our prof. is in position.
Phase B has begun.
Ready, Dolos?
Snap
It's time to find our wild card!
A-one, and a-two, and a one-two-three ~
I spy ~ I spyyy ~

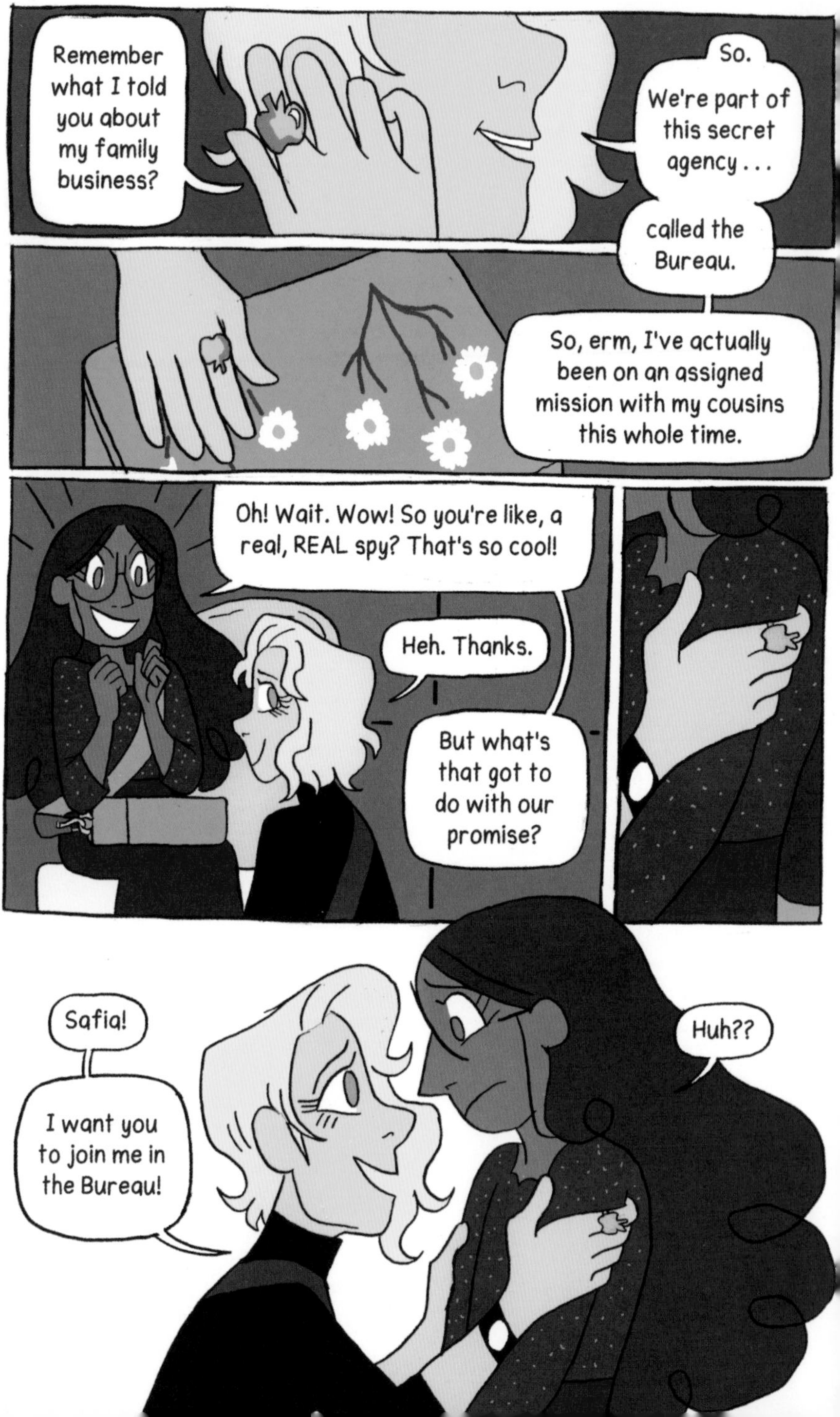
Remember what I told you about my family business?
So.
We're part of this secret agency . . .
called the Bureau.
So, erm, I've actually been on an assigned mission with my cousins this whole time.
Oh! Wait. Wow! So you're like, a real, REAL spy? That's so cool!
Heh. Thanks.
But what's that got to do with our promise?
Safia!
I want you to join me in the Bureau!
Huh??

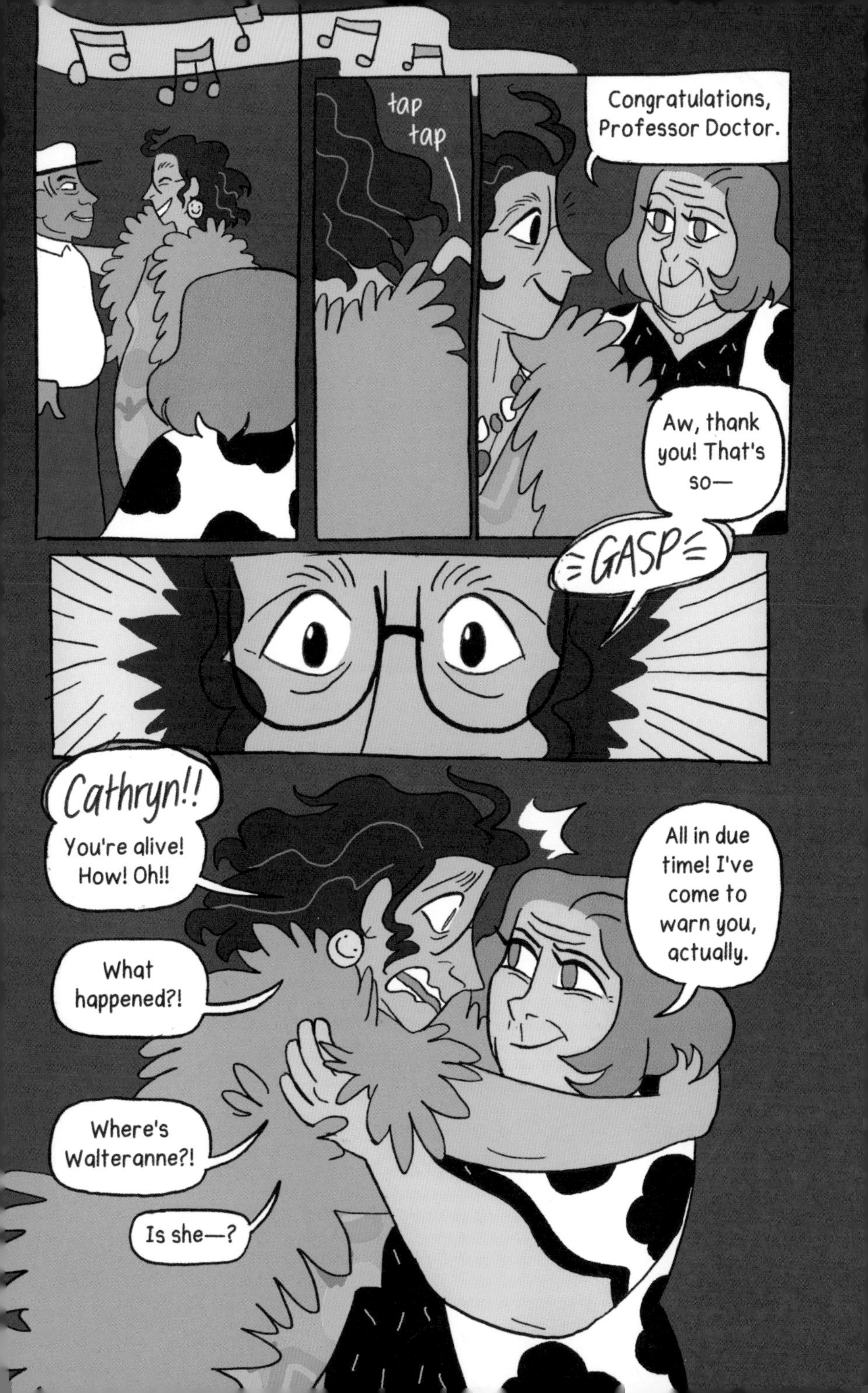
tap
tap
Congratulations, Professor Doctor.
Aw, thank you! That's so—
GASP
Cathryn!!
You're alive! How! Oh!!
What happened?!
Where's Walteranne?!
Is she—?
All in due time! I've come to warn you, actually.

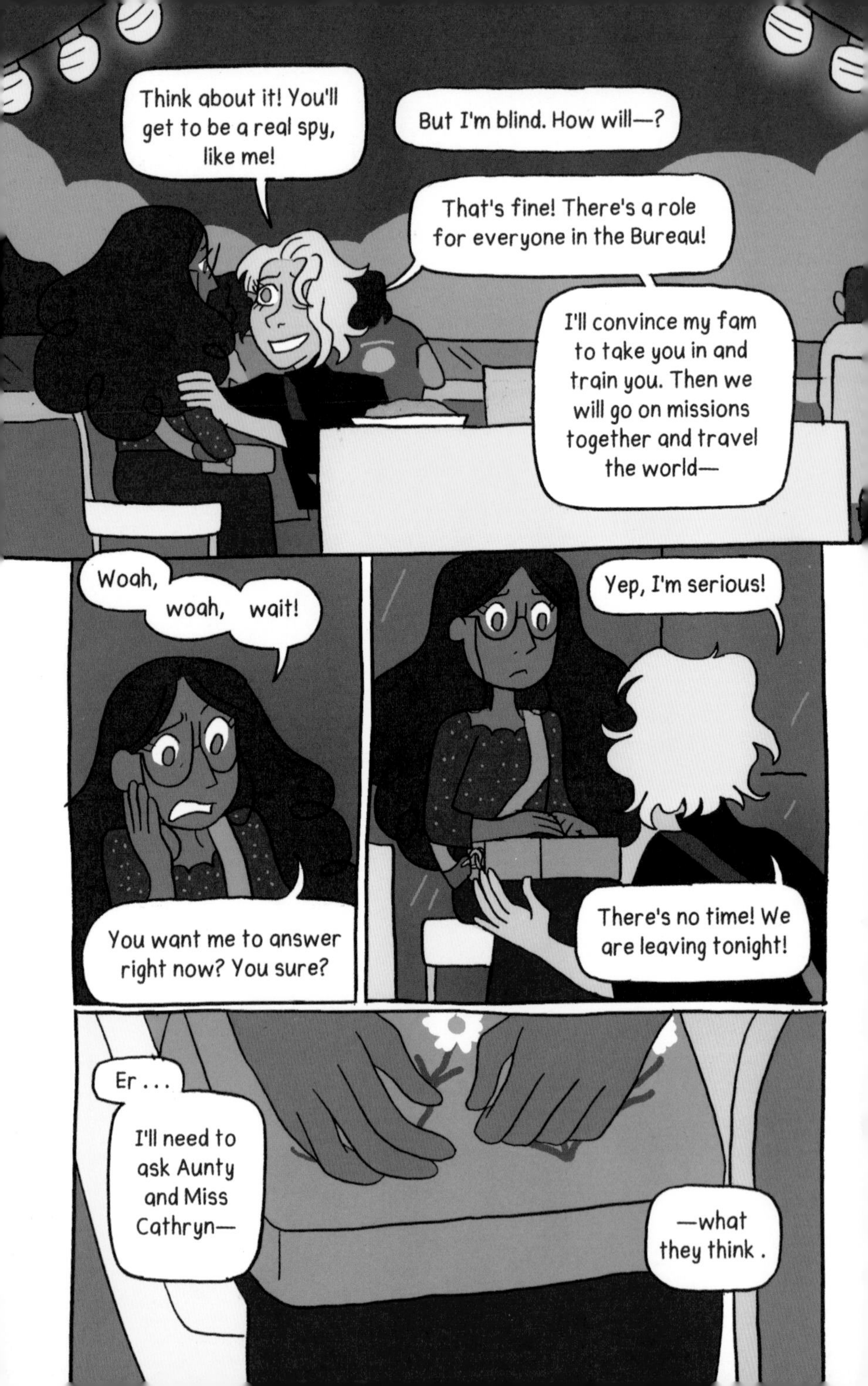
Think about it! You'll get to be a real spy, like me!
But I'm blind. How will—?
That's fine! There's a role for everyone in the Bureau!
I'll convince my fam to take you in and train you. Then we will go on missions together and travel the world—
Woah,
woah,
wait!
You want me to answer right now? You sure?
Yep, I'm serious!
There's no time! We are leaving tonight!
Er . . .
I'll need to ask Aunty and Miss Cathryn—
—what they think .

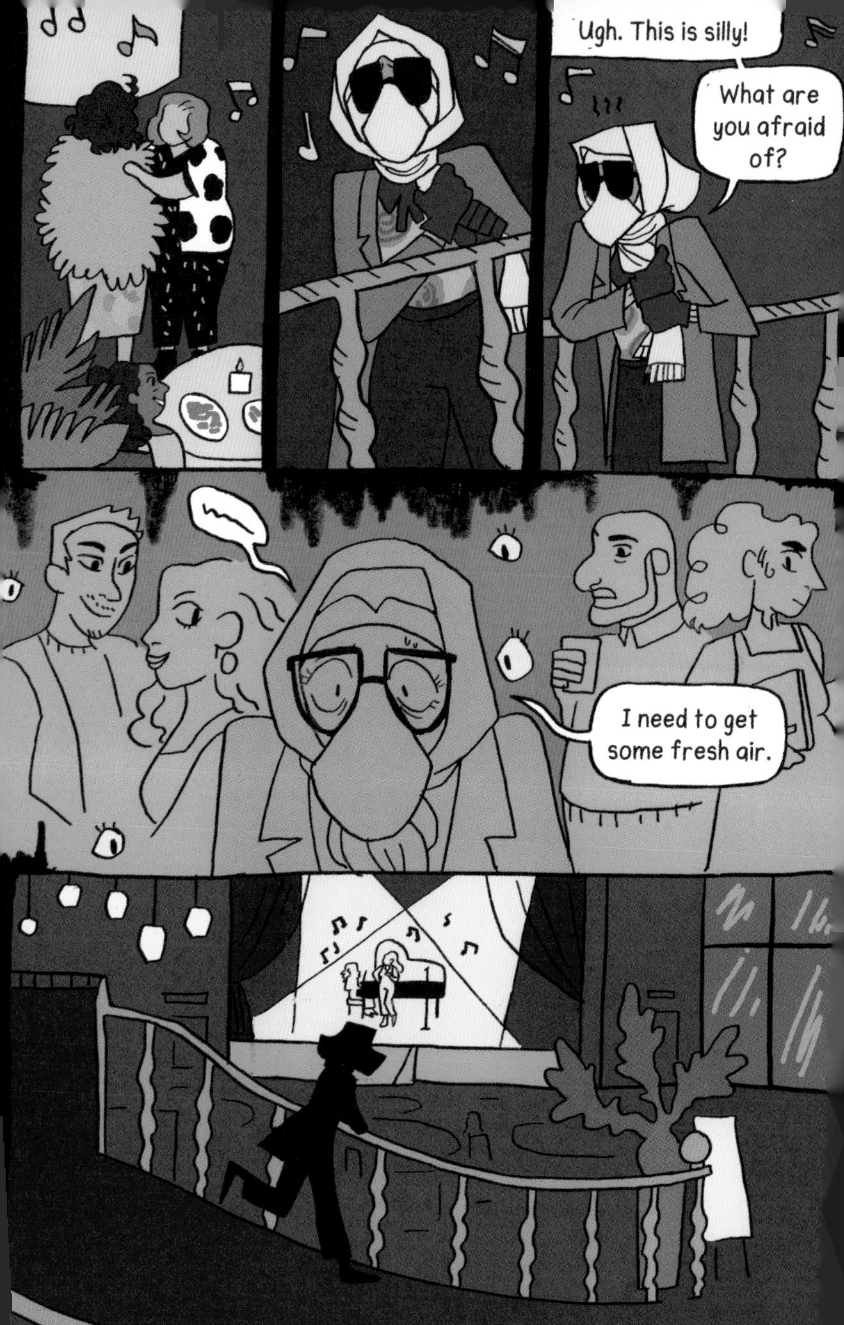
Ugh. This is silly!
What are you afraid of?
I need to get some fresh air.

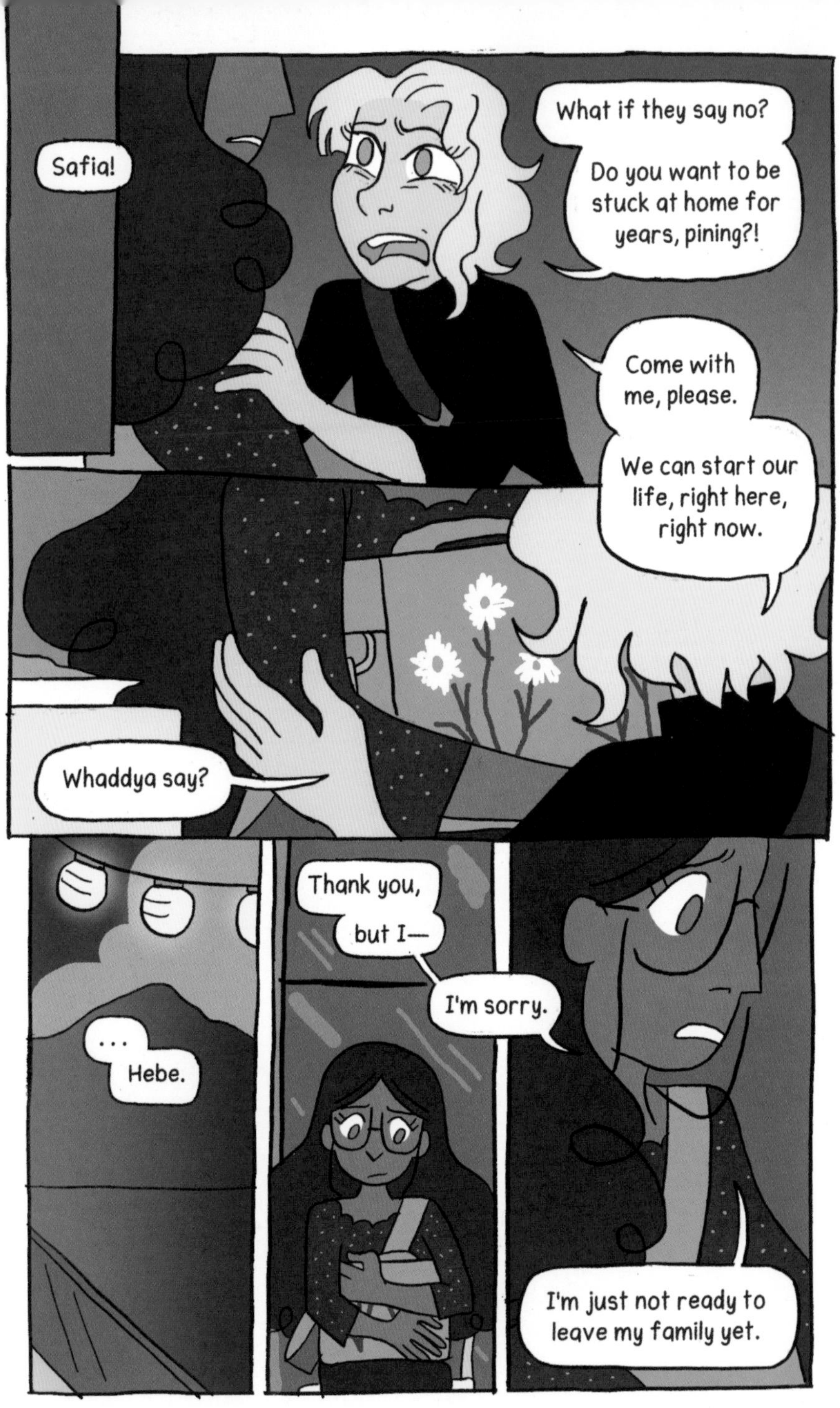
Safia!
What if they say no?
Do you want to be stuck at home for years, pining?!
Come with me, please.
We can start our life, right here, right now.
Whaddya say?
...
Hebe.
Thank you,
but I—
I'm sorry.
I'm just not ready to leave my family yet.

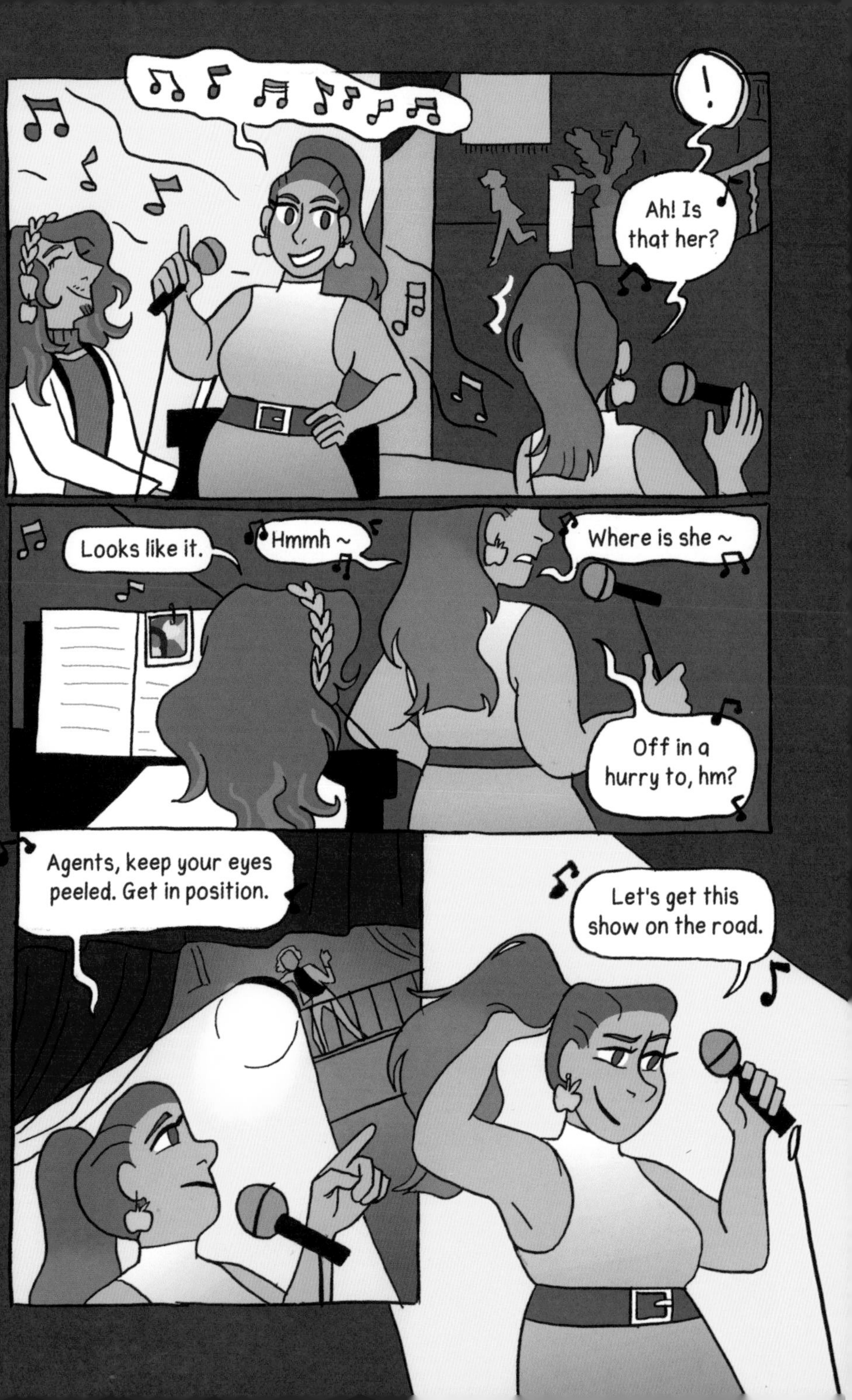

!
Ah! Is that her?
Looks like it.
Hmmh ~
Where is she ~
Off in a hurry to, hm?
Agents, keep your eyes peeled. Get in position.
Let's get this show on the road.

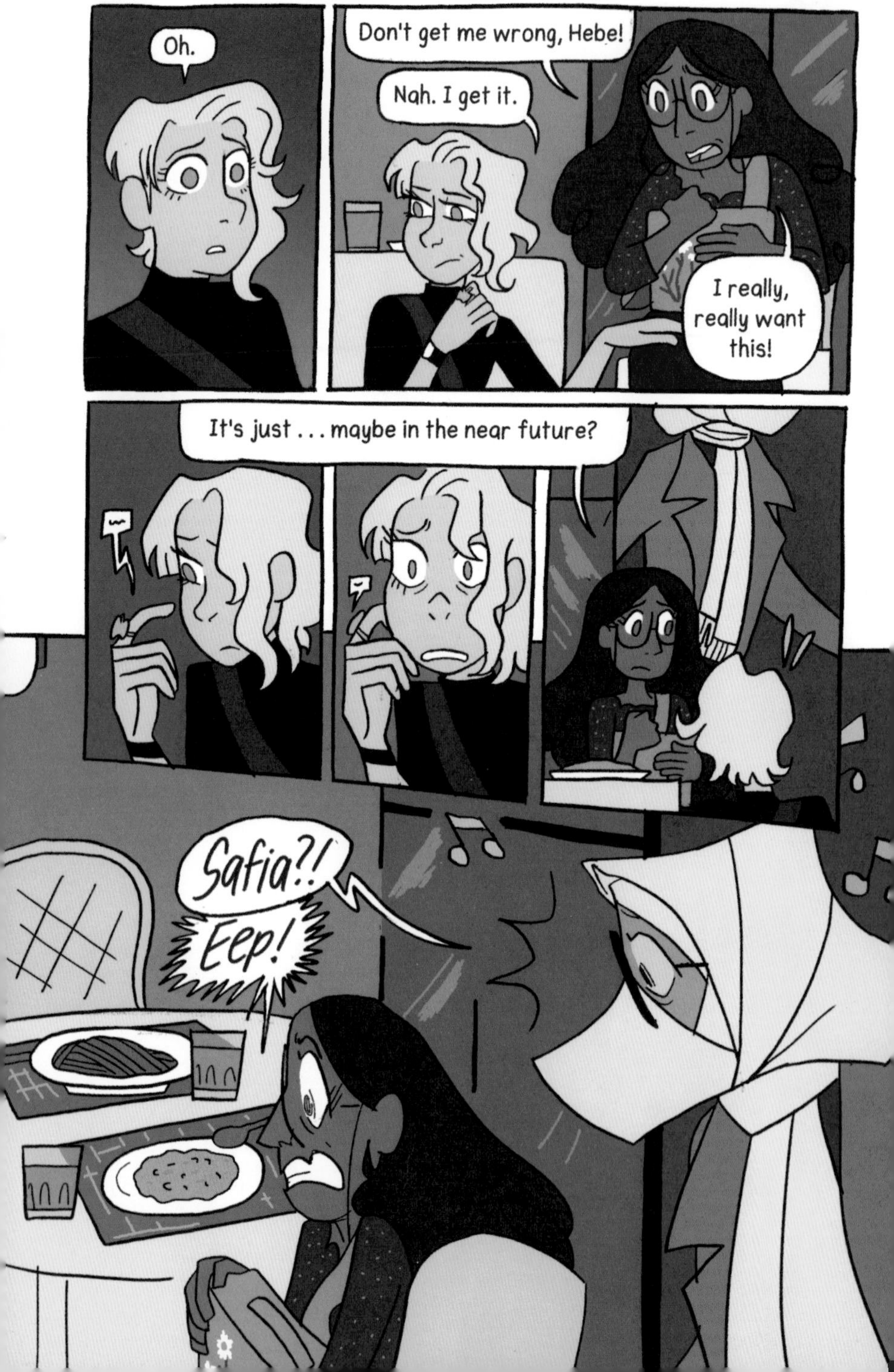
Oh.
Don't get me wrong, Hebe!
Nah. I get it.
I really, really want this!
It's just . . . maybe in the near future?
Safia?!
Eep!

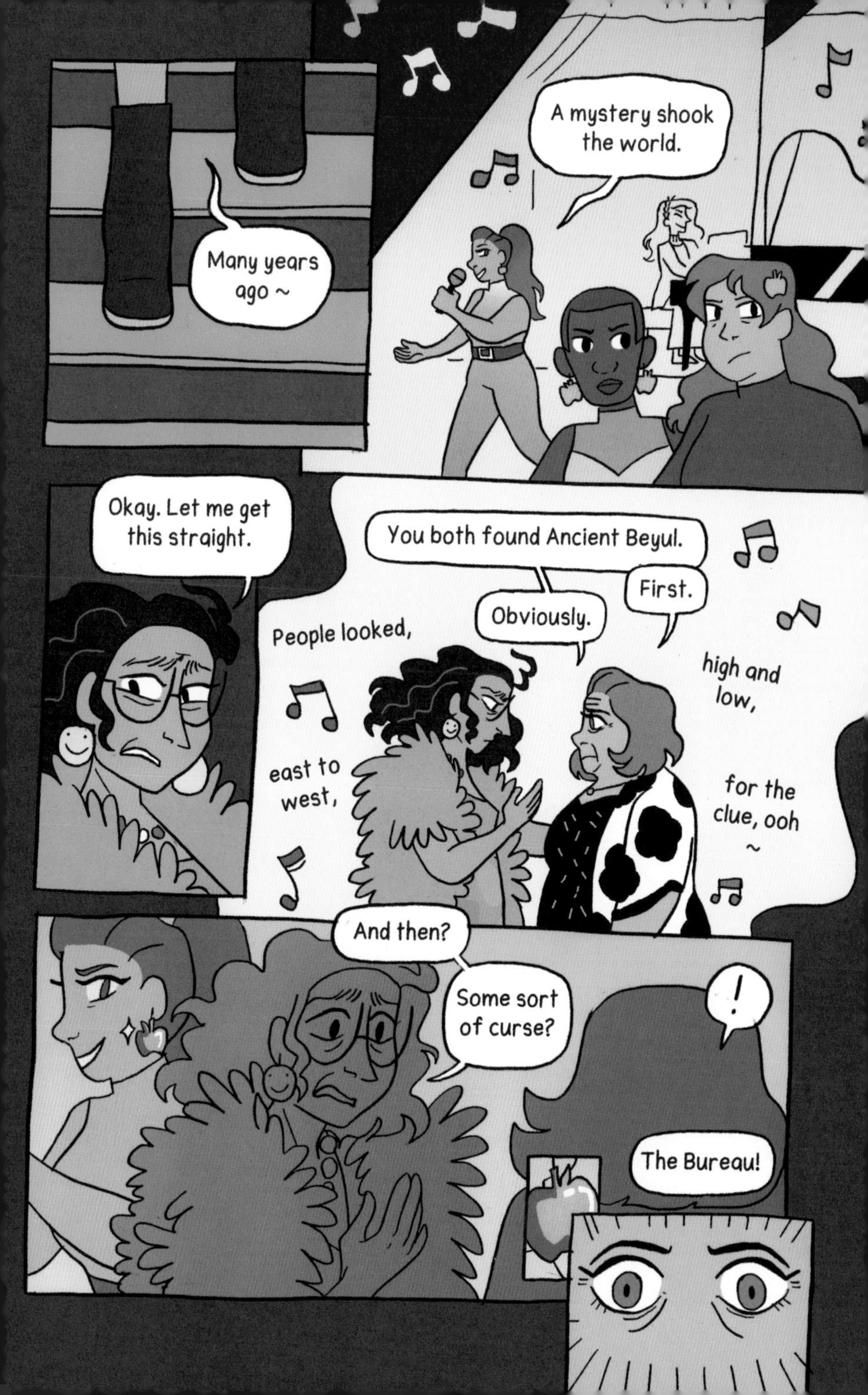

Many years ago ~
A mystery shook the world.
Okay. Let me get this straight.
You both found Ancient Beyul.
Obviously.
First.
People looked,
high and low,
east to west,
for the clue, ooh ~
And then?
Some sort of curse?
!
The Bureau!

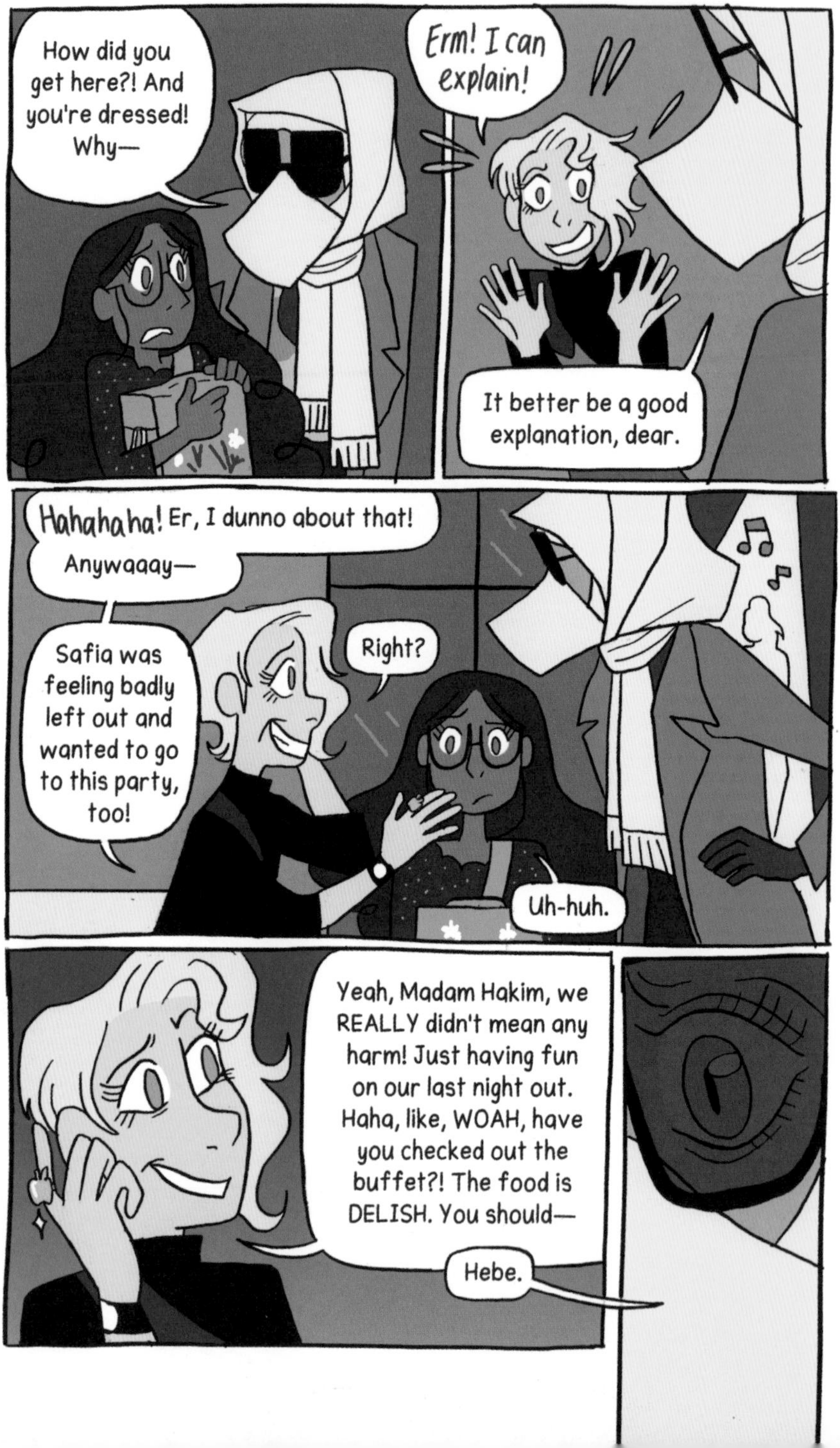
How did you get here?! And you're dressed! Why—
Erm! I can explain!
It better be a good explanation, dear.
Hahahaha! Er, I dunno about that!
Anywaaay—
Safia was feeling badly left out and wanted to go to this party, too!
Right?
Uh-huh.
Yeah, Madam Hakim, we REALLY didn't mean any harm! Just having fun on our last night out. Haha, like, WOAH, have you checked out the buffet?! The food is DELISH. You should—
Hebe.

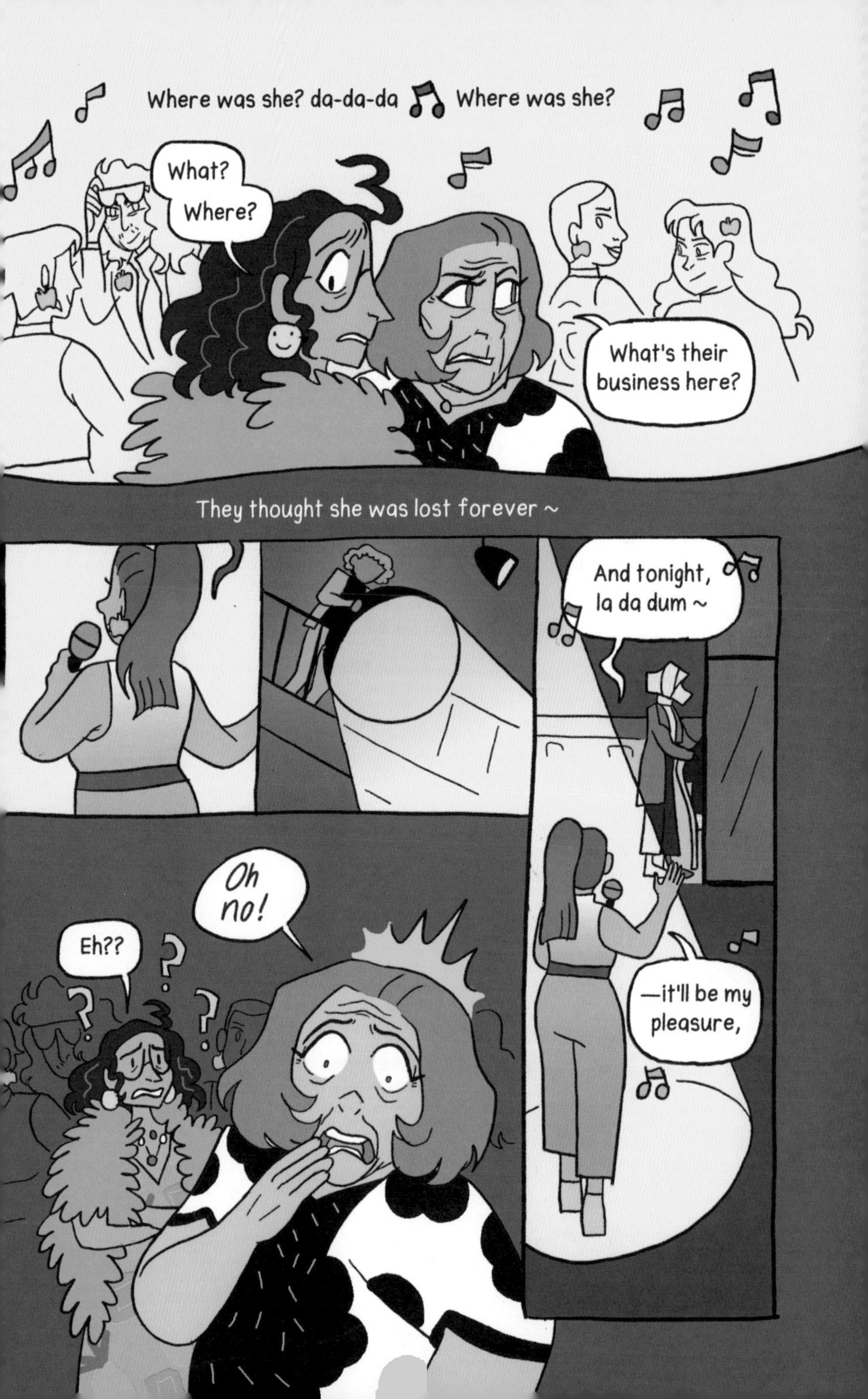
Where was she? da-da-da Where was she?
What?
Where?
What's their business here?
They thought she was lost forever ~
And tonight, la da dum ~
—it'll be my pleasure,
Oh no!
Eh??

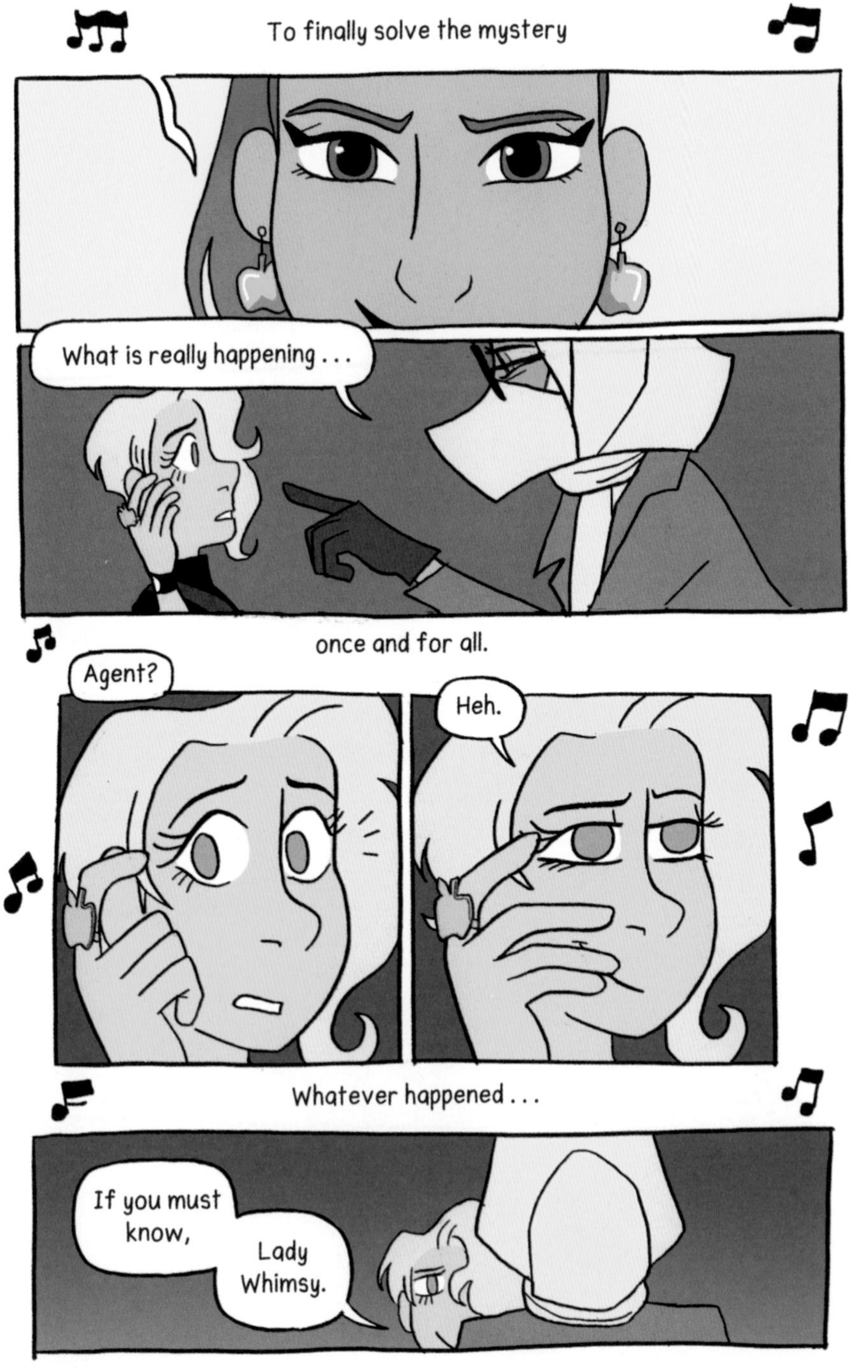
To finally solve the mystery
What is really happening . . .
once and for all.
Agent?
Heh.
Whatever happened . . .
If you must know,
Lady Whimsy.

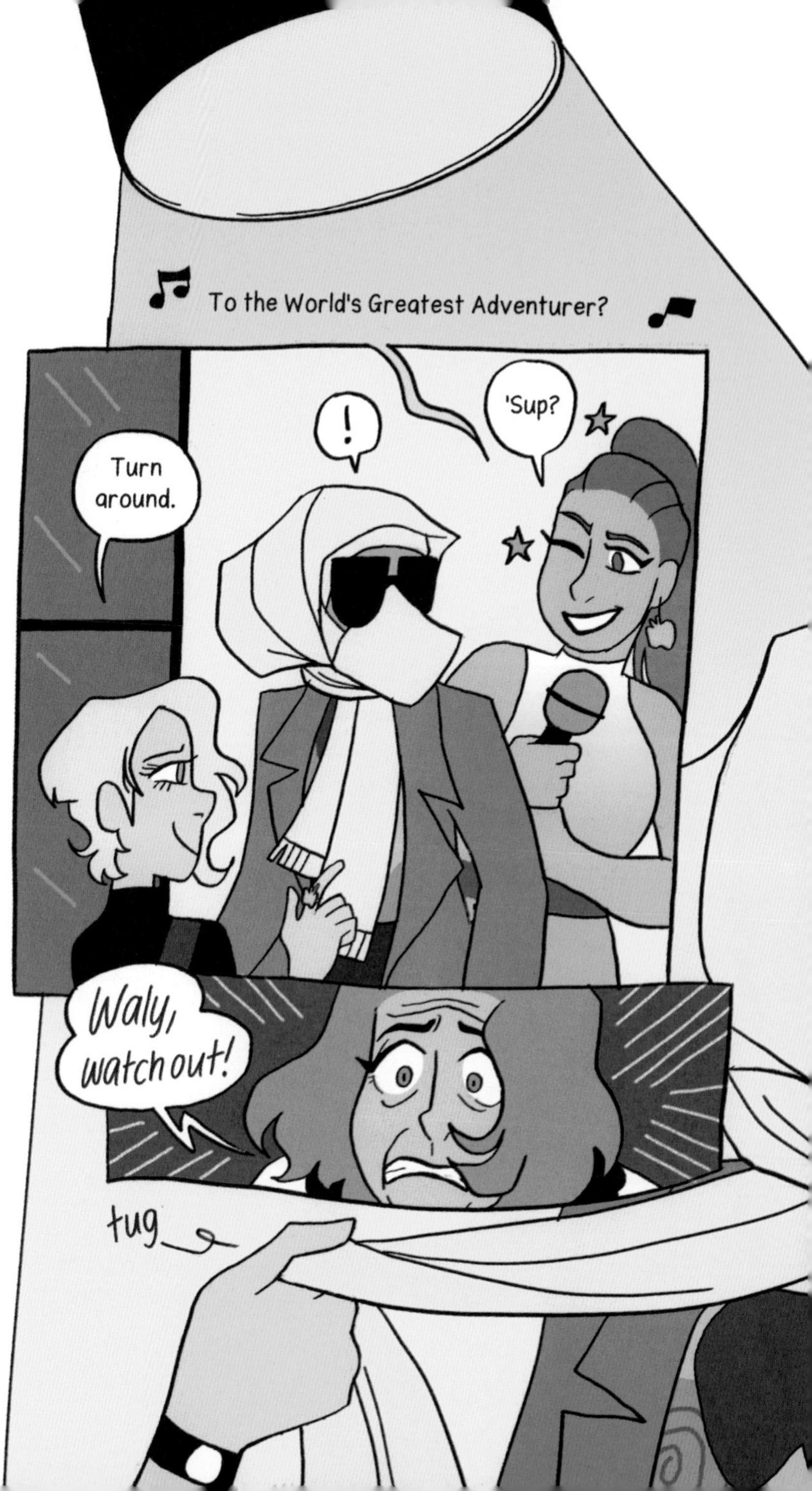
To the World's Greatest Adventurer?
Turn around.
!
'Sup?
Waly, watch out!
tug

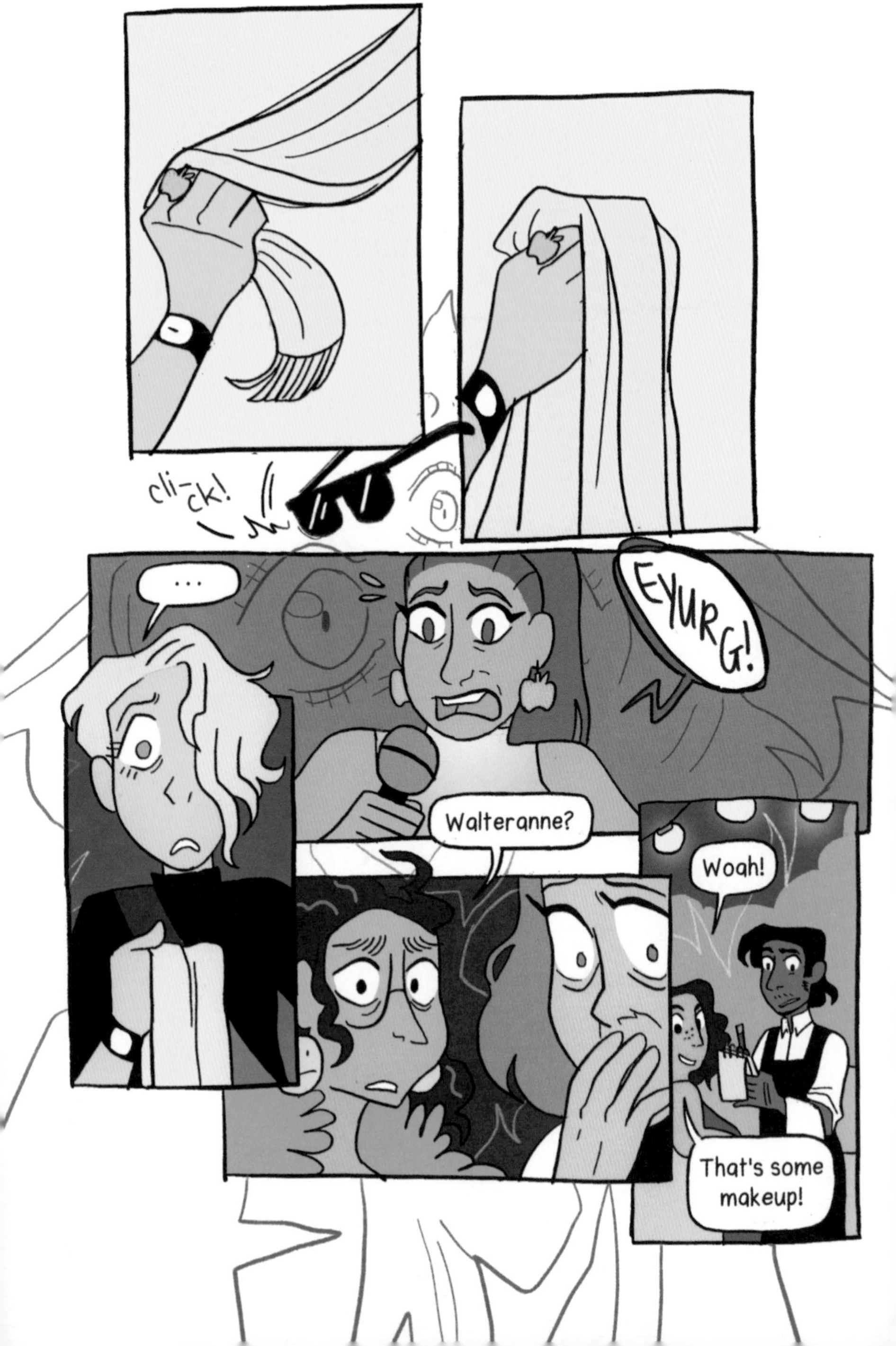
cli-ck!
...
EYURG!
Walteranne?
Woah!
That's some makeup!

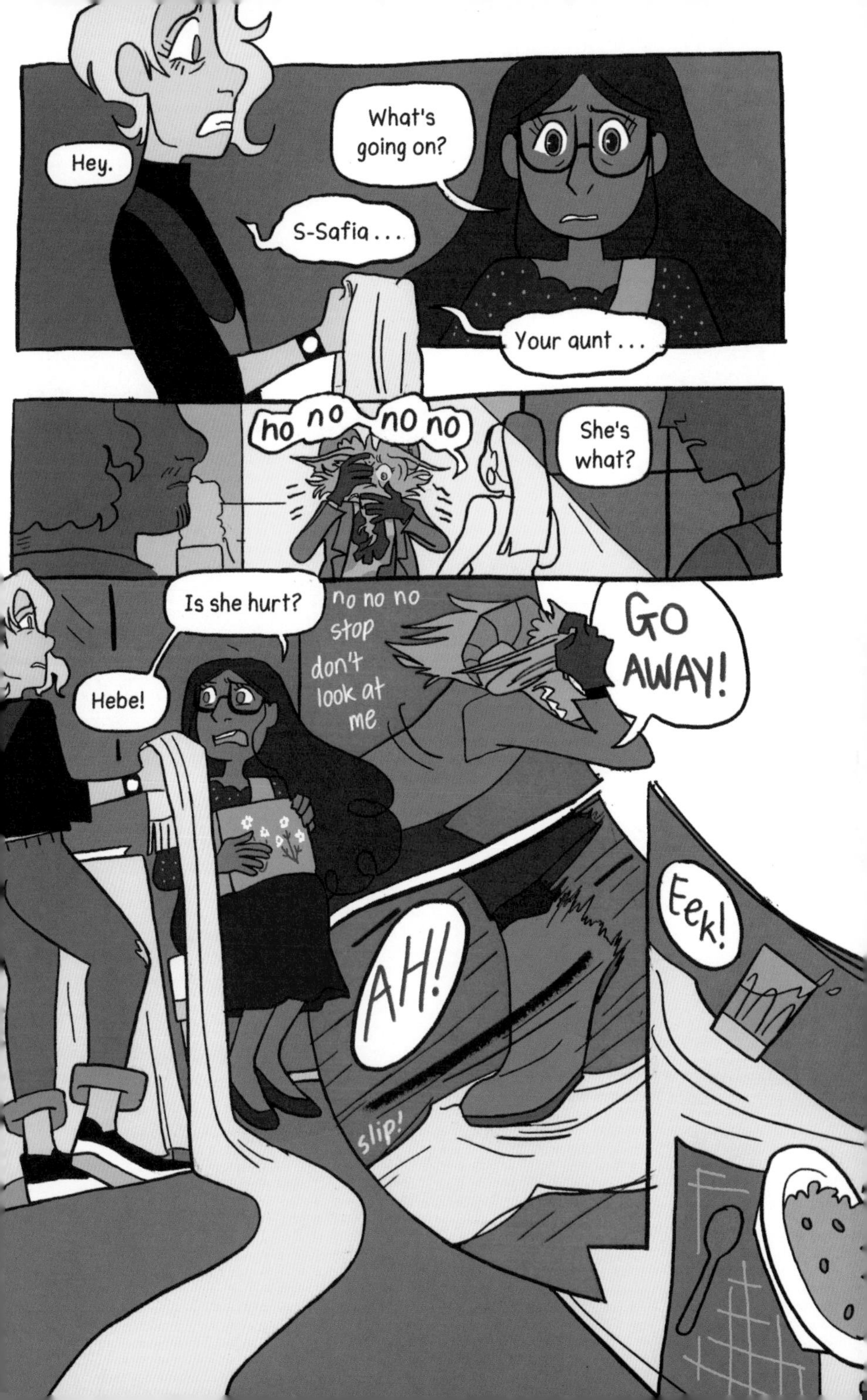
Hey.
What's going on?
S-Safia . . .
Your aunt . . .
no no no no
She's what?
Is she hurt?
Hebe!
no no no
stop
don't
look at
me
GO AWAY!
AH!
slip!
Eek!

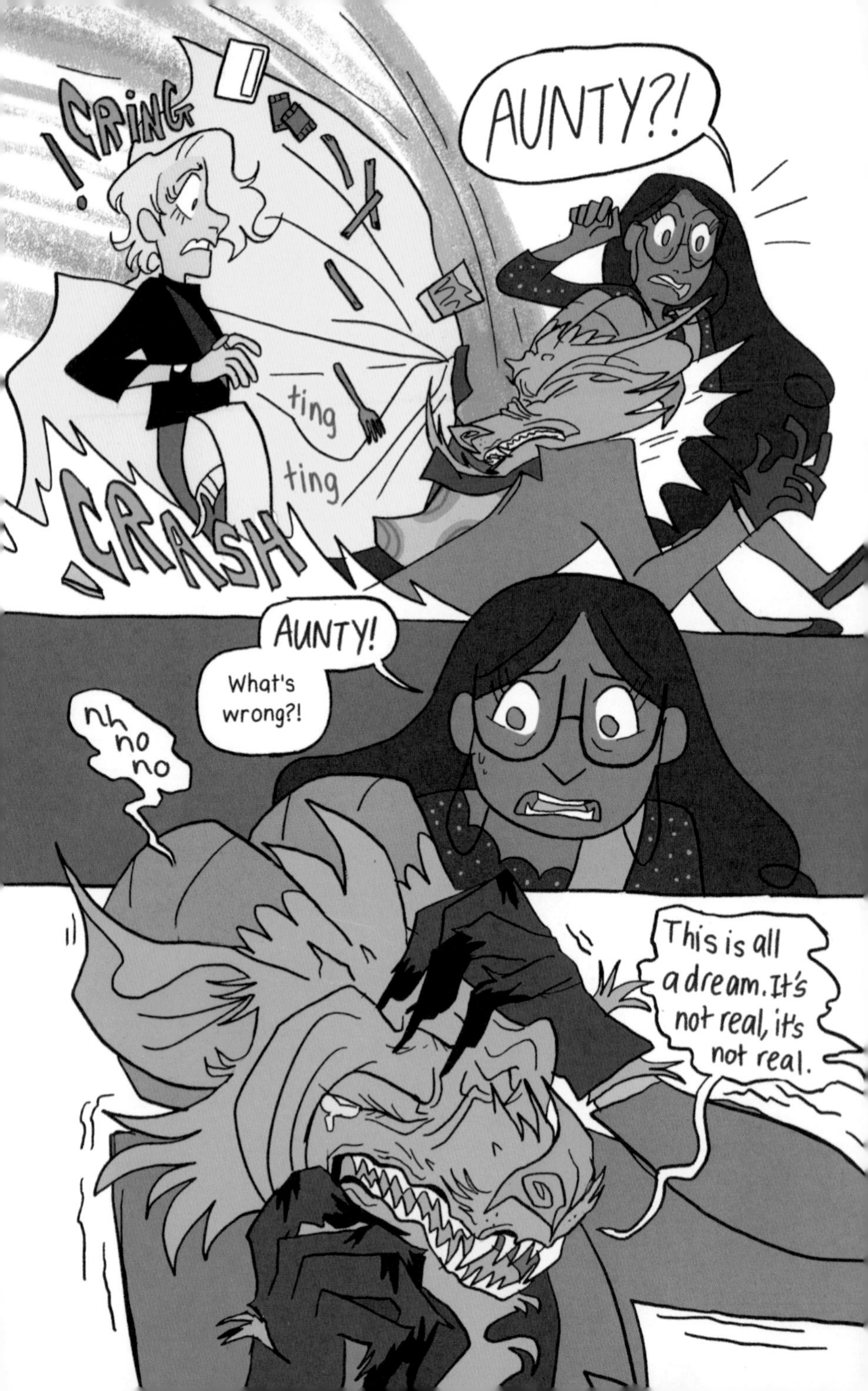
CRING
CRASH
AUNTY?!
ting
ting
AUNTY!
What's wrong?!
nh no no
This is all a dream. It's not real, it's not real.

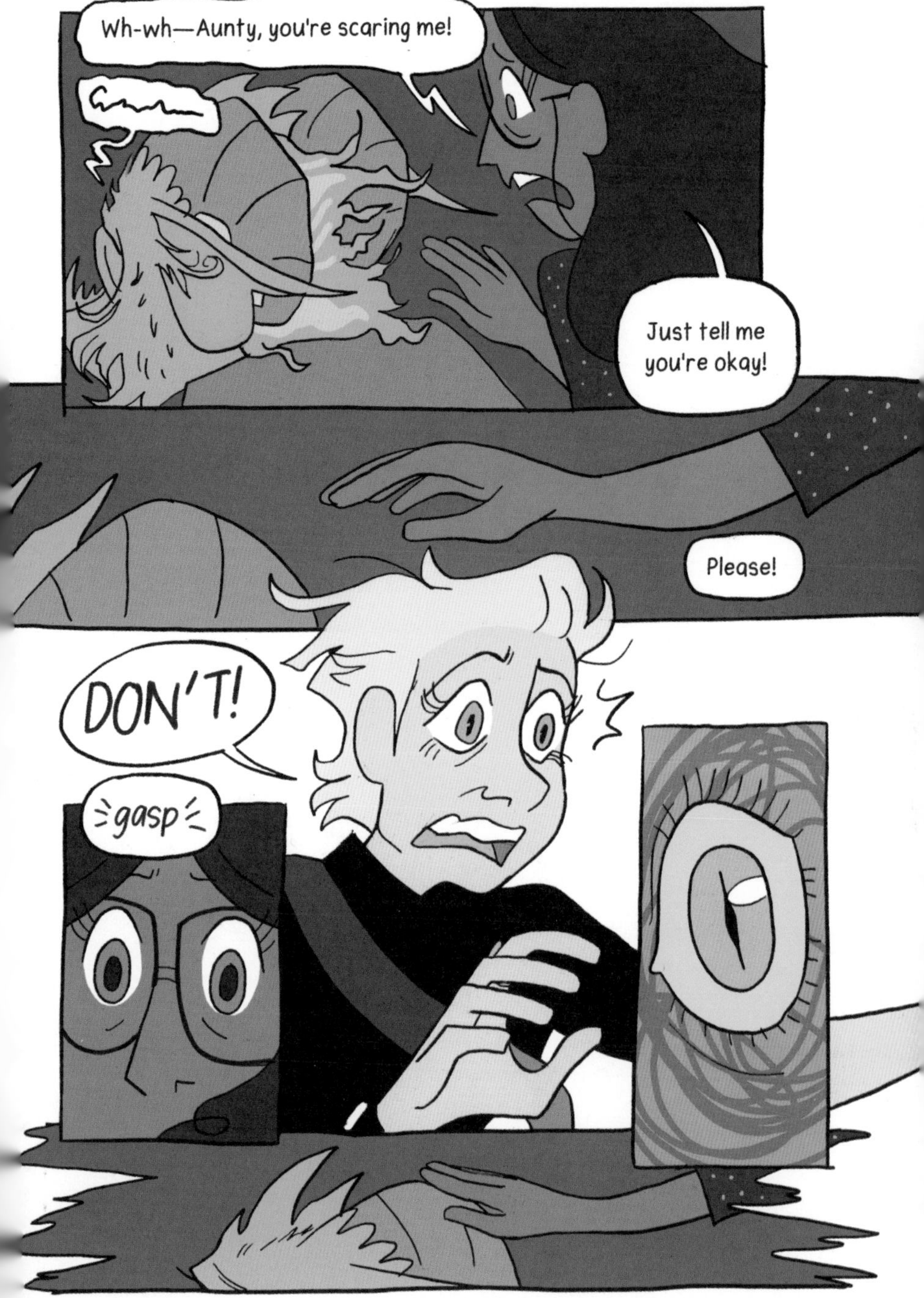
Wh-wh—Aunty, you're scaring me!
Just tell me you're okay!
Please!
DON'T!
gasp

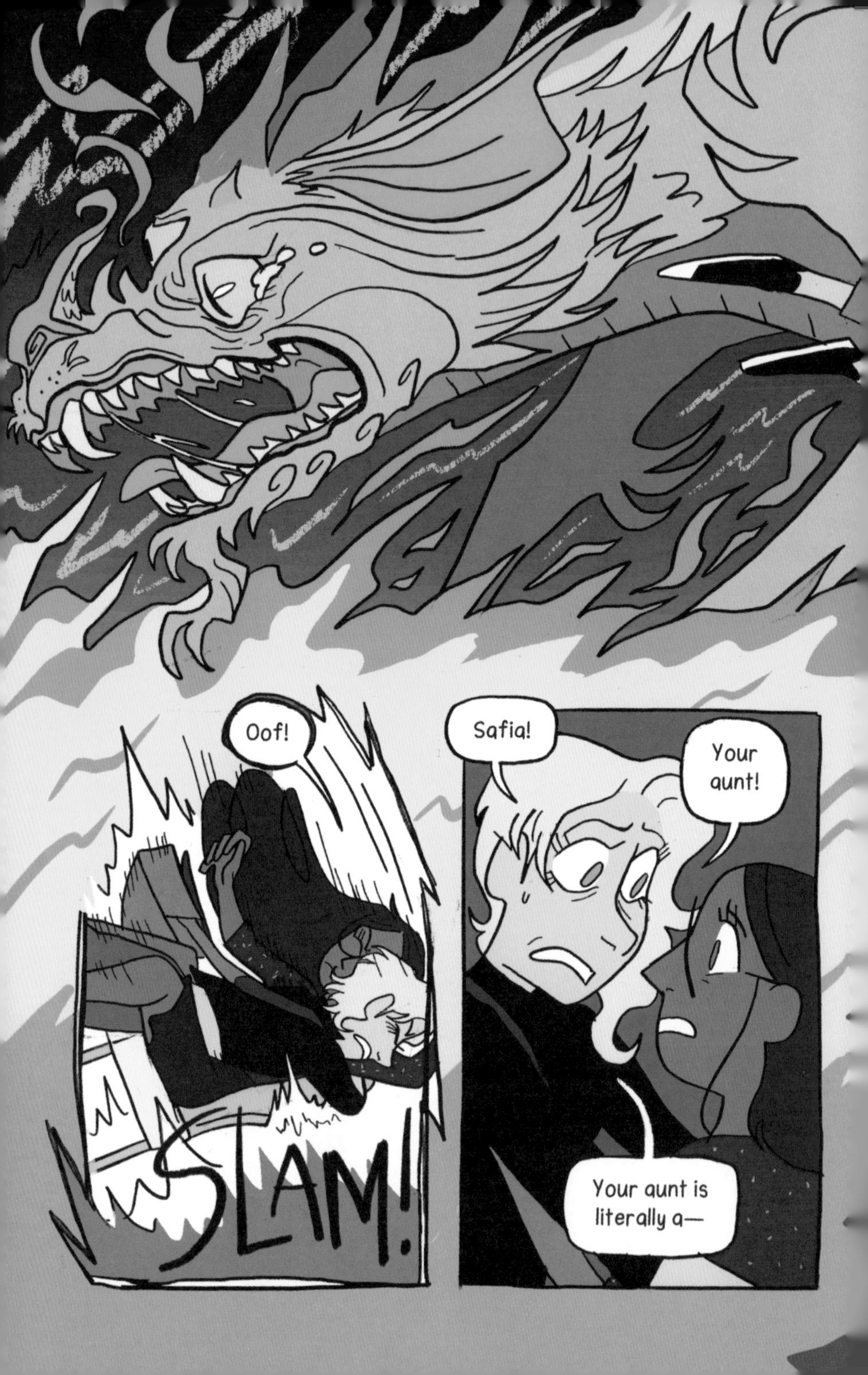
Oof!
SLAM!
Safia!
Your aunt!
Your aunt is literally a—

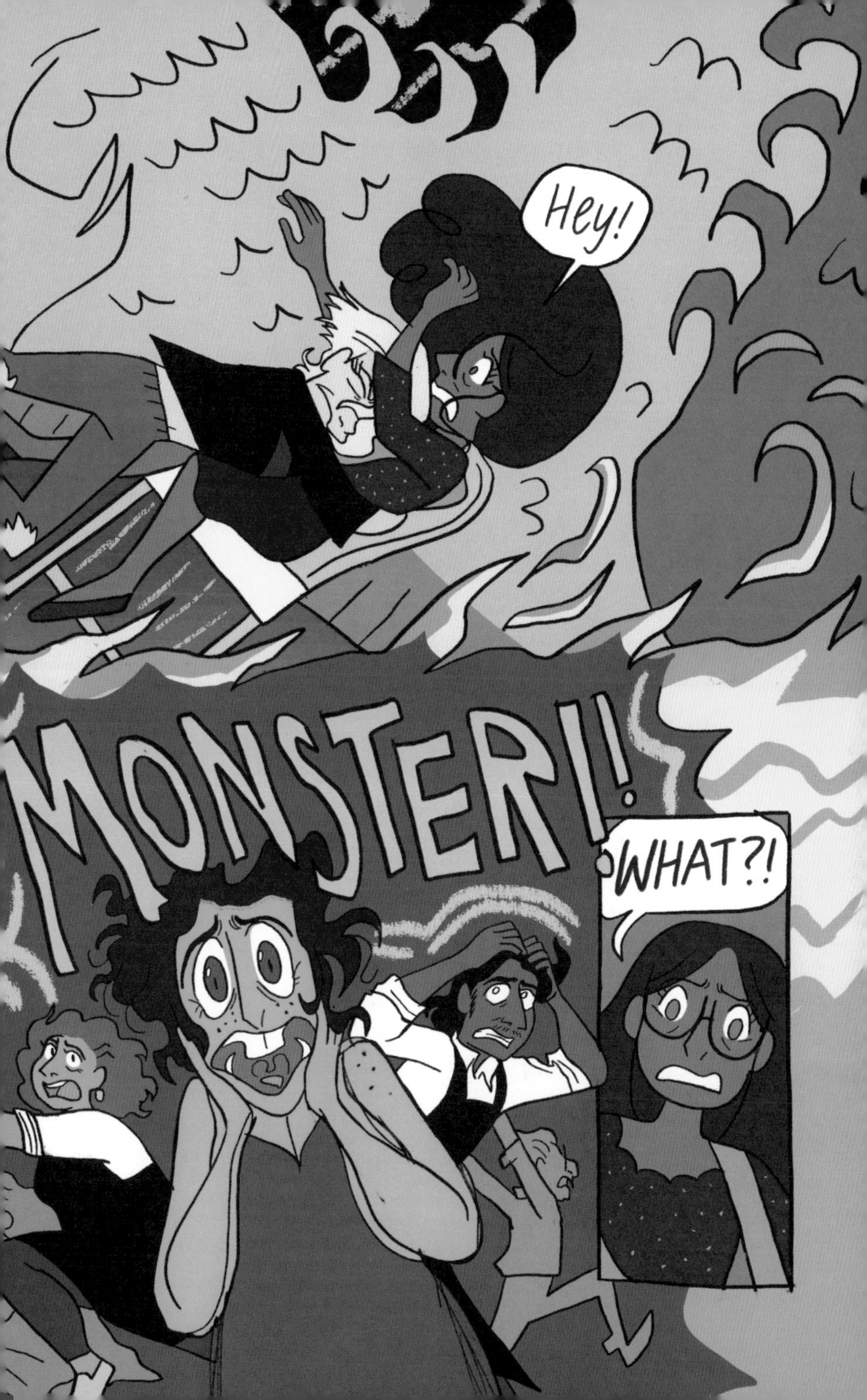
Hey!
MONSTER!!
WHAT?!

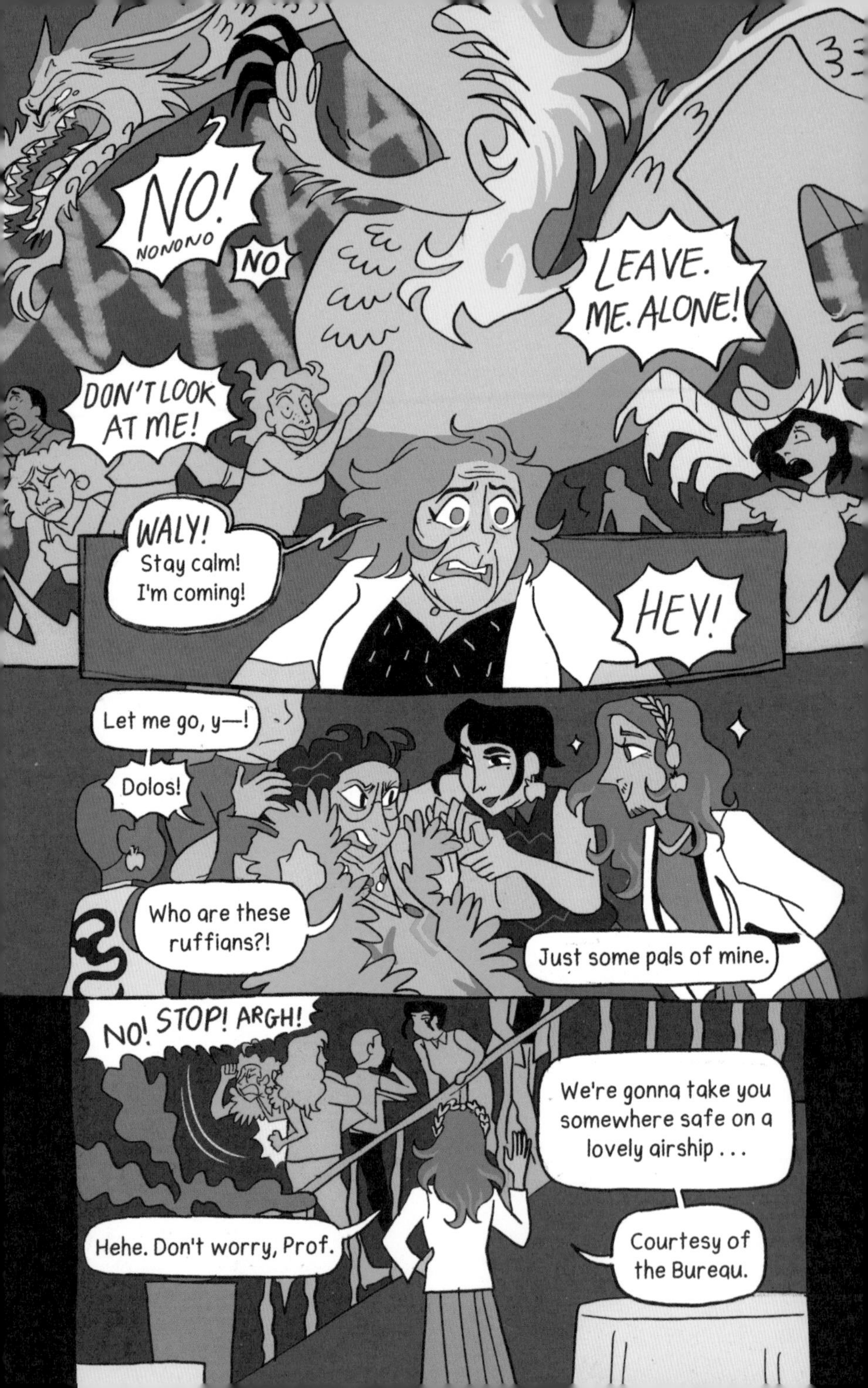

NO! NONONO
NO
LEAVE. ME. ALONE!
DON'T LOOK AT ME!
WALY! Stay calm! I'm coming!
HEY!
Let me go, y—!
Dolos!
Who are these ruffians?!
Just some pals of mine.
NO! STOP! ARGH!
We're gonna take you somewhere safe on a lovely airship . . .
Hehe. Don't worry, Prof.
Courtesy of the Bureau.

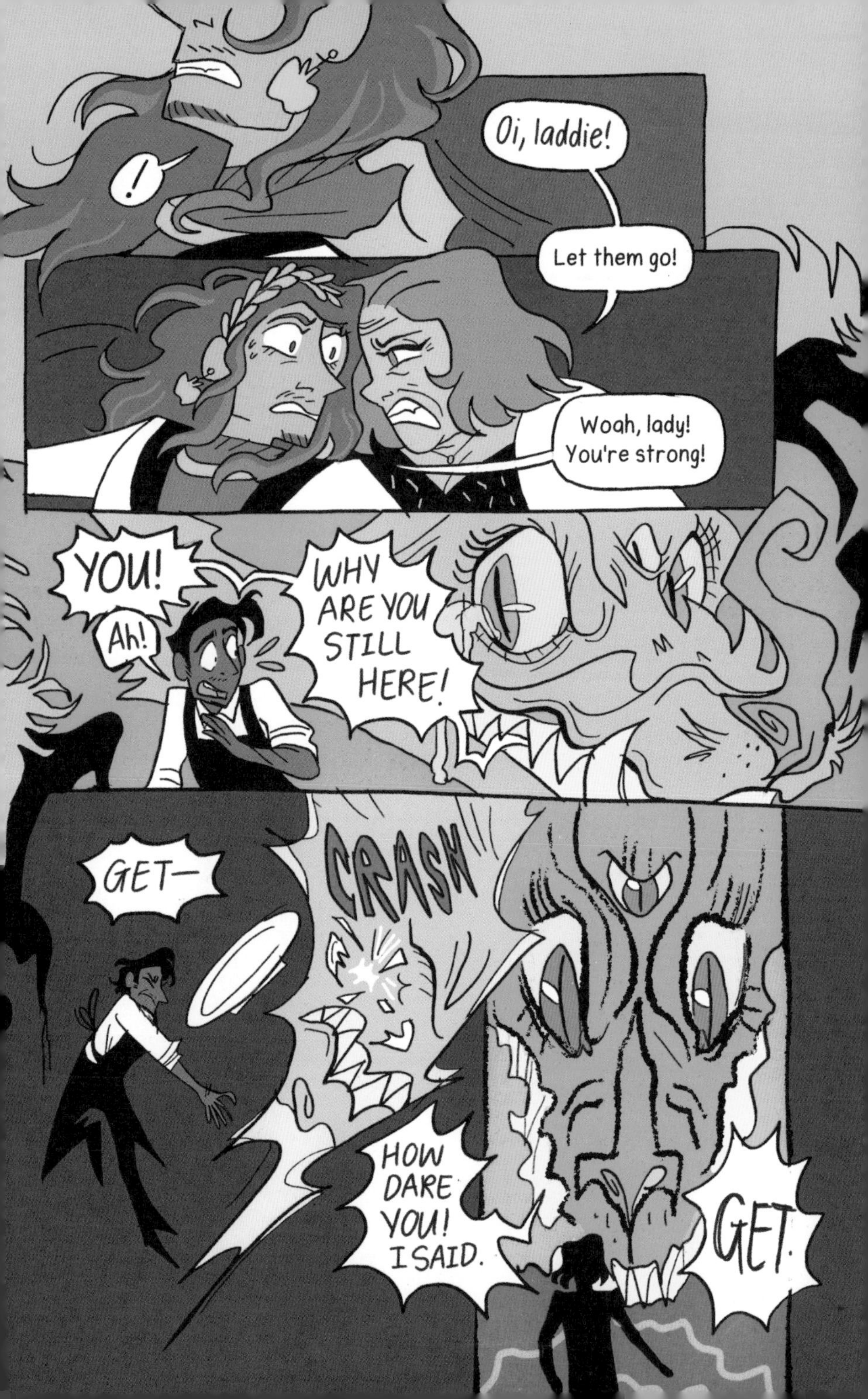
!
Oi, laddie!
Let them go!
Woah, lady! You're strong!
YOU!
Ah!
WHY ARE YOU STILL HERE!
GET—
CRASH
HOW DARE YOU! I SAID.
GET.

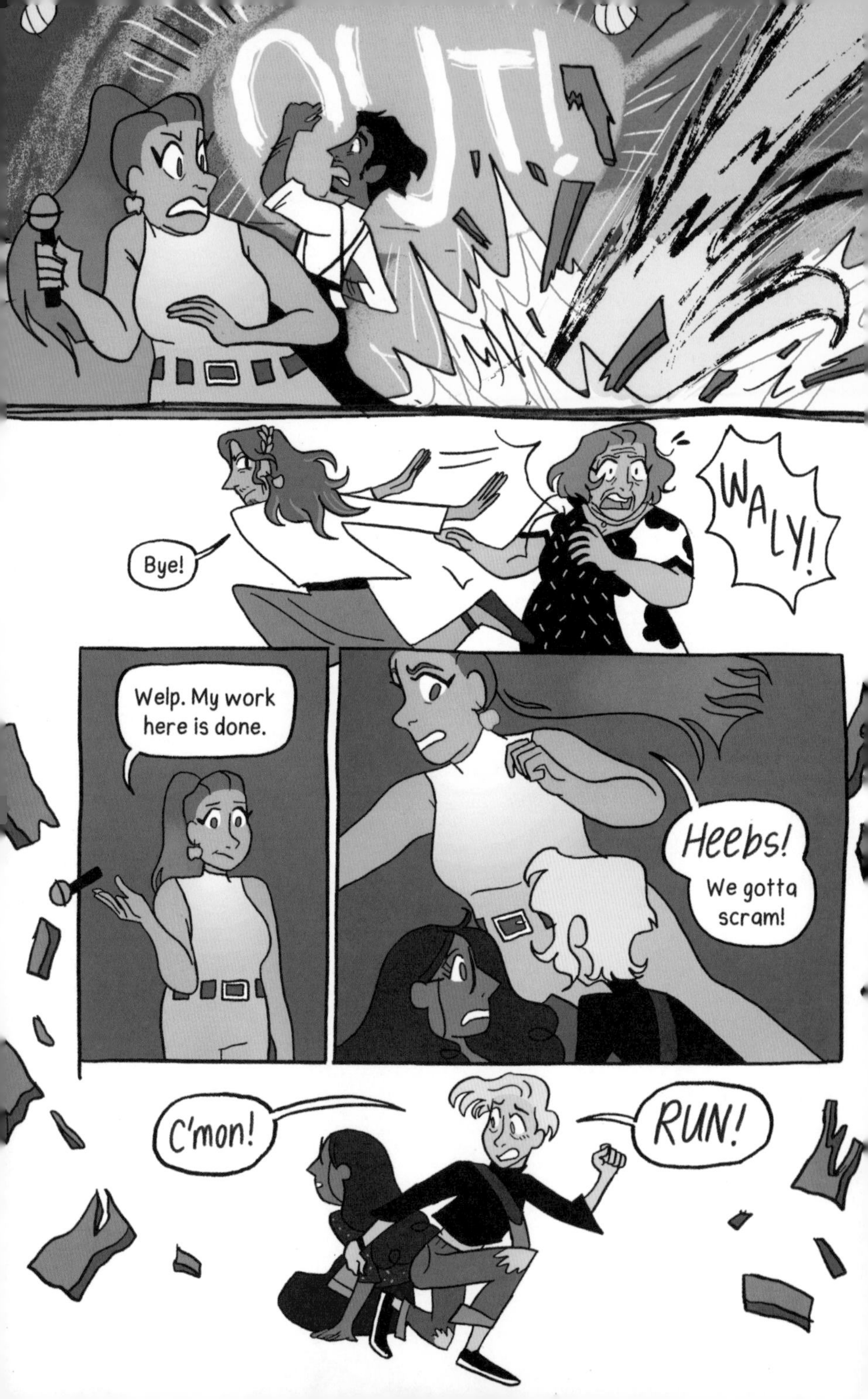
OUT!
Bye!
WALY!
Welp. My work here is done.
Heebs!
We gotta scram!
C'mon!
RUN!

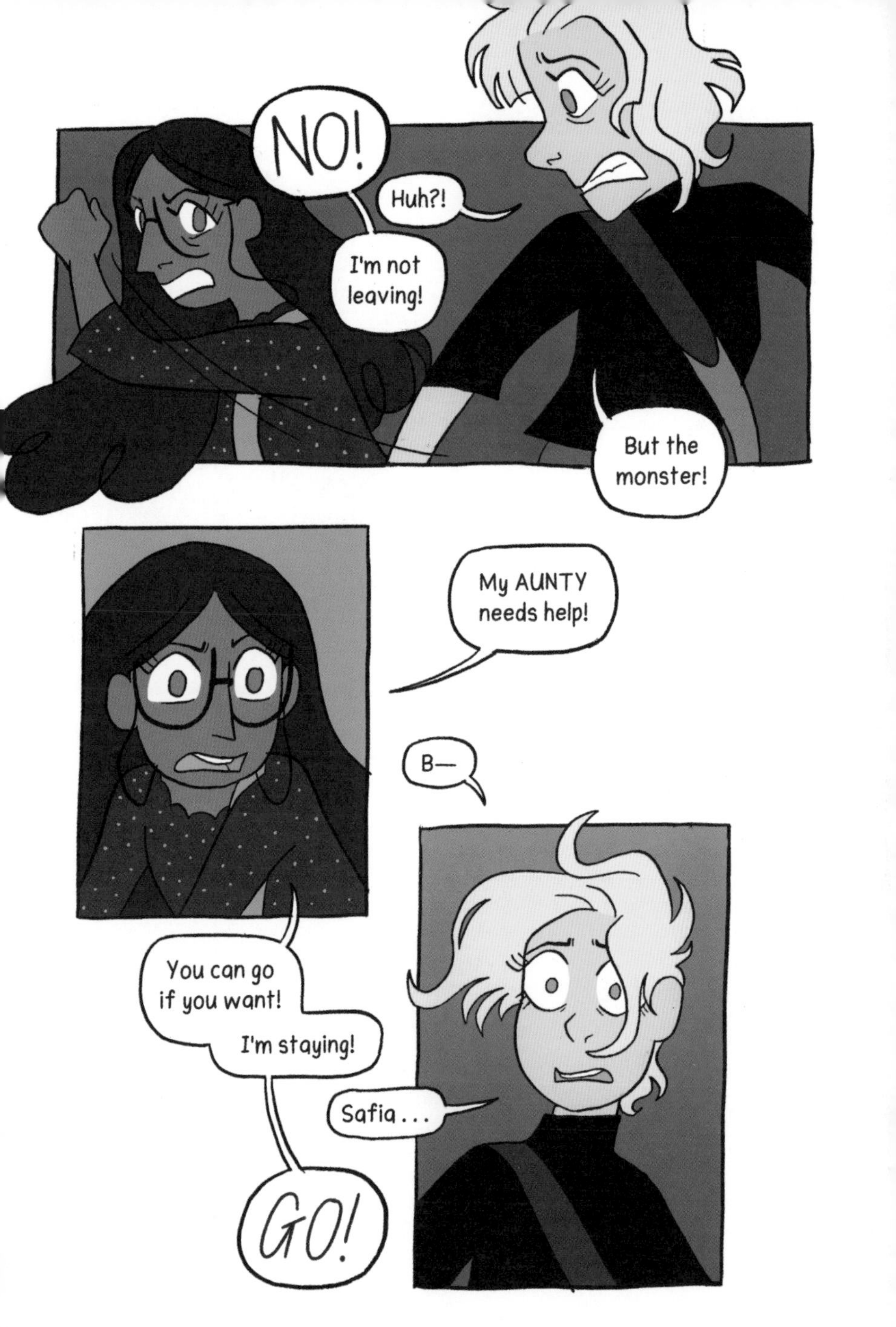
NO!
Huh?!
I'm not leaving!
But the monster!
My AUNTY needs help!
B—
You can go if you want!
I'm staying!
Safia . . .
GO!

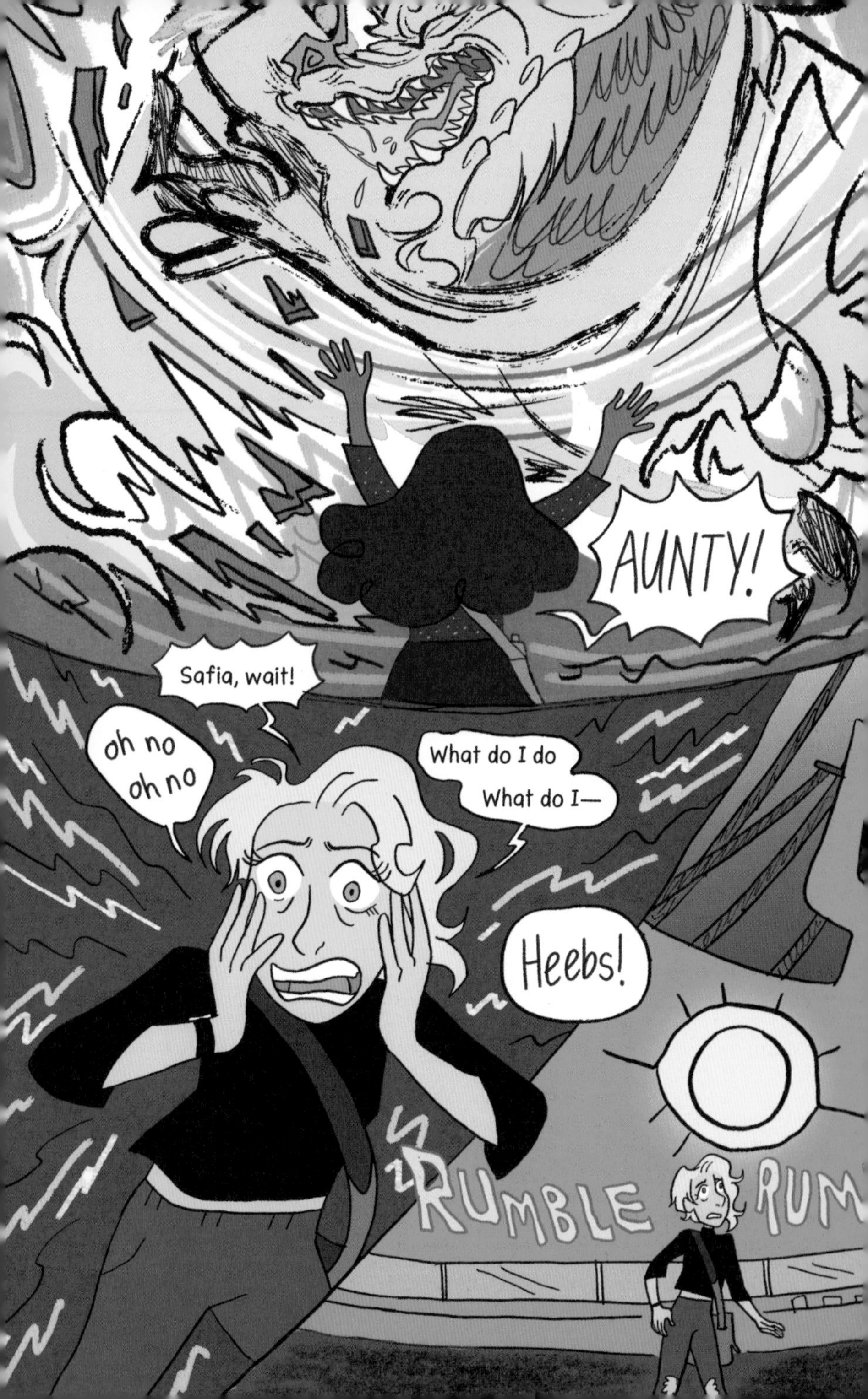
AUNTY!
Safia, wait!
oh no
oh no
What do I do
What do I—
Heebs!
RUMBLE RUM

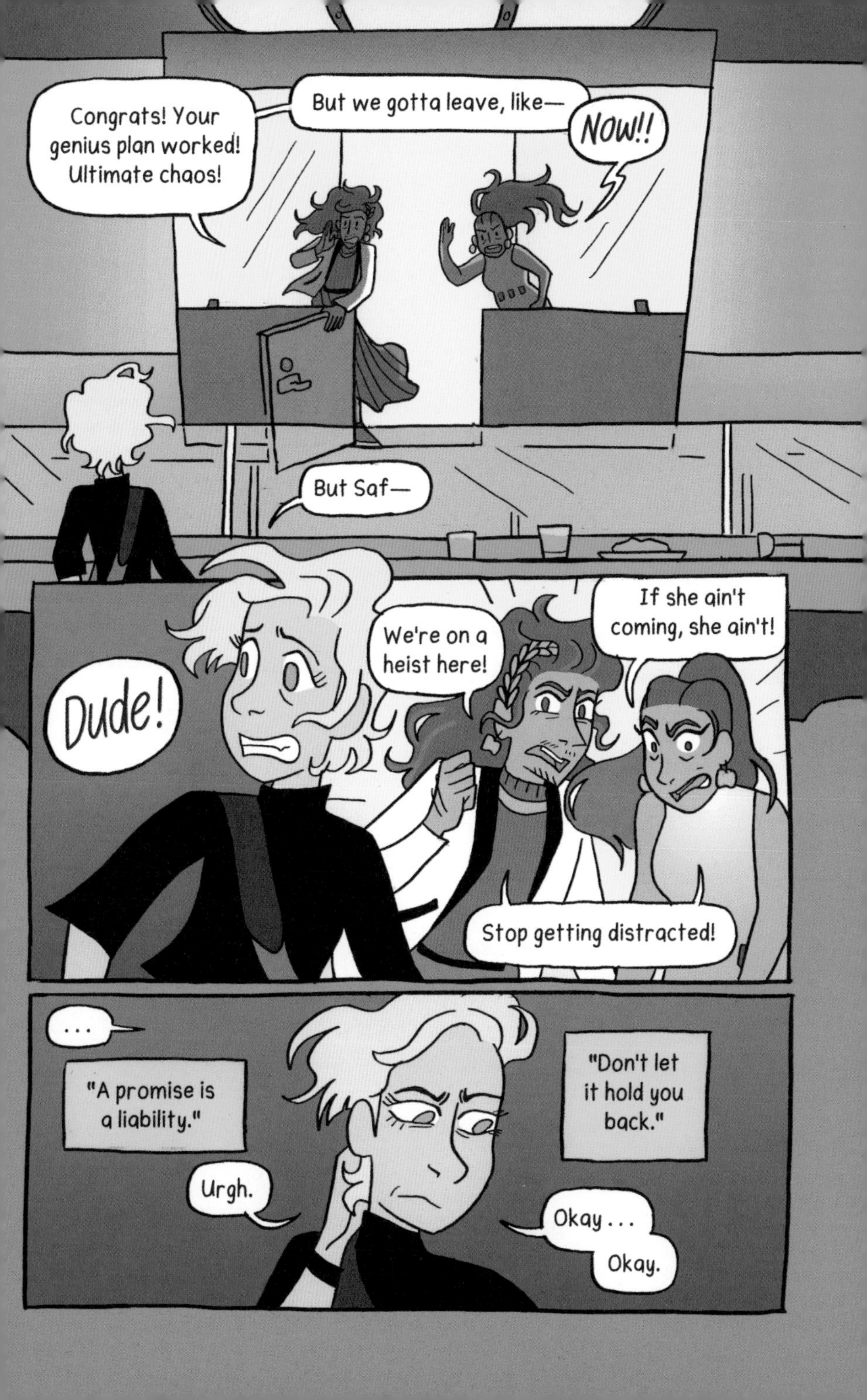
Congrats! Your genius plan worked! Ultimate chaos!
But we gotta leave, like—
NOW!!
But Saf—
Dude!
We're on a heist here!
If she ain't coming, she ain't!
Stop getting distracted!
. . .
"A promise is a liability."
"Don't let it hold you back."
Urgh.
Okay . . .
Okay.

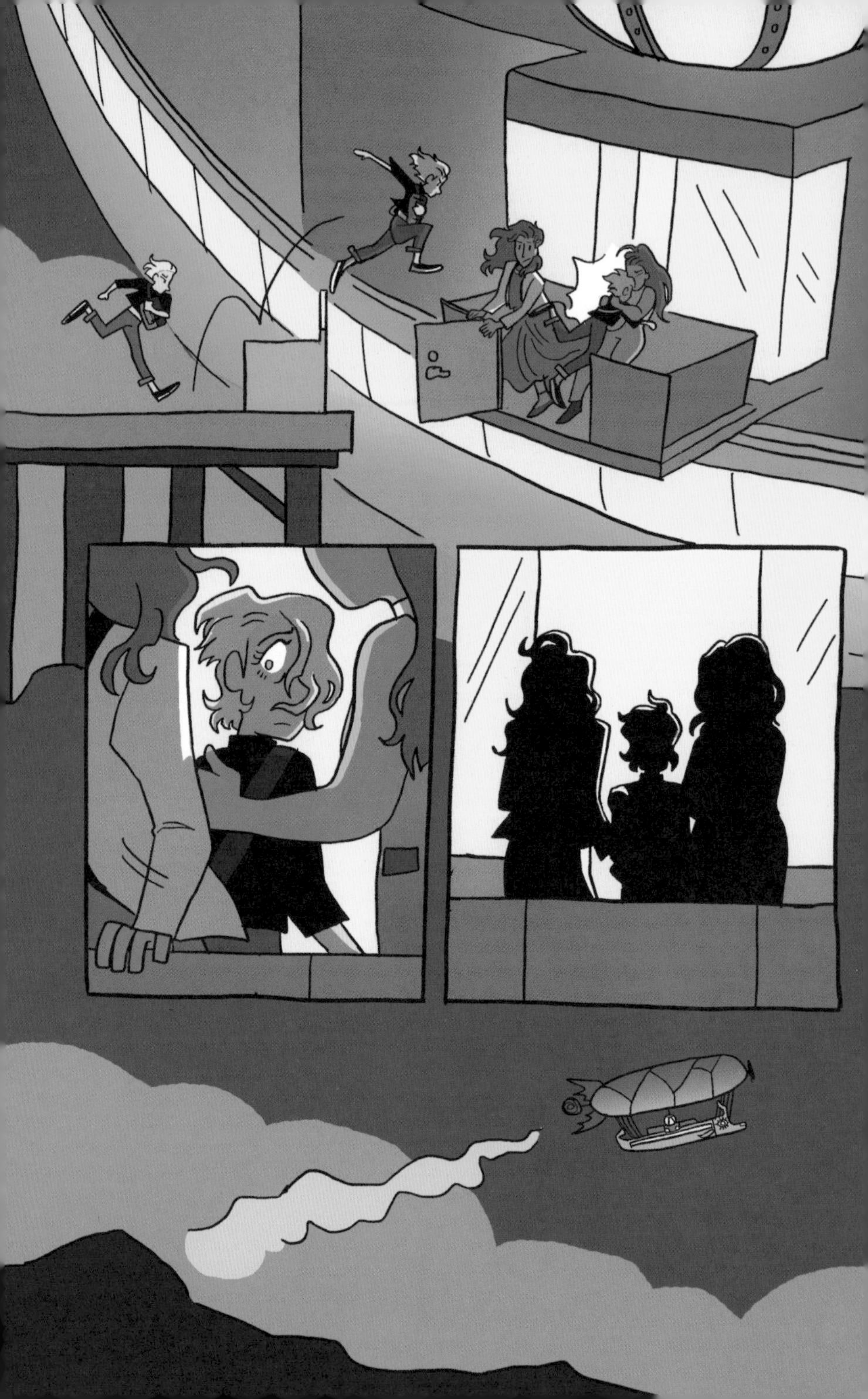

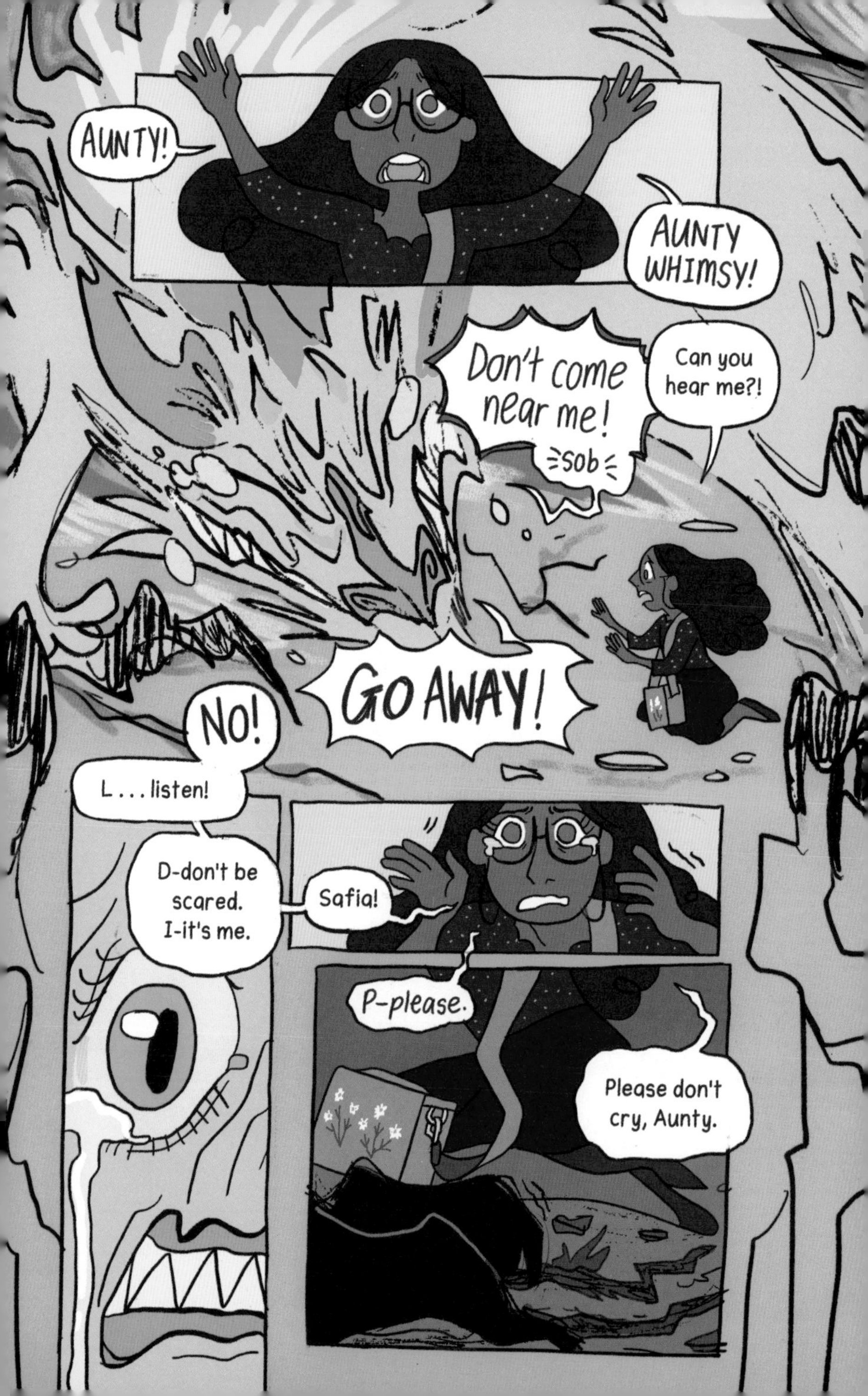
AUNTY!
AUNTY WHIMSY!
Can you hear me?!
Don't come near me!
sob
GO AWAY!
NO!
L . . . listen!
D-don't be scared. I-it's me.
Safia!
P-please.
Please don't cry, Aunty.

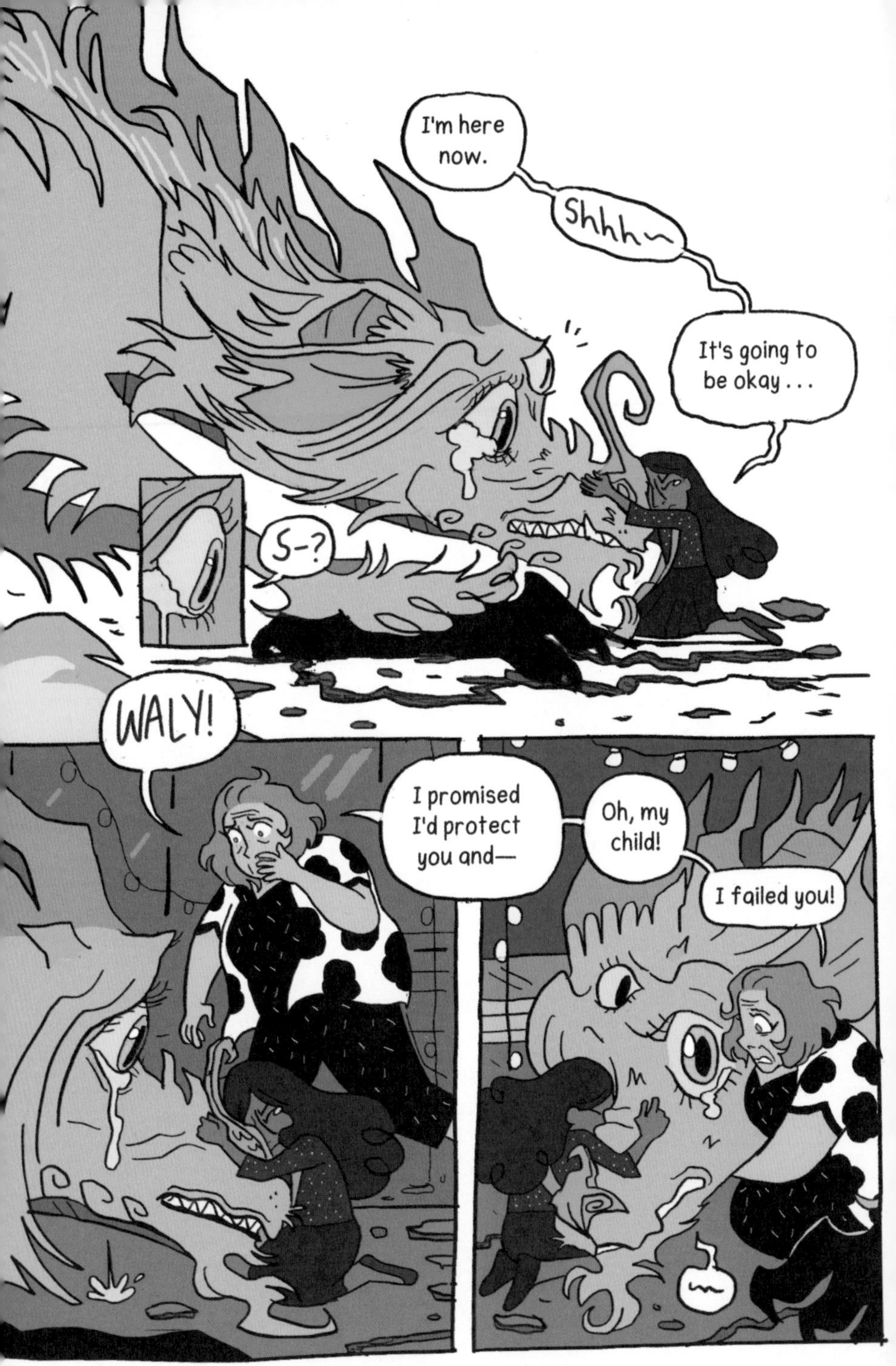
I'm here now.
Shhh~
It's going to be okay . . .
S-?
WALY!
I promised I'd protect you and—
Oh, my child!
I failed you!

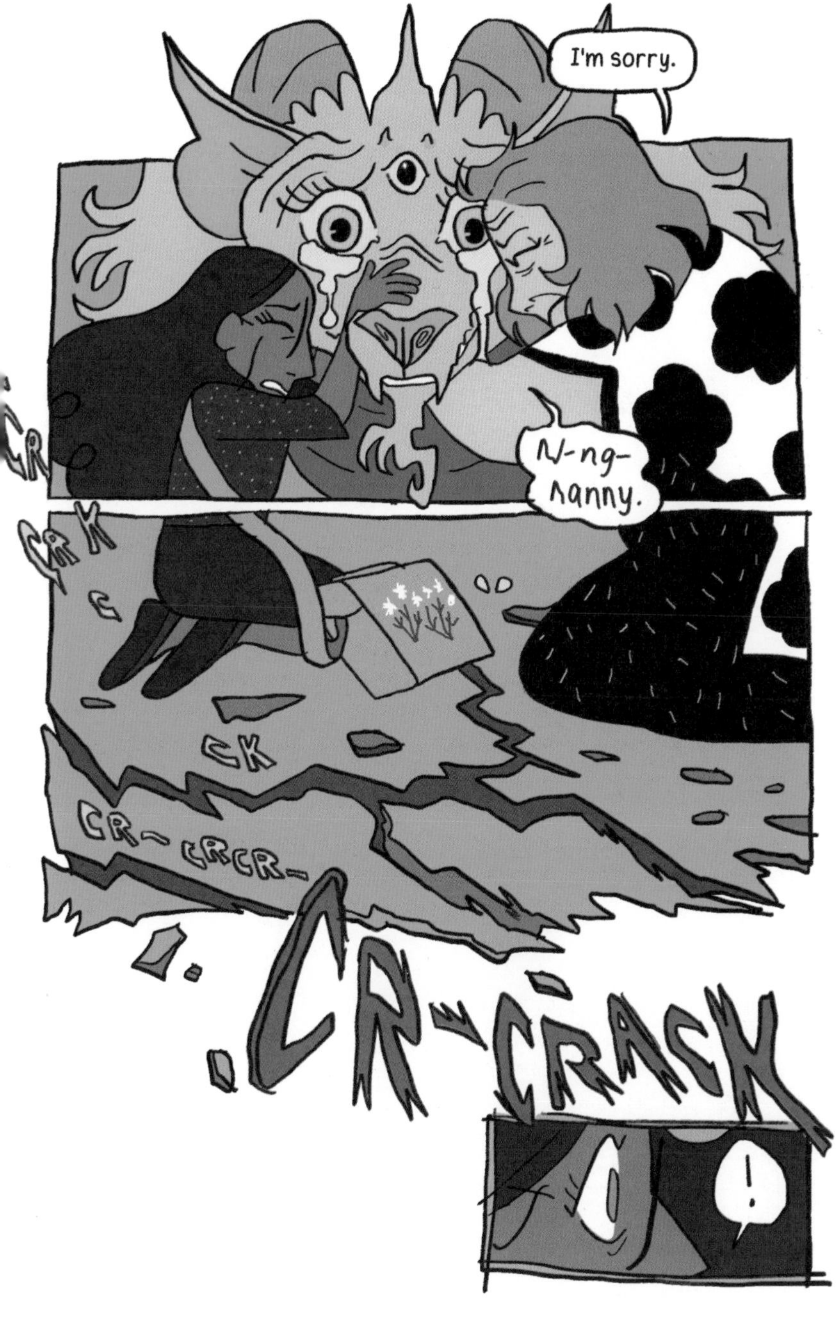
I'm sorry.
N-ng-nanny.
CR
CRK
C
CK
CR-CRCR-
CR-CRACK
!

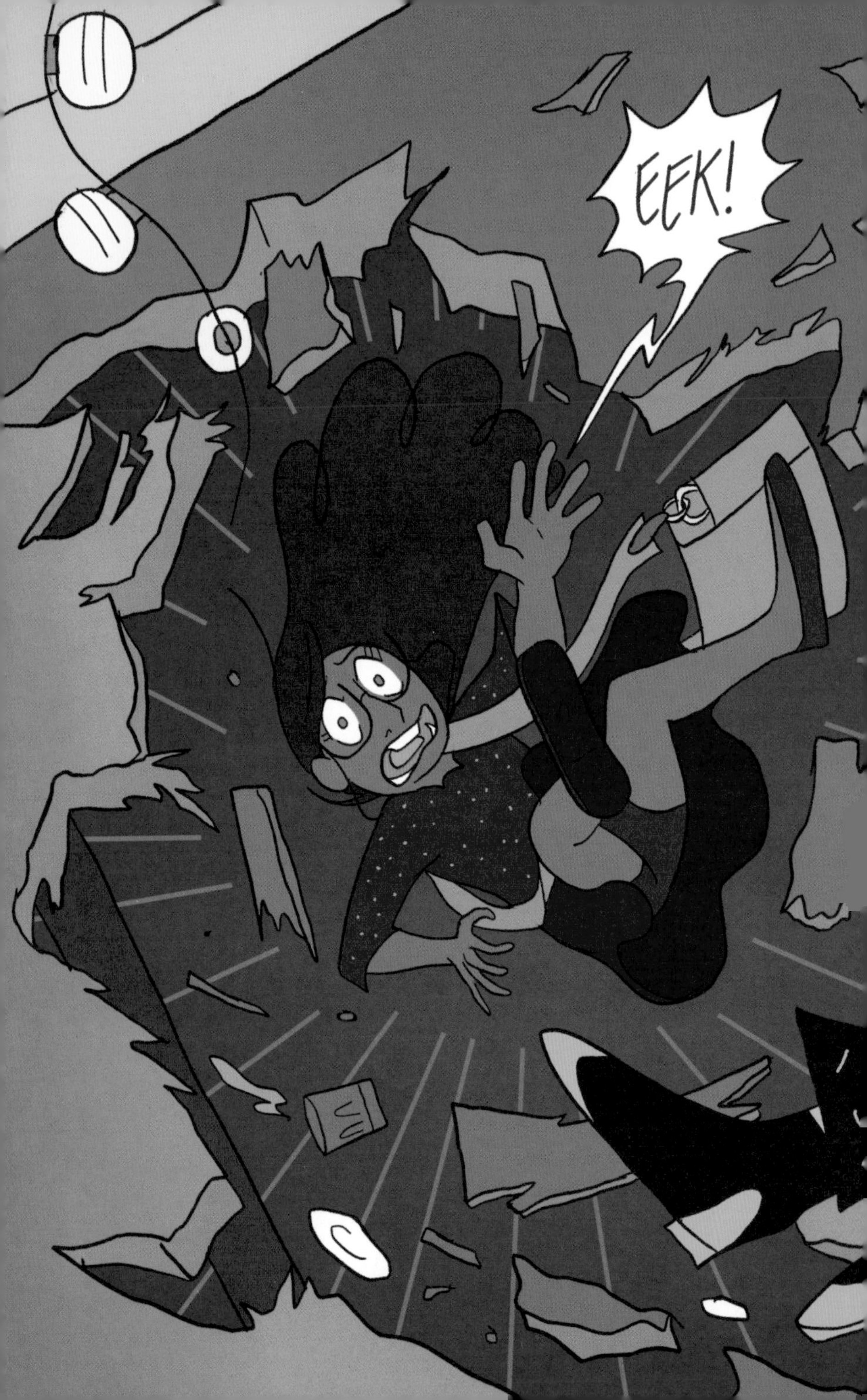
EEK!

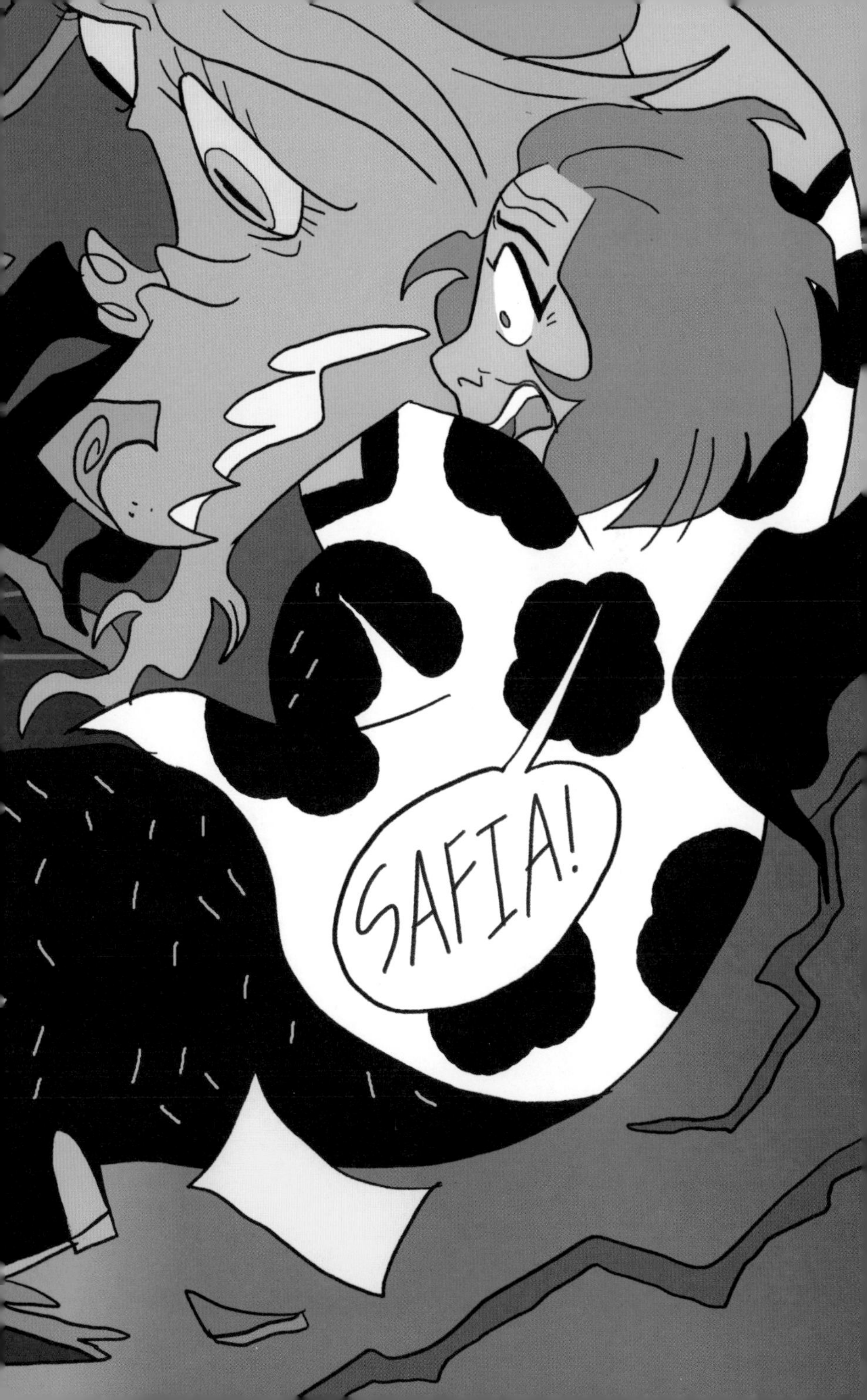
SAFIA!

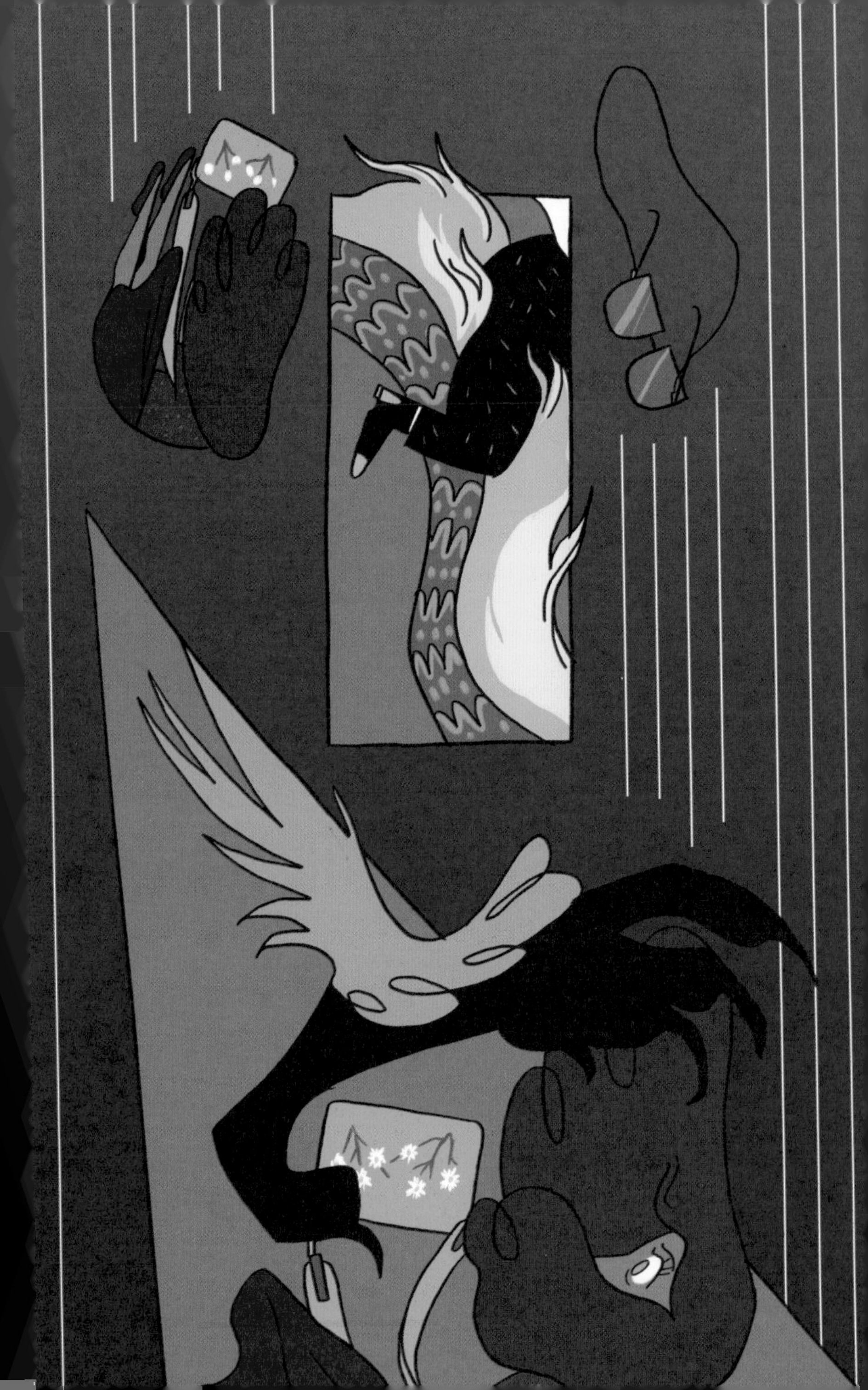

Chapter Eight

Safia . . .

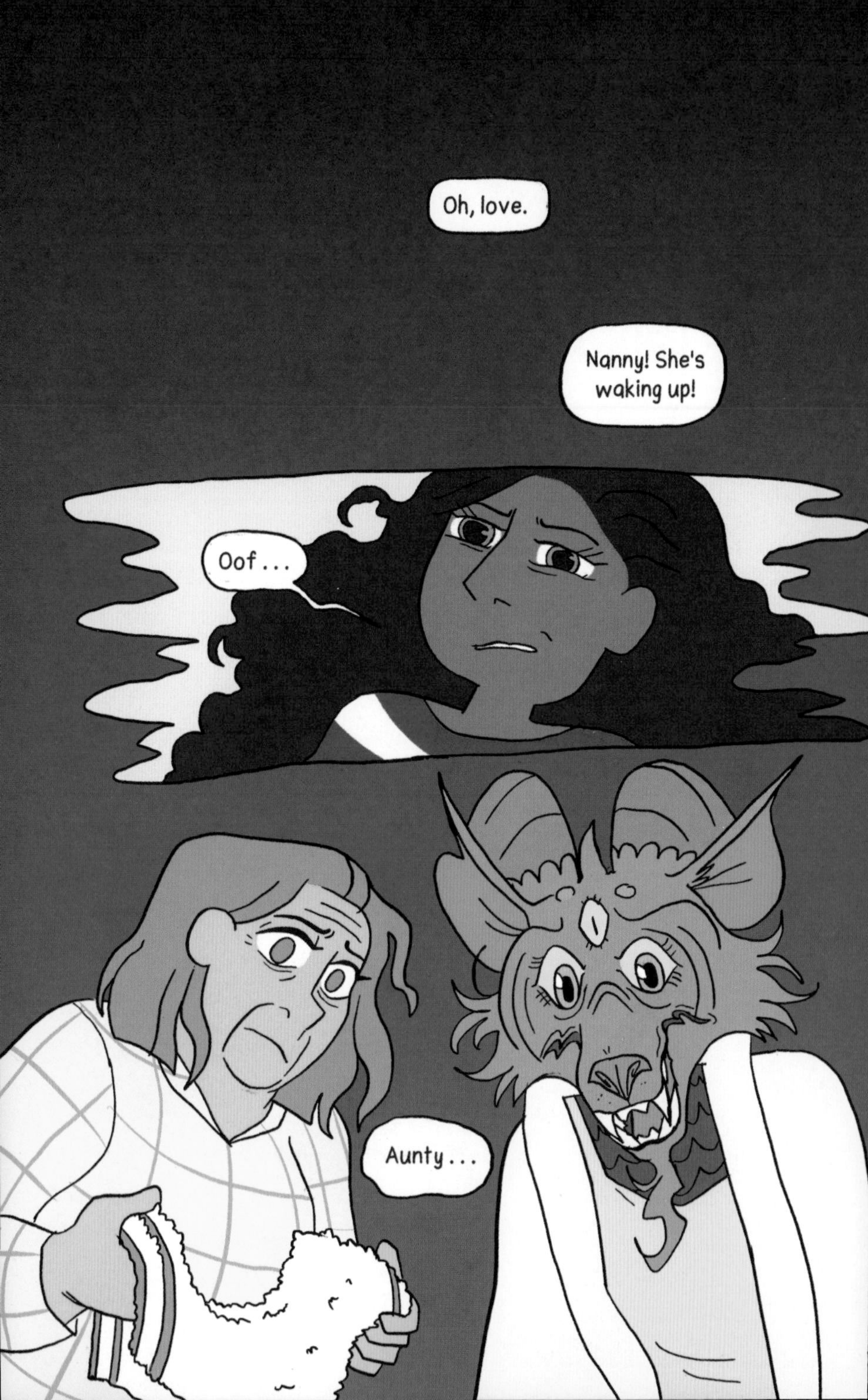
Oh, love.
Nanny! She's waking up!
Oof . . .
Aunty . . .

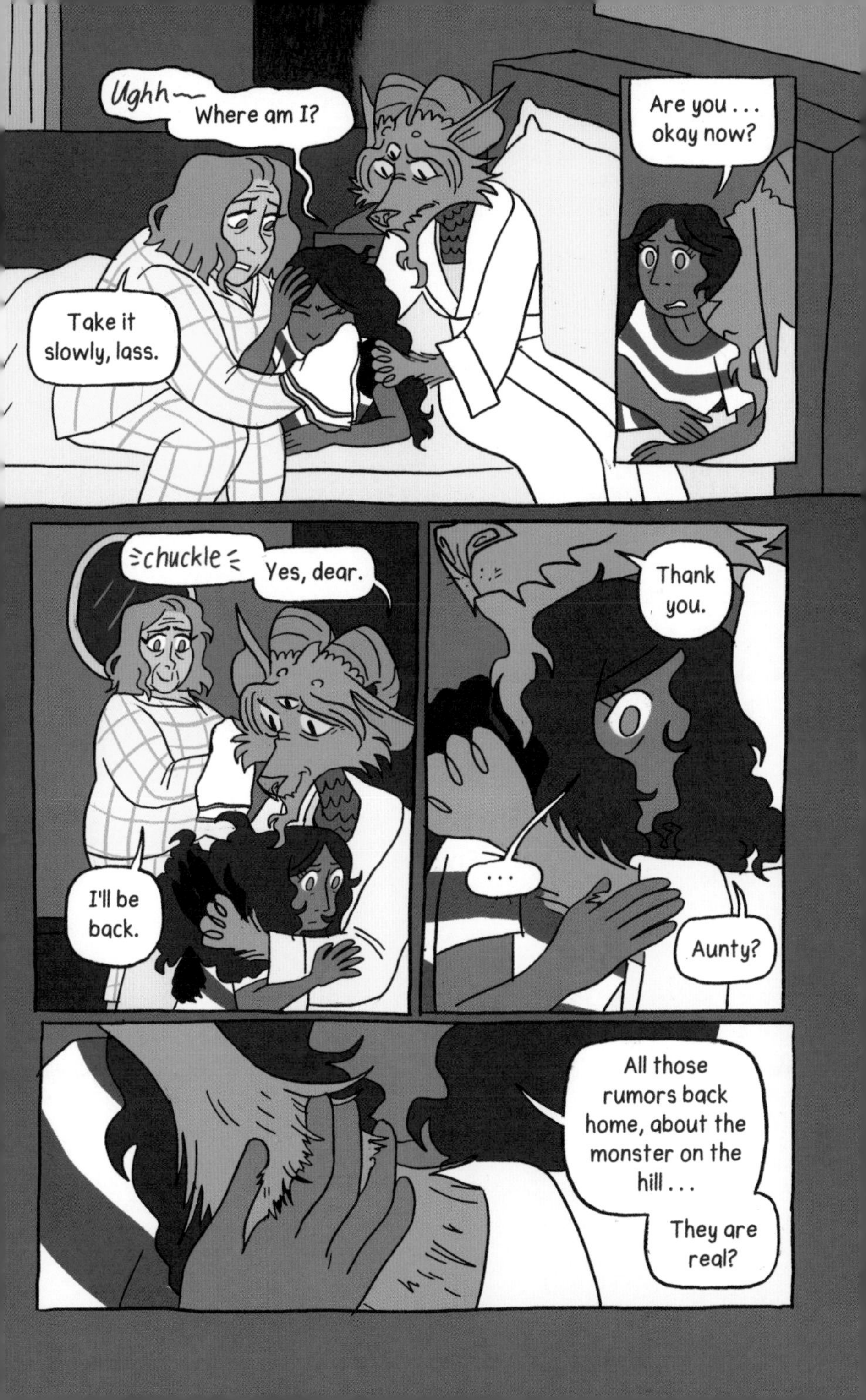
Ughh— Where am I?
Are you . . . okay now?
Take it slowly, lass.
chuckle
Yes, dear.
I'll be back.
Thank you.
. . .
Aunty?
All those rumors back home, about the monster on the hill . . .
They are real?

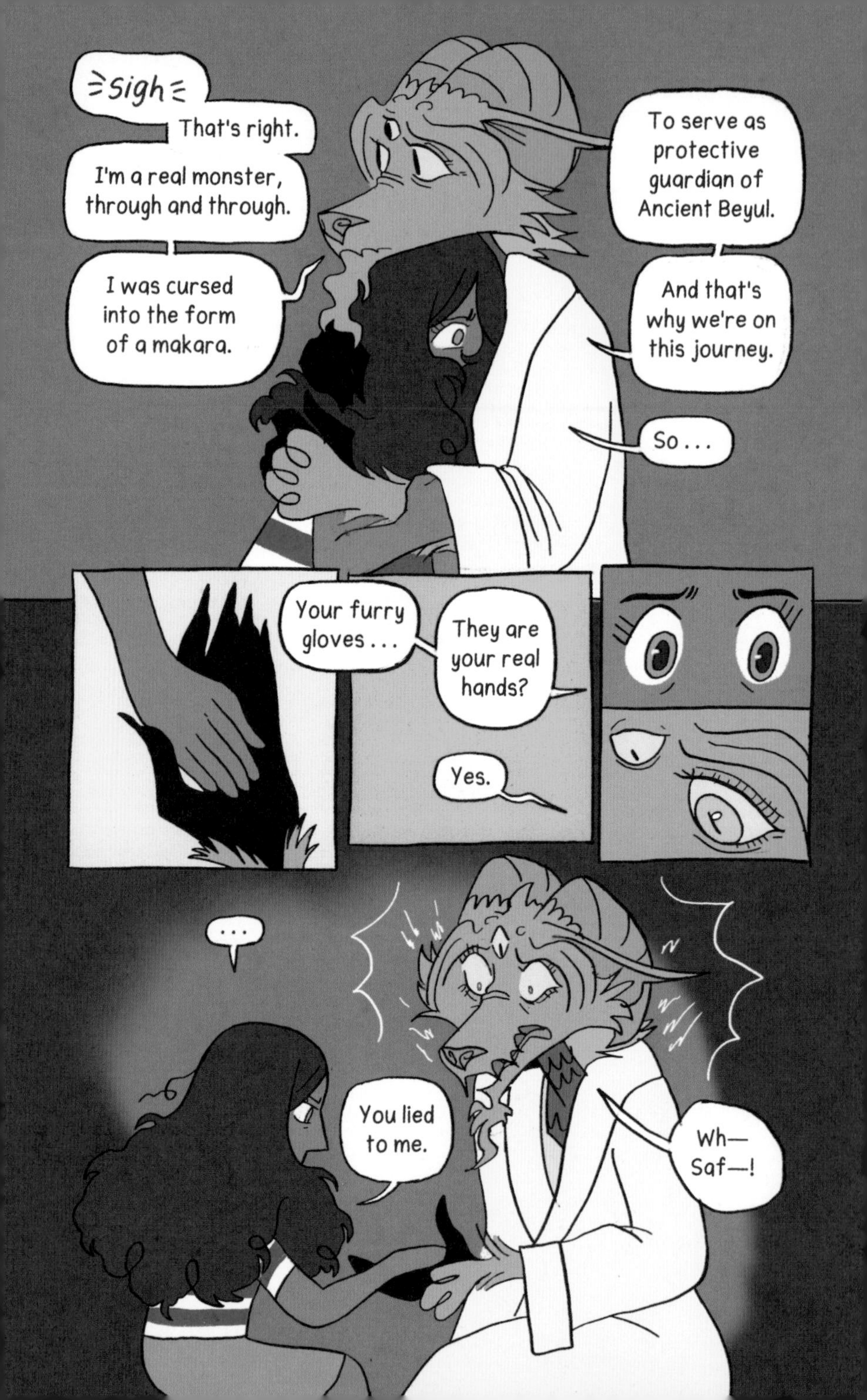
Sigh
That's right.
I'm a real monster, through and through.
I was cursed into the form of a makara.
To serve as protective guardian of Ancient Beyul.
And that's why we're on this journey.
So . . .
Your furry gloves . . .
They are your real hands?
Yes.
. . .
You lied to me.
Wh— Saf—!

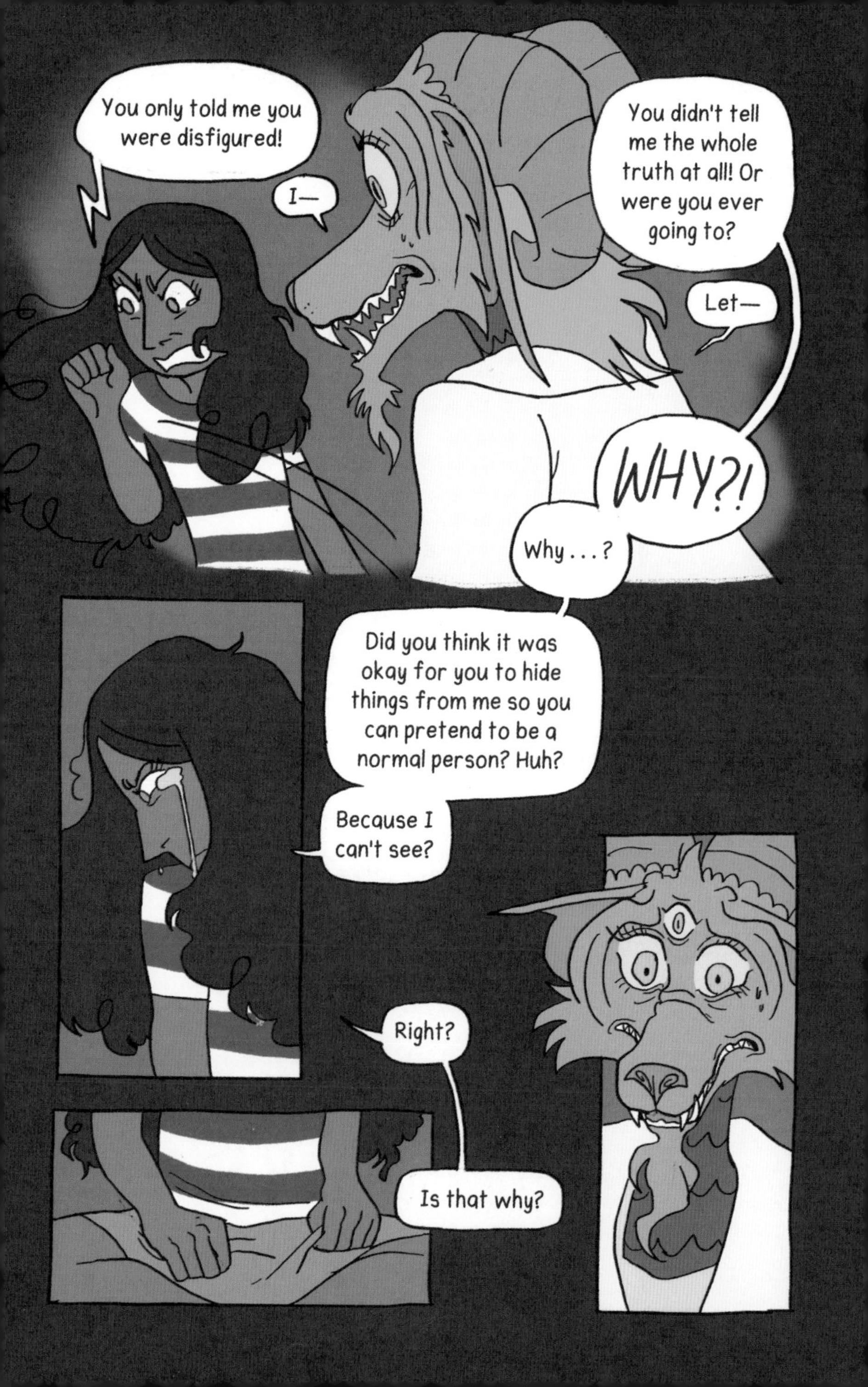
You only told me you were disfigured!
I—
You didn't tell me the whole truth at all! Or were you ever going to?
Let—
WHY?!
Why . . . ?
Did you think it was okay for you to hide things from me so you can pretend to be a normal person? Huh?
Because I can't see?
Right?
Is that why?

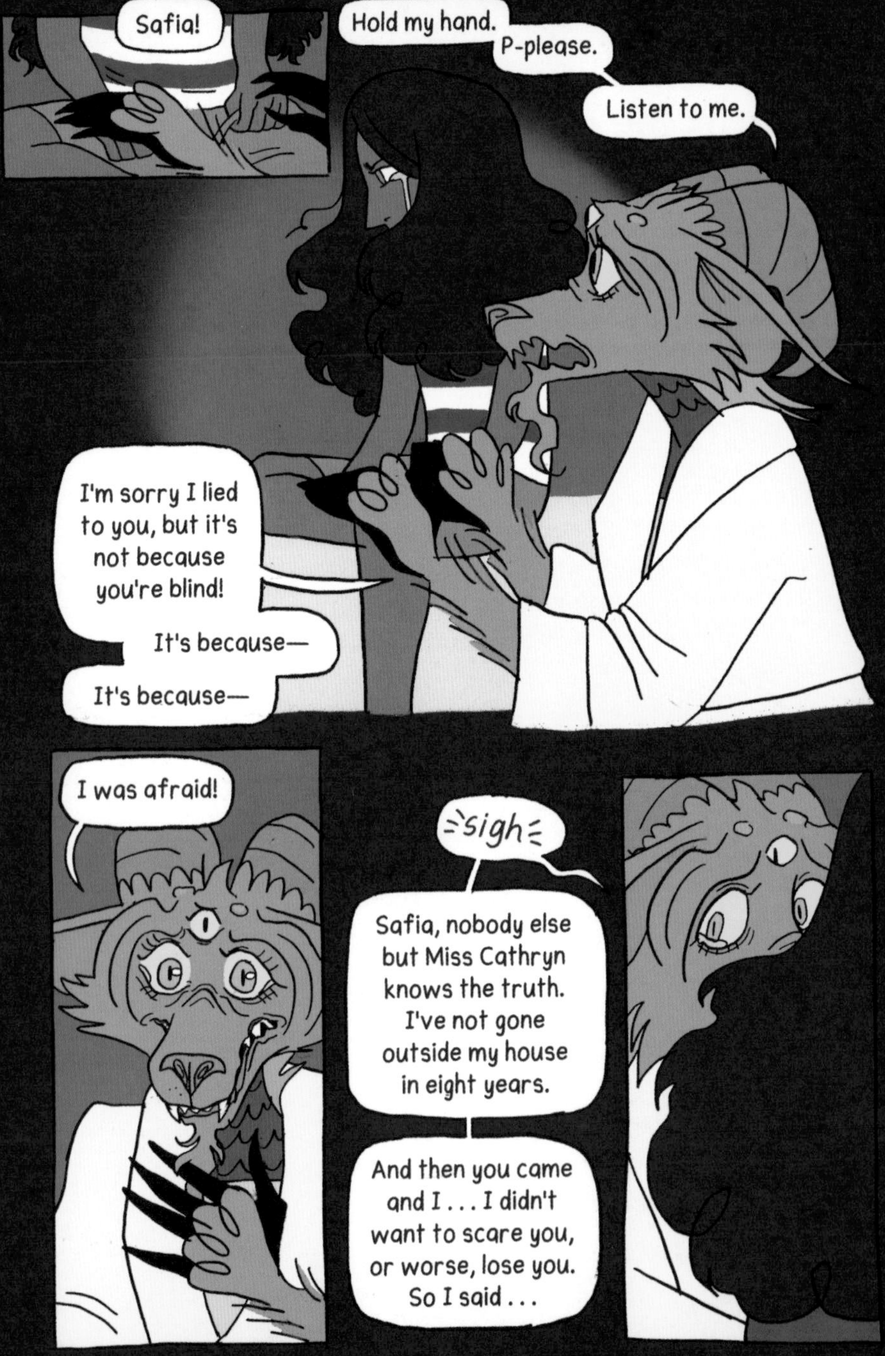
Safia!
Hold my hand.
P-please.
Listen to me.
I'm sorry I lied to you, but it's not because you're blind!
It's because—
It's because—
I was afraid!
sigh
Safia, nobody else but Miss Cathryn knows the truth. I've not gone outside my house in eight years.
And then you came and I . . . I didn't want to scare you, or worse, lose you. So I said . . .

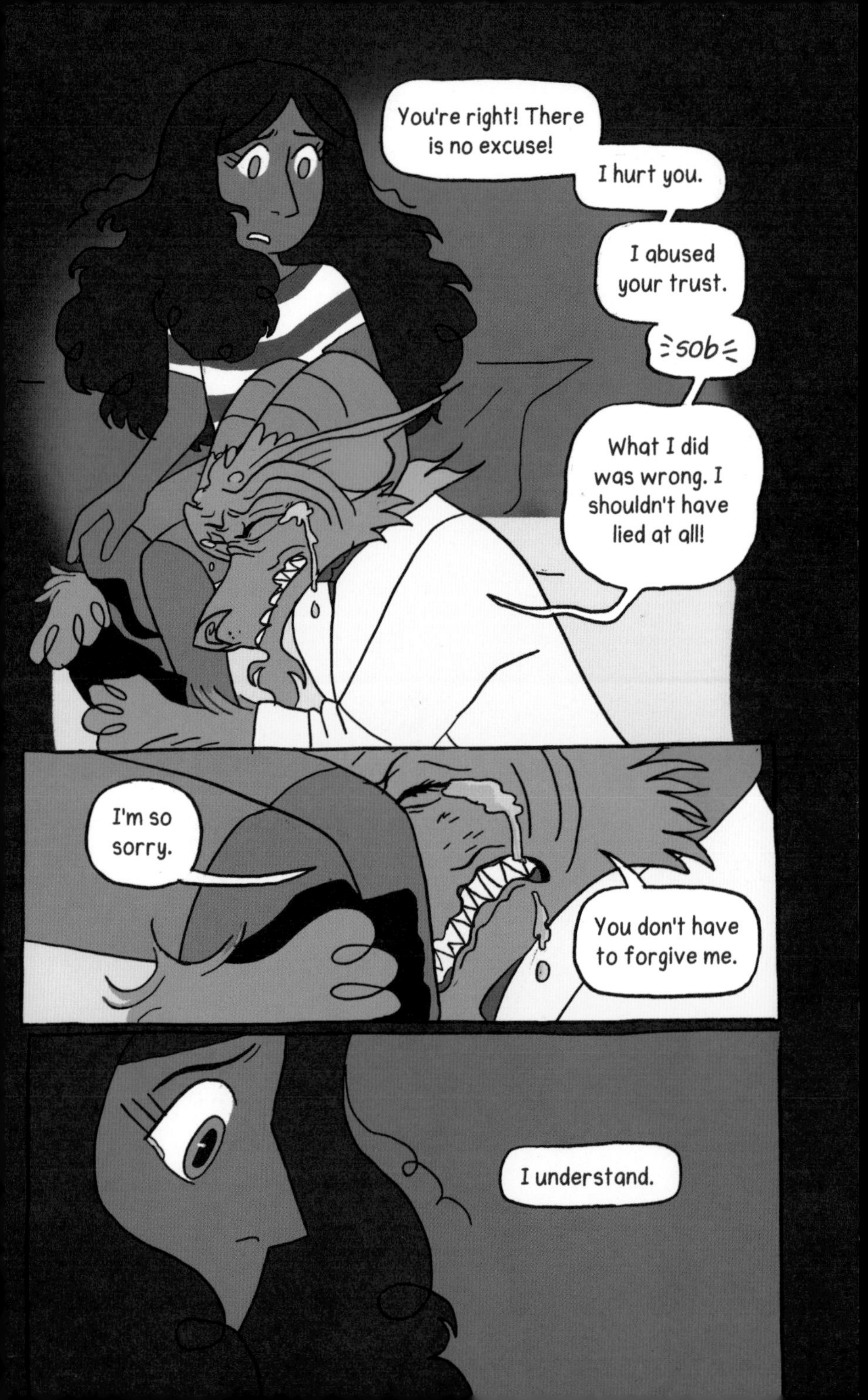

You're right! There is no excuse!
I hurt you.
I abused your trust.
sob
What I did was wrong. I shouldn't have lied at all!
I'm so sorry.
You don't have to forgive me.
I understand.

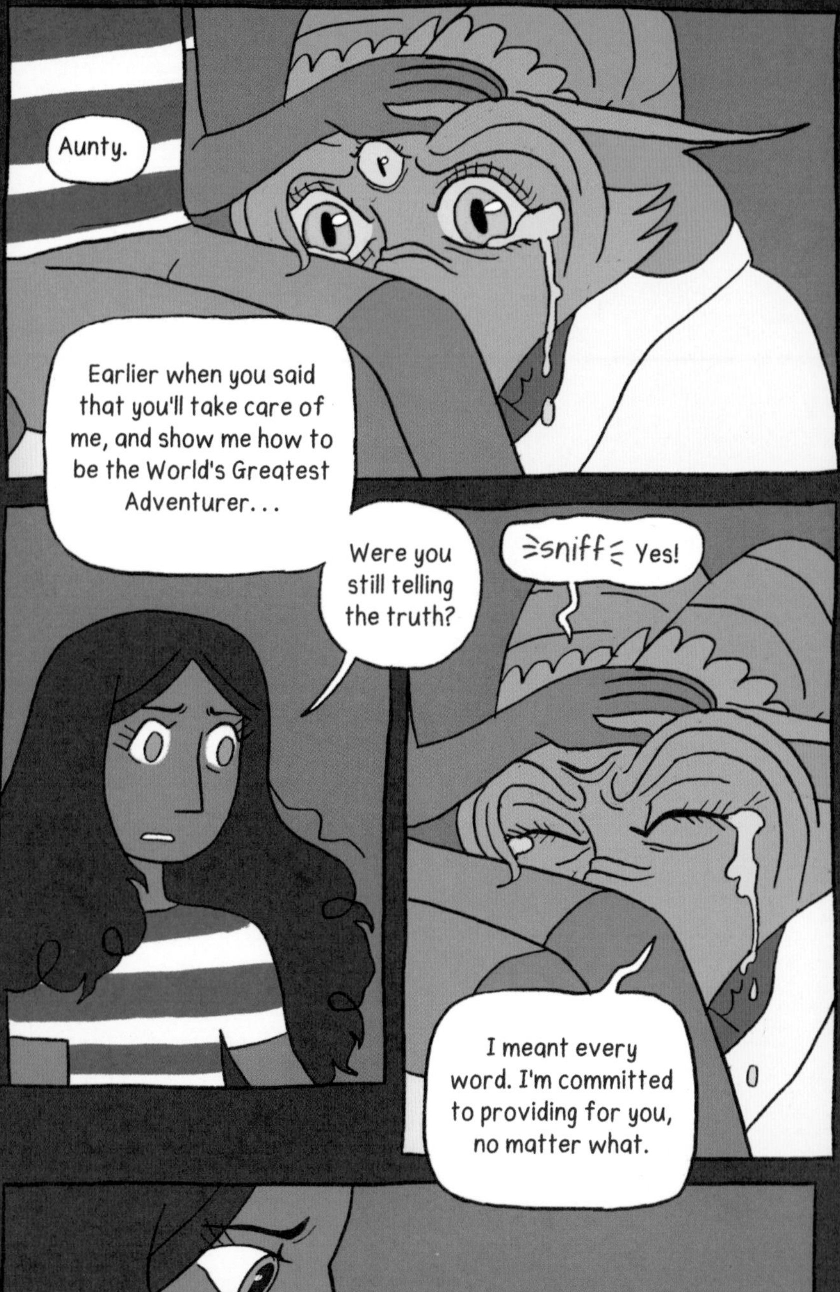
Aunty.
Earlier when you said that you'll take care of me, and show me how to be the World's Greatest Adventurer. . .
Were you still telling the truth?
sniff Yes!
I meant every word. I'm committed to providing for you, no matter what.

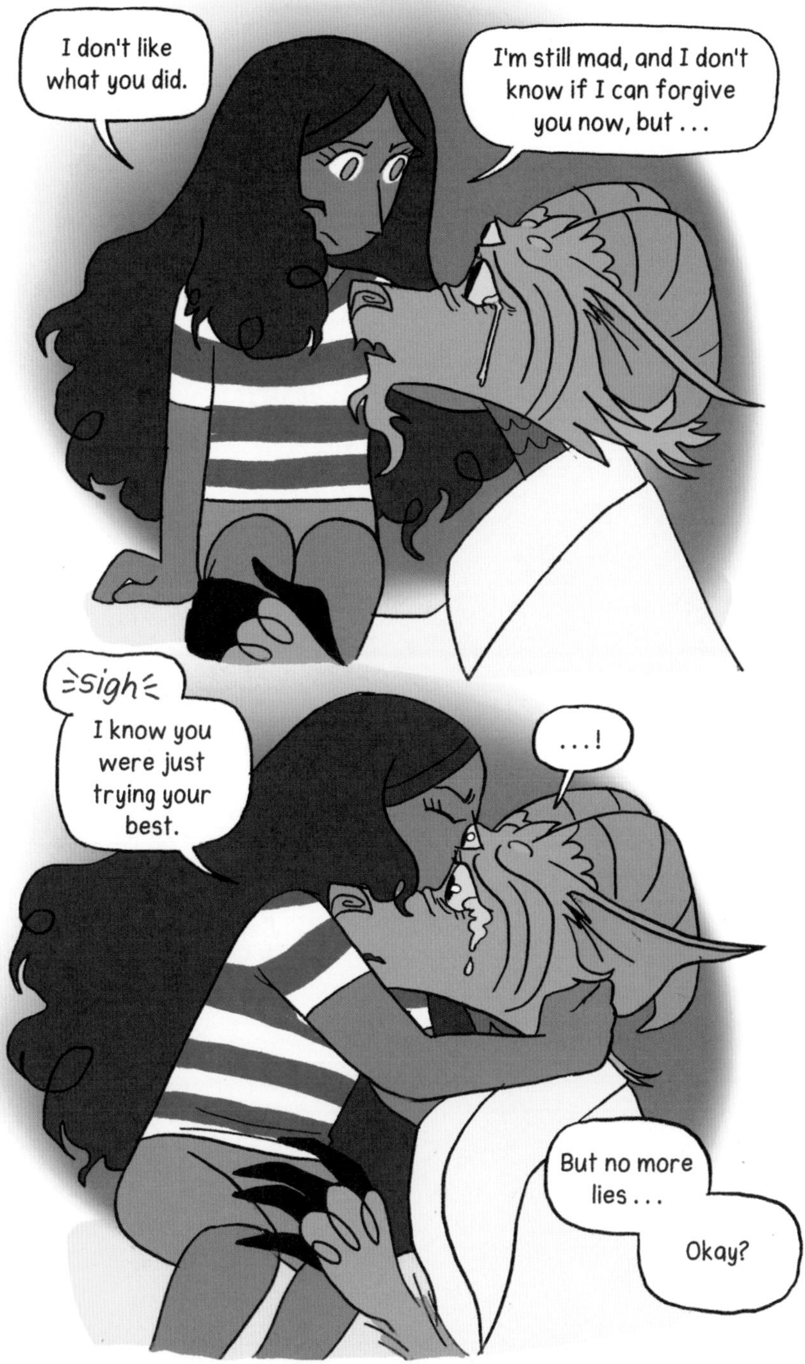
I don't like what you did.
I'm still mad, and I don't know if I can forgive you now, but . . .
Sigh
I know you were just trying your best.
. . . !
But no more lies . . .
Okay?

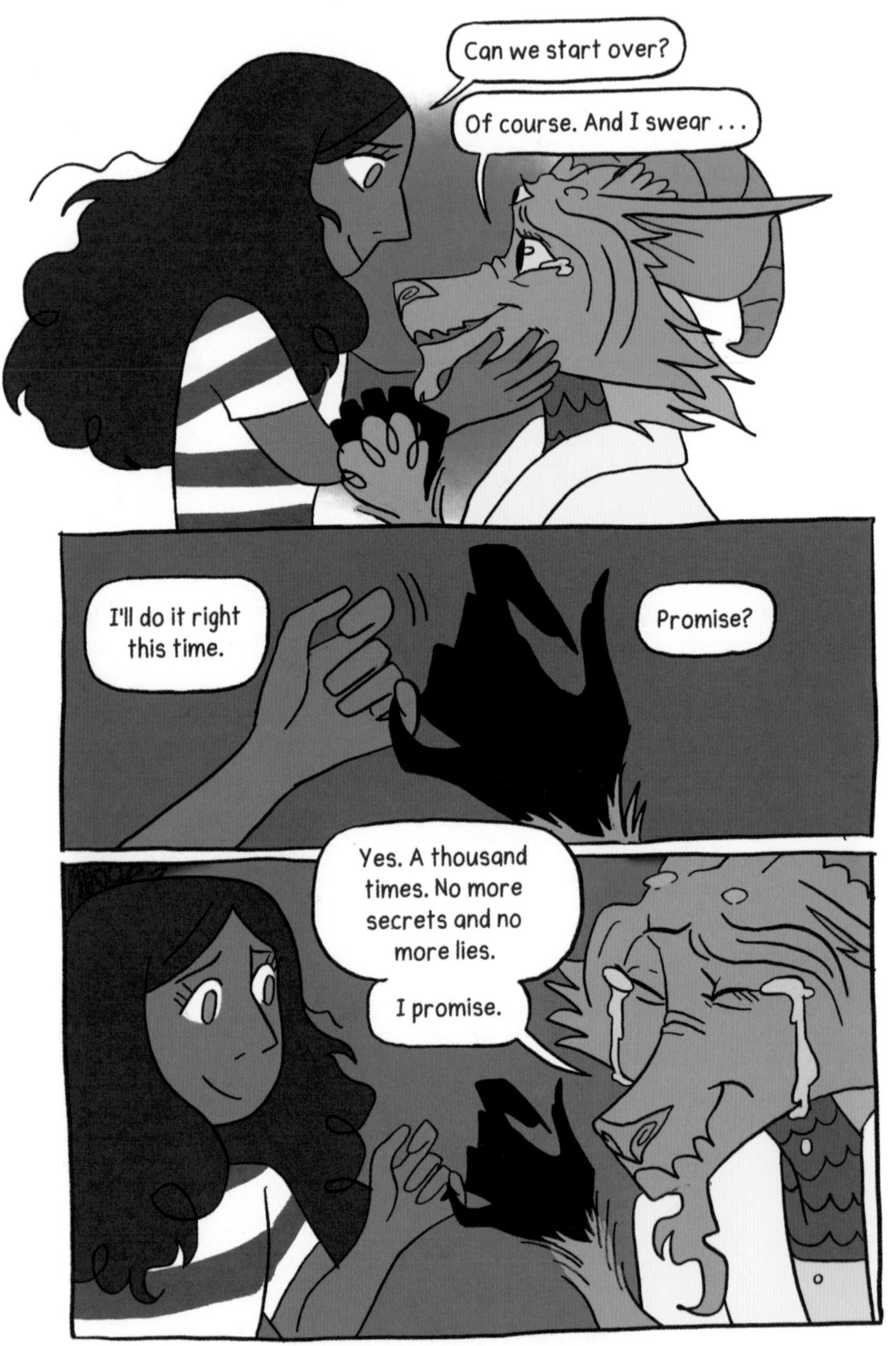
Can we start over?
Of course. And I swear . . .
I'll do it right this time.
Promise?
Yes. A thousand times. No more secrets and no more lies.
I promise.

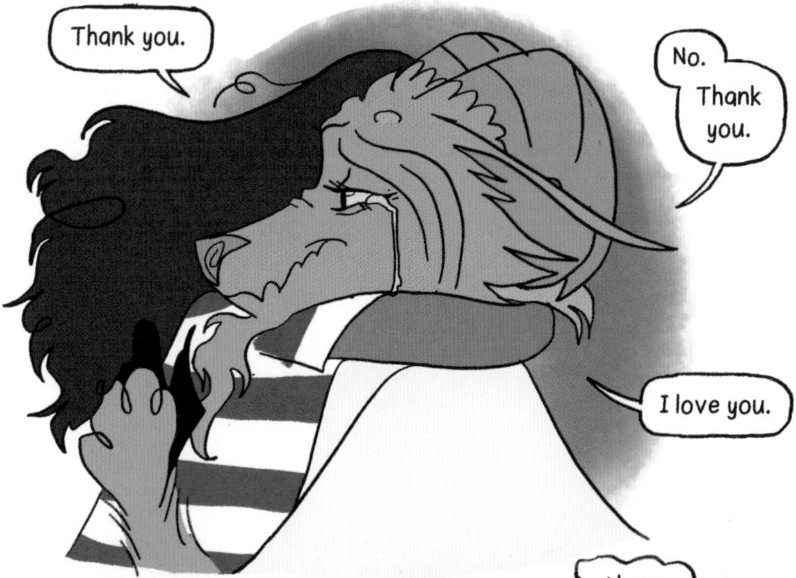
Thank you.
No.
Thank you.
I love you.

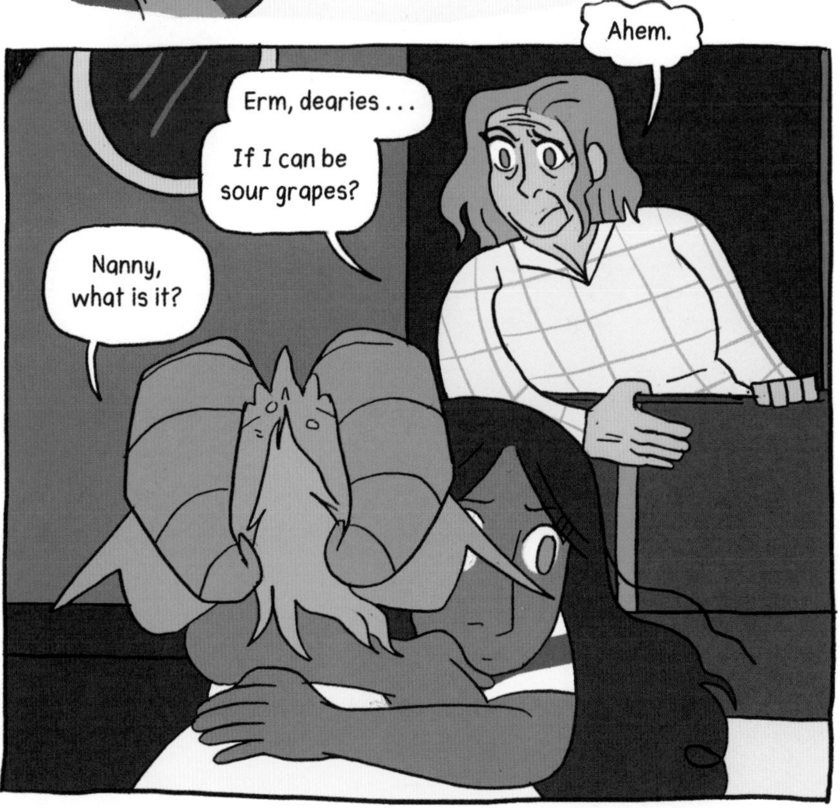
Ahem.
Erm, dearies . . .
If I can be sour grapes?
Nanny, what is it?

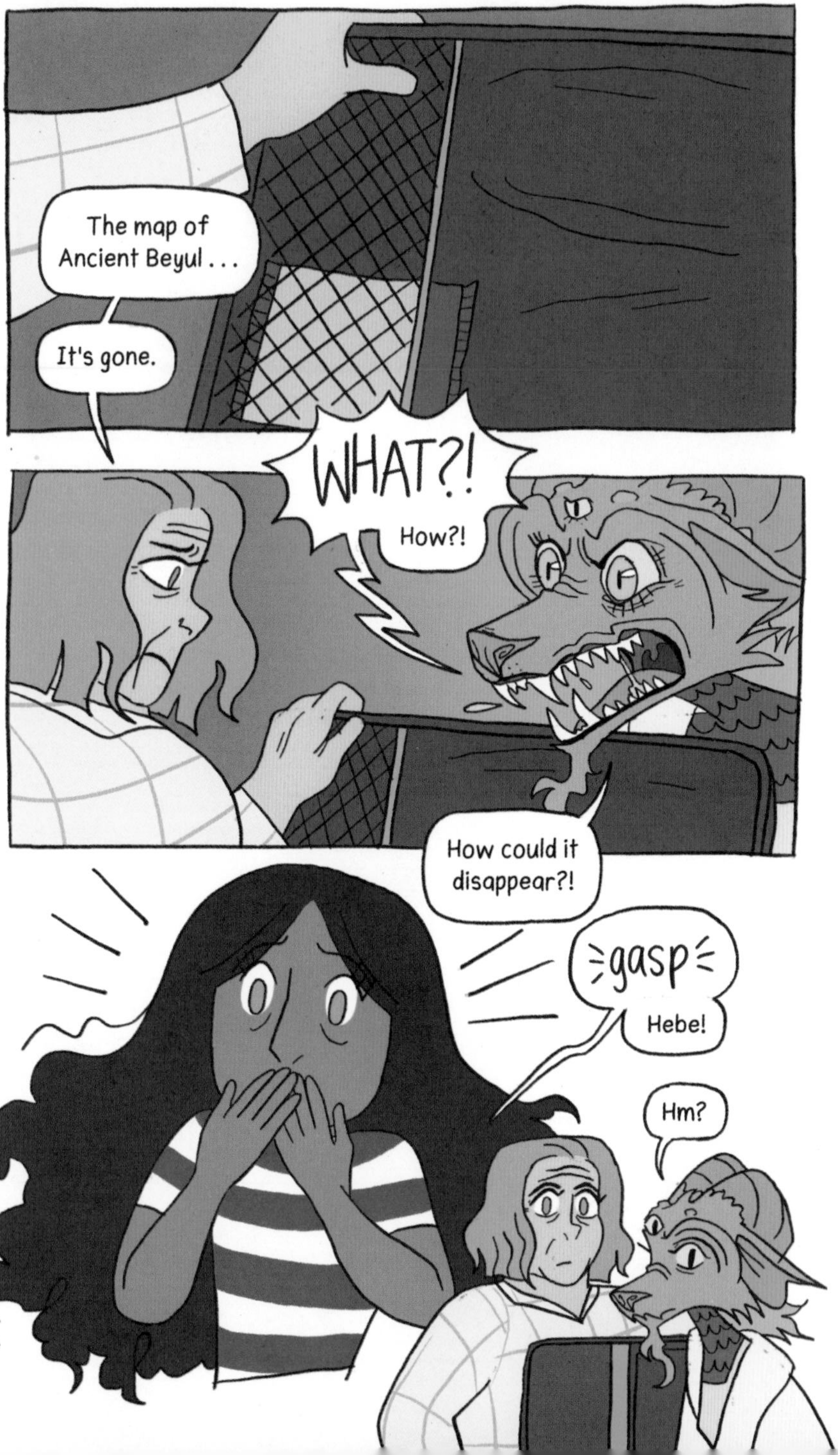
The map of Ancient Beyul . . .
It's gone.
WHAT?!
How?!
How could it disappear?!
gasp
Hebe!
Hm?

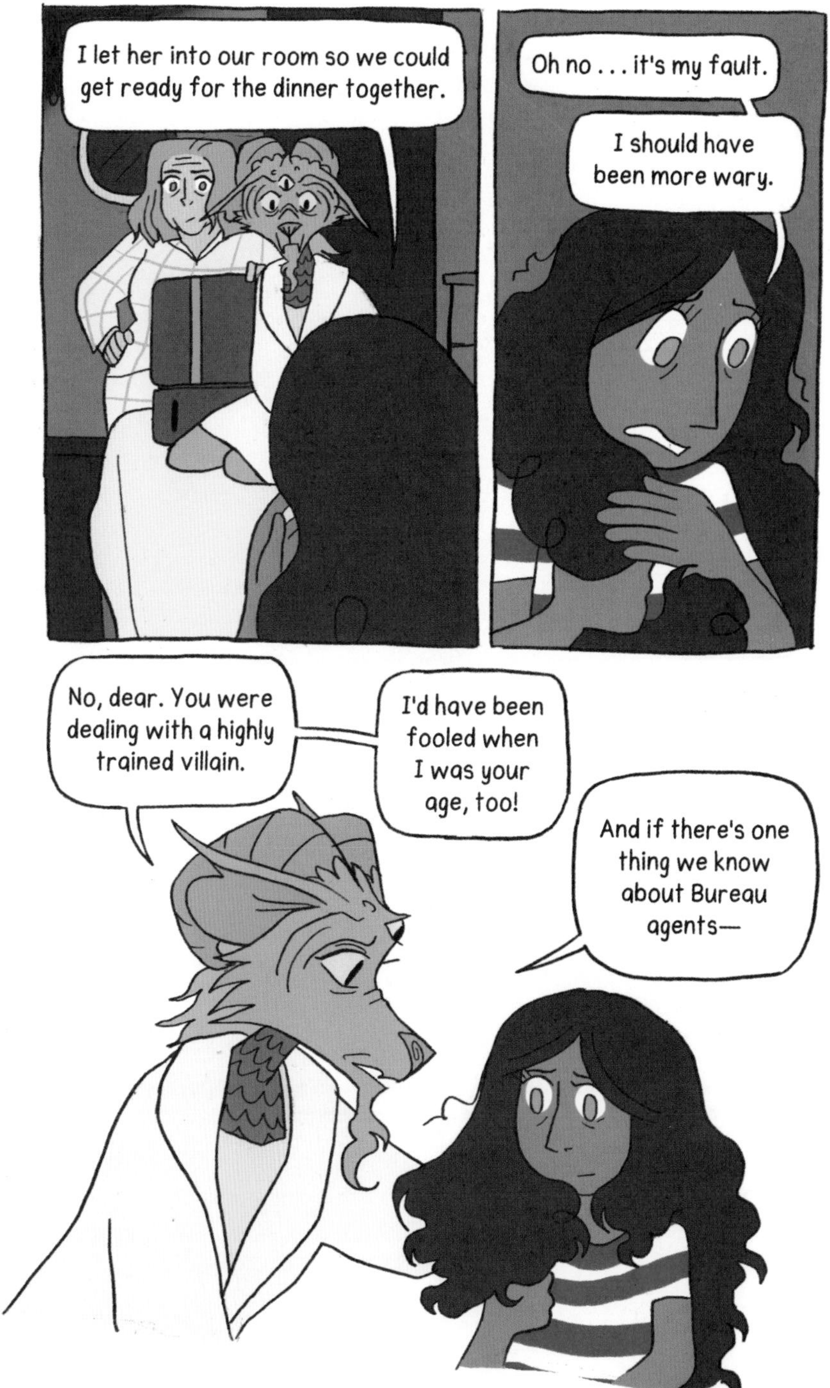
I let her into our room so we could get ready for the dinner together.
Oh no . . . it's my fault.
I should have been more wary.
No, dear. You were dealing with a highly trained villain.
I'd have been fooled when I was your age, too!
And if there's one thing we know about Bureau agents—

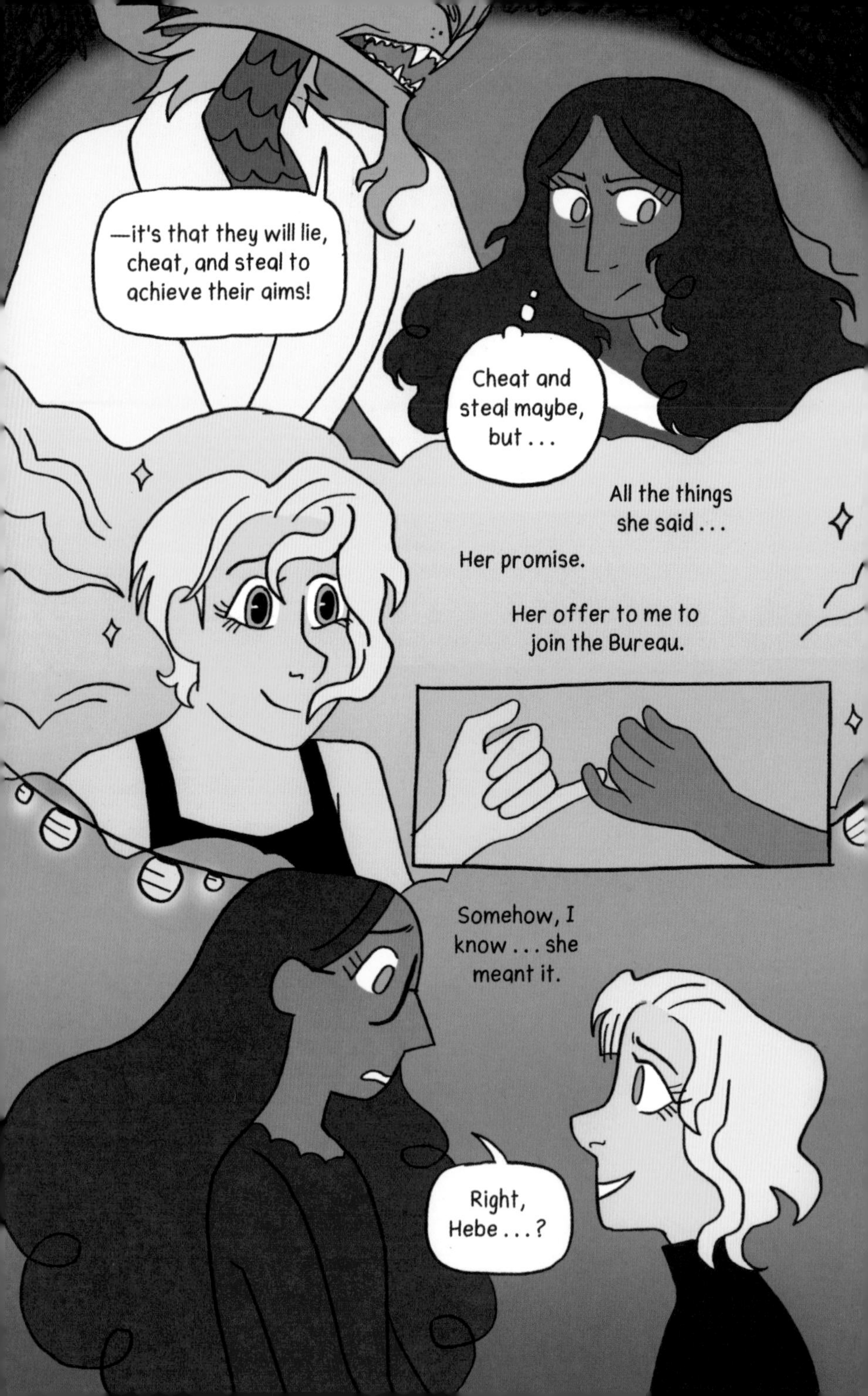
—it's that they will lie, cheat, and steal to achieve their aims!
Cheat and steal maybe, but . . .
All the things she said . . .
Her promise.
Her offer to me to join the Bureau.
Somehow, I know . . . she meant it.
Right, Hebe . . . ?

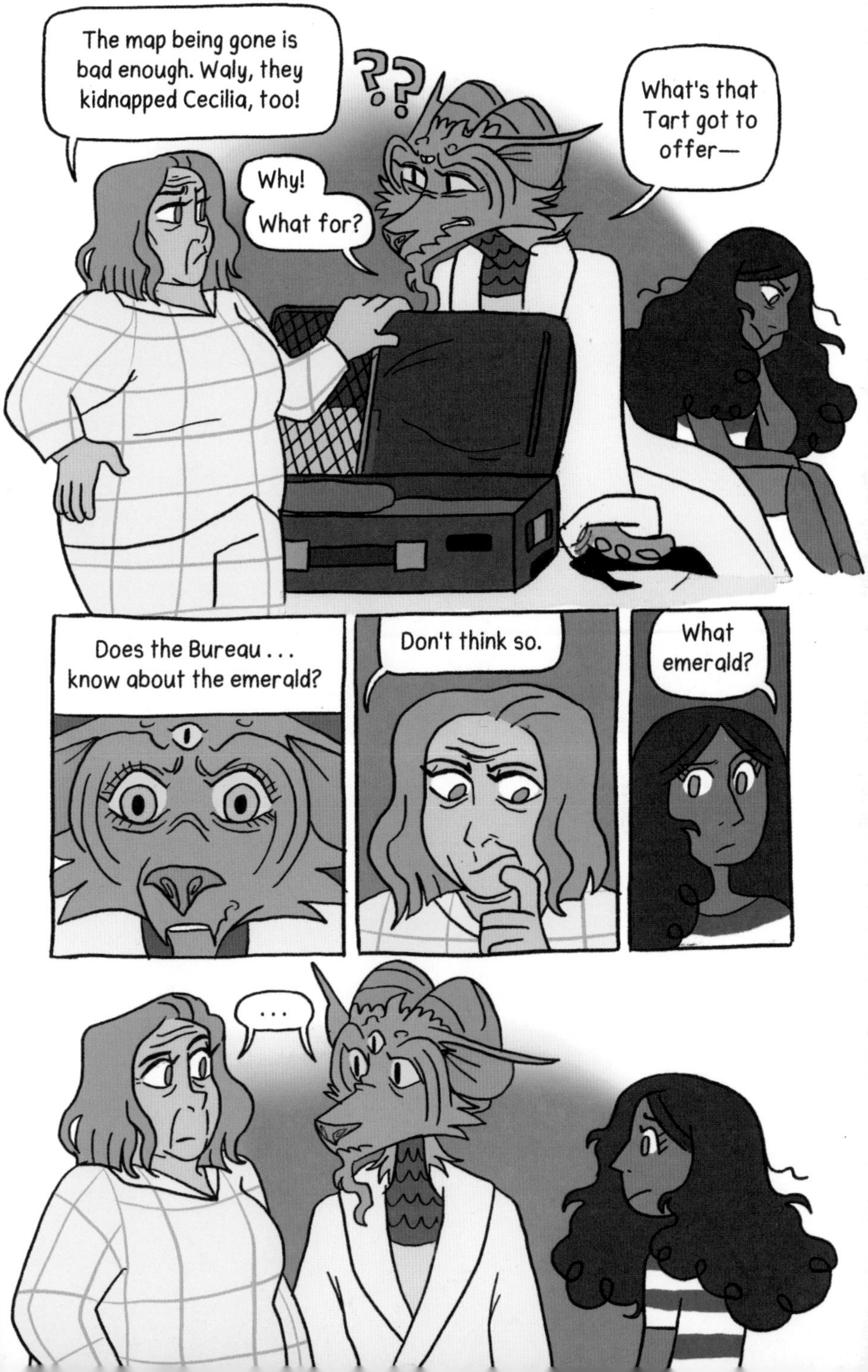

The map being gone is bad enough. Waly, they kidnapped Cecilia, too!
??
Why!
What for?
What's that Tart got to offer—
Does the Bureau . . . know about the emerald?
Don't think so.
What emerald?
. . .

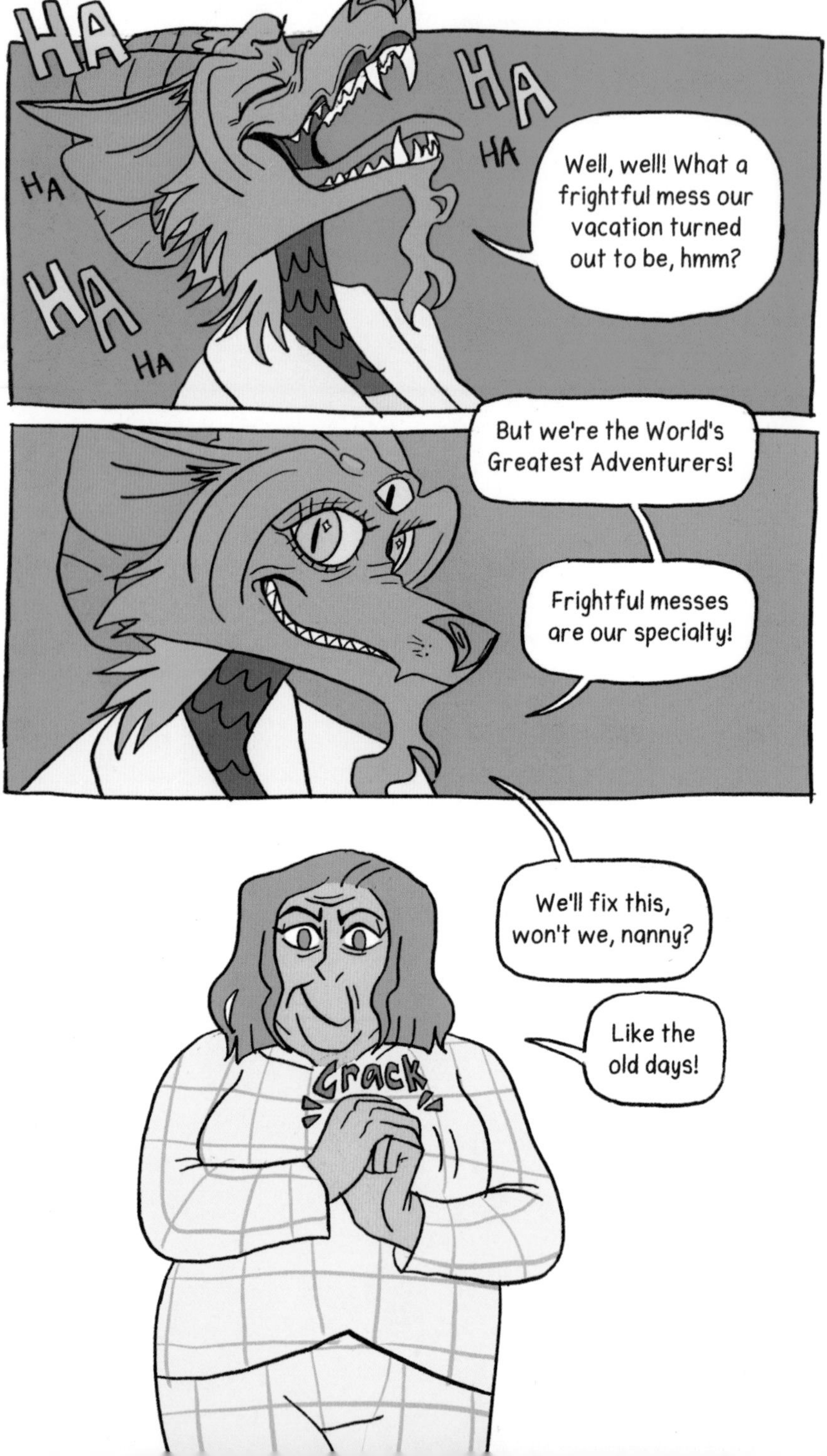
HA
HA
HA
HA
HA
HA
HA
Well, well! What a frightful mess our vacation turned out to be, hmm?
But we're the World's Greatest Adventurers!
Frightful messes are our specialty!
We'll fix this, won't we, nanny?
Like the old days!
Crack

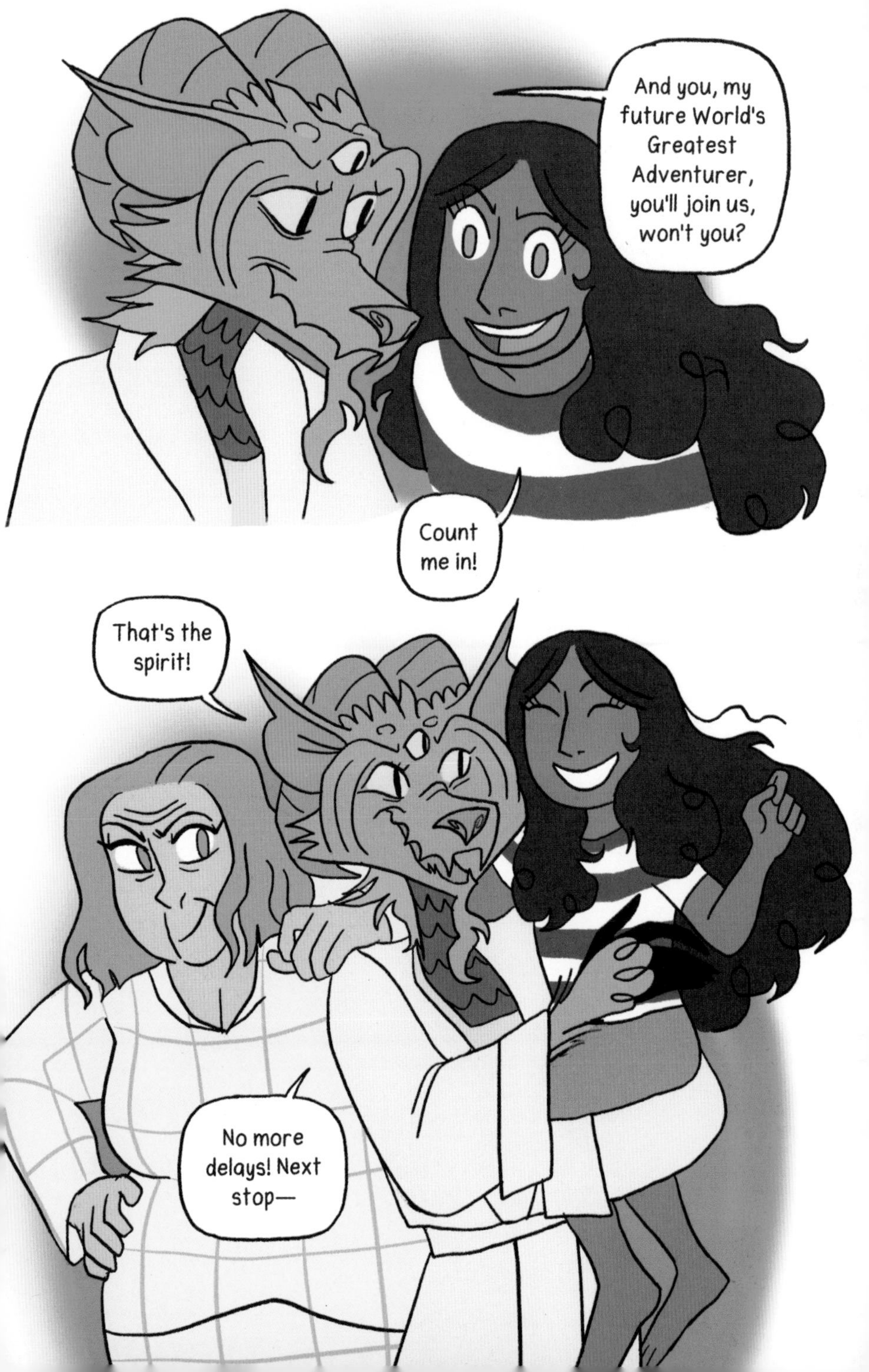
And you, my future World's Greatest Adventurer, you'll join us, won't you?
Count me in!
That's the spirit!
No more delays! Next stop—

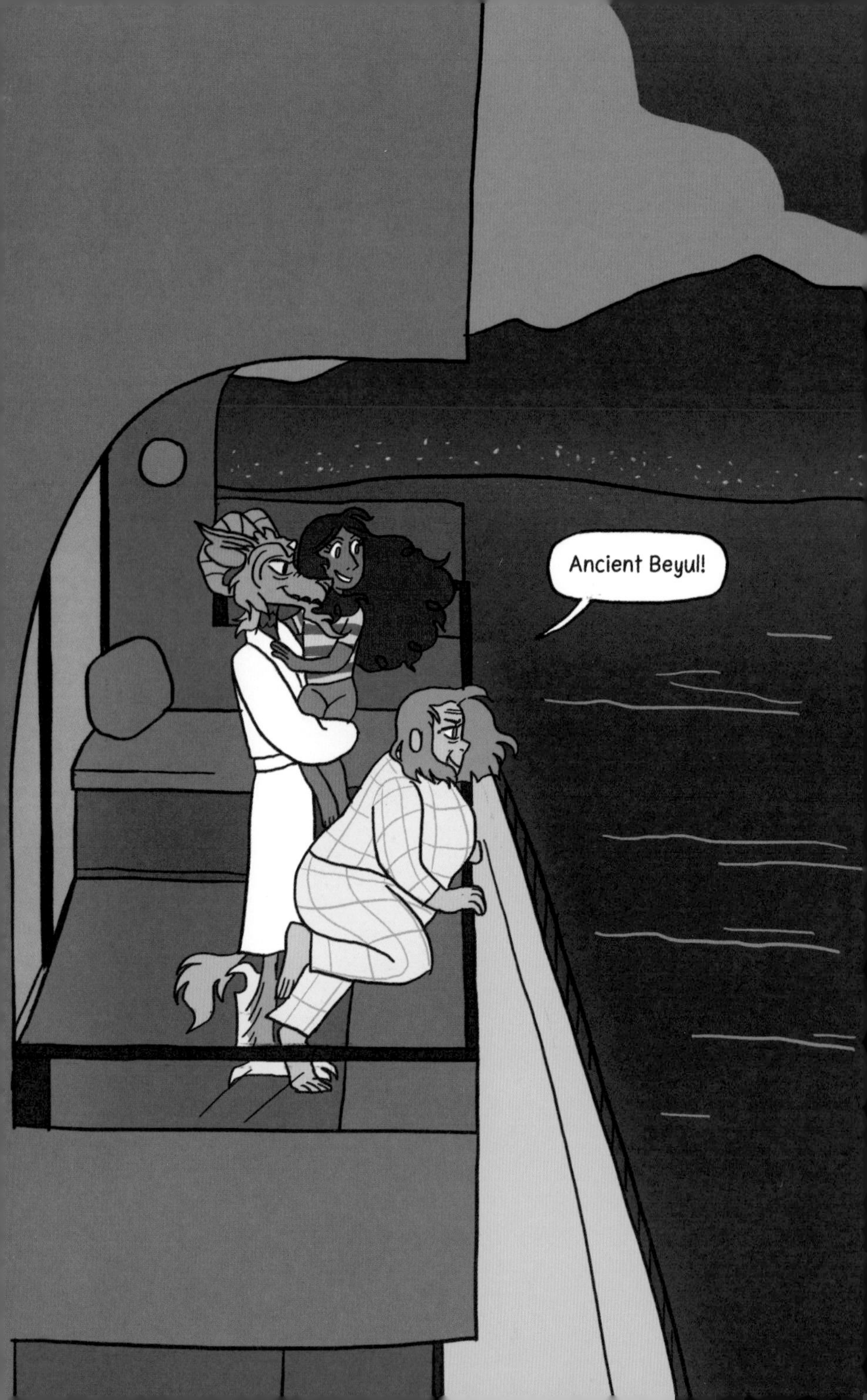
Ancient Beyul!

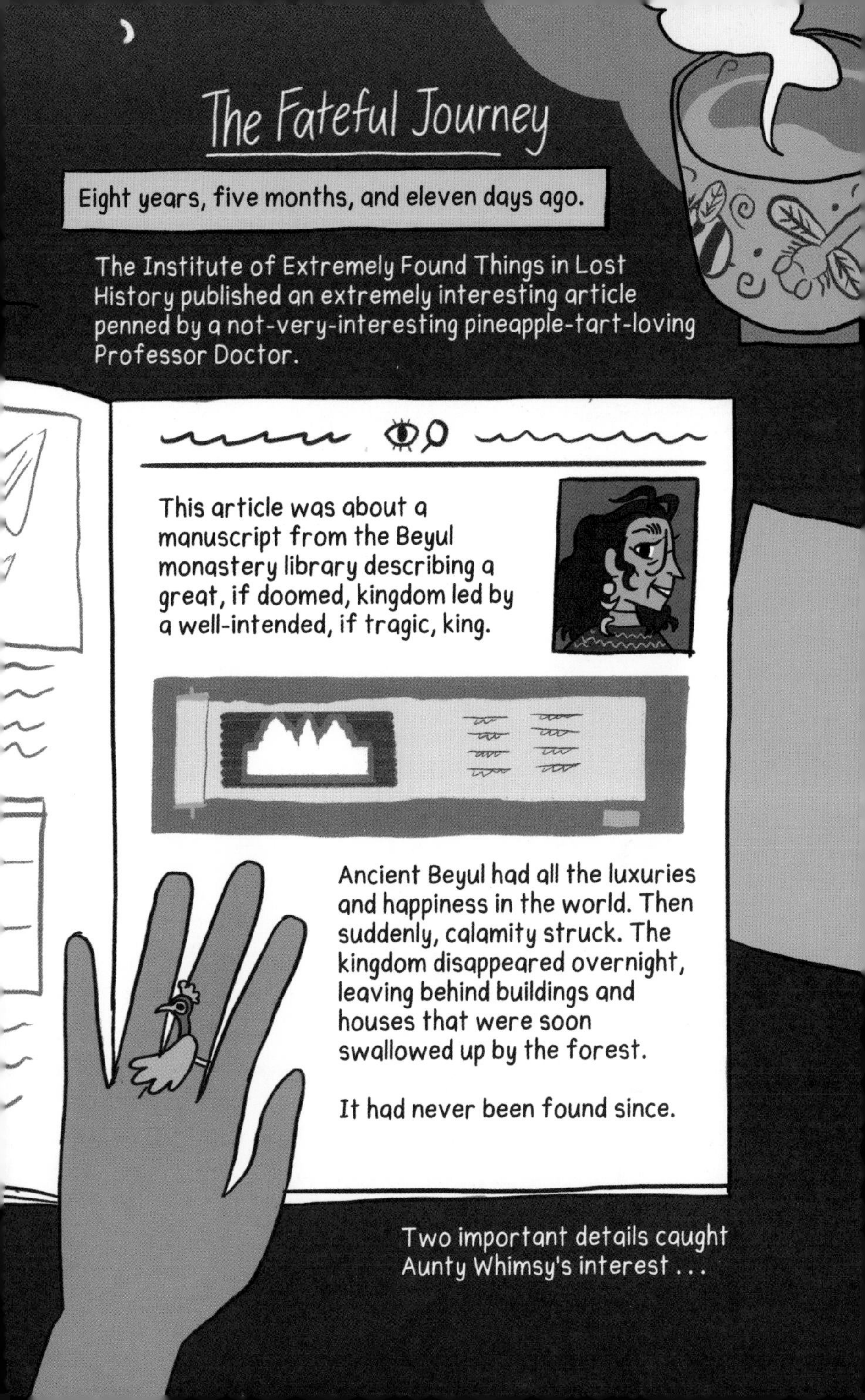
The Fateful Journey
Eight years, five months, and eleven days ago.
The Institute of Extremely Found Things in Lost History published an extremely interesting article penned by a not-very-interesting pineapple-tart-loving Professor Doctor.
This article was about a manuscript from the Beyul monastery library describing a great, if doomed, kingdom led by a well-intended, if tragic, king.
Ancient Beyul had all the luxuries and happiness in the world. Then suddenly, calamity struck. The kingdom disappeared overnight, leaving behind buildings and houses that were soon swallowed up by the forest.
It had never been found since.
Two important details caught Aunty Whimsy's interest . . .

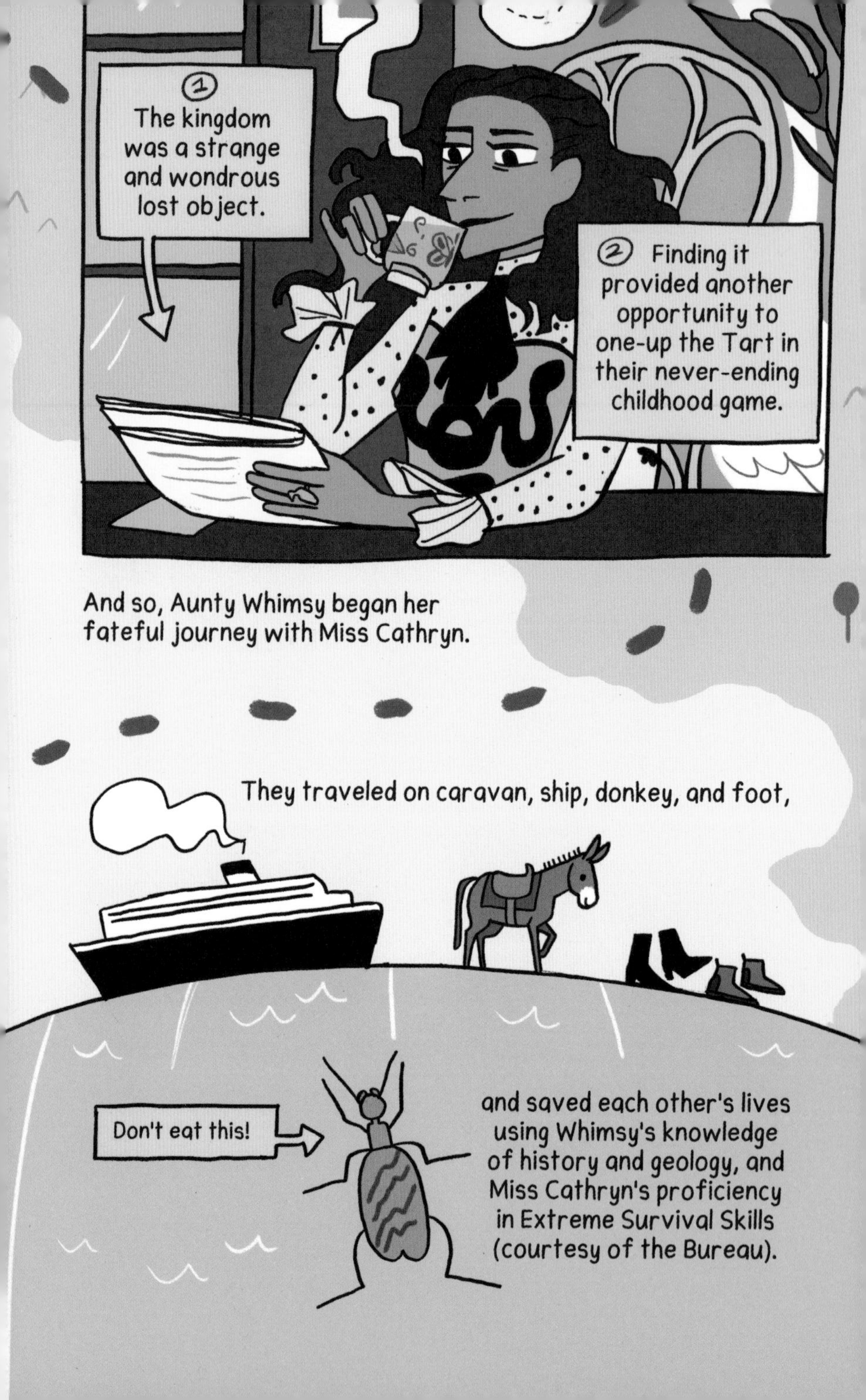
1 The kingdom was a strange and wondrous lost object.
2 Finding it provided another opportunity to one-up the Tart in their never-ending childhood game.
And so, Aunty Whimsy began her fateful journey with Miss Cathryn.
They traveled on caravan, ship, donkey, and foot,
Don't eat this!
and saved each other's lives using Whimsy's knowledge of history and geology, and Miss Cathryn's proficiency in Extreme Survival Skills (courtesy of the Bureau).

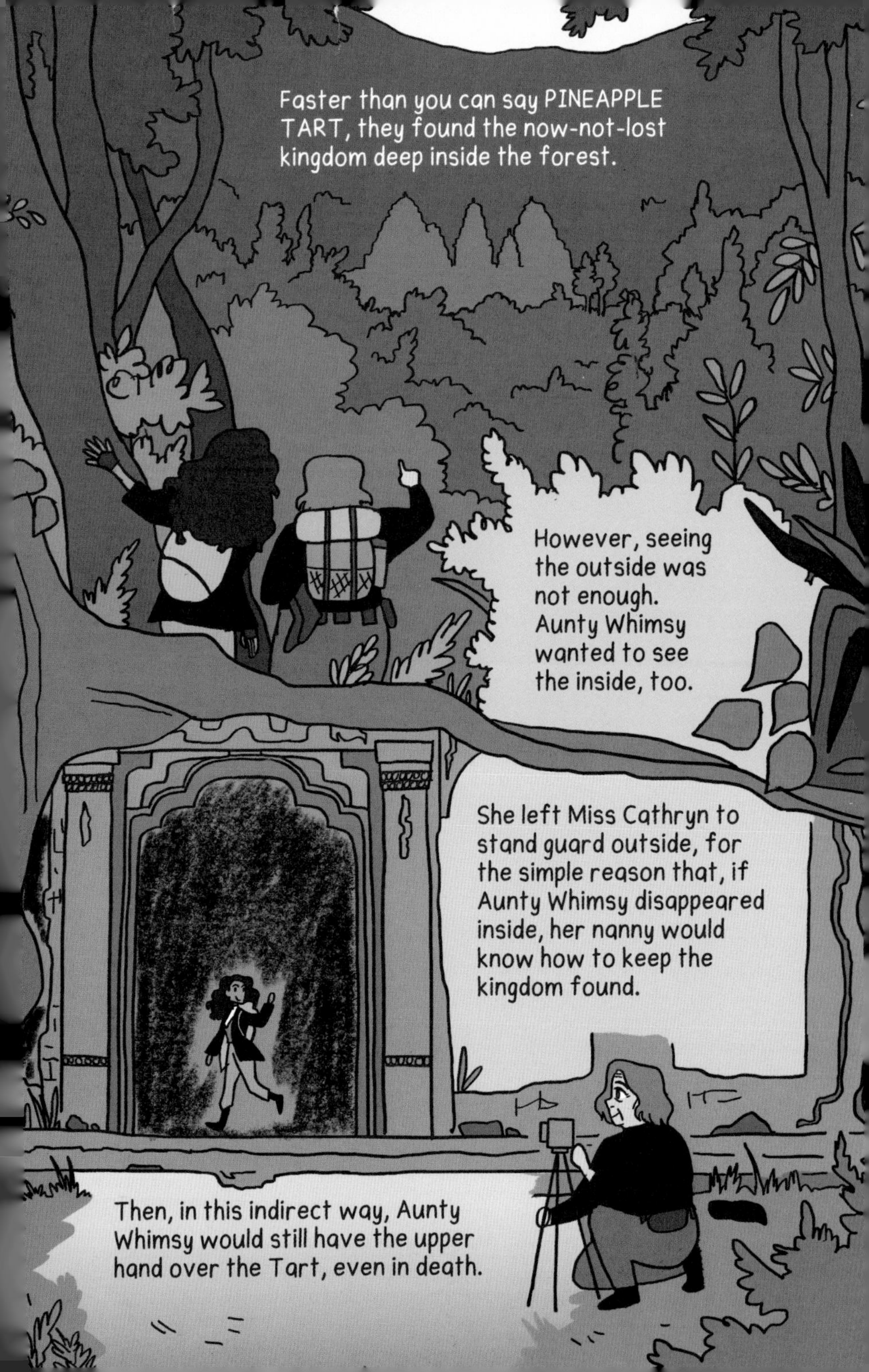
Faster than you can say PINEAPPLE TART, they found the now-not-lost kingdom deep inside the forest.
However, seeing the outside was not enough. Aunty Whimsy wanted to see the inside, too.
She left Miss Cathryn to stand guard outside, for the simple reason that, if Aunty Whimsy disappeared inside, her nanny would know how to keep the kingdom found.
Then, in this indirect way, Aunty Whimsy would still have the upper hand over the Tart, even in death.

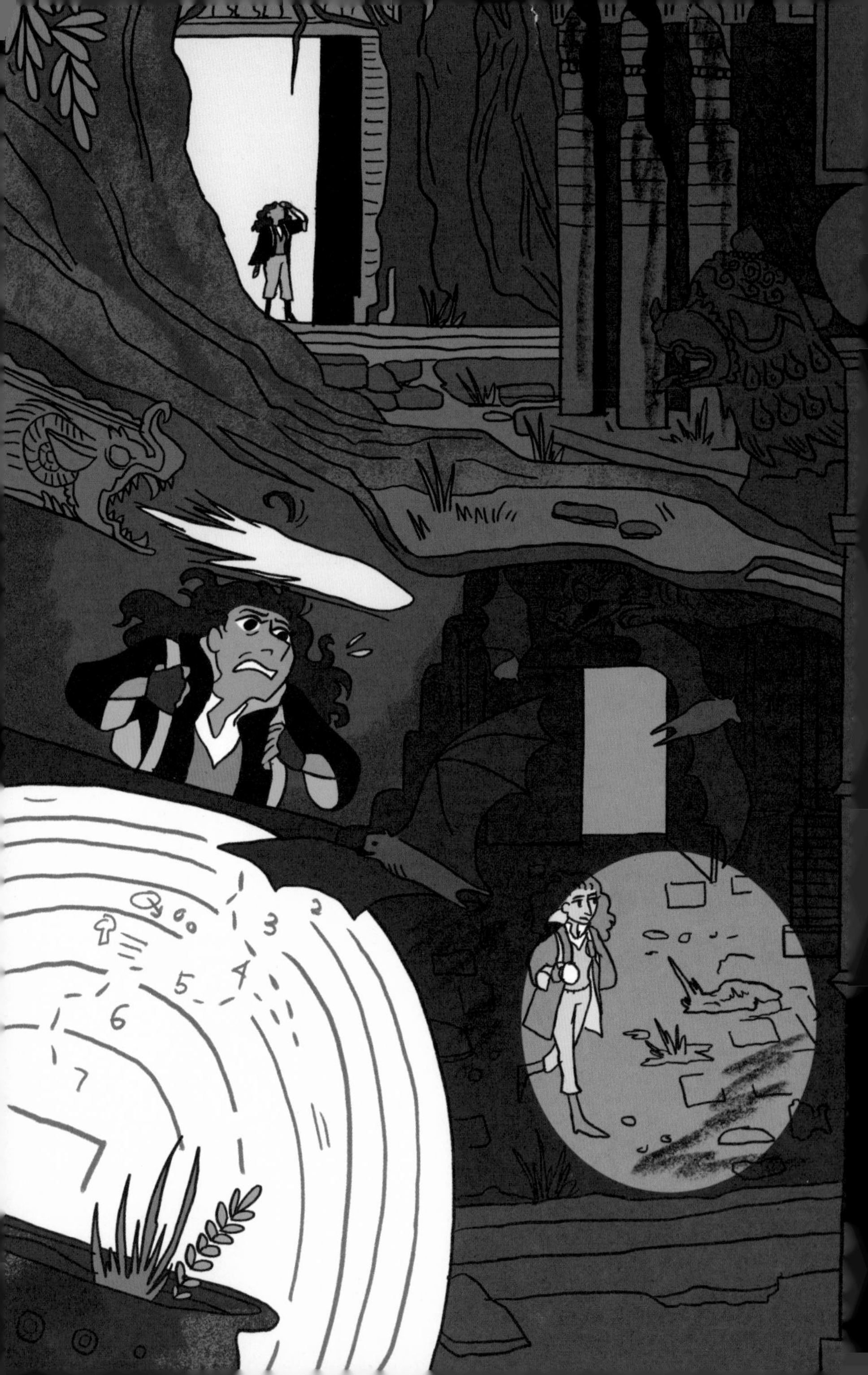
2
3
4
5
6
7

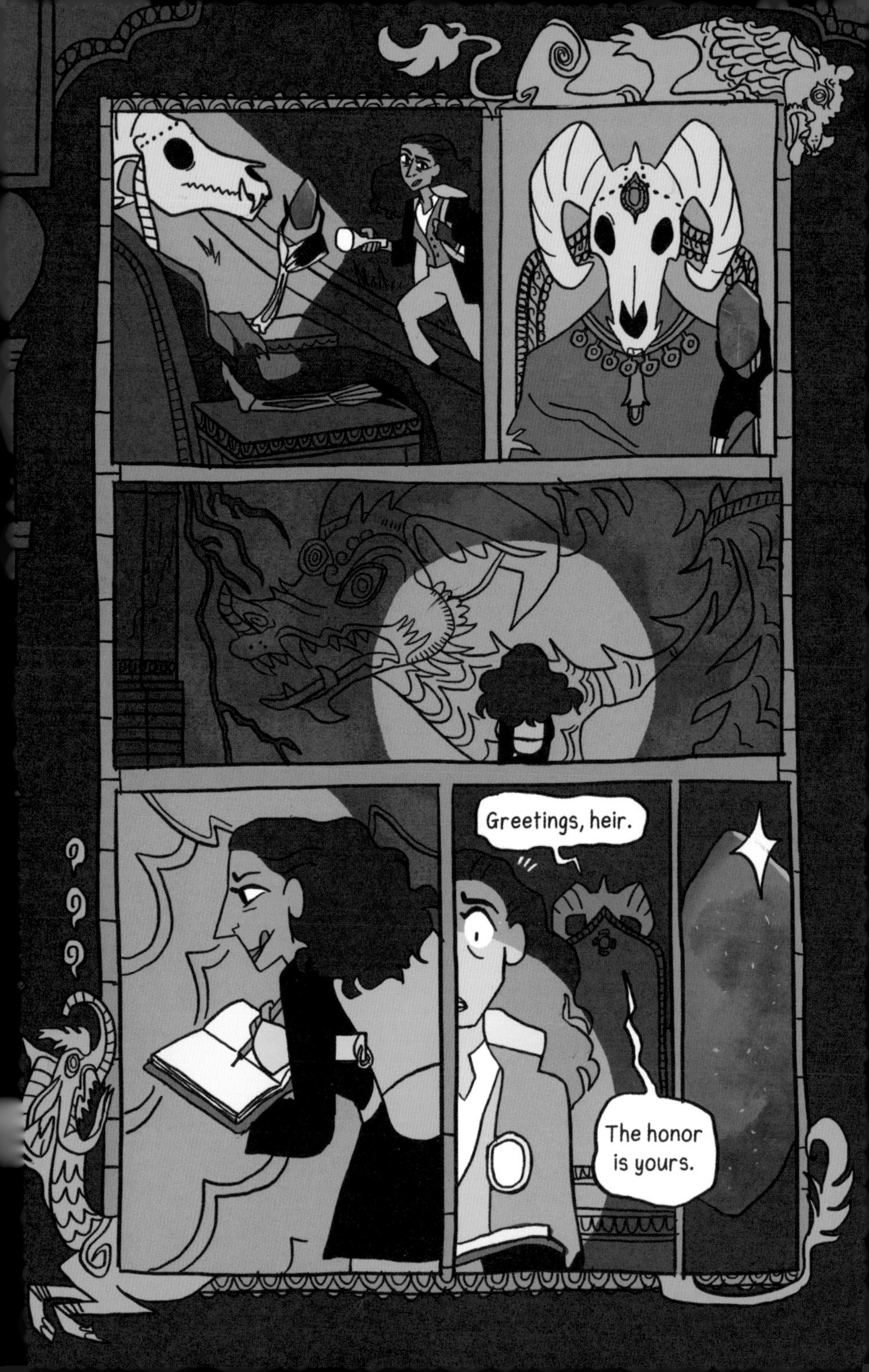
Greetings, heir.
The honor is yours.

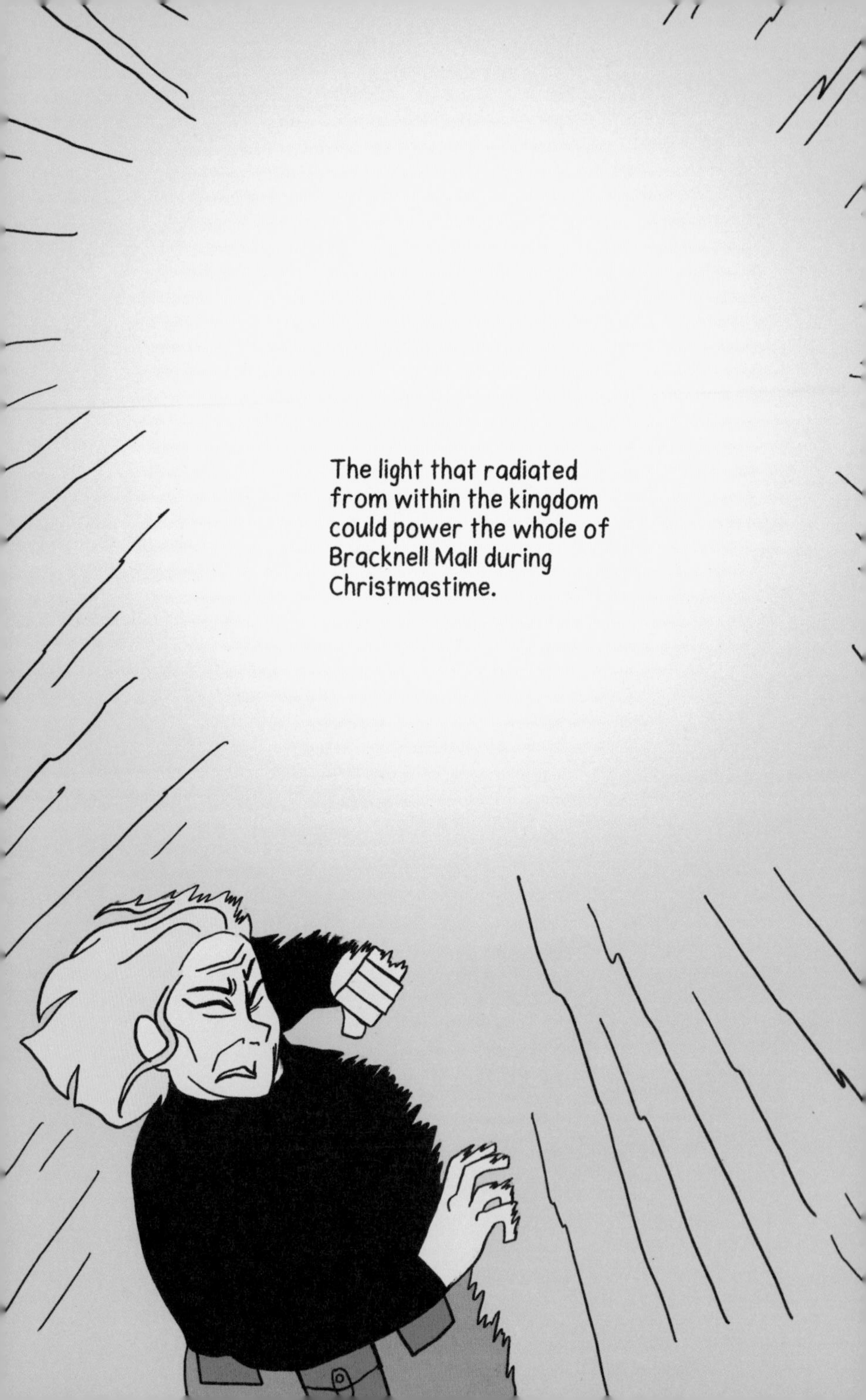
The light that radiated from within the kingdom could power the whole of Bracknell Mall during Christmastime.

Miss Cathryn was prompted to go
inside and rescue Aunty Whimsy,

but the creature she brought out . . .

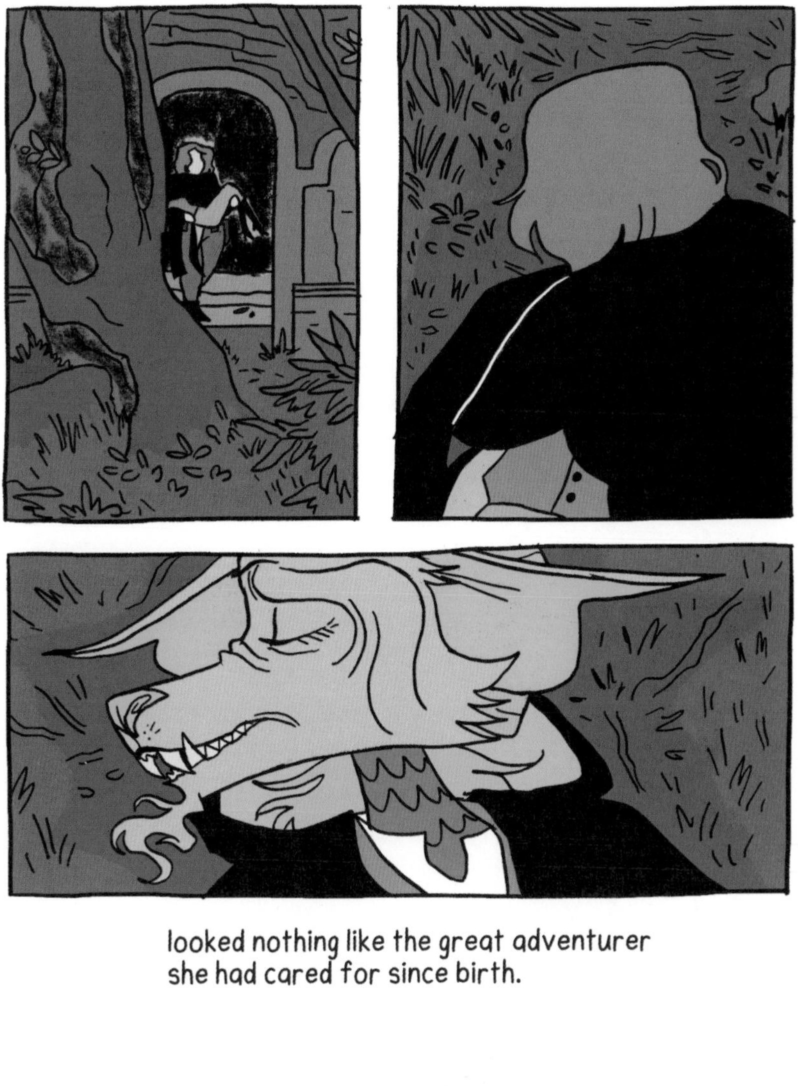

looked nothing like the great adventurer
she had cared for since birth.

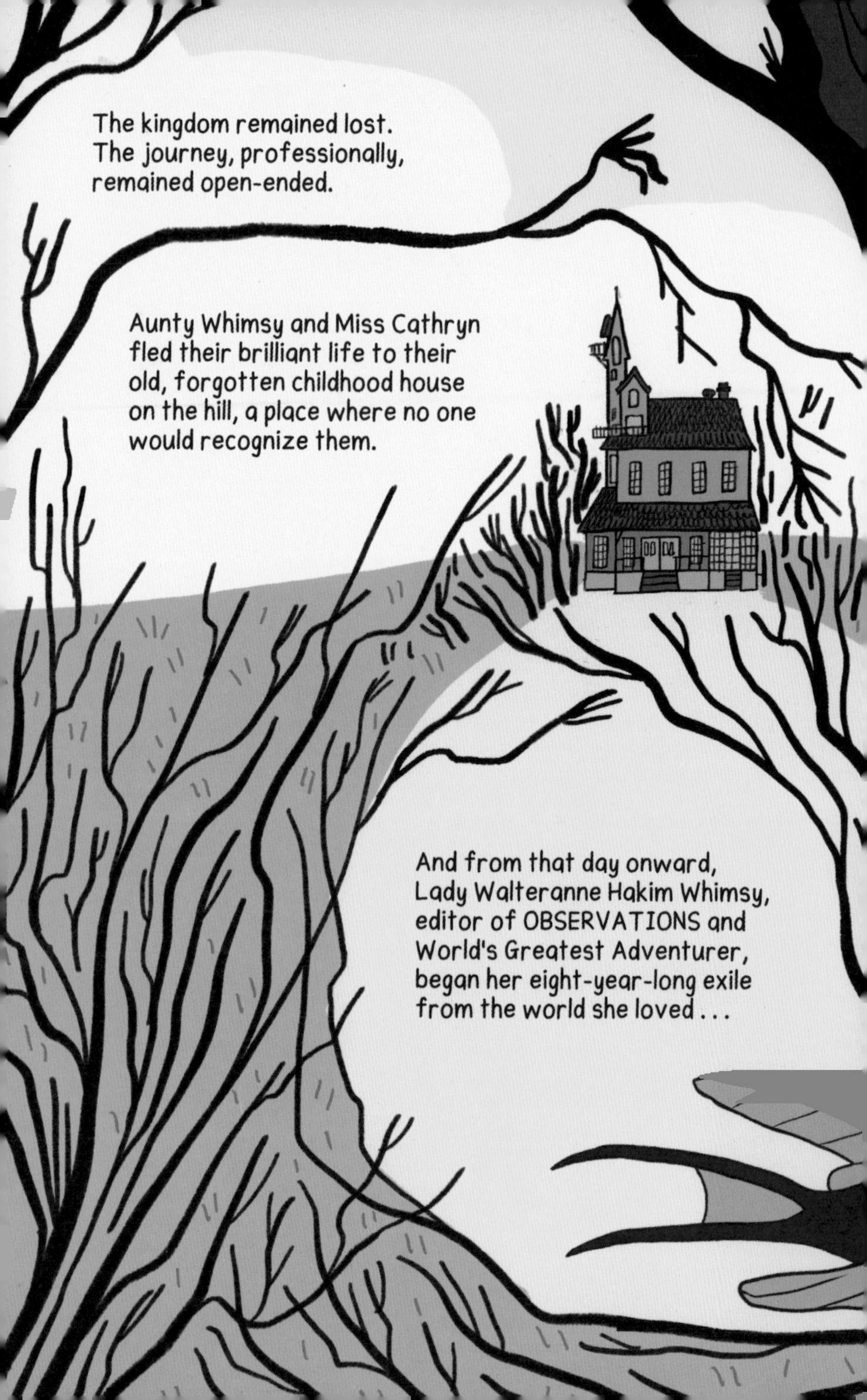

The kingdom remained lost. The journey, professionally, remained open-ended.
Aunty Whimsy and Miss Cathryn fled their brilliant life to their old, forgotten childhood house on the hill, a place where no one would recognize them.
And from that day onward, Lady Walteranne Hakim Whimsy, editor of OBSERVATIONS and World's Greatest Adventurer, began her eight-year-long exile from the world she loved . . .

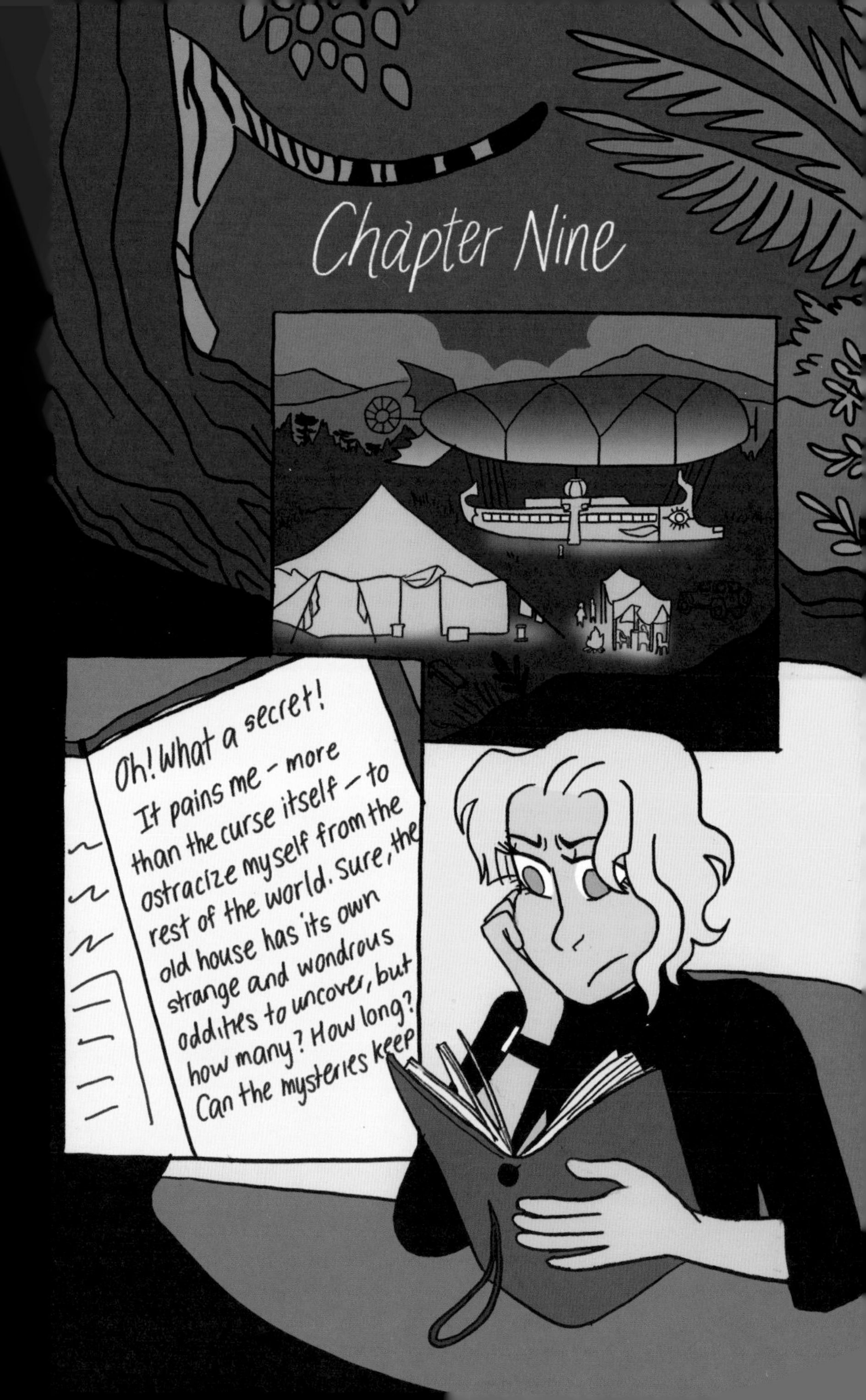
Chapter Nine
Oh! What a secret! It pains me - more than the curse itself - to ostracize myself from the rest of the world. Sure, the old house has its own strange and wondrous oddities to uncover, but how many? How long? Can the mysteries keep

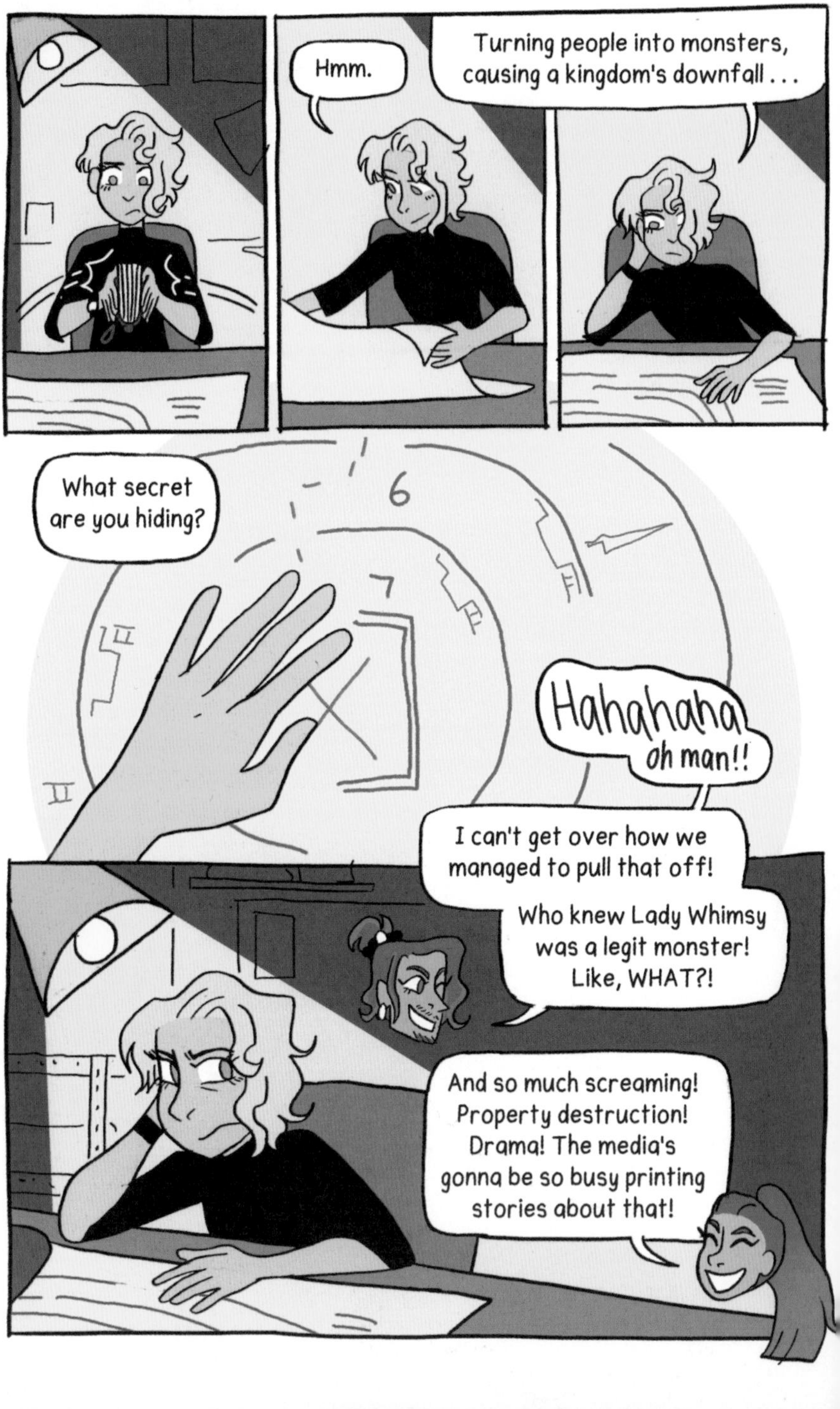
Hmm.
Turning people into monsters, causing a kingdom's downfall . . .
What secret are you hiding?
Hahahaha oh man!!
I can't get over how we managed to pull that off!
Who knew Lady Whimsy was a legit monster! Like, WHAT?!
And so much screaming! Property destruction! Drama! The media's gonna be so busy printing stories about that!

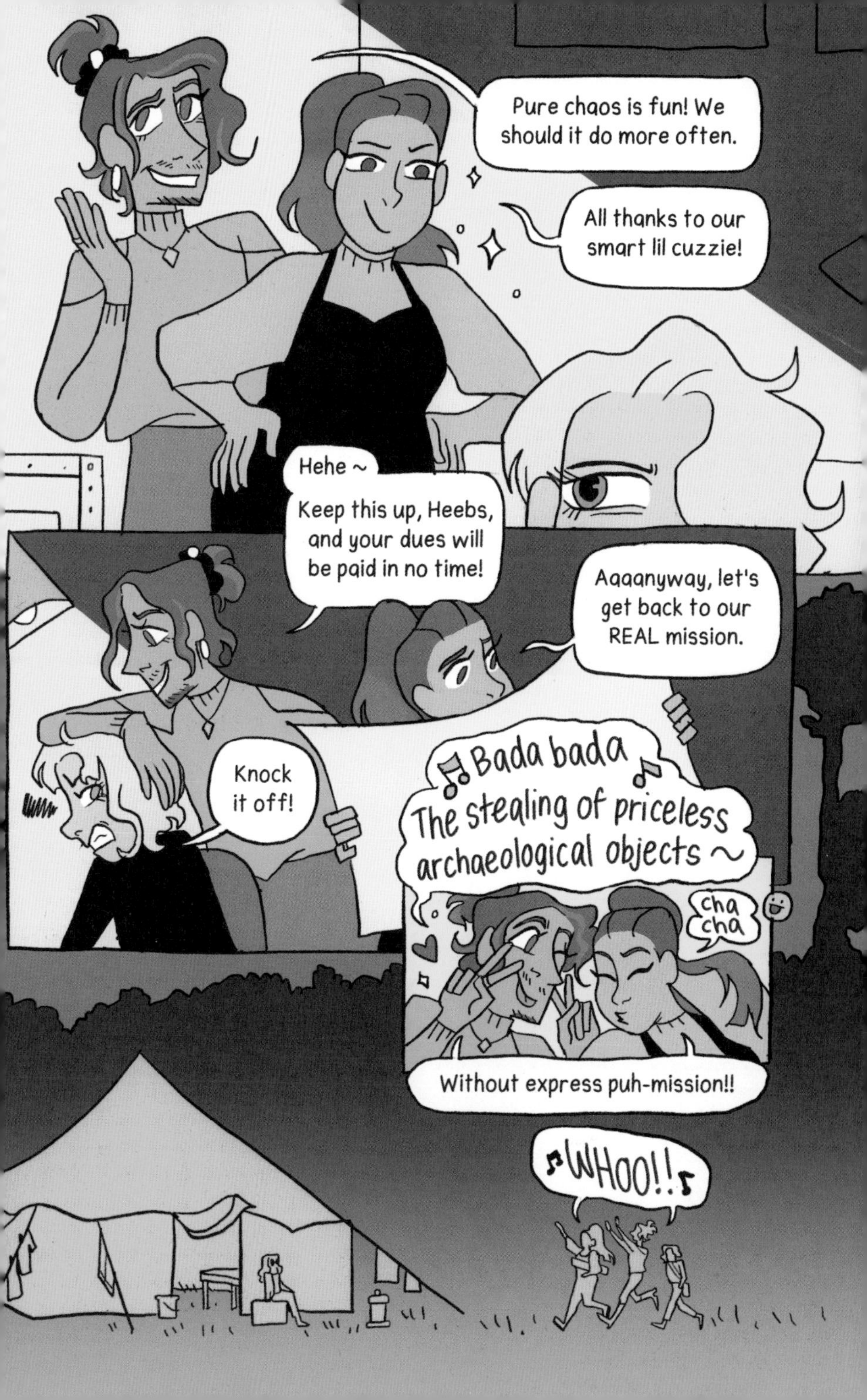
Pure chaos is fun! We should it do more often.
All thanks to our smart lil cuzzie!
Hehe ~
Keep this up, Heebs, and your dues will be paid in no time!
Aaaanyway, let's get back to our REAL mission.
Knock it off!
Bada bada The stealing of priceless archaeological objects ~
cha cha
Without express puh-mission!!
WHOO!!

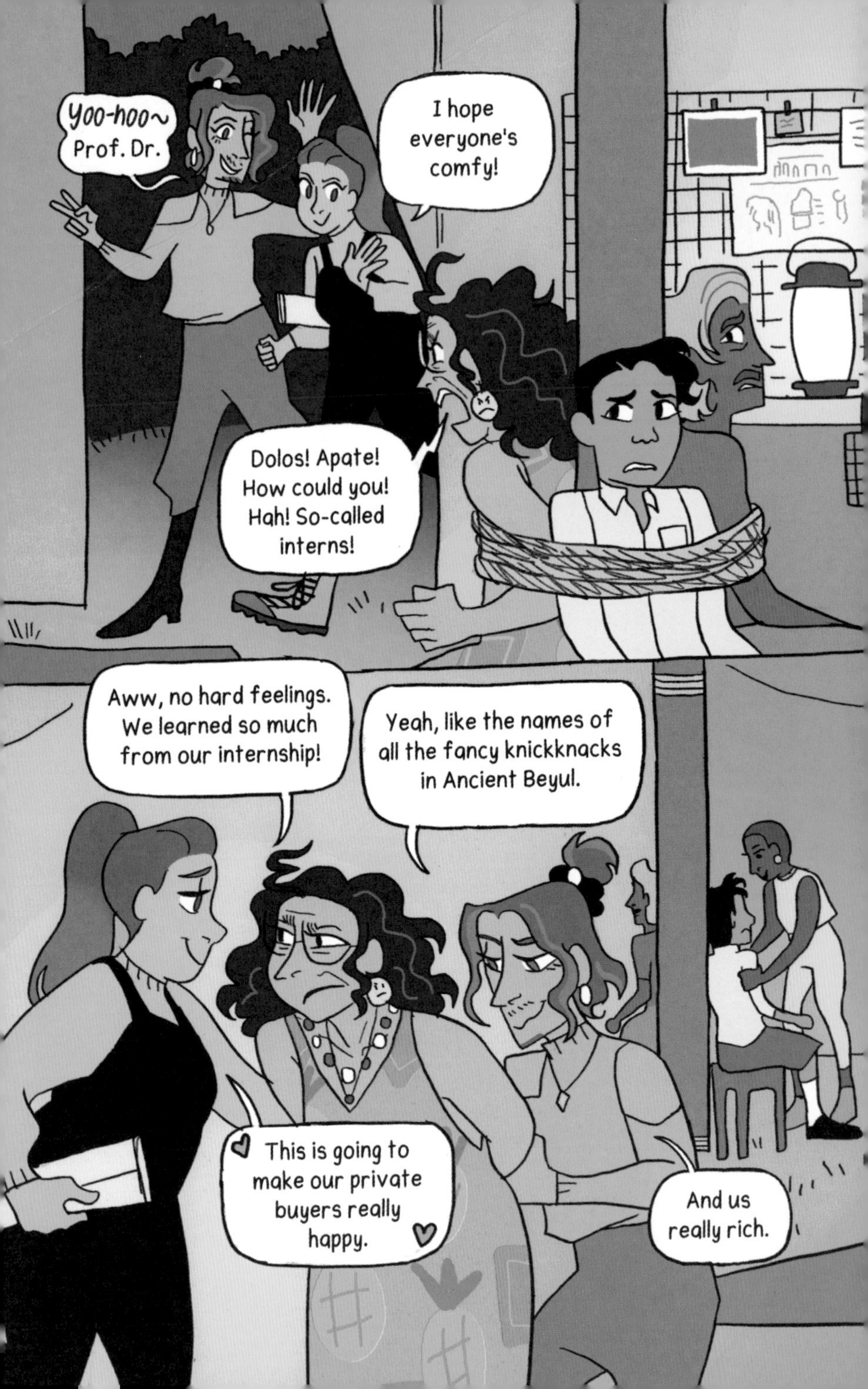
yoo-hoo~
Prof. Dr.
I hope everyone's comfy!
Dolos! Apate! How could you! Hah! So-called interns!
Aww, no hard feelings. We learned so much from our internship!
Yeah, like the names of all the fancy knickknacks in Ancient Beyul.
This is going to make our private buyers really happy.
And us really rich.

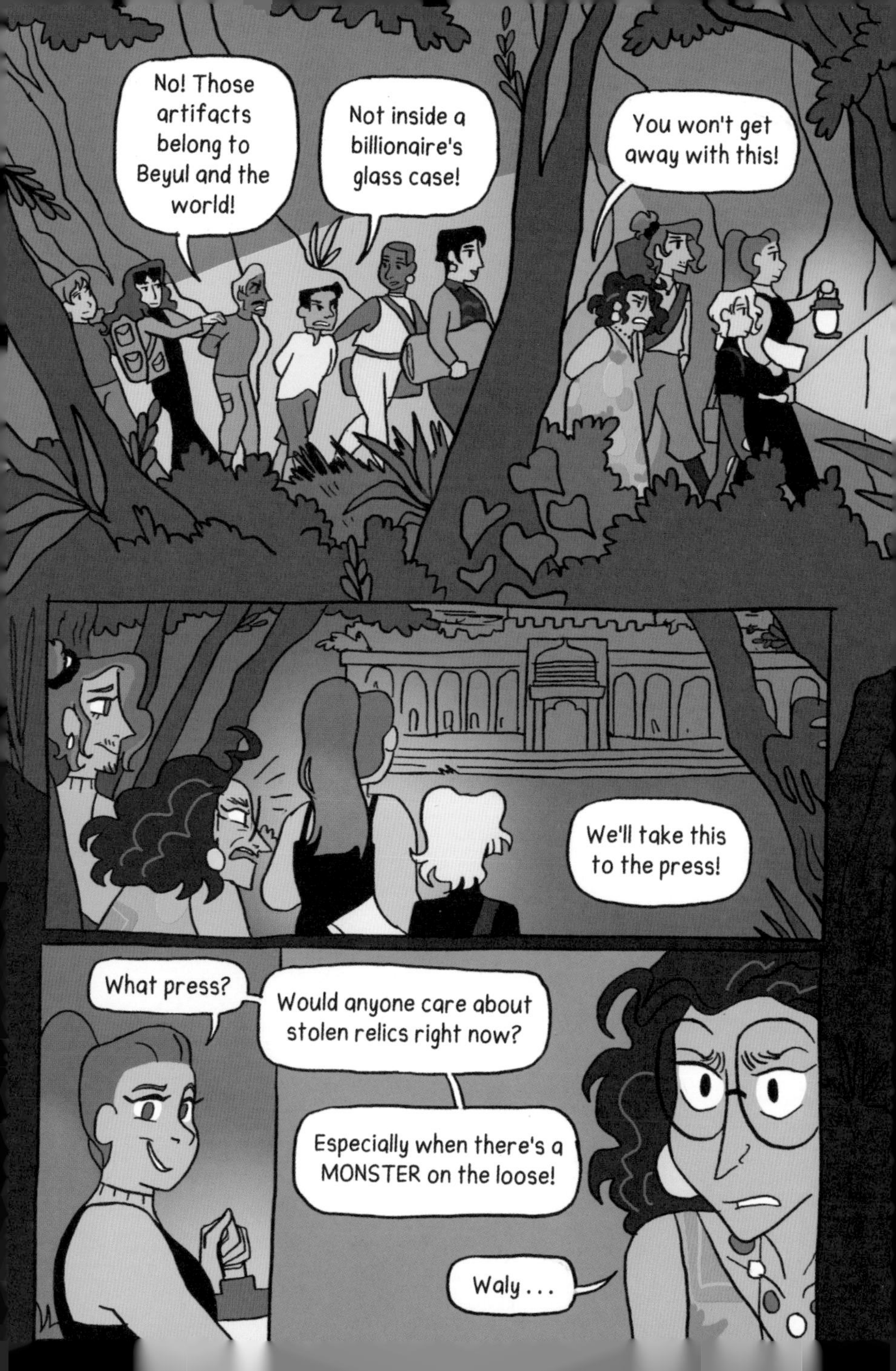
No! Those artifacts belong to Beyul and the world!
Not inside a billionaire's glass case!
You won't get away with this!
We'll take this to the press!
What press?
Would anyone care about stolen relics right now?
Especially when there's a MONSTER on the loose!
Waly . . .

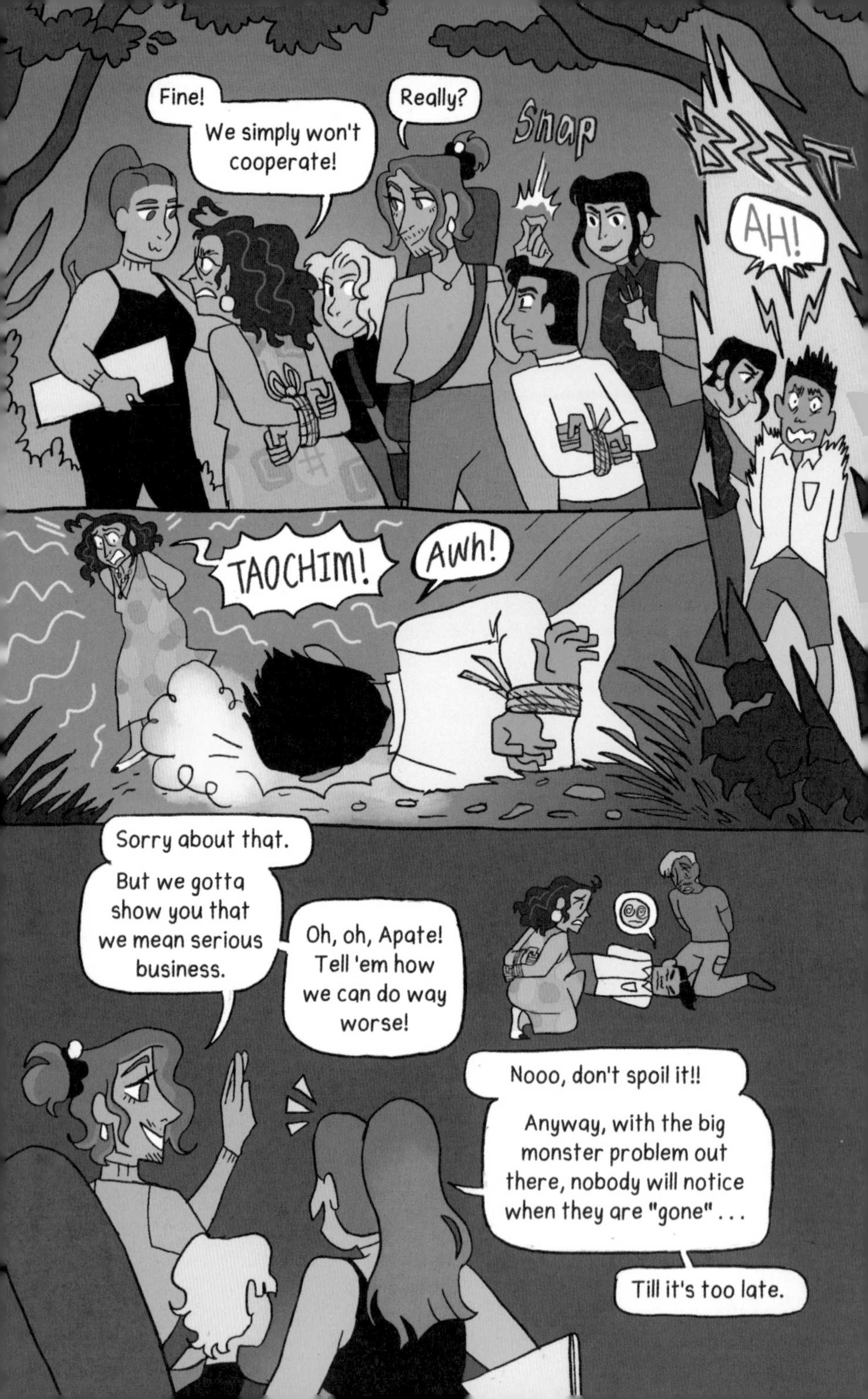
Fine!
We simply won't cooperate!
Really?
Snap
BZZT
AH!
TAOCHIM!
Awh!
Sorry about that.
But we gotta show you that we mean serious business.
Oh, oh, Apate! Tell 'em how we can do way worse!
Nooo, don't spoil it!!
Anyway, with the big monster problem out there, nobody will notice when they are "gone" . . .
Till it's too late.

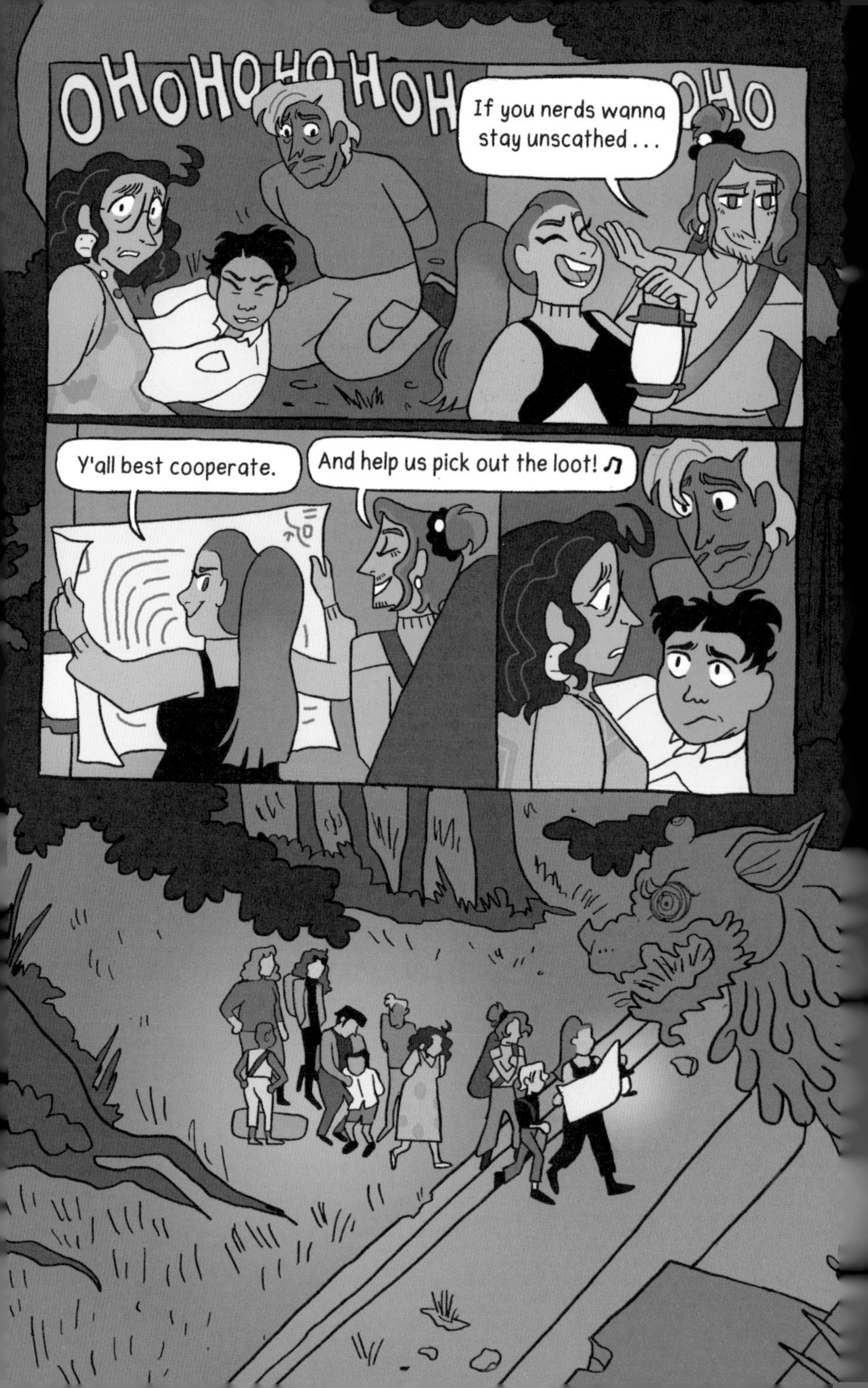
OHOHOHOHOHOHOH OHO
If you nerds wanna stay unscathed . . .
Y'all best cooperate.
And help us pick out the loot! ♫

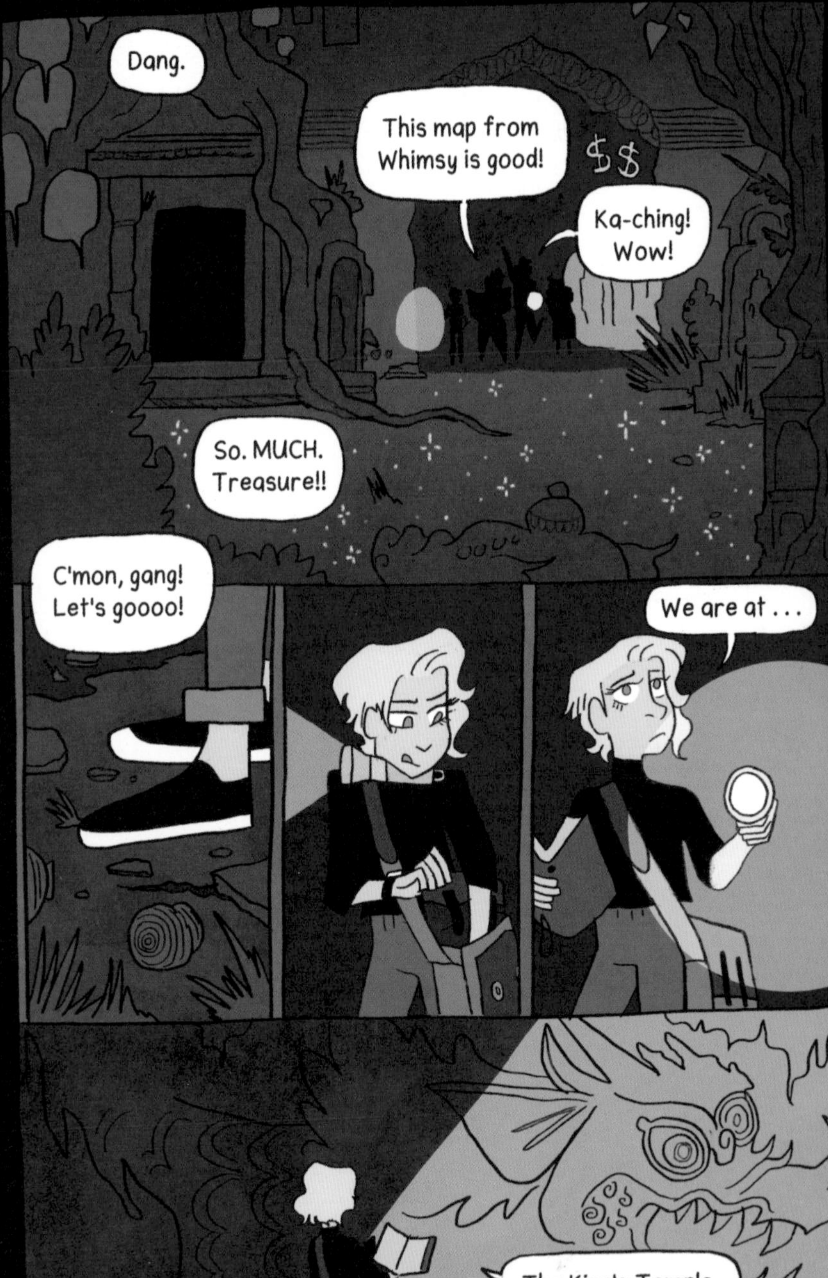
Dang.
This map from Whimsy is good!
$$
Ka-ching! Wow!
So. MUCH. Treasure!!
C'mon, gang! Let's goooo!
We are at . . .
The King's Temple.

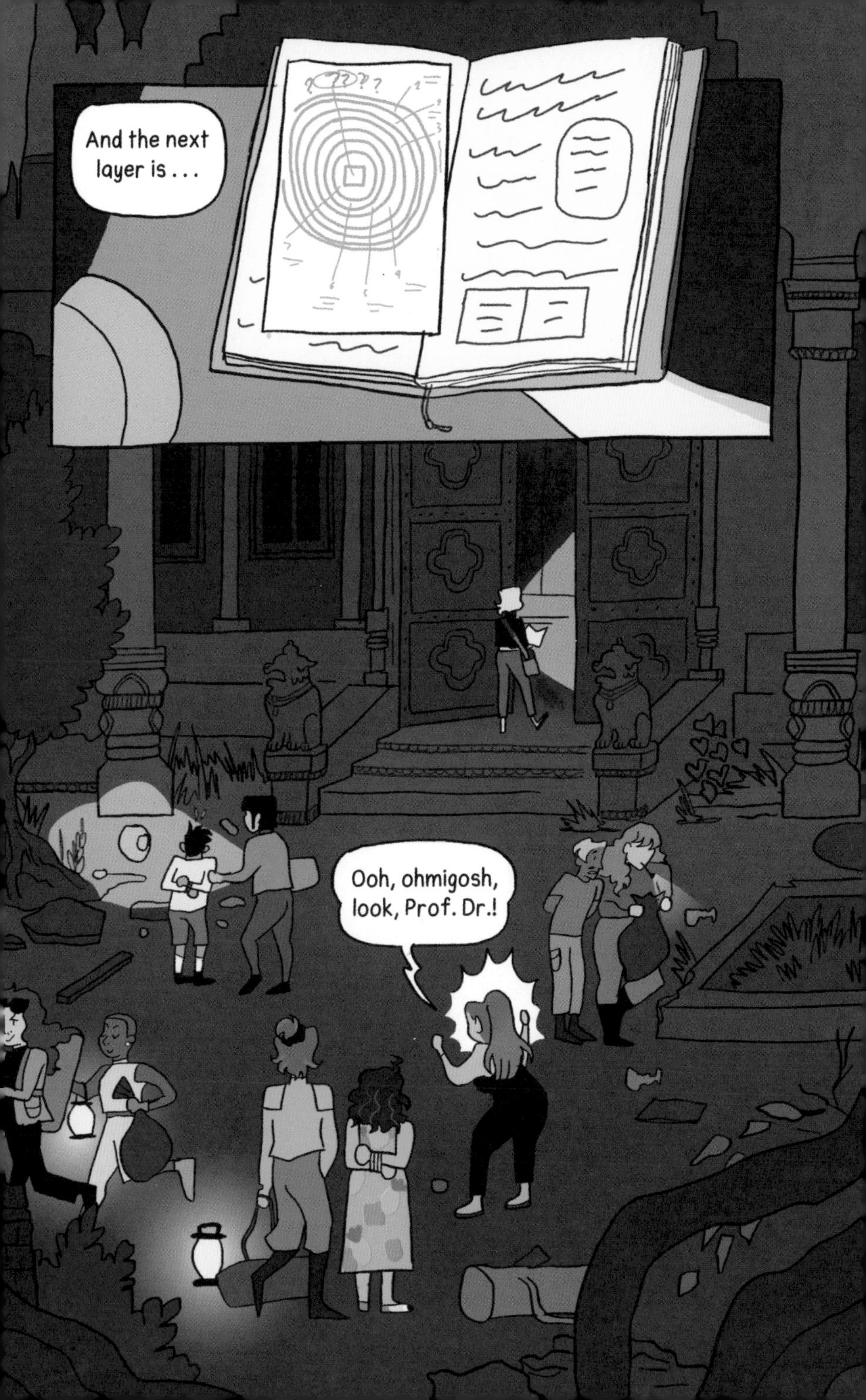
And the next layer is . . .
Ooh, ohmigosh, look, Prof. Dr.!

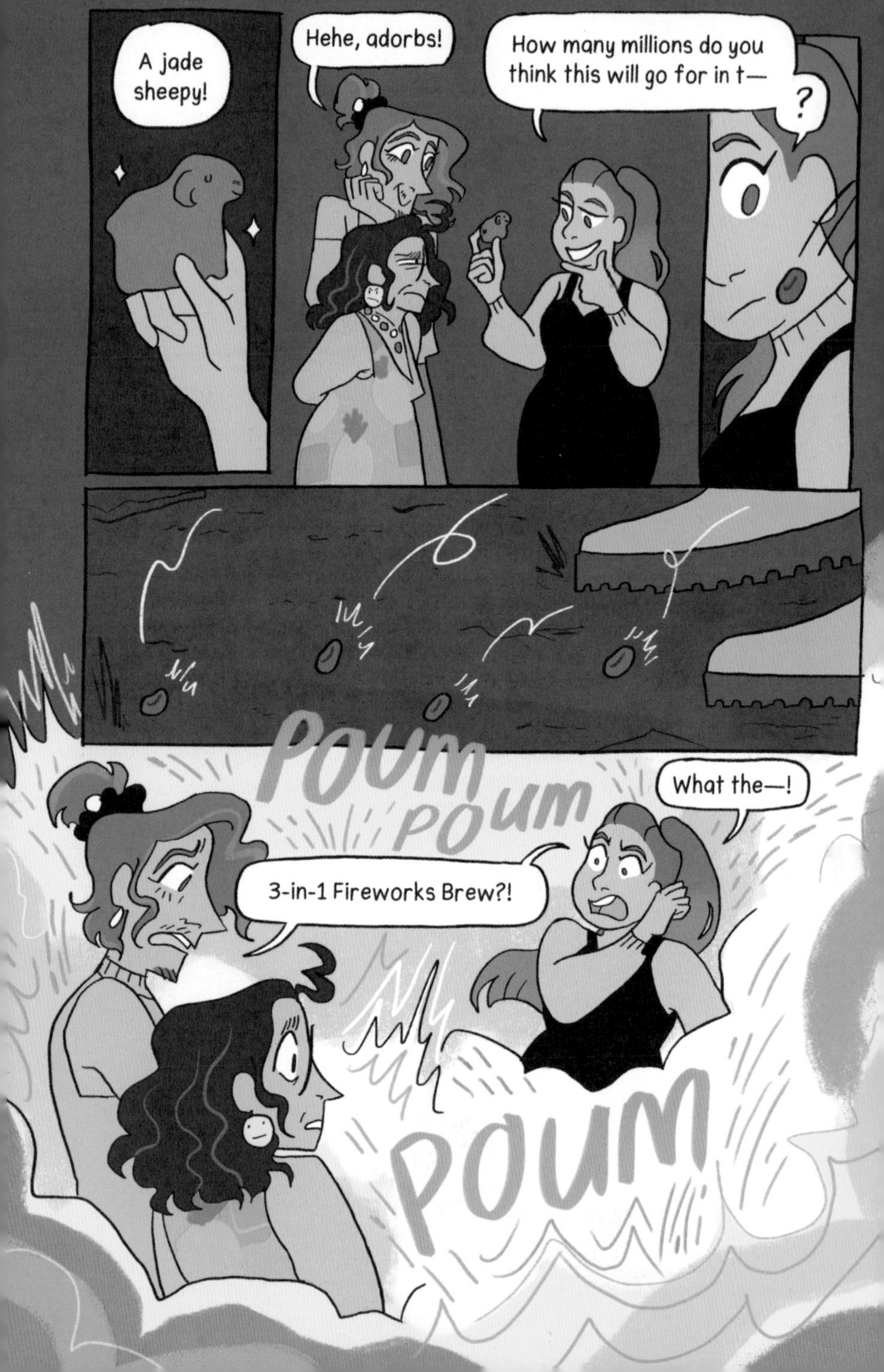
A jade sheepy!
Hehe, adorbs!
How many millions do you think this will go for in t—
?
POUM
POUM
What the—!
3-in-1 Fireworks Brew?!
POUM

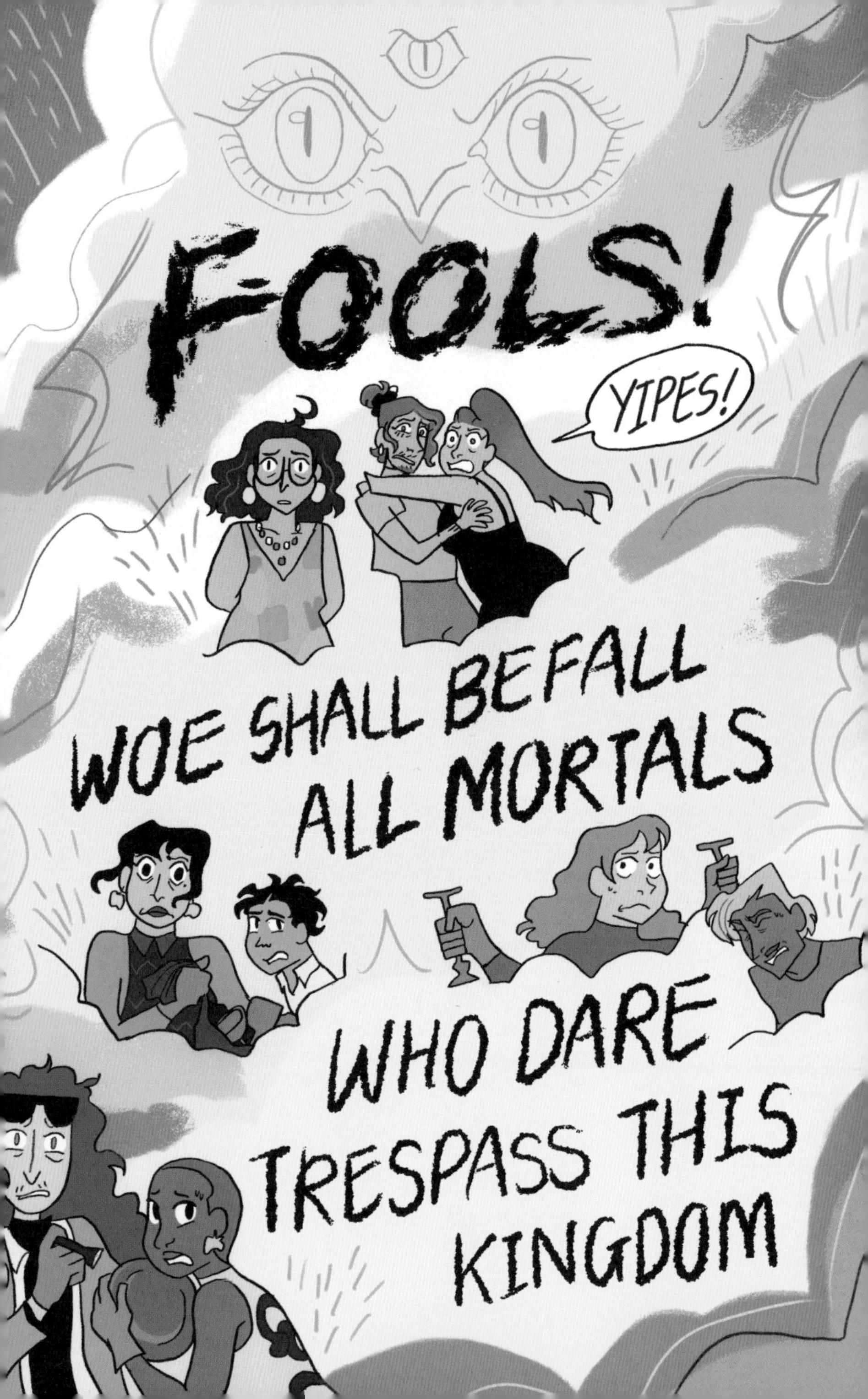
FOOLS!
YIPES!
WOE SHALL BEFALL ALL MORTALS
WHO DARE TRESPASS THIS KINGDOM

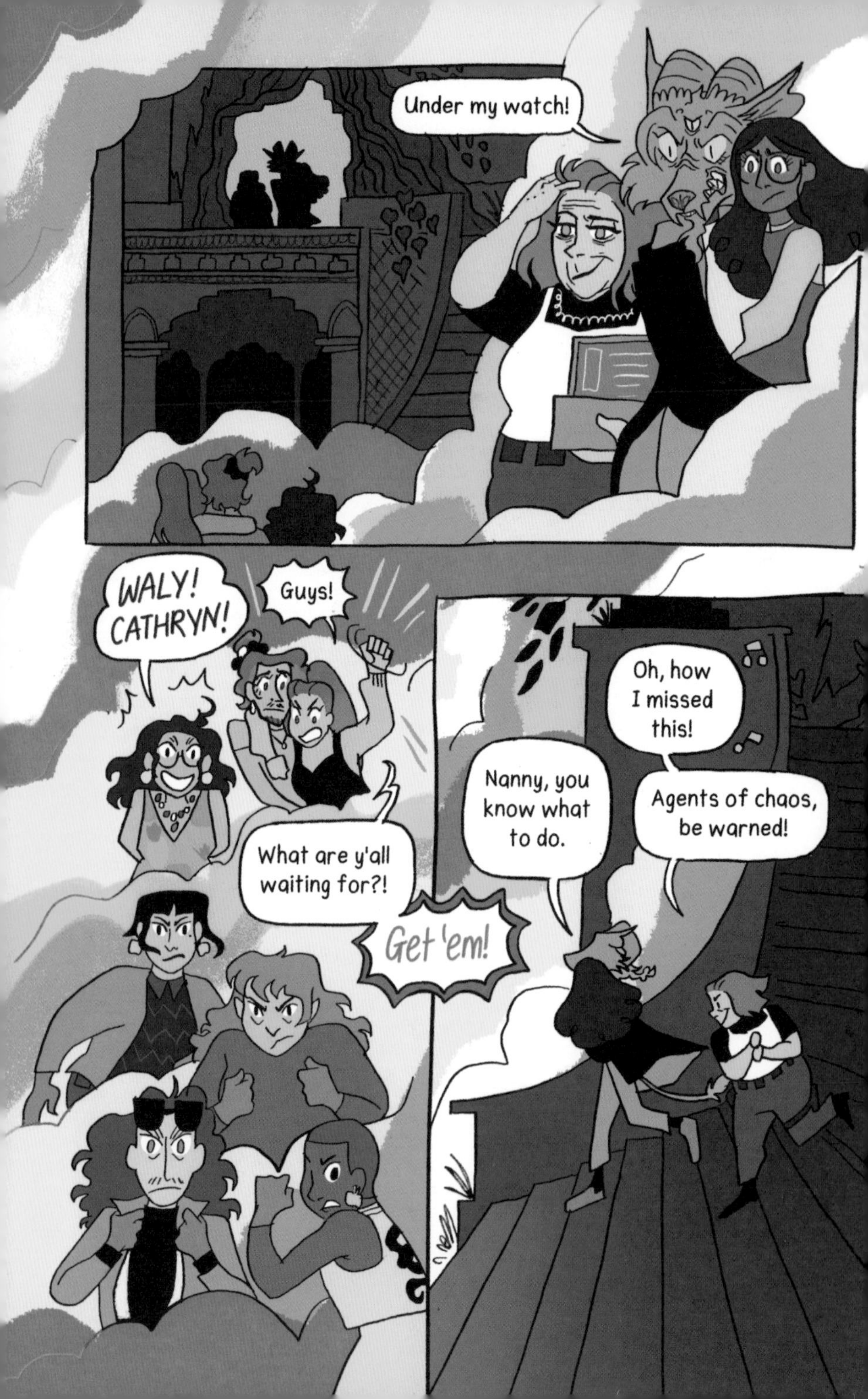
Under my watch!
WALY! CATHRYN!
Guys!
What are y'all waiting for?!
Get 'em!
Oh, how I missed this!
Nanny, you know what to do.
Agents of chaos, be warned!

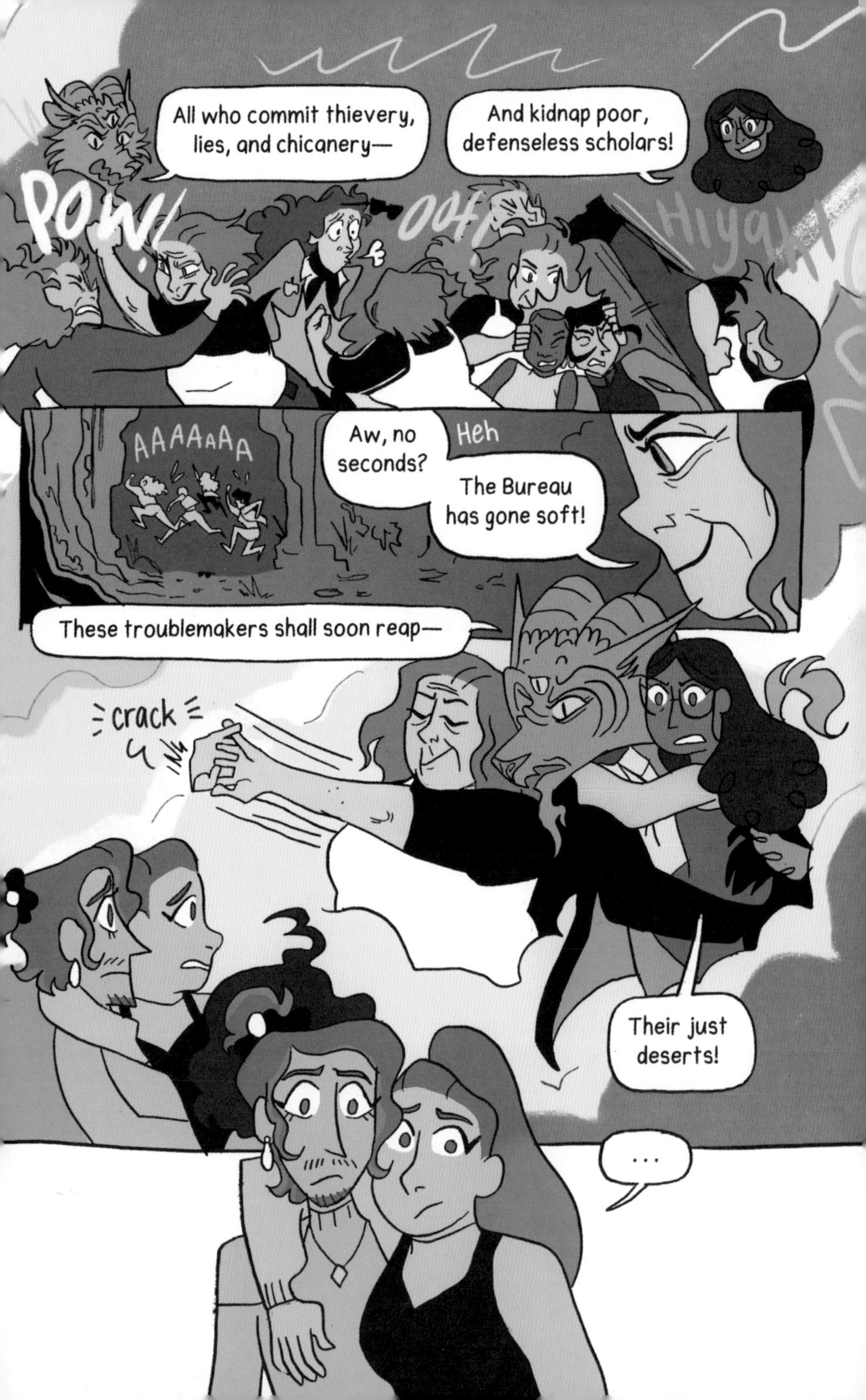
All who commit thievery, lies, and chicanery—
And kidnap poor, defenseless scholars!
POW!
OOF!
HIYAH!
AAAAAAA
Aw, no seconds?
Heh
The Bureau has gone soft!
These troublemakers shall soon reap—
crack
Their just deserts!
...

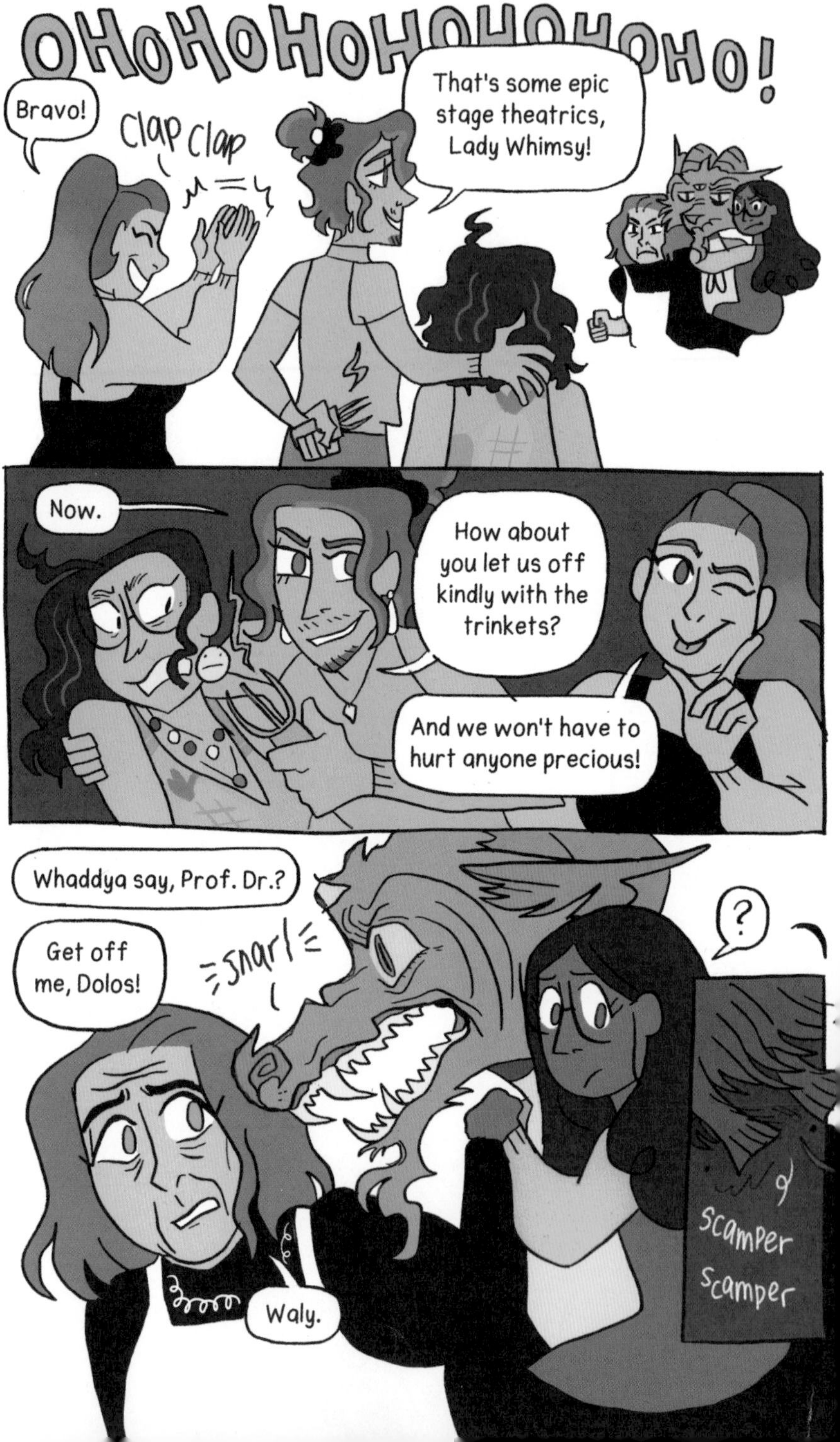
OHOHOHOHOHOHOHOHOHO!
Bravo!
Clap Clap
That's some epic stage theatrics, Lady Whimsy!
Now.
How about you let us off kindly with the trinkets?
And we won't have to hurt anyone precious!
Whaddya say, Prof. Dr.?
Get off me, Dolos!
snarl
?
Waly.
scamper scamper

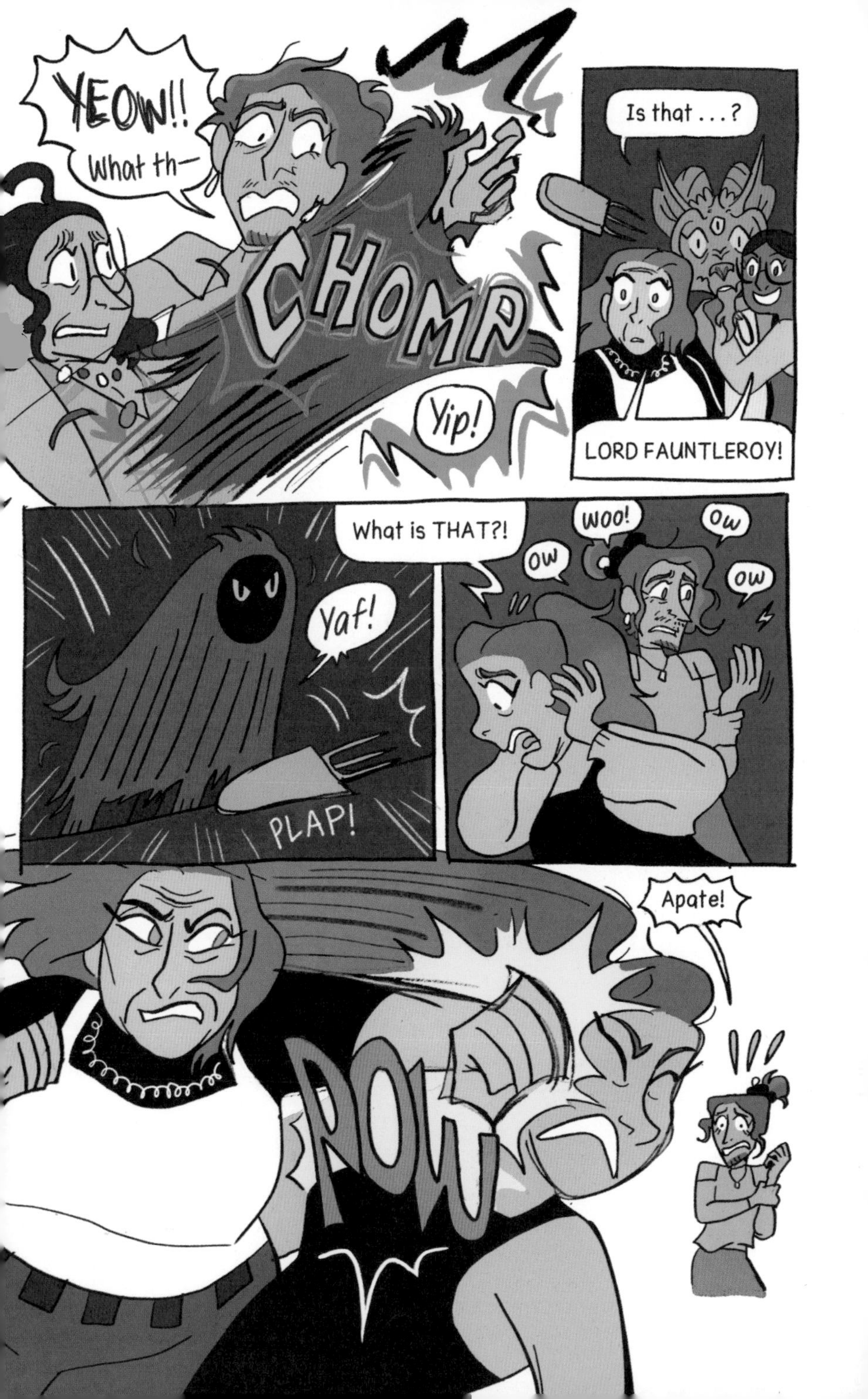
YEOW!!
What th—
CHOMP
Yip!
Is that . . . ?
LORD FAUNTLEROY!
Yaf!
PLAP!
What is THAT?!
WOO!
OW
OW
OW
Apate!
POW

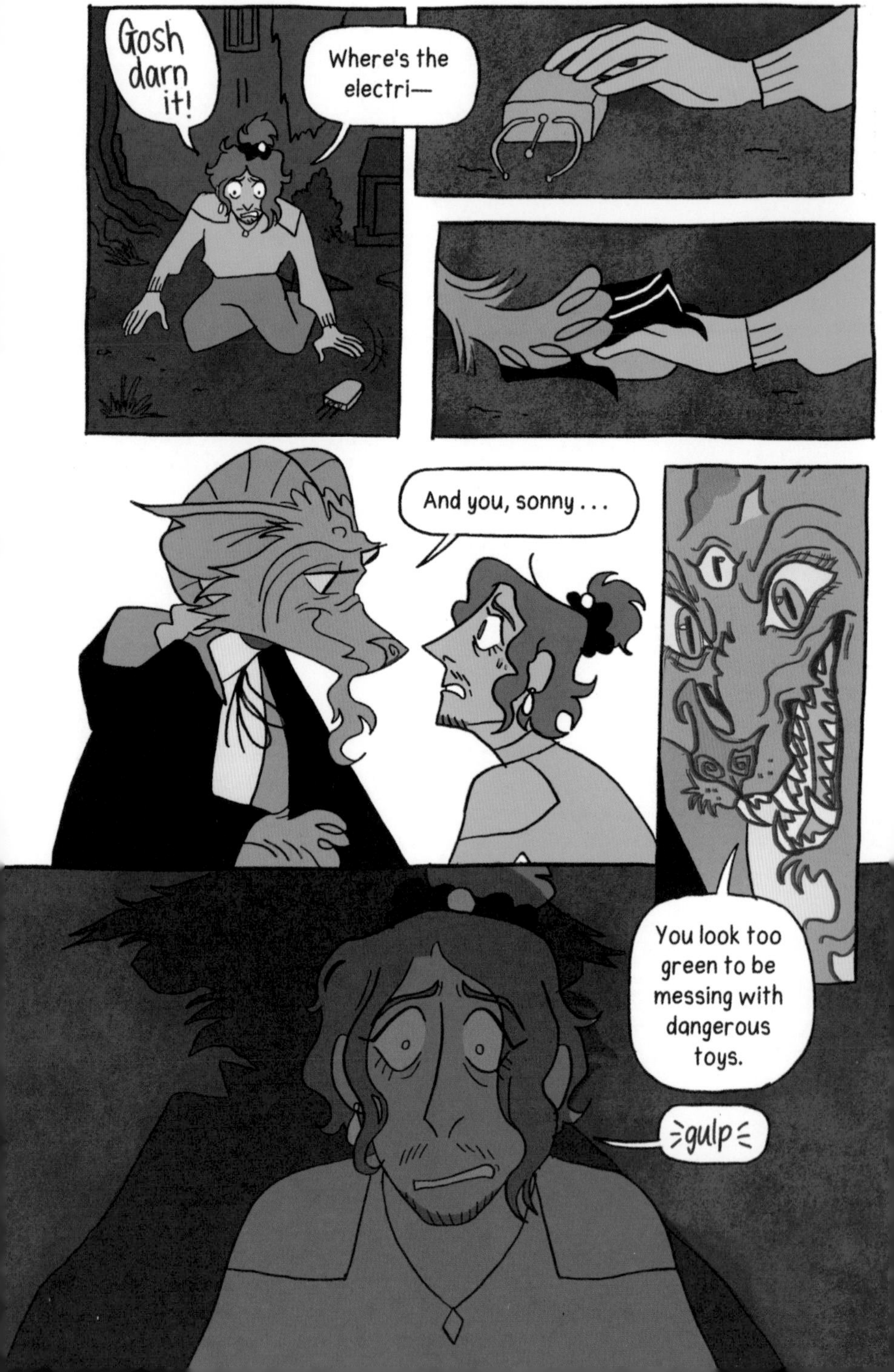
Gosh darn it!
Where's the electri—
And you, sonny . . .
You look too green to be messing with dangerous toys.
gulp

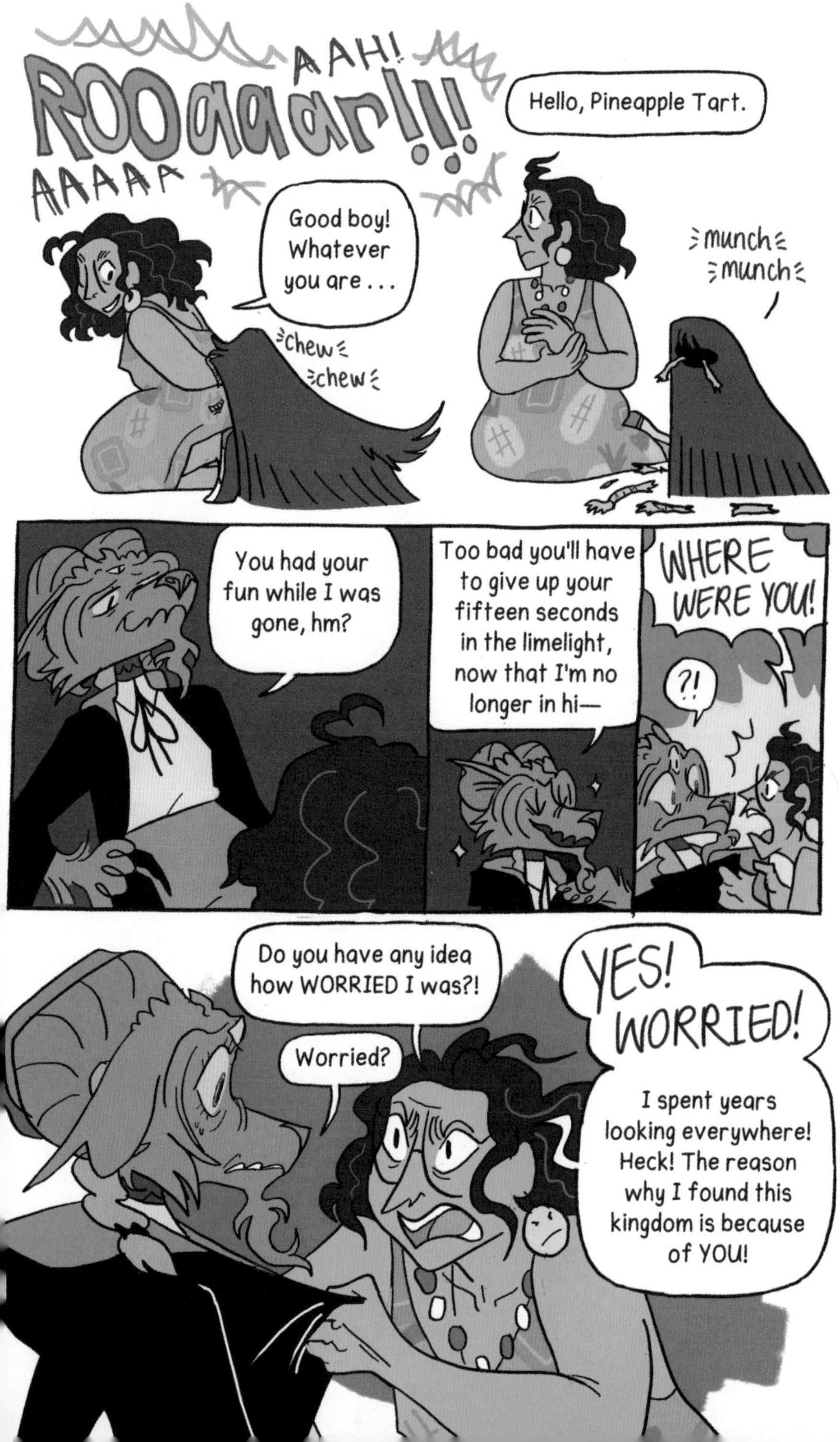

ROOaaar!!!
AAH!
AAAAA
Good boy! Whatever you are . . .
chew chew
Hello, Pineapple Tart.
munch munch
You had your fun while I was gone, hm?
Too bad you'll have to give up your fifteen seconds in the limelight, now that I'm no longer in hi—
WHERE WERE YOU!
?!
Do you have any idea how WORRIED I was?!
Worried?
YES! WORRIED!
I spent years looking everywhere! Heck! The reason why I found this kingdom is because of YOU!

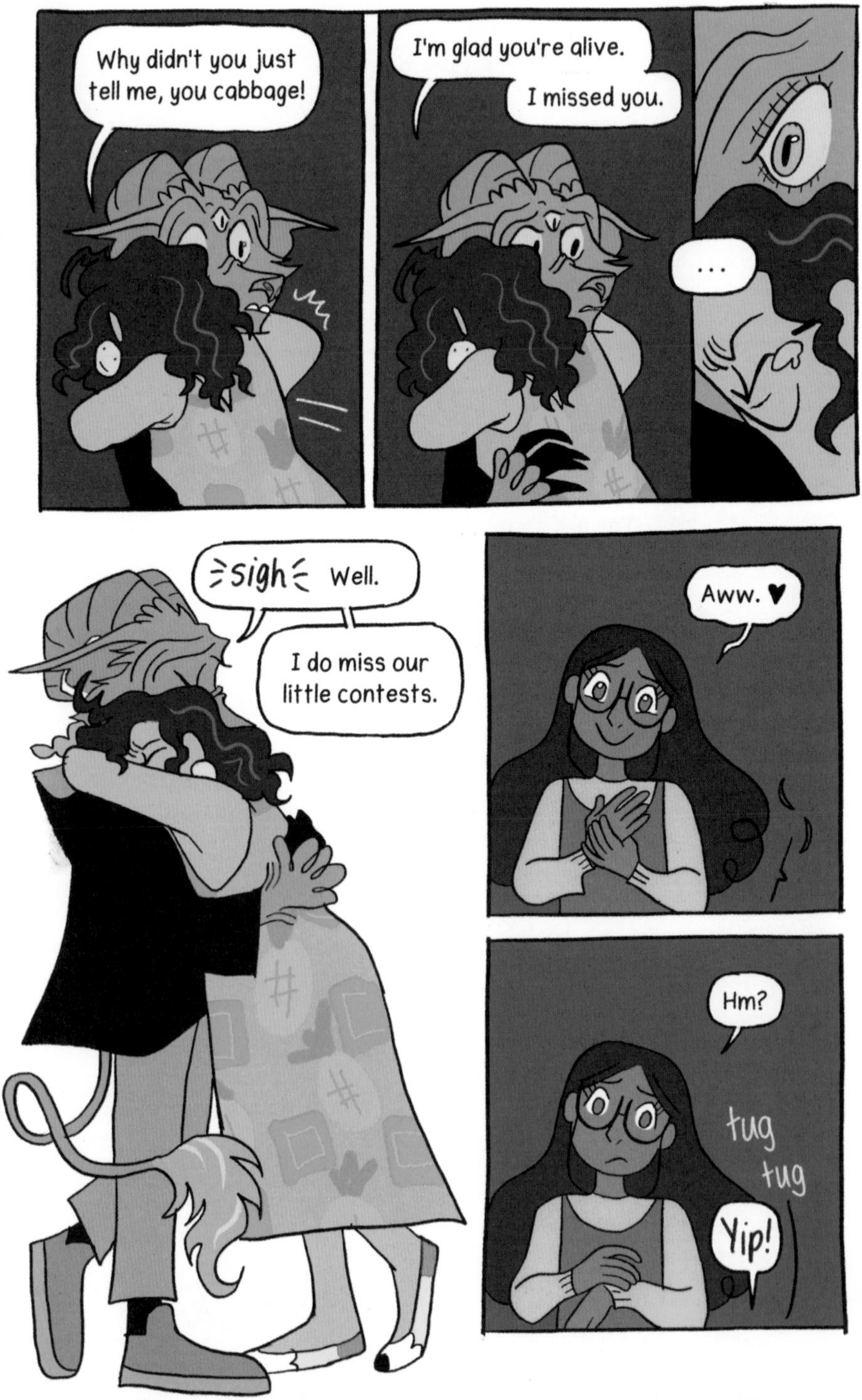
Why didn't you just tell me, you cabbage!
I'm glad you're alive.
I missed you.
...
sigh Well.
I do miss our little contests.
Aww. ♥
Hm?
tug
tug
Yip!

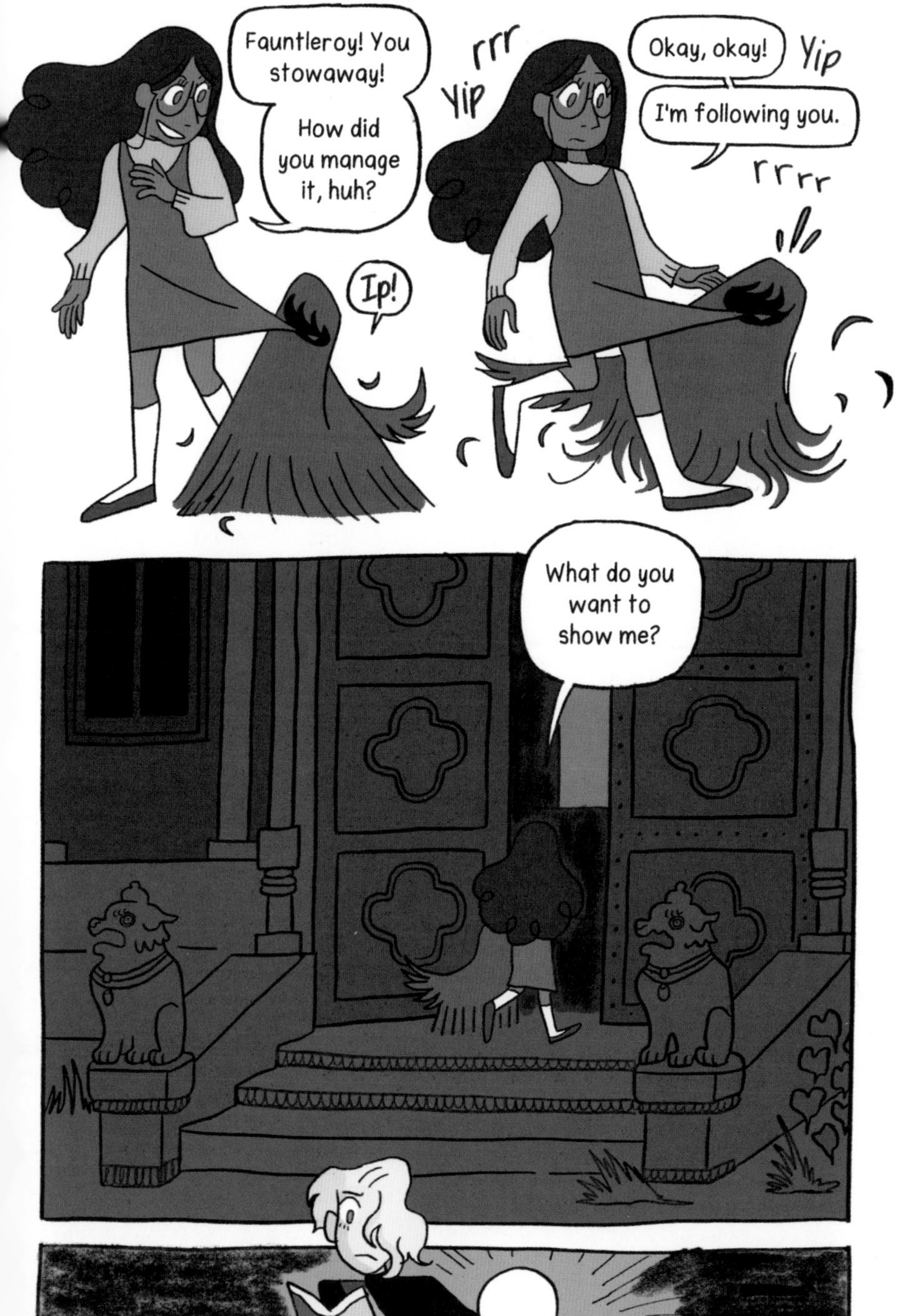
Fauntleroy! You stowaway!
How did you manage it, huh?
Ip!
rrr
Yip
Okay, okay!
Yip
I'm following you.
rrrr
What do you want to show me?

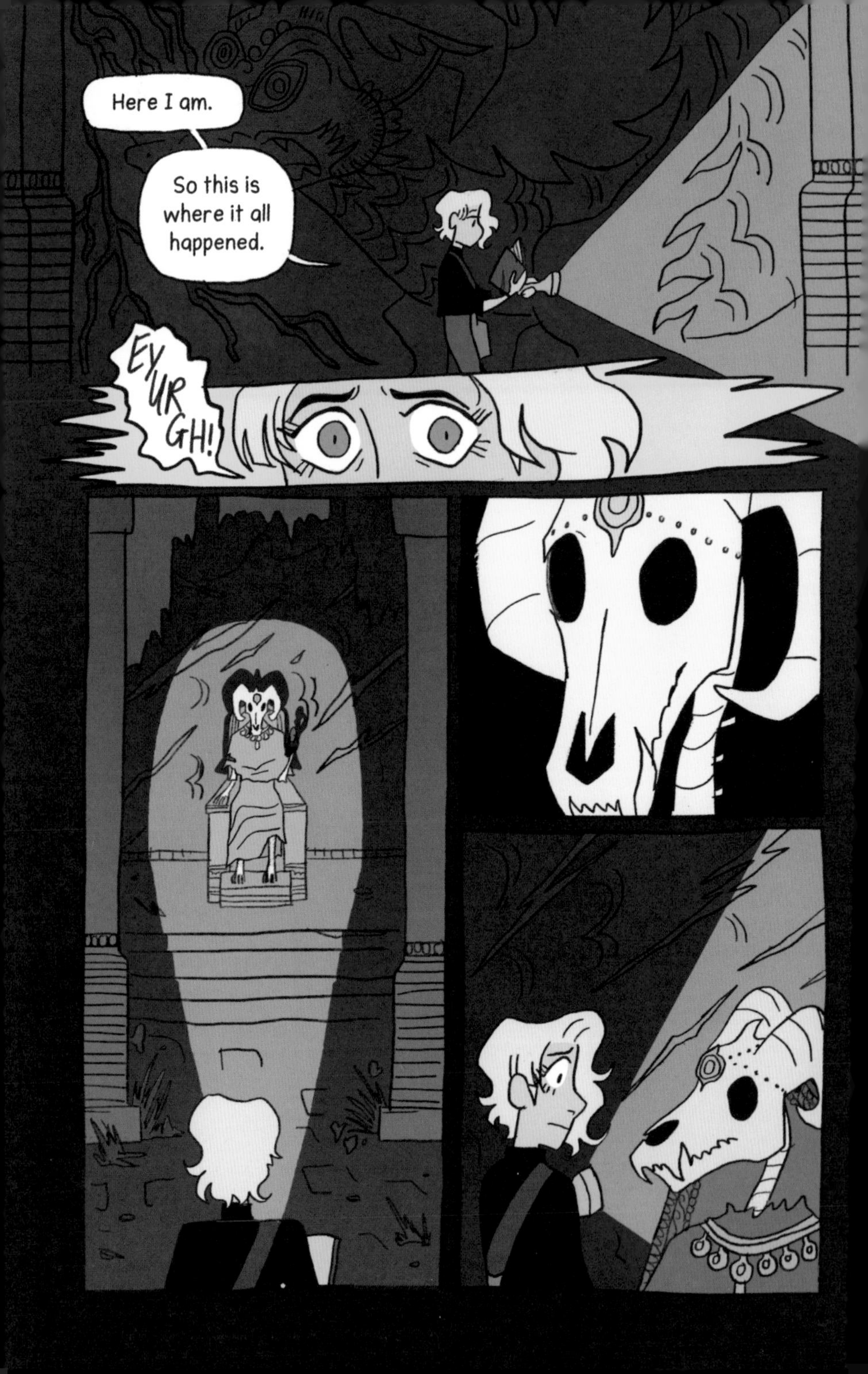
Here I am.
So this is where it all happened.
EYURGH!

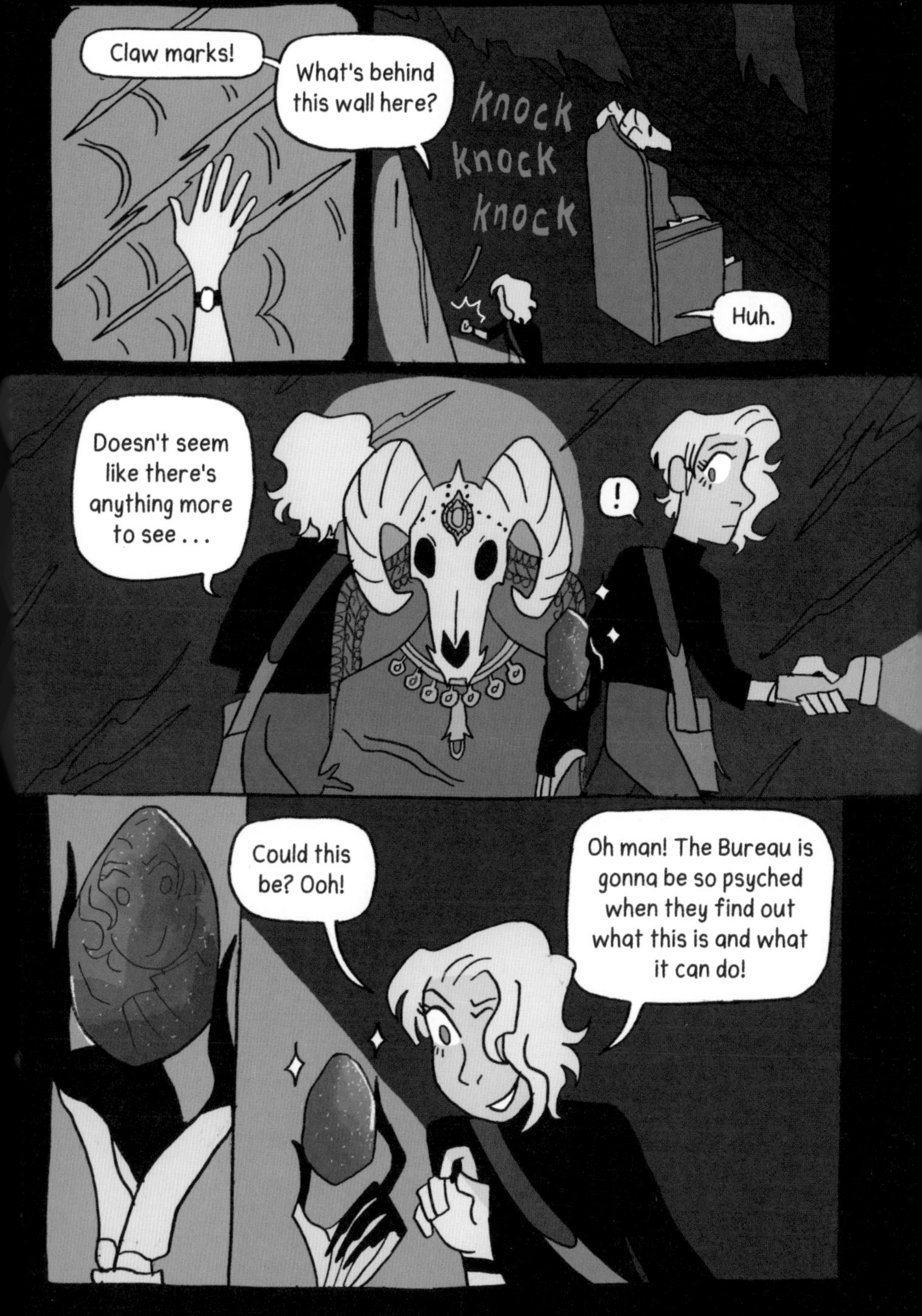
Claw marks!
What's behind this wall here?
knock knock knock
Huh.
Doesn't seem like there's anything more to see . . .
!
Could this be? Ooh!
Oh man! The Bureau is gonna be so psyched when they find out what this is and what it can do!

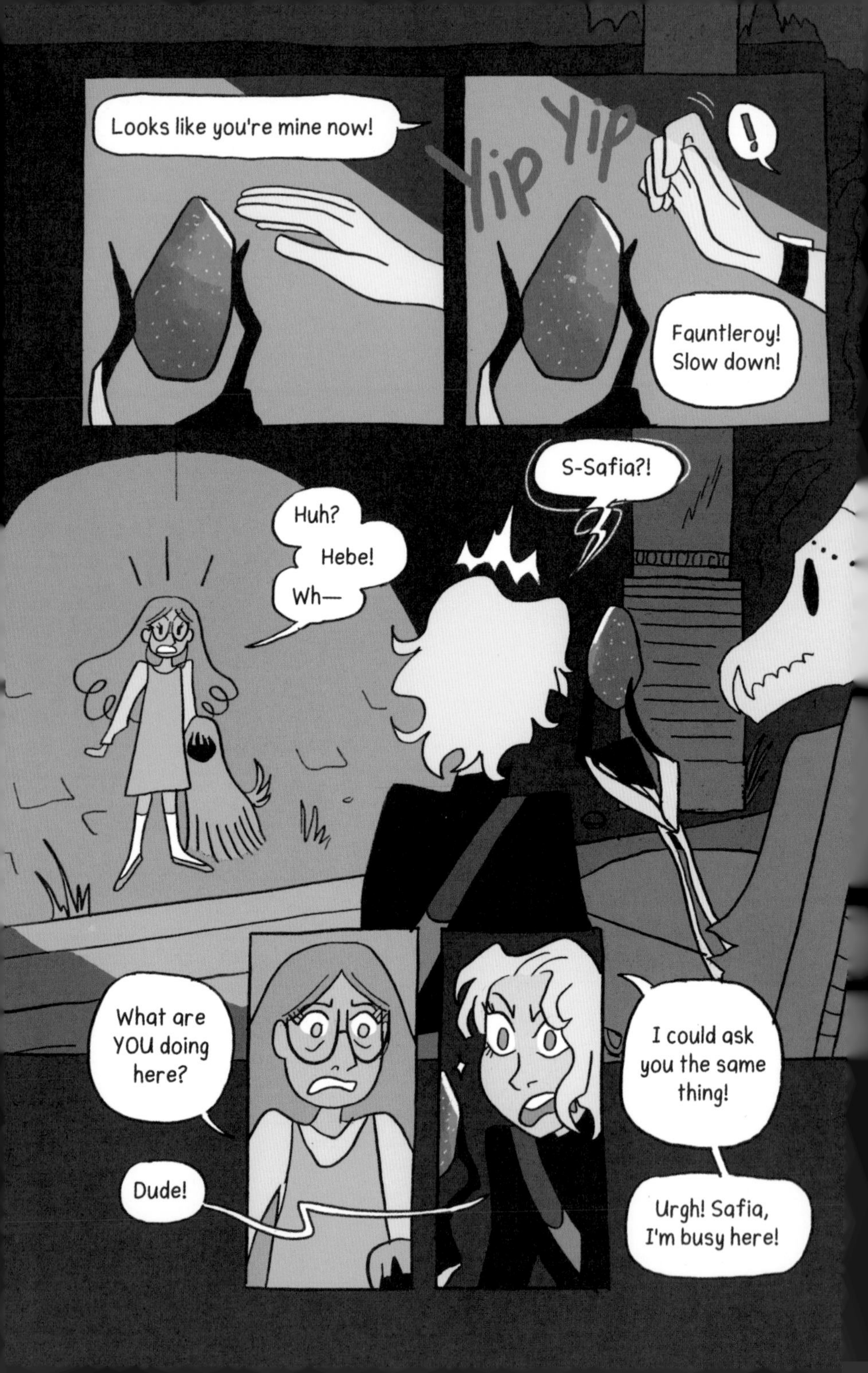

Looks like you're mine now!
YIP YIP
!
Fauntleroy! Slow down!
Huh?
Hebe!
Wh—
S-Safia?!
What are YOU doing here?
I could ask you the same thing!
Dude!
Urgh! Safia, I'm busy here!

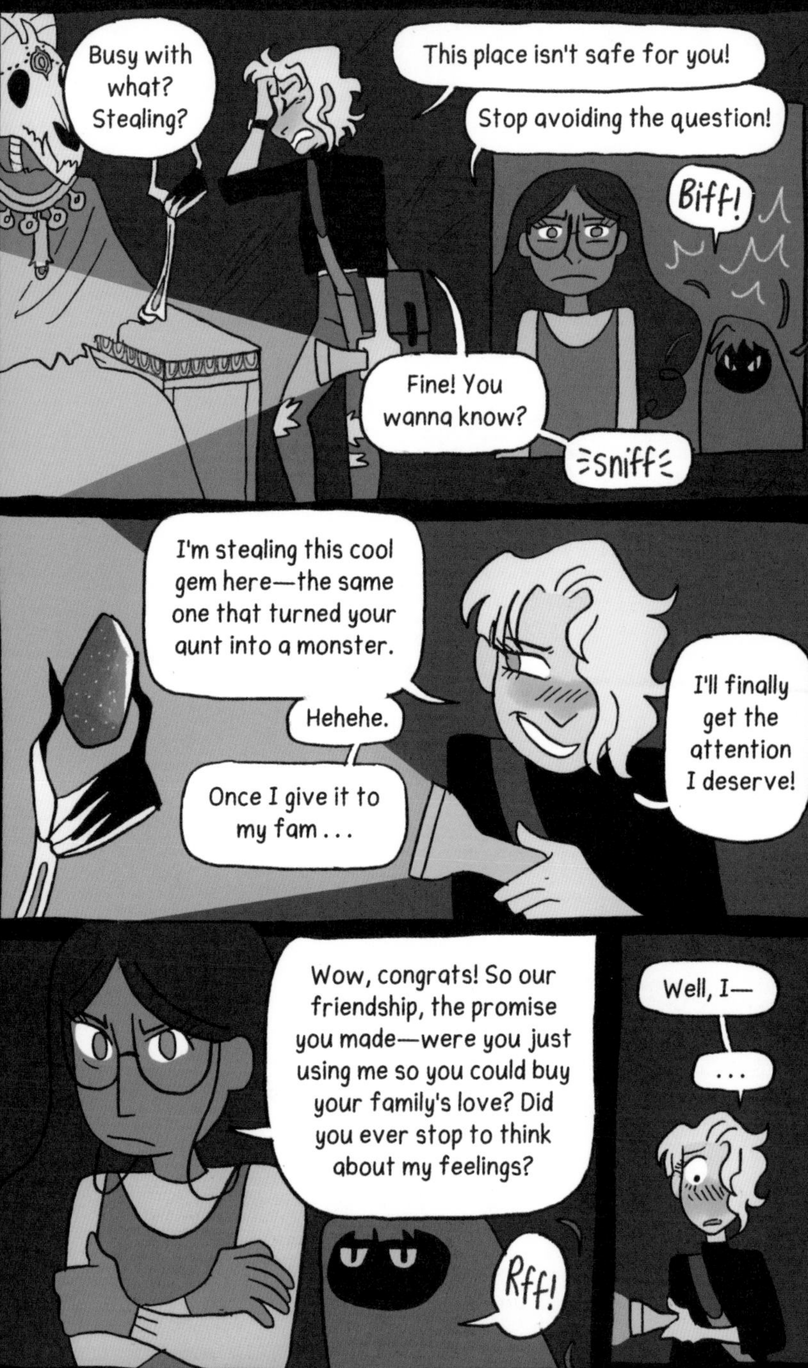
Busy with what? Stealing?
This place isn't safe for you!
Stop avoiding the question!
Biff!
Fine! You wanna know?
sniff
I'm stealing this cool gem here—the same one that turned your aunt into a monster.
Hehehe.
Once I give it to my fam . . .
I'll finally get the attention I deserve!
Wow, congrats! So our friendship, the promise you made—were you just using me so you could buy your family's love? Did you ever stop to think about my feelings?
Rff!
Well, I—
. . .

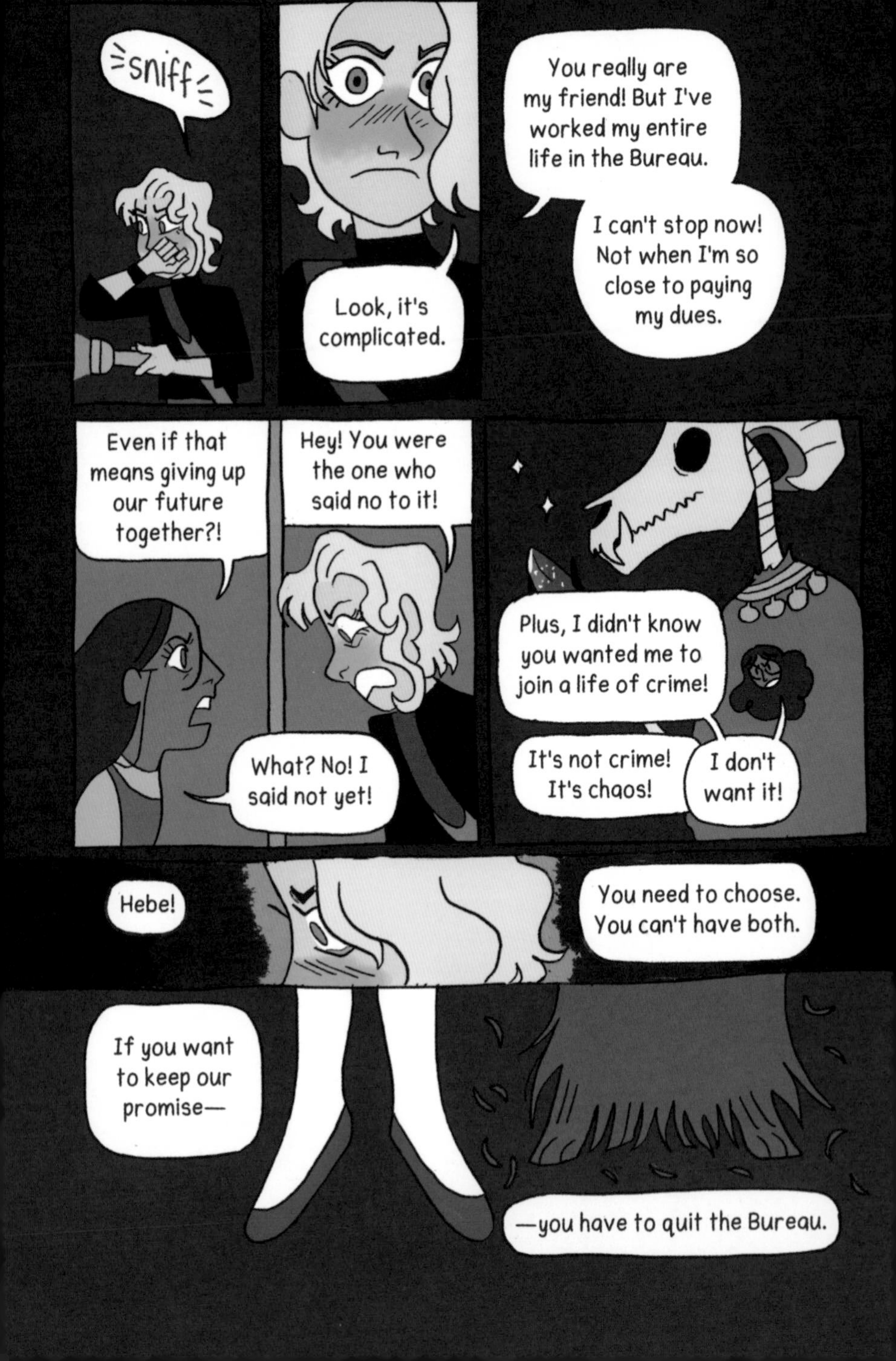
sniff
Look, it's complicated.
You really are my friend! But I've worked my entire life in the Bureau.
I can't stop now! Not when I'm so close to paying my dues.
Even if that means giving up our future together?!
Hey! You were the one who said no to it!
What? No! I said not yet!
Plus, I didn't know you wanted me to join a life of crime!
It's not crime! It's chaos!
I don't want it!
Hebe!
You need to choose. You can't have both.
If you want to keep our promise—
—you have to quit the Bureau.

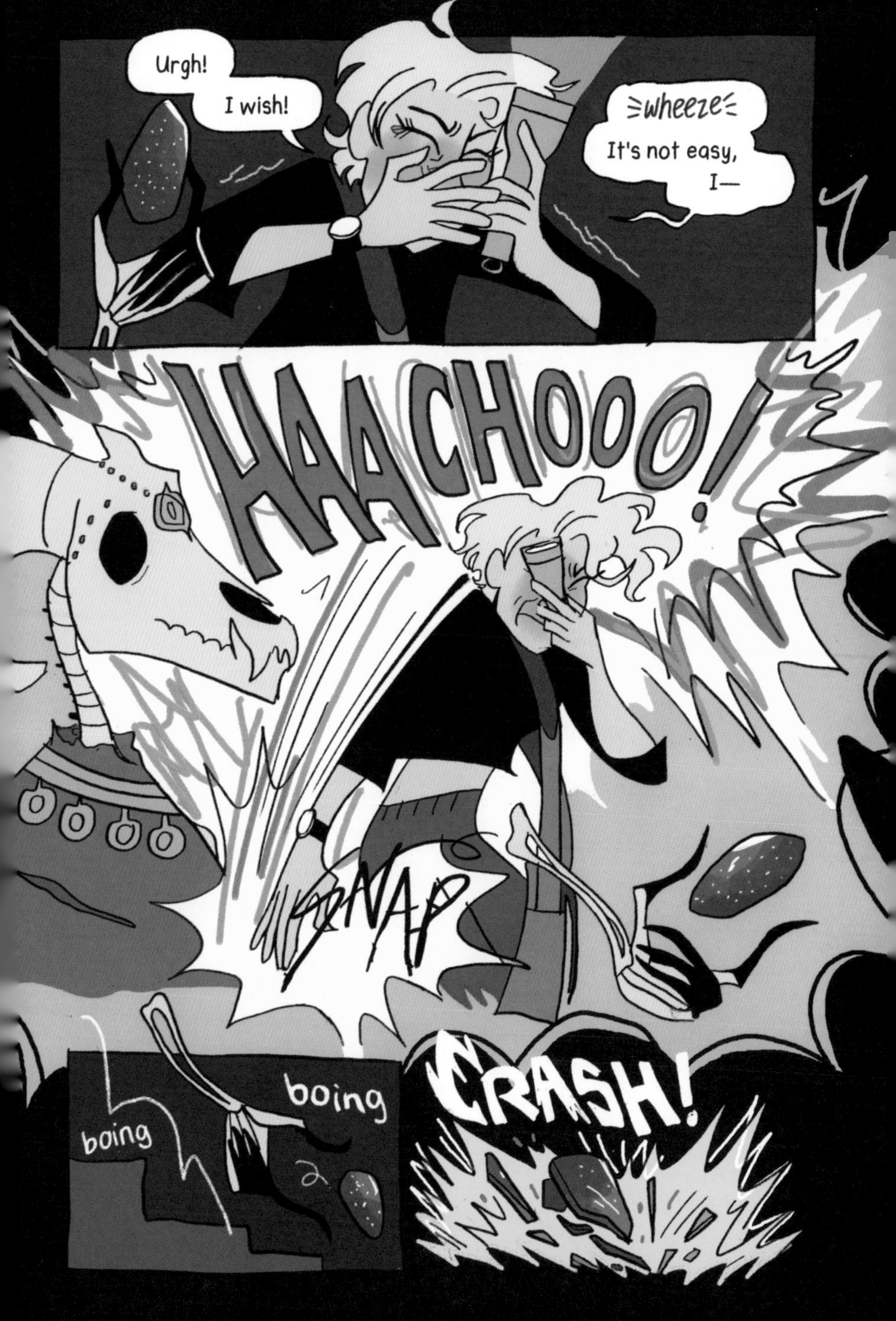
Urgh!
I wish!
wheeze
It's not easy,
I—
HAACHOOO!
SNAP
boing
boing
CRASH!

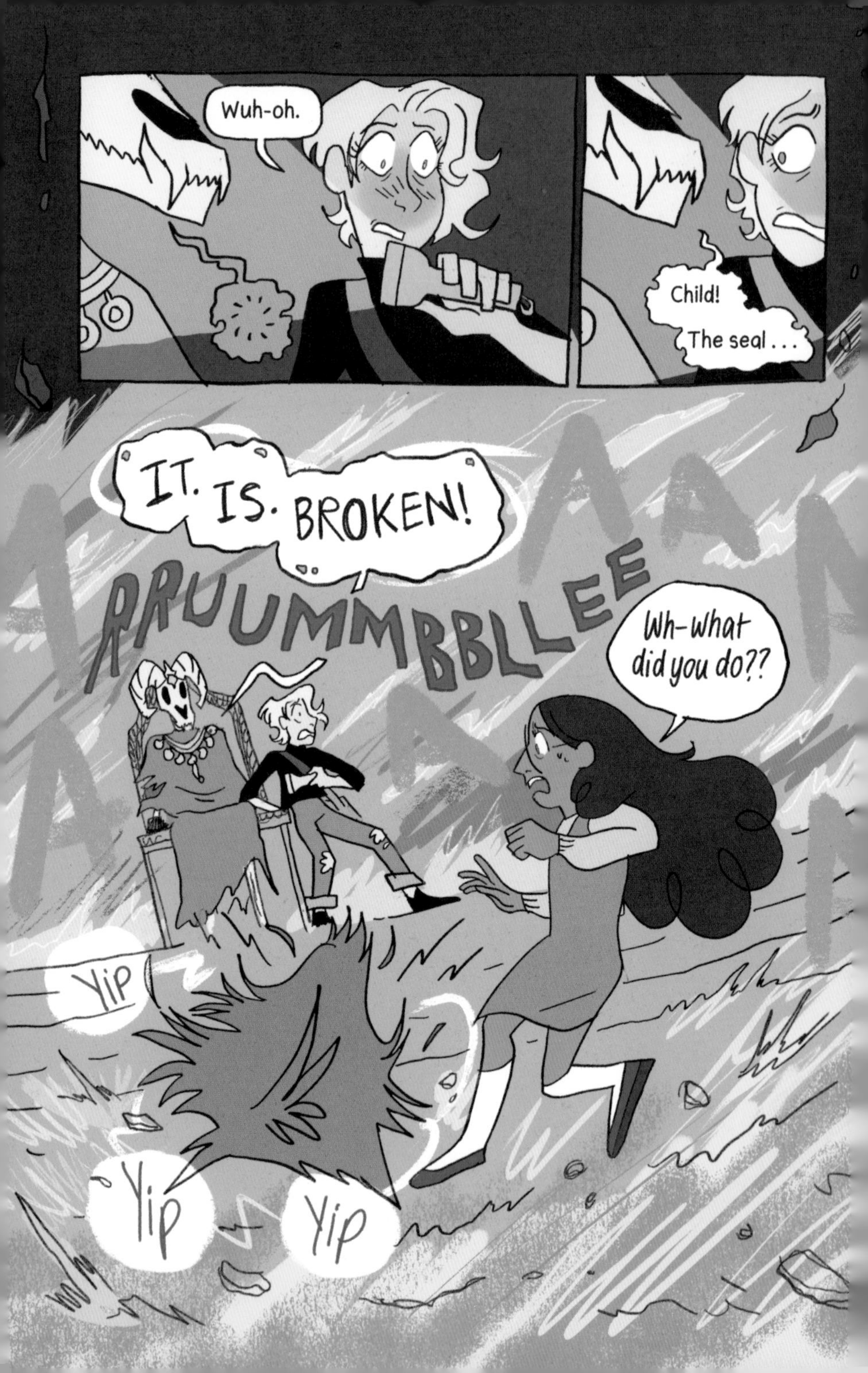
Wuh-oh.
Child!
The seal . . .
IT. IS. BROKEN!
RRUUMMBBLLEE
Wh-what did you do??
Yip
Yip
Yip

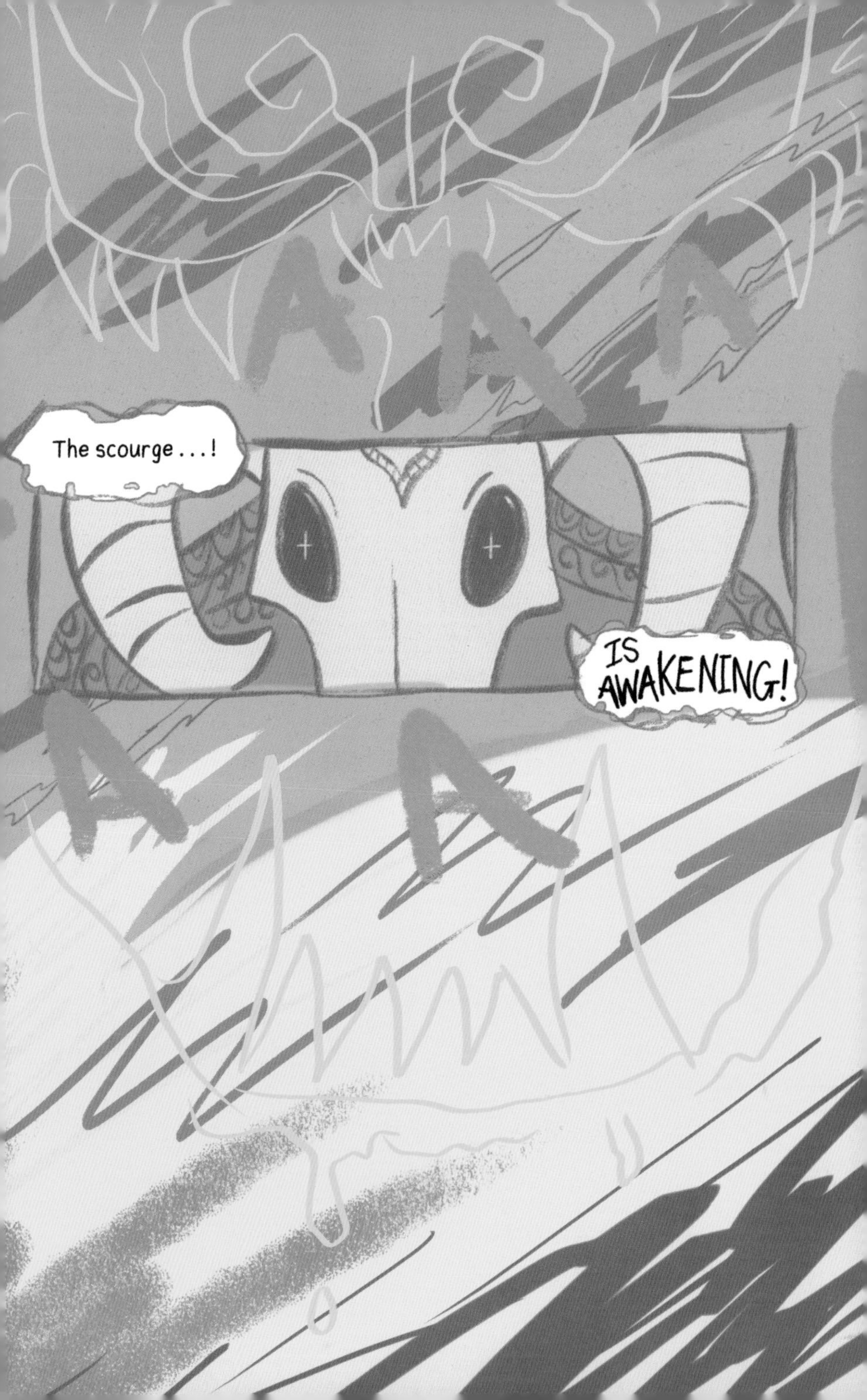
AAA
The scourge . . . !
IS AWAKENING!
AA

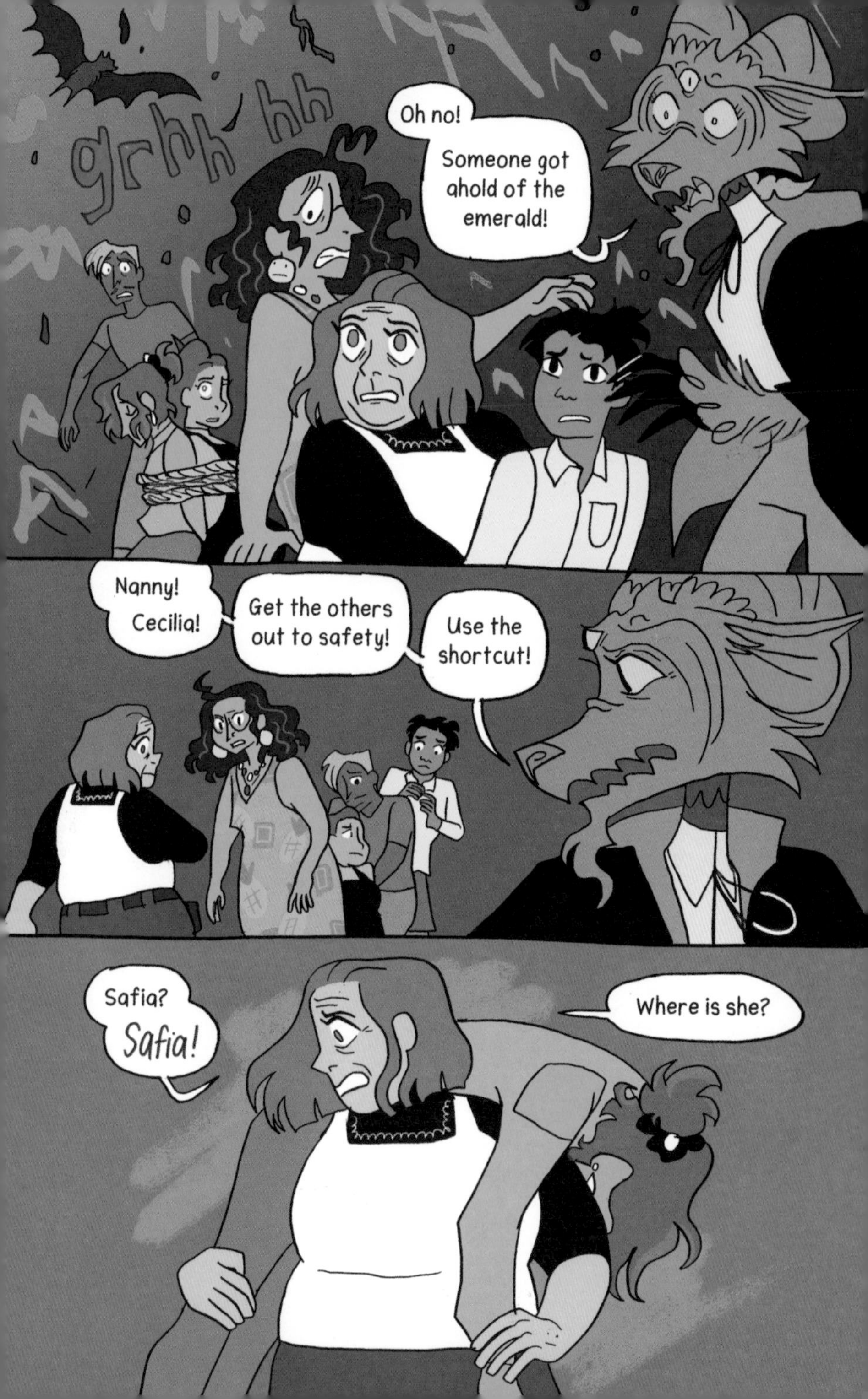
grhh hh
Oh no!
Someone got ahold of the emerald!
Nanny!
Cecilia!
Get the others out to safety!
Use the shortcut!
Safia?
Safia!
Where is she?

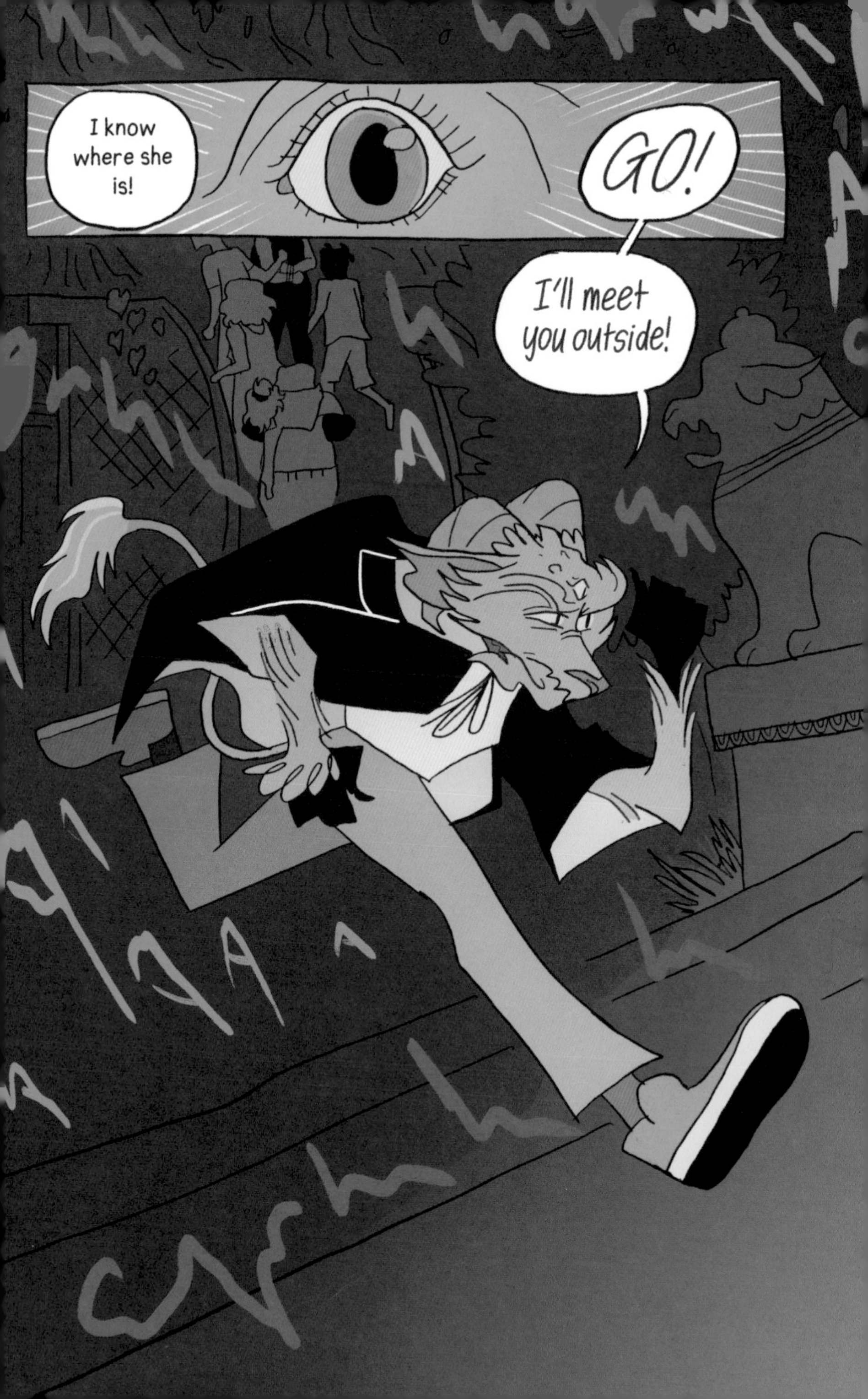
I know where she is!
GO!
I'll meet you outside!

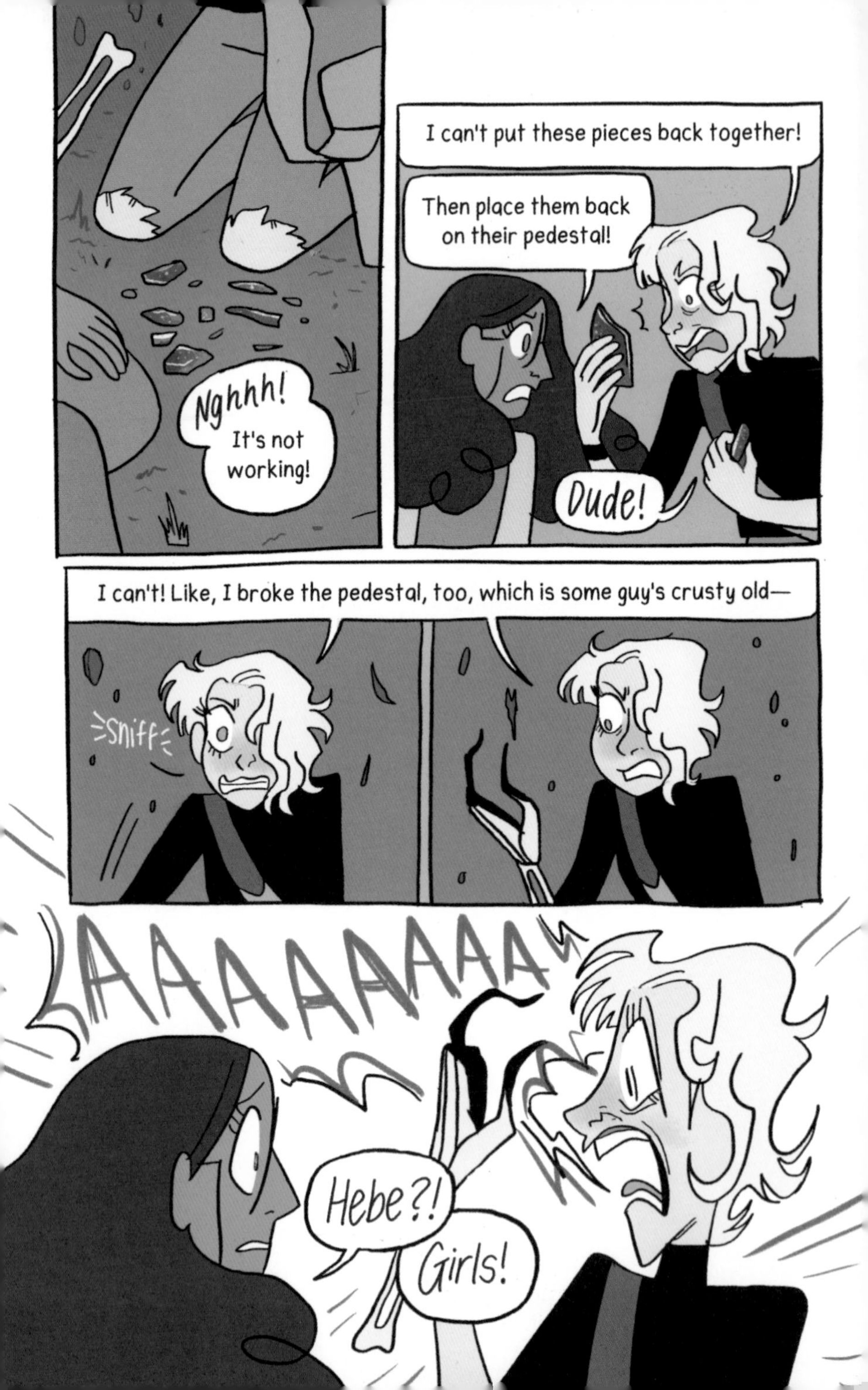
Nghhh!
It's not working!
I can't put these pieces back together!
Then place them back on their pedestal!
Dude!
I can't! Like, I broke the pedestal, too, which is some guy's crusty old—
Sniff
AAAAAAAAAA
Hebe?!
Girls!

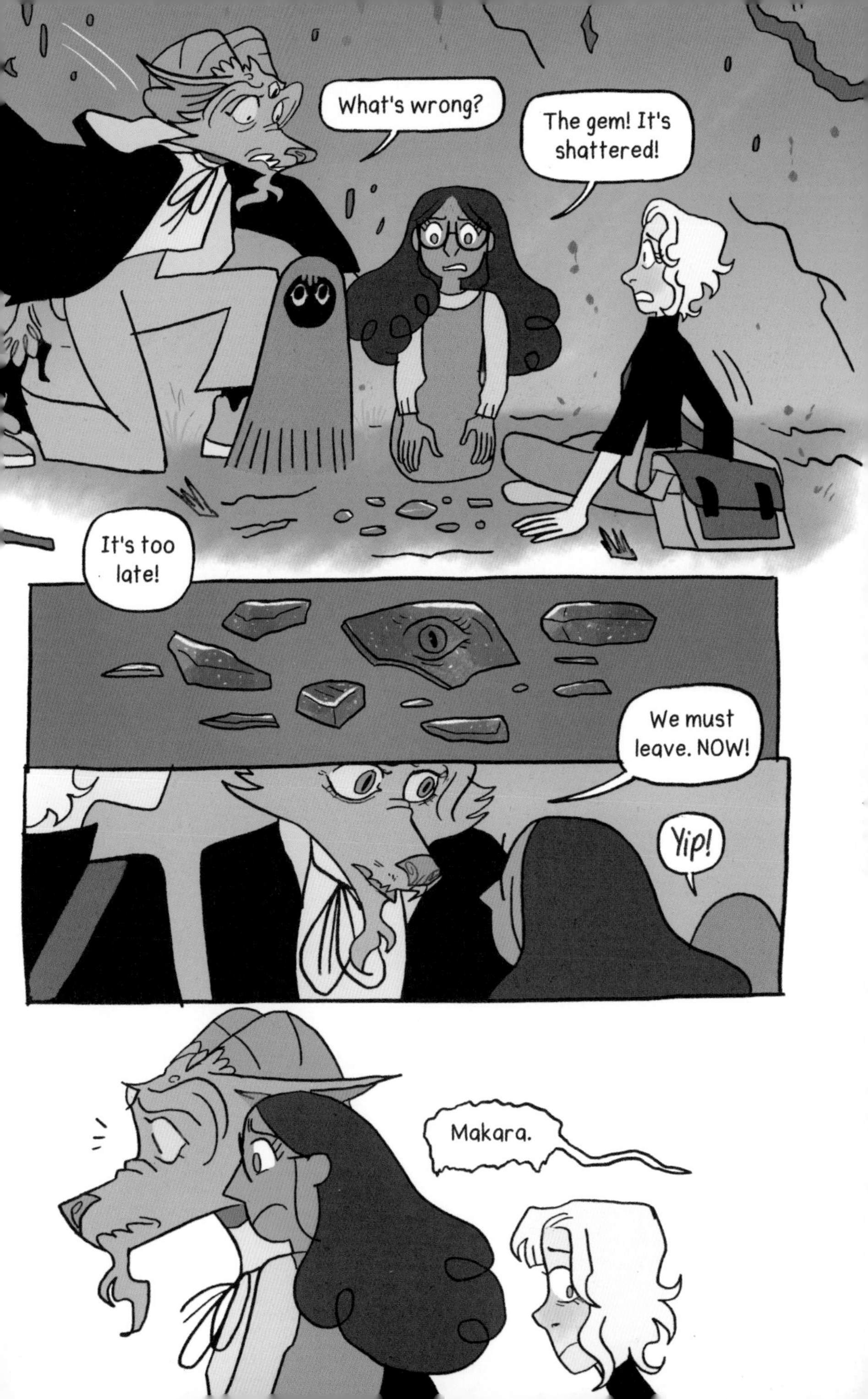
What's wrong?
The gem! It's shattered!
It's too late!
We must leave. NOW!
Yip!
Makara.

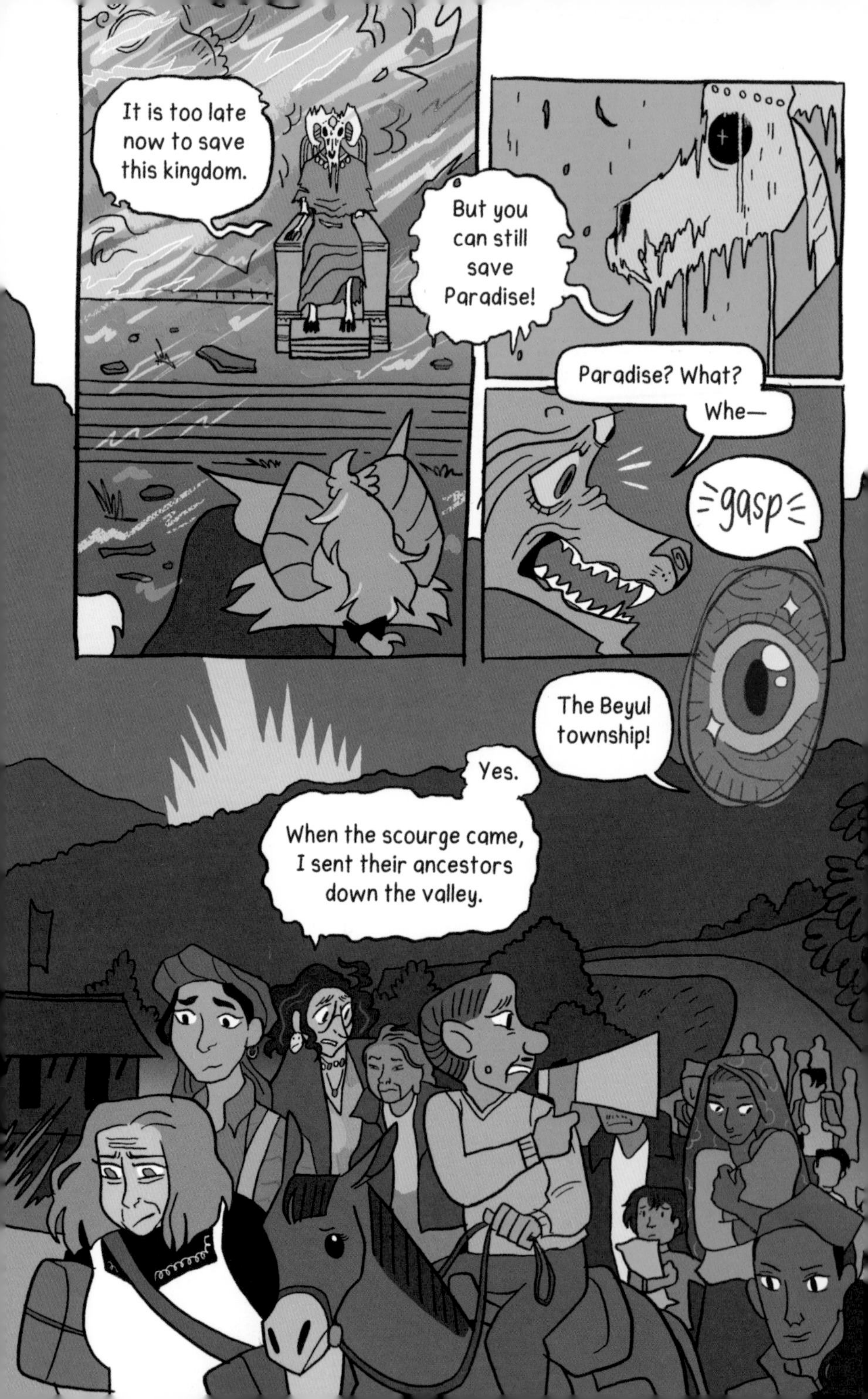
It is too late now to save this kingdom.
But you can still save Paradise!
Paradise? What? Whe—
gasp
The Beyul township!
Yes.
When the scourge came, I sent their ancestors down the valley.

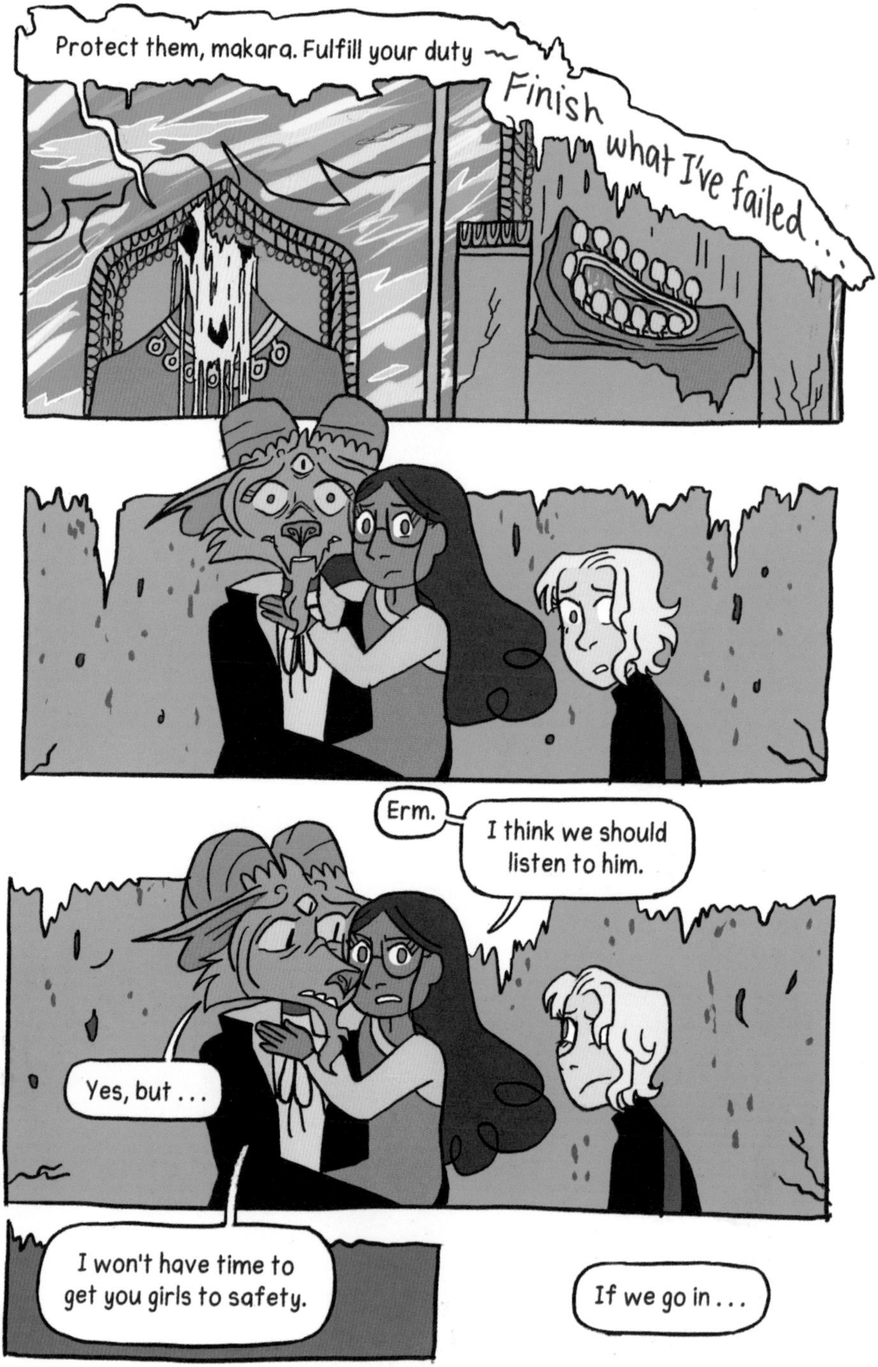
Protect them, makara. Fulfill your duty
Finish what I've failed . . .
Erm.
I think we should listen to him.
Yes, but . . .
If we go in . . .
I won't have time to get you girls to safety.

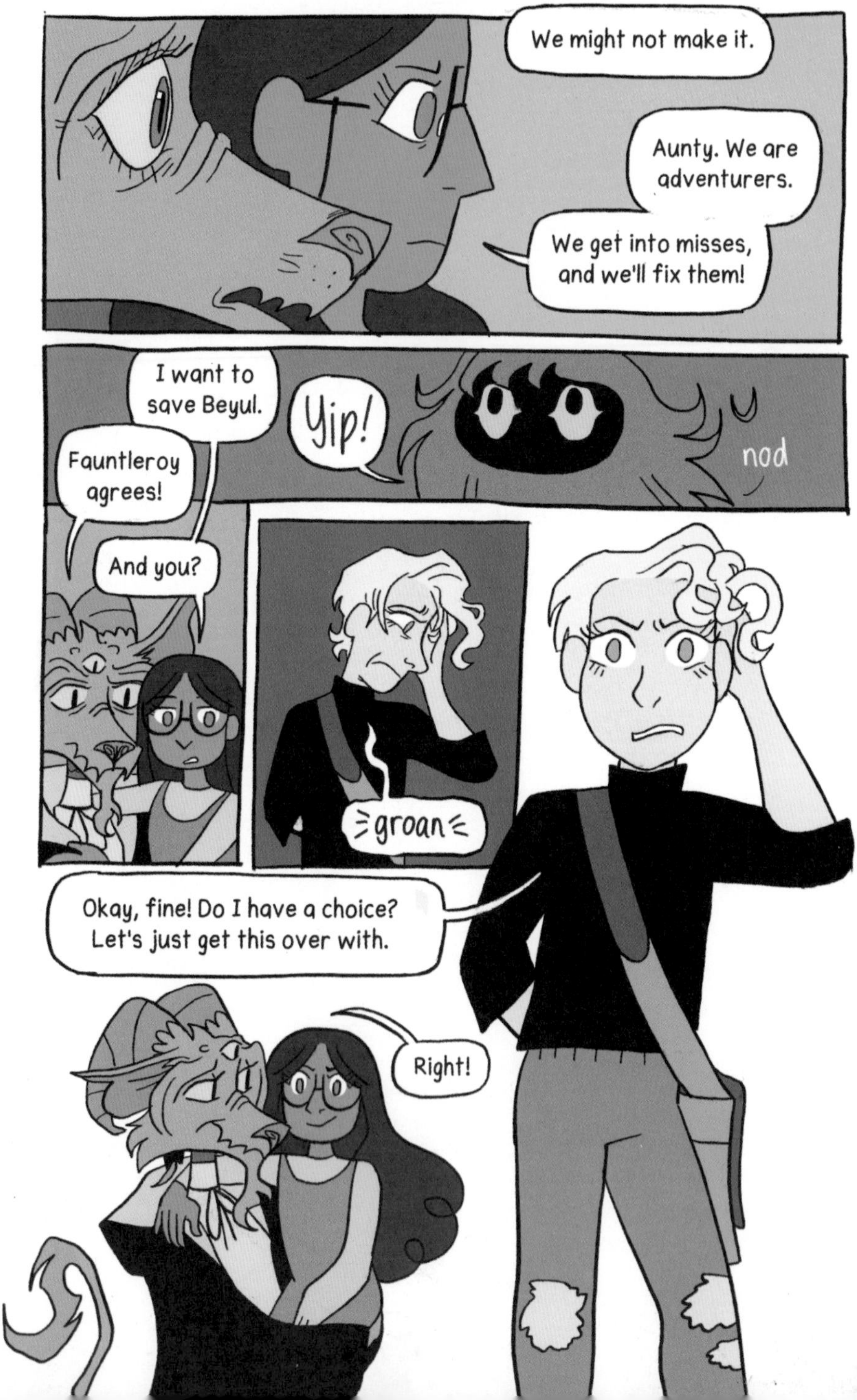
We might not make it.
Aunty. We are adventurers.
We get into misses, and we'll fix them!
I want to save Beyul.
Yip!
nod
Fauntleroy agrees!
And you?
groan
Okay, fine! Do I have a choice? Let's just get this over with.
Right!

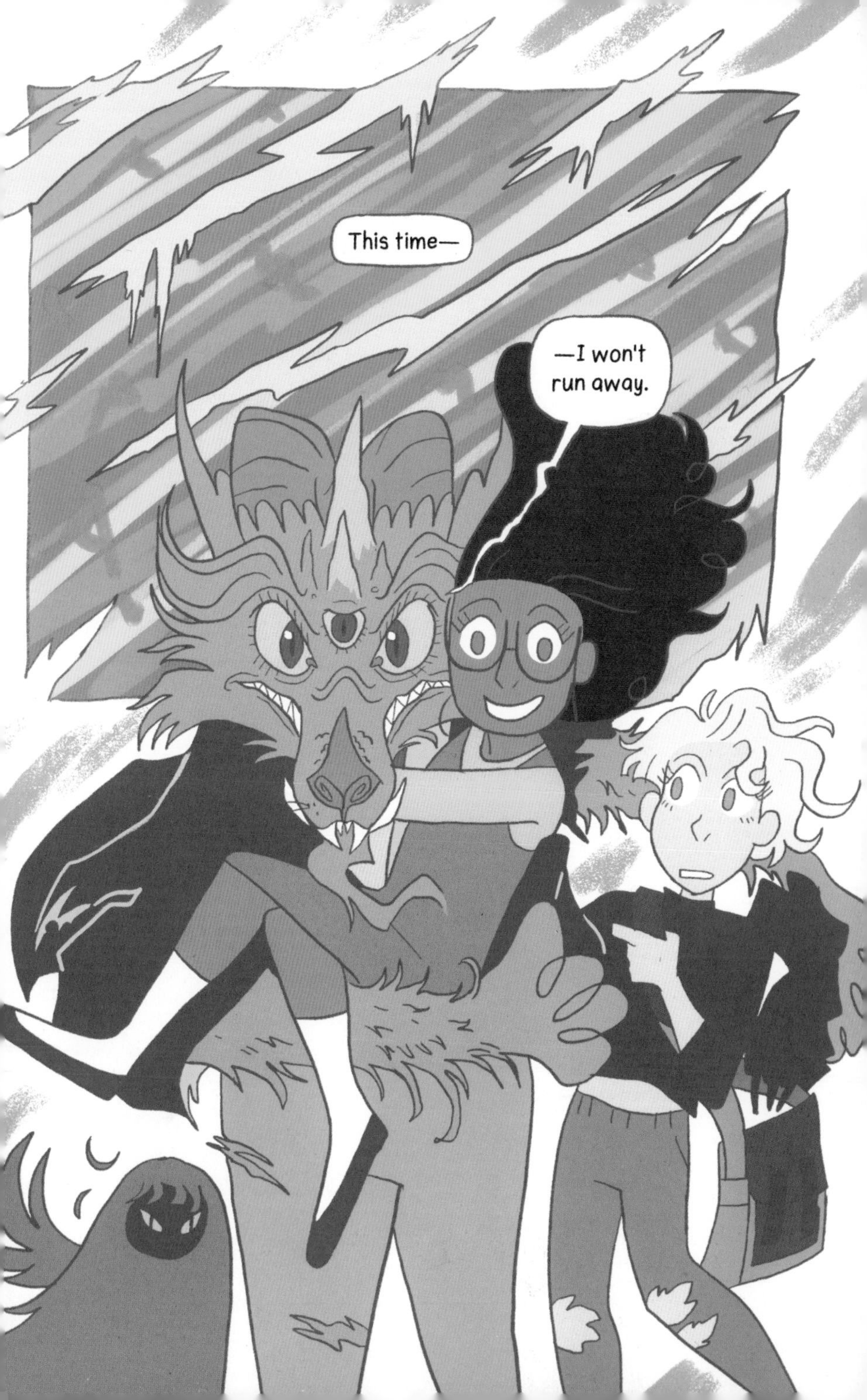
This time—
—I won't run away.

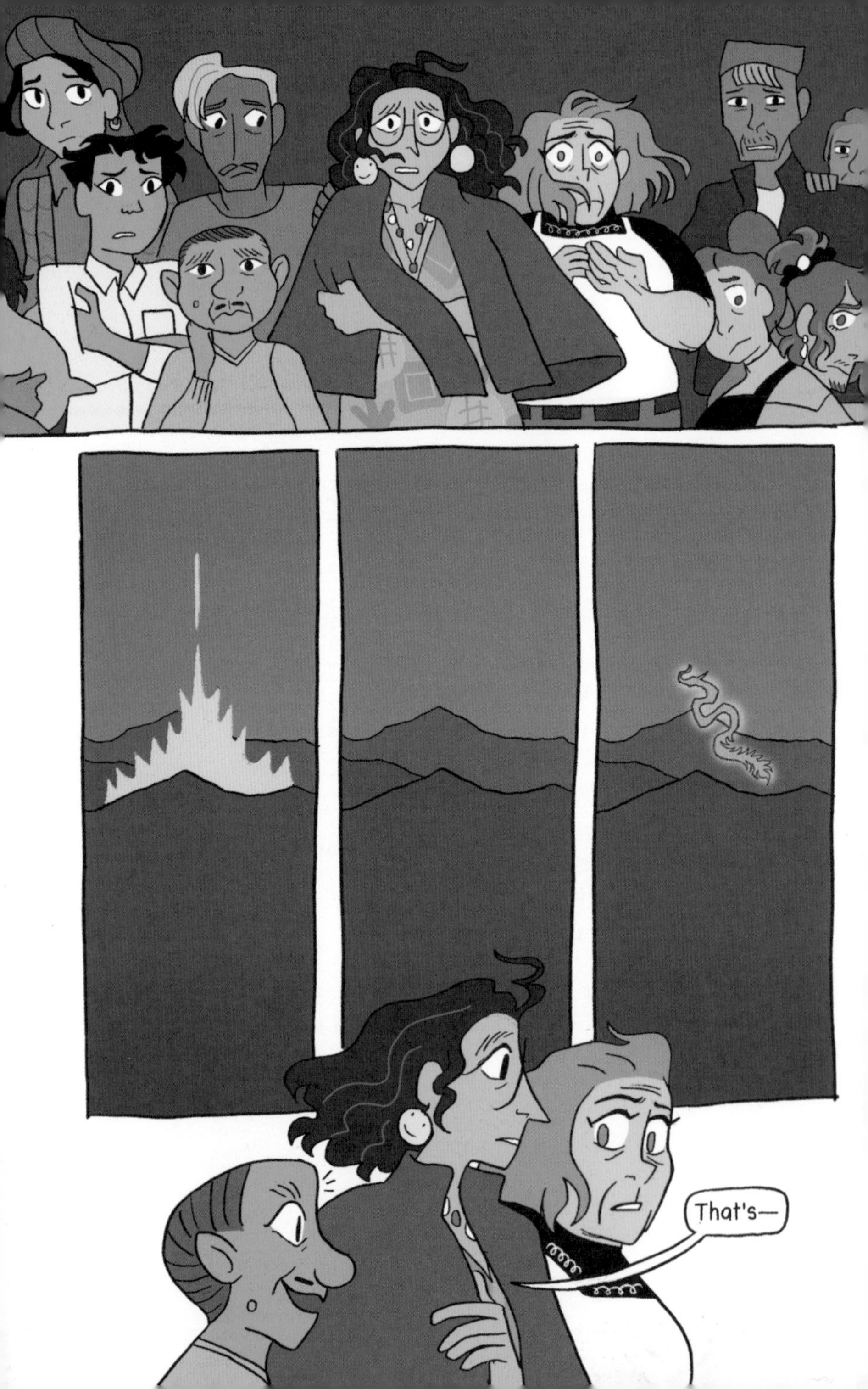
That's—

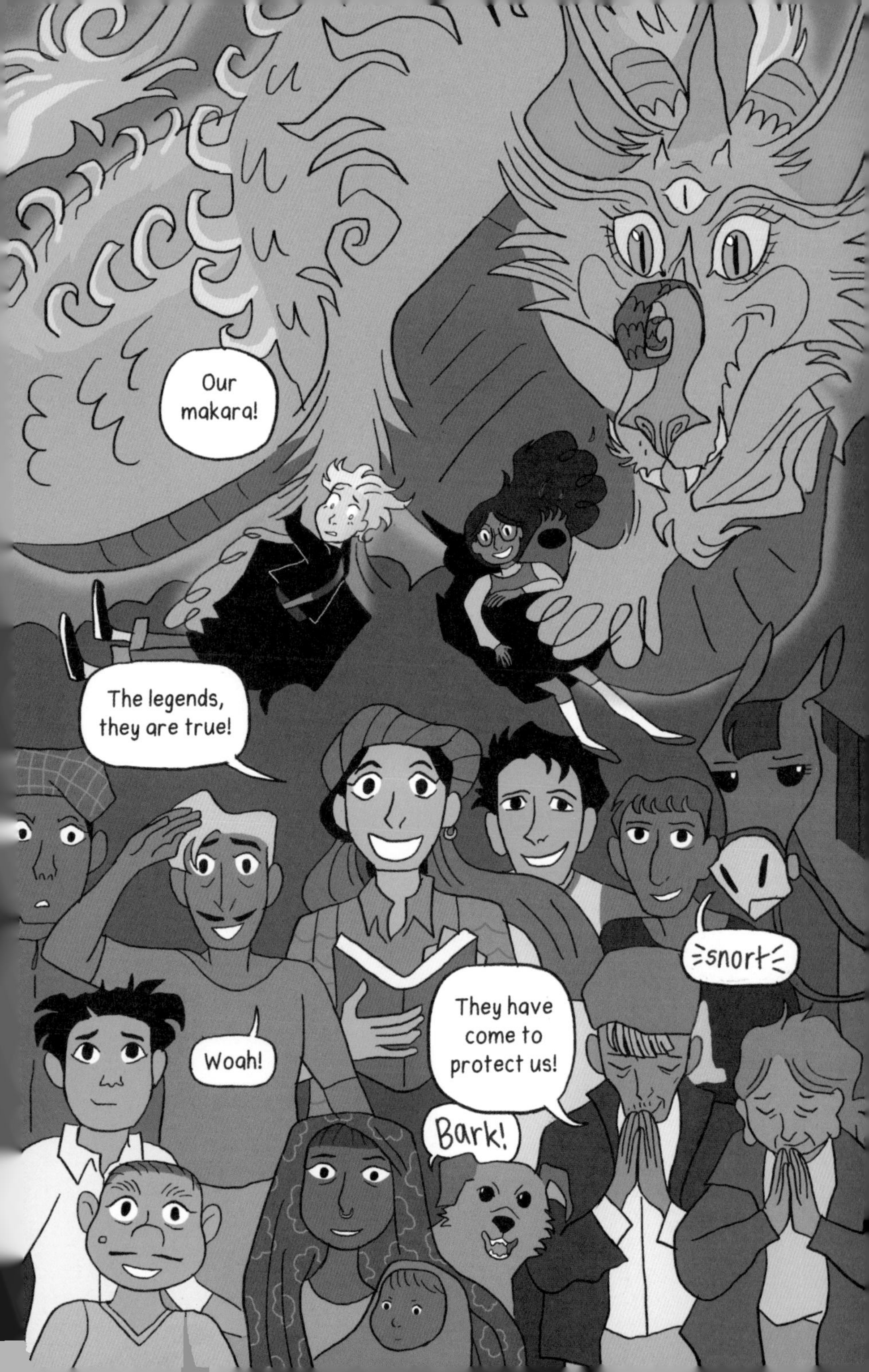
Our makara!
The legends, they are true!
snort
Woah!
They have come to protect us!
Bark!

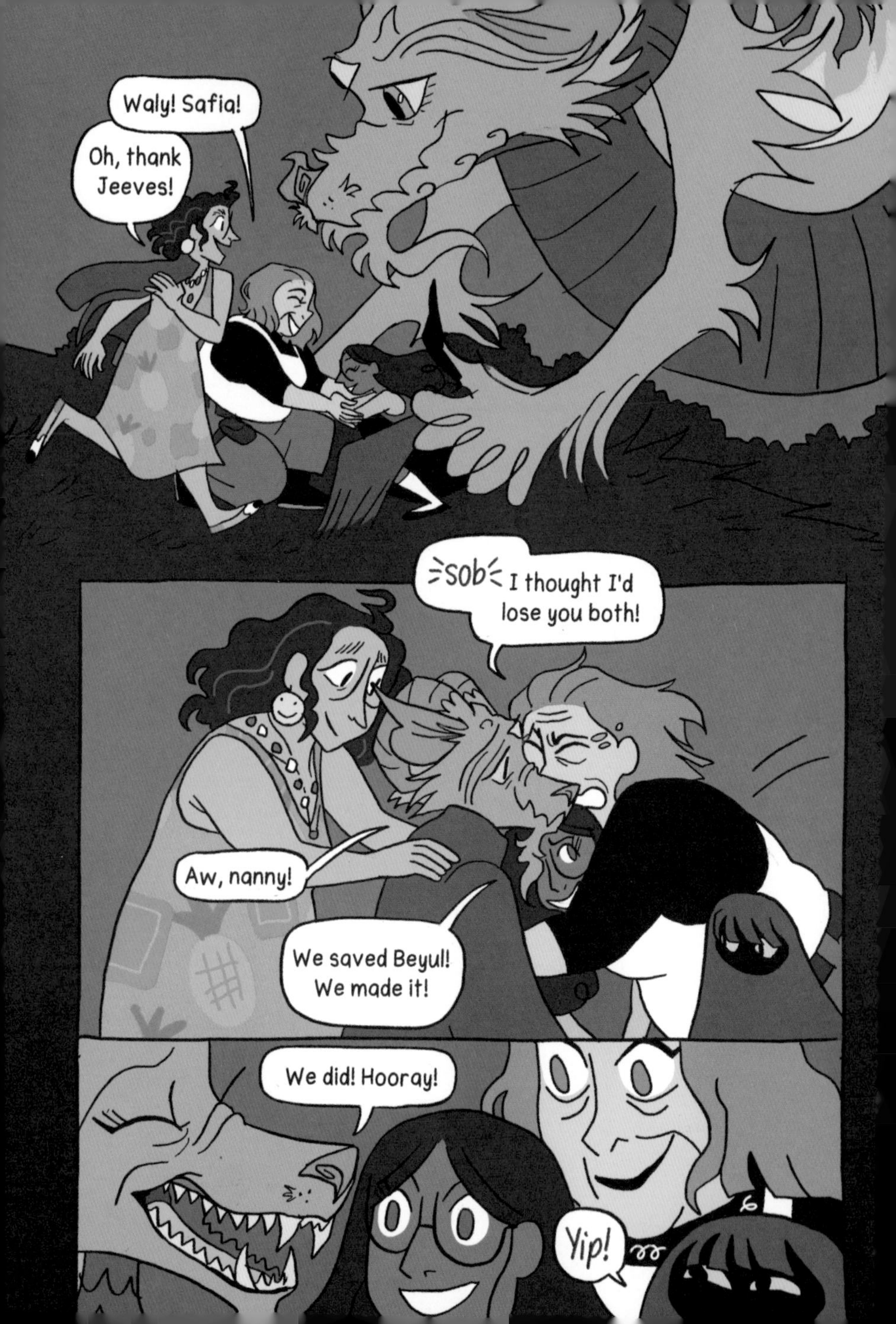

Waly! Safia!
Oh, thank Jeeves!
SOB I thought I'd lose you both!
Aw, nanny!
We saved Beyul! We made it!
We did! Hooray!
Yip!

Thank you, dear guardian.

Our township is indebted to you for your service.

It's an honor, Mayor.

And please, call me Lady Whimsy . . .

?!

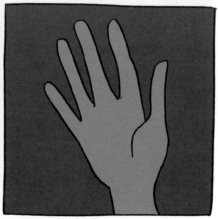

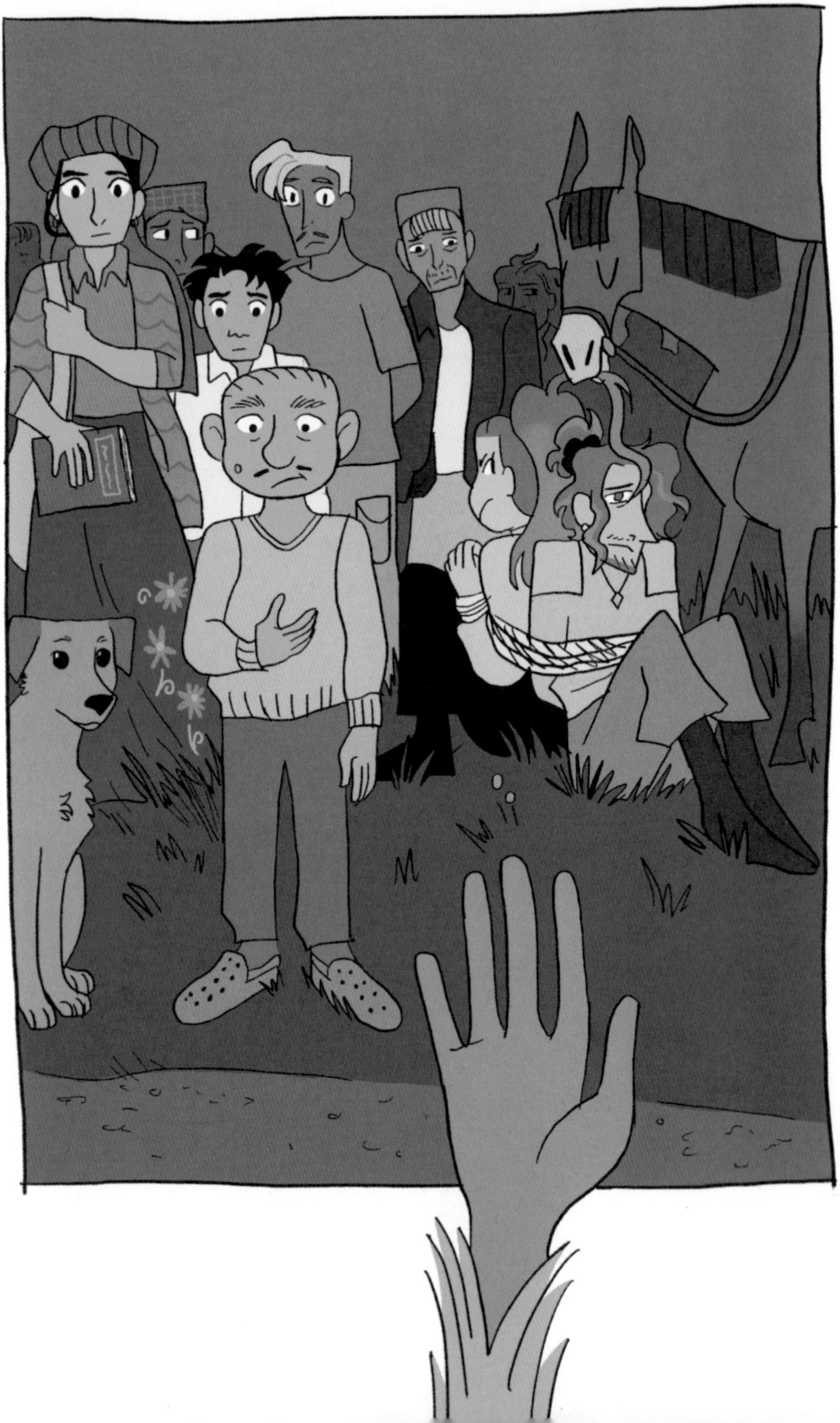

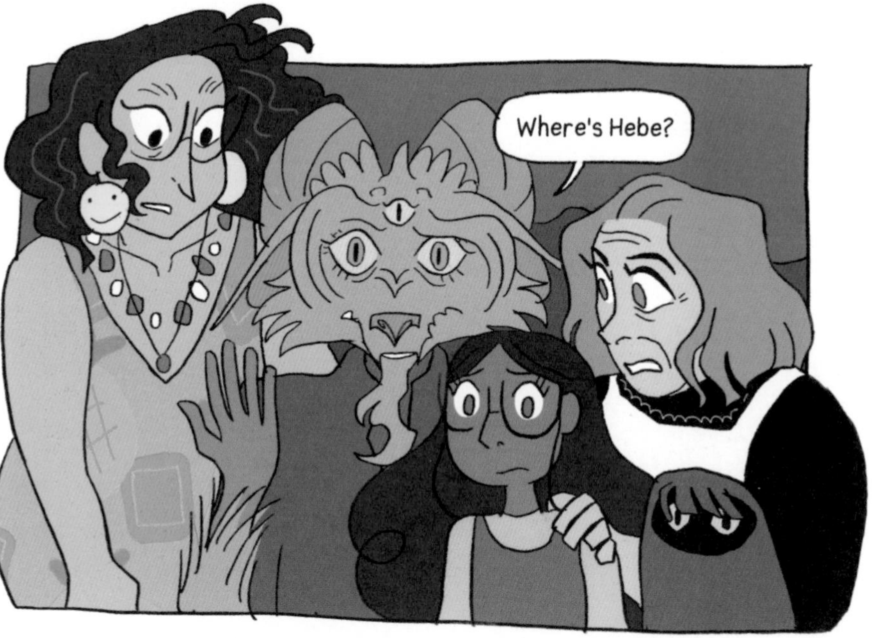
Where's Hebe?

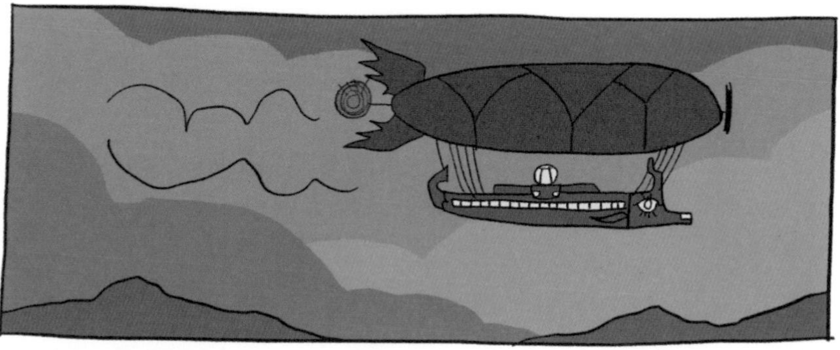

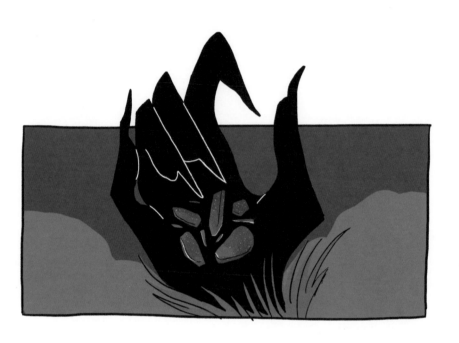

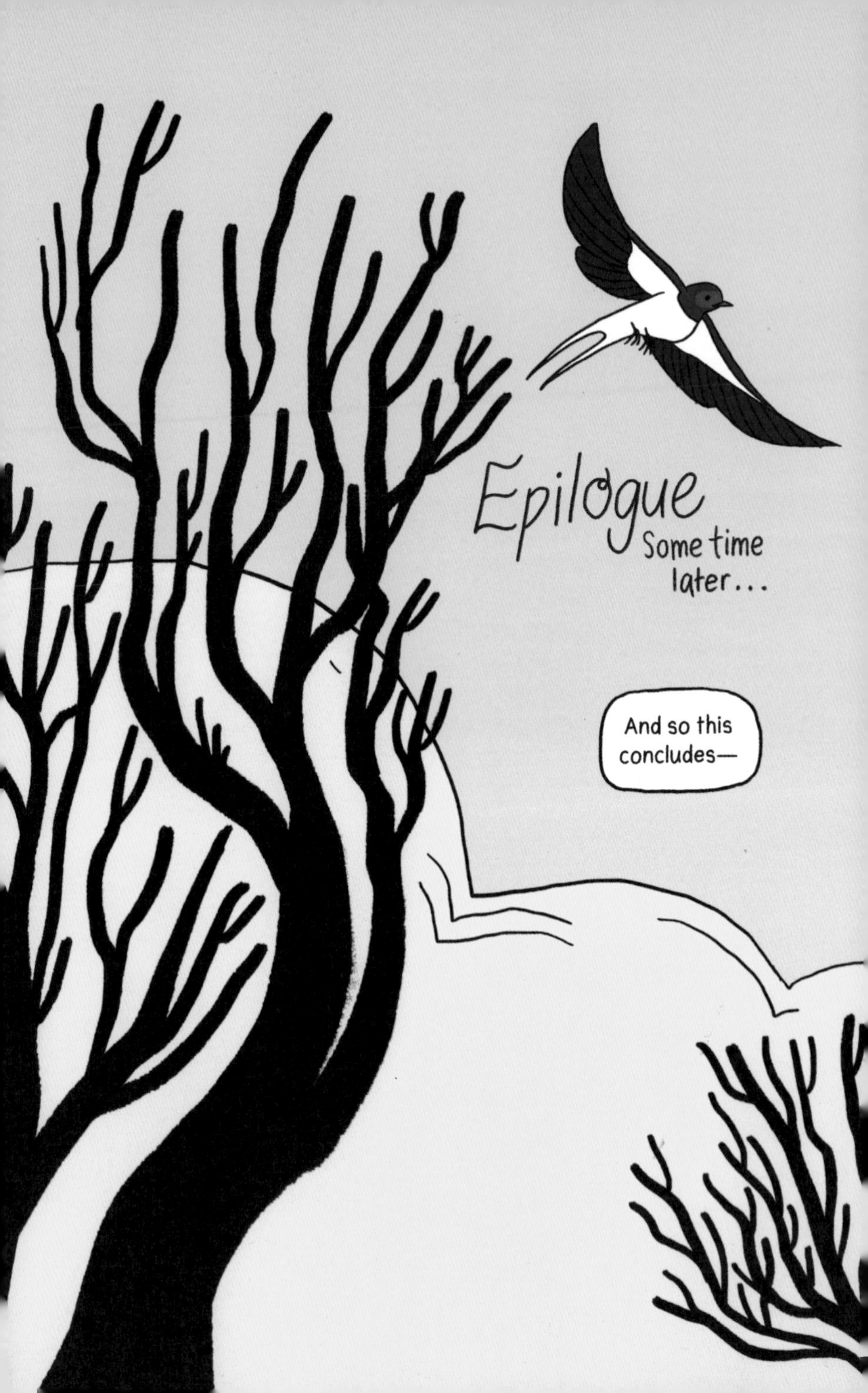
Epilogue
Some time later...
And so this concludes—

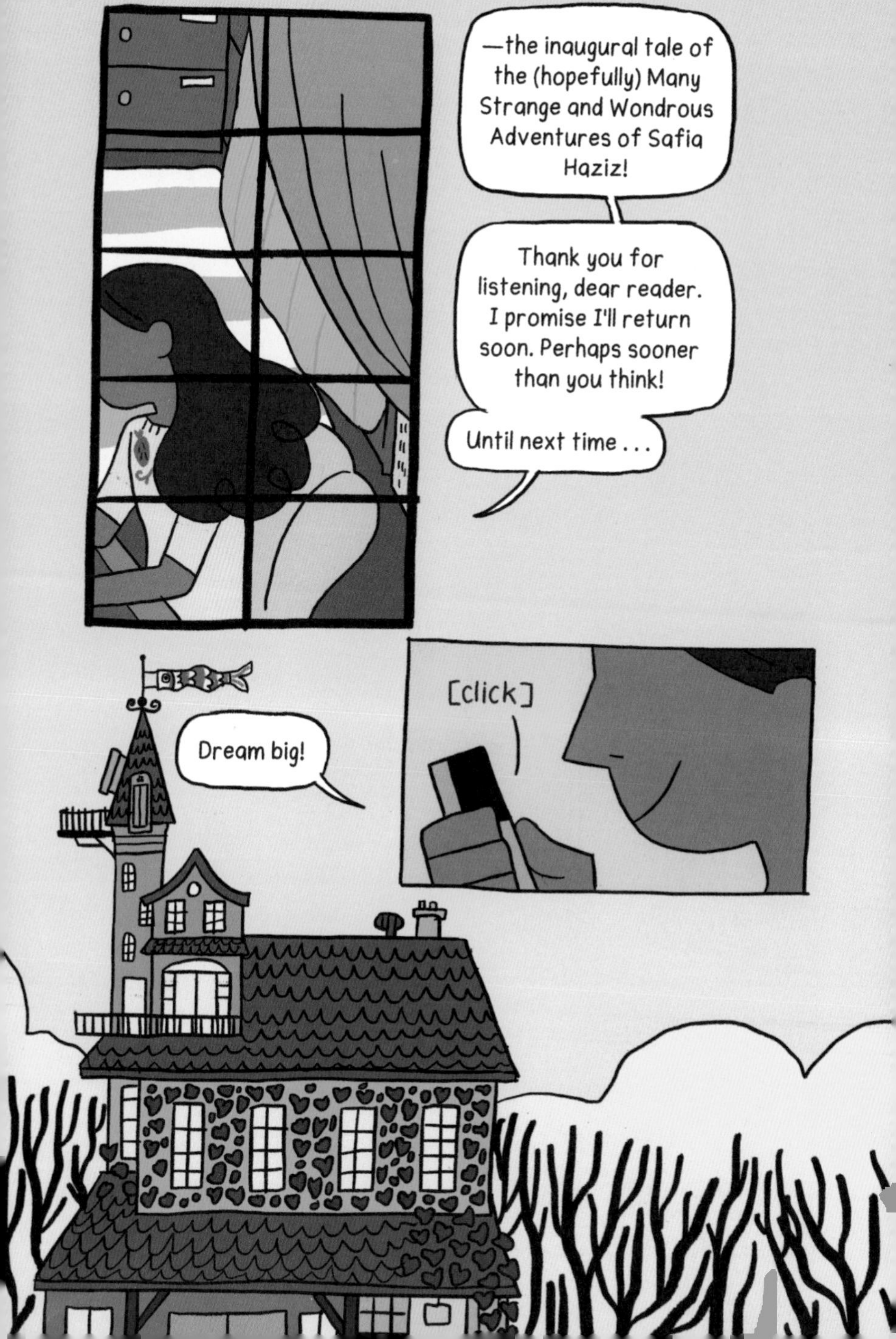
—the inaugural tale of the (hopefully) Many Strange and Wondrous Adventures of Safia Haziz!
Thank you for listening, dear reader. I promise I'll return soon. Perhaps sooner than you think!
Until next time . . .
Dream big!
[click]

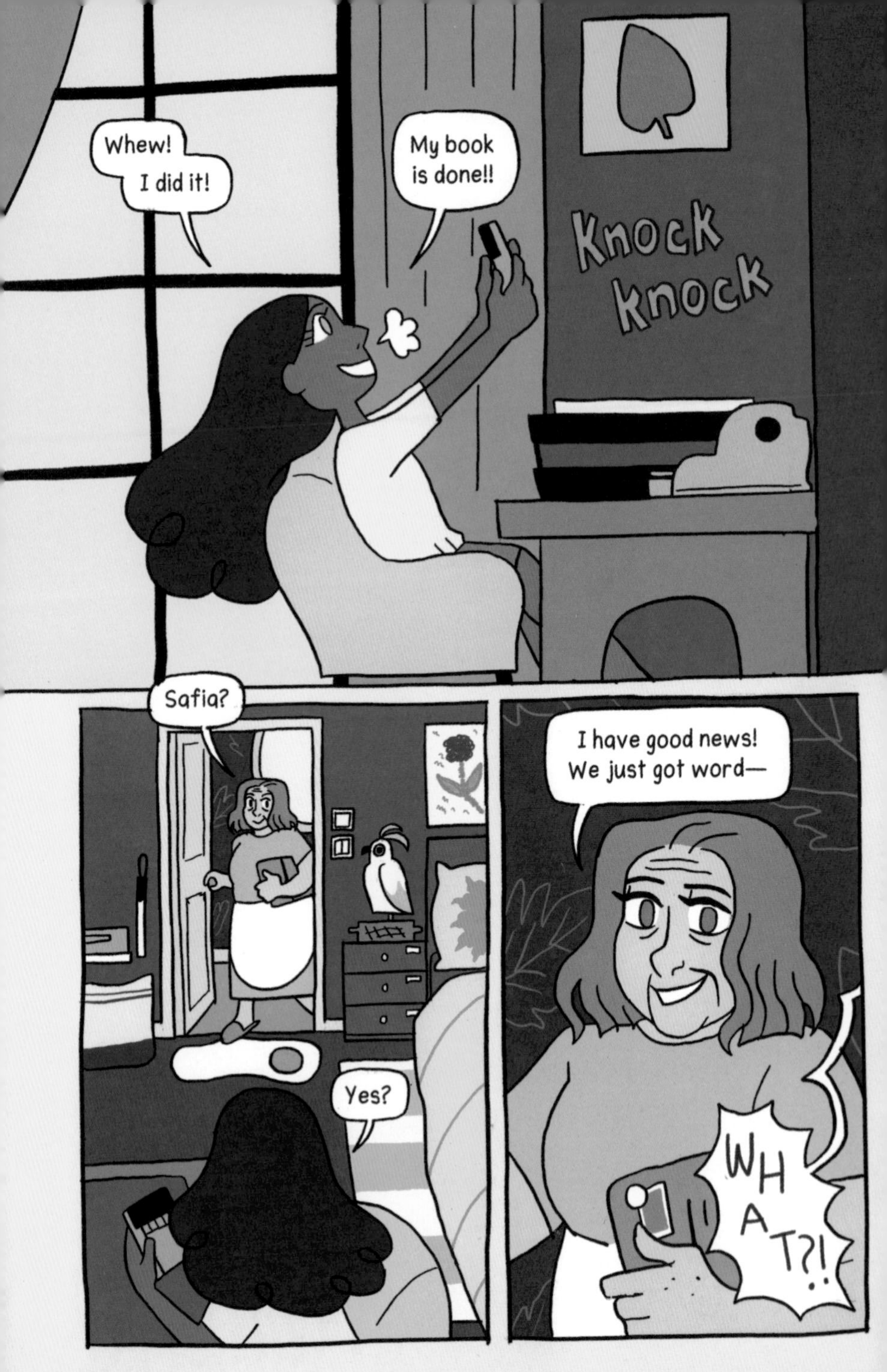

Whew!
I did it!
My book is done!!
Knock knock
Safia?
Yes?
I have good news! We just got word—
WHAT?!

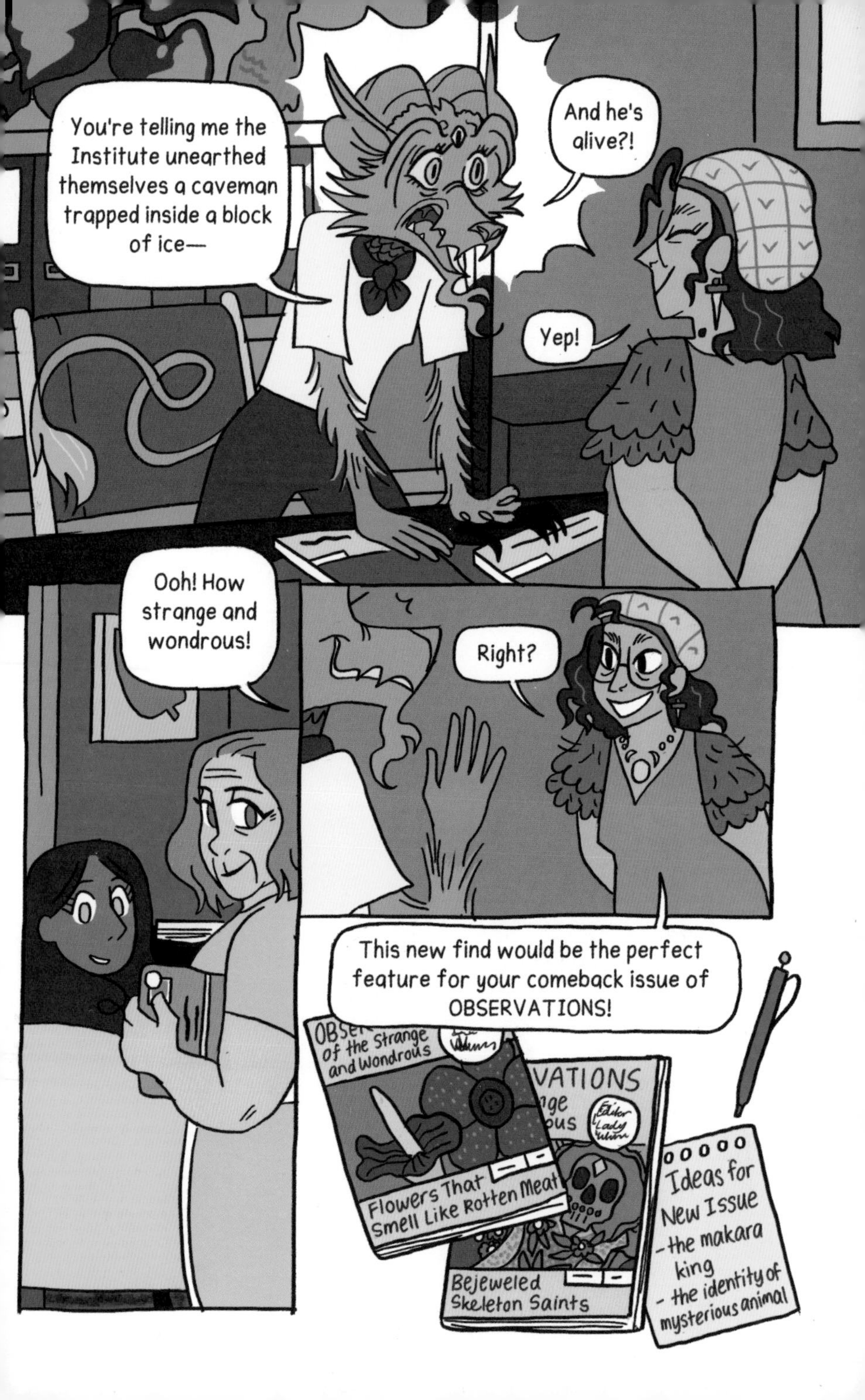
You're telling me the Institute unearthed themselves a caveman trapped inside a block of ice—
And he's alive?!
Yep!
Ooh! How strange and wondrous!
Right?
This new find would be the perfect feature for your comeback issue of OBSERVATIONS!
of the Strange and Wondrous
Flowers That Smell Like Rotten Meat
VATIONS
Bejeweled Skeleton Saints
Ideas for New Issue
- the makara king
- the identity of mysterious animal

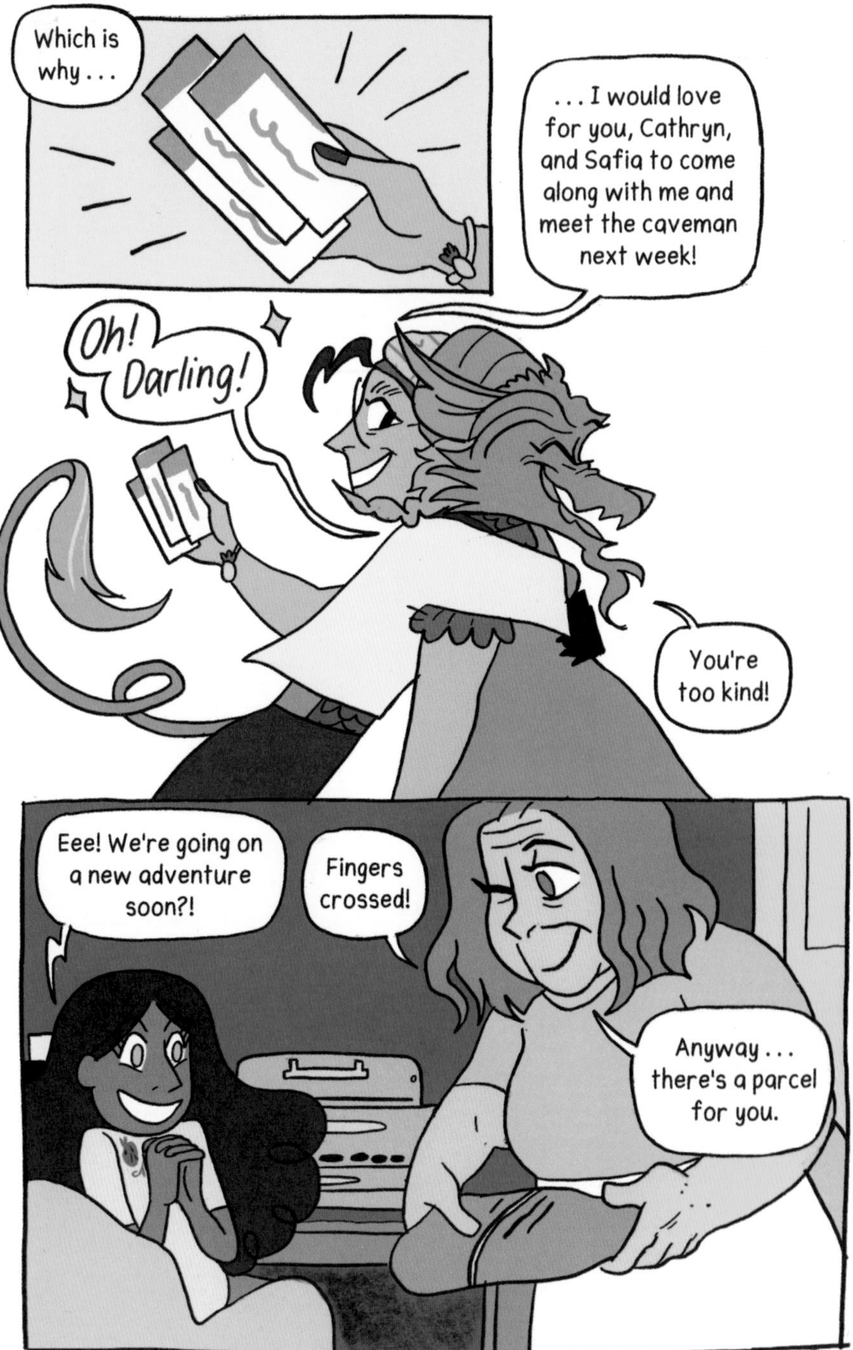
Which is why . . .
. . . I would love for you, Cathryn, and Safia to come along with me and meet the caveman next week!
Oh! Darling!
You're too kind!
Eee! We're going on a new adventure soon?!
Fingers crossed!
Anyway . . . there's a parcel for you.

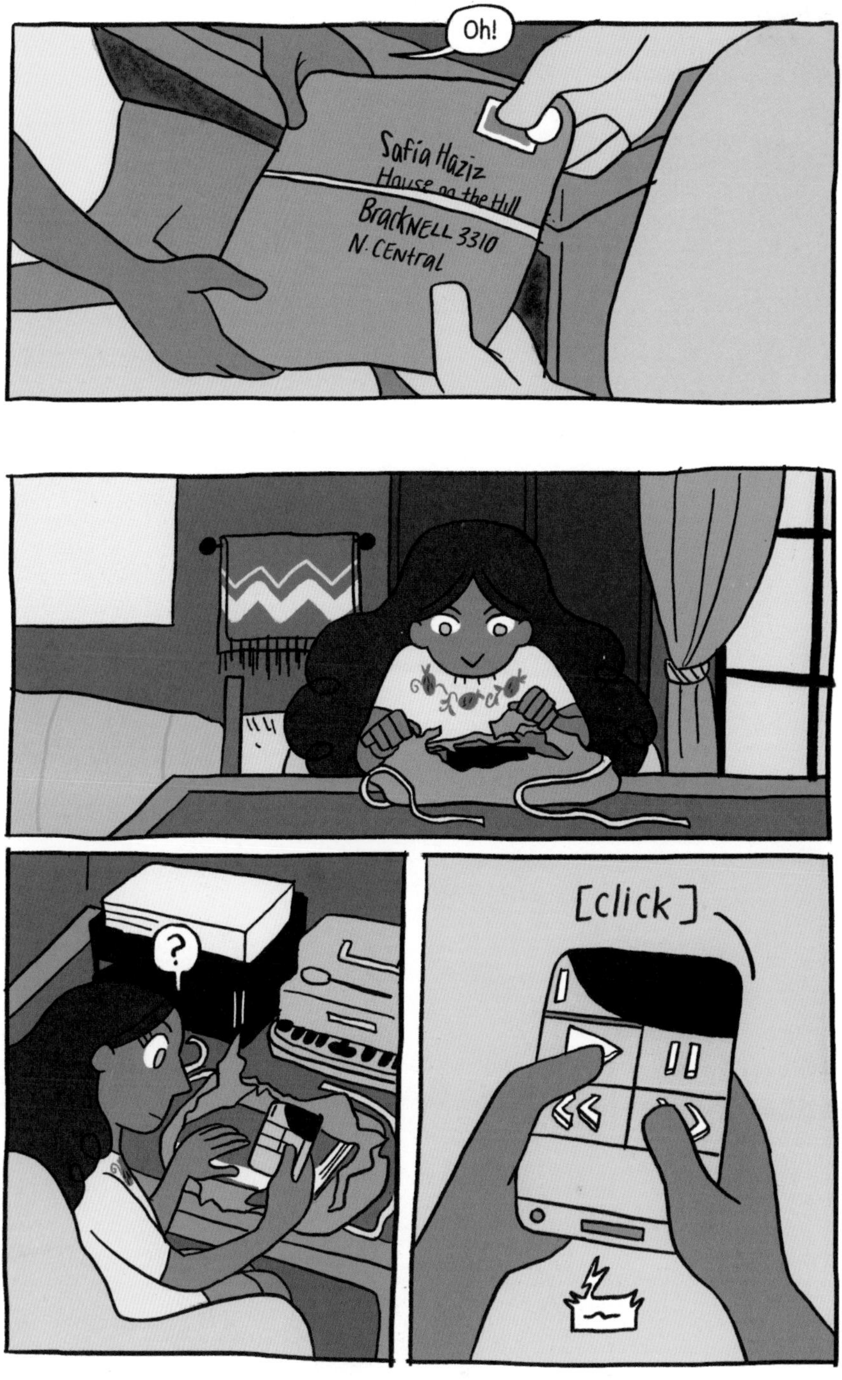
Oh!
Safía Haziz
House on the Hull
BrackNELL 3310
N. CENtral
?
[click]

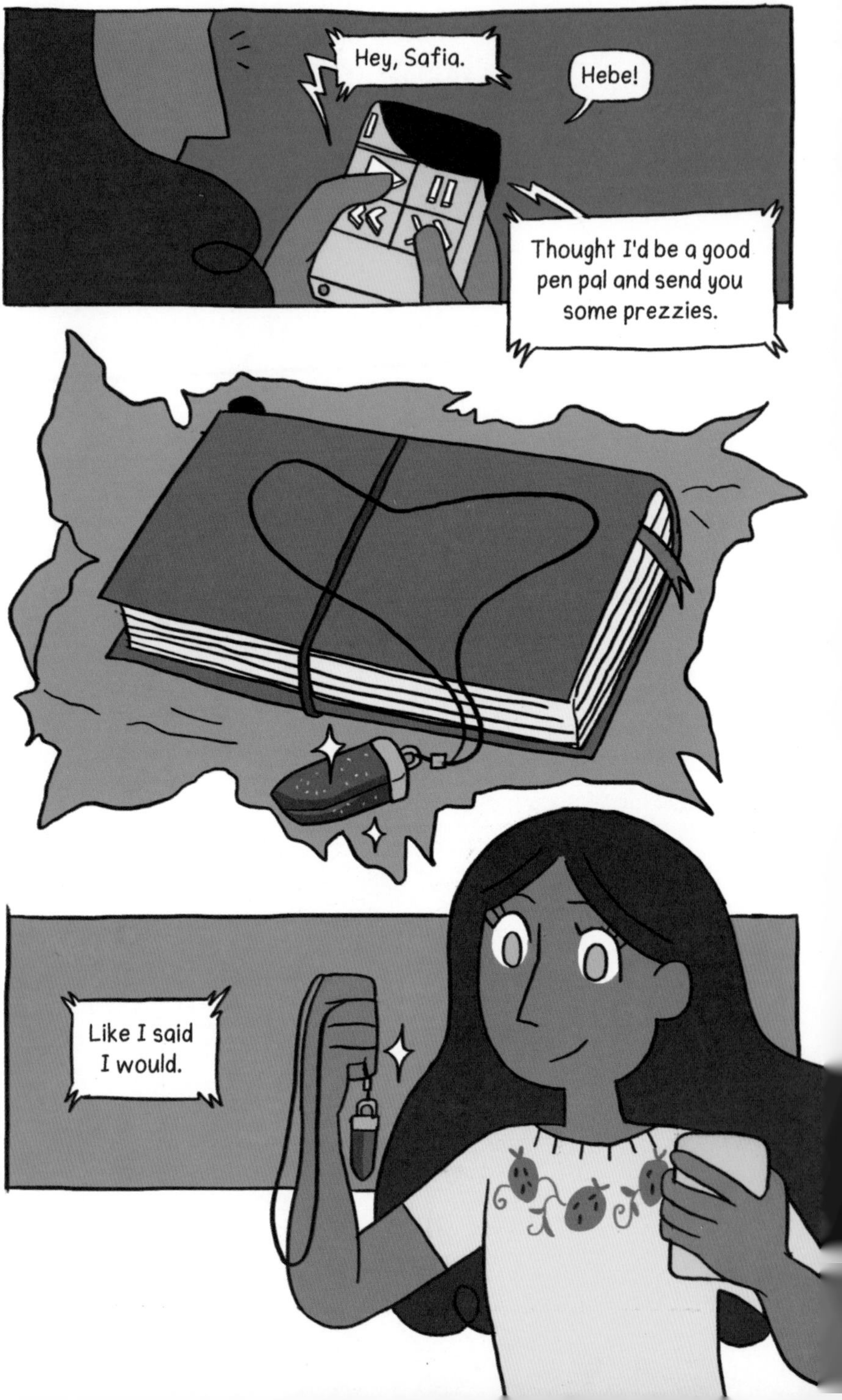
Hey, Safia.
Hebe!
Thought I'd be a good pen pal and send you some prezzies.
Like I said I would.

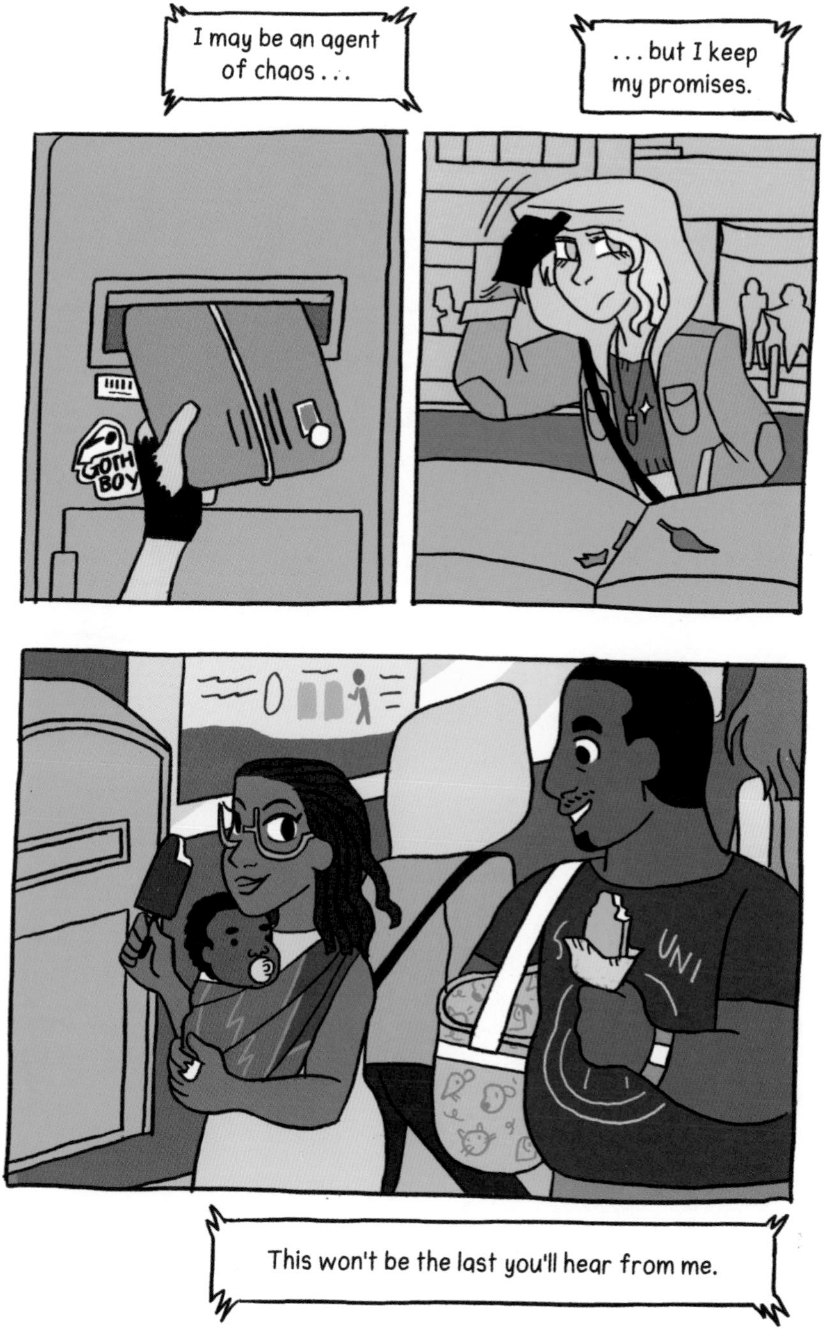
I may be an agent of chaos . . .
. . . but I keep my promises.
GOTH BOY
UNI
This won't be the last you'll hear from me.

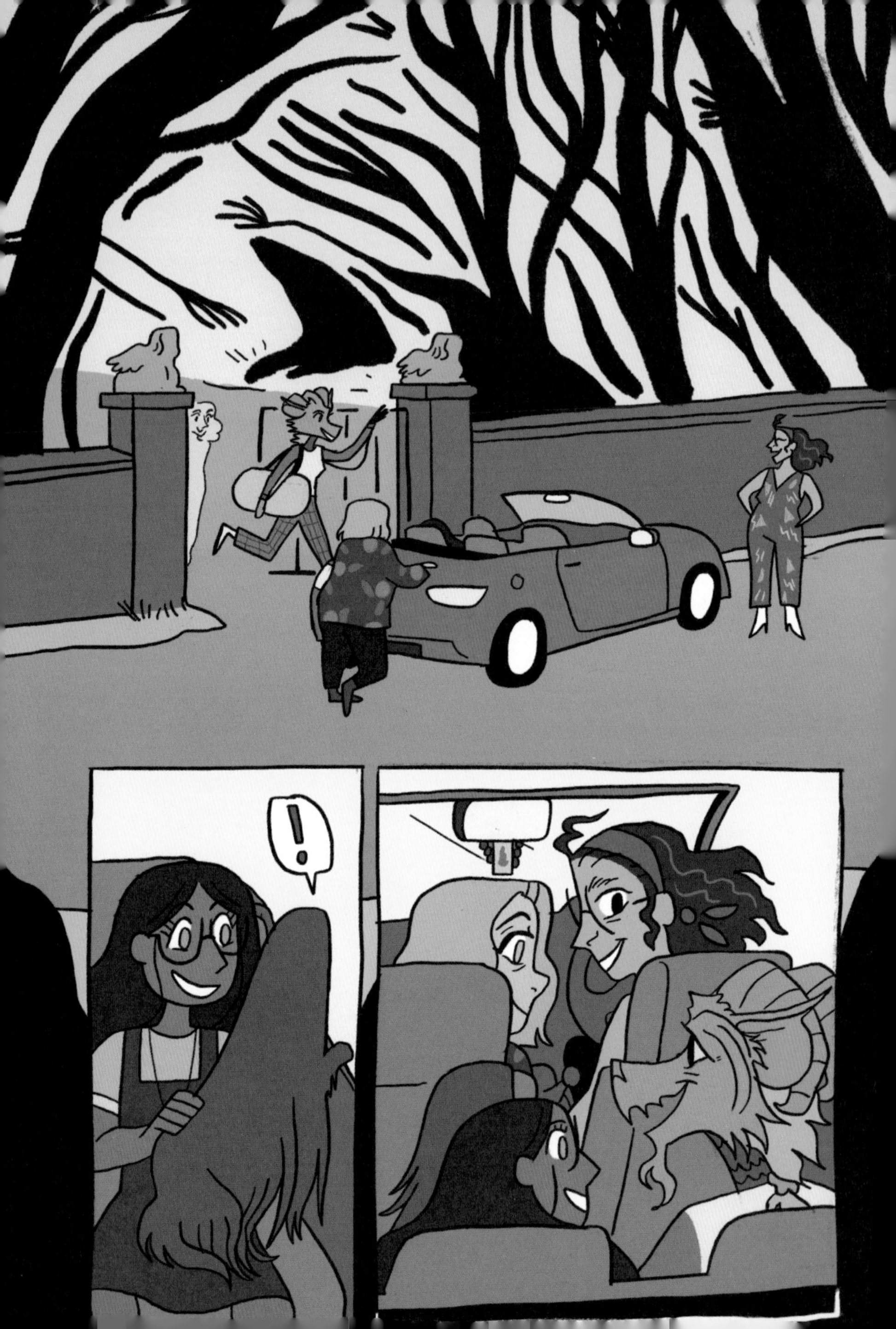
!

Once upon a time . . .

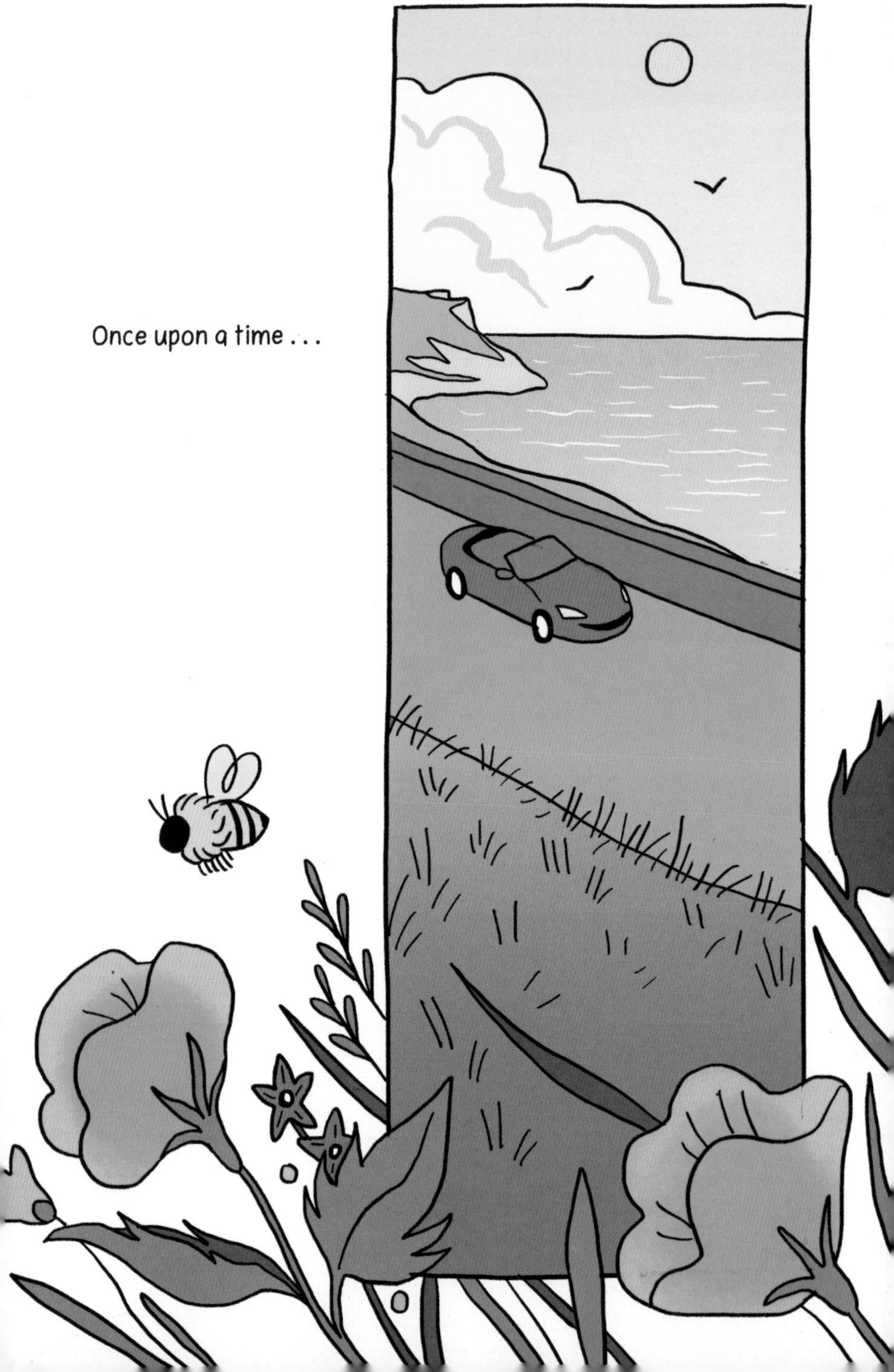

There was a little girl (who has a bright future as a writer), her aunt (who is a monster and the World's Greatest Adventurer), their nanny (who is an ex-agent of chaos and champion baker of apple pie), and their dog-undog (who loves a good chew).

They lived together in a house on a hill, a place where the world is strange and wondrous and where endings . . .

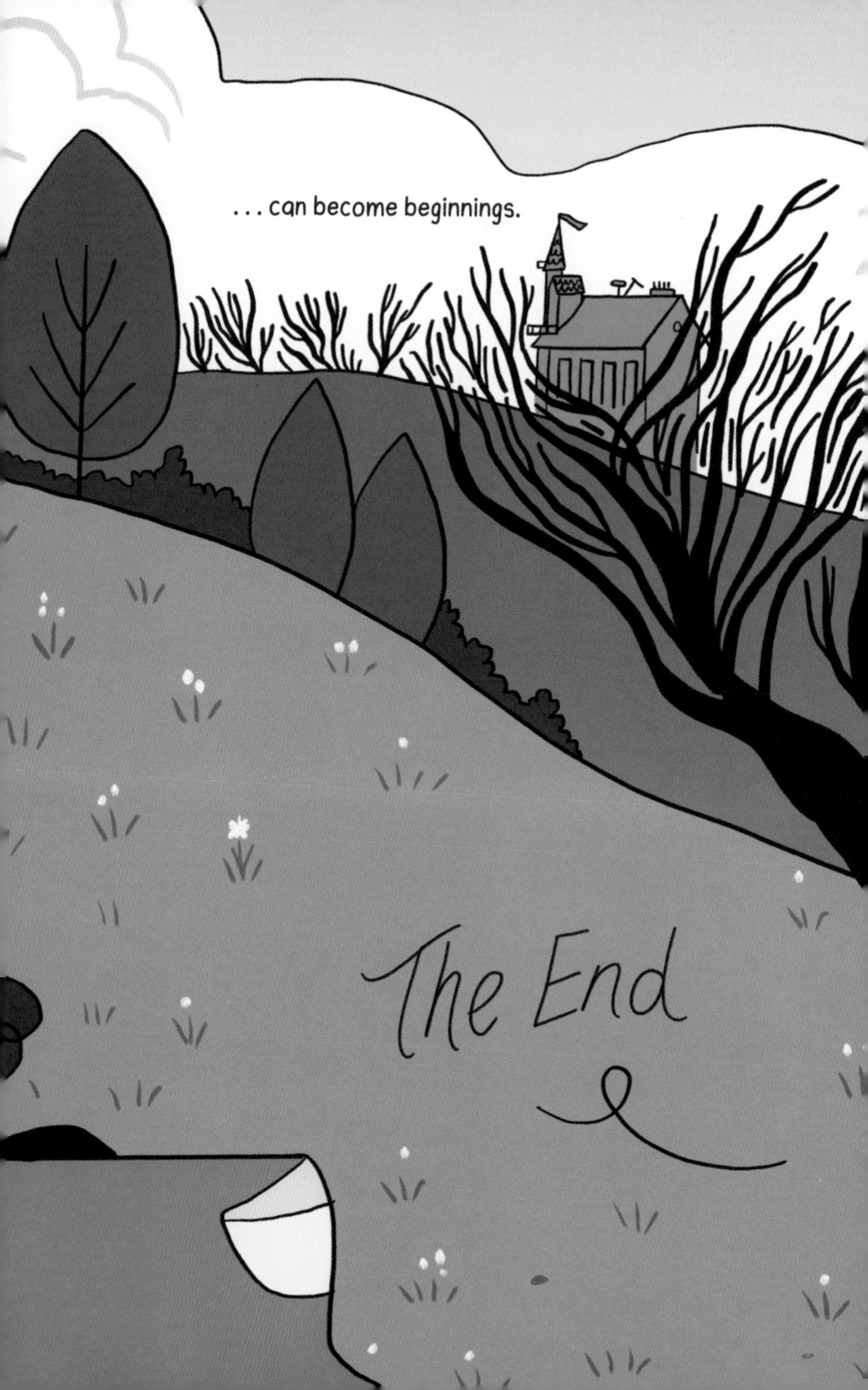
. . . can become beginnings.
The End

Cover Art!

These are my initial sketches for the cover.

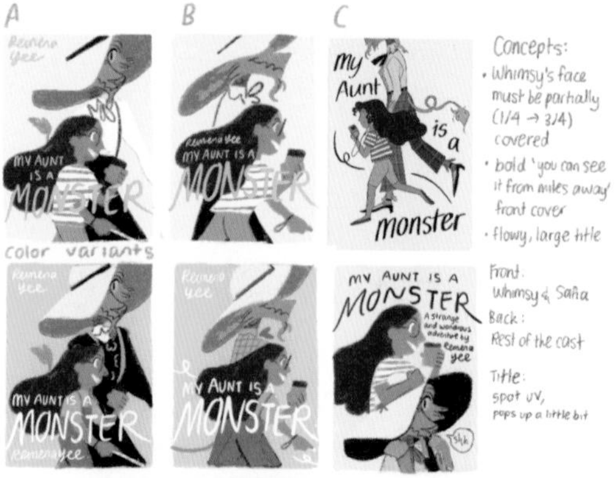
A
B
C
MY AUNT IS A MONSTER
My Aunt is a monster
color variants
MY AUNT IS A MONSTER
Concepts:
• Whimsy's face must be partially (1/4 → 3/4) covered
• bold 'you can see it from miles away' front cover
• flowy, large title
Front: Whimsy & Safia
Back: Rest of the cast
Title: spot UV, pops up a little bit

Notes for the title art for my designer, Patrick Crotty (he does title art better than me)

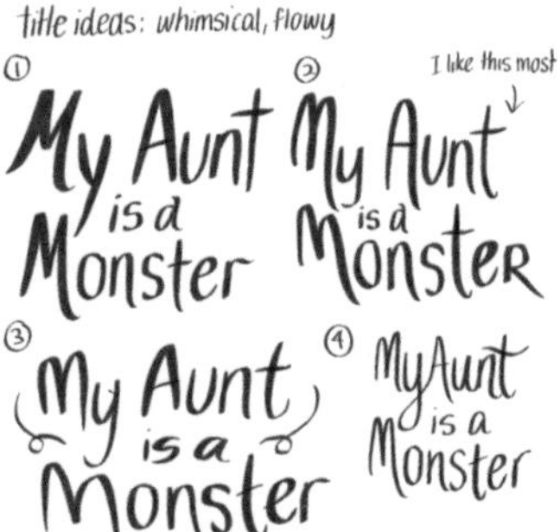
title ideas: whimsical, flowy
①
My Aunt is a Monster
②
My Aunt is a Monster
I like this most
③
My Aunt is a Monster
④
My Aunt is a Monster

New sketches featuring Patrick's title art

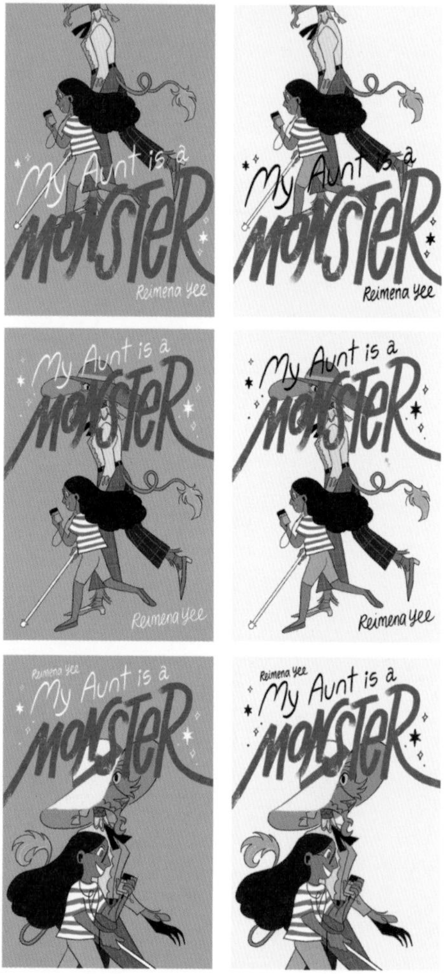
My Aunt is a MONSTER
Reimena Yee

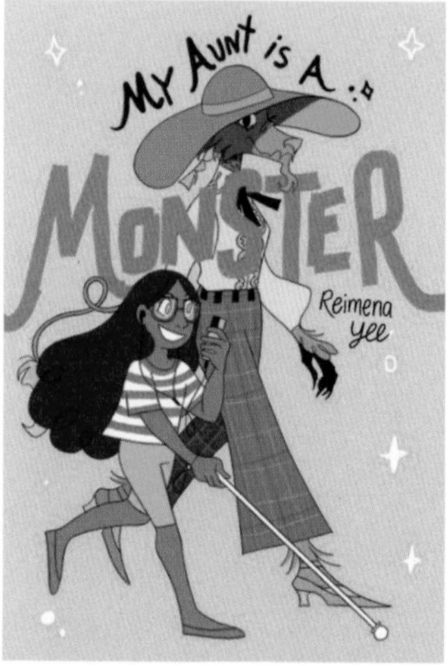
MY AUNT IS A
MONSTER
Reimena Yee

The close-to-final cover

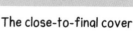

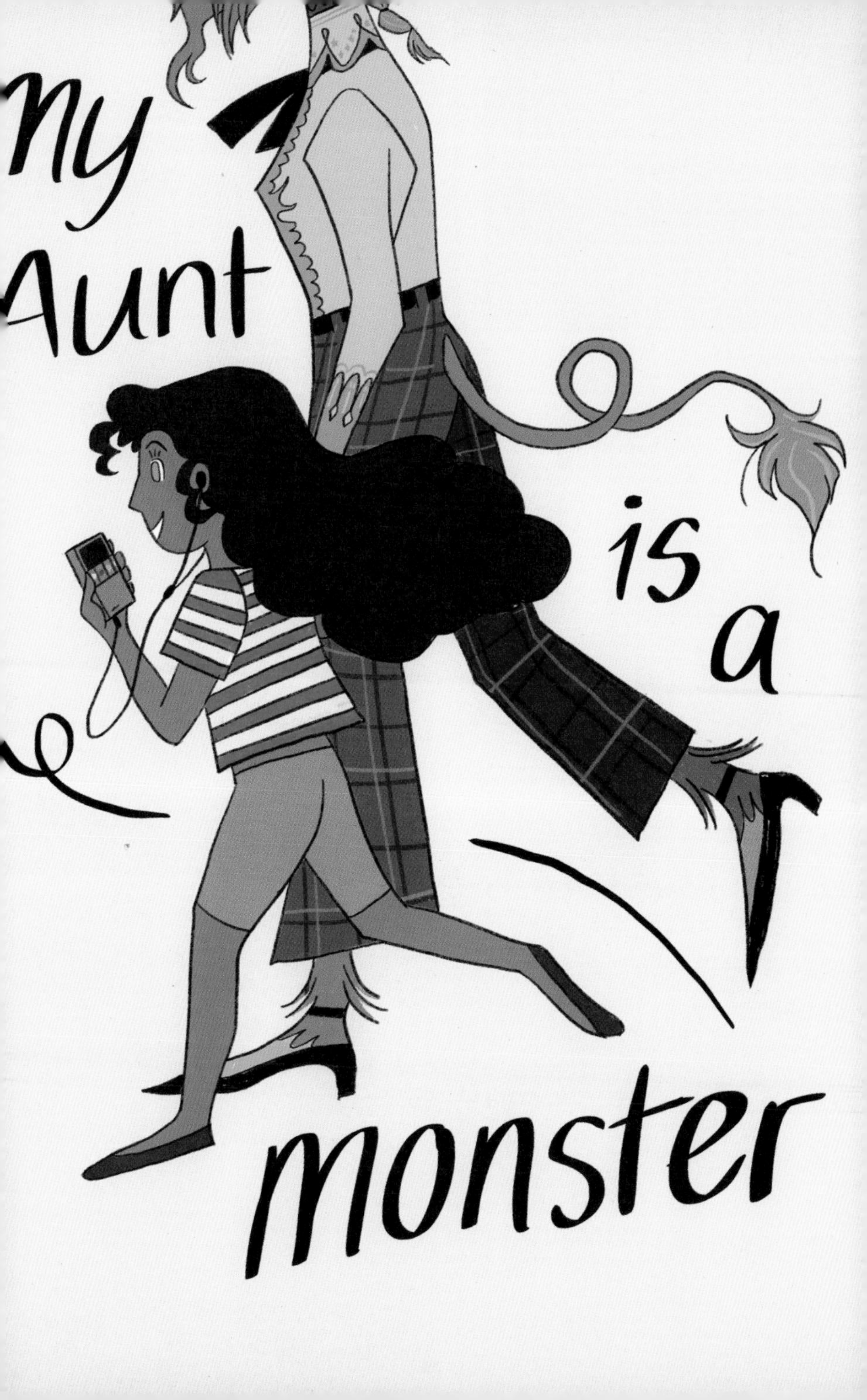
ny
Aunt
is a
monster

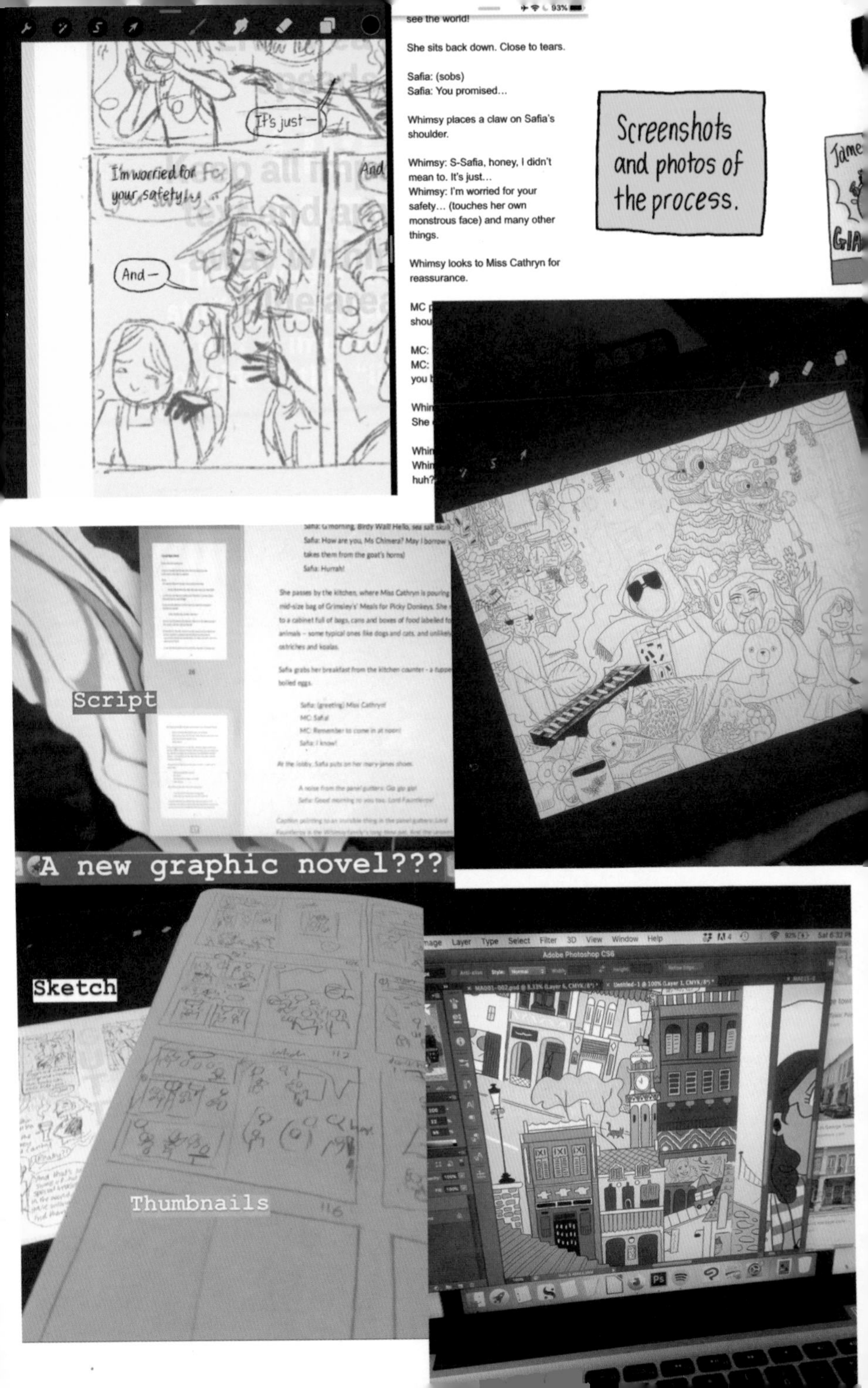
It's just –
I'm worried for your safety...
And –
see the world!
She sits back down. Close to tears.
Safia: (sobs)
Safia: You promised…
Whimsy places a claw on Safia's shoulder.
Whimsy: S-Safia, honey, I didn't mean to. It's just…
Whimsy: I'm worried for your safety… (touches her own monstrous face) and many other things.
Whimsy looks to Miss Cathryn for reassurance.
Screenshots and photos of the process.
Safia: How are you, Ms Chimera? May I borrow
takes them from the goat's horns!
Safia: Hurrah!
Safia grabs her breakfast from the kitchen counter
Safia: (greeting) Miss Cathryn!
MC: Safia!
MC: Remember to come in at noon!
Safia: I know!
At the lobby, Safia puts on her mary-janes shoes.
Script
A new graphic novel???
Sketch
Thumbnails
Adobe Photoshop CS6

Writing and Drawing the Book

How long does it take to make a comic?

Number of pages: 324

Writing the script: February–August 2020
(5 months spent in writer's block)

> Writer's block:
> A temporary inability to tell a story due to a variety of troubles.

Thumbnailing: July–August 2020

Sketching: August–December 2020

Inking: August 2020–April 2021

Coloring: May–July 2021

} visual storytelling

I work very fast compared to most creators* who make your other favorite comics. But it still takes me a long time and a lot of work!

*A graphic novel takes two to five years from start to finish.

I work in six stages: Outline, Script, Thumbnails, Sketches, Inks, and Colors.

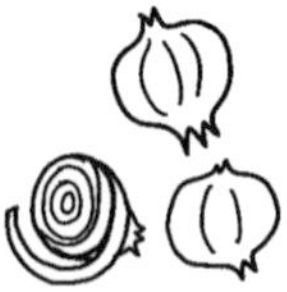

When I'm planning and writing a story, I use the Onion Method (you can search it online or visit my site to learn more). I spend a lot of time thinking about character and theme before I commit to drawing.

After what seemed like forever, they arrive at their destination.

> (off-panel)
> Steph: Oh! Thank Jeeves!
> Sound effect: Ding-dong.
> Steph: We're *finally* here.

They wait outside front door of the house. Steph is uneasy, while Rob looks like he's 100% done with the experience.
Whimsy's abode is a tall, American-style Victorian house. The path opens to a large circular gravel patio, framed by a natural but neat lawn and the dead trees. The trees are eerily flush against the boundary of the lawn. The tower we saw earlier is attached to the house; it's an observatory for stargazing.

> (off-panel)
> Rob: (getting the heeby jeebies) E-erm, Steph?
> Rob: I just had a thought.
> Rob: (gulp) Like y'know, what if... the rumours are true — and

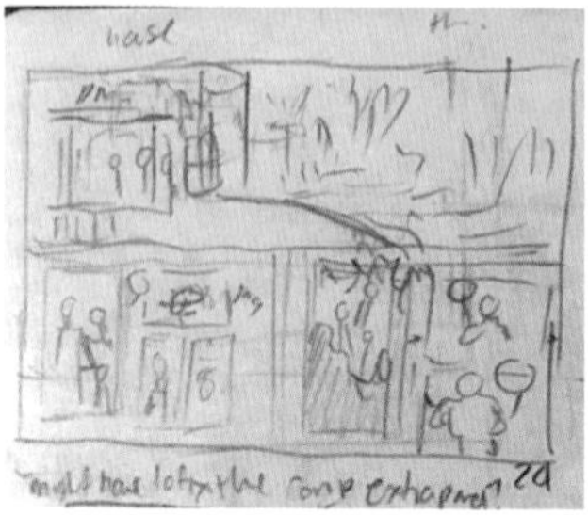

My scripts are usually bare (more bare than this), with minimal art direction.

Once I'm happy with the script, I move on to thumbnails. These little sketches help me pace and edit the script as I draw.

Then I flesh out the details.

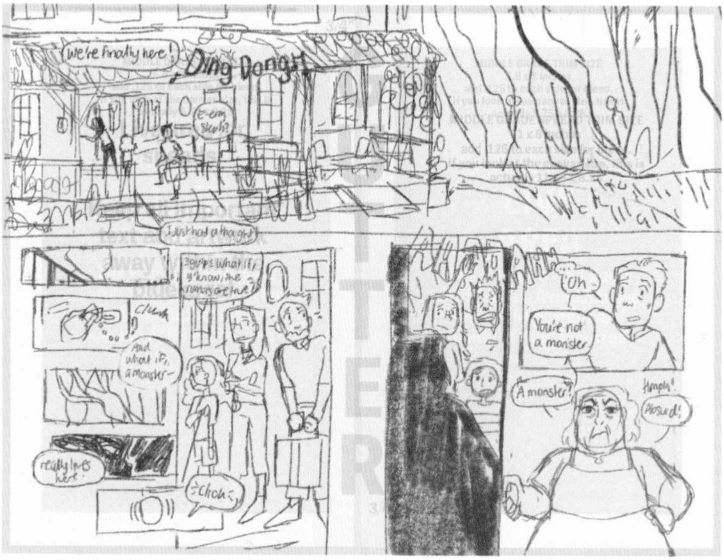
We're finally here!
Ding Dong!
E-erm Steph?
I just had a thought
And what if, a monster—
Click
Oh
You're not a monster
A monster?
Hmph! Absurd!

Later, I add inks on top of it.
By the way, except for thumbnails, everything is done digitally.

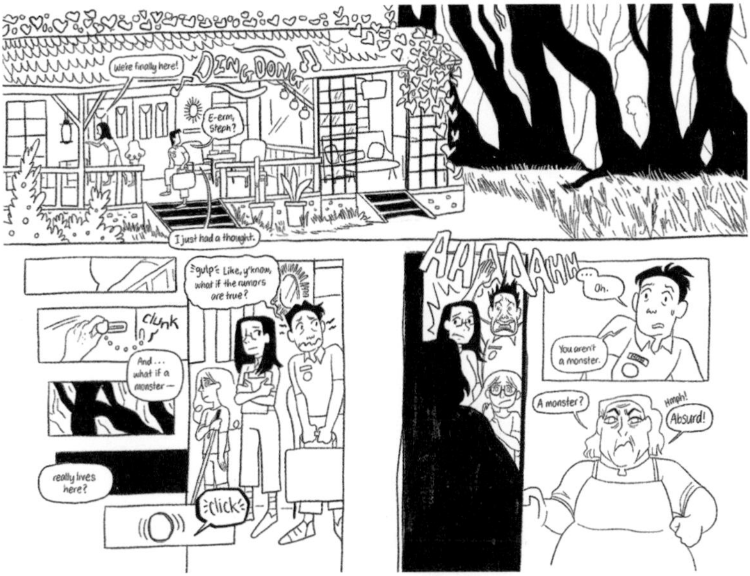
We're finally here!
DING DONG
E-erm, Steph?
I just had a thought.
gulp Like, y'know, what if the rumors are true?
clunk
And... what if a monster—
really lives here?
click
AAAAAHH
... Oh.
You aren't a monster.
A monster?
Hmph! Absurd!

And lastly, colors.

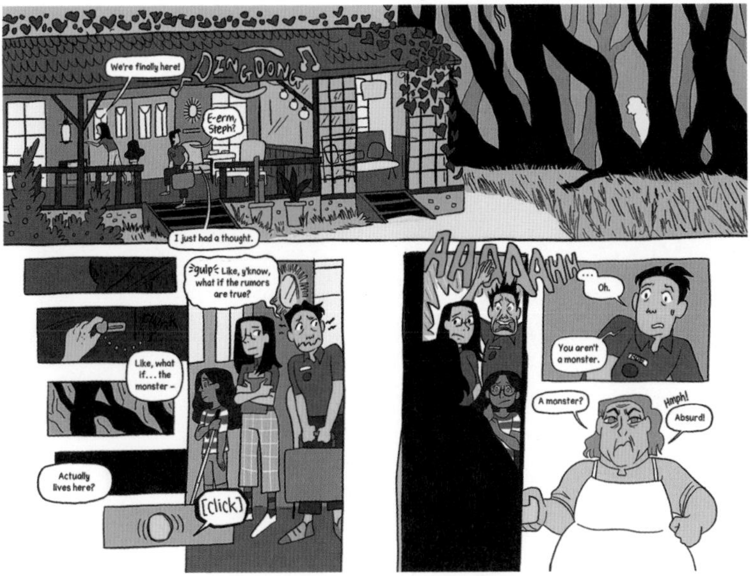
We're finally here!
DING DONG
E-erm, Steph?
I just had a thought.
gulp Like, y'know, what if the rumors are true?
Like, what if... the monster—
Actually lives here?
click
AAAAAHH
... Oh.
You aren't a monster.
A monster?
Hmph! Absurd!

Reimena Yee is an illustrator, writer, and designer who hails from the dusty metropolis of Kuala Lumpur, Malaysia. She once was a STEM student, but left to pursue her passion for the world and all its histories and cultures, which she weaves into her art and stories. She is the cofounder of UNNAMED, a comics collective that builds community and resources for visual-literary creators in Southeast Asia.

She is the author-illustrator of the gothic comics *The World in Deeper Inspection* and the Eisner- and McDuffie-nominated *The Carpet Merchant of Konstantiniyya* and the graphic novel *Séance Tea Party*.

@reimenayee
reimenayee.com